THE CIPHER MASTER

YU ZHIYAN

Translated by
Dennis and **Hui Cooper**

SINOIST

ACA Publishing Ltd
University House
11-13 Lower Grosvenor Place,
London SW1W 0EX, UK
Tel: +44 20 3289 3885
E-mail: info@alaincharlesasia.com
Web: www.alaincharlesasia.com

Beijing Office
Tel: +86(0)10 8472 1250

Author: Yu Zhiyan
Translated by Hui Cooper and Dennis Cooper

Published by Sinoist Books (an imprint of ACA Publishing Ltd) in arrangement with
Guangdong Flower City Publishing House co., Ltd.

Original Chinese Text © 密码破译师 *(Mi Ma Po Yi Shi)* 2016, People's Literature Publishing
House, Beijing, China

English Translation text © 2021 ACA Publishing Ltd, London, UK

Paperback ISBN: 978-1-910760-67-3
eBook ISBN: 978-1-910760-68-0

A catalogue record for *The Ciphermaster* is available from the National Bibliographic
Service of the British Library.

THE CIPHERMASTER

YU ZHIYAN

TRANSLATED BY

HUI COOPER & DENNIS COOPER

SINOIST BOOKS

PROLOGUE

One day in 1967, in city B, a man in his fifties took out a transceiver from a dark corner of his house. Shutting the door and windows tight and throwing a thick quilt over himself, *click-clack*, he started sending messages.

From the analyses done afterwards, at that very moment he was deeply immersed in what he was doing. Following various changes to the sound of the tapper (telegraph key), his face successively showed the full range of human emotions, and his fingers did not leave the tapper the whole night.

At daybreak, when a group of policemen forced open a window and entered the room, he, being intoxicated with himself, was sending messages with his left hand while writing down messages with his right hand. Having seen telegraph clerks either sending or receiving messages, these police officers had never seen anyone who could do both at the same time. They were dumbstruck. At this very moment, as quick as lightning the man picked up something from the desk and shoved it into his mouth. Raising the transceiver, he smashed it on the ground; then jumping on the desk and dashing past the double bed, he landed in the corner between the walls. Turning around, he stood still, leaning his back against the wall. These few movements had won him the time needed to chew what was in his mouth.

Initially, two police officers had intended to pounce on him from left and right, never thinking that this old chap would jump on the desk. They had to run past the bed and pin him down. Seeing the scene, the director of the Public Security Bureau (PSB) groaned inwardly: "We're facing a veteran covert agent. He chose his route of retreat swiftly and precisely, and his movements were quite professional." The police officers quickly used a gun barrel to open his mouth and pulled out a mash of paper. After working on it, except for some strange faintly recognisable symbols and characters, the technical staff could not recover the original script.

After a thorough investigation of the man, the PSB found no indications that he was linked in any way to counterrevolutionary spying activities. They could not declare him guilty just because he was fiddling with a transceiver, a piece of training equipment that could not send out any signals (a fact confirmed by some wireless experts called in to give their professional opinion). However, in a pair of shoes they found four sheets of paper completely covered with utterly clueless numerals. At once they sent them to the related department in charge of confidential work, where no one could decrypt the numerals. The PSB had to lock them in a cabinet for confidential documents, and later transferred them to the NSB archive office. The numerals could not be decrypted and the PSB lacked absolute proof to convict the man, so he was never arrested or put in prison, and this case has been shelved ever since.

Quite by chance in 2013, the four pages of numerals were deciphered by a young female maths teacher and a mysterious old person in city B, where the NSB office treated it as a special case and submitted a report to the related state department. A few months later a memorandum arrived. Of the four higher-level leaders in charge of national security, three drew a circle on the report and one gave a written instruction:

> During the war, there was indeed such a profession and such a person working in this field; these secret numbers are not false but authentic; he is not guilty but a man of special talent; the profession was a true historical existence and the spirit of those working in the field will never die; preserve and pass the spirit on, so that future generations will not forget them; this case has been settled and must not be reopened; and some day public opinion will be the best judge.

Not until then did some people become aware of the existence of the cryptography (codebreaking) profession in our army's history, or come to know that the man was a cryptographer who had made great achievements in the war. It is said that because of a mysterious error he had committed, he was called to account and dismissed from his post. Ever since then he had stayed at home doing nothing. On the day in question, his interest in his old job returned and he was itching to have a go, so he dug out a teaching transceiver to have some fun, never thinking that the old lady living next door would report him to the police. Nobody could understand a cryptographer and the fact that, despite his occupational interest having been suppressed for over ten years, it could have been rekindled all of a sudden. What he was sending and writing were the contents of the paper in the shoes, which were written in code he had produced himself.

That female maths teacher might have known that the methods of hackers and a certain country to steal secrets were awesome (at the time, Edward Snowden had just brought to light the many espionage programmes and other snooping activities of the US government). Hence, after she decrypted the four pages of numerals, she did not use a computer to send or print her script, but wrote them down neatly on paper and delivered them to the NSB of city B in person.

Later her entire script was included in Report Issue 3 (2013) of the security department of city B. The following is a reprint, to which no changes have been made.

Page One: In the history of the Chinese revolutionary war there was a category of people who were mysterious and little known to the public. Those who knew their secret commented: "They made a tremendous contribution to the victories of the Red Army's resistance against Chiang Kai-shek's encirclement and suppression campaigns, the Long March, the War of Resistance Against Japan and the Liberation War, but they kept their identities hidden, mentioning nothing of their great meritorious service. This legendary unit hidden behind the cloak of war was an important force for our army to defeat enemies when we were outnumbered and weaker, turning danger into safety. No history of the Chinese revolutionary war would be complete without mention of what they did in the wars."

Page Two: Although they did not kill any enemies in person, they saved astonishing numbers of officers and men, repeatedly hastened the enemy's defeat, and many times they changed the course of the war; their military service was performed with distinction and their contributions were great, but they sought neither fame, nor gain, nor any return; they were in combat all their lives but what they were showing were always their backs; to help the revolutionary wars to achieve victory, they were able to offer everything and sacrifice everything, including their blood relations, love, fame, positions and even their lives; their outstanding feats did not depend on their fighting or being killed on the battlefield, but their unique professional techniques and unusual methods of subduing the enemy, as well as their powerful convictions; they followed in hot pursuit right up to the enemy's headquarters, destroying the enemy's nerve and taking the enemy's heart and guts. This is a group of people who used their wits to open the gate of victory.

Page Three: Historical events passed through their fingers every day. They knew many wartime secrets and the longest length of service was thirty years up to and including today (1967). Over the years, this group of people, who knew 'too much', remained loyal to their pledge of not telling their parents, spouses or children about what they had done, so none of those around them knew their true identity. When the day came that their profession was declassified, and they were praised and received the historical conclusion that they 'had performed indelible feats for the People's Republic', and the honours came one after another, all of this had lost some practical significance. To those still alive, they seek nothing but to cast away all the taboos and precautions, to be like a child frolicking about in the open, breathing in and out to their hearts' content, then shouting to people all over the world: "At last I am myself! At last I am free of secrecy!" But the majority of them could not wait this long; with a giant rock pressing against their mouth they died, carrying with them all their secrets.

Page Four: Yes, these mysterious people were called codebreakers (or cryptographers). They, along with their occupational actions, were involved with many famous battles and major events during the war years. A lot of associated generals had always spoken extremely highly of these people, their undertaking, their work and their achievements. In fact, their unique professional efficiency, counting on the revolutionary high-ranking commanders' remarkable wisdom and distinguished stratagems, made a great contribution to the victory of the revolutionary wars, making their role irreplaceable.

In her report she wrote a remark: "At the home of the author of the cipher paper, a painting was found. It is 480 centimetres long and 160 centimetres wide, almost with the style of a national treasure, the famous painting *'Along the River During the Qingming Festival'*. It is named *'War Gallery'*, painted using fine brushwork, deploying the method of scatter perspective mapping, portraying vividly a dozen or so classic battles in various revolutionary wars. The key point is that I suspect there is some important information hidden in the painting, more detailed and colossal than the four sheets of paper. With my current capacity I am unable to decipher the whole painting, but on a rear corner I found an encrypted phrase, which I have successfully decrypted. As to whether there are more secrets, I earnestly request the related state department to carry out an investigation, and to organise the leading expert cryptographers to come and analyse and decipher them."

However, things did not go the way she expected. Due to the four leaders' written instruction and the circles on their report, no one from the PSB and the security department wanted to carry out any further investigation into the case, nor did anybody bother to enquire about the *'War Gallery'*, a mysterious painting containing unanswered questions.

PART 1
CIPHER TEXT

1 / THE DUEL

SINCE MY STORY originated from the love between a man and a woman, let me begin from the 1930s. The romantic affair was nothing unusual on The Bund, but it eventually developed into an event involving secret societies and loss of life, something people could never have imagined.

One midday in December 1931, after finishing work Ji Zhenren walked out of the telegraph office building. A gust of wintry wind made him shiver subconsciously so he threw his scarf over the back of his neck; unfortunately, as luck would have it, it touched someone's face, who unexpectedly grabbed the scarf and pulled it with a sudden force; unstable on his feet, Ji Zhenren staggered.

Startled, he was about to shout, but that person covered his face with his hands and called out viciously: "Don't you know when you hit people, you don't hit them in the face? Why did you humiliate me?" He then saw that this person was his colleague Gao Q, who went on shouting: "Why do you always attack people by overt and covert means? It's fun, isn't it? How about we settle our headache in a simple and direct way? Two o'clock this afternoon, under the bell and drum tower at the railway station square, let's fight it out. Afterwards the loser must behave and only be Jiang Xiaodian's colleague, and the winner can openly be her boyfriend. This is a duel for love and honour. Don't recoil in fear if you are a man. I tell you she will come to witness the duel." Gao Q then marched off.

Ji Zhenren's mind was blank, then he flew into a rage: "At work everybody knows that Jiang Xiaodian only loves me. How could Gao Q come to take away my woman by force, and threaten to have a duel? How absurd!"

He ran back to the building and dashed upstairs to see Jiang Xiaodian, but the office was empty. He went to the nearby restaurants, cinemas and shops, but there was no sign of her there, either.

He hurried to the railway station, seeing in the distance that the shameless rat was already standing together with Jiang Xiaodian under the tower, and he even went so far as to give her a hug!

With the tolling of the bell, Ji Zhenren dashed over to them, pushing away the villain. Gao Q sneered: "A gentleman uses his tongue, not his fists. Look at your aggressive posture, want a fight?"

Jiang Xiaodian cried out angrily: "Ji Zhenren, why did you ask Gao Q to come here to fight a duel with you? Do we really need to come to an open break in our friendship?"

Hypocrite! Ji Zhenren did not expect that Gao Q would make such a groundless counter charge. He grabbed Gao Q's collar, demanding an explanation.

Suddenly, waving his fist, Gao Q hit Ji Zhenren in the face. The two came to blows and they fought until their faces had been bashed in.

Jiang Xiaodian tried to stop them, but she was pushed to the ground. She wailed: "I'm too ashamed to live!" But at this moment who would listen to her wailing?

Suddenly all the onlookers' eyes turned to the inside of the enclosing wall on the left, where a six-storey foreign building stood. At the edge of the roof stood Jiang Xiaodian, who was covering her face with her hands and wept loudly. Out of the blue a few gun shots broke out and sparks flew in all directions along the edge of the roof. Jiang Xiaodian fell to the ground.

Meanwhile, some more gun shots were heard in another direction. People cried out in alarm and fled in panic.

Gao Q dashed to the main gate and Ji Zhenren also took to his heels at once. At this very moment, somebody fired at Ji Zhenren, who then lost consciousness.

But he was conscious of two things.

First, the instant he fell to the ground, he realised that what had happened was nothing but a plot. When he charged at Gao Q with his bare hands, the plot had determined the ending: he would definitely be finished! On this point Gao Q's wish was fulfilled. But nobody expected that a new problem would crop up: Jiang Xiaodian also died. Although Ji Zhenren realised where the plot lay, he had no chance to find out the truth.

Second, the circumstances at the railway station on that day were not the slightest bit different to any other day. No one would have noticed that the station toll was mixed with gun shots; neither would anyone have wondered about what grievances lay behind the plot that had cost two young lives. Because in those days the atmosphere in Shanghai was rough and ghastly. Fighting over nothing was a common sight, and schemes and intrigues were everywhere.

With such public morals and mores, people were not surprised by anything unusual. The strange afternoon ended, as well as Ji Zhenren's short life.

The next day the *Da Wan Bao* newspaper reported the incident, saying: "This was a murder for love triggered by a relationship between two men and a woman", and then it emphasised "it had the background of the black evil forces of a secret society, making the case complicated. It must have been hard to give a verdict and that is why the police remained silent. Looking back on public events in recent years, it is not difficult to discover that the secret society forces in Shanghai have expanded viciously, having developed into powerful and influential organisations with considerable political status and economic strength. They have had a bad and far-reaching influence on society, and people from all walks of life must be vigilant and keep a watchful eye on such a phenomenon."

Such news from *Da Wan Bao* added one more layer of mystery to the very odd afternoon.

Some people might think there is more to this case than meets the eye. Anyone familiar with the situation in Shanghai knows that the press at that time had a noted peculiarity. Members of the press were not only deeply affected by the political power of the authorities and the economic influence of financial groups, but also constantly subjected to coercion by secret societies. Some secret society members used the newspapers to promote their influence and to serve their evil ways. But it was extremely rare for the press to use such harsh words to criticise the black evil forces of the secret societies, as had happened on this occasion. So, what was their intention by using the shooting to slap the secret societies in the face, or using the slapping of the secret societies' faces to cover the shooting? Why would a seemingly ordinary shooting motivate the secret societies to act in such a shameless way? How much filth and intrigue were hidden behind it? Only the devil knew the answer!

For a matter only the devil knew the answer to, Ji Zhenren would naturally have no capacity to explore it clearly; but he was certain of one thing, and that was that the newspaper had irresponsibly classified the incident as a 'murder for love'. Because although Gao Q, the fake rival in love, fought fiercely with him in the name of winning love, he had no affection for Jiang Xiaodian at all, not even a scrap of desire for her. Also, Jiang Xiaodian had no sexual relations with Gao Q. Since there was no loving relationship between Jiang and Gao, it was obvious that the press had wagged their tongues too freely to say that it was a murder for love.

Ji Zhenren would die without any closure as to the nature of the case!

In fact, what he could not get out of his mind was the messy, awful love itself. If he were alive, he would often have remembered this love began from a strange telegram.

A new post, it was his first day on duty at the Shanghai Telegraph Office. Near the end of the day, he received the last customer. A telegram draft was handed to him with only one word on it.

In the early 1930s, telegraphy was new in China and a one-word telegram was even more odd. Puzzled, he raised his head, glancing at the customer. This glance immediately got him into the conventional pattern of falling in love at first sight. He, who was always independent in mind and action, and worried that he would be labelled vulgar, would never have imagined that the hormones in his young body could let his scruples completely depart from him on that day. For the first time in his life, he experienced the sensation of falling in love at first sight. Standing in front of the counter was a young girl. Instantly two phrases flashed through his head vulgarly. 'As fervently passionate as gold' were her eyes when she looked at him; 'as gentle as silver' was her voice when she spoke to him. He was so smitten that he felt that such words were far too inadequate to describe her beautiful looks and charming temperament.

How beautiful she was! Her facial features, eyes, nose, mouth, ears, hair style, the height of 170 centimetres, her curvaceous feminine figure, her waist, bottom, legs and feet, she was stunningly attractive.

Her attraction was not the sort of 'beauty that is in the eye of the beholder', but a universal attraction, the sort that everyone found 'attractive'.

Usually he was a man that was overly reserved and not cheerful enough. But on that day he was so self-indulgent that he risked overturning his temperament and destroying his image. He was entirely unlike his former self, and maybe not his future self. He felt that this 'love at first sight' was a feeling that he could not have experienced in a hundred years, and that this attraction was also something that he could not have encountered in a hundred years. Ha-ha, before he knew who this beauty was, he had lost himself in a wishful dream, fitting into a common saying - shameless!

But it wasn't too bad. He hadn't been struck dumb by this rarely seen female charm, as some senses remained in his body.

"Only one word, Miss?"

"OK."

"Does it clearly express what you want to say?"

"OK."

"I mean, are you sure the recipient will understand what this 'OK' means?"

"OK."

"You can send seven words for a telegram. Are you sure this is what you want to say?"

"Then add six OKs, or I'll be taken advantage of."

Normally under such circumstances people would think that there was something wrong with the girl's brain. But at this very moment, to Ji Zhenren, anyone uttering such a thing would have been a blockhead.

"Shall I send it as it is?"

"OK." The beauty had a cunning expression in her eyes, but it disappeared in a flash. "People from Henan like this word very much," she said.

"Oh, I've never had any friends from Henan."

"No wonder it took me such an effort to talk to you."

"……" Trying hard, Ji Zhenren then muttered: "Hey, Liu Hai'er. What an interesting name. Your signature is quite elegant. It is said one's handwriting reveals so much about a person."

"My name is alright. As to 'elegant' or 'the handwriting being revealing about a person', you'd better forget about it. My handwriting is too 'Ah Zha Cai', ah, it is slang for 'rubbish' in the Henan dialect."

Once flattery was out in the open, it became unbearably tasteless. Ji Zhenren was too embarrassed to speak, but he hastened to deal with the telegram.

It started raining outside. Having no umbrella with her, Liu Hai'er stood at the door waiting. Holding an umbrella Ji Zhenren stepped out. Again, he showed poor taste, saying: "Miss, if you don't mind, you can share my umbrella." Giving him a sweet smile, she said: "OK."

While walking along the road, he deliberately talked about his job in the telegraph office. From his tone she did not feel that he was showing off, but he certainly meant it; nevertheless, it was she who started the subject.

"Telegraph clerk, a good job."

"Not bad, a very sought-after job. Like working in a bank, for the customs and on the railways, it is an unbreakable golden rice bowl."

"Living off a government salary, so the wages must be good."

"On average, an ordinary clerk earns about 100 yuan per month, and the payment is never delayed. Compared to other common industries, we telegraph clerks receive decent wages and benefits; even compared to our counterparts in Europe and the USA, the salary for us is also high. The annual salary for a British telegraph clerk is less than six pounds sterling, an American telegraph clerk only earns fourteen US dollars a month."

"So unusual for a Chinese telegraph clerk."

"It is mainly because we work more laboriously than our foreign counterparts. This involves telegraph codes. English has 26 letters, German 30 and Italian only 21 while Japanese mixes Chinese characters which can also be expressed using alphabets with 50 sounds. As long as these letters are provided with the corresponding telegraph codes, it is relatively easy to encode and decode. But for the Chinese it is much more complicated. Because the Chinese telegraph codes use the individual Chinese character as the basic unit, and there are 6,800 commonly used characters. One may well imagine the difficulties by using only the dots and the dashes to arrange them into thousands of different combinations. Oh, forget it, you will not understand this specialised subject."

"You are right, I don't understand what code is, but I understand anyone who does a dignified job will be held in high esteem."

"People from Henan are master speakers. Which bus do you want?"

"Bus 2. Let's say goodbye. I'm a stranger to you, but you've given me shelter from the rain. Thank you very much."

"I also take Bus 2."

"Oh, that's great."

Getting on the bus they sat side by side. When chatting, Ji Zhenren couldn't restrain his curiosity and inquired about her telegram. Smiling lightheartedly, she said: "Should a clerk ask that much? You're breaching a customer's privacy. Ha-ha, only kidding. I can tell you if you want to know. A very touching love story is behind this word 'OK'." She stopped, looking at him with a broad grin.

What stirring eyes she had! No time for him to look away, he warned himself not to be flustered. "My job is to send telegrams for customers who decide the contents. I have no right to ask about them, so if you don't want to tell me, that's fine," he said.

A newsboy was pushing through to sell newspapers. Ji Zhenren bought two copies and passed one to Liu Hai'er. One news item was about an old library that would be reopened tomorrow after a refurbishment. He asked her what books she liked to read. "All kinds of books, but I'm particularly interested in ancient Chinese prose and poems, as well as modern verse and prose. Do you want me to recite a couple?" She asked. He nodded. She then said: "Actually, I'm not from Henan. But a Henan accent is not difficult to imitate. Anyway, I'm not going to recite the following two new verses in a Henan accent." Stunned, he felt that he was being fooled. He was so in shock that he failed to hear what she was reciting.

The bus arrived at Liu Hai'er's stop. After seeing her off, Ji Zhenren got back on the bus and travelled back to the telegraph office building by the original route. He lived in the living quarters for staff behind the building, so how could he go the same way as her?

It was Sunday the next day. At the behest of supernatural powers, Ji Zhenren went to the library the newspaper talked about. As soon as he stepped in, he saw Liu Hai'er reading a book. He went to greet her, seeing that she was reading a book with a blue cover called *The Sad Record of a Strategy for Peace*.

At lunch time he went out and bought some snacks for them both. She wanted to pay him, but she felt embarrassed because she did not have enough money with her. He said they were only some pastries, and that he was happy to pay for them. She said OK and went on reading and taking notes, absorbed in what she was doing. In the evening, when the library was about to close, he asked her if she had enough money for her bus fare. She grinned, embarrassed. He handed her the money.

A week later they met again in the library, and Liu Hai'er was reading the same book. At lunch time, she invited him to have noodles with her. The cost was exactly the amount for the bus fare. He guessed that she must have been struggling to make ends meet. During the meal, they chatted cheerfully, and the feeling of 'falling in love at first sight' intensified in his mind. In a probing manner, he expressed that he would like to be friends with her. She was so mischievous that she grinned while tilting her head to one side, saying in that fake Henan accent: "Okay! I agree." After the meal, he saw her off and walked with her part of the way, thinking all the way about the touching love story behind the one-word telegram. What was it?

Once back at work on Monday, Ji Zhenren went to the third floor to deliver report forms to the technicians. He was still new to the building and after searching here and there, he finally found the room. He knocked on the door and went in. A girl raised her head from the desk. Instantly his mind went blank. It was Liu Hai'er. Dumbfounded, he passed the forms to her and turned to leave. She said: "My name is Jiang Xiaodian. Liu Hai'er is a friend of mine in Suzhou. I sent that telegram for her when I was at work." He didn't know what to say. Again, she said: "The reason for me to know you in such a way is that the expression in your eyes when you looked at me on that day aroused my interest in you. I only followed my mood, not intending to play the fool with you. I hope you won't take offence." Her voice, no matter how hard he tried, had none of the feeling of being 'as gentle as silver'.

In private some colleagues commented that Jiang Xiaodian was a spoilt girl from a wealthy family, driven to work by chauffeurs, spending money lavishly, and now and then going to the best restaurants in the city with her female friends.

Ji Zhenren was then truly dumbfounded, choking with resentment and feeling very bad. Before long, he heard another remark and found out that before the one-word telegram, he had already had dealings with her, only he knew nothing about it, but she knew it very well. He thought to himself that if this was the case, she, who had played such a prank on him, was an extremely self-willed woman.

Before finding the job as a telegraph clerk, Ji Zhenren had received two years' training at the Shanghai Telegraph School. The telegraph business adopts a system whereby the school and the office cooperate with each other, and after graduation the students automatically get to work in the office as clerks. Their salary was decided by the credits they received at school. Ji Zhenren's professional strength was in transcribing and sending telegrams, quickly and with few errors. In his year at school he was the best at transcribing and sending plain and coded messages in Chinese and English.

After reporting for duty, he passed the professional skill tests. Transcribing and sending telegrams were skills that called for great effort, which showed the strength of a clerk. He achieved 'A grade' in transcribing Chinese coded messages at 123 words per minute and English plain messages at 147 words per minute. He made no errors in the five-minute test, despite the one per cent error allowance for both transcribing and sending. This speed was not his best, yet nobody else could do better than him.

In the test for sending telegrams, his performance was also extremely good. He sent 138 words per minute for the Chinese plain messages and 159 words per minute for the English coded messages. But the result was not taken as his grade, because the fastest speed in transcribing for the clerks in active service was 119 words for Chinese messages and 141 words for English messages. The test authorities could not find anyone fast enough to transcribe his messages, so his test results were decided as 119 and 141 words respectively.

It is said that for the test, the telegraph office intended, through strict screening, to select the fastest transcriber and sender as chief examiners, but the result showed that it was the same person who had come to the telegraph office two years before. When the test began, the examiner sent messages from the third floor, while the examinees received the messages in the main hall on the ground floor. The examinees did not know who the examiner was, but the examiner knew the examinees very well. Jiang Xiaodian, the technician, whose position was higher than a clerk, was the examiner. She had not expected that among the examinees would be a guy called Ji Zhenren whose professional skills were amazing. Her own speed was not fast enough to test his best result, which embarrassed her badly. Only after she had played the fool with him when she sent that one-word telegram for her friend, did she feel better. Recently whenever she saw him, she had a triumphant expression on her face.

Ji Zhenren's mental sensation of 'falling in love at first sight' came to an end. But Jiang Xiaodian convinced him still. Despite the fact she had failed to examine his fastest transcribing speed, her consummate sending skill and unique 'handwriting' were unforgettable to him. Afterwards he would listen to her sending messages and each time he would have a new experience.

Every telegraph operator has his or her own distinctive style of sending messages. Once you are familiar with it, you know the characteristics of the sound and the operating habit, and know who the operator is as soon as you hear the sound. Just as people have different voices, to those who know each other, they know who is speaking when hearing their voice.

Jiang Xiaodian could send messages beautifully, just as beautiful as herself. In the test, Ji Zhenren transcribed her wonderful *click-clack* sound, feeling extremely cosy inside. At one point he was even struggling to guess whether the examiner was a man or woman, old or young. Such a sound was very easy for a receiver to transcribe with high speed and high quality. This sound was beyond the telegraph technique, having a strong artistic element to it. It was enjoyable to transcribe such a message. However, despite his good opinion of her skills, it did not eliminate his aversion to her playing a prank on him. He could not understand how a fair lady from a rich and influential family could have behaved in such a way.

Afterwards he met her again in the library. He pretended not to see her. But she walked toward him, waving *The Sad Record of a Strategy for Peace*. She said: "This is a good book. There are only two copies of it in the library. I suggest you have a read."

He smiled: "I've already read it. I don't think it is that good."

"All right, it is me who cannot tell what is good." But as soon as she left, he got up and went to borrow the other copy.

The room for special collections was the most imposing and mysterious place in the library with row upon row of camphorwood bookcases the height of a man. The book titles were marked on the carved doors and columns of thread-bound books yellowed with age were neatly arranged in the compartments. Some of the collections were the only copies in existence - the treasure of the library - so all the books in this room were naturally closed to the general public. *The Sad Record of a Strategy for Peace* could be borrowed from this room.

In fact, Ji Zhenren had never read this book before. He found it difficult to read because the book had made no impression on him after trying to read it twice. After another two attempts, he gradually came to understand the book, not because the book itself was difficult, but because at that time he was often absent-minded and lost concentration.

During the Republic of China, what did young people think of 'falling in love at first sight'? Ji Zhenren went to look up the phrase in the dictionary because he wanted to know what exactly his very first romantic affection was. Staring passionately at the girl who was reading, his mind was racing, and he felt that his life had reached its most wonderful moment.

But the good times didn't last long. A few days later, he was dubious about whether the thousand-year old term, 'falling in love at first sight' worked or not! In short, it was Jiang Xiaodian who was untrustworthy!

Yes, there was so much about Jiang Xiaodian that was difficult to understand. For instance, in the Republic, it was not unusual for a woman to look for a job to support her family, but how could a girl from a wealthy and influential family come to the telegraph office every day and work hard for such a small amount of money? He found out afterwards that it had something to do with her life experience.

In the latter years of the Qing dynasty, secret societies in Shanghai were in disorder but despicable, and their worst evil was that they had turned the city into the biggest gathering and distribution centre of opium in modern China. Jiang Zhijing, a leader without a title, had got up to all kinds skulduggery in his youth, but later he wanted to repent in middle age. He suddenly declared that he would cut himself off from the opium trade. After that the restaurants, tea houses, ballrooms and hotels run by him were no longer involved in prostitution, gambling and opium. Soon, the Jiang family disappeared from the scene.

It is said that after the gang masters from all sects gave their promises, the Jiang family reached an agreement with the secret societies: the Jiang family would donate their businesses in exchange for the resignation of Jiang Zhijing from the secret societies, and for his son, Jiang Daming, to achieve honest social status. According to investigation, after finishing school, Jiang Daming worked for the telecommunication and postal service of the Qing court in Shanghai, and then he was sent to work in the Chinese Embassy in Japan, truly becoming a law-abiding person on a government salary.

However, he did not work for long in his government post, not because the Jiang family regretted abandoning wealth and wanted to return to the secret societies, nor because the gang masters failed to protect Jiang Daming from doing the government job, but because he stirred up big trouble that couldn't be settled by the gangs in Shanghai. The Qing court was defeated in the Sino-Japanese War of 1894-1895. Afterwards an accusation was made against Jiang Daming which the Jiang family unexpectedly agreed was not unjust.

It was truly incomprehensible how, after such a major defeat, one person with no power and who only did a lowly job could be blamed. However, looking at the job that Jiang Daming was doing, it did influence the development of the war. If he had performed his duty scrupulously, even if some incident as big as heaven had happened, fingers would not have been pointed at him; but if he failed to observe the job regulations and was slack in his job, the chances of facing an imminent disaster were great.

Jiang Daming was a minor official in charge of telecommunications in the Chinese Embassy in Japan, in fact a confidential secretary. In the last years of the Qing dynasty the Chinese were only beginners in telecommunications, knowing nothing of the specialised knowledge of coded telegrams, and in practice they could only operate by following what they had been taught by foreigners. However, the Japanese were quite advanced in telecommunications development, having set up a department to monitor and decipher telegrams.

In 1894, the war between China and Japan was about to break out. The Chinese envoy to Japan sent a long-coded telegram to the State Council at home, and the content was about his talks with the Japanese Foreign Minister, including the full transcript of the statement of the Japanese breaking off relations with China. The problem was with the statement. According to daily practice, the statement should have been in Japanese, which would have been translated into Chinese by the confidential secretary who would then have encrypted it and sent it to China. But the statement the envoy received had already been translated into Chinese, and the translation was perfect, smooth and correct.

At the time, diplomacy between China and Japan had broken down, and the situation was extremely critical. The envoy saw that the Japanese statement was ready in Chinese; not worrying whether there was anything amiss, he hurriedly ordered the confidential secretary to encrypt it and send it to China, which completely played into the Japanese's hands. Initially, Jiang Daming thought something was not quite right and tried to delay the sending of the message, but he did not insist and sent it after the envoy pushed him, saying it was a matter of utmost urgency. At the time, he was restless with anxiety, and a fit of inexplicable fear welled up in his mind. But soon he was afflicted with the feeling that he was above the crowd, and the ominous premonition was brought upon him by his own useless reasoning and extra worries.

However, he did not worry too much. Look, the telegram had to go over the Tokyo-Nagasaki-Shanghai telegraph line, and it was obvious that it would be transferred to Tokyo and Nagasaki. During the transfer process, as expected, the Japanese Foreign Ministry juggled things and they got hold of a copy of this encrypted telegram. By comparing the original transcript, the Japanese telecommunications department studied the Chinese telegram and finally decrypted it, from which they discovered the cipher that the Qing court was using. What was more terrifying was that the Qing court was unaware that their cipher had been cracked, and during the whole war with Japan from 1894 to 1895 they frequently used this cipher. One may well imagine the consequences, almost all the Chinese troop deployments and the Qing government movements were laid bare on the office desks of the Japanese. This was a serious breach of Chinese intelligence and data; besides there were many fundamental problems with Chinese politics and the military, so the Chinese suffered a crushing defeat in this war.

A year after the war ended, the telegraph incident was discovered by high-level officials in the Chinese government, and the Chinese Embassy in Japan was of course blamed. In the end, Jiang Daming became the sole scapegoat and was sentenced to prison for his "failure to do a good job, slack work, and serious failure to do his duty." Since then people have become aware of how formidable ciphers are. Businesses could not be managed without telegrams so telecommunications had to guard against theft and to guard against theft, ciphers had to be used; ciphers were more important than life, and life depended on keeping secrets.

The gangsters in Shanghai still cared for Jiang Daming. But they could not do so openly because it was too big a deal. So, in secret they bribed the prison authority and got Jiang Daming out of his cell. The Jiang family would, of course, not return to the secret societies, neither did Jiang Daming want to make a change and find other public employment, so he stayed at home doing nothing but thinking and repenting. He thought it was his own fault and that he deserved the punishment. He had no complaint at all but regretted that he had not done more. He had failed to do his job to the best of his ability which led the country to lose the war. He took the disaster of losing the war upon himself, and he was unable to get rid of the grief. He fell ill as time went by, spending his days in poor health.

Jiang Daming's health collapsed, as well as his mind. The obvious symptom was that he went down a dead end and was unable to extricate himself from the unreasonable matter. After shutting himself away to reflect on his mistakes for several years, one day he became obsessed with ciphers; no matter how hard he tried he could not get it off his mind. All day long he turned the Chinese and foreign ciphers over and over in his mind. People all knew that there was no point in him doing so, other than to try to clear up the pent-up knot in his mind, which was the only thing he was interested in doing.

Later he had a daughter whom he named Jiang Xiaodian. Once she could read, she showed an unusual interest in classical Chinese prose and ancient books. He was delighted and would teach her from morning till night, guiding her to read many books above the level for her age. Except for reading books, he used his cipher knowledge and made some easy-to-understand word games and riddles to lure her into walking along his path, and he even spent money on employing foreign teachers to teach his daughter Japanese and English.

After she grew up, he sent her to study at the telegraph school. She was addicted to books. To her, it was alright to go without food and drink, but it would not do to have no books to read. It could be said that she was fascinated by the literal meaning of characters and the expressive fantasy of the graphics behind the characters and the strange symbols.

Later Jiang Xiaodian finished her studies at the telegraph school. And perfectly justifiably, the Jiang family got her a just and honourable social identity - a member of staff at the Shanghai Telegraph Office.

To the staff at the Shanghai Telegraph Office, there were some taboos that could not be broken. Ji Zhenren did not anticipate that his one covert touch would bring on a disaster that would change the fate of several people.

At the time many people had realised the value of coded telegrams. No matter whether they were government organisations, Chinese or foreign public or private mass organisations, or eminent or important personnel in all walks of life, they began to use coded telegrams to send messages. Apart from a plaintext codebook, anyone with social status would also have a private codebook in their pocket. When there was an important matter, they would encrypt the message themselves and then take it to the telegraph office to be sent. These telegrams were only meaningless numerals or letters when handed to telegraph clerks, who must never have been curious and tried to decipher them. Telegraph offices stipulated that their clerks had no right to break their customers' codes and ciphers, and forbade the able staff from deciphering encrypted telegrams, otherwise they would be sacked or put in prison for violating the law.

But Ji Zhenren was not a man who could behave himself, and he quietly infringed the rule. As he was usually timid and overcautious, no one would have thought that he could have acted so recklessly. In fact, during that period of time he was rather a conceited man. Before he went to the telegraph school, he had a sound knowledge of the Chinese language, and he had also learned some English and Japanese. In the telegraph school, he studied hard for two years. He himself reckoned that his Chinese had reached the level of a literary scholar; his English and Japanese were good enough to qualify him as a translator of the languages; besides, he had achieved top grades in the tests established by the telegraph office, so this made him very arrogant. After the day's work, he would begin to secretly decipher some of the customers' encrypted telegrams. In the beginning he thought it was fun, and later, from these telegrams he discovered many secrets, feeling that he had broadened his mind and horizons; besides, he had sharpened his code decrypting ability, thus becoming more addicted to it. For a period of time and almost every night he admonished himself to stop, but he could not resist the temptation of the mysterious codes and ciphers. He sighed: neither for fame nor for profit, why did he take the risk of doing such a thing?

On that day Jiang Xiaodian appeared. For some time Ji Zhenren had been trying to avoid her. Of course, he did not bear a grudge for her playing the fool with him, nor did he cold-shoulder her for her family background, nor despise her for showing off her wealth, still less was he jealous of her professional ability, but he just felt that this woman was too complicated, not straightforward to make friends with. He did not want to live in other people's traps.

But this time she was very straightforward. She called him to her office. Closing the door, she threw a three-page telegram on the desk, saying: "Let me come straight to the point. It's our job to send and receive telegrams, and between you and me I can't tell who is better. If you think you are better, let's have a competition after work. If you win, I'll concede defeat." Her voice was still as soft as silver, and her eyes were still as piercing and powerful as gold. No, more powerful than gold!

When she was straightforward, he thought inwardly: "I'd better be cautious!"

"Are you a man? Do you not dare to accept the challenge?" She patted the papers.

He picked the papers up. As soon as he threw a glance at the message, he knew it was encrypted, and as long as a thousand words. Experience told him that such a lengthy telegram must be an open telegram to the nation. But according to the regular pattern, any open telegram to the nation was never encrypted. He then had another think, it was not his customers' telegram, so he quickly decided this was not a trap. But he was still cautious, saying: "It is an encrypted telegram. I don't understand it, and I've never had any interest in touching such a thing."

"Who would believe you? A telegraph clerk has no desire to probe a cipher? Nonsense! We must do it to see who is better. Come on, man!"

Ji Zhenren said nothing but stared at her. Whether she had any sinister motives or not, she was really an attractive woman, and it was indisputable that the more you looked at her, the more beautiful she was. But this rare beauty was exhibited in a manner that suggested she would keep him at arm's length.

"Don't just look at me. If you have the capability, let us fight to see who has more guts and who is smarter. Scared out of your wits? Oh, maybe my false Henan accent fooled you; you paid for a few snacks for me, making you feel that I have taken advantage of you, so you don't want to battle it out with me?"

Any words from his mouth would be wasted. Ji Zhenren grabbed the telegram and left the room.

It was not difficult; it took him only one day and one night to decipher the telegram.

A few days later, Jiang Xiaodian came again, with a lengthy telegram but in English. As soon as he saw it, he knew that it was not one of his customers' telegrams, so it was not a trap. Looking calm, he could not resist the itch to give it a try. He took it from her, and this time it took him five days and five nights to decrypt the message.

After handing her his deciphered text, there was a cold smile in her eyes. She then circled some words and lines on every other page, and translated them into Chinese. She linked these words into sentences according to the order and wrote them down in the blank space on the paper, which read: *"For the negotiations this time, our bottom price is 1,100 yuan per machine. Try to achieve a higher price. No negotiation and no deal if the price is below our minimum price."*

He read her translation, feeling that he had come across it before, but unable to remember where. Was it a trap? She gave him a bizarre grin. Taking out the three pages that he had decrypted a few days ago, she circled and linked the words into the following sentences: *"Evildoer Chen fights me, but you stand by watching. Soon after I am finished, you will be finished too."*

At once his whole body broke out in a cold sweat. This was the telegram that he had successfully deciphered after he broke the rules and entered the storage room for the used telegram forms.

The backstory for this telegram was that the Shaanxi military governor of the Anhui Clique, Chen Shufan, had waged war against general Guo Jian of the Army for National Peace, whose troops could not resist the fierce attack by Chen's troops. Guo went to seek help from Zhao Ti, the military governor of Henan. At the time, Guo stopped in Shanghai, so he went to the local telegraph office and sent this telegram, which was concise and comprehensive, despite being in common but refined language, which was reckoned to be extraordinary. When he deciphered it, he felt it had been great fun so he still remembered it.

It was obvious that Jiang Xiaodian had used this telegram's cipher and hidden the words in her lengthy and meaningless telegram to test him. He then went back to read that English telegram, and his whole body broke out in a cold sweat again. It was an encrypted telegram from a British business in Shanghai that he had handled a few days ago. He had deciphered it in secret, and Jiang Xiaodian also hid the message in her lengthy telegram to test him, which deceived him.

He then saw the light. Jiang Xiaodian had set an extremely sinister trap for him. As expected, she said: "You secretly deciphered encrypted telegrams and this is the evidence. You have contravened a strict regulation. What punishment do you think you deserve? Are you going to the director to make a confession, or should I go and report this illegal activity of yours?" He was dumbstruck. Again she said: "You refused to contact me recently. It turns out that you did a lot of thinking about how to break the law and violate discipline."

Quickly Ji Zhenren returned to normal. He got his brain in gear and tried to crack the problem he was facing. In an instant he also presented her with the same amount of words: "Stabbing people in the back, you are treacherous. Soon after I am finished, you will be finished too."

At last he could see some light at the end of the tunnel. He let out a wild laugh: "Miss Jiang, you used our customers' codes and ciphers to write these two lengthy telegrams, which shows you did it before me. You cannot get away with it, either. What do you think? We suffer as a result of our own actions, are we going to meet our death together? Or are we goint to have some self-respect and never do it again?"

Jiang Xiaodian burst out laughing, and her fine manner completely disappeared: "You have not been beaten out of your mind. All right, you won in your counterattack. It seems we share the same hobby, which is hard to come by. How about we do it together? As for breaking the regulations and violating the ban, no one knows about it except you and me. It is fine to have some self-respect, but why should we wash our hands of it? For the long-term enjoyment of life, it is worth taking the risk."

But he did not buy it: "I'm sick of doing things in a roundabout way! I don't agree with you, so it's hard to keep your company!"

She was not in a panic. Smiling faintly, she said: "For all these years, I've only been good at reading books, which is what I understand best. I'm quite poor at interpersonal communication. I will not force you to keep my company."

"Behave yourself!" He lifted his feet and began to leave.

"Goodbye!" In a bad mood she crumpled the papers into a ball and threw it into the wastepaper bin.

A dark light flashed through his mind. He stopped and, lowering his voice, he asked: "Except for you and me, do walls have ears?"

"Overcautious, as timid as a mouse!" She sneered.

The next day the technical section chief, Gao Q, called them to his office. Gao Q was only transferred to Shanghai from Nanjing two years ago. Pulling a long face, he assigned them a task, to set up a few sets of examination papers in Chinese, Japanese and English for the staff.

Ji Zhenren and Jiang Xiaodian had to make contact with each other. He seemed to have changed his feelings toward her. Before long, he met her in the library where they had a chat in the tearoom. He would recall afterwards that books dissolved the misunderstanding between them. If they had not both been infatuated with books, they would not have sat in the tearoom talking about books all day that day.

Many years later, emotionally Ji Zhenren wrote an article to recall the incredible chat on that day. He used Caesar (to commemorate Caesar's invention of the Caesar Code) as his pen name, and the article was published in the *Journal of Construction*, an official Communist Party newspaper in Yan'an.

Books and Life
(By Caesar)

There is a kind of affection, that seeks not to be together day and
*   night,*
But that seeks moral support.
The affection can be as deep, and last as long as one wishes.
This affection must have books as its matchmaker,
One book can hold up heaven and support the earth;
Yet ten thousand volumes can hardly fill in a corner of
*   loneliness.*
How deep and how long, depends on the volume of the heart.

There is a kind of bosom friendship,
That seeks not to keep one another's company all the time,
But wants only encounters beyond love.
The relations can be as much as they wish, and they can do
*   whatever they want.*
For this predestined relationship,
They must make their decision in accordance with heaven's
*   will.*
One person can help them to go anywhere around the world,
Yet millions of people cannot solve their lifetime of frustration.
What course to follow depends on how much good fortune they
*   have.*

One horizontal stroke sends me away,
One vertical stroke makes me a man of integrity,
One stroke paints my life with colour,
One left-hand stroke sends me on my journey,
One tick is the rugged road,
One dot is to search for eternal reading.
How great a mind is judged by one's fate in books,
The broadness of the sky is propped up by the vigour of writing,
The depth of affection is presented in brilliant writing,
The purity of the soul is vouchsafed by words.

This is a story that happened many years ago. I made friends with a book lover through literary activities and we increased our friendship through books.

She said then that she liked a couplet of the grand scholar Wong Tonghe: "A noble family with hundreds of years of history does nothing but good deeds whenever possible; the first and foremost good thing in the world is to read books." In her world, books were her life. She had a tough reading life, so tough that she could overcome all the other issues. Her grandfather was an illiterate man of physical prowess. When he was young, he joined the secret societies in Shanghai, eking out a life of violence; but someone who was juggling with words made him a nobody in the end. He burst into tears, wailing: "We must read books all our lives, so that our lives can become better and better." This was what he came to realise after years of struggle in the secret societies. Then her father, despite being well-read, lacked the power to understand human affairs, and was thus unable to save himself from being punished. He had no more illusions about reading books. When it came to her generation, since childhood, she had developed the hobby of reading books; also it was in her blood, so nothing was on her mind except reading books. Books were her world, and she would read books every day. She was determined to pave her path through life with books.

She worshipped books. I had never seen a woman that crazy, self-confident and at ease when talking about books. She said: "In my life, the friends I am most grateful for are books. It might be that heaven has rolled the wrong dice, bestowing books along with happiness upon me. A book is my lover who will never grow old and my best companion whom I can depend on for survival."

Then I said: "Let me recommend a good book to you, in which

valuable feelings are stored in words, and the only copy extant as far as love is concerned. When reading alone, the reader sees no words; but when two people read together, they can see the content. And it is before your eyes."

Startled, she asked: "Before my eyes? There are so many good books on the shelves, which one do you want to recommend?"

I replied: "To a person who loves books, it is predestined that he or she will not own a good book in a real sense. A good book is always waiting for you to read it."

She said: "Recently I have read a secret book full of god's instructions. Its language was so disorganised, not a maze in the general sense. It has become a barrier to my year-old ambitions, and it smashed my dreams in the fast running rapids. It is wordless with endless pages, as difficult as a book from heaven."

I asked: "Who was the author of this weird book?"

She replied: "Warmongers! Murderous lunatics! Opportunists! Hermaphrodites!"

I muttered: "I understand. This book is called cipher."

She said: "In the past there was no book that I could not understand. But now this kind of wordless book often makes me dizzy and confused."

I said: "Books in libraries are for readers to understand logic, but books written in code and ciphers do the opposite. They deliberately hide the logic deep, and their aim is to prevent readers from understanding them. If someone wants to understand words written in code and ciphers, which are designed to prevent people from understanding them, they must read and understand all the books that they can understand."

She exclaimed: "What a wonderful explanation! You've explained clearly the secret of interpreting ciphers from a certain angle."

Then inattentively, I said: "This book is before your eyes. Stretching out your hand, it is a book. If you have no inclination for it, you will see no image of the words."

She understood what I meant, giggling: "Forget it. You are a man of too much literary talent, but not enough emotional quotient. Let's end our chat for today." Instantly, I could not hold back the happiness from welling up in my mind. It was the fruit grown from reading books, and you never feel lonely when you are in possession of it.

It was unprecedented for the journal to publish such an article, yet it was well received by readers. Someone even commented that it was a love letter, which had spoken out 'my and her' deep affection for books, as well as 'my love for her'. The article was published, but how to interpret it was other people's business. In fact, Ji Zhenren was indeed attracted by Jiang Xiaodian's love for books, throwing the woman of innate character into his book of life.

But unexpectedly, the article triggered an espionage case. Strictly speaking, it was the following contents of the article that accidentally revealed the secret. (Initially, the article was already perfect. But Ji Zhenren might have felt that he had not enjoyed himself to the full, so he ruined it by adding a story, not knowing that he would lay a trap. And this will be taken up later.)

The extra story was added to the article under the following circumstances: soon after their chat in the library, Ji Zhenren asked Jiang Xiaodian to go to a western restaurant for a meal. He ordered a medium steak for himself, while she ordered her steak rare. While eating, she had a bloody mouth and looked savage. "The fondness for rare or well-done steak is determined by a person's character. I will not eat unless the steak is rare," she said.

He tried to add some warmth to the eating, while tactfully saying some sweet nothings: "I've been wanting to know the love story behind that word 'OK' for a long time."

She quickly swallowed her food, saying: "This is an excellent story!"

My good friend Liu Hai'er was from Suzhou, but she would often go to Shanghai to read books. She told me that her family's private library was substantial; besides, it was incomparably mysterious. Any book you can find in the libraries in Shanghai, you can find in her family library. I was puzzled, why does she travel so far to read books when she can find them in her own home? She gave me an irrelevant answer but praised her family's library. It was in the style of the Suzhou gardens, composed of ancient wooden buildings with three entrances. They were built in the 45th year of Emperor Jiajing's reign in the Ming dynasty (AD1567) and were named Luobilou, Guoyunge and Tianyixuan respectively, having tens of thousands of books in a collection of ancient and modern works. After hearing this, I was so envious, but I still wanted to know why she needed to travel to

Shanghai to read books. Seriously, she said that it was a story that had been engraved on her bones and heart, and must not be passed on to others after I heard it.

However, after leaving some bits out, Ji Zhenren wrote this story in his article *"Books and Life"*, which obviously went against Liu Hai'er's urges for Jiao Xiaodian.

The Lius' library in Suzhou has three rules that have never been violated for generations. First, no matter how bad their circumstances are, they must not sell their collection of books; second, only family members can go inside the library; third, women are not allowed to read in the library. Hence, since the library was built, except for burglars, only ten non-Liu family members were allowed to enter, and no women, no matter whether they were from the Liu family or not, had ever entered it. It was said that in the early years of the Qing dynasty, a talented female scholar in Suzhou called Tang Ruyun loved books so much that she married into the Liu family. But she could not violate the rules to get what she wished for, and she died of depression a few years later. After her death, she turned herself into a strong-scented herb *yuncao* (rue or *Ruta Graveolens*), which could repel insects and prevent moths from eating books. Every year the Liu family would use the herb in the library, therefore Tang Ruyun's spirit finally walked into the library, and she was able to stay there reading day and night.

Although Liu Hai'er had the same interest as her ancestor, no matter how hard she tried, she could not get near the library. She was so distressed that she was thinking about finding a non-Liu family member to help her.

In Suzhou city there was a well-known scholar called Zhang Jiayin, who had been given permission to go and read in the library by the Lius. He was a man with astonishing talent as well as appearance. Liu Hai'er, who was hungry to go inside the library, saw him and fell in love with him instantly. Only then did she realise that books are nice, as well as men. After some time, Zhang Jiayin noticed the hidden eyes of the young girl that were full of tenderness and love. One day he asked: "Why do you look at me in this way? Do you think that I am going to steal your books?"

Embarrassed, but not afraid, she said: "It's me who wants to steal the books. But before I steal them, I have stolen a heart."

Not in a panic, Zhang Jiayin said: "I heard long ago that your family has a talented female member who is not allowed to read her family's books. I feel so sorry for her. These old rules and regulations are evil. I have met you today, and you are truly a book lover and you are as beautiful as a fairy." Having read *The Romance of the Western Chamber* and *A Dream of Red Mansions*, Liu Hai'er knew the stories very well.

Not feeling nervous at all, she said: "You can go to the library, and I have been longing to go from morning to night, which means we are both book lovers. My looks are before your eyes, so let's be straight. If you are happy, we can make a deal. You can have my heart and my body and in return you give me your heart and body as well as a book from my family's library every week. How is that?"

Zhang Jiayin understood and, losing no time, he said: "I agree."

But unexpected things may happen at any time. One year later, the Lius found out what was happening. Zhang Jiayin was from Henan province. He was in Suzhou on his own, so the Lius were looking after him. There was no way that he could break the rules and steal books. Besides, he had forgotten the Lius' kindness, but committed adultery with the Lius' daughter, which angered the Lius, who then terminated their assistance as well as contact with him. It was hard for him to find a job, or go to school in Suzhou, so he travelled far to Guangzhou. Liu Hai'er found it hard long ago to part with the man who had stolen books for her, so she selected the best master stroke from novels, and she put it into practice. In an eye-catching spot outside the Luobilou, she formulated a suicide note, saying: "1. Give back my sweetheart. I want to marry him, and then I will flee to a faraway place. I will have neither complaints nor regrets! 2. Open the library door for me. Then I will spend the rest of my life with the books! 3. Prepare a coffin for me. I would like to die and be reborn among books. Please choose one of the above three. I have no other requirements, otherwise I will kill myself tonight."

Wearing a shroud, Liu Hai'er stood under this suicide note the whole night, arms folded across her breast. Before daybreak, a response came, also written on a piece of paper. Stuck beside the suicide note, it read: "1. The library rules have never been broken. 2. We have a gifted daughter who loves books, which is the result of our ancestors cultivating virtue and doing good deeds, but we can never send her to her death. 3. A common interest in books helps those who are in love, and the duration of their love depends on their fate in books. Zhang

Jiayin has been to our library, and he has thoroughly read all our collections. He can pass them on to his wife by word of mouth, and the couple can enjoy the books and pursue self-support."

The Lius' decision was very clear. The rules could not be broken, nor should there be a loss of life, so they allowed Liu Hai'er to marry the man she loved. As for Liu Hai'er, this would both satisfy her thirst for books and save her life as well as provide her with a husband.

Jiang Xiaodian also told Ji Zhenren that, by chance, she was in Suzhou to visit Liu Hai'er the day after Liu ripped down her suicide note. As soon as they saw each other, Liu Hai'er burst into long tears of joy. She tore off a corner of her suicide note and wrote down 'OK', asking Jiang Xiaodian to send it for her by telegraph after she returned to Shanghai, so that her lover in Guangzhou could know about the good news.

Deeply touched by the love story, Jiang Xiaodian asked: "How are you going to thank me after I send it for you? You must let me use the name of your ancestor. The spirit of the bookworm Yuncao is profound, and I want very much to use this name as my nickname." Liu Hai'er readily agreed. And later Jiang Xiaodian did take 'Yuncao' as her nickname.

This love story spawned by a shared interest in books was memorable. The couple married, and three days after their marriage Ji Zhenren was lucky enough to come to know Liu Hai'er and Zhang Jiayin.

As a good friend, Jiang Xiaodian went to attend the couple's wedding in Suzhou. When chatting, she recommended the ancient book *The Sad Record of a Strategy for Peace* to the couple. Being linked by books, and regarding books as their priority, the newly-weds went to Shanghai to read it at once.

Jiang Xiaodian then introduced Ji Zhenren to them and they had lunch together. During the meal, Ji Zhenren drank a lot of wine. When he was looking at Jiang Xiaodian, the expression in his eyes showed that he fancied her. Grinning, Liu Hai'er pinched Jiang Xiaodian's hand. Feeling shy, Jiang Xiaodian blushed. Liu Hai'er then said: "There is so much grief in history, as well as erratic relationships between gifted scholars and beautiful ladies. In the world, sentimental people suffer the most mental anguish, and magnificent writing always contains sadness. But fortunately, *The Sad Record of a Strategy for Peace* is not a book about such sentiments and grief; otherwise, inside and outside the book, people would all have irrational passion all over the city of Shanghai." Jiang Xiaodian pinched Liu Hai'er's hand, who gave out a weak cry.

Mention of *The Sad Record of a Strategy for Peace* drew Ji Zhenren's attention away from wine. He said: "I am not singing my own praises. For years, whenever I finished a book, I would write down my explanatory notes on the background of the book, including *The Sad Record of a Strategy for Peace*. Have a look at my notebook. The lines are thick, and the words are thin, but they are clear to read." Clumsily he took the notebook out of his pocket.

During the Warring States Period (BC475-221), there was an eccentric man called Kai Qie. Born into an aristocratic family in the State of Qi, he worshipped his senior Mozi and studied with his teacher Xunzi, becoming a thinker and statesman who was well-known among the seven states for his intriguing wit and cunning intellect. He gave priority to the long-term construction of the world but denounced the calamity of wars and spurned the use of force. He advocated mutual respect and mutual benefit between countries, regarding peace as of paramount importance, while opposing the strong bullying the weak, nobles being arrogant to those from humble origins, or the clever swindling the foolish. He absorbed the essence of the thoughts of famous people from all states and all times, and he attached particular importance to the application of the teachings of the Taoist, Confucian and Mohist schools of thought on making a state prosperous and stable, and regarding harmony as the goal for society. He engaged in detailed consultation, investigation, research and analysis of the seven states' politics, military and relations formed through geographical links and the will of the people. After ten years' hard work, he presented each individual monarch of the seven states with a secret book about a strategy for peace, and each book specifically stressed what this state should do to avoid being attacked, emphasising that they should seek common ground, move forward together and enjoy peace. The seven books were: 'A Strategy for Peace for Qin', 'A Strategy for Peace for Qi', 'A Strategy for Peace for Zhao', 'A Strategy for Peace for Wei', 'A Strategy for Peace for Han', 'A Strategy for Peace for Chu' and 'A Strategy for Peace for Yan'. He used an extremely unusual way to deliver the books. He cut off his own eyes, ears, nose and tongue, put each piece in a book and sent them to the seven states, trying to use his sincerity to urge the seven monarchs to accept his strategy for peace.

But the result was a great disappointment for the man who had lost his eyes, ears, nose and tongue. Some monarchs discarded the book after reading it, with no intention of adopting his ideas at all, while several of his books never reached the monarchs but were held back by their military officials or advisors. One Qin advisor read the book. He shouted abuse and then laid the book aside. Then two cats began to fight for an eyeball among the bamboo slips[1] and a scholar discovered the book, and secretly hid it in his room. This scholar had a strong admiration for Kai Qie's talent, sincerity and propositions. For many years afterwards, he travelled back and forth among the other six states and secretly looked for copies of the other six books. In the end, after scouring every corner, he found them. He compiled them into one book and recorded the remarkable story of Kai Qie cutting off his own eyes, ears, nose and tongue in his sincere quest for world peace, and how his books were cast aside by the seven monarchies. He named his book 'Eyes, Ears, Nose and Tongue - Do Not Attack Others – a Strategy for Peace'. He secretly sent his book to the seven states. At the time, Kai Qie was able to endure the physical pain of losing his eyes, ears, nose and tongue, but he could not take the humiliation that his strategies for peace had not been adopted, let alone witness the callous use of force, the rising scale of chaotic warfare and the worsening calamity inflicted on the people. He was sad and depressed, went on a hunger strike and died.

By AD213, Qin, the state that had fed Kai Qie's eye to the cats and who had exterminated the other six states, united China, carried out the burning of books and buried scholars alive. Most of the handwritten copies of the 'Eyes, Ears, Nose and Tongue - Do Not Attack Others – a Strategy for Peace' were burnt, and only some loose slips were passed on among the public. When it came to the early years of the Qing dynasty, by accident a scholar acquired those bamboo slips. Based on the key thoughts and the thread of the story, he began to write a book, portraying Kai Qie as the anti-war god, a fighter for harmony and a messenger of peace. He named his book 'The Sad Record of a Strategy for Peace'. Later, as time went by, most of the copies ceased to exist, and in the period of the late Qing and the early Republic of China only two copies existed in China.

After reading the notebook's contents, Liu Hai'er and Zhang Jiayin hurriedly got up and said: "It really is a good book. Both the existing copies are in a library in Shanghai. Hurry, let's go."

They left. But Jiang Xiaodian took Ji Zhenren's notebook away. After some time, she returned it to him, saying: "I would like to pay my respects to you. You are a true scholar. I only use my eyes to read, but you use your brains to reveal the true implications in books." He could hear that her words were sincere.

Flustered, he bowed quickly: "I feel ashamed by your compliment. You are from a family of scholars, and your reading capacity developed since childhood has enabled you to read more than ten thousand books. I am no match for you."

After a moment's silence she said, solemnly: "Today I want to ask you a favour. When my father died, he left no last words, but fished out a wrap from his bosom and handed it to me. Then his head dropped to one side and he died. There was neither treasure nor cash nor deposit books in the wrap, but a stack of paper in a jumble. The paper was completely covered with numbers and words that nobody could read. I knew that my father's last words were in them. I have been studying them all these years, but I could not hear my father's voice. I know it is beyond my capacity to decipher these secret words, so I want you to join me to enable my father to open his mouth."

Ji Zhenren had an unusual feeling all over his body. That was the excitement of being trusted by somebody. Under Jiang Xiaodian's solemn eyes, he sat down and buried himself in these secret papers.

A few days later, he told her that he was completely in the dark and could not see any light. She said: "Let me tell you something about my family. I think it is the best way to find some cracks among these chaotic codes and ciphers." In a kindly and informal fashion, she told Ji Zhenren everything about her family. He listened and was absorbed by what she said, and he truly regarded himself as a Jiang family member. Together with Jiang Xiaodian, he sifted out a few major events that would have been worth writing on the paper. Then he tried to decrypt them, but he ended up without any result after a few attempts.

For some time later, he had no more time to think about this wrap because he needed to finish the assignment handed down by Gao Q.

He and Jiang Xiaodian had prepared thirteen sets of examination papers for Chinese, English and Japanese telegrams to test the speed of sending and transcribing a telegram, the speed and accuracy of deciphering plain text, and all sorts of general knowledge and required skills concerning the telegraph system. Gao Q was unhappy with the question papers and asked them to redo them. He gave them the green light, allowing them to consult the old telegram drafts that had been stored up over the years, to use them for reference and to open up their thinking.

The old telegram drafts were stored by year and by plain text or coded. Ji Zhenren and Jiang Xiaodian were only allowed to read the plain-text telegram drafts. But the cipher-text telegram drafts were next to the plain-text telegram drafts, so they could pick them up easily. Gao Q's green light made it convenient for Ji and Jiang to get up to their monkey business. In the past, when they read a few coded telegram drafts, they had to be very careful and read them in secret. But now these drafts were all before their eyes. The rules were there, but it all depended on their conscientiousness. The mutual monitoring turned into mutual keeping guard and it was a very safe method for them. What Gao Q saw was that they worked overtime every day to prepare the examination papers, but in fact they worked on the question papers in normal working hours and secretly read the encrypted telegrams when they were on overtime.

This time they got the job done with flying colours. They prepared high-quality examination papers for the next two years. Gao Q was very happy, so he let them have two days off.

On bicycles they wandered beside the Huangpu river. Jiang Xiaodian was unusually charming, saying: "In the two-day holiday, we will not talk about heaven or earth, books, telegraphs, parents or Yuncao. You decide what we talk about, but I'll decide how we talk."

He decided: "Let's talk about love."

But she set up a rule: "Only talk, nothing physical."

Outside the small eastern gate near the stone bridge, the sun was warm and genial. Along the river bank the willow leaves were either green or yellow, and the sandy beach was shining under the sunlight. Ji Zhenren felt a tidal surge of emotion, and his ears could not hear the noise of the surging waves of the Huangpu river in the autumn season. Timid and shy, he stretched his hand outward, trying to touch Jiang Xiaodian's hand, but failed.

A small boat was approaching them. A young fisherman sang a song in Shanghai dialect as he rowed the boat. Ji Zhenren could not understand what the fisherman was singing, but Jiang Xiaodian blushed, turning her head to the bank, and as expected she saw a young girl standing on the stone bridge, smiling and waving at the fisherman, her soft eyes exuding tenderness and love.

Jiang Xiaodian chanted casually: "Willows are green and the river water is smooth, I hear my darling singing on the river."

At once Ji Zhenren understood, and he chanted: "The sun is coming from the east and it's raining in the west, you might say it is *wuqing* (no sunshine), but it isn't."

Boldly he held her hand. Looking at the small boat, she said: "But there's no rain in the west!"

Greatly excited, he said: "Neither are there any clouds in the east!"

She muttered: "My phrase '*wuqing*' has a double meaning (no sunshine, or unfeeling)."

"In my phrase," he replied, "it means '*youqing*' (there is sunshine, or to have feelings/to be in love)."

In her soft voice she said: "It seems that principles can be broken." She then scratched the centre of his palm a few times. Hot with passion, he fixed his eyes on her face, but she lowered her head.

She took her hands from him and ran towards the shallow waters of the river. Impatient, he caught up with her, saying everybody says that waves the size of a mountain sweep along the Huangpu river in mid-autumn, but why didn't they see them today?

"Your trembling voice tells me that you don't want the answer," she murmured. "Your mind is not on the waves."

He said: "Over there at the river bend in Tangyan, the camphor trees are gorgeous, let's go and look at them."

"OK," she said, throwing him a glance.

That day Ji Zhenren felt that the most beautiful place under the sun was the camphor tree forest on the Huangpu river bend at Tangyan.

The autumn scenery in the camphor forest was captivating. The trees stretched away into the distance and the red and yellow oval-shaped leaves were flying in the wind, like beautiful butterflies dancing in the air. The trees were studded with berries like black pearls, and flocks of birds were happily chirping in the woods. Blasts of delicate fragrance wafted into their nostrils before they approached the woods, and the scent freshened their minds and made them excited. Yet they ignored the charming scenery. Misty-eyed, Jiang Xiaodian was leaning against an old tree. Arms raised above her head, she held the tree trunk tight, not letting her body fall downward. He was almost out of his mind. Her body scent was heavy, but not strong; it was pervasive but not unchecked. The scent had overwhelmed the fragrance of the camphor trees, like a fine and colourless mist drifting in the air. In short breaths, Ji Zhenren breathed it all into his lungs. Her face was at its most beautiful. He thought a woman's beauty must be measured in such a moment. Stretching out his hands, he held her neck, and they had their first kiss.

At this moment she uttered her famous remarks: "Love will come in time. Be sincere, but don't take advantage of me. Reasonable and good desire should be allowed between a man and a woman." As she spoke, her eyes stopped his impatient lust. Turning around, he took a deep breath of the camphor scent. Driving away her gorgeous body from his mind and breast, he calmed down and said:

"Yes. Love between a man and a woman is like all sorts of things in life. It should depend on reading books to cultivate one's moral character and polishing one's character to discipline one's temperament."

"That's right," she said. "And in the end, we all depend on our reading, and reading great books, and reading extensively and thoroughly so that we can be self-restrained when alone and exercise self-discipline."

"Good books, good poems and good temperament and interest," he continued. "Ha-ha, it is truly the sun rising in the east while it rains in the west. You might say it is not sunshine, but it is."

The fire of desire ignited by youth gradually dissipated, and their passion and excitement finally cooled. They spent the two-day holiday with restless minds and a dubious relationship. After they went back to work, Gao Q sized them up with a curious look in his eyes, saying:

"Have a good rest? Did you spend your days together, or not? Let me guess. If either of you spent the two days alone, you must have been to the library to read books. If you spent the days together, the camphor woods at the river bend in Tangyan would have been a good place to go. The woods are thick, and you don't have to worry about being seen."

Jiang Xiaodian blushed up to the temples, while Ji Zhenren had his heart in his mouth. Had they been tailed? Shanghai has so many beautiful places, but why did he only mention the camphor woods? Humph! In appearance, he looked casual, arrogant, straightforward;

but, in fact, he was not a simple man. He might have been a bad guy, deep and very crafty.

But Jiang Xiaodian thought otherwise. Her feeling was that Gao Q was not that complicated, merely the sort like a reed on a wall or a bamboo shoot in the mountains, shallow on the inside despite their pointed sprouts and robust cortexes. But why did Gao Q give himself such a nondescript name. She had no idea, but guessed that it might have something to do with his profession.

No matter what, this Gao Q, as his name would suggest, was fond of doing things very ostentatiously.

GAO Q STUCK to his old way of doing things no matter how others might be prejudiced against him. Why should he bother ? In the telegraph office building he himself was a man with a double character.

Some years ago he was in Nanjing where his open identity was Deputy Director of Section Two, Telecommunications Department, Ministry of Communications of the Nationalist government. Now in Shanghai and in the open, he was the technical section chief of the Shanghai Telegraph Office, dispatched by Nanjing. Yet his covert identity was a secret agent of the Special Secret Wireless Section (SSWS) of the Military Council. It was a top-secret unit, even within the upper echelons of the Kuomintang (KMT). So few people knew about it that in Shanghai, no one, not even the director of the telegraph office, knew anything about his undercover identity.

He was sent to Shanghai for two secret missions: first, to keep watch on and check all the telegrams sent by foreigners; second, to secretly search for qualified personnel for the SSWS. There were two reasons why the KMT attached such importance to these two missions: first, the Japanese had not given up their wild ambition to subjugate China, and their spies were all over Chinese territory. Skilled at carrying out clandestine activities, they used local telegraph offices to send coded intelligence, and even violated international laws by secretly installing transceivers in their embassy and consulates to send coded telegrams, in blatant disregard of China's sovereignty. The KMT Military Council responded by quietly sending agents to all the major telegraph offices in China to keep watch on the telegrams sent by the Japanese; besides, they set up a special wireless reconnaissance unit, assigning technical personnel to monitor the private Japanese stations and to decipher their coded telegrams. Also, some years ago, during the war between Chiang Kai-shek and Feng Yuxiang and Yan Xishan, Chiang was one move ahead. He paid attention to improving his army's ability to encrypt and decipher wireless messages, and they were successful in intercepting Feng and Yan's coded telegrams. The result played a role in the battles, as well as in the application of battle tactics, helping Chiang's troops take the initiative in launching offensives against Feng and Yan's troops. It became the key factor for Chiang's swift defeat of Feng and Yan and conquest of China's central plain. The armies under Chiang's command became well aware of the benefits of this technology, sparing neither human nor financial resources to secretly recruit wireless talent. Chiang Kai-shek specifically wrote the following instructions: "It is easy to acquire a frontline general, but hard to find a cryptographer. Even if it is as difficult as climbing to the sky, we must try at any cost, either to recruit by force, or to win them over by any means. We must do our best to find them. Special cases need special measures. Act swiftly without delay." Thus, Gao Q went all out, taking measures, as well as some rare and underhand tricks, to find the people he wanted.

Being a man with a double character, it was normal for him to act one way in public and another in private. In the eyes of his colleagues, he was outwardly strong but inwardly brittle, behaving frivolously every day, so no one took him seriously. In the telegraph office building, only Jiang Xiaodian was regarded as important, and was everyone's favourite. The reasons were: first, because she was highly professional. Second, her family background was profound; despite the fact that they had quit the secret societies, in the eyes of ordinary people, they were still under the cover of that 'force'. Third, she was well behaved and got on well with everyone; although aloof and extravagant, as well as having quite a high level of professionalism, she never showed off or bullied others; she had never been involved in any wrongdoing, but was eager to help and generous to those in need. Fourth, she was beautiful. In those days, not many women went out to work, so female staff were highly valued in the telegraph office building; besides, she was a girl of exceptional beauty with the qualities of a movie star on The Bund.

Without making any particular effort, a beautiful woman could expect opportunity to come knocking at her door. That day, the director called Jiang Xiaodian to his office to make her an offer. Nobody else knew about it. Seeing her entering the director's office, and hearing the director's loud voice, Gao Q could guess what was going on. Besides, the director's phone book knew about the secret. Due to the importance of the matter, the director had made a record of his telephone conversation with his superior, and because it was a secret, he had locked the phone book in a drawer.

In the phone book it said: "Instructions from the Telecommunications Department, Ministry of Communications. We want to approach technician Jiang Xiaodian to go and work in Nanjing. Although it's a special assignment, she cannot be coerced to transfer. You must talk her into coming to Nanjing willingly. The reason for the transfer is that the party and the state need her. If she has any doubt, you can tell her that her future vocation is related to her present profession. I'm handing the matter over to you, so be sure to get the job done."

A special assignment from the government department. Anyone who gets such treatment will be sure to have a great future. The director tried to curry favour with Jiang Xiaodian, saying: "I'm sure you won't object to going to work in Nanjing, the headquarters of the party. It's a rare opportunity." Contrary to his expectation, Jiang Xiaodian did not jump with joy, but laughed:

"Really? I don't know if it's such a good thing. Let me have a think."

The smile on the director's face disappeared and he said: "Special assignments are always sensitive, so don't tell anyone else."

The next day Jiang Xiaodian declined the offer, throwing the opportunity in the bin, not even giving it a second thought. "Nowhere is better than Shanghai. I want to work here all my life, so I don't want to go anywhere else," she told the director.

Before long, another entry was added to the director's phone book: "Notice from the Telecommunications Department, Ministry of Communications: an extra quota is allocated for the special assignment, but Jiang Xiaodian must decide who will be the person."

The director was really confused by this. He had never come across such an odd thing before. So he passed on the instructions to Jiang Xioadian.

Once again she refused the director.

A few days later, the director received another phone call from his superior. The contents were almost identical to the first phone call he received, the only difference was that Ji Zhenren would replace Jiang Xiaodian. It was very clear to him that his superior was targeting the pick of his technical staff.

Surprisingly, Ji Zhenren also said no to the offer. Jiang Xiaodian has the capital for her refusal, but how dare Ji Zhenren refuse, a country bumpkin from Jiangxi?

However, the people in Nanjing were not annoyed: "We don't want to just get two able-bodied people. They must feel happy to come, otherwise it is a waste of time. OK, they can stay in Shanghai and we will get them transferred at another opportune time."

It was obvious that love had made the two young people muddleheaded.

The Shanghai summer was really unbearable. In previous years, Jiang Xiaodian was able to put up with the heat, but this year she felt unbelievably suffocated. She knew she could not lay all the blame on the weather. She had fallen in love, which made her mentally hot and dry; then she was targeted by Nanjing, which made her feel irritated. She thought that Ji Zhenren could help her, but he did not want to go out with her to enjoy the cool air. He had no time, as his mind was all on his books.

The friends who had eaten meals with her at the western restaurant understood her very well, so they often asked her to go out with them to enjoy the coolness of the open air, and after a few times, she found the outings enjoyable.

Gao Q also joined them a couple of times, and the most memorable time was when they went swimming. That day they went to a private swimming pool. They were the only ones in the pool, so they thoroughly enjoyed themselves. Gao Q did not do much swimming but busied himself taking pictures of the group. Before leaving the pool, Jiang Xiaodian said to Gao Q that she must have every single shot and film of her. A few days later, Gao Q went to her office and gave her the photos. He flushed before opening his mouth.

Jiang Xiaodian was composed, saying: "Feeling guilty? You've kept some of my photos, haven't you?"

"No, not a single one."

"But why did you flush?"

"Recently, I have been in a confused state of mind. It seems that I have a lot to say."

"This summer, friendship has grown out of our going out together, which is not something unusual. When the time is right, we can go out again."

"Can you and I improve our relationship one step further?"

"I have a form that needs to be taken upstairs. See you later." She went, and did not return.

The frequent contact between Gao Q and Jiang Xiaodian finally caught Ji Zhenren's attention, particularly a picture of her in a bathing suit gave him quite a shock.

It really showed a dubious relationship between Gao Q and Jiang Xiaodian, therefore it was like a thorn stabbing his eyes. The picture was taken at the moment when Jiang Xiaodian's upper body was out of the water and she was ready to move forward. Her long hair was crammed inside her swimming cap and her face was very smooth and clean. Her mouth was slightly open and her eyes were as sharp as tacks. An understanding smile that was only vaguely discernible lingered on her lips. She raised her right arm in the air like an archer while pushing her left arm down into the water. A fine wave was formed by her fingers pushing through the water. Such a posture completely exposed her body shape and features, particularly her right breast sticking up with her waving right arm, while her left breast stood out more with her left arm moving backwards. The water splashes were glistening on her flat, tight belly; her snow-white thighs pulled her straight calves, and her pointed toes showed off the charm of unbound feet. It was simply an image of a water goddess. And the key point was that even a fool could see that the picture was taken up close and in front of the swimmer, and that the photographer had ignored everything else in order to catch the moment more clearly. Only ghosts could imagine how the photographer had pushed himself into the water, raising the camera high in the air to avoid it getting wet.

Ji Zhenren could have imagined whatever he liked about the photo, but he stayed in his room reading his books all day. No matter how hard he tried, he could not conjure up in his mind any of the wonder of Jiang Xiaodian in a swimming pool. However, he did try to prevent her from having a new sweetheart, taking her to the cinema, which would push their love to a climax. An air-conditioned cinema was a good place for fashionable young people to go, where they watched movies from midday to evening, and from evening to midnight when the cinema closed for the day. Afterwards, their relationship was more resolved.

The situation was pressing for Gao Q, so he used a trick to make a final attempt to win Jiang Xiaodian over. It was a simple trick. He found her and grabbed her hands, saying: "You've driven me mad this summer. Let's go somewhere far away. I can help you leave Shanghai and work and live in a better place."

Pushing his hands away, she gave him a cold smile: "Elope? Stop making trouble, or we won't even become ordinary friends." Gao Q turned and left, tears in his eyes.

Before long, the Jiang family met with a major mishap which meant that Jiang Xiaodian then had no time to be concerned about love and romance.

A British business in Shanghai called Reading Overseas Trading (Ruitong Yanghang) was planning to sell forty-five units of machinery for cotton mills. These machines were ten times more efficient than manual machines, and those who knew about textiles were very clear that whoever owned them would greatly improve the technological efficiency of their cotton mills.

Among the bidders, there were three main competitors: Zhang's Cotton Textile Company, Jingchuan Cotton Mill and Jiang's Cotton Mill, which was owned by Jiang Xiaodian's grandfather, Jiang Zhijing. The competition was so intense that it naturally hurt everyone's feelings, yet it had not reached the point where the veneer of mutual respect was being torn off. Zhang's Cotton Textile Company had a background of belonging to a secret society, and therefore displayed a slightly overbearing attitude. It fixed 1,600 yuan as the ceiling price for a unit of machinery, saying openly that no matter how the talks went, this was the maximum price they would pay. Whoever could settle on this price would own the machines, and afterwards no more interference from the other two parties would be allowed. Anyone who violated the agreement would be punished by the market, as well as by the secret society under their rules. So the three companies reached an agreement, signing their names and stamping their finger prints on the documents. Each company had a copy and kept it in a safe.

Afterwards, the three companies went to their own talks with the British company. However, an odd situation appeared. The Chinese kept their purchase price at around 1,100 yuan per machine, but the British company had raised its price to 1,600 yuan. They talked and bargained, but no agreement could be reached.

Later they found out what had happened. The British company had obtained a photograph of the original agreement of the three Chinese companies and was well aware of their ceiling price for buying the machines; on the other hand, the three Chinese buyers had also got the British company's base price for selling the machines. It was said that an unknown person had secretly sold the information to both sides.

Therefore both the seller and the buyers knew what to do and were confident of winning. They would not complete a deal until an ideal price was agreed. Each of the three Chinese companies thought they knew the base price of the British company, so they all pressed for 1,100 yuan for a unit of machinery, and the British company naturally raised its price to 1,600 yuan.

These see-sawing talks went on for several days, then suddenly the British company sold all its machines to a Japanese textile firm, the Midoriwamaru Co Ltd for 1,250 yuan per unit. It turned out that the Japanese had obtained photographs of the original documents for the ceiling and floor prices for both the Chinese and British. They showed them to the British. It couldn't have been more clear that the Chinese would not agree to a deal until they had pressed the price down to 1,100 yuan. Under such circumstances, the Japanese set their offer at 1,250 yuan, a price the British had to accept. This is how the Japanese plot succeeded and they benefited themselves by taking advantage of the situation, thereby strengthening their position as the leading enterprise in Shanghai's textile business.

Shanghai was the centre of the textile industry in the Yangtze delta. The Chinese and the Japanese each shared half of the textile business in Shanghai. The Japanese were combating and suppressing Chinese national enterprises, so if these machines fell into Chinese hands, they would not only have improved the efficiency of their mills, but could also have become models on which the Chinese could have made their own, which was what the Japanese feared most. They breathed a sigh of relief after the Chinese failed to buy the machines.

Such a result was the worst for both the Chinese and the British, so they swore to find out who this unknown culprit was.

A few days later, a rumour was spreading that in order to seek self-interest, a Chinese company had sold the photographs of the Chinese agreement to the Japanese and the British, but there was no mention of the company's name. So the three Chinese companies began to speculate and accuse each other. No one could justify themselves, so they resorted to violence. People from all sides got hurt and one member of staff from the Zhang's company died. Meanwhile, the British did not rest, either. They rushed to find out who had leaked their information.

At this very moment, some reliable information appeared, saying that a manager from Jiang's Cotton Mill had concealed his identity and done the dirty deal. What surprised everybody was that he even had a photograph of the British telegram from London: "*Our base price is 1,100 yuan per unit of machinery; try to get a higher price; no negotiation and no deal if it is below this price.*" He sold this photograph to the three Chinese bidders and also to the Japanese company along with a photograph of the Chinese agreement, then he had run away after taking the money.

The whole truth had come out. It was the vile man from the Jiang's company who had caused the trouble. The owner, Jiang Zhijing, knew nothing about it, but they demanded that he hand over his manager. Then the police found a man's dead body near the Huangpu river; it was the Jiang's manager, who had died of multiple knife wounds and on whose body the photographs of the telegrams were found. Consequently, the Jiangs were accused of silencing their manager by killing him, an accusation they found it difficult to defend.

Calamities come in succession and before long, new evidence emerged against the Jiangs. An examination showed that the British telegram was transcribed by Jiang Xiaodian.

Jiang Zhijing was desperate. Many years ago, after paying a huge sum of money, the family managed to withdraw from the secret societies. He was baffled as to how they could have fallen into such misfortune, being harassed by the underworld as well as the British. What could he do?

It was a grave matter, but he kept it a secret from Jiang Xiaodian, as he did not want the family's affairs to distract his granddaughter's focus from her job, which was a priority to him, and only when he could not conceal it any more, did he tell her about the matter.

He confronted her with the photograph of the British telegram. She was puzzled: "It's my handwriting, but I can't remember where I threw it away. How did you get hold of it?"

"Somebody has engaged in a dark plot to go against us," said Jiang Zhijing. "We can't wash our hands of it. This time it's going to be difficult for us to avoid disaster, but keeping your job is my priority." He then went on: "We mustn't get your work place involved, or you could lose your job, or be prosecuted. You must insist that you got it from me, then let me find a way out." Stupefied, Jiang Xiaodian was lost for words.

She went to see Ji Zhenren, who was also dumbstruck after being told what had happened. Together they began to analyse the telegram, and gradually they started to remember some details about it. At the time, they were arguing about something and she was in a temper; crumpling the telegram into a ball she threw it into the waste bin. She could not understand how this crumpled paper could have flown out and landed in the hands of someone with an axe to grind. Normally, only she had the key to her office and she would do all the cleaning herself. Every day, at nine o'clock in the morning the cleaner would wait in the corridor to collect the rubbish from her. She really could not recall on which day she threw the telegram away, and if she had thrown it away, who would then have opened and read it? The cleaner or someone else? And after reading it, they then delivered it to the related people? Who could it have been? It was so odd.

Ji Zhenren gave it another analysis: "At some stage that crumpled piece of paper accidentally fell into the hands of someone who was mad about making money. In secret, he investigated its intended recipients and discovered how valuable it was. He then made some further investigations, and came to know about the links, subsequently carrying out his plan to make money. The most noted feature of the plot is that it was not aimed at your family, and you were found out only after the police examined the telegram and confirmed it was your handwriting." Jiang Xiaodian's mind was in turmoil, so Ji Zhenren added: "We cannot rule out another possibility, which is that from the beginning the person was targeting your family, and their sole aim was to bankrupt your family and seize your property. If that was the case, the waste bin was not emptied by you, but someone entered your office and dug it out of the waste bin. They then carefully carried out their plan."

Jiang Xiaodian's mind returned to normal and she shouted

abruptly: "That's it. I'm a hundred per cent sure that's what happened. That's it. That must be it. Because when I used the cipher of the British company to create those several pages of disordered words and numbers, I only put in a few sentences of the telegram. What you decrypted and I wrote down was the core content of the telegram, with only the base price, no mention of the goods, or the sender and the recipient of the telegram. Who would have known that this was the British company's base price for cotton machines? So, I can say this person must have known about the telegram and specially gone to my office and stolen it. This person was targeting me and my family."

Simmering with rage, Ji Zhenren cried out: "Which means that apart from you and I, a third person knew that we were deciphering our customers' telegrams. That person must be the chief culprit, the arch enemy of your family. Who can it be? And why?"

Jiang Xiaodian was trembling with terror, but she still held out some hope: "The three Chinese companies came to blows and people were killed. Once people are killed, where a foreign company is also involved, the police have to deal with it. I wish heaven had eyes. Let us wait for news."

That afternoon Gao Q went to see Jiang Xiaodian at her home. She was touched by his display of concern about her. She was implicated in a sensitive case, so she could not talk too much about it. Gao Q then suggested that they go to a restaurant for supper; she did not refuse him.

Having not eaten properly for several days, she ate her fill of the best dishes in the restaurant. During the meal, her eyes glistening with tears, she said: "Although the police are investigating, the secret societies are controlling the situation. Our family is in a very bad situation from which it's hard for us to emerge favourably." Showing that he was genuinely worried about her, Gao Q said:

"You know about my family. We have some influence and contacts in both the government and the underworld. Let me try and get you some help." Jiang Xiaodian thought that once the conversation reached this point, except for the fact that her deciphering of the customers' telegrams could not be talked about, she could tell him some other information about her family, so she briefed him roughly about her family's circumstances.

"What you've said is pretty much the same as what I've learned from other sources," said Gao Q. "The situation is really very serious."

Then Jiang Xiaodian said: "You may not know that our director is a womaniser, and he has been trying to get at me for a long time. I did not tell Ji Zhenren about it, because I was worried that he might not be able to contain his anger."

Showing no sign of surprise, Gao Q cut her short: "I'd already guessed that. Let me come straight to the point. From the first day you came to work, our director has been fascinated by your beauty and his mind has been disturbed. Now the opportunity has finally come, not once but twice. When the Nanjing government wanted you to go and work in Nanjing, the old fellow wanted to use the offer to lure you. But you declined the offer. This time your family was in trouble. You wanted him to give you some support. No problem, but you had to satisfy his desires. On that day you told him: 'At the worst, I might die! I would rather die than submit! I know you cannot escape the responsibility for my family's recent trouble. You might have been the cause of the trouble.' He listened, waving his hand, and muttered: 'Go, go, go. I don't want to see you again.' You said: 'Wait, I will never let you go unpunished even if I have to die. You must explain clearly how you have collaborated with the Japanese and brought calamity to my family!'"

Jiang Xiaodian was dumbstruck. What Gao Q had described was as though he had seen it with his own eyes and heard it with his own ears.

Again, Gao Q said: "You said that you did not tell Ji Zhenren, only me about that old fellow's attempts to sexually harass you. But I don't feel that you trust me more than you trust Ji Zhenren, because you love him too deeply to hurt him. Am I right?" Jiang Xiaodian did not want to answer the question, so she swiftly changed the topic of conversation:

"Some words can be heard by eavesdropping, but how did you know about the other matters? For instance, the Nanjing government wanted me to go to Nanjing. I was told that no one else except me and the director knew about it, but you know. How do you explain that?"

After a moment's silence, Gao Q said: "It is obvious that your family affairs have been the immediate reason for your family and the underworld to have brought this situation to a head, the immediate cause of which was that piece of paper with your handwriting on it. I suspect that that piece of paper has something to do with that old womaniser chap. As to how he got it, and how he used it in the incident, we have no way of finding out the details. But how did he know that you had that piece of paper? It might be that somebody called his attention to it, or tipped him off unintentionally."

After hearing his words, Jiang Xiaodian became panicky: "You mean somebody else is behind him? Who might that be?"

Gao Q muttered: "What concerns me most right now is that you really love Ji Zhenren but not me!"

He did not reply to Jiang Xiaodian's query but found a piece of cloth to cover it up. She thought it was better to remove this cover today: "Forget it, man. Like I said I am a person who has made the ultimate achievement in reading books, and my views on things can be pretty close to the truth. You keep saying that you love me, and want me to love you, but I am more than clear that from the depths of your heart you simply do not love me. You are dominated by a more powerful desire, and I just can't figure out what it is!"

Gao Q was scared stiff by her remarks and fear filled his eyes: "This monstrous thinking of yours is really scary. Who said that I do not love you?"

"Why do you pretend you love me?" she said.

"I must go now," he muttered impatiently, "or I will be crushed to death by this repetitive talk of yours."

After Gao Q left, for a long time Jiang Xioadian was unable to hold back her tears.

The next day, Ji Zhenren went to see Jiang Xiaodian. It might have been because of the encounter with Gao Q the night before that she kissed him extremely passionately. However, he said: "I have been studying the materials left behind by your late father. Not bad, I've made some new discoveries." Incompatible with the present needs, he talked about her father.

"One day, I thought of the coded telegram that destroyed your father. I restarted my research and I discovered a very special material in the wrap. I firmly believe it was a duplicate of the Japanese statement severing ties with China before the Sino-Japanese war in 1894-1895. What was your father's intention in leaving this duplicate to you? We have tried many ways but we could not decipher the materials in the wrap. Are the ciphers the ones used by Chinese diplomats in those years? So, like the Japanese in those years, I compared the statement with the materials in the wrap and tried to decipher it. After a few days, I deciphered a long encrypted telegram. I had a read and it was the telegram the Chinese Embassy in Japan sent back to the Qing court. I imitated what the Japanese had done and revealed a corner of the ciphers in your father's wrap. I was very excited, because it means that I have the same deciphering level as the Japanese in those years. I carried on and I found that some of the coded materials in the wrap used identical ciphers. Among them there was a letter, your father's will to you. He said:

> "My child Xiaodian, you must bear in mind the following two things all your life. First, work hard and go all out to achieve success, devote yourself heart and soul to the nation and dedicate yourself to the service of the country to make up for your father's mistakes. Second, our Jiang family absolutely cannot be reconciled with the Japanese, who have never given up clinging to their aggressive ambitions towards China. The Japanese devils are our nation's sworn enemy and our Jiang family's sworn enemy. If you do not avenge your father, you are unworthy of being a descendent of the Jiang family."

Now I'm handing you your father's will in both cipher and plain texts. And I'm also handing you the Japanese statement severing ties with China, as well as the plain and coded texts of the telegram of the Chinese Embassy in Japan as a memento. Besides, some of the materials in the wrap have not been deciphered, and I am sure they were encrypted by one or several different ciphers. At the moment I don't have the capacity to decipher them. But I can get the job done if I am given more time. So I want to keep them with me. After I get them done, I'll return them to you. Please grant me this request."

Immersed in her father's will, Jiang Xiaodian nodded her consent without giving it a second thought.

Carrying the unsolved mysteries with him, Ji Zhenren left the Jiangs' house.

No one could have imagined that before long a duel between Ji Zhenren and Gao Q would take place at the railway station square, and that Jiang Xiaodian and Ji Zhenren would be lying in a pool of blood.

3 / XISHI

IN FACT, Jiang Xiaodian jumping off a building was a hoax single-handedly conducted by Gao Q.

It happened like this.

The Jiangs were in a hopeless situation. With his family's influence, Gao Q tried everything to help reverse the trend, but to no avail.

The underworld, a Japanese firm and a British business establishment were involved, and especially a man from Zhang's Cotton Mill was killed, so they would not let the Jiangs off easily. In the end, the related parties reached an agreement, deciding to hand the matter over to the underworld to deal with. They would then share the Jiangs' businesses and properties to compensate for the profits they deserved but had failed to obtain. Jiang Zhijing was old, so he could be driven out of Shanghai to live a life of vagrancy and suffering. Since Jiang Xiaodian was the source of the trouble, she had to be eliminated. A life for a life, fair and reasonable, a satisfactory result in accordance with the rules of the underworld.

To the director of the telegraph office, the matter was really a headache. It was his staff who had leaked the contents of the customer's telegram. Illegally deciphering a customer's telegram was against the law and was also damaging to the reputation of the telegraph office. It might even have stirred up an international incident if the matter had not been dealt with properly. For the time being, all he could do was to try and make the related parties believe that the piece of paper with Jiang Xiaodian's handwriting on it had nothing to do with her job, nor was it anything to do with the telegraph office, so he had no right to punish her. Coincidentally, the Jiangs took the same stance. So the telegraph office would not meddle in the underworld's dealings with Jiang Xiaodian, because if he had intervened, he would have been bogged down with trouble. He even sent money to the related parties, making them firmly believe that the telegraph office was innocent and that the Jiangs were to blame. Jiang Xiaodian was guilty, so the others had a reason to share her family's property; in addition to that, her family had to hand over all the profits it had made during all these years.

Therefore, the underworld teamed up with the British company; overtly and covertly they applied all sorts of tricks and got their share of the Jiangs' businesses and property, driving Jiang Zhijing and Jiang Xiaodian to the end of their tether.

The Jiang family had been living in Shanghai for generations. Jiang Zhijing would rather have died than leave the city. He burst into floods of tears: "Leaving my hometown in my old age is as good as dying in a strange land. It will be difficult for my spirit to return, and my ancestors would be very sad." He regretted getting involved with the underworld and having done unjust things; and now he had got himself into such a gloomy state with no chance to prove his innocence; besides, he had dragged his granddaughter down the road of perdition.

One day, Gao Q went to see the Jiangs again and they discussed how they could avoid Jiang Xiaodian being killed by the underworld gang.

At first, she would rather have died than leave Shanghai. Jiang Zhijing urged her to give it further thought, as keeping her alive was a priority. "The choice to leave is either because we have no alternative, or a conscious choice on our part to show that we absolutely cannot be reconciled to the underworld. Please leave, whoever understands the times is a wise person."

Gao Q then conceived a plan, and together the three of them worked out the key steps and the specific details. To put it briefly, in a certain location Jiang Xioadian would appear to 'die for love'. Of course, her death would be faked, but they had to make people believe it was real to stop the gangsters from taking matters into their own hands.

The reason for her to take her own life had to be sound, which was not an issue because people believed she had no choice but to die:

firstly, she had upset the underworld, causing them to gang up against her; secondly, the womanising director had taken advantage of her and added to the misfortunes of someone who was already unfortunate; thirdly, she was driven to desperation by love. It is easy to fall in love with a beautiful woman, as well as to get into trouble. There was no way for her to free herself from the emotional entanglement with two men, so she chose to end her life.

Then the location had to be right. It had to be open and highly visible, and suitable for the trick to be played yet for no flaws to be spotted. After examining a few locations, they decided the railway station square was ideal. Nearby was an abandoned courtyard house. It was said that after the family members died of illness, or a series of accidents, a *fengshui* master had counted on his fingers and concluded that the trains running past day and night had upset the Earth Dragon and all the demons, therefore the house was punished as a deterrent to others. It became a haunted house which no one dared to live in, nor was there any maintenance, so it was in a dilapidated state. It was less than two hundred metres from the square and its interior was hidden from view by a high brick wall around the perimeter. The double doors were on the verge of collapse, and half of the door was crooked. Anyone who dared to go in could only enter it by walking sideways. In the courtyard stood a dilapidated six-storey building, the lower part of which was out of sight, while the upper part towered above the wall. One day, Jiang Xiaodian, Gao Q and some of his friends got some rope, net and quilts, and they went inside the courtyard where Jiang Xiaodian tried twice to jump off the roof of the building. She was unharmed except that she had sore legs. They worked out how long it would take for people to run to the house from the square, and to reach the back of the six-storey building. There was time enough for them to remove the rope and net, and sprinkle blood around to make it look as if a head had been split open.

Thirdly, the prelude leading to the suicide had to be realistic, which needed the participation of Ji Zhenren. To make his performance either in the telegraph office building or at the railway station square look realistic, Gao Q thought that they had to keep the true situation from Ji Zhenren, but would explain to him afterwards, which he would understand as it was for the sake of saving a life.

And fourthly, the follow-up work had to be meticulous. To stop people smelling a rat, Jiang Xiaodian could not be left lying in blood for too long. As soon as people entered the site, she would be put into a car and driven straight to the hospital, where Gao Q had connections. He had discussed with the doctors that they needed to pretend that they had been unable to save her and had issued a death certificate. Then the funeral had to be simple but detailed, and after that she was to be secretly sent to Nanjing. Gao Q promised Jiang Xiaodian that he would choose an appropriate time to tell Ji Zhenren the truth, and then work out a clever way to transfer him to Nanjing.

Once everything was ready, they triggered the plan. As expected, Ji Zhenren was enraged by Gao Q, so the result was good. But nobody could have expected that when Jiang Xiaodian was standing on the edge of the roof about to jump, a gunshot would ring out. Startled, she fell, but into the net prepared beforehand. Apart from faking a head injury as planned, she grabbed some blood and applied it to her breast. At least this extra action successfully deceived Gao Q. When he ran over to her and saw blood on her breast, he really thought that she had been shot by a gun. He wailed while shaking her body, then he carried her to his car, which was driven to the hospital. He held her tight in his arms. Closing her eyes, Jiang Xiaodian pretended that she was dead. She dared not open her eyes, either fearing that someone would enter the car and give the game away, or that she was glad to see Gao Q distressed. Hearing his heart-breaking wailing and feeling his tears (or sweat) falling on her face, she had an inexplicable feeling of passion running through her heart, accompanied by a sort of happiness.

Afterwards Gao Q told her what had happened outside the courtyard. As soon as the gunshot rang out, he knew that it had been done by gangsters. It seemed the duel between him and Ji Zhenren, as well as her crying and shouting, had convinced the gangsters. When they saw her standing on the roof, they did not know whether she was trying to scare the two rivals in love, or really wanted to kill herself. A god-sent opportunity, better to open fire and finish her off. But the gunshot drew another group of armed gangsters to the site. The two groups knew nothing about each other's circumstances, so after shooting at each other, they all took to their heels. And no one knew who the second group of gangsters were.

For the whole thing, the most astonishing result was that Ji Zhenren was hit during the chaos of shooting. It was said that he had been moved away by his fellow villagers. Very soon reliable information emerged that he was dead. His fellow villagers went to the telegraph office, demanding an explanation. Tapping the 'Da Wan Bao' (Big Evening News) newspaper, the director said, "He was murdered for love, done in by gangsters. His death has nothing to do with his work. Please restrain your grief and accept the inevitable." The country folks were honest, not being very worldly. With due care and respect they took the newspaper, as if it was an official document. They stopped bothering the director but went to collect Ji Zhenren's items for daily use and the bookcases. They then carried his remains to a cargo ship bound for Jiangxi. Before the ship departed, in a symbolic gesture, the director took a few people from the telegraph office to the port to see them off, handing them some benefit payments, thereby finally sending off the spirit of the deceased Ji Zhenren.

Gao Q said that the news printed in the 'Da Wan Bao' newspaper could pull the wool over those country bumpkins' eyes, but not his. He believed that someone was behind that piece of news, because it could either have allowed the telegraph office to evade responsibility or have elevated the status of the underworld. The description of such a powerful underworld gang, exceptionally adept in trickery, had in fact given them publicity. These gangsters had no fear of being exposed or cursed, so both the gangs and the government departments would vouch for the article.

Jiang Xiaodian could not take any more of Gao Q's long and pompous speech. She asked: "You promised that you would deliver Ji Zhenren to me. Where is he now? You promised that nothing would go wrong, but how could he have died?"

Facing the angry Jiang Xiaodian, Gao Q could do nothing but listen. When he was so annoyed by her complaints, he cried out: "A life for a life. Kill me so I can go to heaven to apologise to him."

Embarrassed, she muttered, "My family is indebted to you for two lives, how can I demand your life?" She meant he had saved her and her grandfather.

But how her grandfather had been saved was quite fishy.

Jiang Zhijing sold his businesses and property. After paying off the related companies, he still had some money left, so he divided it into two parts. He took his part and went to Guangzhou, in an attempt to seek help from his friends and to bide his time pending a future comeback. He left the other part to his granddaughter.

The owner of Zhang's Cotton Mill had accumulated considerable rancour against the Jiangs, complaining their punishment had been too lenient. Feeling that he hadn't vented his hatred, behind the back of the gangsters and the other companies, he got the information about the ship that Jiang Zhijing was about to take. He sent a coded telegram to his diehard friends in Guangzhou, demanding that they kill Jiang Zhijing and take his money as soon as he arrived. But he did not know that Gao Q would secretly change his telegram, so his friends never met Jiang Zhijing at the port.

When Jiang Xiaodian heard about it, she thought of showing her gratitude to Gao Q for saving her grandfather's life. But then she was pondering an extremely important question, namely, that Gao Q had also secretly marked the customers' coded telegrams, and he had even broken some of the codes. How else could he have understood the Zhangs' telegram in such a short time and successfully changed the date from the 12th to the 13th?

She asked herself: in the telegraph office, how many pairs of eyes were on her and Ji Zhenren? When Ji Zhenren had warned her to be aware of eavesdroppers, she had not taken his warnings seriously. It seemed that apart from the old womanising director, Gao Q had also been watching them.

She was so scared that her whole body broke out in a cold sweat.

Could it be that Gao Q had been the orchestrator of the whole incident? Was there an unknown or tightly hidden relationship between the Gao family or Gao Q himself and the Jiang family's misfortunes? In all honesty, she really did not want to imagine such a thing.

Gao Q had to end his job in Shanghai. Somebody said that the Telecommunications Department of the Ministry of Communications had recalled him to Nanjing; or that he was sacked because he had created a very bad impression due to his involvement in the duel, which caused the death of his girlfriend, so that he went to seek his connections who then helped him return to Nanjing; or even that he had offended the gangsters in Shanghai so that he had to flee the city.

Nothing was significant, no matter how the rumours were spreading. But one thing was true. He returned to Nanjing soon after the incident and was assigned as Technical Chief of the Nanjing Telecommunications Bureau.

After Jiang Xiaodian arrived in Nanjing, she rented a small apartment in Wanchong Street, south of the city. After resting for a few months, she changed her name to 'Gao Yuncao' and started her new life.

In Nanjing she became a technician, doing the same kind of job she had done in Shanghai, an easy job for her. And of course, all of this had been arranged by Gao Q.

Although she could not understand, nor could she get an answer from him as to what had happened in Shanghai, she generally had a good opinion of him, and he was now a completely different person to the one she had known. His usual frivolous behaviour, the boasting and prattling, had all gone. Before her was a young man who could go about things steadily and was well behaved, amiable to staff, experienced, careful and reliable in business. She would often look at his back, wondering how a man could manage this? Did he have a split personality?

One day, all of a sudden, she called to mind Liu Hai'er and Zhang Jiayin. "The couple are my good friends. Should I tell them that I am OK? When they are free, they may go to Shanghai to visit me, and they will surely hear what has happened to my family, so they will definitely cry, and find an empty space to burn paper money for me." When she thought of this, tears welled up in her eyes. She then picked up a pen and had only written down 'Hai'er and Jiayin, last night I received the paper money you burned for me' when Gao Q entered the room and saw it.

His usual affability vanished. He snatched the paper from her and tore it to pieces, bellowing: "Don't you think your handwriting has caused enough trouble? It has only been a few days since your misfortunes ended and you have forgotten all about them? I tell you, Jiang Xiaodian is dead, so you must not have any contact with anyone you knew in the past otherwise, sooner or later, Gao Yuncao will be exposed, and your life will be in danger again."

Stupefied, she looked at him, crying miserably. She could not stop crying no matter how hard he tried to soothe her.

Gao Q's anger turned to worry. "To be honest," he muttered, "I did think of bringing your grandfather to Nanjing, or finding you a job in Guangzhou, so you could live with a relative. But after thinking about it again, I just couldn't bring myself to do it. Your grandfather used to make a living by wandering from place to place, so he knew all sorts of people. The probability of him being recognised is great, so for the time being we have to keep the situation as it is. Wait for a few years, and once the situation takes a turn for the better, we will find a way for you to be reunited with him."

With tears streaming down her cheeks, she sobbed, "But I am lonely. I need love. My grandfather is too far away, but you are close to me. Why don't you love me? I mean it. It'll be OK, just like in Shanghai when you pretended that you loved me."

Walking over to her, he held her in his arms, "I cannot be a substitute for your grandfather, nor can I be a substitute for Ji Zhenren; besides, I can't give you my love. I hope you understand." But she persisted with her silly talk.

"So you will not love me? But why?"

He then said: "How about this? I will love you as I would love my own younger sister."

She calmed down, muttering: "Sorry, I've scared you, brother."

One day she called to mind the poem 'Mooring on the River Qinhuai' by Du Mu in the Tang dynasty, wanting to see the river. She found Gao Q: "Brother, tomorrow is Sunday. If you don't spend the day with me, I'll go to the Qinhuai river and become a singsong girl. What do you think about it?"

Without giving her a glance, and in a bad mood, he said: "I don't have time. You go as you please."

The next day she naturally was in no mood to go to the river, but to the library instead. Some time ago, she had read the *History of the Southern States of Wu and Yue*, and now she was reading the *Random Episodes of the History of the Southern States of Wu and Yue*. Frustrated by reading, she wanted to find someone to have a lengthy discussion with about the books, but she knew that she would have difficulty finding a soul mate. These days, who liked to read such dull history books? She sat in her seat in a trance.

The woman next to her turned to look at her with curiosity. "Hello. We've been sitting next to each other for half a day. I noticed that your facial expressions are so rich when you read. It's because of the magic power of the book, isn't it?" she said softly. Gao Yuncao cast a sidelong glance at her, feeling inwardly surprised.

Subconsciously, she turned a few pages of the book, saying: "I thought that Xishi had flown out of the book. You gave me a start. You are...?"

The woman laughed: "Oh, I come here and read a lot. I noticed that you were very absorbed in your reading, as if there were only you in the room. I really admire you, a genuine reader. Well, I've read the *History of the Southern States of Wu and Yue*, so we might as well exchange views about what we have learned from this book."

They went to the lounge where they chatted until evening when the library closed for the day.

This gorgeous woman had a beautiful name Zhen Yanli (Yanli means beautiful). She worried that Gao Yuncao might not believe her, so she took out her library card. Gao Yuncao laughed: "You should be called Zhen Piaoliang (very beautiful)."

Then Gao Yuncao, from the point of view of love, talked about why she liked King Fuchai of Wu but despised King Goujian of Yue. But Zhen Yanli said that she liked neither of them; on the contrary, she liked Xishi very much. The wars between Wu and Yue made the commoner Xishi reveal her talents. As a tribute, she was offered to King Fuchai of Wu by her own King Goujian, who at the time was enduring hardships and tempering himself in order to accomplish his goal of revenge. Fascinated by her charm, Fuchai did what she wanted, and at her instigation he forgot all about his state affairs and in the end his country was defeated, and he committed suicide. A completely unarmed little woman had become an irreplaceable pawn determining victory or defeat during the process of toppling the Wu state, thereby achieving fame as being the first female spy in the human history of war. So, beautiful woman or not, she had to be tested in war, and being a war spy was the best thing for a beautiful woman to do.

Gao Yuncao was amazed by this woman, who had become emotional about the topic, as tears were welling up in her eyes. How could she shed tears over such a thing?

"I have no doubt that your tears are real. But I tell you that all the stories about Xishi and war were made up. We know that the historical facts of the Wu and Yue contending for dominance were mainly from the records of *The Commentary of Zuo, Discourses of the States'*, and *'Records of the Grand Historian'*. But none of these records mentioned Xishi, so I would say that during the wars between Wu and Yue, if there was a woman who had such magical power, all these books would have recorded it. I think you are wasting your tears," said Gao Yuncao.

Zhen Yanli wiped the corner of her eyes. Waving her hand, she said:

"No, no, no. It's absolutely true, I am completely convinced. In ancient Chinese war history, Xishi led the way, and after her, there were Yu Ji, Wang Zhaojun, Diao Chan, Liang Hongyu, Chen Yuanyuan and Li Xiangjun. These women were closely linked to victory or defeat in war. As a woman, particularly one that can be called a great beauty, we must follow the example of these ancient women. Only by serving the war, can our beauty no longer be cheap but have some significance; otherwise, it is a waste."

"Your view is quite interesting. But I feel that it is horrible when a beautiful woman forms a tie with war, and all her original beauty gets lost," argued Gao Yuncao.

"But in fact, in many battles in history, the later generations could not tell whether they were tragic war history, or sad romantic affairs. Or we can say that many historical events were the history of tragic wars filled with sad romantic affairs. Since this is the case, Miss Gao, can you say a war can be won without a beautiful woman?" replied Zhen Yanli.

Although Gao Yuncao had read books about war, she really could not answer this question, still less exchange views with Zhen Yanli under circumstances whereby she herself was filled with true feelings. However, this did not prevent her from having a good opinion of Zhen Yanli. She thought that Zhen was a special girl, a very interesting book reader, worthy to be associated with.

They became friends, and then close friends.

A gorgeous woman she met by chance had enriched her life in Nanjing. What a bit of luck when she was living on her own! she thought to herself.

Zhen Yanli did not appear in Gao Yuncao's life by accident, and her comments about Xishi being the first female spy in human history was not some casual remark, either. She told Gao Yuncao that she was an English teacher in Jinling Women's College. Her English was indeed good, but she was not a university teacher, but a secret agent of SSWS of the Military Council of the Nationalist (KMT) Government. Her purpose in approaching Gao Yuncao was to recruit her.

The recruitment had to be a complete success. Because once it was brought out into the open, there would be no turning back. If she failed, she had to remove the secrets from Gao Yuncao's head, which meant she would either have to kill her or turn her into a zombie, an iron rule in this business.

Yes, Zhen Yanli was Gao Q's colleague. The reason for her rather than Gao Q recruiting Gao Yuncao was that Gao Q had repeatedly stated that he could not kill Gao Yuncao if the recruitment was a failure.

But Zhen Yanli was experienced in this respect. She went into great detail and started to work professionally and, with extraordinary skill, she got the job done. When the last curtain was removed, Gao Yuncao was not taken by surprise. Keeping her calm, she told Zhen Yanli that she needed to give it some further thought. Zhen Yanli said, "You can go and discuss it with your good friend Gao Q." This reinforced what had stayed in Gao Yuncao's mind, namely, that Gao Q was a man with a complicated political identity. As expected, he told her that he was a member of SSWS of the Military Council. She didn't feel flabbergasted, although she was startled a bit. Again, she said that she would give it some further thought.

She then thought of Ji Zhenren. How nice it would have been if he had been here, so she could have sought his advice, even if her life was threatened. But he was dead. However, she had her father's last will that was decrypted by him. She took it out and for two days and two nights she had no sleep but consulted her late father and Ji Zhenren. Her father's opinions were very clear: He wanted her to repay the country with her service to remedy his life-long regret, and for her to set herself against the Japanese devils to the end.

But she needed the right environment to fulfil his last wishes. At the time, the Mukden Incident that happened on the 18th September 1931 had already infuriated her compatriots, and the Battle for Shanghai had taken place on the 28th January 1932, soon after she left the city. The environment was right, and now someone was providing her a platform. Was she going to take it? Zhen Yanli had fully explained it to her so there was no need to imbue her with anything else. In the final analysis, her late father's will played a key role in her decision.

"Yes, I will do it!" she said.

The ensuing process can be simplified as follows: before she was officially admitted to SSWS, she was sent to the Juntong's[1] training base where she received one year's intensive training. Firstly, she was subjected to political brainwashing. She had to pledge to devote herself heart and soul to the party and the state. Secondly, she was trained in the basic skills of being a secret agent. As to the third area of training, the basics of telegraphy, she had already mastered these skills.

At the base, the method for political teaching and cultivation was unique and strict. According to her superior, "In this base, we can make a human into a demon, and vice versa." The principles and ideologies were novel to her, but she learned them quickly and well. Of her own free will, she experienced the sanctity of the cause of the party and the state. In the end, she was awakened. Even if she was required to be like Xishi and lay down her life for the party and the state, she would have had no complaints whatsoever. "While I'm alive, I am a woman of the party and the state; after I die, I will be a spirit of the party and the state."

Juntong's basic skills training for being a spy was also strict and harsh. But she did not feel that she had had a hard time. She trained like mad, wrestling, hand-to-hand combat, shooting with rifles and handguns, as well as some other basic training. She invested more time and thought than the others. According to the training instructor, "This woman is mad, no matter how hard I try, I can't diminish her enthusiasm for training."

One year later she appeared in the SSWS office. With a frosty and mysterious demeanour, she frequently smiled sweetly, which made her look more icy and indifferent to fame or gain, but mentally she never felt disheartened nor down on her luck. Quite the contrary, at heart she possessed the latent energy of a volcano about to erupt. The lofty aspiration of engaging in a great undertaking was surging in her heart and sustained her.

She worked as a technician in the telegraph office as a cover for her identity as a spy. Except for SSWS, no one else knew about her new profession and new identity. Well, no one had told her exactly what to do yet, she was only tasked with some individual assignments. She knew that she was being tested.

But there was one thing she wanted to do immediately, a private matter between her and Gao Q. She wanted him to tell her how many secrets he had concealed from her. She wasn't happy after she discovered that he had been an SSWS member for many years.

She complained to Zhen Yanli: "Who on earth is this Gao Q? I know now that everything he has done has been for the sole aim of making me willingly become an SSWS member. But I want to clarify some issues."

Zhen Yanli's facial expression was complicated. She said that she could clarify one thing on behalf of Gao Q.

"He had no affection for you, but why did he chase you? The situation was like this. When in Shanghai, you were offered a transfer to Nanjing, to SSWS. But because we are a top-secret unit, therefore it is openly referred to as the Telecommunications Department of the Ministry of Communications. Both you and Ji Zhenren declined the offer, so the transfer failed. Now you know that anybody doing the SSWS job must do so entirely of their own will. There was no other way we could get you to come to us, so we used this clumsy trick, namely, to let Gao Q pretend to love you. If you had fallen in love with him, you could not have lived without him, so you would have followed him to Nanjing. However, you did not love him! This is the true reason why Gao Q pretended to be in love with you. I'm in Nanjing but I know about everything that happened in Shanghai."

"But after I arrived in Nanjing, why didn't he stop this, which resulted in me having the illusion that he still loved me? Ji Zhenren is dead, and I am very lonely. I still cherish hopes for Gao Q."

"This is not his but his superior's problem. His superior has not clearly ordered him to refuse you, so he can only maintain a lukewarm relationship with you. Yesterday, he went to his superior for instructions and, unexpectedly, his superior said that he should have ordered him to stop chasing you after you came to Nanjing, but he forgot to."

"What he has done is really disgusting. But I have decided that from tomorrow I will launch an offensive to get him to love me!" cried Gao Yuncao.

Zhen Yanli's voice started to tremble a bit, "Impossible. Because he is to marry soon, and I am the bride."

"Really? He never told me that you were his girlfriend."

"He only received instructions to refuse you yesterday!"

Gao Yuncao was a little irritated: "You…"

"We can do nothing about it, they are our orders."

Beside herself with rage, Gao Yuncao went to Gao Q's office.

"Before I break off my friendship with you, I want to know how many things you have concealed from me?" she shouted.

Gao Q went to close the door tight, then in an unhurried manner he began to tell her.

"I worked in the telegraph office firstly to cover my identity, because to attend a public occasion I needed this cover; secondly it was for supervision, because certain work we secretly carried out in the telegraph office had something to do with the military. As to what I concealed from you, I can tell you all about it now.

"You know that according to laws and rules, foreign embassies and consulates in China must use Chinese telegraph services. But the Japanese violated international law and they secretly installed wireless transceivers in their embassy and consulates in China and had their important telegrams processed by these transceivers. They only used the Chinese telegraph service for a small amount of plain text or coded telegrams. This disregarded the sovereignty of China. They knew very well that the Chinese police could not search their embassy and consulates, and the practice was economical, fast and safe.

"Regarding the Japanese actions, our true approach was that we were openly angry but secretly delighted. We had to maintain our sovereignty and protest at their violation of the law. Of course, they denied it. We were delighted, because the Japanese had set up a network of transmitters and receivers operating a unified system for its embassy and consulates in China and its Foreign Ministry in Tokyo. We had carried out surveillance, transcribing and decrypting messages sent by these transmitters. Their service began every day at eight o'clock in the morning and four o'clock in the afternoon. It was a very concentrated service, which helped us intercept them quickly. So, from the point of view of gathering intelligence, we wanted these transmitters and receivers to continue working, which helped us gather all their codes and ciphers over time.

"But a small quantity of their telegrams was sent via local telegraph offices throughout China, which our intelligence organisation could not immediately put under surveillance. So I thought of a method, an equivocal and not very clever trick, namely, to create an incident to let them know that in the Chinese telegraph offices, somebody was secretly deciphering customers' telegrams. Once they felt it was unsafe to use the local telegraph service, they might have all resorted to using their private services.

"I had a thorough grasp of the situation in Shanghai. You may still remember that once, in the name of producing examination question papers, I opened the telegram storage room for you and Ji Zhenren. I had already sensed that you two were secretly deciphering our customers' telegrams. So I deliberately revealed this behaviour of yours to Director Yang Tianhu without mentioning your names. I knew that Director Yang had always been on friendly terms with the Japanese, and that he had some sort of association with both the Japanese 'Company Faction' and 'Native Faction' in Shanghai. I was hoping that he would reveal this news to the Japanese, who would then fall into my trap.

"But things didn't proceed according to plan. Director Yang started to suspect that you were the one who had secretly deciphered our customers' telegrams. He sneaked into your office to search for evidence, and he found that piece of paper, on which was the telegram of the British company you had deciphered. As if he had found a treasure, he went to report to the Japanese. So the Japanese knew that as long as the British telegrams could be deciphered, theirs would not be safe either. From then on, including Shanghai, all the Japanese in China began to use their private installed transmitters to send messages. However, they carried on making an issue of that piece of paper. They bribed your grandfather's manager and created the disturbance in your family, so that they could have all those cotton machines for themselves.

"So, now you know that I was the creator of the bad precedent in your family, of course, unintentionally. This was not the end of the matter. The underworld gangs wanted to punish your family, while I had promised that I would help you. But I told you afterwards that I could not help. The truth is that I used my family influence and controlled the gangs. Their original agreement was: 1) Half of your family fortune had to go to compensate them; 2) Your grandfather had to be crippled by breaking his legs, keeping him alive but letting him suffer; 3) Your face had to be disfigured to make you feel you'd rather die than carry on living, which meant using two disfigured bodies of your family in exchange for the death of one underworld figure.

"I felt it was too cruel to have your grandfather crippled, and even more evil to have you disfigured. I then came up with a strange idea that I would use the underworld to force you to join us, falling on the protection of the military.

"So my family stepped in and the underworld gave us due respect. The final result was that there was no change to article 1 of the agreement. As to article 2, it was changed so that you and your grandfather moved out of Shanghai in exchange for not being physically hurt; and you were not to return to Shanghai on pain of being captured and summarily executed, the condition being that the Gao family would take care of all the underworld factions.

"Hang on, I haven't finished yet. My family demanded that the underworld disseminate different information, that is, that your grandfather had to leave Shanghai and you had to pay with your life for the death of a gangster. The reason I let them release such information was because I had a dark purpose. I wanted to force you and your grandfather to leave Shanghai for the sake of survival. Because your grandfather might have chosen to become crippled rather than leave, but he would have agreed if he could have saved your life, which is what happened.

"What happened afterwards you already know.

"One bad result of all this is that the Japanese got those cotton machines, which disadvantaged the Chinese textile companies. I am guilty of this and I have made a self-criticism in my report to my superior.

"This is the truth. I have no complaint no matter how you regard me or treat me, but I don't want to lose you as a friend. Meanwhile, I hope you will not leak what you know to other people and will be sure to keep all this secret to the end!"

Grief-stricken, Gao Yuncao cried: "You are sick beyond description! I don't want to see you again!"

4 / ASSASSINATION

At this stage of the story's development, there's something I should say.

After an investigation, I found that four generations of my family were involved in the story.

My great-grandfather Ji Huizhong and my great-grandmother Zhang Chengfeng died long ago, but their images are engraved in my mind forever.

My grandfather Ji Zhenren spent his life seemingly clear-cut, but with an unusually distinguished feature. Seventeen years of warfare had left him with two gunshot wounds and one shrapnel wound. Afterwards, he spent twenty years sitting at home painting one picture. After that, he would only do one thing over the next thirty years, telling his children and grandchildren stories about battles. Successively, eighteen primary and middle schools had invited him to be an extra-curricular activities counsellor; apart from this he was interested in nothing else. He had a touch of weirdness, giving the impression that he was a dull man. He looked dignified, proud and very strong-willed, but whenever he was approached, he was very reserved and cautious in every word and deed, as if symptomatic of some kind of occupational disease, which he would say was a certain kind of revolutionary occupational disease.

My grandmother Xia Yuhe was over ninety years old. Despite being in poor health and confined to a wheelchair, she still had an extraordinary disposition, looking frosty and mysterious. From time to time, she would keep people at arm's length. Let me put it this way, she was just like a very rusty, iron-mouthed gourd, that could neither be opened, nor smashed; seamless, but a rather hard lump. During all these years, her children and grandchildren's attempts to look into her inner world had all failed.

Regarding my father's generation (including my mother), my parents had a similar disposition, seemingly mute, and both were archaeologists of few words. They undertook fieldwork in other places, thereby spending less time with the family, meaning that they never fulfilled their duty to bring up their children, who were brought up by their grandparents. Our neighbours would comment: "We have never seen such parents, only giving birth to their children, but never bringing them up." As far as I can see, they didn't have much to do with the family, so there's no need to mention them in this story.

With regard to my daughter's generation, Ji Shan was a university mathematics teacher in city B. In her spare time she studied cryptography, and surprisingly she mastered the subject and reached a professional level. Every now and then she would represent her university to attend domestic and international academic conferences. She was really mad about the subject, and she would spend all her spare time studying abstruse material and had little communication with other family members. But strangely she would pester her great-grandma whenever she had a chance. Of course she had her own reasons for going into her great-grandma's inner world to see her secrets. From childhood to adulthood this had been her dream and that of other younger generations of the Ji family, but none of us could get anything interesting out of Xia Yuhe.

The following miraculous stories were told by my grandfather's former comrades-in-arms, which were published in the magazine *Military Documentary Writing* entitled: *The Life Story of the Family Who Told Lies.* Some of the details cannot be told here. If a new policy on declassifying information is unveiled, I will undertake an investigation and revise and supplement my story.

We were all bustling in and out due to wars, and up until the end of the Korean War, the Ji family members could not find time to search for their father who they had not heard any news of for years.

Ji Huizhong was from the Chinese Soviet Area, and he ran away from home. For the following decade no news of him reached his family, who gave up all hope of finding him, thinking that he had died in the war. However, during October 1950, news came from an unknown source, saying that deep in the mountains of Yunnan lived an old blind man who looked like Ji Huizhong. Although the source was unreliable, everyone was excited. At the time the Korean War was about to break out, so the Ji family members put this matter to one side.

After the war with the Americans ended, they remembered their father. A certain leading cadre of the central authorities came out, saying: "Our revered Mr Ji has made two contributions to the revolution. First, when the Red Army was having its most difficult time, with high political awareness he generously donated all his family wealth to the Central Soviet Area. Second, the Ji household has produced many rare talents, and Mr Ji's children are all loyal and sincere to the Party's cause, and have made many contributions to the revolution." So let us go and find him. As the central leadership had given instructions, what was initially regarded as unlikely became a reality, and he was found. After Ji Zhenren carefully examined the blind old man and asked him many questions, he confirmed that this was his father!

Ji Zhenren flopped onto his knees.

But no one could have expected that as soon as he heard that his wife had been dead for many years, the blind old man would have had a heart attack. After emergency treatment, his life was saved. What needed to be said could not be held from him forever, so Ji Zhenren told his father that his little sister had also died, almost at the same time as his mother. Hearing this, the blind old man uttered a mournful cry and fainted, which scared Ji Zhenren so much that he dared not mention any more of the sadness that had befallen the family members. But his father was a strong-willed man. After he recovered consciousness, he made detailed enquires about the whereabouts and the safety of the other family members. Ji Zhenren explained that his brothers, sisters and their spouses were all very well, and at the moment they all had urgent business to attend to, so they couldn't come to visit him.

Afterwards they all came. Mr Ji could not see, so he felt them one by one until they were all in tears. Having not seen his children for a decade, he could not recognise their voices, but enjoyed listening to them talking. What he really wanted to know was the circumstances in which they had joined the revolutionary ranks. To this question, his children seemed to have some painful secrets. They hummed and hawed, and no one could give a clear answer. Mr Ji misunderstood them, thinking that they had been good-for-nothings and had achieved nothing, therefore they were too ashamed to answer him. Impatient, he sat up in his bed, shouting:

"Tell me! Where were you when everyone was on the battlefield fighting for the survival of the country?"

"Tell me! When the revolutionaries shed their blood and laid down their lives to combat Chiang Kai-shek and to eliminate the Japanese invaders, where were you hiding and how did you keep yourselves alive?"

Questions! Criticism! Blame! The roars of the veteran hero of the wide world stunned his children.

Then choking on his phlegm, Mr Ji fainted.

Doctors and nurses rushed into the ward. They drove away Mr Ji's children and applied emergency treatment to him.

Mr Ji's children then hurried to exchange views:

"Did you see how after so many years, our father is still imbued with the same revolutionary sentiments and heroism. He will not be pleased if we don't have any decent revolutionary experiences and combat performances to tell him about."

"Although we had little combat experience, we were well aware of many of the battles. We could relate what we knew, combining truth and falsehood, and we could place ourselves in these battles, and then tell him stories about them. This trick could be vital for him to fulfil his wishes as well as to maintain his health."

It worked. Mr Ji was very pleased with his children's revolutionary adventures and he applauded every act of bravery on the battlefield. His children then breathed a long sigh of relief.

Afterwards the related department arranged for Mr Ji to live in a nursing home for disabled servicemen. But his children refused the arrangement, saying that Mr Ji had lots of children and that if they let their father stay in a nursing home, they could be blamed for unfilial behaviour toward their father. So every one of them tried to take their father to live with them. Mr Ji was a sensible man. He personally arranged a timetable and took it in turns to stay with every one of his children for a year, showing complete impartiality in the matter. His children looked after him extremely well and he was also extremely happy. After the first cycle ended, Mr Ji ended his happy life and died peacefully.

Only then did the Ji family's lies come to an end.

On that day, after Ji Zhenren told his father about the death of his mother and little sister, he knew that he could not carry on telling the truth. If he told his father the truth, that except for him, all his brothers and sisters had died, his old father would definitely not have been able to wake up again. At once he thought of a plan. He went to see his colleagues, asking them to pretend that they were his brothers and sisters, and to go to the hospital to visit his old father. He planned to slowly tell his father the truth once he got better. However, his colleagues thought that the lie had been told, so they'd better carry on with it, and only by doing so, could his old father spend his old age in happiness.

His colleagues all knew about the sad status of his family, which made them sad whenever they thought about it. The most unforgettable and tragic thing was the recent death of his twin brother Ji Zhenyi. The hardships of war had ended and the good life was on the way, yet he left the world in a hurry, and in such an unusual, tragic, but heroic way.

It was said right before everybody's eyes, that seven enemy agents had opened fire and that Ji Zhenyi's body was riddled with bullets. The crackling bullets penetrated Ji Zhenyi's flesh, but each one of them hit the bottom of Ji Zhenren's and his colleagues' heart. How could such a tragedy happen so easily? It was so odd!

At the time, New China had only just been founded, and the KMT secret agents were still running wild across the mainland. In November 1949, the related department of the new government intercepted a mysterious coded telegram. At once they assembled the top cryptographers to take emergency action to decrypt the telegram, and the result was that the KMT secret agents were planning to assassinate Chairman Mao on his way to visit the Soviet Union!

Afterwards all the coded telegrams between Taiwan and the secret agents on the mainland were intercepted and deciphered by the national intelligence department. In the following few months, centred on assassination and counter assassination, the two sides carried out a secret life-and-death battle. The end result was that on 27 February 1950 Chairman Mao returned to China safely, declaring the visit to the Soviet Union a success. According to official news, the new government had captured all the KMT secret agents who had participated in the assassination operation in one fell swoop, and the Taiwan secret agents on the mainland suffered a crushing blow.

Decades later the related files were declassified, and the truth of this incredibly shocking case was able to be made public. However, what the public did not know was that one more case was related to this one, which was called 'Case 5387'. Until today, we haven't seen any official information about it. Is it because this case cannot be declassified, or is just unworthy of being declassified? Or was it basically sheer fiction? People had heard different versions of the events, and one rumour said that three enemy agents related to that incredibly shocking assassination attempt had avoided being captured and went into hiding. Soon they received a second assassination order - to kill the CPC's expert cryptographer Ji Zhenren at any cost. This order was not sent through a transmitter, but in a most traditional way, hand-carried to the agents who were hiding in city B, although it took more than two months to deliver the message. But they headed off danger several times, and in the end they avoided being discovered by the Communist intelligence department.

It was said that in the meeting room of the Baomiju (literally: the KMT's Bureau of Secrecy Preservation, formerly known as Juntong and later renamed Military Intelligence Bureau) in Taiwan, Director Mao Renfeng smashed a teacup on the ground. Exasperated, he roared: "While Ji Zhenren is alive, we at the Baomiju can't keep any secrets! If Ji Zhenren is not killed, we at the Baomiju can get nothing done! If we don't kill him, our secret agents on the mainland will be discovered and killed one by one."

Another teacup was then smashed to the ground and he cried out, "Don't be smug with the little achievements we have made on the mainland; as long as Ji Zhenren and co still have their eyes and ears open, all the results for us are only a process. Only a process, do you understand?"

It was obvious that in the eyes of the KMT Baomiju, Ji Zhenren was a major scourge who had given them no peace of mind day or night.

It was March 1950 when Mao Renfeng smashed teacups on the floor after that shocking assassination operation failed. So he vented his anger on Ji Zhenren.

The main difficulty for them to kill Ji Zhenren was that he was off the beaten track. The Taiwan Baomiju could only infer that he was in city B but had little contact with the outside world; besides they did not know his specific address. There were too many important classified locations in the city, so where to find him? Or even if they knew where the site was, how could they access it and kill him?

Then the Baomiju got the news that Long Yun, the KMT's governor of Yunnan, had made an open statement in Hong Kong saying that he was to break away from the KMT and would travel to Beijing to take up the position as vice chairman of the National Defense Commission. Originally it had nothing to do with Ji Zhenren, but in the Baomiju there was a former subordinate of Long Yun called Lao Kai. For no specific reason, Long Yun reminded Lao Kai of Ji Huizhong, who was a former friend of Long Yun. Ji Huizhong went to Long Yun for shelter after he was purged in the Communist Soviet Area. Lao Kai vaguely remembered that a few of Ji Huizhong's children had joined the Red Army. Ji Huizhong and Ji Zhenren both shared the surname Ji. Were they father and son? It was somehow possible in theory. Lao Kai also remembered that Ji Huizhong had stayed in Yunnan to treat his illness, but he did not know if he was still alive or not. Well, better to make every possible effort, so after Mao Renfeng nodded his head, Lao Kai made contact with their hidden agents in Yunnan.

All Lao Kai's efforts paid off. In a mountain township in Yunnan, his agents found a blind old man called Ji Huizhong, and they learned that he was that former friend of Long Yun. What made their eyes light up with delight was that a son of his was called Ji Zhenren, who had joined the Red Army. He had not heard from his son, so he had no idea if his son was alive or not. The agents had a photo of Ji Zhenren, but it was utterly useless under the circumstances. The agents had no choice but to take this old blind man's son as the Ji Zhenren whom the KMT hated to the very marrow of its bones.

Although old Ji Huizhong could not see, he knew very well the evil ways of the world, and from then on he wouldn't even say a single word about his children any more. He made up his mind that he would keep his mouth shut until he saw his family members. After eight months, and by some very invisible ways, Lao Kai's men cleverly spread news to city B that Ji Huizhong was still alive. It was clear that these agents had followed the clumsy strategy of 'drawing a snake out of its hole'. By October 1950, through a convoluted route the news reached the ears of Ji Zhenren and Ji Zhenyi.

As soon as the Korean war ended, the Party organisation quickly arranged to send people down to Yunnan. They followed that peculiar clue, and they soon brought the old man to Beijing. Ji Zhenren was then taken to a hostel by a special car to meet the blind old man from Yunnan.

The scene of Ji Zhenren identifying the man, kneeling down and calling him 'Father' was clearly seen by the secret agents, who had tailed theblind old man to Beijing. Comparing Ji Zhenren with the photo, yes, this was the demon they wanted to kill. Only top-level security prevented them from taking action.

After being identified as the genuine father, Ji Huizhong, along with a man call Liu, was taken away by Ji Zhenren's work unit. Liu was Ji Huizhong's neighbour in Yunnan where he had looked after the blind old man for some years. This time he was given permission to come along and look after him again. The car took them to a large, heavily guarded courtyard house. After getting the luggage out of the car and getting Ji Huizhong settled, Liu was driven away and sent back to the hostel before he could clearly see anything in the courtyard house. But each day he would be driven to the courtyard house where he would spend some time with Ji Huizhong, because Ji Zhenren's work unit was concerned that old Ji was a newcomer who needed time to get used to a new place, so it was better for him to have someone he knew with him. The mysterious courtyard house and the amazing scenery of the capital impressed Liu every day; it was a real eye-opener. After being driven back to the hostel, he would talk to the guest staying in the next room about the novel things he had seen. A careless word can reveal much to an attentive listener because this guest was Lao Kai's man.

In grief, Ji Zhenren told his father about the death of his mother and little sister. His father immediately had a heart attack. The medical people inside the courtyard house resuscitated him but sent him to the main hospital outside. In hospital, Ji Huizhong was treated as an important official, and he was put in a single-bed ward. Liu was of course called to look after him but, anyway, there were doctors and nurses, so Liu had nothing else to do but chat a little with Ji Huizhong once his condition improved.

Ji Zhenren's twin brother Ji Zhenyi was a cadre in charge of logistics support to the troops, and he was still in Korea to finish his job. So Ji Zhenren's colleagues who had pretended that they were Ji Huizhong's children would often come to the hospital to visit and look after the old Mr Ji, which made the old man very happy. However, it provided the opportunity for the secret agents to carry out their assassination.

Four more secret agents were called, making seven in total. They confirmed the car which Ji Zhenren would be in, as well as the security arrangements. After an analysis, they thought that as soon as Ji Zhenren arrived at the hospital, the building and the corridors would be the most guarded, so it would be hard for them to act there. The only possibility for success was when the car was passing the main entrance.

It was 7 August 1953. In the drizzle, one after another, two cars drove towards the hospital. The front one was for guards, while the black one behind was for Ji Zhenren. After the guards passed the entrance, the barrier suddenly lowered, forcing the black car behind to stop. Instantly the secret agents hidden on either side dashed to the car and opened fire.

Unexpectedly, a man in the car suddenly opened the door and got out. Looking startled and confused, he ran towards an alley. The secret agents saw clearly that it was Ji Zhenren, so all of them chased him into the alley.

The guards knew instantly what was happening. They followed and ran to the alley. Soon fierce gunfire was heard from the alley, and the man running in front was riddled with bullets. The guards then opened fire and shot four of the secret agents, while three fled.

A few days later, Ji Zhenren's work unit held a grand funeral in the Babaoshan Cemetery. Several hundred people either in plain clothes or in army uniform came to attend the funeral.

Nearby, a different funeral was being held. Three men mingled with the crowd, and they were the three secret agents who had run away a few day ago.

A black Soviet-made ZIS-110 limousine was now seen to be slowly driving to Ji Zhenren's funeral. Someone gave a silent cry, saying this limousine was only for important central leaders!

The front door opened and out came a guard. Then the back door opened and out got a man who looked like a secretary. They walked to Ji Zhenren's remains, laid flowers and bowed to pay their respects to the deceased.

A mourner commented quietly: "The central leader's secretary and guard also came, and they must be representing the leader himself. Ji Zhenren was really somebody!" The three secret agents clearly heard it, and they released the grip on their pistols. Holding back their wild joy, they witnessed the whole process of Ji Zhenren's funeral. They firmly believed that the assassination of Ji Zhenren had been a complete success.

They soon withdrew from the city and made a detour to the border between China and India, trying to sneak out of China. But they were discovered by the Chinese border guards, two were shot dead and one fled back to Taiwan.

Later intelligence showed that the commander of this action was a man called Gao Q, who was highly skilled in the business and extremely crafty. In those years he travelled between Taiwan, Hong Kong and the mainland and he had never been defeated in action. His superior gave him handsome rewards for his successful killing of Ji Zhenren. Some would say that Gao Q was redeeming himself by good service, because he was responsible for the failure of a plan earlier in the year to embed a sleeper mole, codenamed 'Grasshopper', into the enemy camp. He was in charge of the plan, but it hadn't worked as expected. 'Grasshopper', who had access to a CPC department in charge of confidential work, did not respond to headquarters' requests and contributed nothing to several important actions after being in hibernation for many years. It made Mao Renfeng very angry with Gao Q. Luckily, through other means he thought he had found the target and killed Ji Zhenren (in fact it was his twin brother Ji Zhenyi that was killed), the sworn enemy of the KMT.

Old Ji Huizhong recovered and left hospital. He first stayed with Ji Zhenren for a few months. Ji Zhenren's wife had long been absent from home, so he was looking after his mischievous little son. Having taken on the responsibility of looking after his blind old father, he felt his ability was falling short of his expectations. In particular, he was a top-level cryptographer, and he would often forget things when he got to work, allowing the blind old man and his young son at home to sometimes go hungry. Afterwards his colleagues, who pretended to be his sisters and brothers, would take the old Ji as well as the young boy to their home and take turns to look after them for a year. Old Ji could not see and did not feel that anything was unusual. Besides, they were all his children so he was happy no matter whom he was living with. There was no problem for the little boy either. It did not matter whether he had a father or not. Wherever he was living, the male host would be his father, so he felt as free and easy as at home.

Yes, Ji Zhenren, who was neither able to fulfil his duty to look after his father, nor was he up to the requirements of being a father, did not die!

The assassination that took place on 7 August 1953 was codenamed 'Case 5387' by the higher authorities. It was highly classified so as not to let the Taiwan spies know the truth. In fact, the man who was killed by the secret agents' indiscriminate gunfire was Ji Zhenren's twin brother, Ji Zhenyi.

On that day he had just returned to China from Korea and hurried to see his father. So Ji Zhenren went with him to the hospital by car. They were attacked at the entrance. At the time the one who reacted quickest was the guard. Sitting beside Ji Zhenren, he pressed Ji Zhenren down below the seat almost as soon as the first gunshot was heard and threw his own body on top of Ji Zhenren. Ji Zhenyi had just returned from the battlefield and the gunpowder smoke had not completely dispersed from him. He got himself combat ready straight away. Instantly he was conscious that it was an assassination attempt and the target was his brother. Without another thought, he opened the car door and went off, pretending to be his brother, he drew the enemy agents to him. The agents did not know that Ji Zhenren had a twin brother. At this moment, turning the car around quickly, the driver sped back to their base and straight to the internal hospital. The result was not too bad; Ji Zhenren was unhurt, but the guard had been shot twice in the back and died.

After the incident, the leader of the department immediately sent people to investigate and very quickly they formed a clear picture of the case. They managed to beat the enemy agents at their own game, took Ji Zhenyi for Ji Zhenren and gave him an elaborate funeral at the Babaoshan Cemetery.

The reason for making a show of holding such an elaborate funeral was to convince the covert agents that Ji Zhenren had been killed. During the funeral, the related department had already spotted the three agents, but they did not arrest them on the spot, only secretly shadowing them to the border between China and India, where they were able to kill all three of them. But in the plan there had to be a living witness who could furnish information to Mao Renfeng in Taiwan that Ji Zhenren had died.

Many years passed and to verify the accuracy of the above account, I went to the related department and consulted some documents, which coincidentally would soon be declassified, making the consultation process much easier.

One document was a biography. According to what was written, there was indeed a funeral for my grandfather. In the *Biography of the Personnel of the CA Army* there was a brief introduction to my grandfather, and on the 15th page there was *The Memorial Speech for Comrade Ji Zhenren*. A note at the bottom of the page read:

Editor's note:

> Comrade Ji Zhenren was a prominent figure in the CA Army. He and his comrades-in-arm comprised the core technical and military competence of the CA Army. If judged by his important standing, role and contributions, he should have been the first to be introduced, but due to the lasting effects of the serious political nature of his wife's misconduct in her job, after a discussion with the leadership of the CA Army, his name was dropped to 13th in this book. We hereby testify."

After reading this page, two questions struck me.

The first one was the memorial speech itself. It was uniquely short at only 199 words. The contents looked highly concise, but they were actually ambiguous. I made an enquiry about the issue to the current leader of the political department of the CA Army, whose reply was: this speech was drafted by Comrade Ji Zhenren himself and approved by the leadership of the CA Army. Despite it containing no words such as 'repeatedly performing outstanding service' or 'making tremendous contributions', it lost none of its impact and authority, yet very precisely described comrade Ji Zhenren's unusual destiny as well as his unique contributions.

Later I heard from veterans of the political department who said that at the time, they had specially arranged someone to write an eleven-page memorial speech, but after my grandfather read it, he had raised his hand in the air, powerfully and rousingly, and said: "This is full of praise about me! You can use this 6,000-word memorial speech next time when I am really dead. I won't be able to hear it then, so my heart won't grieve over it. But this time, it must not exceed 200 words."

Shattering his heart, each piece is loyal. In his life Comrade Ji Zhenren unremittingly pursued the truth and gave his undivided loyalty to the Party, accustomed to being incognito and staying silently in the background. With his formidable political conviction and a high level of political consciousness, he was always loyal to the lofty spirit of the Party, grateful to the Party and followed the Party.

Behind the scenes he exhibited great ability, wisdom and sharpness. Comrade Ji Zhenren had always been ruthless with his enemies. In his life he fired not a single shot, but through his consummate professional manner and impressive professional accomplishments, he held back wars, saved the lives of generals and soldiers, and fought for peace and tranquility.

The Party's secrets meant more to him than life itself. Comrade Ji Zhenren was always discreet in word and deed. He scrupulously abided by the rules of his professional work, exercising strict self-discipline, never committing a single infraction against the rules, and cultivating a mindset of keeping a secret so that it became instinctive. No matter what the circumstances, he never revealed secrets in exchange for life, honour or self-interest.

My grandfather then said: "If you agree with this speech of mine, the funeral will be for me. If you insist on using those eleven pages, I will not die, but you can revert to the truth and mourn my brother Ji Zhenyi, the real dead one."

The second thought to enter my head was the editor's note. I had never ever heard that my grandma had done something improper which could have implicated her politically. What had she done? How serious was it? What was the impact? I wanted to be clear about these questions. I found all the people in the know, but they all refused to speak, keeping their mouths shut more than once. All right, I would not ask them any more. In all these years my grandma had lived a peaceful life. I did not see any issue unless she was really disciplined in the early years?

Besides, I consulted some newspapers issued during the Korean war. One paper gave the following account:

In the front line, Ji Zhenyi was responsible for supplying goods and materials to the troops. Before the truce was signed, his convoy was targeted by an enemy aircraft. He then drove a truck and sped away from the convoy, successfully drawing the aircraft deep into the mountains, thereby safeguarding large amounts of combat supplies, but he and his vehicle were destroyed and burnt. He died on the battlefield in Korea and his remains could not be found and brought back to China.

I linked this report to my grandfather Ji Zhenren: to support his faked death by a coordinated action, without anybody knowing, the newspaper published this false news. One can well imagine the strength of the operation behind it, where there was a considerable probability that the high-level leadership could have been alerted, which also indirectly demonstrated that the life and death of Ji Zhenren could have had a big impact on certain things.

5 / A SCHEME

JI SHAN REMARKED that the peculiar things that had happened to our family's older generations really made her scratch her head. But they had aroused my interest so much that I made some deep enquiries about them. After some investigations, I discovered that the mystical nature of the Ji household started in Huai'en township in Ruijin during the Chinese Soviet period. It was Ji Huizhong's and Zhang Chengfeng's totally different judgement of the situation and their weird actions that set Ji Zhenren and his siblings down a mysterious path.

When Ji Huizhong was on his deathbed, Ruijin was in its heyday during the Soviet period.

At the time, the county, which would be called the 'Red Capital' by later generations, was the capital of the Chinese Soviet Republic, where the political climate was unimaginably flourishing. State power! The Communist Party of China (CPC)! The inexhaustible energy attracted and appealed to all living beings. Many men and women with high ideals were amazed by the phenomenon, and they were overwhelmed with admiration for the Red Republic.

Ji Huizhong was one of the admirers, despite the fact that he should have been on the opposite side to that of the toiling masses. An influential man from Ruijin, who used to make a living away from home. He had almost died several times in the carnage of war and was unshakable in his determination to follow the CPC. In his study, books about Marxism and Leninism filled one side of the wall, and he could absolutely be called a Marxism believer. If this was not enough, have a look at this fact: as the saying goes, great men's sons seldom do well. But the Jis had been prosperous for five generations, being well known in the villages and townships of Ruijin for their wealth. When it came to Ji Huizhong's generation, he was famous for another imposing reason. He earned a name for himself in the region for his financial help as well as political support for the Chinese Soviet Republic, and several times he donated his family wealth to the Red Army.

When he was critically ill and on the brink of death, his family could not figure out what he meant when he raised two fingers in the air and refused to breathe his last breath.

He was dying of an acute attack of tuberculosis. His health had been going down and several times he nearly died, so his family feared that he would not get over it this time. Repeatedly his wife put her ear to his mouth, but all she heard was a rumbling sound like the air puffing out of an old pair of bellows. No last words. Several times she used her fingers to dig out the red and white, thick phlegm from his smelly mouth, then bent down to listen, but she still could not hear any words. Yet with absolute stillness he raised his arm, and the two fingers stuck up even higher.

Unprecedentedly panic-stricken, the family members crowded round the bedroom door. In silence they prayed for him as he was on the verge of dying at any moment. Ji Huizhong had two sons and three daughters. Ji Hongying was the eldest daughter after her two elder brothers. The other two girls were Ji Hongmei and Ji Xiaomin. Ji Hongmei was the most educated among the three sisters, having received both private and public education and was now a teacher in an evening school. She had twice read the novel *Unofficial History of the Scholars*, and she remembered the description in Chapter Five of an imperial college student called Yan, a miser who refused to breathe his last breath when he saw two rush sticks burning in the oil lamp. She looked around, but she could not see an oil lamp with two rush sticks. Suddenly she cursed herself. Her father was an enlightened man and generous all his life; how could she think of him as an old miser?! Then the mother's knitted brows turned smooth. She muttered: "I know what he wants. He wants us to call back his two sons."

Ji Hongying mumbled, "Are you sure, Mother? But it was he who drove them away from home."

Ji Hongmei was a quiet girl with a quick temper. "Father is raising two fingers, so he must mean it. Let us hurry and bring them home!"

"Hongmei, you are mad to think of your brothers," teased Ji Hongying. "They are thousands of miles away, how can we find them? It's not easy. Look at you, so impatient. We all know this selfish little calculation of yours." Embarrassed, Ji Hongmei flushed.

Hongmei was born into the Liu family. When she was three years old, there was a catastrophic flood in Ruijin. A pig, which her parents had made a huge effort to raise, was washed away by the flood water. When her father, Mr Liu, jumped into the water to search for it, he saw Ji Zhenfu, the eight-year-old son of the Ji family from of a nearby village township. Holding a tree branch, the boy was washed toward the rapids and would have been swept away by the flood water. Mr Liu threw himself into the water. After he became exhausted and pushed the boy to the bank, he was engulfed by the waves. Mrs Liu was four months pregnant. Overanxious and grief-stricken, as well as rushing around to search for her husband day and night, she had a miscarriage. It was a boy. The Lius had already been in dire straits with two young girls to raise. Now the pillar of the family had died, it was even harder for them. The Jis suggested that they pay a debt of gratitude. Mrs Liu said that she would like to send her daughter Hongmei to the Jis to be Ji Zhenfu's child bride. But the boy's mother said that it wouldn't do, because she could not let her benefactor's daughter be a child bride. She promised that she would bring Hongmei up like her own daughter, and marry her to a good husband with a house and a dowry. Mrs Liu did not agree, saying that she did not want the Jis to bring up her daughter for nothing. If the Jis were happy to take Hongmei in, she could only be a child bride. Mrs Ji had no choice but to let Hongmei and Ji Zhenfu kneel down and kowtow as a token of being husband and wife. Only then was Mrs Liu's mind put at ease. Before long, Mrs Ji gave birth to twin sons, Ji Zhenren and Ji Zhenyi, and she made the decision to give Ji Zhenyi to the Lius as an adoptive son, named Liu Kailai.

After Hongmei came to the Ji family, outsiders regarded her as a child bride, but the Jis raised her just as if she were their own daughter, even changing her surname to Ji. Not only did she suffer little discrimination, but she was the most spoiled among the Ji children, living like a person of noble birth. When Hongmei was little, she had no intention of being the Jis' daughter-in-law. Only when she grew into a pretty young lady did she have such a mindset, thereby intentionally or unintentionally distancing herself from Ji Zhenfu. She stopped acting spoilt in front of him, and when the two of them were alone together, her face would become flushed for no reason. Sometimes, when Ji Zhenfu was sent by his father on business trips for three to five days, she would become dispirited and missed him very much. It went on like this until Ji Zhenfu left home for a faraway place.

Ji Zhenfu, who was eighteen, and Ji Zhenren, who was not yet seventeen, left home on the same day. Their father, who had fallen out with their mother, made the resolute decision to send his sons away to make a living, saying that a true man should be ready to offer his services wherever they are needed; if they wanted to amount to something in the future, they had to temper themselves anywhere in the country, to endure suffering and to gain extraordinary skills.

The father himself was like this when he was young. The next day after his wedding, he left home with several hot-blooded young men. His new bride Zhang Chengfeng, the daughter of a wealthy and influential family, was abandoned at home. At the time, the Boxer Uprising was happening in the North. Burning with righteous indignation he and his friends rushed to join the boxers. Later, they heard that Sun Yat-sen had risen in revolt in the South, so they went there to join in the fun. After some life-and-death encounters, he seemed to be disillusioned with the world, pulling back his ambition of carving a niche for himself. He then remembered that he had a wife at home. When he returned, he was 36 years old and his wife 28, but she had no problem in giving birth, and in the following years they had three sons and a daughter. After living a stable life for some years, his ambitions overtook him again. He left home and drifted for a few years. After he returned, he and his wife had one more daughter.

Years later a succession of unforeseen events happened in the country. Again, he failed to restrain his restless heart. However he suffered from tuberculosis; apart from illness, he was old and could no longer endure any physical suffering, so he turned his eyes to his sons. After thinking for a few months, he decided to drive his middle-school-student sons Ji Zhenfu and Ji Zhenren into the outside world. Threatening suicide, the mother tried to stop her sons leaving. But one morning after she woke up, she saw that the boys had gone. Ji Zhenfu was sent to Liu Yiping, Ji Huizhong's former accomplice in the United League of China. Liu had taken part in the Baise Uprising in Guangxi in 1929, then he joined the Red Army's 7th Army. With his help, Ji Zhenfu became a foot soldier in the 19th Division of the 7th Army and went on to fight in Guangdong, Hunan and Hubei provinces. Ji Zhenren went to Shanghai. He asked for help from an old sworn friend of his father, who had accomplished fame and fortune in the city. Feeling that he did not have enough education, he chose an interesting course to learn. He went to register at the telegraph school. At the time, a telegraph clerk was a most fashionable job, and he was able to work in the Shanghai Telegraph Office as soon as he graduated from the school.

The two sons hadn't visited their family for three years, mainly because their father had stopped them from doing so. He wanted them to focus on their work.

On that day, seeing her husband raising two fingers on his death bed, Zhang Chengfeng decided to send Ji Hongying and Ji Hongmei to go and bring Ji Zhenfu home from the Red Army base between Hunan and Hubei. Feeling nervous the two girls were reluctant to go. After a lot of dawdling, they still had not embarked on their journey. Kicking a stool away, Zhang Chengfeng howled: "Your father wants to see his sons before he dies, what is wrong with that? Taking part in revolutionary activities has made you two unruly. Is it that people in the revolutionary ranks are not raised by a father and a mother? Today, I want to see who dares to prevent your old father from fulfilling his last wish!" Looking at each other, the two girls agreed immediately. But who would be sent to Shanghai? Zhang Chengfeng thought about it for a while. She then went to see Mrs Liu, telling her that she would like her son Liu Kailai to make the trip. Mrs Liu was a sensible woman. Liu Kailai was originally the son of the Jis, so there was no reason for her to stop him from going. But Liu Kailai had joined the army, so what she said did not count. Zhang Chengfeng knew that Liu Kailai had been recruited by the Red Army when they were expanding, so she went to see the senior officer. Surprisingly, the senior officer readily agreed; besides, he sent a medical officer to the Jis to treat Ji Huizhong.

Tears welled up in Zhang Chengfeng's eyes. "What an affectionate army!" When she had finished saying the words, she gave a strange smile that no one noticed.

Then she prepared the girls' travel money and two letters for her sons. Before she saw the girls and Liu Kailai off, she urged them again and again: "You must not open the letters until you see your brothers in person. I have consulted the fortune teller Gao and he said that if the letters are opened before you see your brothers, your father will die straight away. Pay attention to what you are told!" The three youngsters lowered their heads and, seeing 'To Be Opened Personally By My Son' on the envelopes, they felt that it would be a weighty trip.

The army medical officer treated the dying Ji Huizhong for seven days until he was finally out of danger. Lowering his two stiff fingers, he muttered: "Go and find Zhenfu and Zhenren. I want them to join the revolution in Ruijin!" As soon as his wife heard it, she said: "I've already guessed what you wanted and sent Hongying and Hongmei to find them. I didn't realise that you wanted them to come home and join the revolution. I thought you only wanted to see them and that they could leave again. All right, you have the final say."

Ji Huizhong was still weak. Turning to the doctor, he muttered, out of breath: "It is not that I miss my sons. In my life, I used to make a living from place to place. In recent years I came into contact with the Red Army, and I realised that the truth is in the hands of Zhu De and Mao Zedong. The Communist Party is trustworthy and the Red Army has the most promising troops. Today, if I don't call back my two sons and let them join the revolution in the centre of the Communist base, I am the biggest fool under the sky. I cannot set my mind at rest until I hand them to Zhu De and Mao Zedong, otherwise I will die unhappy! As well as this, I will donate more of my property to the Red Army."

The army medical officer saved Ji Huizhong's life, and he also passed on his words to Zhu De and Mao Zedong. "How open-minded Ji Huizhong is! His words are more precious than the property he has donated. Expropriating local tyrants and distributing their land among the poor is not our final goal, but to have people's support is a matter of great importance!" So said a leading cadre in a meeting.

Normally, when a matter came to this stage, it ran extremely smoothly. Ji Huizhong finally turned the corner; if everything went well, his two sons would be home to be reunited with the family and make revolution on the doorstep. What a wonderful thing!

But it was not that simple, because three schemes had been planned behind the whole affair.

The first scheme was devised by Zhang Chengfeng.

Let me say some more about Zhang Chengfeng. From a wealthy and influential family with a Hakka background from south Jiangxi, she never considered herself an ordinary woman; and indeed she had some capacity for dealing with things in society, a woman with wide experience. The first setback in her life was that her husband left home

after their wedding day. In desperation she resolved to make the
decision that she must neither regret marrying him, nor kill herself, nor
leave. No matter how long it took, she would stay and keep waiting
until this heart-breaker came home, to see what kind of person this
lousy man, who had done such a thing to her, was. For a newly-wed
young woman, it was hard for her to bide her time. Although her body
stayed idle, her eyes, ears and head were busy. By enquiring, paying
close attention and thinking over the major events that were happening
in the country, she visualised the condition of her fickle-hearted man,
counting on her fingers this bastard's life and death. Although she had
not heard from him for many years, she firmly believed that this
damned man was still alive. One day the cursed one came home at last.
Although she had wasted so much of her beautiful youth, she also
gained a lot from this extraordinary and painful experience, which
tempered her insight as well as giving her the capacity for seizing
opportunities. Feeling that she had a precise grasp of the recent
situation inside and outside the Soviet Area, she came to a gloomy
conclusion: that the thriving and prosperous scene of the capital of the
Soviet Republic was temporary. Ruijin might soon become a scene of
bloody red; the Red Army's fate was sealed. It was only her
imagination, which could make her lose her head if she made a slip of
the tongue. Luckily, she kept her thoughts to herself. When she said to
the leading cadre "The Red Army is absolutely invincible", she was
obviously telling lies, but the strange smile reflected her true thinking.
She, who had spent so many nights thinking about her life, believed
the Red Army would meet three calamities.

Calamity one: the determination of Chiang Kai-shek to eliminate
the Red Army and his powerful military force. Combat effectiveness is
the key statement for a military commander. Between the Red Army
and the KMT (Nationalist Army), anyone with any sense could see
easily who would be the winner.

Regarding herself as a reasonably discerning person, she then
foresaw the second calamity, which could happen within the
Communist Party, whose political movements frequently went too far.
Like the campaign to purge the 'AB Tuan' or 'Anti-Bolshevik Group'
elements which had plunged the whole Soviet Area into chaos, causing
many innocent officers and soldiers to be wrongly killed. The reason
for the Jis' safety was firstly due to their many donations to the Party,
as well as their son Ji Zhenfu being in the Red Army fighting in Hunan

and Hubei. But Zhang Chengfeng regarded these merits as unreliable. Because no matter how, the Ji household could not shake off its history of being landlords and rich gentry, and therefore some time in the future they could still be knocked down by a political movement.

The third so-called calamity seemed even less worthy of being taken seriously, but Zhang Chengfeng felt that she could foresee it. The Soviet Area in south Jiangxi and west Fujian was originally founded by Mao Zedong, Zhu De and Peng Dehuai. But after the Central Committee began to send senior cadres to the base, the original organisation system underwent a change, and Mao Zedong and the other leaders were no longer able to be the *de facto* leaders who had controlled the base before. There was an indication that they had been pushed to one side and cold-shouldered. Someone made a prediction that conflict between the two leadership groups would be unavoidable.

So, Zhang Chengfeng, who was a grass widow (a woman whose husband is absent for prolonged periods) when she was young, and who used to ponder minor matters when she had nothing else to do, slipped back into her old ways. She abandoned her life of tranquility, but was tormented by the affairs of the Chinese Soviet Republic and, being frantic with worry, she had no appetite and was unable to sleep. When her husband was critically ill, she watched over him. The worst calamity she sensed was not that he was going to die, but that the dark line of calamity that ran in the blood of the Jis was becoming thicker and thicker. Having been a bastard all his life, his death was not to be regretted. But if their children were unshakable in their determination to follow the Communist Party, the consequence would be that they would not only lose their ancestral estate, but their lives.

Therefore, she planned a plot in response to her husband's request to bring back their two sons, seizing the opportunity to attain her own goal. She had no intention of calling her two sons back; instead she would send her two daughters away from a place where she thought they were likely to get into trouble. She wrote two letters and handed them to the girls, in which she explained why she was sending them away and did not want them to return. Her stance was poles apart from that of her husband's, sending out a message that she had little confidence in the Communist Party and the Red Army. She firmly believed that as long as she could keep her children far away from Ruijin, they would be far away from calamity. When she had finishing writing, she bit her finger and wrote down at the end: " You will live as long as you leave Ruijin, but you will die if you return. The Jis' children must never be associated with the Communists!"

Besides the above reason, there was another reason for her to send Ji Hongmei away, which she wished to hide. So she planned a second scheme.

In the previous two years, the women's liberation movement was carried out in a spectacular way in the Soviet Area, and freedom of marriage was the most distinguished achievement. For a while the young men and young women were the most active, and the freedom to choose their spouses was slow to happen. A folk song become popular: *"Let me tell you, there is no sharing of wives in Communist society. A boy and a girl must love each other and be willing to marry each other; it doesn't matter if you don't have a matchmaker."* Ji Hongying liked to sing this song very much, and Ji Hongmei would also hum it when she returned home from work. Zhang Chengfeng would stop Hongmei singing the song, because the neighbours all knew that she would marry Ji Zhenfu sooner or later. The more Hongmei sang it, the more turmoil it caused in Zhang Chengfeng's mind, worrying that Hongmei would be taken by another man. So this time she took the opportunity and sent her away to marry Ji Zhenfu. Hongmei was nobody else's but Ji Zhenfu's. Earnestly and clearly she stressed this point in her letter to her son: the day when you see Hongmei is the day you marry her.

The two girls had no idea about their mother's secret plan, nor could they disobey her and open the letter before they met their brother, but of one mind they travelled day and night. Compared to their formidable mother, the youngsters seemed novices in scheming. But, it was not exactly the case. Liu Kailai, who was usually simple and honest, also hatched a plot, which was the third secret scheme I am going to talk about.

Someone encouraged Liu Kailai to plan the scheme, and this was Gao Yueming, an unusual figure in the Red Army. What made Gao stand out was that he was the chief of a mysterious unit of the Red Army, codenamed 'Red Star Unit 2 (RSU2)', a special department that always accompanied the Central Committee. Except for the highest commanders, no one else knew about its function and nature, which was classified as top secret.

As a matter of course, Liu Kailai knew nothing about this secret, either. What he knew about his mission was that he had to get Ji Zhenren back to Ruijin in perfect condition at any cost and by any means. RSU2 was in urgent need of a telegraph operator like Ji Zhenren. Chief Gao told Liu Kailai that the Red Army had tens of thousands of officers and soldiers, and that adding or losing one more was not a big issue, but that people like Ji Zhenren were indispensable, extremely rare for the Red Army. Getting someone like Ji Zhenren might be more significant than recruiting several companies of combat forces. This was the real reason for the Red Army commander readily agreeing to Zhang Chengfeng's request and sending him to Shanghai. Of course, he had to keep his mission secret. He was well aware that he was firstly a Red Army soldier, then secondly a relative of the Jis. He knew it and he was able to keep to his vow of loyalty to the Party.

After he arrived in Shanghai, he went to see Ji Zhenren. When they saw each other, both felt their eyes were blurred. Although they differed in many ways - one dressed in Western clothes, the other rustic; one fair-skinned and delicate, the other dark and tanned; one softly-spoken and mild-mannered, the other rough and ready; one with a reserved, ambivalent smile, the other simple, honest and direct - yet it was not hard to tell the striking similarity in their figures and facial features. If they had been wearing the same clothes and had the same skin colour, they could have passed as the same person.

After Ji Zhenren opened his mother's letter, he was even more surprised. It turned out that he and Liu Kailai were twin brothers. Dumbstruck, they hugged each other passionately, tears streaming down their cheeks. Liu Kailai then talked business, saying that their father was critically ill and he wanted to see Ji Zhenren for the last time, so Ji Zhenren had to go back to Ruijin with him. But Ji Zhenren said that their mother had said the opposite. They had a heated argument, with neither willing to concede.

Liu Kailai then said that the Red Army needed him urgently. But Ji Zhenren said that he had no intention of serving in the army at all. Liu Kailai argued that their mother had been shrewd all her life, but that she was muddleheaded in two respects. Firstly, she had carelessly let their father leave home and run wild outside for so many years, which had destroyed her shrewdness for half of her lifetime; secondly, she had carelessly determined the nature of a revolutionary army, concluding that the days for this army were numbered; she thereby pulled the wool over her children's eyes, leading them down the wrong path. Ji Zhenren responded that no one could make him change his mind, and he wanted to stay in Shanghai to be with the woman he loved.

The two brothers parted in discord. Liu Kailai then followed Chief Gao's third plan and contacted the Shanghai underground, the *Hongdui* or the Red Brigade of the Central Committee. At once they carried out a secret investigation into the telegraph office as well as Ji Zhenren and the woman he said he could not leave. They then drew up two plans: either to persuade Ji Zhenren to leave or to take Ji Zhenren by force. But before they could put their plans into action, something serious happened to Ji Zhenren.

That day, Liu Kailai and several *Hongdui* members followed Ji Zhenren to the railway station square and found him fighting with another young man. But the girl, Ji Zhenren's lover, appeared on the roof of a six-storey building nearby, was shot and fell to the ground. Unexpectedly Ji Zhenren was also hit by a bullet. Resolutely, the *Hongdui* members fired back, and in the end they took Ji Zhenren's body away from the scene. A few days previously, Liu Kailai had himself indulged in wishful thinking that if he could get Ji Zhenren as well as his lover to Ruijin, he could achieve the task he had been assigned. He hadn't expected that, in the twinkling of an eye, both of them would suffer a sudden misfortune.

But Ji Zhenren did not die. He fainted after the bullet went through the lower part of his left shoulder. The *Hongdui* members sent him to a hospital where they had connections. Liu Kailai and the *Hongdui* members then changed their plan regarding how to take Ji Zhenren to Ruijin. They organised some people and in the name of Ji Zhenren's fellow villagers they went to the telegraph office to report that Ji Zhenren had been shot dead, which tallied with the *Da Wan Bao* newspaper report, and demanded an explanation. But they left while the going was still good.

Director Yang went to the port to see them off. The corpse lying in the boat was Liu Kailai who had disguised himself as his brother. Director Yang had a look at the corpse and didn't notice anything wrong. For all this time, Ji Zhenren was hiding in hospital receiving treatment. Two weeks later, his wounds had healed. He then had to follow his brother's arrangement and was escorted by the *Hongdui* members out of Shanghai, although he told his brother that it was all right for him to go home, but that he would certainly not join the army.

At home, he intended on leaving. He said to his mother: "Out of a hundred reasons, I have one reason to stay in Shanghai. If I must die, I want to die in Shanghai with the woman I love. I want to be near the city, to accompany the soul of my beloved all my life."

Hearing her son's words, Zhang Chengfeng said: "It's obvious that your mood and mind are very bad, too far away from what is normal. However, staying in Shanghai is better than waiting for death in the Red Army's nest!"

She was not only paying lip service; she also made ample secret preparations to send him away from Ruijin.

But it was impossible for him to leave. According to Chief Gao's arrangement, Liu Kailai kept a secret watch on him.

After Liu Kailai came back from Shanghai, he stayed at home with his brother. He would enlighten Ji Zhenren about what Chief Gao said. Fed up with his brother's mumbling, Ji Zhenren selected a few books from his father's study and began to read. He picked up Karl Marx's *Das Kapital* and threw it at Liu Kailai, who then dug out a book on his person, saying, "We not only read Marx and Lenin, but also books written by Americans."

Taking hold of the book, Ji Zhenren did not put it down until he had finished the whole book. He then found Liu Kailai, saying:

"With your education level, you can't read this book."

"Chief Gao said that you can explain it to me."

"Since this Gao has racked his brains to try to get me to take his bait, I have decided to let him fulfil his wish. I am going to meet him."

"But you must treat him well. I am afraid of him, because I have done something awful and he uses it as leverage against me."

"He does things in such a roundabout way. I can see at once he is the sort who is fond of schemes and plots."

"He is not to blame. I reap what I sow. Two years ago, I was in the vanguard unit in the battle for Xiziling. When I charged the enemy headquarters, they had all run away, but I heard a *di-dah, di-dah* sound coming from a big metal box and somebody's voice coming from a different metal box. I wondered who could be hiding in them. I thought they were boxes for monsters, so I smashed them until they were silent. Afterwards I realised that they were a transceiver and a radio, valuable items that we wanted very much. I was disciplined for my blunder. But the punishment can be terminated if I do well in my work in the future; if not, I will live with it all my life."

"You are funny, and the Red Army is also funny. How can an army that can't recognise a transceiver win battles? Ah, has your punishment been terminated?"

"Not yet. But if I can keep you from running away, I will be considered to have succeeded in my task. Chief Gao promised me that if I could persuade you to join the Red Army, they would surely end the disciplinary action against me."

"Good Lord! The Red Army is a human trafficker. Isn't it the Red Army which also applies a policy of implicating one's close relatives?"

Ji Zhenren then went to see Chief Gao. He went prepared for a long talk, but Gao got straight to the point. "Leave or stay? If you decide to leave, you cannot go in a matter of days. At least we'll keep you thinking about it for two or three years. If you decide to stay, you can wear our uniform immediately."

"I want to leave," replied Ji Zhenren, "but I can't. However, I really don't want to stay. How about this: you take me to your place and let me have a look, then I'll decide."

"But once you see my place, you won't be able to leave," said Chief Gao, "and you'll have to work for me. Once you've seen my place, and you say, oh no, I don't want to come here and work for you, then only one result awaits you; we'll have to kill you."

Ji Zhenren's face grew grave and he said, "After hearing your words, I'm in a cold sweat. Am I worth such a painstaking effort and such ruthlessness on your part?"

"I'm resolved to win you over," said Chief Gao. "Please don't blame me if I have offended you."

"In that case, I'll go for it!" muttered Ji Zhenren.

Chief Gao laughed. "It's all right once you understand the times we live in!"

After Chief Gao told Ji Huizhong about his son's decision, the old man was extremely excited: "All three of my sons have joined the Red Army. Wonderful! Glorious!"

"No," replied Chief Gao, shaking his hand. "Your family has more than three Red Army soldiers. You have two beautiful and energetic daughters in the Red Army too."

Some days ago, Chief Gao had asked all the troops about the Ji children's circumstances and he did get some news about them. Ji Zhenfu had been fighting with the 7th Army in Guangdong, Hunan and Hubei. Later his troops engaged in guerrilla warfare in east Hubei. He was wounded and left behind with the guerrilla troops in Wushan mountain and became the leader of his brigade. His two sisters came to look for him. But after several months' trekking, they went the wrong way, so they joined the local Red Army troops.

"We carried out a search for your children in secret, so they knew nothing about it," Chief Gao told Ji Huizhong. He then urged, "We must keep it secret that Ji Zhenren has joined RSU2, the fewer people that know about it, the better. Ji Zhenren is a talented man, and the army will make adequate arrangements for his life and work." The old man breathed a long sigh of relief, while his wife's face flushed scarlet, feeling as if a knife were piercing her heart. She had tried hard to prevent her children from joining the Red Army, but all of them had joined it now. The Jis' fate had really been sealed; she sighed.

After Ji Zhenren joined RSU2, he wasn't given any specific work to do. He wasn't even taken to the office to look around but to a small courtyard house where a special team tested him for two weeks. They then drafted a political review about him and presented the report to Chief Gao, who skipped the parts about the family background, work experience, social contacts, character traits, political views and reasons for joining the army, and went straight to the attachment part, *"Ji Zhenren Talks About What He Has Learned from Reading Books"*:

Book One: *The Sad Record of a Strategy for Peace*

I have read some books about war and what I don't accept is the fascist viewpoint. I have always thought that military men must have more wisdom, better plans and more strength for a strategy for peace. On this foundation, 'The Sad Record of a Strategy for Peace' has been imprinted in my memory, making me believe in the ideology of 'in the world harmony is above all'. I believe that if one more military man reveres the ideology described in *The Sad Record of a Strategy for Peace*, there will be one more force for antiwar and universal love. I am neither gifted nor capable of becoming a tactician for a peaceful strategy like the man who was willing to cut his ears, eyes, nose and tongue, but I can applaud and appeal for his ideology. In China, at this very moment, for those who have power as well as the will to unify the country, why do they have to attain their goal by the cruel use of force? I cannot work it out. Since I cannot get my mind around it, I have to do something to the best of my ability, therefore I want to join the Red Army.

Book Two: *The American Black Chamber*

The author of this book was Herbert Yardley, the authoritative cryptographer in the 1920s, and the father of American cryptography. The cryptographic organisation the American Black Chamber led by him decrypted nearly 50,000 coded telegrams from Japan, France, Germany and China, to serve America's military, politics and foreign affairs. What he wrote in his book were these shocking stories, as well as his unusual experience of indulging in the powerful countries' political schemes and plots. It was published in 1931 in the United States, causing a huge stir around the world. It was soon translated into Chinese. I heard that as soon as the Shanghai underground got a copy, they passed it on to Chief Gao. Surprisingly, the book became a super bait and I bit on it tight but felt no pain. It gave me a substantial understanding of cryptography, making me wish that I could enjoy myself to the full in cracking codes and ciphers one day, and work wonders like that American did. Meanwhile, Chief Gao's act of giving me the book to read also made me form an association: Does he also have a mysterious black chamber? He made a thorough investigation of me and racked his brains to get me. He must have wanted me to work for him. Why not go ahead? I became obsessed with cracking codes and ciphers and it became the source of my strength. Yes. I decided to join the Red Army!

When he finished reading this attachment, with one stroke of the pen Chief Gao wrote, "Ji Zhenren is a man with an honest character, particularly having read the classics so intensively. He has wide and extensive knowledge of the Chinese language, he is skilled in telegraphy techniques, having a quick and keen sense of codes and ciphers. He also has a good command of the English and Japanese languages. With some training and tempering under battle conditions, he will become a man of considerable accomplishments, and certainly an extraordinary talent in our army, a sharp sword. No amendment to this report. Please present it to the higher-level organisation without delay." He then wrote a note: Be quick to consult the 3rd Company to transfer foot soldier Liu Kailai to RSU2's Guards Company. Terminate the disciplinary action on Liu Kailai without delay.

Very soon Ji Zhenren's political review report was officially approved. It was said that Chief Gao personally went to see a certain senior leader. In an overbearing manner, he said, "I take responsibility for recommending Ji Zhenren. If you find anything wrong with him politically, gouge my eyes out. If he fails to become a great talent, cut out my tongue. But if you bureaucrats delay the approval procedure, holding up my use of him and spoiling the opportunity to win a battle, I will snap your head off your neck!" The senior leader knew very well Chief Gao's style of handling affairs, and that it must have been a matter of great urgency. Without demur, the senior leader wielded a pen and endorsed the organisation, security and the headquarters departments to quickly carry out the recruitment procedure.

In less than three days, Ji Zhenren put on an army uniform and officially became a member of RSU2.

6 / CIPHERS HIDDEN IN A PAINTING

THE WARTIME EXPERIENCES of my grandfather Ji Zhenren and grandmother Xia Yuhe had puzzled me for many years. While they never talked about it, little historical materials were available. As for the roundabout way in which word about their deeds reached me, there was no way I could verify what I heard about them by doing textual research. The situation had really put me on the spot. However, my daughter Ji Shan would later solve some of the puzzles.

I mentioned in my previous chapters that Ji Shan was a university maths teacher, and that she had a profound interest in cryptography. Some experts commented that her level on the subject was professional. Once she went to a dinner party, where some friends remarked that people like her who specialised in maths and were fond of deciphering codes were extremely boring, although they looked mysterious; they were OK as a workplace colleague but not to have a romantic relationship with. She had just experienced such a disappointment, the seventh in a row, her profession having made her boring in life. Anyway, she wasn't annoyed by her friends' remarks but, taking advantage of the euphoria from drinking, she gave a full list of things that she found interesting in maths and cryptography. She was satisfied with herself, but her friends could not see anything interesting in her repetitive words. She said: "Those who often think in a mathematical way are the most interesting people. Those who cannot appreciate such fun are the dullest people. Learning maths and decrypting codes and ciphers is like writing a happy song or reciting a beautiful poem. Especially after you rack your brains, you enter a fortress of codes and ciphers, and instantly you ruthlessly and mercilessly destroy the fortress. It is so much fun and it can be called one of life's treats."

One friend sat in a corner, rarely speaking but quietly watching her and listening to her tipsy talk. He had a different opinion about her and thought she was an interesting girl with a full understanding of the subject she was talking about. After dinner he sent the tiddly Ji Shan home.

A few days later, this friend called Wu Yuan came to see Ji Shan. He worked in a state department in charge of confidential work. He had some encrypted material that he could not work out, so he came to her for help. Ji Shan decrypted it very quickly. Later he would often come to bother her with some insignificant classified materials. She then understood that he was interested in her and she began to go out with him.

One day, Wu Yuan came again. Ji Shan laughed, "I've been your girlfriend, so why do you still play games with me?"

Wu Yuan did not laugh, saying, "I truly have a hard nut to crack."

Some time ago, the security department in Chengdu submitted some material to city B, saying that when they did maintenance work on an old church, they discovered a mummified carrier pigeon with a coded letter tied on its foot. Judging from the capsule and the paper, it must have been from the wartime period before 1949. The paper was covered with nearly a hundred groups of code, each consisting of four or five numerals. Wu Yuan's department spent two months trying to decipher them, but to no avail. Thinking that the letter could be seventy or eighty years old and that there was not much point in decrypting it, they put it to one side and no one bothered about it any more. Wu Yuan then thought of Ji Shan, so he brought her the photographs of the remains of the pigeon and the capsule, as well as the letter he had reproduced from the original.

Ji Shan asked: "You duplicated them all right? Was the original legible?"

"My boss gave me permission to ask you for help," replied Wu Yuan, "but said not to give you the original letter nor to take a photo of it. I checked several times and every group of numerals that I duplicated are correct."

One month later, Ji Shan told Wu Yuan that she could not decipher them, but that she would seek expert help, saying that her great-grandfather Ji Zhenren was a veteran cryptographer. Pretending to remember something, Wu Yuan said that he did not know that Ji Zhenren was her great-grandfather. He had heard that in 1967 Ji Zhenren was put in police custody because a transceiver and four pages of coded messages were found in his house, that the four pages were still kept in the reference chamber of the department for national security, and that no one could decipher them.

Ji Shan was surprised. How could she have known nothing about it? She went to ask her great-grandpa, who was alert and resourceful. He replied, "Why ask? It was a trivial matter that happened a few decades ago. The state has left it alone but you, little girl, are reviving old scores again. You want me to tell you stories? Sorry, I have none to tell you!" From then on, no matter how hard she tried, he wouldn't say another word about it. During all these years, her great grandparents were like this, if they did not want to say anything, they wouldn't, not even if the sky were to fall.

It seemed that it was truly hard to get the two elders to open their mouths. Ji Shan then said, "You don't want me to ask you about things. But here is an odd thing, which has nothing to do with our family. Do you want to know about it?" Taking out the photographs of the carrier pigeon, she then told them the ins and outs of the matter.

After Ji Zhenren examined the photos, he said:

"I can conclude this was a cipher used by KMT troops in the late 1930s, and book-based. This kind of cipher has little repetition, so it's hard to crack. Besides, the limited information makes it even harder to decrypt the message. Regarding the cipher, three to four decades have passed, so there is no way to find out the primary information about the sender and receiver. The code book and the encryption system will have been destroyed long ago. Without any background information, I don't know where to start, so it is indecipherable."

But Xia Yuhe was more optimistic. With a weird look in her eyes and a strange smile on her lips, she looked into her husband's eyes, saying, "Did you say this to Ji Shan or to me? If to me, then you should carefully look at the ciphers. Once you see through them, these decade-old irritating things will all be cleared up before your eyes." She took the paper from her husband and examined it for a while, saying: "You are right. This is exciting. It could make people very, very happy." She turned around and left the room.

But two days later, her optimistic zeal vanished. She said to Ji Shan:

"What your great-grandpa said is true. I tried for two days, but to no avail. You'll have to tell Wu Yuan that we can't help."

Disappointed, Ji Shan went to see Wu Yuan, muttering, "I thought we had a chance. Anyway, I haven't given up hope yet. I want to have a go with my great-grandpa's four pages." Wu Yuan thought it would be okay, saying that several decades had passed, and some of the state classified secrets had been declassified, so what secrets would be known by an old man who had been staying at home doing nothing for half of his life? So he followed procedure and asked for instructions from his superior, and in the end Ji Shan got those four sheets of paper.

But, confronted with them, Ji Shan was at a loss what to do. In three months, she hadn't decrypted a single word. She knew that with such material, for which she had neither the background nor the related information, she would get nowhere by just shutting herself inside the house and wrestling with it. Let he who created the problem resolve it. She then tried some clever ways to get something out of her great-grandpa, but she got nothing.

The carer took Ji Zhenren to Qingdao for a holiday. In a wheelchair it was not convenient for Xia Yuhe to go, so she stayed behind. Ji Shan had an idea. She took the four pages to her great-grandma, whose expression became more and more complicated when she read them. "What is all this about? Make a clean breast of things! These are in your great-grandpa's handwriting. When did he encrypt them? Where did you get them from?"

Ji Shan smiled, "You are playing hide and seek, aren't you? Why do you ask me about it?" Ruffling the papers noisily, Xia Yuhe said, "Cut out that cheeky grin!"

"It seems that you really don't know about it. Great-grandpa encrypted this in 1967 and he even used a training transceiver to send and receive it himself. He was caught on the spot by police. You know nothing about it?" Ji Shan then told Xia Yuhe what had happened that year.

"I wasn't home at that time," muttered Xia Yuhe, "so how could I have known what happened in this house? But your great-grandpa never mentioned this to me."

Ji Shan quickly asked: "If you didn't live with Great-grandpa, then where did you live?"

Waving her hand, Xia Yuhe said, "Don't ask about that if you want me to help you. And you must keep it a secret that I am helping you. If your great-grandpa finds out that I am deciphering his work behind his back, we will definitely fall out." Ji Shan promised resolutely not to tell.

"How did you get them?" asked Xia Yuhe. "Through private connections, or through official channels? This is a matter of principle. If it was via private connections, you'd better send them back quickly. Although they were written by your great-grandpa, as long as they were kept by the public and national security departments, they are national archives, so no individual can touch them."

Ji Shan had no choice but to ask Wu Yuan to show Xia Yuhe the photocopy of the letter of approval. Only after Xia Yuhe read it word by word, and examined Wu's staff card, did she agree to help. Ji Shan then added: "This is a job handed down by his work unit. He is my boyfriend, so helping him is helping me." Xia Yuhe had been concerned about Ji Shan's love life and marriage, so at once she said she would do her best.

Xia Yuhe then asked the nanny to cook two more dishes and she insisted that Wu Yuan stay for lunch. During the meal, Xia Yuhe looked Wu Yuan up and down. Seeing the old lady constantly looking at him with her piercing eyes, Wu Yuan felt uncomfortable, and he wanted to sneak off after the meal. Xia Yuhe whispered into Ji Shan's ears: "I want to test him on your behalf. I'd like to have a chat with him." Ji Shan did not want her great-grandma to meddle in her private affairs. Xia Yuhe said if not, she would stop meddling in the affairs of codes and ciphers. Ji Shan had no choice but to leave the room. When she returned, Wu Yuan had left.

"This boy is not bad with ideas," said Xia Yuhe. Then she switched the conversation to another subject: "What is hidden behind these four pages? You want to know, I want to know, so does Wu Yuan. Or to put it bluntly, the public security and the national security institutions want to know. Once they are decrypted, what does that mean for your great-grandpa? I'm not so certain. But what I am sure of is that he had no political issues, and he never did anything wrong regarding security regulations, for which I trust him beyond a shadow of doubt. If he did have a problem, I would not shield him. Never! I have such political awareness and sensibility, which are with me forever!"

After Xia Yuhe's words, Ji Shan felt nervous, "Am I going to bring trouble to Great-grandpa? I think we'd better stop."

Looking more serious, Xia Yuhe said, "He was retired, but he still did it in secret, so insensible. If he is guilty, that's it. He must take responsibility for his actions. Never say that I'm not strictly impartial or heartless. In the war years, compared to political issues and army secrets, individual ties of friendship were worthless! Besides, I am curious, and I want to know what he has done behind our backs. If I don't clarify things, I won't be able to sleep."

Suddenly Ji Shan felt that she was facing imminent disaster. Feeling ill at ease, she looked into Xia Yuhe's eyes, which were deep-set, and with no sign of the usual turbidity of an old person but focused and piercing. Disrespectfully Ji Shan thought inwardly, "They are like an old monkey's eyes!"

Looking away, Ji Shan said, "I have a dim feeling that this crumpled bit of paper bodes ill rather than well for Great-grandpa. I'm very frightened."

"No matter what, the lid must be taken off," said Xia Yuhe. "If not, I will never let him get by."

"I really have a bad feeling about this," muttered Ji Shan.

Then Xia Yuhe said, "I also have a story about a carrier pigeon, which happened in Yan'an. Let me tell you the story, so you can relax a bit."

That year, after careful planning, a certain KMT espionage department sent a senior spy to Yan'an, who successfully infiltrated our department that was in charge of confidential work; their mission was to evaluate our capacity to decipher the KMT army's codes and ciphers, and particularly to find out about our key cryptographers.

This spy was the young and beautiful Gao Yuncao. She got what she wanted, but she could not send her intelligence out of Yan'an. The compound where she worked and lived was heavily guarded and the department had many strict disciplines and rules. For instance, without permission the staff could not make any contact with the people living outside, even normal contact with ordinary military personnel from non-confidential departments had to go through the process of approval and be put on record. If they had to leave the compound, for either private or business reasons, they were obliged to go through the process of examination and approval at three levels, and there had to be three people going together; and once they were out, they could not move about alone.

The KMT secret agent who was responsible for getting in touch with Gao Yuncao finally entered Yan'an, but he was unable to make contact with her. Before the agent was sent, Gao Yuncao's superior had prepared a plan B. If she could not contact the agent, she had to find a way to go to the market in Chigangzi township and establish contact with a one-eyed chicken peddlar called Li. The market was held every five days and Li would only go for the one at the end of the month. To ensure the operation was secure, she was tasked not to pass any intelligence to Li but only to receive instructions from him. For several months, Gao Yuncao racked her brains to find an excuse to go to the market, but to no avail.

The opportunity finally came. A female colleague called Ding Lili was six months pregnant, and therefore receiving care from the department. Besides, she was the wife of the leader of a certain department, making it easier for her to leave the compound. Gao Yuncao had a good relationship with her and after she became pregnant Gao Yuncao helped her out with this or that. Noticing that Ding Lili showed signs of undernourishment, Gao Yuncao talked to Ding to cook something good for herself rather than eating in the mess. In Yan'an, the leaders' wives could not enjoy preferential treatment, and if they wanted to have a better meal, they had to buy and cook food for themselves. A single woman, Gao Yuncao spent little each month, so she gave Ding Lili what she had saved from her allowance by way of a loan.

That day, the department leader, a reasonable man, said that it was no good for a pregnant woman to stay in the compound all the time, so Ding Lili was able to go out for a walk and go to the market to buy some chickens and eggs to supplement her diet. He gave permission for Gao Yuncao and Ji Hongmei to accompany her to the market.

Excitedly, the three women walked twice around the market from one end to the other. After Ding Lili bought some cloth for her unborn baby, Gao Yuncao and Ji Hongmei walked with her to a one-eyed peddlar. Compared to the chickens and eggs of the other two peddlars, his were not inferior but cheaper, so Ding Lili bought a hen and a kilo of eggs from him. The peddlar was good at doing business. He was pushing to sell four young hens, saying that he was going to leave home for some time so he could not look after them. They could take them home and the young hens would grow into big fat hens in a few months' time. Gao Yuncao said what a good idea, when the young hens grow into adult hens, the baby would be born, so the mother could have meat and eggs to eat. The four young hens only cost Ding Lili half of the money she had paid for the adult hen. Flapping all over the place, the hens' feet were tied together. The three women were very happy because they had bought them so cheaply. Gao Yuncao also bought a kilo of eggs, saying that she had diarrhoea, and it had not cleared yet, so she needed to eat some eggs to supplement her diet.

At the compound gate there was a checkpoint. Despite the fact that the sentry knew the women, and one of them being a leader's wife, he had to fulfil his official duty. He examined the items the women were about to bring in. Cackling, the women were chatting and laughing, and the hens were also clucking and flapping their wings. In the ensuing chaos the sentry couldn't make head or tail of what was going on with the hens. When he checked the eggs, he got some chicken poo stuck on his fingers. He found nothing unusual, so he let them in with their shopping. Returning to their dormitory, the women found a cage and put the hens in it. They then saw a black-and-white pigeon half the size of a hen among the hens. Laughing, Ding Lili said that the chicken peddlar was going on a long journey, so he had sold everything with wings that he had in his home. Gao Yuncao said that they had the advantage of having bought a fat pigeon for the price of a young hen.

The next morning, they found that the cage door wasn't closed properly and the hens were all in the yard looking for food, but the pigeon was nowhere to be seen. It was bought cheap, so Ding Lili wasn't annoyed: "It's OK that it flew away. It can be compensated for as long as I look after the other three hens well."

So that was the end of the matter. But Ding Lili and Ji Hongmei could never have imagined that Gao Yuncao had done something behind their backs. First, right under their noses, she had exchanged code words with the one-eyed chicken peddlar, cleverly taking away from him the carrier pigeon and the eggs hidden with intelligence; second, on the way back to the compound, when taking a break, she had stealthily changed her eggs for Ding's eggs, and after entering the compound, she had secretly changed her eggs back. So, at the compound gate the problematic eggs were in Ding's hand, while Ji Hongmei carried the hens, so even if the sentry had found something, it would have been easier for Gao Yuncao to absolve herself from blame.

Among the eggs that Gao Yuncao bought there were some cooked eggs. She peeled the shells and exposed the egg whites that were covered in writing. They were written in code, so even if they were found out, they could not reveal any intelligence. A certain KMT secret agent often used such a method to communicate with other agents. The method was simple. Acetic acid was used to write the intelligence on the eggshells. After the acid dried, the eggs were boiled. The acid would go through the eggshell and leave marks on the cooked egg white, yet no trace of writing could be seen on the eggshell itself.

The intelligence for Gao Yuncao this time was a rigid order from her spy superior: use the carrier pigeon to send out intelligence as soon as possible. If this failed, she had to kill the communists' key cryptographers, even if her own life was put at risk.

That same night, in cipher she wrote her intelligence about the communists' main cryptographers and their technical skills, and the status of their decryption of coded messages of the KMT troops and the secret agency; and the communists' new garrison locations. She also expressed her loyalty and allegiance to the KMT party and the state. Then she made a capsule. Putting her intelligence in it, she released the pigeon.

When Xia Yuhe finished the story, she asked Ji Shan, "What do you think of the story? Exciting, isn't it? But Gao Yuncao did not carry out the assassinations. Afterwards, they organised some other agents to assassinate your great-grandpa. I had always thought that the reason that the KMT secret agents knew very well that your great-grandpa was the key cryptographer for the communists was because the carrier pigeon had brought out the intelligence."

Xia Yuhe's mood began to swing violently, with her bursting into a flood of tears one moment, then giggling uncontrollably the next. She spoke equivocally, illogically, not knowing what she really wanted to say. At last Ji Shan understood what she was saying. In brief, she said that a species of carrier pigeon for night travel was impressive; its wings had more than eleven feathers and it could fly extremely fast. But no matter how impressive they were, they were afraid to meet hawks, especially the black hawks which were the pigeons' natural enemy. These hawks would hide in the dark, and when the carrier pigeons began to descend, they would seize an opportunity and suddenly fly at the pigeon and kill it with one bite. Then they would fly to a quiet place and eat their prey.

Xia Yuhe said the pigeon released by Gao Yuncao was a high-quality carrier pigeon for night flight. It had 13 feathers on its wings. Under the moonlight, with its piercing eyes and straight posture, it looked like a well-trained soldier, very imposing.

Seeing her great-grandma describe the carrier pigeon with such affection, Ji Shan asked her how she could know that Gao Yuncao had released the pigeon that night. Xia Yuhe said that she had heard it from other people afterwards. Ji Shan said that since the news about releasing the pigeon had spread, it means Gao Yuncao's identity as a sleeper had also come to light. Xia Yuhe said that was probably so.

Xia Yuhe's mind was entirely on the ending of that pigeon. She said, "Although it was a high-quality bird, there was still the possibility of it being caught by a hawk. I had studied this kind of hawk. They had a very powerful catching capacity, particularly the rate of success with a solitary pigeon was very high. For some years I was mad about my studies, and my aim was to draw a conclusion that the pigeon released by Gao Yuncao had certainly been caught by a hawk, and the intelligence it carried had failed to reach its destination. The information about Ji Zhenren that the KMT secret agency wanted to know did not come from that pigeon, but from some other channel. Ji Zhenren was later repeatedly subjected to attempted assassinations by the KMT, yet it had nothing to do with the intelligence carried by that pigeon."

Ji Shan laughed: "Why is it that this pigeon must have been caught by a hawk? It might have ended like the pigeon in Chengdu, falling into the chimney of a church."

It seemed that Xia Yuhe's thinking was really confused. It was Gao Yuncao who tried to send out intelligence via carrier pigeon, why was she bothering about whether the pigeon reached its destination or not? An old lady of ninety years old, she was nostalgic about the past. She got worked up without rhyme or reason and easily got confused about timing. Xia Yuhe was like an old well with cloudy water that was too deep to see the bottom. Ji Shan thought that in a heavily guarded military area, where intelligence could be sent in and out by using eggs and carrier pigeons, it showed that the KMT espionage agents were crafty.

Afterwards Xia Yuhe showed her guilty conscience again. Ji Shan said to her, "It is nothing extraordinary for us to decipher these four pages. If it affects your mood and health, we'd better stop doing it now. That carrier pigeon in Yan'an had nothing to do with you so why do you have such a guilty conscience about it? I don't know how much guilt you will feel because you directly fiddled with Great-grandpa's stuff this time. Let's stop here. Don't do any more."

Staring at Ji Shan, Xia Yuhe mumbled, "Only a crumpled bit of paper, why did you use such a method to prod me into doing it? You've had your way. But I've made it clear that I can't provide you with any specific method. You are a university teacher and you have a lot of advanced methods to apply. My old, cumbersome method is outdated. All I can do is to provide you with the possible background information. Without that, no matter how good your maths is, or even if you use a super-computer, you will be unsuccessful in decrypting the information."

Listening to this, Ji Shan called out, "Great-grandma is wise."

As expected, afterwards things were much simpler. When Ji Zhenren was in Qingdao for a month, Ji Shan and Xia Yuhe spent twenty days working out his four pages of ciphers.

They were encrypted in English. After working strenuously for several days, Ji Shan and Xia Yuhe failed to decipher them. Dejected, Ji Shan was in tears. Suddenly Xia Yuhe had a violent coughing spasm. Then, as though she had remembered something, she said breathlessly, "Humph! Playing tricks on me, you don't want to court death, do you? You old monkey, seek your doom! *Willows are green and the river water is smooth, I hear my darling singing in the river.*" Then she gazed at Ji Shan, chuckling. Ji Shan wiped away the tears from her eyes, staring blankly at Xia Yuhe, who carried on, "*The sun rises in the east and the rain falls in the west.*" Ji Shan gave no reaction.

Shaking her head, Xia Yuhe said, "You are no good, because you are a person with little comprehension of love between a man and a woman. It seems that you wasted your time going out with Wu Yuan. The next line should be '*You might say it is wuqing (no sunshine) but it isn't*', which is the key word for deciphering the message. Ha-ha! Inspiration comes out of a fit of coughing. Aren't I remarkable?" Then she went to her bed and took a nap.

Like dismantling a fortress, armed with the key word, Ji Shan prised open cracks, separated stones from cement, shattered stones, filtered out dust, and this fortress of codes and ciphers was finally dismantled. After Xia Yuhe woke up from her nap, she laughed, "You are doing maths, so it's excusable for you not to know the poem of the Tang poet Liu Yuxi. But now you have the key word, if you still fail to decipher them, I'm not going to play the game with you any more."

After reading what Ji Shan had deciphered, Xia Yuhe said, "This is nothing important but some comments on cryptography. The higher leadership had openly acknowledged this conclusion in the early days of the revolution, and no one had ever underestimated the importance of this profession. This old fool deliberately mystified things. He gave the state more trouble, didn't he? All the effort for the arrest and the examinations."

Ji Shan went to see Wu Yuan, saying that she had a result, and that she'd better write a report so that he could reply to his superior.

When she was at home writing her report, she discovered a giant painting hanging on the wall in her great-grandpa's studio. It was in the style of the painting *On the River During the Qingming Festival* from the Song dynasty. The name of the painting was *War Gallery* and it was signed by Ji Zhenren. At first she didn't suspect that tricks had been played in the painting. But accidentally she found a coded text on the back corner of the painting. She decrypted it in three days, it read:

> I learned to speak in several years, but I learned to be tight-lipped all my life. I retired dumb and mute, and young talents will surpass us of the older generation. I yearn for Dian's affections, no one could understand my heartfelt feelings. The political situation made us walk on the path of killing each other, the time to resolve the issue is when I meet Q again.

She was lucky. The letter 'Q' was flawed when the text was encrypted, and sharp-eyed Ji Shan spotted it. The following deciphering work was simple, and she got it done all by herself. But she said nothing to her great-grandma about this text.

In a wheelchair, Xia Yuhe seldom went to the studio upstairs. Even if she had seen the painting, she wouldn't have thought that secrets had been hidden in it. In recent years, her health had been deteriorating, so Ji Shan thought that it was better not to let her know about the secrets upstairs.

In her report Ji Shan included the possible secrets in the painting. She did not expect that she would receive the following official reply: "No change for this case. No further examination of the matter."

She turned her attention to Wu Yuan. Her dating him was the sweetest experience she had ever had. They were passionately in love. Like cracking a cipher, once you dig into it, there is no going back, either you advance smoothly and decipher everything, or you achieve nothing. The final attempt, which is full of impatience, eagerness and madness, is usually the most satisfactory and memorable. For the time being, she and Wu Yuan were at such a stage in their relationship.

But before her relationship with Wu Yuan had reached a conclusion, she still failed to resist the temptation of the *War Gallery*. Initially she didn't want to bother Xia Yuhe again, but she had failed to decipher a single code after spending so much time and effort. Banging her head several times on the wall and pulling a handful of hair from her head, she still could not find a tiny gap to crack the codes. Having no choice, she went to pester her again.

This time the progress was nowhere near as smooth as last time. Of course, they still did it behind Ji Zhenren's back. Ji Shan spent all her spare time and made the most use of her great-grandma. Three months went by and they made little progress except that they discovered secrets in the surface layer of the painting, namely, the length of the grass and branches, the size of the fruit, the colour of the birds, the vertical and horizontal gaps between the bricks in the city walls and the blockhouses, the height of the soldiers and the shape of the weapons represented dots and dashes of code; so within the painting were hidden thousands upon thousands of groups of code, which prevented Ji Shan and Xia Yuhe from making any further progress. The scale, structure and density of the numerals were far more complicated than those on the four sheets of paper. They made countless analyses of the circumstances associated with Ji Zhenren, with Ji Shan even using some advanced decryption methods, but to no avail.

Xia Yuhe declared defeat. Ji Shan was so disappointed that she leant on Xia Yuhe's knees and cried her heart out. Xia Yuhe muttered, "The old fool spent twenty years painting this picture, and he encrypted his life's calculations into it, so how can we outsiders decrypt them? But Shan, wait, I will pry his mouth open."

A few days later, Xia Yuhe said to Ji Shan: "Rather than making him say something, I have made him so angry that he has stopped talking to me. Shan, you go and beg him. Don't argue, because arguing with him is a waste of time. On this matter he reckons nothing is justifiable. There is one thing you can do. Go and sit in his studio crying for three days and three nights."

Weeping and wailing, Ji Shan went to pester her great-grandpa, who flew into a rage, cursing her and smashing a teacup on the ground. But Ji Shan neither dodged nor withdrew from the room. She said nothing but went on weeping, the true mingling with the false.

Her heart-broken wailing, and Xia Yuhe's moaning and groaning, and their refusal to eat or drink, filled the air of the house. Since he had no choice, Ji Zhenren took a bowl of apples to the studio, saying, "OK, listen to my story while you eat an apple." Sounding hopeful, Ji Shan picked up an apple and gave it a bite.

Ji Zhenren said, "Let me tell you how the Allied forces broke the German army's code during the Second World War, a fabulous story."

Waving her mobile phone and patting the keyboard of her computer, Ji Shan said, "Great-grandpa, I'm tired of listening to this story. Look, I am using an Apple mobile phone and an Apple computer."

"I can tell you what is the most important component on your phone and computer," said Ji Zhenren. "The keyboard!" Ji Shan stopped chewing the apple and seemed lost in thought.

Ji Zhenren passed her another apple, saying, "The apple tastes good, doesn't it? But it definitely does not taste as good as the apples in my painting." Pointing at the apple orchard in a corner of the painting, he left the room.

Looking at the apple in her hand, then at the apple orchard in the painting, Ji Shan shook her head, "It's so absurd."

But standing under the painting, and under the apple orchard, she was lost in deep thought.

A light was on in the studio all night. When the morning sunlight shone through the window, Ji Shan dashed downstairs and pushed open the door of her great-grandparents' room. Ji Zhenren had gone out to do his morning exercises. So she said to Xia Yuhe, "In that apple orchard on the left corner of the painting, the size of the apples represent the dots and dashes of code. They formed several dozen groups of code, which you and I have already found out but failed to decipher. Last night I had another try and I worked it out. They are: breaking the other party's code into hundreds; making the deciphered codes into charts; searching for hidden secrets according to the tracks; an old hero still cherishes high aspirations."

Solemnly, Xia Yuhe looked hard at these words, saying nothing. Ji Shan then told her how she had deciphered them.

"Yesterday, the conversation between Great-grandpa and I seemed ordinary, but it really gave me a lot of food for thought. After he left, I thought over and over about his words, feeling that there was more to them than met the eye. He seemed to be giving me a pointer. From what he had said I sifted out three key words: apple, mobile phone keyboard and computer keyboard. It was only a hypothesis, of course, but I decided to have a go.

"First, according to the size of the apples in the painting I formed numerous Morse codes, a secret you and I discovered long ago. But Great-grandpa knew nothing about it, so his talk of apples gave me a pointer. I based it on the Morse code table and converted these codes into numbers, which was also easy to do. Anyone who has learned telegraphy can do it. I wrote these numbers on a piece of paper and there were thirteen lines, the head and the tail linking, thickly dotting the paper. Taking a look, I was in a hopeless tangle and could not get anything out of it. But after careful examination, one thing was dazzling, the number frequency was clearly unbalanced. Starting from number 1, when I marked the position of the numbers, the digits of the even numbers were always less than or equal to 4, which was an interesting phenomenon.

"My preliminary judgement was that these numbers might not be codes in Chinese, but I could not come to a conclusion until I made, step by step, some careful guesses and judgement calls. I was short of patience and time. Afterwards I noticed that if I divided these numbers into different groups with two digits, the basic unit in every group was less than or equal to 4. I remembered the mobile phone keyboard, on which only the keys 7 and 9 have four English letters, the other digits all have three letters. I tried to write out the letter from every two digits, for example, number 23, the third letter under digit 2 was C; number 94, the fourth letter under digit 9 was Z, and so on. I converted those thirteen lines of numbers into the respective English letters. But they were not readable. It was obvious that this was not the original plain text but an encrypted one. What was the methodology behind it? No need to guess, even a fool could think of Great-grandpa's third key word: computer keyboard. Anyone who has used a computer would know the order of the letters on the keyboard. Correlating the order of the 26 English letters to the location of the specific alphabetic keys on the computer keyboard, it then constituted a conversion table.

"However, after I used this table to convert the thirteen-line encrypted text, these letters still did not form any words, which meant that the text had a second encryption. If this was the case, the same method must have been used. Then what was the key word? And where was it? Since Great-grandpa had intended to give me a pointer, this key word must have been one of the words he had spoken to me. Hence, the English words for apple, apple tree, and orchard came into my view. One by one, I used them as the keyword. After following the corresponding steps, I formed a conversion table. I tried to decipher the text, but to no avail. However, I was more certain that something else was in this orchard in the painting. The size of the apple representing the length of the Morse code might not be the only secret, and the possibility that this is where the key was from was also great.

"I decided to try every possible way. I used the conversion tables composed of three key words to decrypt the text respectively, then I tried using the conversion table comprising the letters of the computer keyboard, and the dawn appeared. The conversion table which had 'fruit tree forest' as the keyword worked, and the result was those sixteen Chinese characters. Great-grandpa's pointer hadn't been in vain, otherwise I would have been too embarrassed to go weeping to his studio again. But I could not precisely guess what these words meant. Was Great-grandpa expressing his thoughts and feelings? Or keeping a secret? Or was it an introduction to the decryption of the whole painting? Can you give me some advice?"

With eyes brightening and mouth tightly closed, Xia Yuhe listened attentively to Ji Shan until she had finished speaking. She then breathed a long sigh of relief. "I never expected that this old fuddy-duddy would have resorted to high-tech, secretly using the mobile phone and computer keyboard letters. When did he have such a thought? I have no idea whatsoever about it. You are right, Shan. Viewing these words, this painting is certainly expressing his thoughts and feelings. My instincts tell me that they might really be an introduction and the key to the decryption of the whole painting. We need to interpret them by analysing the circumstances of his related background in the war years."

She went on, "During the Red Army's campaigns against Chiang Kai-shek's encirclement and suppression (1930-1934), the Long March (1934-1936) and during the War of Resistance Against Japan (1937-1945) as well as during the Liberation War (1946-1949), your great-grandpa and his colleagues had successfully broken hundreds and thousands of enemy codes and ciphers, so many that after they broke a hundred, they would add them to a chart to display their achievement. They called it the *Chart of a Hundred Beauties* and would stick it on the office wall to boost their morale, as well as to vividly inspire their fighting spirit. The chart was on the wall, and also engraved in their hearts, unforgettable. So *'breaking hundreds of the other party's codes'* certainly expresses such a meaning.

"Then how to explain *'making the broken codes into a chart'*? I think it might be that he had selected one chart from many of the *'Charts of a Hundred Beauties'*, or selected a hundred codes from all the charts, using their encryption methods for reference to construct his giant painting. I am certain of one thing. He painted this painting by using the cracked enemy ciphers. And that is why you and I have not been able to make a breakthrough in the last six months, because we used our own army's ciphers to unlock the mysteries in this painting. We made an orientational mistake, therefore our efforts were all in vain. So if we dived straight into a particular method, our efforts were destined to be futile.

"*'Searching for hidden secrets according to the tracks'* is more obvious. To interpret it by following the original meaning of this idiom, that is to search for the hidden stories by following the clues.

"*'An old hero still cherishes high aspirations'* expresses a state of mind, which shows that in old age, he still aspires to great deeds. When he was young, he was quite accomplished and did many great deeds. Although he is old now, he still has the aspiration and wants to do what he can. Or, more specifically, this is the only way for him to impart and inherit the professional spirit and fine traditions of codebreaking.

"But I have an issue regarding maintaining secrecy. He painted this picture at home using the enemy's decrypted ciphers. Has he violated security discipline? Although he does not directly reveal the related secrets, if this painting is found by somebody who then deciphers them, doesn't that amount to leaking state secrets?

"I feel that this painting does involve some secrets. Otherwise, how could he have made such an effort and spent twenty years to paint it? What for? He is always overconfident or self-important, which is his problem. But fortunately it is truly difficult to decipher this painting and those four pages. If it were not for my knowledge of his professional background and habits, and the other circumstances surrounding him, the four pages would be forever locked in the iron cabinet of the Security Bureau."

After Xia Yuhe gave her interpretation, Ji Shan dared not hide anything else from her. Hurriedly she told Xia Yuhe what she had found at the back of the painting.

After reading the text, Xia Yuhe said nothing. She went for lunch and then took a nap. She still said nothing after she got out of bed. Only the next day did she tell Ji Shan what interpretation she could place on the text.

"'I learned to speak in several years, but I learned to be tight-lipped all my life' means that to learn to speak is easy but to keep one's lips sealed tight and tell no secrets is hard. A person can learn to speak in two or three years, but guarding one's mouth from releasing secrets is a lifelong matter. He wrote this on the back of the painting, which means that he has already sorted out the issue of guarding secrets.

"'I retired dumb and mute, and young talent will surpass us of the older generation'. Hey, look Shan, the first part seems to say that he wanted to be dumb and mute and say nothing. The second part seems to say that young talent will come to decipher the secrets. If no secrets are hidden, how can the later generation do it? Which shows secrets are indeed hidden in the painting. Besides, for young talent he must mean you.

"'I yearn for Dian's affection, no one could understand my heartfelt feelings'. This is clearly pure sweet nothings from him. The word 'Dian' must be for Jiang Xiaodian. He wanted to say that he admired and cherished the memory of the intimate relationship between him and her, but these memories were only between him and her, no one else could discern them.

"'The political situation made us walk along the path of killing each other, the time to resolve the issue is when I meet Q again.' This text has a very strong political flavour. He borrowed it from a poem of Cao Zhi of the Three Kingdom Period (220-280AD), which reads as follows: 'People burn beanstalks to boil beans. The beans in the pot cry out, we are born from the same root, why must we hound each other to death with such impatience.' He meant that the KMT and the CPC are two political parties of the same state. In the age of rapid change they struggled against each other for many years. When would they stop being swayed by past personal resentment? And how would they untie this knot in their hearts? The time might come when he met this man called Q. The Q is for Gao Q, a senior KMT secret agent, an arch enemy of the communist cryptographers. He may not live in this world any more. A disgusting fellow, how can he outlive your great-grandpa and I?"

• • •

When things developed to this stage, it basically paved the way for the decryption of the *War Gallery*, as this was the general background to the painting. Since Ji Shan and Xia Yuhe had unveiled a corner of the secrets of the painting, they were in high spirits. Yet they kept their progress a secret from Ji Zhenren, who was often indifferent about what they were doing. Probably he firmly believed that even if he had given Ji Shan a pointer, no one could decipher the core secrets hidden in the painting, and the stubborn old fogey and youngster were wasting their time. Therefore he did not bother, but let them busy themselves with this family game, otherwise they would have felt lonely with nothing to do.

But Ji Shan and Xia Yuhe did not waste their time. One day, putting on grand airs, Xia Yuhe said to me, "My grandson, you cannot write your novel without the contents of the painting. It is exclusive historical data, so you must seize it. Go and ask your daughter for details."

Instantly I knew that the one-track-minded oldie and youngster had completely undone my conceited grandpa.

When I talked about it to Ji Shan, she said, "Great-grandpa's pointer was the starter, while Great-grandma's knowledge of the background and the former deciphering methods were the cornerstone, and my new way of thinking and the new technology were the winning lots.

"In the painting, Great-grandpa used an unusual method to encrypt his text, changing all the time. Only by making an organic combination of the related elements, and using every piece of my mind to make a clever overall arrangement, thinking backwards, linking top to bottom, and in a roundabout way, did I, corner by corner, area by area, layer by layer, reveal the secrets until I had a full grasp of the whole painting.

"Looking back, his encryption was tight, high and deep, nearly perfect except for two flaws. First, he overused one of the enemy code compiler's ciphers. He might have been partial to Gao Q's method of encryption. The codes encrypted by this man were perfect, easy to use and smooth, making cryptographers enjoy deciphering his codes, and leaving a deep impression on them. Although Great-grandpa did not indiscriminately copy Gao's ciphers, he creatively broke the structure, cleverly taking the essence and, after multiple alterations, he made changes of his own. However, sharp-eyed Great-grandma spotted them one by one, hardly imagining that she knew Gao Q like she knew herself. She said that even if Gao Q's bones had been smashed to pieces, she could have told which piece was from which part of his body. She also told me that, of course, Great-grandpa had no idea that she knew Gao Q so well.

"Second, Great-grandpa overused the love phrase when he dated Jiang Xiaodian for the key word. He might have intended to commemorate this unforgettable love, so he narrated his tender, sweet regards and the pains of lovesickness to the greatest extent in his painting. The love of the past was really alluring and touching, which made Great-grandma cry and laugh when she decrypted the texts. She was so familiar with the love story in the painting that when she made a start, she could tell what would happen next.

"So when Great-grandpa's two flaws met Great-grandma, they were not flaws but fatal loopholes. And that's why Great-grandma would often say that in this world, only she could confront Great-grandpa on many issues for many years.

"In her nineties, Great-grandma's sensibility to ciphers is not inferior to that of a young maths teacher. She still remembered vividly some of the ciphers used in the war era, particularly those cracked by Great-grandpa and the other senior cryptographers. As though she had done them herself, she could precisely tell how they were cracked.

"When we began to decipher the painting, Great-grandma set up a rule that she would only do some elementary work, while the main work would be done by me. Her reason was, 'A cipher sets up the same labyrinth for everyone, and every mature cipher is a reticular blockhouse full of traps. What I will do is to put up a signpost at every crossroad, leading you to cut across all sorts of obstacles, pass through the dangerous sites and reach the victorious destination.' She achieved this goal. When we finished the work, I reaped substantial benefits.

"I knelt down and kowtowed to Great-grandma to express my heartfelt thanks and respect. I then raised my head, saying, tearfully, 'As far as the revolutionary wars are concerned, you have made outstanding contributions. Your extraordinary life is something that is rare to see in this world.'

"Great-grandma replied, 'Shan, we have deciphered the codes hidden in your great-grandpa's painting. We must keep it a secret from him forever, otherwise he will have a mental breakdown!'"

· · ·

After listening to Ji Shan's account, I was amazed and also deeply moved. Each cryptographer was an exquisite talent, which made me interested and in awe of them. Ji Shan then told me about a strange thing that happened to her, which pulled me from the story of the older generation back to reality.

"At the beginning of this year, Wu Yuan accepted a special assignment from the first-in-command of his department: to undertake an overall investigation of our family. The leader said to him that Ji Zhenren had played with a transceiver many years ago, and the matter could not be left unsettled for decades. He also said to him that the method of his investigation could be flexible and diverse, as long as it did not break the law or violate discipline.

"After Wu Yuan did some research on our family, he drew up a plan. He thought it would help him to get twice the result with half the effort. His plan was to be close to me in the name of dating me and to go deep into our family and find out what made us tick.

"Without anybody knowing, he made friends with a friend of mine. As he got on well with this friend, he slowly became closer to my circle of friends, then he naturally appeared at my side. Step by step, we became acquainted with each other, and came to know and love each other. When we were head over heels in love, he would frequently turn up at our house. He had an easy conscience about dating but felt uneasy about spying on the progress of my great-grandma's and my deciphering of the painting.

"I made an accurate judgement that he was truly and deeply in love with me. I knew nothing of his initial motive or his mission. After the painting was deciphered, I told him the excited contents just as though I was telling him some interesting stories, without any awareness of guarding against other people's ill intentions. He kept my stories in his head, and he even secretly read my notebooks about the results of what had been deciphered. After he discovered the main circumstances of our family, he wrote a report and submitted it to his superior.

"Love between a man and a woman is one of the most difficult things in the world to work out. Once he had fallen so deeply in love with me that I had completely occupied his mind, he voluntarily told me about his secret mission and the related circumstances, asking for forgiveness. Meanwhile, the related department at a higher level made no settlement of the matter regarding our family, which meant that his mission had not ended. He told me everything about it, and it was obvious that he had violated discipline. Well, faced with a choice between love and discipline, he chose love.

"Regarding this matter, I told him what was on my mind, 'First, I never expected that this modern story of a secret agent could have happened to me. If you had said nothing, I would never have known your real identity. Was this a honey trap like I had heard about in stories? If you want forgiveness, I need time; besides, I want to see what damage it brings to my family. Second, it takes time for the higher-ups to examine a case, and before the final verdict is reached, the relationship between you and I can stay the same; no cutting down on the time we see each other, no restriction on how far we can go. If the time for marriage comes, but the final verdict for this case has not been reached, we can still wed and have kids. Third, if an unfavourable verdict is reached on my family, I will absolutely break my relationship with you. To me, and for a certain period of time, love must give way to the dignity of my ancestors. This is my principle.'

"Listening, Wu Yuan sighed, then said, 'Shan, there's one more thing that I've hidden from you; or, to put it more precisely, something about your great-grandma that I've hidden from you.'

"What he meant was the conversation between himself and Great-grandma, during which not a single word about my relationship with him was mentioned. Great-grandma took out her deciphered script of the letter carried by the carrier pigeon many years ago, telling him that as soon as she got it, she decrypted it. The letter was encrypted using an ancient book called *The Sad Record of a Strategy for Peace*, and from the contents it could be said that a covert agent codenamed 'Grasshopper' had released this carrier pigeon in Yan'an. The real name for this 'Grasshopper' was Gao Yuncao, and what she sent out was information about RSU2, its technical strength, its key cryptographers and the circumstances about its deciphering of the KMT armies' codes. Because Great-grandpa was mentioned in the text, and besides it was a case handed down by the state department for security, she told Wu Yuan that I must not be told about the details of the text. She then told Wu Yuan an even more important bit of information, asking him to pass on to his department that since the carrier pigeon and the text were found in a church in Chengdu, it meant that the intelligence had failed to reach its destination, so it was not related to the later assassination attempts on Great-grandpa by the KMT secret agents. At once Wu Yuan made known his position by saying that what she had said was reasonable, and he would report it to his superiors accurately. Great-grandma burst into tears, her voice trembling, as she muttered, 'Little carrier pigeon, you were a great hero. You died a worthy death, which was as heavy as Mount Tai!' Her condition frightened Wu Yuan. Picking up the paper, he left like a rat avoiding a mouse.

"After Wu Yuan told me about this, I said to him, 'It is hard for me to understand why my great-grandma was so emotional; as to the cursed secret agent, Gao Yuncao, her failure in her evil plot does not mean that she was a good person. We don't know if this pigeon was the same pigeon, or this text was the same text. Drawing a conclusion based only on the result of what my great-grandma deciphered is not a perfect way of doing things, and especially concerning the intelligence involving my great-grandpa. So we must handle it with greater care. My great-grandma was able to decipher the text so easily, which makes someone like me, who understands cryptography, think of the factors beyond cryptography itself. It seems that she was no stranger to the text. Maybe she had some relationship with it, otherwise she could not have deciphered it so quickly.

"Sincerely, Wu Yuan praised me, 'Your reasons are remarkable and professional. Shan, I love you!" He held my hands tight.

"'You must truthfully report my words to your boss! If not, your dirty covert mission may not be a perfect one.' At that moment I pulled him into my arms."

In those days, I expended some of my energy on Ji Shan's personal life and marriage. But soon I turned my attention to my creative writing and decided which parts of the *War Gallery* should be included in my book. I adopted the stories made up by my grandfather's twenty codes (or groups) and ciphers into my novel, which would be Part Two 'Plain Text', meant to make them the rich soil in which to breed the main characters of my novel.

I have neither the intention, nor the qualification, to write our army's war codebreaking history, but only try to reference my grandfather's painting and the related background, as well as the professionalism of codebreaking so that I can increase the artistic appeal of my novel. No more, no less!

PART 2
PLAIN TEXT

RSU2 WAS STATIONED on a small mountain ridge extending outward and surrounded by water on three sides.

Thirteen courtyard houses were built in the style of local dwellings to deceive the public. The vegetation on the ridge was luxuriant, linking the forest on the slope at the back of the mountain and making the ridge like a natural extension of the mountain forest. What was different to an ordinary forest was that aerials were installed in the crowns of trees, among the barley fields and the vineyards. Camouflaged and all over the ridge, they blended well with the natural environment.

When Ji Zhenren was taken to this village where neither common people nor soldiers were visible, he was at once attracted by the picturesque scene. He wanted to walk around, but was stopped by hidden guards. He found out it was free from tension on the outskirts but tense towards the centre where in every corner of every street and lane, or in the shade of trees and bushes, guards would suddenly jump out at any moment. He realised that this mountain ridge was a very secure place.

He had received six months' preparatory training, giving him a glimpse of what his future job would be. Personally in charge of his training, Chief Gao abandoned conventional training methods, instead adopting the most demanding and intense ones, which no ordinary trainees could have completed, but he demanded that Ji Zhenren persevere and succeed.

Before the training started, Chief Gao warned, "A cryptographer may only be requested to decrypt one or more enemy ciphers, but at all times he must be mindful of the enemy and everything about the enemy. We let you monitor troops, but more likely we let you guess about and exploit the whole world. To crack a cipher is to guess about the world! An excellent cryptographer must have the breadth of vision, manner, courage, insight and capacity to embrace the whole world. These mandatory qualities are not innate but acquired through hard training and hard work. So, before taking on the post, the numerous, diverse, tough and tortuous training is beyond your imagination. You must be mentally prepared for the crushing process of it."

The training began and was exactly as Gao had described.

Within the first eight hours, Ji Zhenren had routine training on military drill regulations, how to keep secrets, political studies, telegraphy and cryptography.

For professional skills training, the subjects were:

Interception. Apart from the basic knowledge about telegraphy and ability to monitor and transcribe, he had to have good knowledge of the KMT's head station and substations, their distribution of staff, communications network, call signals, wavelengths and ciphers used by them. He also had to carefully learn the type, function and frequency change patterns of the enemy transceivers, and every enemy operator's sending technique and style. He had to be capable of skilfully operating his equipment and handling a general transceiver breakdown; and of improving his monitoring skills, mainly of improving his ability to capture enemy signals amid fast-changing frequencies, and particularly of training to optimise his transcribing ability in bad weather and in unexpected situations.

Decryption. He was required to learn by heart the 'New Chinese Telegraph Codebook' and memorise the four-digit numbers for more than 10,000 Chinese characters. During this period, some KMT troops' telegrams were encrypted directly by using this codebook. He had to know very well the Chinese map and memorise the names and locations of all jurisdictions at or above county level. He had to have a good grasp of the enemy's thinking on encryption and get to know their encryption regularity; to learn the enemy code compilers' way of thinking, academic background, work experience, special areas, individuality and habits, as well as to learn and master the basic techniques of cracking ciphers, to cultivate unique skills of his own, to perfect his capacity to guess a Chinese character and to attack a thorny problem, striving to reach the pinnacle of 'guessing a whole text'.

The extracurricular activities were also formidable. To put it simply, it was to practice well three subjects.

The Chinese Language: to read and memorise one thousand or more classical poems, prose and literary compositions; to memorise by heart the verses in the beginning, at the end or in the middle of classical novels; to know a large amount of rarely-used or unusual words; to learn the forms and formulas as well as the usage of ancient official documents; to know the order of classical rhymes for Chinese characters and to memorise the contents of the entire *Kangxi Dictionary*.

The Enemy Situation: to know the enemy troops' military and political terms, the forms and formulas of all kinds of official documents, their customary terms and their procedure for document submission to superiors; the disposition of enemy army units, the deployment of troops, their relationships, all enemy troops' current situation, history, commanders' distinguishing command characteristics, modus operandi and internal relations; the KMT army hierarchy's strategy, military ideology, operational patterns and features, guiding principles, and short-term and long-term operational targets.

Our Own Situation: to have a good general knowledge of our army, good knowledge of each army unit, their function, responsibility, troop disposition, state of combat readiness, relationships, garrison locations and garrison duty dynamics; to have detailed knowledge of the domestic situation and general knowledge about major international events.

Every day, day and night, people in charge of specific subjects took turns to bombard him with their own training regimes. The trick was for each of them to fill him with their own stuff until he was full. Then they stopped. Anything he could chew he had to swallow; anything he could not chew he could not spit out either. He had to chew, swallow and digest everything, even if they were bricks and tiles. He would often swear inwardly, but also give himself encouragement: "Guess about the world! Come on! I am not afraid! Bring on all the books from the library in Ruijin. Go and find all the information about the civil and military situation of the Red Army and the White Army, I can swallow them all alive. Evil, cruel Chief Gao, I'm not afraid of you!" He was resolved to take on the challenge. In full swing, for 16 to 17 hours a day, he soaked up the training and reading.

One day, feeling that he really couldn't take any more, he went to see Chief Gao. Before he opened his mouth, Chief Gao said: "Want to throw in the sponge? You coward! Worrying the spring in your head is going to snap? I tell you, what we are doing is taking special measures in special times. I don't have the time to carefully ascertain the limit, but to slowly try everything on you one by one. After I determine the limit, I will then gradually tighten up the spring even more. It is obvious under such intensive tests which ones are well above the average scale; the possibility for you to get wrecked is great. But I have no choice. I need a man who can take on the major duties as soon as the training is finished. I must take the risk. And I firmly believe that you can do it! And you must do it!" He then threw a glass of cold water in the dispirited Ji Zhenren's face, which chilled him, and made him swallow what he wanted to say. Turning around, he left the room.

In the end he withstood Gao's style of training, and surprisingly he achieved good results in every subject. In the last training session, Chief Gao gave him a detailed account of RSU2's function, responsibility, the nature of their work and related matters regarding confidentiality.

He then understood that RSU2 was an intelligence unit working for the Red Army headquarters, to gather enemy information by means of wireless surveillance. Such information was intercepted from the enemy's leading centre, the core of secrets, so they were authoritative, precise, reliable, economical and safe. It was much quicker and more effective to decipher the enemy's coded messages than to obtain information by any other means. Someone had described the deciphering of codes as picking the jewels from the imperial crown, the highest state of intelligence warfare. In view of the above facts, this trade occupied a decisive status in the eyes of the Red Army's senior commanders, and it was irreplaceable. And such status was gained by the excellent performance and top quality intelligence obtained by all staff during the second and third campaigns against Chiang Kai-shek's encirclement and suppression.

Burning with righteous ardour, Ji Zhenren believed this was the evidence that he could bring his telegraph skills into full play in wartime. Allured by the temptation, he cried inwardly, "To guess about the world, I'm coming! To guess about the world, I'll go all out!"

Next morning after reporting for duty, full of enthusiasm, he got up early and went to the woods to recite some short essays from the Ming and Qing dynasties. He immersed himself in reciting. Suddenly, a gunnysack flew out from nowhere and covered his head, followed by someone pouncing on him and tying him up tight.

At the complex, he had no sense of guarding against attack. By the time he realised that disaster was imminent, he had been put in a dark room in the woods. He heard the door being locked and footsteps receding into the distance. He called out loudly, but there was no response. Not knowing how many hours had passed, he heard someone opening the door. The gunnysack was removed from his head, and he saw Chief Gao and two female soldiers standing in front of him. Flushed in the face with anger, he bellowed, "Why did you do this to me? Who did it?"

Chief Gao roared with laughter, "Who can explain, you two women soldiers?"

One girl said, "This morning when we passed the woods after the night shift, we heard something unusual. We quietly closed in, seeing a peculiar stranger wagging his head and chanting some old texts to himself. It was just after daybreak and few people come into these woods; besides, we were in an important military site. Especially as what he was chanting seemed inappropriate, we became suspicious and took action."

"Quick, untie him," said Chief Gao to the two girls. He then took the book from Ji Zhenren and the smile on his face completely vanished, "It's true, it's not an appropriate book. No wonder they apprehended you. You should know that you must read more books related to your profession. For every day earlier you go on duty, that'll be one day less for our soldiers to die in the front line. Do you understand?"

Choking with resentment, Ji Zhenren flew into a rage, "What old texts? What is not appropriate? All scholars in the Ming and Qing dynasties, and in the early days of the Republic of China, were fond of reading and also good at writing such short essays. We cannot guarantee no Nationalist army officers who were nurtured by such essays would not incorporate such an eccentric style of writing into their telegrams. If they do, how can we decipher their messages? If we cannot decipher them, more generals and soldiers would die in the front line. So it is my job to recite these essays." When all the ill feelings built up in the training sessions broke out, it could also eject a few sharp nails. "Chief Gao, everyone says you have shown great foresight, but I never thought that you could be so shortsighted."

Chief Gao was speechless. One girl soldier roared, "How outrageous! Tie him up again!"

Chief Gao stopped her, "Let him finish."

Straightening his neck, Ji Zhenren said, "If you ask! It is very important to understand the enemy's learning structure and their writing habits. What is in their mind must also be in our mind. Otherwise, it will be hard for us to crack open the shell and cut through the wrapping to get the contents of their codes and ciphers."

Chief Gao laughed, "Look at your aggressive and murderous bearing soaring skyward. After you perfect your skills, you will definitely be a man who can make a showy display of your ability, perhaps like the Monkey King in the novel *Journey to the West* you will often wreak havoc in my place. Not bad, the profession of cryptographer will not do without this heroic spirit of fearing nothing and supreme self-confidence." He turned to the two women soldiers, "All right, can you please apologise to him?"

The Number 8 courtyard house was located in the central area of the south ridge, where the 4th monitoring team was stationed. Chief Gao took Ji Zhenren to report for duty. On the way, Ji Zhenren took out a red Parker pen and handed it to Chief Gao, saying, "This is a pledge of love from my girlfriend before her death. I'll leave it with you. I want to completely banish any distractions from my mind so that I can devote myself to my job here." Chief Gao took the pen, seeing Jiang Xiaodian carved on the cap.

He said, "The pen is precious, the love between you and your girlfriend is precious, and your trust in me is precious too. You can rest assured. I will defend the pen with my life!"

After entering the office, Ji Zhenren met with two surprises: the team leader Song Daxiong was one of the women soldiers who had tied him up in the woods, and there were three pots of begonia on the window sill opposite the work desk.

Song Daxiong was a beautiful and sensitive girl. At once she knew what the new colleague was curious about, saying, "I'm the fifth daughter of my family. My parents had no sons, so I was given a boy's name and brought up like a boy. I planted these begonias, only wanting to add some charm and peace to the tense and bustling atmosphere in the work room."

Ji Zhenren was still looking at the flowers, his attentive expression showed an innate self-importance, but his face revealed sadness: "Actually, the begonias have a quiet nature because they are depressed. The flora emblem for begonia is pangs of love, and the ancients called them heart-broken flowers. Recently I liked this flower very much. Could it be that team leader Song also…"

Chief Gao stopped him and, turning to Song Daxiong, he said, "Your work desk is a battlefield, not suitable for planting flowers. Little Song, move the flowers away." Flushed, Song Daxiong asked a colleague to move the flowers out of the room.

Casting a sidelong glance at Ji Zhenren, Chief Gao knew that he was the kind of person who could feel things very deeply. He had asked for the flowers to be removed because he did not want Ji Zhenren every now and then to think of the woman in Shanghai. How could Song Daxiong have known about this? She thought that Chief Gao had given her an out.

After Chief Gao left, Ji Zhenren discovered that the second woman soldier who had tied him up in the woods was also in this team. He said to the two girls, "You two owe me an apology. Make it up now."

"It's office time," said Song Daxiong. "We mustn't do anything unrelated to work. This is discipline. Chen Xiaohua, come with me to the maintenance room and let's get our transceiver back." As soon as they stepped out of the room, they burst into laughter.

The 4th monitoring team was allocated two transceivers. Three people shared every one and did a 24-hour monitoring shift. After Ji Zhenren began to work, he would not leave the transceiver and worked more than 12 hours a day, taking up other people's time, so the others complained about him. He gave no thought to the problem, which was left to be sorted out by Song Daxiong, who handled the issue carefully and skilfully. She generously let Ji Zhenren take some of her hours, while she spent the time doing management work. Afterwards she would often plug a headphone into the transceiver Ji Zhenren was working on, as she noticed that his way of monitoring was very strange, not conforming to common practice, but it looked like he was fooling about with the transceiver. She had to supervise him because it was her duty to do so.

A monitor had to perfect two basic skills: the ability to capture radio signals and the ability to transcribe the signals after catching them; otherwise he or she had low-grade professional skills. Song Daxiong was an expert monitor, having rich experience in actual combat situations; her ability to monitor and transcribe in a complicated signal environment was clearly well above the others, so she was eminently qualified to supervise Ji Zhenren.

In a sea of radio signals, to catch the useful ones was like being in a forest searching for tree leaves that looked the same superficially but had different patterns underneath. The usual way was to start from one edge of the forest, leaf after leaf, tree after tree, row after row, until one reached the other edge, then to turn around and do the same again, covering the whole area without missing a single tree or a single leaf. During the process, when monitors found what they were looking for, they transcribed the information using standard writing symbols and then handed the transcript to cryptographers for decryption. Song Daxiong noticed that Ji Zhenren did his monitoring in a completely different way. He would hammer here and batter there, jumping, or attacking a vital point, or searching without any order, and his transcription method was particularly unorthodox; no one could understand his random numbers and strange symbols.

She questioned him and ordered him to strictly follow the standard operating procedure. Promising that he would, he carried on using his own method. When he was pressed too hard, he would say: "My way is faster, more efficient and more precise for catching useful signals. For the time being I cannot explain clearly how it works, nor can I explain the method to the others. Let me do it and I will explain later."

Song Daxiong reported Ji Zhenren to Chief Gao, who called Ji Zhenren to his office. "Although you can't explain what you're doing, I still trust you because I never intended to make you adhere to conventional methods. All I want from you is that you are able to stand out, make a spectacular display of your ability and sweep away all obstacles. How you achieve this is entirely up to you. I just want results!"

However, Ji Zhenren still tried to explain, "My method is quick and precise. In the same amount of time, I can search a much larger area. My method suits all types of transceivers and operators with different techniques and changing signals. I tried this method when I received my training, and I am grateful that you still support me."

Chief Gao tried to give a smile, but didn't, saying, "You are grateful. You are a special case. You plough your own furrow! But we found and summed up our current effective procedures and practices through years of actual combat experience. Except for you, all the other comrades must follow these procedures and practices, no one can act recklessly."

In some respects, Ji Zhenren was too insensitive. What he said next ultimately annoyed Chief Gao.

"I jumped among the related frequencies, accurately attacking the vital ones and scanning them section by section. I didn't do it recklessly. I summed up my method after my unrelenting testing and the result is not inferior to our orthodox practices; therefore only treating me as a special case is not enough. More people should be given the opportunity to blaze new trails in their own way. What is Chiang Kai-shek's technical efficacy? What is our technical efficacy? Isn't it perfectly clear in our mind? If we don't let every one of us exploit our brain power to make full use of it, there will be no hope for us no matter what the circumstances."

Pounding the table and glaring at Ji Zhenren, Chief Gao yelled, "Don't push your luck! We've worked day and night for two years to reach our present position. You've only been here for a few days, so how dare you challenge my authority? That I support you does not mean that everything you do is correct. Don't come to me and cry that you are more brilliant than me until you catch the golden rat, open its chest bone and pull out its evil guts." Ji Zhenren was dumbstruck by Chief Gao's tirade. Taking a breath, Chief Gao went on, "You are not the only staff in our unit. All your actions must be understood by the others. Without understanding, there would be no support. Do you understand?"

Ji Zhenren seemed to comprehend, saying, "When I do something, it's not enough that I myself understand it, or that the leaders understand it. I must let everyone understand it and support me." He did not return to his office, but went to the Number 1 courtyard. He wiped the propaganda text off the blackboard, then filled the board with his own words. The contents were mainly about how he followed the generality and particularity of the wireless signals, tuning in to the frequency at the most appropriate time, and writing the information down in shorthand by writing an index. He openly declared that to intercept enemy radio communications and to decipher enemy codes, as well as having an exceptionally good memory, comprehension, imagination, and ability to crack ciphers, a cryptographer had to cultivate a manner of immortality and wisdom. A super-intelligent genius and his attacking posture of half immortal and half human might enable him to defeat all enemies. At the end he wrote, "Please understand me, believe me and support me!"

His writing caused a sensation in all the courtyards of the complex. Everyone seemed to have understood what he had said, but they all felt that they could not follow such a style, saying it might only suit people like him. But the phrase 'half immortal and half human' was denounced, and in private someone gave Ji Zhenren the nickname 'Ji the half immortal'.

But 'Ji the half immortal' did live up to his name!

A few days ago, something unexpected had suddenly happened to the 4th monitoring team. The radio signals for the KMT 121st Division, 2nd Brigade, 3rd Brigade and the Huang Gu Independent Regiment, who were stationed east of Qingchuan, suddenly disappeared. These troops had all been using the *LEI* cipher to communicate with each other, but they all suddenly stopped using it at the same time. The 4th monitoring team's two transceivers made an emergency search but failed to find any signals. In the end Song Daxiong handed the task to Ji Zhenren, who made an analysis of the related circumstances. In the past, the wireless communications between the enemy's 121st Division and the two brigades shared a common feature; the implementation of security regulations was not strict. In their coded telegrams, they often mixed in plain text, and particularly the names of their commanders and their unit designations were often sent by plain text. The monitoring team followed this feature to search for enemy signals, but to no avail. He judged that it was because the enemy might have tightened up their discipline, banning their operators from mixing coded messages with plain text.

So he was on duty for 13 to 14 hours a day, focusing on monitoring the signals without any plain text. Soon he captured six suspicious targets. After consulting the other monitoring teams, verifying, classifying and sifting through, he logged on to two key signals. However, to ascertain whether they were the target transceivers, he needed to transcribe more encrypted messages so as to decipher and therefore verify them.

Chief Gao pressed for results, and Song Daxiong was also restless.

In the day time, when Ji Zhenren was on the transceiver, Song would stand by his side watching, and no one could drive her away. Ji Zhenren then asked her to replace him. He sat next to her, plugging headphones into the machine, listening, watching her transcribing and thinking. According to regulations, whenever a telegram was transcribed, it had to be sent to the decryption office to be deciphered at once. Ji Zhenren always made a copy for himself, and comparing them with those intercepted previously he would often be lost in thought.

On the day in question, he sat there holding some telegrams in his hands. Out of sorts, he looked like he had fallen asleep. Suddenly he patted on the desk, crying out, "Yes. This signal we are monitoring is not the one used by the enemy's 121st Division but by their logistics brigade stationed in Ganku township."

Song Daxiong was startled, knowing that from his analyses of the headings and endings he must have found the flaws in the telegrams, thereby coming to the conclusion where they were sent from. She ordered him to concentrate on monitoring another signal, while they both knew that the remaining signal was basically the one they were looking for.

Song Daxiong was very excited. Sitting beside him, she constantly looked sidelong at him, and she even held up her thumb in praise. Having no time to pay attention to her, Ji Zhenren hastily transcribed a message. When he had finished, he signalled her to make a spare copy.

They both relaxed a bit after they only needed to monitor one signal. Ji Zhenren wrote on a piece of paper, "You go to sleep and come back tonight. I have no confidence in the others." Giving him an understanding smile, Song Daxiong turned and left the room.

That evening, she came to take her turn on duty. Ji Zhenren picked up a few copies of the spare telegrams and clutched them to his chest. Song Daxiong showed that she had seen nothing. Ji Zhenren knew that she had given tacit consent to what he was doing. According to security regulations, they were not allowed to make a spare copy of intercepted telegrams and they were not to be taken out of the office. No matter whether it was tacitly approved by the team leader or not, he had already violated the regulations, because at her level she had no authority on such a matter. He thought that she had neither stopped him, nor exposed him, which meant that she had guessed what he was thinking.

Although he had sat at the desk monitoring radio signals all day, he did not feel tired. In high spirits he walked out of the room. Behind him a voice said, "I've boiled some chicken soup and it's in your dormitory."

Grateful, he replied, "Let me bring those begonias back tomorrow."

She called out, "How dare you? You pay me the money for the chicken."

After Ji Zhenren finished his supper, he began to feel tired. He went to bed with his clothes on, but was woken up by his own dreams. Picking up the telegrams he turned the cipher over in his mind, feeling it was different to the other ciphers he had met before. Unlike a hard rock, it could neither be broken nor opened; a solid piece, neither soft nor hard force could penetrate. It was more like a rubber ball; a knife could not cut it and fingers could not break it either, but it bounced when it was thrown to the floor, or caved in if it was pressed. Bouncing means there was a reaction, caving in means it could change shape. This gave people hope, temptation, making them feel that they could break it. Why did he have such a feeling? He finally confirmed that this cipher was encrypted on the basis of the master copy of the plain text codebook, and that was why he felt he had met it before. After he found out the cipher type, he was one step closer to the target.

At midnight he went to the office. Song Daxiong said to him urgently, "The enemy's 121st Division has communicated frequently with the two brigades and the regiment. It seems that something is happening. I transcribed five telegrams and have sent them to the decryption office. I've kept the spare copies, so you can have a look at them." Looking at her, Ji Zhenren felt grateful. He knew she had violated the rules to keep the spare copies for him, which showed she had confidence in him, as well as great expectations of him. Taking the copies, he left the office.

Early the next morning, Song Daxiong did not see Ji Zhenren in the office but found a note on the desk, "I'm free today, but don't look for me." However, it was impossible for her not to look for him, because he had those telegrams she had kept without permission. After not seeing him all day, she was in a panic. She searched all the buildings and yards in the complex but failed to find him. Where could he have gone? Patting her head, she dragged Chen Xiaohua and they ran to the wooded slope.

They pushed open the door of the small dark room. It was empty, and there was no furniture inside but an oil lamp was burning. A man was sitting on the floor in the centre of the room. It was Ji Zhenren, who was gathering a pile of paper with codes and ciphers written on it. Seeing someone entering, he staggered to his feet. Song Daxiong rushed to support him, "Sitting on the cold floor with no food or drink for a day and a night, you are the biggest fool in the complex."

Extracting a few sheets of paper from the pile, Ji Zhenren said, "I've cracked it. The cipher used by the enemy's 121st Division is *MIAN*. Hurry, take these three telegrams to Chief Gao. It's very urgent! Wait, send the instructions how to decipher *MIAN* to the decryption office. Quick!"

Song Daxiong sped away.

After delivering the telegrams to Chief Gao, Song Daxiong went back to the office. Ji Zhenren was there and said, "You might not have read those three telegrams. They were combat orders for operational preparations from the enemy's 121st Division to the 2nd and 3rd Brigades and the Huang Gu Independent Regiment. Early tomorrow morning they will encircle and attack our 2nd Regiment in Qihe Village. But it's not too bad, our troops have one day to prepare for battle."

In high spirits and excited, Song Daxiong said, "Yesterday, after the 2nd decryption team got those telegrams, they spent the whole day and night but failed to decipher them. But you sorted them out in that small dark room. You are marvellous."

Ji Zhenren laughed, "When my head was wrapped in a gunnysack and I was thrown into that room, I felt it was a tranquil, solitary and inspiring place."

Putting one hand over her mouth, Song Daxiong chuckled, "You are a narrow-minded man, still harbouring resentment toward us."

They went to eat their breakfast, but in the mess they saw not a single person from the decryption teams. Song Daxiong said, "Chief Gao has taken all the cryptographers to test *MIAN*. Perhaps they are holding meetings to discuss the result. I'm afraid they will miss breakfast. But how can they eat?"

Ji Zhenren did not understand. "Why?"

"Because of you. How could they stand the humiliation?"

"It can't be. They are cryptographers. If they are so narrow-minded, how can they face the mighty enemy force?"

"I don't know what Chief Gao was thinking," said Song Daxiong.

"He should put you in the decryption teams to display your skills to the fullest. But he put you in my place to transcribe telegrams; what a waste of your talent."

"It's probably because he wants me to be a good vegetable farmer, and then a good cook," replied Ji Zhenren. "To be a good cook, I must learn how to grow vegetables first."

Song Daxiong shook her head, "It's not fitting, not proper, and you did it covertly; what the hell is this?"

Ji Zhenren laughed, "This is not the first time I've been in this position. I used to secretly decipher telegrams when I was in Shanghai." A sensitive man, he went quiet at once when the past event in Shanghai was mentioned.

After breakfast, he returned to the office. Song and Chen were on the transceiver so he sat beside the desk watching them working. With no sign of joy on his face, his expression showed that something was weighing on his mind.

He asked, "What do we usually do with the important telegrams we decrypt?"

"When we decrypt a telegram, we lose no time in sending it to the senior leaders in the general headquarters," replied Song Daxiong. "The intelligence from us played a big role in previous campaigns against Chiang Kai-shek's encirclement, so generally the senior leaders at the headquarters trust us very much."

Ji Zhenren looked pensive. After a silence, doubt and worry repeatedly showed in his eyes. With ease and fluency, he said, "The enemy's 121st Division terminated its communications with the two brigades and the regiment. But it suddenly resumed the communications, and corrected its previous mistakes but used a higher-level double-cipher substitution table to encrypt their messages. Why? I don't see any problem with the MIAN technique, but I feel there's something not right about the enemy's action this time. I need to go to the other monitors to see what they have got, to see if any communications among the other enemy troops are related to this action, particularly whether the enemy's 121st Division has submitted a request to its superiors for instructions to encircle and attack our 2nd Regiment, or any operational orders to the 121st Division from its superiors. This enemy transceivers' practice was a longstanding practice, and they had always been ignorant of their stupidity. But they suddenly terminated the service of their transceivers and changed their cipher and enforced discipline. Viewed from the scope of the technique and common practice, there is a strong possibility that the enemy has smelt a rat that their cipher has been broken. Is it necessary for us to warn the senior leaders of the general headquarters about it?"

Song Daxiong did not agree with him at all, saying, "You had no sleep for a whole day. Why not go and take a rest? Don't sit here pondering and worrying for nothing. I am puzzled what kind of a woman in Shanghai could have tempered you into such a disposition. I always say the first thing that comes into my mouth, and I am frank and outspoken, so I hope you won't take offence."

Ji Zhenren's eyes became blurred, terrifying, and he gazed at her, "From the telegram, the time for the enemy troops to launch the attack is six o'clock tomorrow morning, which means they must make a long-range raid by moonlight to Qihe village, then go and hide in the woods in Jumao mountain on the eastern outskirts of the village, and wait for daybreak. Then they can suddenly appear in front of the barracks of our 2nd Regiment and launch an offensive. If the telegram is true, this is what the enemy will do." Song Daxiong realised he had not taken in anything she had said.

"If the enemy 121st Division's military deployment is a hoax, its intention must be to test if their wireless communications are safe or not. Therefore, ahead of time they will definitely send out scouts to observe our 2nd Regiment. If our 2nd Regiment moves away for no reason, it will tell the enemy that their cipher has been broken and we have obtained their battle plan." He persisted, "If the enemy battle plan is true, but our 2nd Regiment doesn't move away in advance, they will be completely surrounded when the enemy makes a surprise attack. Meanwhile, the enemy can also figure out that if we have truly cracked their cipher, we will most likely send troops to reinforce our 2nd Regiment. Therefore the enemy will definitely lay an ambush and attack our reinforcements. When I did my training, I memorised all the names of the Chinese counties and cities on the map, and I also did some research on the villages, townships, mountains and rivers in the Central Soviet Area and its surroundings. I noticed that from Ruijin to Qihe village, the Jiahe mountain path is the only route, so the enemy can lay an ambush on the mountain path and attack our reinforcements. My guess is that, based on the three telegrams, our headquarters will deploy some of our main forces to go firstly along the Jiahe mountain path, then they will split and go to Wangouling and

Yangcun to ambush the enemy's 2nd and 3rd Brigades respectively, as well as to Mashan to counterattack the enemy's Huang Gu Independent Regiment, which is over there to surround our troops. If the three telegrams sent by *MIAN* are true, the above plan is the best for us. If it is a trap, the enemy must have made preparations. So if we follow the above plan, we will definitely come to grief!"

Song Daxiong laughed loudly, "It seems that my team is too small a place, even Chief Gao's office will fail to do justice to your talents. You should go and report for duty at the general headquarters. I hear they are short of a chief of staff."

Ji Zhenren also laughed, "It's true this *MIAN* is making me feel uneasy. I must go to every team and check every transceiver."

Song Daxiong stopped him. She said, seriously, "I've already violated regulations to let you keep copies of the enemy telegrams. Now you want to go to the other teams and check their transcripts. You have no right to do so, nor do I, that is our chief's job. As I see it, you'd better stop poking your nose into the matter. In the past, the ciphers cracked by all the teams played a good role; besides, every cryptographer wants the ciphers they crack to be more valuable, so they can attract more attention from the higher-ups. But you are different. Before the decryption teams did anything, you had already broken *MIAN*, making a crucial contribution to obtaining three important pieces of intelligence, so your achievement has been greater."

Ji Zhenren remained silent for a while, then he said, "I know *MIAN* is the first cipher I've cracked, which is a memorable thing. But I still believe I'm not worrying too much. I will go and see Chief Gao."

"He's gone to the headquarters with those telegrams," said Song Daxiong. "They're going to discuss the deployment of troops."

Ji Zhenren was more fidgety, muttering, "Team leader Song, I am going to get you into trouble again."

He left in a hurry. On the pretence of Chief Gao ordering him to check all the enemy telegrams, he went to every team but he saw nothing to worry about except a few telegrams showed that the enemy troops were doing some military drills in a mountainous area far away from Qihe village. None of these activities had anything to do with the enemy's plan to encircle and attack the 2nd Regiment of the Red Army.

Song Daxiong was furious, "How dare a monitor use his chief's name and violate regulations to go and check the telegrams?" She then placed Ji Zhenren in confinement, putting Chen Xiaohua in charge of guarding the room.

In less than the time needed to eat a meal, Chen Xiaohua ran to Song Daxiong reporting that Ji Zhenren had escaped by climbing out of the window, and he had also taken a horse from the messenger squad.

Without a moment's hesitation, Song Daxiong mounted a horse and rushed to the headquarters which was located in a high-walled, three-entry landlord's residence. When Ji Zhenren arrived, he slipped out of the saddle and tried to get in. But guards stopped him. No matter how he explained, they wouldn't let him in. Song Daxiong arrived and she pulled him away.

Ji Zhenren simply refused to go back, shouting, "Song Daxiong, you either shoot me or help me to break in. This time you must believe me."

Song Daxiong told him, "Things are normal, but your unbridled behaviour could disrupt the senior commanders' combat determination, which will be a serious black mark against you."

Ji Zhenren replied, "After I thinking about it over and over again, I felt that the situation might really not be very encouraging."

Clenching her teeth and stamping her feet, Song Daxiong said resolutely, "Ji Zhenren, you can even read those short essays from the Ming and Qing dynasties, which shows that your professional achievements are not inconsiderable. I believe you this time. Go, I will cover for you."

Leading the way, she lowered her head and forced her way in. When the guards came to stop her, she made an exaggerated gesture of drawing her pistol. How outrageous! The guards at once threw her to the ground.

While the guards' attention was on Song Daxiong, Ji Zhenren took the opportunity to get through the entrance, but he was stopped at the gate of the back yard. Picking up a brick, he thew it at the door of the room. Immediately two men, Chief Gao and Assistant Chief of Staff Li, ran out.

Held back by two guards, Ji Zhenren called out, "If I am not allowed to finish my words, I will bang my head against the wall and kill myself today."

Like a machine gun firing, he said, "There is a strong possibility that those three enemy telegrams encrypted by *MIAN* are false and that the enemy has laid a trap to ambush our troops en route to Qihe village. The enemy seem to be doing drill far away from Qihe village, but their main force is advancing by a roundabout route. I have checked the map, and all the enemy troops doing the drill have a shortcut to take.

"This enemy action is a long-planned, large-scale military action. But the conditions for us to fight the battle are not ripe. If we engage the enemy, we will be broken up into pockets at the Jiahe mountain path and Wangouling, Yangcun and Mashan villages, and we'll be wiped out by the enemy one by one. If my guess is right, you've just decided on this route for our troops to advance.

"Our safe plan should be like this: to the north of Qihe village is Limaozi mountain where the tree cover is extremely thick. At about 4 or 5 o'clock tomorrow morning, our 2nd Regiment can send some people to the mountain and secretly light a few big fires, so that the troops and the villagers can go to the mountain to fight the fires. If the enemy's 121st Division's action is just a hoax to test if we have broken their cipher, then our troops' and civilians' departure from the village will not make them think that we have done so. Besides, they may follow us to the mountain, where we can ambush them."

Assistant Chief of Staff Li roared, "As I see it, there is a strong possibility that you are a lunatic!"

Chief Gao added, "My goodness, only on the basis of your own judgement, with all these 'possibilities' and 'maybes' but no hard evidence, how dare you create such havoc at the general headquarters? You really are a Monkey King."

Ji Zhenren opened his mouth again, "There's no urgency, nor is it strategically necessary for the enemy to make such a long-range raid on our 2nd Regiment. What do they want then? One thing is clear, that this long-range enemy raid is not just to wipe out our 2nd Regiment. From Ruijin to Qihe village, the physical features of the terrain are favourable for a formidable enemy to ambush a weaker army, and it's easy to separate a weaker army into pockets, or to surround them. The hills are easy to enter but hard to get out of, so the door can be closed very quickly."

Waving his hand, Assistant Chief of Staff Li stopped Ji Zhenren. "By only seeing your neighbour having a good wok, you're making a judgement that they are going to slaughter a pig and cook pork. Is this how RSU2 has got all your intelligence? Absolutely ridiculous. You came here to disrupt our decisionmaking. What a nerve you've got! Get him out of here!"

Two guards pulled Ji Zhenren out of the compound. Stamping his feet he cried, "Brother soldiers, life is as precious as Heaven. We can't let our soldiers lose their lives for nothing." Seeing that Song Daxiong's hands and arms were being tied behind her back with a rope looped around her neck, he dashed across to her. But he was tightly pressed to the ground by the guards.

Many days afterwards, whenever Ji Zhenren thought of MIAN, he would feel uneasy, but he was reluctant to ask for information. However, he paid close attention to the radio signals of the enemy's 121st Division, finding no new changes. He admitted that he had been so oversensitive that he had overcomplicated the enemy situation and got it wrong, making quite a scene. When he saw Song Daxiong again, he felt embarrassed. He pushed the money for the chicken soup into her hand but she refused to take it.

One day RSU2 held a meeting for all staff. The general headquarters specially sent Assistant Chief of Staff Li, who was in charge of intelligence, to attend the secret commendation meeting, in which a tribute was paid to Song Daxiong and Ji Zhenren, who were called to the podium and had a big red paper flower pinned on their chests. The scene took Ji Zhenren by surprise, and he looked dumbstruck. He then realised the enemy intelligence encrypted by MIAN was genuine, and not intended to test the Red Army. The three telegrams he had deciphered must have played a role in saving the lives of the Red Army troops as well as those of the villagers in Qihe village.

The ferocious expression previously on Assistant Chief of Staff Li's face had vanished. Gently he announced the award winners' achievements. First, he mentioned that Song Daxiong's monitoring team had recaptured the enemy 121st Division's radio signals and successfully transcribed the encrypted telegrams; and, in particular, Ji Zhenren had broken MIAN, which was of profound technical significance. He then said, "But I want to tell you that the benefits of the intelligence we obtained from those three telegrams was zero. Because they were all false intelligence."

Buzzing was heard under the podium. The expressions on Song Daxiong's and Ji Zhenren's faces changed, and sweat was dripping down their backs.

Waving his arms, and Li went on emotionally, "But it is these three false intelligence signals that have tested the military and political quality, as well as the professional skills that a cryptographer should have. After comrade Ji Zhenren deciphered the messages and reported them to his superior, he did not stop there; instead he did something that no one else has ever done before. Upholding his opinion, he used a scientific attitude to analyse the enemy situation and our situation, thereby capturing the facts hidden behind the enemy telegrams, and he worked out that they were false. The enemy's aim was to lure us into their trap, so that they could find out if we were monitoring their radio signals and trying to break their ciphers. What is even more frightening is that the enemy had laid out a tight encirclement, planning to ambush our troops, at which point Ji Zhenren forced his way into the general headquarters to remind us commanders to withdraw our combat plan, and to introduce a new countermeasure to deal with all aspects of the situation. We weren't fooled by the enemy. We successfully secured the radio monitoring channel, the source of our intelligence; and, in particular, we prevented our troops from being surrounded and annihilated. So we should give Ji Zhenren one more accolade. Apart from this, his suggestion to light fires on Limao mountain was also adopted by the headquarters, with good results. Therefore, this time Ji Zhenren has received top marks for monitoring, deciphering and reporting. He has won a clear victory, which I hereby praise him for by way of encouragement."

Ji Zhenren was dripping with cold as well as hot sweat. His legs trembled nonstop, so Song Daxiong had to quietly help him stand still.

8 / THE YING CIPHER

It was during an informal discussion that Song Daxiong unwittingly revealed her romantic inclination towards Ji Zhenren.

Some time ago, the 'comparative study method' collectively worked out by RSU2 had produced a conspicuous effect under battle conditions. At one stroke they had broken three enemy ciphers. After the battle ended, in the summing-up meeting, Chief Gao read out the appraisal given by the higher authorities, "The mastery of codebreaking techniques has brought a revolutionary leap forward in the Red Army's reconnaissance capacity, underscoring the unique advantages of wireless reconnaissance. RSU2 shoulders a heavy responsibility. One word, one code can decide the future of the Red Army and our soldiers' lives. The merits and achievements of the unit are evident, yet they will forever go down in history as silent, truly unsung heroes. The miracle of killing three birds with one stone created by RSU2 in this battle has been completely proven."

Obviously the remarks were immensely encouraging. At once everyone was in high spirits and burning with righteous ardour. Unexpectedly, as soon as Chief Gao finished speaking, Song Daxiong talked of her feelings, too impatient to wait. Normally, in an informal discussion anyone could speak out freely, but this meeting was about tackling codes and ciphers, so the cryptographers had to speak first. As a monitor, under the circumstances she should have said nothing or spoken less. But her lengthy spur-of-the-moment talk was beyond everyone's expectations.

"Millet plus rifles are always linked to the Red Army, while aircraft, artillery and tanks are always linked to the White army. No matter how, we cannot rival them in weaponry. Therefore we must make the most of at least one or two strong points. So what are our strong points? One is obvious, the Red Army officers' and men's firm political faith, high level of class consciousness and fearless spirit of giving their lives for their cause. No matter how, the White army cannot rival us in this respect.

"Next is our fast-increasing understanding of wireless reconnaissance technology. In intelligence-based warfare, we can be more advanced, or even better than our enemy. But where do our killer skills come from? The most crucial thing for us is that we have people like Ji Zhenren, who is exceptionally gifted at breaking codes and ciphers. He is our backbone, a real treasure for us.

"The three enemy ciphers, their relations and internal regularities, the dots of the rarely used characters, the faces of the commonly used characters, the shadows of the horizontal lines, the flavour of the vertical lines and the voices of the angled lines, at every key moment and link, Ji Zhenren was able to follow the changes in frequencies, capturing the enemy signals one by one and getting the cipher cracked. With him I truly witnessed what invisibility is like."

Rash in her manner, she spoke without a break. The whole room was silent. When she had finished, she realised something, so she added, "Of course, he is not the only one who should be credited with the three wins over three battles. I only want to express my feelings about the wonderful achievement made by our rare talent Ji Zhenren. What he has done is something I have never seen before."

Chief Gao stopped her. "It seems that comrade Song Daxiong has been aroused by this victory. The rest of you, don't just sit there, you can also say something."

After the meeting was over, Chief Gao let the mess prepare a victory feast with food and wine. Calling it a feast, each table actually only had a bowl of wild herbs, a mixed stew of aubergine, beans and taro, and a large bowl of assorted stewed fish, freshly caught from the river and ponds - all filled to the top.

They had just finished the night shift, so everyone was hungry and tired. The food went quickly. Some staff then went to bed to sleep.

Chief Gao kept Ji Zhenren behind and had a chat with him. Too fatigued, Ji Zhenren leaned on the table and fell asleep.

Song Daxiong was helping with the washing up in the kitchen.

Walking over to them, she used a towel and gently wiped Ji Zhenren's face. Then putting his arm around her shoulder, she said: "Every cipher is as heavy as a thousand *jin (catties)*. It's impossible for him not to be crushed under the pressure. I'll take him back to his room."

"Let me do it."

"You are a leader. It's not proper for you to help a drunk."

"He only drank a little."

"He gets drunk as soon as he touches alcohol."

"It's not proper for a woman to hold a man's arm on her shoulder."

Hearing Chief Gao's remarks, Song Daxiong arched her back and Ji Zhenren was on her back. "Now his arm is not on my shoulder. A leader shouldn't let their imagination run wild," she muttered.

Carrying Ji Zhenren on her back, Song Daxiong turned around and walked away while muttering, "What is wrong with me? Why is my mind so confused where Ji Zhenren is concerned? It confuses me and confuses others. How could I have lost control over my own mind?"

Watching the shadow staggering away into the distance, feeling apprehensive, Chief Gao followed them.

A few days later, Song Daxiong boiled some chicken soup for Ji Zhenren. On the way to his dormitory, she met Chief Gao. Deliberately, she put the pot on top of her head and entered Ji Zhenren's room. She meant to leave as soon as she had put down the pot, but seeing Chief Gao still standing outside the window looking around, she just sat down on Ji Zhenren's bed and chatted with him for a while. Then she said to him, "I'm going. Can you see me off?" When they were outside, she said again, "We are not relatives, but you see me off outside the door." Cheerfully she touched his face with her fingers, saying, "Look at you, you've still got chicken soup on your chin." Seeing the scene, Chief Gao went off in a huff.

Song Daxiong then broke into a wide smile.

Her tender loving care did touch Ji Zhenren, whose heart was as warm as spring sunshine. That night he warmed up the last of the chicken soup and drank it. Then he added a bowl of hot water and, shaking the pot, he drank that too. At the time supplies were extremely scarce, but she made chicken soup for him. Such a show of affection was firmly embedded in his mind.

Ji Zhenren had missed his normal bedtime for quite a period of time. That night, after drinking the chicken soup, as soon as his head touched the pillow he was fast asleep. The soup warmed his stomach, while the person who had cooked the soup came into his dreams. It was a scene he had never experienced in his dreams before. To his heart's content he gave free play to expressing his complicated yet clear affection for her. A few times he turned her body around but what he saw was not her. Who was she? It was an indistinct face. She walked away. He did all he could to chase. And at last he caught up with her in a forest. Madly he kissed that indistinct face. Suddenly the weather changed. There was a violent storm with flashes of rolling thunder and lightning. He had nowhere to take shelter. He then clearly saw that he was in the camphor forest by the Huangpu river. Against the wind, the rain, the thunder and the lightning she ran away from him. Again he chased. Exhausted, he could not catch up with her no matter how fast he ran. When he finally caught up with her, it was on a battlefield, which was filled with continuous gunfire, the sound of bombs going off, the whistling of bullets and the screams of women. He threw himself at her and her warmth embraced him again. Trembling with excitement, he was seized by happiness, feeling her love interwoven with him. Holding her tight in his arms, he slowly felt the warmth on his chest turning cold. Stretching out his hand, he touched her. He cried out in alarm. The warmth he felt was the blood pouring from her breast. He fainted and sank into sleep.

Too tired, he slept until the first glimmer of dawn the next morning. Throwing on his clothes, he went to attend the morning shift.

It was cold outside. The sky was overcast; drizzling with fine rain, puddles were all over the road. He suddenly remembered he had heard thunder in his sleep. Then thunder came into his ears from the mountains in the distance. He paused and was scared into a cold sweat. Instantly he thought of a fatal question: thunder in the rain was a wireless monitor's natural enemy. My goodness, it thundered last night.

Normally a thunderstorm could badly disrupt a monitor's work. A succession of the ear-piercing noises in the headphones make it impossible for monitors to hear signals clearly, and therefore they are unable to fully transcribe messages. Sometimes the signals disappear, consequently monitors can only transcribe some incomplete or useless messages. Moreover, continuous loud thunder claps can almost pierce the ear drum and damage the ear canal. For monitors who have been in the profession for a long time, many suffer from tinnitus or loss of hearing, a professional disease. While the worst danger is to be struck by lightning. Electricity follows the aerial and gets into the transceiver and the earphone, instantly damaging the transceiver and possibly killing the monitor. However, no matter what the weather conditions, a monitor must never leave, never remove their headphones and never stop monitoring for one second.

Quickening his pace he ran to the office. But a terrible accident had happened.

He saw Song Daxiong sitting at the desk with her headphones on, her left hand turning the channels, her right hand holding a pen poised above the paper, but her whole right arm was soaked in blood. Under her feet the floor was covered in blood dripping down from her wrist. When she heard someone coming, she said, "Hurry up and replace me," and she then slipped under the desk and fainted.

Without hesitation, Ji Zhenren carried her on his back and ran to the medical unit.

Afterwards he found out what had happened. Song Daxiong was on night shift. Before he arrived, she had been working all night; even after she was struck by lightning and her right ear was bleeding continuously, she kept on working by using one ear for over three hours, during which time she didn't miss a single message.

She achieved this under such adverse weather conditions, demonstrating that her determination, professional skills and experience were sensational; particularly her skills were very admirable. Amid the lightning and thunder, the weak *click-clacking* sound of radio signals was hidden amid thousands of noises and many other *click-clacking* sounds; however, her brain and the good ear were able to subconsciously eliminate the interference, filter out the noise and precisely pinpoint the signal. She transcribed without missing a single symbol for hours.

Through her loyalty, incredible ear and first-class skills she miraculously didn't miss a single telegram in the stormy weather conditions, going down in RSU2's history as an exemplary model of how to behave in battle.

However, unexpectedly, for the first time since joining the army, Ji Zhenren was disciplined for taking Song Daxiong to the medical unit and thereby failing to balance the relationship between his duty and saving a life.

The reason was very simple. He spent 15 minutes taking Song to the medical unit, leaving the transceiver unattended for 15 minutes. If the enemy had sent out any important messages during these 15 minutes, the Red Army would have missed them.

This incident left Song Daxiong impaired in one ear. Ji Zhenren fell into despair and for a long time he could not get his mind around the events.

Chief Gao asked Song Daxiong to talk to Ji Zhenren. Since the incident, she had never expressed her gratitude or any feeling of sorrow toward him. From the bottom of her heart she felt that he was wrong for abandoning his post, which was an indisputable error, and that the loss caused by his action was also irreparable. As to how wrong he was and what kind of loss had been caused, there was no way of checking because, under the circumstances where there was only one transceiver to monitor one or several target signals, it was impossible to know whether the enemy had sent out any messages during those 15 minutes and, if so, what messages had been sent. But RSU2's rule was that as long as there was a possibility that messages could have been lost, it entailed dire consequences; as long as Ji Zhenren was at fault on the matter, he was in the wrong.

She reasoned things out for Ji Zhenren most sincerely, but he flared up in anger, "So you want me imprisoned or executed, don't you?"

Covering her left ear, she said, "The hearing in my right ear is impaired. I can't hear what you are saying. But I can tell you, I was the first to suggest that you be punished. You'd better get your head around this."

His tone became mild, "I deserve it no matter how harsh the punishment is. Compared with my affection for you, the work discipline is not worth a damn. It's worth shit!"

Many days later, Song Daxiong said to Ji Zhenren, "I didn't know that in your eyes I was that important." He understood she had clearly got the message on that day!

Before long the atmosphere in RSU2 became tense, which started after the interception of two enemy telegrams. One was a circular concerning the arrival in Nanchang of Chiang Kai-shek, and the other was a general order about Chiang Kai-shek concurrently being the Commander-in-Chief of the Encirclement and Suppression Army in the border area of Jiangxi, Guangdong and Fujian, and that he would personally command the fourth campaign to wipe out the Red Army. Although a few days previously they had already intercepted intelligence about the KMT army moving large numbers of troops from

Hubei, Henan, Anhui and Hunan to Jiangxi, the contents of these two telegrams still made RSU2 anxious and panicky, as they heralded a fresh and more perilous KMT campaign against the Red Army.

To crack an enemy's new cipher was always the most difficult and important task. During this period of time, the KMT's campaign headquarters at all levels and the field headquarters of Chiang Kai-shek in Nanchang had introduced some new codebooks and tables, which were extremely difficult to decipher, and which put huge pressure on the Red Army cryptographers.

War was around the corner. It was a busy scene for the frontline troops and their commanding officers, getting ready for the coming battles. RSU2's life-and-death fight had already begun a long time ago. They had to break the enemy's new ciphers before any confrontation started. They had to exhaust their brains and take great pains, yet never balk at any sacrifice, even if it cost them their lives. They had to work full time to monitor every aspect of the enemy situation, and to predict the enemy ciphers in combat circumstances so as to decrypt the enemy's important and urgent telegrams, while answering the Red Army general headquarters' questions concerning strategy and tactics.

Technically speaking, the most frightening thing for a monitor or a cryptographer was for the enemy to suddenly change to a new cipher on a new frequency when a battle was in progress. The signals you were monitoring and transcribing could instantly disappear without a trace. Both the warring sides were frequently sending out messages to deploy troops for battle, but suddenly you could hear nothing from your opponent. Anxiously you tuned in and searched, but all you could hear were dozens or hundreds of signals. You did not know which was the one you had just lost. The enemy transceivers you were monitoring had changed all of their frequencies, call signs and code. All the familiar clues had gone, like a drop of water hiding in the ocean, or a leaf concealed in a forest, you did not know where you could recover it, or where you could catch it.

This time, soon after the enemy began its fourth encirclement campaign, RSU2 lost all the signals of the communications between the KMT Central Route Army Headquarters and its 1st, 2nd and 3rd Columns. Meanwhile, following the Central Bureau's line of active offense, the Red Army's main forces were storming Nanfeng city, which was defended by the KMT's 8th Division under commander Chen Cheng, but failed to take the city after a long battle, and casualties were on the increase. At this critical moment of hostilities, RSU2 lost the enemy signals in this direction, thereby cutting off wireless intelligence resources.

The Red Army general headquarters frequently pressed RSU2 for information.

At the time, Chief Gao was organising the cracking of a new cipher used by the enemy's Left Route Army. After Song Daxiong's report, he wielded his pen and wrote down 'Ji'!!!

Chief Gao himself was a master cryptographer. He both personally cracked ciphers and made sure that the other cryptographers spared no effort to focus on the task in hand. This time, he adopted new measures. Apart from the normal system, he organised a special security team, led by Song Daxiong. Liu Kailai and another twenty soldiers were transferred to RSU2 to safeguard the cryptographers' supply and security needs. After the formation of this special team, he was able to spend more of his energy on supervising technical work.

So when Song Daxiong gestured to Liu Kailai and another soldier, they at once propped up Ji Zhenren, who was in his dormitory bent over the desk decrypting messages. He had not had any sleep for four days and three nights, and felt extremely weak. He did not know what had happened when he was held by two soldiers and forced to run. Song Daxiong explained to him about the situation while running beside him. Hearing her words, his spirit was aroused. Throwing off the two soldiers, he ran to the stream beside the road, plunging his head into the icy cold water. He got up and ran to the office.

Chen Xiaohua was on duty. Her face streaming with sweat, she was tuning in for signals while choking with sobs, "I've lost it. I've lost it. I beg you, uncle, where have you run to? Come out quick, OK?" She was from south Henan and always had a strong sense of responsibility, never allowing herself to make an error. She was the sort that when she missed a word or a numeral it was like she had lost her life. That day, the communications between the enemy's Central Route headquarters and all the columns were busy. She was contentedly transcribing the messages and every one of them was a top-quality job. But suddenly after she received the enemy coded message "All transceivers to use frequency 7, wavelength 8, code 14", her headphones went silent. She was at a loss. In her anxiety, she went so far as to call Chen Cheng uncle.

With the bearing of a general, Ji Zhenren was unusually calm.

Wiping Chen Xiaohua's face with his icy cold and wet sleeve, he said, "Calm down. Stop crying. Don't worry, let me have a go. You sit down and assist me."

Taking his seat, he put on the headphones. His left hand tuned and his right hand held a pen. Eyes flashing, he was immediately in his extraordinary and unique state of action.

All sorts of call signals could be heard. Dozens or hundreds of long and short signals, and all kinds of strange noises were also appearing and disappearing . Which one was the target signal? This member of the family whom he had never met before, but had changed into new clothes, a new gender and a new voice, was somewhere playing hide and seek with him.

According to operating rules, each team and its team members monitored and transcribed their own target signals. It was impossible for the monitors to immediately familiarise themselves with signals outside their own team, therefore these transceivers would be the jamming transceivers for him. Besides there were many unidentified signals, not for military but for civilian use. They could be either in plain code or in cipher. Also there were the *click-clacking* sounds of telegrams, or communications in local dialect, as well as opera singing and news reading. These signals badly interfered with the search for a target signal; meanwhile the enemy transceivers would also wantonly send signals to cover their new signals, so under such circumstances, to find a target signal with no particular characteristics would be like trying to find a needle in a haystack. No, harder than that. Think about it; searching for a needle in a haystack, at least an iron needle exists and although there is little hope of finding it, there is still a possibility of seeing it. However, in the sea and among countless fish, to find a little fish with the same outward appearance as the other fish, but with different internal organs, one can see how difficult a job it is.

But Ji Zhenren had the capacity to catch this little fish when the Red Army general headquarters could still afford to wait.

The useful signals could pass like a flash while noises and chaotic wavelengths would come into a monitor's ears endlessly. Under such circumstances, the knowledge, skill and experience that Ji Zhenren had accumulated for years could instantly work miracles. The situation of the enemy, the transceiver and the cipher combined to form a wonderful, fast chain reaction in his brain. Swiftly he tuned. Like lightning the signals repeatedly flashed past him. He had no time to think or to make a judgement at all. His brain cells directly told him, yes, no, or maybe. On hearing the enemy operators' different techniques or styles in sending messages, or different transceiver sounds, he was instantly able to discern which operator was using which transceiver. As soon as he heard the plain-code messages, he knew their contents straight away. On hearing a cracked cipher, he could tell what cipher it was and instantly transcribe the message into plain text. On hearing an uncracked cipher, he could quickly and precisely determine its characteristics and generally what type it was. He could distinguish if it was useful or useless, and a general or a key target. Then according to the information he quickly narrowed the search area, jumping and focusing on the key point. Repeatedly he tested and eventually captured the target signal.

He did monitoring, transcribing, comprehension and evaluation at the same pace, and at the same time he could deal with signals from eight enemy transceivers; his left hand swiftly tuned in to select stations, his brain judged the signals, his right hand transcribed; from the cracked ciphers he mirrored the related ciphers and turned the message into corresponding plain text; quickly he appraised the uncracked ciphers, and all these actions were completed in the blink of an eye and almost simultaneously.

Song Daxiong saw that the symbols and plain text read out by him were completely different from what he wrote down, the result of his quick thinking. What emerged from his lips was for Chen Xiaohua to record, who would then put her records on his right hand side so that he could from time to time flash his eyes at them. That is to say his hands, brain, mouth and eyes did different things at the same time, each complementing one another but not delaying his work. His ability to do several things at the same time had reached the pinnacle of perfection.

Song Daxiong was amazed. She exclaimed inwardly: "What a naturally gifted man! He is truly an exceptional person!"

After three hours' intensive work, Ji Zhenren recovered the enemy's new signals. At once he locked onto the communications between the commander-in-chief of the Central Route Army and the commander of the 1st Column. He wrote them down, but what he read out was different: "I've got the following enemy transceivers: Frequency U2 (code name), the enemy No. 2 transceiver of the Central Route Army Headquarters is sending messages to the enemy's 2nd Column;

Frequency B31, the enemy's No. 3 transceiver of the Central Route Army Headquarters is trying to get in touch with the enemy's 3rd Column; Frequency K17, the No. 2 transceiver of the enemy's 2nd Column is communicating with the No. 2 transceiver of the enemy's 1st Column. Hurry up and inform our reserve transceivers to monitor these enemy transceivers and transcribe their messages, and quickly send them to be deciphered by the decrypting team." Chen Xiaohua wrote down what Ji Zhenren said. Standing beside them, Song Daxiong saw clearly and memorised the information then swiftly ran out of the room.

After he had finished transcribing three long messages, Ji Zhenren signalled to Chen Xiaohua to replace him. He then began to decipher them. Chen Xiaohua transcribed two more messages and pushed them to him. He then spread the five messages on the table, sitting upright in his chair and noisily flicking through the papers. Suddenly he stood up. With his hands behind his back he paced up and down the room. Then he went and stood behind Chen Xiaohua, picking up the assistant's headphones and listening. Taking over more transcribed messages, he bent over the table and stayed motionless. Several hours passed. Song Daxiong brought in food but Ji Zhenren did not want it. Putting three chairs in a row he lay down to take a nap. But before long he got up and went to sit at the table, two bright eyes jumping among the numerical groups. Song Daxiong felt that wherever his piercing eyes fell, a hole could be burnt.

During the night, a sudden tinkling sound could be heard. It was Ji Zhenren pushing the food box onto the floor and giving it a few kicks. He swore, "Damn shit! You caused me too much trouble. You fucking wicked trick, pushing me too hard." He then pinched his head hard with his hands, looking like he was about to get two horns on his head. He twirled round a few times. Pulling up a chair, he sat down and fell asleep. It was the first time he had lost his temper and used foul language. Song Daxiong was surprised. She knew that he had come across a very hard nut, and he was on the brink of going mad. All right, let him have a good sleep, better not to wake him up until it is broad daylight, otherwise even an iron head would be wrecked. But after lying down for a short while Ji Zhenren tried to get up. He rolled off the chair and landed on the floor. Song Daxiong hurried to help him up. He then pinched his head hard again and whirled round and round. In a daze he muttered, "Call Chief Gao."

Song Daxiong dared not delay. She hurried to call Gao and the doctor. When the doctor saw Ji Zhenren in a lethargic sleep and unresponsive, he immediately carried out an emergency treatment. Ji Zhenren suddenly sat up, calling out, "Why? Have things changed?"

Chief Gao pulled at his shoulder, asking, "What is wrong with you?"

In a daze, Ji Zhenren said, "Nothing, I only want some sleep. I fell asleep and I dreamt that you were taking me to town to watch a play." Everyone in the room looked at him in amazement. He then said, "Oh sorry, I'm too tired to speak properly. Chief, I've cracked it, the YING cipher. One cipher overlapping with another cipher. It is being used by the KMT Nanchang field headquarters, the KMT Central Route Army and its 1st, 2nd and 3rd Columns. The telegrams show that Chen Cheng has assembled all the columns under his command and these troops are advancing to Nanfeng in an attempt to encircle and destroy our main forces in the city."

Grabbing the telegrams from the table Chief Gao dashed out of the room. Remembering something, Ji Zhenren asked Song Daxiong, "You thought I was ill, so you called the doctor, didn't you? You are smarter than I am, not carrying me on your back and going to the medical unit."

"Ah, you are so narrow-minded." She pressed him into the chair, saying, "I'm glad that you are OK. Hurry up and get some sleep. I will not wake you up unless there are changes to the enemy signals."

Ji Zhenren fell fast asleep. Song Daxiong called some people and they put him into a camp bed in the next room. This was his first sound sleep without interruption for four days.

After he woke up, Song Daxiong told him that the Red Army's main forces had evacuated Nanfeng on a timely basis, shaking off the danger of being encircled by Chen Cheng's superior forces.

Very soon, the Red Army general headquarters adopted a new strategy. One part of the troops pretended to move east to Lichuan, but the main forces secretly withdrew to Luodong, the area west of Guangchang to take cover and bide their time.

All at once the RSU2 staff swooped down to the front line, closely monitoring every movement of Chen Cheng's troops. After a few days' sleepless work, they finally captured the enemy's important messages, knowing that, as expected, Chen Cheng had misjudged the situation and he personally led his three columns to attack Lichuan.

Ji Zhenren was extremely excited. Patting Song Daxiong on the shoulder while stroking Chen Xiaohua's head, he said triumphantly, "Chen Cheng has been fooled."

Trying to push away his hand, Chen Xiaohua cried, "Aiya, comrade Ji's hand is so hot."

Song Daxiong touched his head, and also cried out, "You have a high temperature. Quick, go to a doctor." He refused. Song Daxiong had to call the medics who came and gave him medicine. But the temperature stayed high; besides, he felt chilly all over. Wrapping himself in a quilt, and with a wet towel on his forehead he read the telegrams that Chen Xiaohua put before him. In one breath he decrypted three urgent telegrams. In a weak voice he muttered: "A god-sent opportunity. Eat Li and Chen alive!" He then fainted and fell under the table.

A dozen telegrams intercepted and decrypted by all teams of RSU2 showed that the communications between the enemy's 52nd and 59th Divisions under the command of the 1st Column on the right flank had been blocked and they could not coordinate their operations, resulting in them being isolated on the north and south faces of Geluohe mountain. A rare chance for combat!

Meanwhile, Ji Zhenren's heavy cold had developed into pneumonia. He was in a lethargic state for two days. After he woke up, there was no further improvement in his condition, but he still rushed to the office, where Song Daxiong told him the good news, "The intelligence gathered by us has proved effective. In Jiaoba, Huangxiang and Dengxianqiao our main forces ambushed the advancing yet isolated enemy 52nd and 59th Divisions. After fierce fighting for two days and nights, we achieved complete victory, wiping out ten thousand of the enemy and capturing alive the commanders of the 52nd and 59th Divisions."

After hearing the news, to everyone's surprise the very weak Ji Zhenren jumped into the air. Song Daxiong's eyes moistened. He was that sort of man, as long as there were wireless signals and telegrams before his eyes, he had considerable endurance and amazing strength. His mind, energy and the battle had blended as one.

Suddenly Ji Zhenren became interested in several ordinary telegrams between the enemy's 1st Column headquarters and its advancing division commanded by Li Ming. Meanwhile it was the key moment for Chen Cheng's headquarters to assemble a large number of troops to surround the Red Army's main forces in Guangchang. The Red Army's general headquarters decided to beat Chen Cheng at his own game, trying to cast off the enemy encirclement but to create opportunities for combat. Under such circumstances the enemy frequently sent out all kinds of urgent and special telegrams, so RSU2 was swamped with work. From a batch of ordinary telegrams Ji Zhenren sensed something unusual: two from the 1st Column headquarters hinted to Li Ming that haste made waste, and advancing prematurely would certainly come to grief. But Li Ming ignored the warning. In the end the 1st Column headquarters just ordered Li Ming to move 80km away from Kucaoling.

The enemy troops under Li Ming's command were to withdraw from Kucaoling! So Kucaoling was where Li Ming's troops were concentrated!

Ji Zhenren dared not delay. He wrote down the information and submitted it to the Red Army headquarters, who immediately altered their operational preparations.

Ji Zhenren again went into a state of semiconsciousness. With his eyes half open, again and again he rummaged through the spare copies of the telegrams. He did not find anything unusual. In the small hours of the morning, he was too weak to raise his head. He picked up Chen Xiaohua's sewing kit and used a needle to prick his arms and thighs, while calling out inwardly, "Don't fall asleep. Don't fall asleep. I must not fall asleep." Feeling undecided, he finally stabbed the needle on the name 'Li Ming'.

Ji Zhenren knew this Li Ming inside out. The commander of a crack division, his bearing was always domineering and arrogant. He capitalised on commanding a crack force, striving to outdo the others in everything. A guy who would never say die, nor give up. His pet phrase was "I will never be defeated". So this extremely arrogant Li Ming would certainly not withdraw but fight this battle with the Red Army!

In high spirits Ji Zhenren suddenly called out, "Take me to Chief Gao."

Chief Gao thought that Ji Zhenren's words were reasonable, so he called some people and they carried Ji Zhenren to Assistant Chief of Staff Li, who was not in a hurry after finding out what it was about. Slowly he said, "Again it is a 'strong possibility' expressed by Ji Zhenren. No hard evidence, but some guesswork. I dare not report it to the high command. As far as I know, the troops under Li Ming's command are Chiang Kai-shek's *elite* troops. And all along they have observed strict military discipline, and they would certainly take action as long as there is an order. Li Ming will not defy orders."

"That's true," argued Ji Zhenren. "A crack unit always has the manner of a crack unit. But you should know that the soul of the crack unit is its commander, and this commander is Li Ming. I know him like I know my brothers. He will definitely defy orders and hold fast to his position. The best choice for us is to order a force to feign an attack on the enemy's 1st Column headquarters, making them move farther away from Li Ming's troops. Then we fight at Kucaoling, wiping out the mad man Li Ming!"

Assistant Chief of Staff Li ran out of patience, "Show me how clever you are when you have concrete evidence."

"You bureaucrats only know how to eat a ready-made meal," countered Ji Zhenren. "You can only drink spoiled soup and cold water." Feeling suffocated, he coughed nonstop, then lost consciousness and dropped to the floor.

He was put on a stretcher. Half way to the medical unit he regained consciousness. He simply refused to go to the medical unit. So he was carried back to his office. As soon as he entered the door, he cried out, "Stop two transceivers' work and have all three machines monitor Li Ming's troops."

Song Daxiong did not agree: "We will violate discipline if we do that without permission."

"I will take responsibility if things go wrong."

"I am the team leader, so how can you take such a responsibility?"

Ji Zhenren's voice was feeble: "Daxiong, at this moment what I need most is your support. This pot of rice needs you to cook it."

Song Daxiong's eyes brightened. Not reluctant any more, she said, "Let's do it." For the next part of the night, three monitors with three transceivers separately intercepted telegrams in which Li Ming ordered the follow-up unit and the supplies and gear unit to swiftly move to Kucaoling. "Damn it. Half a night has been wasted. I don't know if we still have enough time. Most urgent! Report to Chief Gao! Report!"

Three days later, Ji Zhenren was on the mend. Song Daxiong went to see him in the medical unit. She brought him good news. After RSU2 obtained intelligence of the movements of Li Ming, it was the Red Army's general commander-in-chief, Zhu De, and the general political commissar, Zhou Enlai, who issued the order to attack. The Red Army troops broke up the enemy into many small pockets and wiped them out one by one. In Kucaoling we wiped out Li Ming, as well as one brigade and one regiment of enemy reinforcements, capturing over three thousand enemy troops.

Listening, Ji Zhenren showed no sign of surprise, but looked indifferent. Sitting in bed, expressionless, he muttered to himself, "Brother soldiers, life is as precious as the sky. Fortunately we have finally removed the butcher's knife, and prevented adversity from happening."

Up to the time when the Liberation War ended in 1949, all our army's generals who had commanded various campaigns spoke highly of RSU2. Several hundred written comments, words or decrees of commemoration, praise and encouragement, merit bulletins and commentary telegrams hung on the walls in all sections under the RSU2 system to display the glorious honour. It was hard to remember them all, but after the victory over Chiang Kai-shek's fourth encirclement campaign, one First Front Army senior officer's not very standard commendation remained fresh in Chief Gao's memory for many years.

This praise, to which the speaker had no time to put the punctuation marks but finished in one breath, had been quoted by him on many occasions, and the impact was that many RSU2 cryptographers would often imitate his tone and say it in one breath. It was passed on here and there for so many years that people thought that Chief Gao was the inventor of this long sentence but forgot the real author.

"In the world no self-labelled highly effective ciphers compiled by the self-labelled highly talented KMT cryptographers are able to avoid the highly talented fatal attack of the highly talented cryptographers led by the highly talented comrade Gao Yueming."

The reason they received such high praise was because they had cracked many ciphers of Chiang Kai-shek's headquarters and his Left, Right and Central Route armies, thereby obtaining a substantial amount of high-quality intelligence. When the battle in Kucaoling ended, even Chiang Kai-shek sent Chen Cheng a 'mournful telegram' which was also decrypted by RSU2: "This time our defeat was so wretched, really the only secret anguish of mine since I was born."

So the KMT armies' fourth encirclement campaign ended up with 'Chen Cheng spitting blood; Chiang Kai-shek sending him telegrams to express his sorrow; and all the KMT troops suffering defeat and pulling out of the red area.'

Several days later, as soon as Ji Zhenren's condition stabilised, he went back to work. But he was poker-faced and silent. No matter where and when, he looked anxious and unsettled. When everyone was jubilant about the victory, he showed no emotion. Another unusual thing about him was no matter whether it was after the day or night shift, he refused to go back to his dormitory, but rested on the camp bed in the room next to the office. No one could persuade him to change his mind.

Chief Gao said it might have been because he had been working so intensely for so long with his brain operating so fast that he was mentally stretched. Besides, he was tortured by illness, so his self control had been weakened, therefore for a while it was hard for him mentally to switch from fierce fighting mode. Meanwhile, the possibility could not be ruled out that something was wrong with him mentally because he had been thrilled by the frequent urgent battle situations, and had burnt the candle at both ends. If one victory wrecked Ji Zhenren, our crack cryptographer, the loss to RSU2 would be great, thought Chief Gao.

That night Chen Xiaohua was working on the night shift. She had been working extra hours when the hostilities were tense, so after the victory she relaxed a bit and fell asleep. After midnight, the *click-clacking* sound suddenly appeared in the transceiver, but it failed to wake her up.

But a miracle happened. In the next room, half dreaming, Ji Zhenren suddenly heard a weak radio signal coming through the wall. Despite being half asleep, he could still faintly tell it was YING, and at once he had the plain text in his head. He did not jump out of the bed and dash to the office, because it could have stopped the electrical waves from flying into his ears, which could have affected his ability to listen to, transcribe and memorise the signals. In his subconscious hallucination, he dared not open his eyes. He raised his ears while his brain smoothed the electrical waves. Gently he got out of bed and walked to the office. Opening his eyes, he slowly sat down, picked up a pen and, shaking his wrist, began to write swiftly. At once the plain text appeared on the paper. As soon as the enemy transceiver finished sending the message, he wrote down the part he had captured in his head. He then slightly closed his eyes, quietly making a fine and detailed recollection of the whole telegram. The text on the paper was accurate, not a word needed correcting. He then woke up Chen Xiaohua, who was frightened to see him sitting by her side in his shorts and vest, thinking that he had truly gone insane. But after she read the telegram, she cried out in shock, as the content truly scared her.

It turned out that after the defeat in his fourth campaign to wipe out the Red Army, Chiang Kai-shek went to inspect the headquarters of Chen Cheng's Central Route Army to boost morale. He planned to take a boat back to Nanchang so that he could do some sightseeing to show that the Nationalist army was not discouraged, and that their fighting spirit remained high despite having been defeated. This top-secret intelligence clearly stated Chiang Kai-shek's travel arrangements, departure time the next morning, the route, the port to be used and the people that would accompany him. Chen Cheng's Central Route Army headquarters encrypted the message via YING and sent it to the Nanchang field headquarters.

That night, Zhu De and Zhou Enlai despatched crack troops to lay an ambush, but for some reason Chiang Kai-shek changed the route for his journey the next morning. Rather than taking a boat he took a car back to Nanchang, thereby avoiding being killed.

When Ji Zhenren decrypted the telegram saying that Chiang Kai-shek had arrived at Nanchang via a different route, he banged his headphones on the table. He was so disappointed that he pinched his own ears and twirled round and round. Seeing this, Song Daxiong said, "Old Chiang is not dead, so your ears will be put to good use. Don't pull them off. If a monitor's hearing is impaired, he is as good as dead. Treasure them." He knew that he had touched her sore spot unintentionally. He handed her the telegram, saying, "Report to Chief Gao. Pull back our troops who have gone to ambush Chiang Kai-shek."

After the incident, Chen Xiaohua requested to be disciplined. Staring at her blankly, Chief Gao took out the telegram, asking, "Why? You transcribed it and you reported it, and your name is clearly signed here."

With tears streaming down her cheeks, she said, "I fell asleep when I was on duty and I missed this telegram. My guilt is unforgivable.

Please give me another chance and I will never make the same mistake again."

Chief Gao called Ji Zhenren to his office. Ji Zhenren didn't agree that Chen Xiaohua should be disciplined, "Judging from Xiaohua's consistent behaviour and her consciousness, it makes no difference whether she's disciplined or not for the incident because she will never commit the same mistake again in her life."

"Ji Zhenren magically captured the telegram," said Song Daxiong. "Kindly, he didn't want to discipline Chen Xiaohua but falsely signed her name to conceal her fault. So he is also guilty and should be disciplined along with Chen Xiaohua."

"Chen Xiaohua must be severely punished!" said Chief Gao. "Ji Zhenren has merits as well as faults. Let him make a self-criticism in a public meeting to see how he behaves." While speaking, his mind wandered to another thought: at that moment the country had narrowly escaped a major incident that could have been significant enough to change the course of Chinese history. It was a pity, but also an element of luck. The lucky thing was that Ji Zhenren's capture of the important telegram in his dream made up for Chen Xiaohua's error. This was enough to prove that there was nothing wrong with his brain.

9 / THE ZHUO CIPHER

ANOTHER OCCASION on which Ji Zhenren was driven to a state of near-death was when the enemy changed to a new code book.

After the Red Army won a resounding victory over Chiang Kai-shek's fourth campaign to wipe them out, all the KMT armies under the direct control of Chiang Kai-shek changed to a self-compiled five-digit code book characterised by a type of cipher that was much more varied, more advanced, and constantly changing. The new practice of the enemy pushed the Red Army cryptographers into an abyss.

Ji Zhenren almost went insane. His days and nights began to go into reverse. He had no fixed time for meals or sleep; ignoring everything and behaving oddly, he would not spend an ounce of energy on anything other than codes and ciphers. Determined, he dedicated his heart and soul to them. What amazed the others was that he could solve some of the technical problems in his dreams.

After a while, and out of his craziness, he indiscreetly wrote his thoughts on the blackboard.

My Dreams and My Days

Normally I spend a quarter, a fifth, or sometimes a sixth of my day sleeping. My work regime from when I get up in the morning until I go to bed at night continues and intensifies in my dreams.

When I crack ciphers in my dreams, it is done with a distinct precision and a mark of depth. It can be calculated and measured. This kind of dream is sometimes a dream within a dream, and sometimes even three dreams within a dream. Like lightning at night, my train of thought flows forcefully. I myself am not sure from which layer of dreams I gain my great awakening. But they are all recorded in my numerous little notebooks beside my pillow, and every one of them has become a stepping stone to my success in cracking ciphers. As far as the significance of this is concerned, dreams are not only day by night, but also night by day. A good cryptographer must have the capacity to attain the power of understanding both during the day and at night; besides, the quality of the attainment in dreams is sometimes higher than what one obtains when one is awake.

Hence, sleep has become my most yearned for and most mystical activity. Yet this sleep should not be actively sought after. The sleep after taking sleeping pills is a meaningless sleep. My birthday present from Song Daxiong was a small packet of sleeping pills. It was not easy for her to get them. It is said that they were seized from a KMT division commander. When she gave them to me, she was beside herself with laughter.

Before long Song Daxiong could not laugh any more. It was not because Ji Zhenren had lost his ability to crack ciphers but because, when he energetically cracked a series of enemy ciphers one after another, he was suddenly seized and taken away by a group of armed men in plain clothes.

When she first heard the news, she thought they must have been KMT secret agents. During the previous KMT encirclement operations, they would send out special teams to hide in the hinterland of the Soviet Area and make surprise attacks on the Red Army general headquarters and other important departments. Although RSU2 was a key unit to be protected and there were troops to guard them, Chief Gao still did not feel at ease. He repeatedly told Song Daxiong to pay attention to the safety of the cryptographers and the all-round monitors. "When the cryptographer is alive, you live; when the cryptographer is dead, you die!" Representing the special security team, Song Daxiong signed the life-and-death certificate.

But now Ji Zhenren had been taken away. She was in a panic. Holding a pistol, she led a company of soldiers and charged out of the barracks. Half way, on horseback, Chief Gao caught up with them, telling her it was the people from the central government who had taken Ji Zhenren away.

On the way back to the barracks, they ran headlong into a group of
local young armed men, singing while marching toward them. They
were very cocky, not wanting to give way to Chief Gao who had to
dodge to the roadside and wait for them to pass.

> It is nineteen thirty-three,
> We are carrying out land investigation.
> Eliminate despotic gentry and landlords,
> We are consolidating the Soviet Area for ten thousand years.

Resonant and powerful, this song was heard widely in the Jiangxi
Soviet Area in recent years. From the words it was easy to see the
extent of the land investigation movement initiated by the Jiangxi
Soviet central government. Later the movement sunk into a 'leftist'
mire, and Mao Zedong was ousted from his concurrent position as
chairman of the people's committee. In many places, without any
principles, the better-off middle peasants were upgraded to rich
peasants or landlords and were cracked down on, while many
landlords and rich peasants were either sent to labour camps, driven
out of the area, or executed on the spot.

The Ji family could naturally not escape misfortune. The
investigation team, formed by the poor peasant league, ignored the fact
that the Ji household had already voluntarily donated their family
fortune to the Red Army, but discovered that previous generations
were landlords and wealthy gentry, so they decided they were a major
despotic landlord family. They came to search but only found a small
amount of money, so they thought the Jis had hidden their money and
valuables. They locked up Ji Huizhong who was riddled with illness
and tortured him, forcing him to tell them where he had hidden his
money. Ji Huizhong's eldest son and two daughters were too far away,
but his younger son Ji Zhenren was serving in the army locally, thereby
becoming a target to be struck down.

The movement brought disaster upon Ji Zhenren and his family, so
Chief Gao had to go and negotiate on Ji Zhenren's behalf. Knowing
very well the current complicated situation of the power struggles in
the leadership of the Soviet Area, he dared not go to the senior officers
of the general headquarters, but went to Assistant Chief of Staff Li,
who felt that it was difficult for him to help, saying that this political
movement was very sensitive, and even Mao Zedong couldn't do

anything, so who else could, and who would dare to? Li understood that the Ji household was clear on the matter as well as the importance of Ji Zhenren. Although he couldn't come up with a sure-fire plan, he agreed to seek a better solution for the Jis within his power. Through his efforts, the final solutions for the Jis were:

1. Ji Huizhong could avoid being eliminated in the flesh, but he must be driven out of the Jiangxi Soviet Area. Having no choice, old Ji decided to go to his confidant and friend for many years Long Yun, the military governor of Yunnan, for help. Of course he said nothing about his plan, or he might not have been able to make the trip and might have been executed.

2. The Jis were to hand out all their property and land, keeping only two storage rooms for tools in the corner of the back yard for Zhang Chengfeng and Ji Xiaomin to live. In fact, after several donations, the family had only an empty shell, with two big courtyard houses and several *mu* of paddy fields, which were now handed to the authorities.

3. Ji Zhenren was banished to the transport corps of the logistics department to become a porter. His mind was completely focused on codes and ciphers, so he was not at all worried about the treatment. "As long as I can crack ciphers, I don't mind how they punish me," he said.

Assistant Chief of Staff Li got around the regulations and secretly transferred Song Daxiong and soldier Zhang Ping to the transport corps. They had three tasks:

1. To secretly safeguard Ji Zhenren's personal safety.

2. To make sure not to lose any of the code material that Ji Zhenren had with him. Taking this material out of the office was the decision reached by Chief Gao after thinking it over and over. Although there was a danger the secrets could be exposed, it was the only solution he could come up with. No matter what the circumstances or how hard the conditions were, as long as Ji Zhenren could still breathe, his work on ciphers must not be stopped. This was unshakable and nobody could change it.

3. If Ji Zhenren was kidnapped, or he himself tried to run away, under the circumstances, he could be shot dead on the spot. He knew too many secrets; if he wanted to leave, he had to die. This was an iron discipline and the bottom line. In private, Chief Gao authorised Song Daxiong to take whatever action was needed, but she was very reluctant, saying, "I can't do that."

"If you don't do it, the revolution may suffer heavy losses," said Chief Gao.

"Why don't we trust him?" she asked.

"In RSU2, we must trust every comrade but also suspect everyone at any moment," replied Chief Gao.

Shaking her head, she said: "I have faith in his conscience! My gun will never fire on him."

After arriving at the transport corps, Ji Zhenren was forced to have his hair shaved in the centre from his forehead to the nape of his neck; a way of preventing forced labourers from running away. He paid no attention to his hair; neither could he find a mirror to view it. He buried himself in ciphers. However, he would still ask Song Daxiong: "A new work unit, a new job and a new look. What do you think of my new hair cut?" Song Daxiong did not know whether to laugh or cry. Her heart was in pain as if it had been pierced by a needle.

The intensity of labour in the transport corps was great. Those who were physically fit and experienced could sustain such an intensity. But Ji Zhenren was physically weak and inexperienced, in addition to being poorly fed. After three to five days' labour he could not even straighten his back. Besides, he would often shift his attention to ciphers and the loss of concentration could cause injuries. Luckily he was often put in the same group as Song Daxiong and Zhang Ping, whose attention was all on him, giving him a hand and doing the work for him, so he could be less fatigued and avoid injury.

One day when he had just put a box of ammunition on his back, two overseers came. They added another box on his back and at once he was pressed face down on the ground. The overseers kicked and punched him. Seeing the scene, Song Daxiong went to remove the load from Ji Zhenren. The two overseers stopped her, at which point she stretched her hands and held both men by the collar, yelling, "You bastards! Don't you dare push him too hard!" Ji Zhenren got up, charging toward the two men and punched each of them once on the ears. The two men picked up wooden sticks and began to hit Ji Zhenren. Song Daxiong tried to stop them but she was hit hard on the back with the sticks.

Ji Zhenren then held a box of ammunition in his arms and charged head-on at the two men, roaring, "If you're going to hit anyone, then hit me!"

Song Daxiong cried out between clenched teeth, "Listen, you two. If this man dies, neither of you will live, and none of your family members will live, and the whole Central Soviet Area will be a bloodbath. If he dies, the happiest man will be Chiang Kai-shek, and his army will come here to kill and burn. If you don't believe me, try it."

The two men were frightened, mumbling, "This woman has gone insane."

Afterwards, Chief Gao carried on bringing telegrams to Ji Zhenren whose mind was occupied by piles of code. He spent what time was available to find solutions for them, and in the shabby room he broke two very difficult ciphers.

One day, when he was bending over his bed focusing on the numerical groups, the two overseers wandered into his room. Carrying two toads, they threw the animals in his bed, saying: "You're weak, so we have brought you two toads to build up your health."

Gazing at the paper, he was deep in thought, unaware that two people had come in and two toads had been thrown into his bed. Feeling curious, the two men stood behind him, watching quietly. The toads hopped among the sheets of paper, but he was aloof and indifferent to them. One overseer was unable to control his bowels and, grabbing two sheets of paper from the bed, he ran to the toilet outside to relieve himself. When a toad jumped on the back of Ji Zhenren's hand, he came to realise that there was another toad on the bed and a man stood beside him. He showed no surprise, but he cried out in alarm when he saw two sheets of paper disappearing, "Who has taken my paper? Hurry, somebody come, my paper has gone."

In the next room Song Daxiong heard his shouts and rushed to his room, asking, "What's happened?"

The overseer grinned, "Two sheets of shabby paper, taken to the toilet to wipe a bottom." Turning around, Song Daxiong ran to the toilet outside.

It was a twenty-metre long ditch. Squatting over it, the man had just finished emptying his bowels. Reaching out his hand he was about to wipe his bottom with the two sheets of paper. Song Daxiong fired two shots at the ditch and the bullets hit the faeces, making the human excrement fly in all directions. The man sat on the ditch, terrified, while the two sheets of paper in his hand were snatched by Song Daxiong in the twinkling of an eye.

How dare a porter carry a pistol?

The pistol had been hidden under Song Daxiong's clothes. Several times when Ji Zhenren was bullied, she almost drew it but finally restrained herself.

Now the corps leader came to deal with the matter.

Calming down, all smiles, Song Daxiong said, "Something is wrong with comrade Ji's brain. He likes doing sums. If he is not allowed to do them, his illness recurs." She then took out her credentials, a special pass issued by Assistant Chief of Staff Li. The holder of the pass was permitted to enter an important military area with a weapon.

The corps leader looked at the pass, saying: "A woman is allowed to carry a gun, showing you have strong backing. A male soldier with a bad class background has his own problems. I don't want to make things hard for you, but you must mind your gun well. If you shoot anyone and harm them, you must compensate them."

Song Daxiong burst out laughing, "I don't grow that stuff, so how can I compensate?"

The corps leader laughed loudly and, turning to the two overseers, he said, "This female comrade is so straightforward. She carries a handgun, while this male comrade often falls ill, gets mad and is unable to control himself. If one day the handgun falls into his hands, are you two aware of the consequences? It won't be just your buttocks being stained with poo. So in the future you two must not bully this landlord's son any more."

From then on, Song Daxiong handed the pistol to Zhang Ping for safe keeping. She was worried that she might cause an accident if she failed to control herself when something happened.

The situation in the Jiangxi Soviet Area became more and more tense. Chiang Kai-shek's preparation for his fifth encirclement campaign was underway. RSU2's cryptographers were under great pressure. The higher authorities pressed for intelligence, but the enemy's self-compiled ciphers were really difficult to crack. The cryptographers lost several layers of skin to crack even one. In the transport corps, Ji Zhenren laboured during the day, and at night he slept as little as he could. He turned to skin and bones and looked like he could be crushed to death under the weight of half a sack of rice.

One morning he went to see Song Daxiong, looking weary. He handed her two sheets of paper, giving her a strange smile, "Have a look on the back of them. They're still stained with the smelly shit from your shooting." Turning the two sheets over, she saw some yellowish stains.

In a mysterious tone, he said, "Your two shots are worth big money now," he said, mysteriously, "no less than shooting dead two enemy commanders. I finally deciphered these two sheets of paper you snatched from that smelly bum. This is an odd cipher, called ZHUO. The contents of the two pages are about the KMT armies' transfer and deployment situation in Jiangxi and Fujian provinces. They are very important intelligence. This is the prelude of Chiang Kai-shek's new campaign to encircle the Red Army. But the key word for this cipher is very interesting, a number of between four and five digits, which I have never come across before." Holding a twig, he wrote on the ground and rattled on.

"6174 plus Q makes 6174Q. It can just be regarded as a quasi-five-digit keyword for a cipher. When I was nearly driven mad, and in that instance I was falling into a deep well in my dream, I accidentally thought of a hidden but interesting phenomenon in this cipher. Its principle is that you randomly select four unrelated numbers, arranging them sequentially with the highest first, then the lowest first, using the highest first to subtract the lowest first. Following this principle and carrying on subtracting, never more than seven times, the final result is the same number 6174. For example, take the number 2851. Taking the highest first, it is 8521 and taking the lowest first, it is 1258. The number 6174 appeared after I repeated the procedure six times. Any numbers, after following this principle and repeating the procedure for at most seven times, cannot escape the number 6174.

"The enemy adds a letter Q after the numbers to form the key word 6174Q. Actually Q is just a distraction, only 6174 is the true key word. ZHUO was encrypted by using this mystical number-repeating principle. I consulted some maths books, but I didn't see any one drawing any conclusions about this phenomenon and put forward the principle. That is to say, on the enemy side there is a capable person who has tested out a rarely known number and used its principle to encrypt ZHUO. Although it only borrows the embryonic form and the superficial knowledge of the principle, it is still mysterious enough."

In high spirits he finished speaking. When he raised his head, he saw that Song Daxiong had gone. It was urgent. She had brought Zhang Ping with her to deliver Ji Zhenren's result to RSU2. Taking the opportunity, she reported to Chief Gao about Ji Zhenren's health, suggesting that he should get Ji Zhenren back to RSU2. Chief Gao found it hard to bring up the matter, saying that he was not afraid of being dismissed from office, nor of being beheaded. He could go to the higher authorities to kick up a fuss, but the result would be obvious, and it might bring calamity to the whole unit.

Song Daxiong had to go back to the transport corps. Some days afterwards, she used every trick in the book to keep a good relationship with the corps leader so that he could give Ji Zhenren some light work to do, or some more vegetable soup to eat at dinner time. The food couldn't be worse, which had affected the porters' health. The majority of them found it hard to stand the hard labour, but Ji Zhenren carried on working with all his mental strength, because if he relaxed, he might just die.

One morning, Song Daxiong could not see Ji Zhenren. She searched the work site and the living area, but she couldn't find him. When she recalled that the day before he had told her that he couldn't endure any more, her whole body came out in a cold sweat. What if he had really run away?

Scanning the surrounding landscape, she asked Zhang Ping to go and report to the corps leader. Taking the pistol from Zhang Ping, she ran towards a valley. She knew that walking along the valley for ten to twelve kilometres and over two peaks there was a road leading out of the Soviet Area. If Ji Zhenren had wanted to run away, he would have chosen this route.

When she ran to the foot of the hill, her stomach rumbled with hunger. Breakfast was a bowl of thin rice congee mixed with vegetables, which could not sustain one until lunch. Grabbing some dried tree leaves she stuffed them into her mouth to chew. She then climbed the hill. After crossing a small hilltop, she saw a man on the slope on the other side. She chased after him. The thin and unsteady figure looked like Ji Zhenren and he had almost crossed the peak. She was too exhausted to catch up. With no more hesitation, she fired two shots at the figure, then huffing and puffing, she reached the summit. She searched and searched, but she could not see the man. Leaning on a tree, she took a rest, feeling a heartrending panic. What if he had really run away?

Suddenly a dark figure appeared and something hard covered her head. She rolled on the spot and freed herself from the cover. Dodging behind a tree she pointed her pistol at the top of the tree. Somebody was straddling a branch; it was Ji Zhenren. Kicking a broken bamboo basket away, she called out: "Behave, you escaped criminal. Come down and be captured." Ji Zhenren threw down another item, which landed in her arms. It was a bag of dried wild mushrooms and wild berries.

"Why did you leave without saying goodbye?"

"If I had said anything, how could we have solved our starvation problem."

"My bullets didn't hit you, did they?"

She began to sob.

It was the first time he had seen her cry. He hurriedly came down from the tree and comforted her. She wept miserably. "It's really hard to live. It's really hard to make revolution. Yesterday when you said that you could not endure any more, I nearly threw away my job here and went back to RSU2. Chiang Kai-shek is pressing us hard day by day, but our internal movements come one after another and go to extremes. I really thought that you had lost confidence and run away."

After some hesitation Ji Zhenren held Song Daxiong in his arms. She also held him tight. When her hands touched his back, she was so alarmed that she withdrew them: "How scary, you are all skin and bones!"

"For the sake of survival, if I really want to run away, what are you going to do?"

Pressing her face against his and moving it up and down, she muttered, "I will fire at you. Attachment is attachment, an assignment is an assignment, the two cannot be confused."

"The more ciphers I crack, the quicker the war ends. For this reason I run away and for this reason I live," said Ji Zhenren.

"Let us wait together for the day when the war ends," muttered Song Daxiong.

Several days later Song Daxiong secretly bought an old hen from a villager and boiled a pot of chicken soup for Ji Zhenren to eat. But the aroma brought the gluttonous demons, the two overseers, to the yard.

Pointing at Ji Zhenren who was sitting there in a trance, Song Daxiong explained, "The soup is for him to build up his health."

One overseer muttered, "A blockhead who can't tell what is a sweet smell and what is a stink, the soup is wasted on him. At the moment we have supply difficulties, so waste is a crime. The soup is confiscated."

Song Daxiong blocked them from touching the pot, begging, "This soup is for saving a life, please show some mercy."

One overseer mumbled, "The poor don't even have any wild herb soup to eat, but this landlord's son acts like a tyrant and eats chicken soup. Is that the way to behave in this world? I will either smash the pot or confiscate it, which one do you want me to do?"

Tears streamed down Song Daxiong's face, then she saw outside the wattled wall a group of soldiers passing, and among them a bearded man who looked like a senior officer. Turning around she saw the two overseers going out with the pot of chicken soup.

Unusually calm, she pushed her hand under her shirt. She then remembered that Zhang Ping had the pistol. Before Zhang Ping could respond, the gun was already in Song Daxiong's hand. Pointing it towards the sky, she fired three shots. Almost at the same time the sound of a pot crashing to the ground was heard. Instantly a row of dark gun muzzles pushed through the wattled wall, and some soldiers rushed into the yard.

With an easy manner, Song Daxiong squatted on her heels. Holding a corner of her shirt she began to pick up the chicken meat from the ground, mumbling, "What a waste, such a nice pot of soup." Beside her feet, smoke was coming out of the muzzle of the pistol.

The bearded officer asked, "Why did you shoot?"

"Because of the chicken! A chicken can save a life," she muttered, holding the chicken meat and walking toward the room. The soldiers halted her. The bearded officer ordered the soldiers to lower their guns, but he followed Song Daxiong to the room.

Ji Zhenren was still bending over the bed gazing at the papers full of numerals. The gun shots failed to draw his attention away from the ciphers.

The bearded officer picked up a few sheets and had a read.

Immediately he called out to the soldiers outside, "Surround the yard. No one can come in or out!"

Song Daxiong pulled Ji Zhenren up. In a daze he looked at the stranger. Then he swiftly gathered the papers; with one stride he stepped across to the fire that was used to cook the chicken soup. "Don't come near me!" he cried, assuming the posture of dropping them into the fire at any moment.

The bearded officer hurriedly gestured to stop him from burning the papers.

"Who are you?" Ji Zhenren asked.

"Who are you? Which unit are you from?" The bearded officer asked in reply.

"It's obvious that I'm a porter of the transport corps. These are the figures for the goods coming in and going out. Supplies and equipment and their amounts are confidential information. Don't come near me!"

"Tell me, which unit were you originally from?"

"I've always been a porter."

"You lack the strength to truss up a chicken, clearly you are a man of letters."

"I'm a landlord element, a scoundrel. You'd better leave now, or you will be implicated."

"Many people from rich peasant, landlord and capitalist families have done a very good job in the revolution. I am one of them."

"But why didn't you have your head shaved like me?"

"I'm afraid no one dares to do that to my hair. Hey, you are from RSU2, aren't you? I know a man called Gao Yueming, who also works with numbers."

"Who is he? Which family's bookkeeper is he?" Song Daxiong asked.

"Don't keep me guessing. I know that only people from RSU2 have papers with random numbers."

Ji Zhenren's eyes brightened. Raising the roll of paper high in the air, he said, "'A man of war going on a punitive expedition sees no sky.'"

Surprised, the bearded officer responded, "'How can we tolerate the beanstalks burning under the cauldron?'"

Ji Zhenren, "'On the moonlit path the bright moon is lonely.'"

The bearded officer, "'Solitary in the field of battle, cold reigns at night.'"

Ji Zhenren, *"Lying on the ground alone, I miss the happy days with my wife.'"*

The bearded officer, *"On the long road crying for blood, men perish."*

Ji Zhenren, *"'I lose my life beside the Immortal Bridge.'"*

The bearded officer, "How many beautiful women cry until their tears dry up."

Ji Zhenren, "Who wrote this melancholy poem?"

The bearded officer, "The division commander of the KMT Army, Li Mo'an."

Ji Zhenren, "Which newspaper published this poetry?"

The bearded officer, "The telegraph carried it to its recipient."

Ji Zhenren, "Who was the recipient of this poetry?"

The bearded officer, *"The beautiful woman Gu Lin longed for her husband to come home."*

Only then did a smile cross Ji Zhenren's face. Clasping the roll of paper to his chest, he walked toward the bearded officer, who remarked, "It seems that Gao Yueming has done a good job on security education. His men have talent, insight and discipline. Besides, they can also beat about the bush! Let me speak directly. Li Mo'an, the commander of the 10th Division of the KMT army, wrote this poem on the battleground during the KMT's fourth campaign to encircle us. His troops followed up the main attacking forces. When he heard the news that the advancing 52nd and 59th Divisions had been wiped out and the two division commanders had been captured by the Red Army, he was sad and he became war-weary. He missed his wife and children, so he penned this poem. He sent it via coded telegram to his wife Gu Lin in Shanghai, and our RSU2 intercepted and deciphered it. I think this poem can be regarded as an excellent piece of battlefield writing, vivid and sentimental about war-weariness, which is the reason I remembered it after I read it."

Ji Zhenren was still cautious, "Very few people know about RSU2, and even less people know about this telegram. You must be a leading Red Army officer, may I know your name, sir?"

"Remember me correctly, and go and ask Gao Yueming about the bearded officer."

The three of them then shut the door and had a long chat.

According to Song Daxiong's recollection afterwards, the bearded officer mainly talked about two issues. One was the importance of RSU2's work. From different angles he stressed that only with a higher level of technique, and being one step ahead of the enemy could the victory of the revolution be assured. The second issue was that we had to have faith in communism, and persevere in making revolution. He also said that Gao Yueming's men had the appropriate technical skills, their thinking was on the right track, and they were also politically sensible. His words gave Ji Zhenren immense encouragement. Excitedly, he said to the bearded officer that as long as he could break ciphers, and as long as his work could reduce Red Army casualties and win more battles, he would remain a revolutionary to the end of his life. Then he shot his mouth off, asking the officer why he grew his beard so long.

"I grew my beard as an expression of my ideals," replied the officer. "Last time we won the campaign against enemy encirclement, an enemy telegram decrypted by RSU2 nearly made me shave." Ji Zhenren then understood that the officer's ideals were to capture Chiang Kai-shek and destroy the KMT.

When they had finished talking, they walked out of the room. Ji Zhenren had his quilt roll on his back. The bearded officer told his men, "Take them back safely to their work unit. And pass on my order, that from now on no matter what their movements, anyone who dares to touch Gao Yueming's men will be court-martialled!"

ONE DAY AT DUSK, Ji Zhenren met the German advisor, Li De (Otto Braun), for the first time. He was extremely busy on that day, going to work before dawn, with lunch being brought to him, and when the sun was setting, he had been working for nearly ten hours without leaving the room.

After he returned from the transport corps, he worked even harder, which affected his health and made him very weak. Getting him to take a break had become difficult. Song Daxiong was so worried that she would often find a way to get him out of the office to take a break.

That afternoon, she saw that Chief Gao was to deliver telegrams to the 'Lone House', so she had an idea, asking him if he could take Ji Zhenren with him. Chief Gao thought it was not a bad idea and a good reason to take Ji Zhenren out of the room, so he agreed.

The 'Lone House' was where Otto Braun lived, the military advisor sent by the Comintern. This foreigner, who wielded real power over the Red Army, was a very mysterious figure, hence many Red Army officers and other ranks were very curious about him. According to working procedures, any important intelligence intercepted by RSU2 had to be sent to Braun as soon as possible, and Chief Gao would often take three members of staff and a squad of guards with him.

This time he took his personal guard, Ji Zhenren and Song Daxiong, while the squad of guards walked behind neither too far nor too close to them.

The 'Lone House' was surrounded by ponds, with a causeway

leading to it. When they arrived, what Ji Zhenren saw first were several dozen lovely ducks quacking and flapping their wings in the ponds. Delighted, he glanced at Song Daxiong. She smiled, understanding what he meant: duck soup would taste better than chicken soup. In a low voice Chief Gao said to them, "Yes, each day there is one duck less in the ponds, not due to stealing, but because Comrade Braun has one duck a day for his meal. The duck minders then add one duck to the ponds, a practice that never stops. The number of ducks must be kept exactly at 66. The guards have to protect not only the host of the house, but also the ducks in the ponds. I know that Song Daxiong has a special way of getting chickens, but you must not think about getting these ducks."

They entered the house, while the guards stayed outside. With a smiling face Braun took the telegrams. While having a drink of coffee, he read them carefully, with a cigar between his fingers which he did not put down as he read. He then sank into deep thought. Poker-faced, he stood up, pacing to and fro before the giant map on the wall. When the cigar burnt to the end, he picked up a ruler and a pencil. On the map he made some measurements and drew here and there. He mumbled something and an interpreter recorded what he was saying. Ji Zhenren clearly heard his last sentence: "Send them to Comrade Enlai."

When it was done, Braun saw that Chief Gao was still in the room. Usually if Braun had no more queries, Chief Gao had to leave immediately. But today he intended to let Ji Zhenren and Song Daxiong see the scenery, so he stayed a bit longer.

Through the interpreter Braun conveyed his words to Chief Gao, "Comrade Yueming, you changed your guards today? Neither the woman nor the man who has no strength to truss a chicken, is guard material."

Chief Gao hurriedly introduced them: "This is Ji Zhenren, our expert cryptographer. Only in the last two months he has cracked several extremely difficult ciphers alone."

"Oh, great, a heroic cryptographer," said Braun. "Then can you tell me what you are good at?"

Ji Zhenren's eyes brightened and, beaming, he said, "The key for cracking ciphers is not to rely only on technique. What is more important for a cryptographer is that one must have an excellent strategic way of thinking, to crack ciphers by taking a leap out of the ciphers themselves."

Expressing more interest, Braun asked: "Cracking ciphers is indeed mystical! Then tell me how does one be strategic, how does one leap out?"

"Actually, a good cryptographer's way of thinking is the same as that of a military commander," replied Ji Zhenren. "One must have an outstanding strategic mindset and often think about strategic issues beyond codes and ciphers. Let me give you an example." While speaking, a faint obstinacy showed in his eyes. Oh, no, Chief Gao cried inwardly, but it was too late for him to stop this strong-willed man.

"For instance the 'Fujian Incident' some time ago. From the intelligence we intercepted we knew that Chiang Kai-shek already knew of the KMT 19th Army's wireless communications and the ciphers they used, and that therefore he was aware of their anti-Chiang strategy and operational plans. We also knew that an assistant chief of staff called Fan in the 19th Army was an undercover agent of Chiang Kai-shek, and he was secretly selling out the 19th Army all the time. However, the 19th Army knew nothing about this situation. What's more, we had intercepted intelligence that Chiang Kai-shek was dispatching 11 divisions to surround and annihilate the 19th Army. We submitted all this information to the higher authorities. At the time the Red Army had already signed an anti-Japanese and anti-Chiang Kai-shek agreement with the 19th Army. But our side failed to take the whole situation into account. We did not inform the 19th Army about the intelligence we had gathered, let alone go to rescue the 19th Army when they were attacked. At the time we had several divisions stationed along the border with Fujian, so it would not have been difficult to dispatch them to the province. This is a matter of military thinking and vision. If we had chosen to be allied with the 19th Army to resist Chiang Kai-shek, there was a fair possibility that we could have successfully broken Chiang Kai-shek's encirclement of us. The 19th Army, the iron army that had fought with the Japanese in the Battle for Shanghai last year, was wiped out by Chiang Kai-shek. When that happened, what were we doing? We were watching. What a pity! How sad!"

Whether the interpreter had given a faithful translation or not was another matter.

Chief Gao pulled Ji Zhenren's sleeves several times but failed to shut him up. He had to shout at him, "I let you talk about cracking ciphers but this, this is not something you can talk about. You spoke like a fool! Let's go!" Pulling Ji Zhenren, he tried to get him to leave. But Ji Zhenren stood still, because he wanted to finish what he had to say. Chief Gao groaned inwardly, as he knew that the Red Army's internal views differed considerably on how to treat the 'Fujian Incident'. Zhou Enlai, Mao Zedong and Peng Dehuai thought that the Red Army should have launched an attack on Jiangsu, Zhejiang, Anhui and Jiangxi, and militarily supported and united with the 19th Army, but the Comintern who held the power, as well as the 'leftist' dogmatists in the Red Army adopted a closed-door policy. Today Ji Zhenren suddenly attacked the Comintern's decision, obviously getting himself into trouble.

After hearing Ji Zhenren's view, Braun, who wielded supreme authority over the Red Army and was usually impetuous, vulgar and dictatorial, gently patted Ji Zhenren's shoulder, smiling, "I know some people in the Red Army leadership didn't agree with my tactics. Peng Dehuai scolded me as 'a subjectivist and a tactician operating on maps'; he also scolded me as 'a son who feels no sorrow when selling his grandfather's land'. But this is the first time I've heard someone from a grass-roots unit complain. This comrade Ji accuses me of lacking strategic vision. Is it fair? I don't want to reply, but the facts in the future will prove everything. We'll see. However, one thing I must stress clearly. The stance taken toward the 'Fujian Incident' is not about military strategy, nor military vision, but is a serious political concern. The KMT's 19th Army was a middle element, a third force, a most dangerous enemy to the Chinese revolution. Every Red Army soldier must bear in mind my words on this!"

Although Braun's tone was stiff, his facial expression was mild and warm. Surprisingly, he saw the guests off out of the gate. Chief Gao did not feel the gesture was encouraging at all. Ji Zhenren had spoken to his heart's content. Already physically weak, his legs wobbled like jelly when he walked. Song Daxiong rushed to support him with her hands, saying, "You've worked too hard, no wonder your health is suffering. As I see it, you are completely tired out and confused, and had no idea what you were talking about. Luckily Advisor Braun did not bother arguing with a person like you." Just at that moment a flock of ducks were crossing the causeway, so they stopped for the ducks to pass. Song Daxiong then cracked a joke, "Look, the ducks are like Comrade Ji, waddling as they walk. The ducks are too fat to move, but Comrade Ji is too starved to support his legs." Otto Braun just turned around and made his way back to his house. On hearing Song Daxiong's joke, he walked back, saying, "It is hard for people doing technical jobs to avoid being ideologically confused, but health must not suffer. RSU2 should improve the quality of food given to their staff." He asked his guard to catch a duck, saying it was for Comrade Ji to build up his health. Chief Gao tried to decline but to no avail. On the way back to the unit, he gave a wry smile, saying: "It seems that Song Daxiong also has a way of getting a duck."

Ji Zhenren had been against the higher authorities' approach to the 'Fujian Incident', and neither was he very happy with their refusal to use the high-quality intelligence intercepted by RSU2. Chief Gao explained to him several times, saying that RSU2 was like a brick maker, whether the builders used its bricks to build a house, how to build it and how many bricks to use, and particularly regarding the design of the house, a brick maker had no say in it, so they ought not to make indiscreet remarks or criticism; no one could talk wilfully about the current situation of the Red Army; a cryptographer's duty was to crack ciphers and crack more; as for other issues, they'd better keep their mouth shut.

Before they entered the RSU2 complex, Chief Gao said, "Keep what happened today to yourselves."

"Daxiong, hurry to the kitchen and cook the duck," said Ji Zhenren, "so Chief Gao can have a bowl of duck soup to help him get over the shock."

"Take the duck to the mess and let the whole unit share it," said Chief Gao. "If Ji Zhenren eats the whole duck, his mouth will be like a duck quacking even more cheerfully."

Just as Chief Gao expected, before the aroma of the boiled duck had dispersed, the higher authorities issued a notice, instructing RSU2 to carry out a special education programme to rectify its staff's undisciplined thinking; Gao Yueming to make a self-criticism to a higher party committee; and Ji Zhenren to be sent to the transport corps for reform through labour for three months. But at the end of the notice, it said that the special education programme should not affect their work, showing that the higher authorities were well aware of the current situation, and that RSU2's intelligence was urgently needed, therefore its work should not be affected. Chief Gao used it as an excuse, bracing himself and arguing to the higher authorities to allow Ji Zhenren to receive his special education at RSU2, so that his work would not be affected. But no one dared to change Otto Braun's decision. So Chief Gao had to send Ji Zhenren to the transport corps. This time he didn't send someone to the transport corps to protect Ji Zhenren, nor did he send Ji Zhenren any coded materials to work on.

During these three months the monitoring teams were short-handed, so Chief Gao gave his approval for the guard Liu Kailai to do some simple technical and office work.

Liu Kailai was an extremely hard worker. He competed with the others to do miscellaneous jobs or heavy work, or machine maintenance, then he would sit down and read. The books he read were often reference books for telegraphy. He told everybody that he preferred doing this job to standing guard. Because he had been to school for a few years, he was regarded as an educated man in the Red Army ranks, with everyone thinking that he could do a good job in this trade. During this period he spent most of his time with Song Daxiong, whose sense of responsibility was so rigid that she would often lock him inside the room. He had to follow her timetable for everything, and no changes were allowed.

But behind all this hid a plot, secretly planned by Chief Gao and Song Daxiong, which nobody else knew about. This Liu Kailai before everybody's eyes was actually Ji Zhenren, while the real Liu Kailai had been to the transport corps to take his twin brother Ji Zhenren's place. Taking the risk, Chief Gao boldly perpetrated a fraud, something he had no choice but to do. He was ready to risk everything. The frontline battles were intense and critical, and they desperately needed Ji Zhenren on duty. He would say to himself, "When the situation improves, I'll go to the higher authorities to offer a humble apology."

Ji Zhenren did not let Chief Gao down. In these particular three months, he cracked 18 enemy ciphers, 11 of which were extremely difficult to crack and quite a few were ciphers compiled by the enemy themselves. The other cryptographers also showed superb skills, so for that moment and a period of time afterwards they achieved a 100 per cent rate of monitoring, transcribing and deciphering. The decryption could be done whenever it needed to be done. They even created the miracle of decrypting a telegram while transcribing it. However, the higher authorities failed to make good use of this reliable intelligence, which disappointed the RSU2 staff.

Otto Braun, a person of power in the Chinese Red Army, did have some knowledge of military theory and experience of regular warfare. But he did not appreciate the Red Army's strategy and effective guerrilla warfare tactics that were in keeping with China's actual conditions. Unrealistically, he adopted the principles of regular warfare to guide the Red Army's campaign to counter Chiang Kai-shek's encirclement. But Chiang Kai-shek had changed his strategy. His troops would advance slowly and entrench themselves at every step, building blockhouses everywhere. Relying on ring after ring of blockhouses as well as roads, they steadily and surely advanced towards the centre of the Jiangxi Soviet Area, nibbling away at the Red Army's base on their way. Under such circumstances the Red Army's decision makers chose to build blockhouses to counter blockhouses and to combat positional warfare with positional warfare. They set up defences everywhere. Their forces were divided, and they made short and brief assaults on the enemy, attacking recklessly, or intercepting passively. They suffered defeat again and again, and in the end the Red Army's casualties were disastrously heavy.

An uneasy atmosphere was spreading throughout the whole of the Chinese Soviet Republic. The Red Army's top leadership were aware of the adverse situation they were facing, but the ordinary officers and ranks knew no details of the general situation. However, many of them had a sort of premonition, worrying that something disastrous would happen, yet not knowing what. At the headquarters and all the other important locations, people coming and going, mysteriously busied themselves with this and that. Poker-faced and tight-lipped, they did more but spoke less. The atmosphere was unusually tense.

Chief Gao spent much of his time trying not to let this uneasy and anxious atmosphere affect his staff's work. He had to make sure all of them focused on their work. Before long he seized an instance and used it as an example to boost staff morale.

The story went like this.

The false Liu Kailai (the real Ji Zhenren) accepted the task of cracking an enemy cipher. After working on it for several days and nights he failed to crack it, so he was extremely irritated.

One morning Song Daxiong brought wild herb congee to his desk. Tired and weary, he stared hard at the bowl. He did not utter a word but clenched his teeth noisily. Song Daxiong was not scared by the strange expression on his face, as she was not surprised by anything unusual he did. Whenever he encountered a problem that he could not solve, he would have such odd expressions on his face, or would act or speak like a patient with a mental illness. Suddenly he picked up the bowl and drank the congee in one go. Then he raised the bowl high and threw it hard at the wall. The wall and the floor were both made of mud, so the pottery bowl did not crack after dropping to the floor and bouncing off the wall. Picking it up, he ran outside. Holding the bowl high in one hand he smashed it on a rock, and it immediately shattered to pieces.

"I just don't believe there is a pottery bowl that I can't break," he cursed. "But I've met a mortar; stinky and hard, I can't crack it. I'm not going to do any more." He returned to his dormitory and went to bed.

When it was about time for lunch, he screamed in his dream. Only in his underpants and barefoot, he dashed out of the room, crying as he ran, "Mortar, mortar, you damned mortar!" He ran straight to the office, seizing a piece of paper and bending over the desk he swiftly wrote and sketched. Standing by his side, Song Daxiong watched the scene in amazement, not knowing what to do. In silence she looked at his back, eyes moistened.

Like a walking skeleton Ji Zhenren's body was propped on the wooden stool like a tight bow. There was no fat at all beneath his rough grey skin, which was barely able to hold the bones together. Without rhythm, his long, bony head of dishevelled long hair, moved from side to side. She was worried that his long, thin neck would snap at any moment due to the weight of his head. She also worried that if somebody came to touch that skeleton, it might collapse and fall apart. Taking off her jacket she gently put it on his thin back. Nose twitching, she began to sob. She restrained herself, trying not to make any noise while sobbing.

Then Ji Zhenren stood up and began to run inside the room, which attracted other people's curiosity. Several underaged soldiers came to watch at the window. Song Daxiong quietly gestured to them not to disturb him.

He sat down at the desk. Three hours went past. Slowly he got up, and the clothes on his back fell to the ground. He was unaware of it. Unhurriedly, he screwed the cap back on the pen. Trying to push the pen into his top jacket pocket, it fell to the floor. Lowering his head he saw that he was almost naked. He cried out in alarm, "Who has taken my clothes? Where are my clothes?" Now somebody pushed the door open and walked in. He hurriedly turned around and went to hide in front of Song Daxiong whose back was toward the door.

She pulled him into her arms and held him tight while calling out without turning her head round to see who was at the door, "Get out of the room!"

She felt Ji Zhenren's trembling, hard chest bones and chilly breath. She held him tighter to give him warmth, strength and love. Her warm face touched his face and her hot tears dampened his cheeks. Slowly he stopped trembling.

"Don't hold back," she said. "Cry and shout. You can't crack that cipher, but you can take me as a porcelain bowl or mortar, and crack me. You can do anything with me as long as you can vent your anger. I beg you, don't make things difficult for yourself. Can you just give up this cipher? Don't put all your eggs in one basket, go and try a different one." He gave her an embrace as his reply.

Then somebody spoke behind them, and it was Chief Gao's voice, "Why have you no clothes on? Put them on quickly."

Ji Zhenren pushed Song Daxiong away. Picking up the papers on the desk, he cried out, "Report to the unit chief, I've cracked the enemy's *YIN* cipher and gathered the following information: four enemy regiments of the 3rd Division under Wang Yijiang's Column are advancing prematurely, trying to infiltrate our interior area of Pinghu and the other two townships, but the other enemy troops have not followed up, so they are isolated at the front. Quick, deliver the telegram to Otto Braun. If this time we still don't make good use of the intelligence, I... I... I am going to be damned..."

Chief Gao took the telegram from Ji Zhenren and had a read. Unbelievably excited he said, "This time, if they..., to hell with it, I'm going to set a fire and burn that 'Lone House' down!" He then dashed out of the room.

Full of emotion, Song Daxiong looked at Ji Zhenren, but he gave no reaction to her gaze. His mind was still immersed in that key word for deciphering *YIN*.

"Medium rare!" In his memory only one person he knew liked medium rare steak and that person was Jiang Xiaodian. Now his thoughts were stuck on the dead Jiang Xiaodian, the sweet love in Shanghai again flooding his mind. But his mind fell on an odd question: the close relationship between *YIN* and the bloody key word, as well as the relationship between eating and being eaten, between Jiang Xiaodian and the medium rare steak. Did Jiang Xiaodian have any relationship with *YIN*?

"Have you been drinking whisky?" he asked Song Daxiong.

She was dumbstruck, "I've never heard of it. What's that?"

He assumed the posture of making a speech, "This *YIN* is baffling, really a big monster. First, the symbols of the code are all in English, which is rarely seen by the Red Army; second, it uses a substitute table to encrypt messages, and successively it uses the English words 'whisky' and 'medium rare' as keywords, twice and double-encrypted messages; third, it surprises me that it uses the format of short essays of the Ming and Qing dynasties.The incorporation of three characteristics into one makes the cypher neither fish nor fowl, neither a cat nor a tiger, but something completely strange. The successful cracking of this cipher is the pioneer for us to crack a cross breed between Chinese and a foreign language, and between modern and ancient writing styles. It has a foul-smelling significance. They even used the damned medium rare steak as a key word, bloody, simply psychopathic!"

Song Daxiong was pleasantly surprised, "Who could know which cloud would rain? I did not expect that the format of the short essays in the Ming and Qing dynasties was truly of use. So please forgive me for tying you up in the woods."

"Not only are you not guilty," said Ji Zhenren seriously, "but you contributed to the cracking of the cipher because, for no particular reason, I suddenly thought of the morning when I first met you in the woods, then the gunnysack and the dark room. Instantly my mind jumped to the short essays from the Ming and Qing dynasties, opening up a gap in *YIN*. You might not believe me when I say I thought that I needed my woman to lend me a hand to crack this cipher, and another woman appeared and a plate of medium rare steak flew to me. But after I cracked *YIN*, I was thinking whether it was the shadow of the short essays or the smell of the steak that reminded me of my two women; or I remembered my two women first and then I thought I should start from the characteristics of the short essays and use the medium rare steak as the key word to make the first try?"

Song Daxiong came back to her senses. Flushed, she muttered, "You wish! Who is your woman?"

After cracking *YIN*, the Red Army amassed a superior force and surrounded and annihilated Wang Yijiang's four regiments, killing and capturing 6,000 of the enemy, and capturing about 3,100 guns. They achieved a rare victory after the beginning of the campaign to counter Chiang Kai-shek's fifth encirclement. The higher-level leaders praised RSU2 for its crucial contribution to the victory.

But for many days afterwards Ji Zhenren showed little excitement or happiness. He had a big secret, and the weight of the matter made him breathless.

That day he was on night shift. He intercepted a grade-A telegram encrypted with *YIN*. It was a notice from the field headquarters of the president of the KMT Military Council in Nanchang to the commanders of all columns involved in the encirclement army.

During this period of time the Red Army was frequently defeated in battles but the KMT Army won a series of battles, therefore some Red Army officers' and soldiers' minds began to waver, feeling that the future was bleak. Apart from defeat on the battlefield, many officers and soldiers were wrongly killed in the campaign to eliminate the counterrevolutionaries within the Red Army and the land investigation movement, which made some of the officers and ranks lose confidence in the revolution, so defections to the KMT were on the rise.

The telegram Ji Zhenren decrypted was a name list of the Red Army defectors, including the time, location and details of how they had defected. The names were listed according to their ranks, and the first one was Kong Yihe, the former commander-in-chief of the Hunan, Hubei and Jiangxi military command, followed by eight division and regiment commanders. Every one of these names scared him into a cold sweat, his hand trembling as he decrypted them. But what startled him the most was the last name. It suddenly appeared, like a ghost. He could not believe what he had decrypted. He did it three times, but each time it was the same name: Ji Zhenfu, the captain of the guerrilla force in Wushan mountain in east Hubei. This junior officer, much lower in rank than those nine names before him, knocked Ji Zhenren out immediately.

Dripping with cold sweat, he collapsed under the desk. Lying on the floor face up, he stretched out his limbs, letting the chilly air on the ground slowly get into his spinning head. The scene of him with his elder brother in childhood flashed before his eyes, and some good images of his brother were shattered to pieces by the wretched scene of him fleeing the battlefield with a wounded leg.

According to the enemy telegram, Ji Zhenfu and his guerrilla force were surrounded and wiped out on a small mountain slope by the KMT force. The members of his force were badly battered, with half of them dead or wounded. He himself was injured and, seeing that the game was as good as lost, he spotted a steep slope and rolled down it, hiding in a hole between the rocks. He stayed in the mountains for three days, and on the fourth day he went straight to the enemy camp, where he wrote down a statement of repentance as well as a statement about quitting the communist party.

The three characters 'Ji Zhenfu' tumbled around in Ji Zhenren's mind. Getting up from the floor, he picked up the pen, gritting his teeth. He wanted to write them down on the paper. But his hand trembled too much to hold the pen. He thought about it a lot and thought realistically. At the moment the life or death of his brother was not important. The problem was that this brother, whom he would prefer to see dead, would bring fatal damage to his siblings in the Red Army ranks. Especially to the two brothers working with RSU2, the damage could be disastrous. Could a traitor's siblings still be able to stay in the Red Army? Particularly with regard to the political environment in the Jiangxi Soviet, his family situation, being a landlord coupled with a traitor, absolutely bode ill rather than well, and there could be no way for them to live. For himself, the misfortune brought upon him by being a landlord element had just passed, and Liu Kailai was taking his place to receive the punishment for his offending Otto Braun. Now he sank in the spiral of his brother being a traitor and a turncoat.

He was aware that if he wrote down the three characters, the telegram might be his last one as a cryptographer. He would then be locked up, isolated, and even shot. Even if his life was spared, he would still be driven away from RSU2 and away from his post.

"Leaving the world of codes and ciphers, I'm better off dead," he said inwardly. Then he thought of his mother and her letter. He did not know whether his mother's letter had reached his brother, who would always do whatever she said. Did he betray the Red Army because of her influence over him? Or were the present defeats suffered by the Red Army what made him lose confidence in it?

"Heavens, should I write down this stinky name? I have plenty of reasons to do it, but also plenty of reasons not to do it.

"For the ten traitors, if I report nine, will the higher authorities find out? The first nine are division and regiment commanders and they are major enough to shock and enrage the Red Army high-level authorities. So who could then think that a little man's name is missing from the report? Besides, the damage this little man can bring to the revolution is too small to take into account.

"Let me remove the numerals for 'Ji Zhenfu' from the original telegram. The wireless signals were poor and missing some numerals was such a normal thing to happen. Late at night why shouldn't I make a mistake? In fact, I can do it in a different way. Without removing the numerals, I can change them. I can add a '0' under '0', turning '0' into '8', or add a horizontal line on the digit 1, turning '1' to '7'. I only need one change on one numeral, to change 'Ji Zhenfu' into some other unrelated character. One move of my finger and everything will be just fine. But how can I do such a thing?"

Ji Zhenren was so irritated that he was like an ant on a hot pan. He truly did not know what to do. Then he thought about Chief Gao, who was his backbone, a brother whom he could absolutely trust, and whose professional skills and political level were very high, and whose principled and flexible management style was also very high. "Let me put myself in his hands. Whether to live or die, I resign myself to my fate," he thought inwardly.

It was at the stroke of midnight, Ji Zhenren wrote down two drafts of the telegram, one with nine names, and one with ten. He went to Chief Gao's office. But before he knocked on the door, he tore the nine-name list to shreds, pushed them into his mouth and swallowed them.

Chief Gao let him in, asking, "Urgent telegrams?" He said nothing but sat down on the edge of the bed.

Chief Gao said, "You look like you are in a bad mood. Is it because you've heard about your brother?"

Ji Zhenren looked surprised.

"I planned to tell you about it a few days later," said Chief Gao, seriously and solemnly. "Our guerrilla detachment in the Wushan mountains in east Hubei was wiped out by the enemy, and the guerrilla leader Ji Zhenfu died bravely. He was hit by artillery, his face disfigured, eyes blinded and belly blown open. Before he died, he thrust his bayonet into the chest of an enemy."

"You mean my brother was killed in action?"

"His identity documents were in his pocket. I understand your feelings," said Chief Gao, by way of comforting Ji Zhenren. "You didn't want him to die, but war is cruel and anyone may die for the revolution, including you and I. The dead cannot come back to life, so you restrain your grief and adapt to inevitable changes."

A picture then flashed through Ji Zhenren's mind: before Ji Zhenfu defected, he pushed his identity documents into the pocket of a corpse whose face was beyond recognition, and then destroyed the documents belonging to the corpse. After the enemy had left, the Red Army went to collect the dead bodies. Seeing his documents, they thought that he had been killed.

Slowly he stood up, saying, "I was overwhelmed with grief when I heard about the death of my brother. I came to you for some reassuring words, and now I have thought it through."

He left Chief Gao's office. Wandering in the courtyard for nearly two hours, he finally knocked on the door again. Taking out the telegram, he handed it to Chief Gao, who was stupefied after reading it. Then he became silent, nodding his head: "You go back and take a rest. Let me deliver the telegram now."

Ji Zhenren said, carefully, "I hope the organisation trusts me and keeps me in RSU2."

Looking at him, Chief Gao said, "I trust you and RSU2 trusts you. But the problem is that it is a very troublesome matter, so you must be prepared for the worst. I will deliver this telegram directly to the bearded officer, telling him about your family situation, and let him decide. Before the higher authorities' instructions arrive, only you, I and Heaven and Earth know about it, understand? The reason I say this is because I view the problem from two different angles. But today I am saying to you that I trust you and I never had any doubts about you, because your heart and my heart are the same!" Finishing his words, he called on his guards and they hurried away.

Standing under the bright moonlight, Ji Zhenren looked into the distant mountains for a long time. He saw that clouds and mist seemed to be spread all over the peaks, and his mind was also in turmoil. But in a flash, the clouds and the mist dissipated, and he caught sight of a clear, resolute and steadfast face in the depths of the bright light in the blue sky, and that was his own face. He felt that in this world nothing could cover his true identity.

That night he slept soundly and when he woke up, it was broad daylight. Chief Gao came and told him, "The higher authorities trust you; nothing has changed. Your brother's defection is top secret!"

He nodded his head. For the moment any extra words were unnecessary. He turned around and went back to work.

Before long, Liu Kailai returned to RSU2 from the transport corps. The two brothers reassumed their own identities, and Liu Kailai was transferred back to the guards squad.

11 /THE QI CIPHER

IN FRAGMENTED FORM, the QI cipher came into Ji Zhenren's view. It might have been because it was a stormy day, so poor signals caused the enemy's operator to fail to transcribe the full text, asking for the message to be resent; at the other end the operator resent the message three times, each time a few changes were made, and finally the complete text made it. According to conventional practice, doing it this way broke the taboo of sending encrypted messages. The same text and the same meaning were sent again and again, while during the process the operator made some alterations to some paragraphs, or slightly changed the beginning and the ending of the message. However, if they were intercepted, the possibility of them being decrypted was several times higher. The reason it happened might have been that the enemy was over confident regarding the degree of safety of this complicated cipher; or the enemy operator was muddleheaded and incompetent. They just did it anyway.

To the Red Army cryptographers, these were pennies from heaven; but after a few tries, they failed to decrypt it, not even a smattering of it. Ji Zhenren was in a panic and getting anxious. With the mentality of fighting to the death, he assaulted the cipher. After working for several days, he was still circling around the surface, not knowing how to make a breakthrough.

Song Daxiong brought him a bowl of vegetable soup. As usual he ate it in one gulp. Hurriedly, she gathered the porcelain bowl in her arms. Standing far away from him, she said, "From your face I can tell you had a hard day today. If you want to vent your anger, you can vent it on me, but don't smash the bowl again. I had to pay for the one you smashed last time."

He walked over to her, saying, "A broken bowl can be glued back together. After putting it in the kiln and baking it, it can be a good bowl again. I ask you, if we want to break it again, is it going to be easier to start mending it?"

Not knowing what he was talking about, she hid the bowl behind her back, saying, "My ancestors were potters. What you said is just the opposite. To glue back the broken pieces and to put the bowl back in the kiln to bake, the repairs become stronger. The same applies to a tree. When a tree is cut, the cut grows into a knot, which is harder to chop than a tree branch."

"I see. I have three fragmentary messages, which make one full message. But this message is not the kind of full message we usually see. Like the mended bowl you mentioned, it looks ugly but it loses none of its strength. I know how to break the cipher now." Bending over the desk, he worked on it for three days and three nights without a break.

At daybreak on the fourth day, Song Daxiong came to ask Ji Zhenren to come for breakfast. Gathering the papers, he pressed his knees together and did not move. Stretching one hand, he said, "Help me get up. I can't strain myself. I didn't pee all night until now. It's so urgent, I can't wait. Something's going to happen. Something very bad is going to happen."

Laughing, Song Daxiong understood, "Don't wet your pants. We are in short supply of garments and there are no spare trousers for you to change into."

"Don't tease me. Give me your hand." Poker-faced, he held her hand and slowly got up. Gently he moved his legs away from the chair.

She saw the seat was wet through, laughing in surprise, "What a shame."

Looking distressed, he said, "Don't laugh. Don't say anything about it. I beg you, sister, keep it quiet." He handed the telegram to her, saying, "Chiang Kai-shek's army is never fussy about what they are doing. It seems that this time they did take one bowl for dual usage." She looked at him hesitantly as he said, "Why are you looking at me in a daze? This *QI* is a self-compiled dual-use cipher. As the term suggests they used a special code book to encrypt both the messages going out and those to be received, but the messages sent out and received were encrypted in different ways. It is the first time we have cracked such a cipher."

When Chief Gao read the telegram in front of Song Daxiong his hands began to tremble; it looked like disaster was looming. Song Daxiong had never seen such a frightening scene and her legs couldn't help shaking. Suddenly she knew what wetting one's trousers felt like. She muttered inwardly, "Could it be that Ji Zhenren was also scared and wet his pants?"

The contents of the telegram were as follows:

Two major Red Army traitors (their names were on the name list intercepted and decrypted by Ji Zhenren) were received by Chiang Kai-shek in person. They gave Chiang Kai-shek the location of the Communist Party Central Committee and a map showing the distribution of the Red Army's main forces. Based on this information Chiang Kai-shek made plans to bomb these locations. As part of the bombing, Chiang Kai-shek's field headquarters in Nanchang will send its frontline task force to cooperate with the action.

The KMT's hidden agents as well as the anti-communist elements in the Jiangxi Soviet will collaborate from within with the KMT's shock troops, guiding the bombers to drop their bombs on selected targets. During the chaos of the bombing they will carry out sabotage activities, such as undertaking surprise attacks on important CPC Central Committee organisation locations, blowing up the communists' strategic points, and assassinating the communist leaders.

The liaison point for the secret agents is in a mountain goods shop called Yuhe in Guyu township. The way for the agents to contact each other is extremely unusual: this liaison spot is in the heartland of the Jiangxi Soviet, where they are unable to set up a transceiver, so they can use the QI code book to write notes for meetings with other agents and passing on information, which means that between the mountain goods dealers and the shop they will only recognise the code. After seeing such a note, if the person could decrypt the message, he will be regarded as being on their side.

The operation will be carried out in two phases: at midnight on the 11th of July, KMT bombers will fly to the air space above the Jiangxi Soviet's strategic points. Some of the secret agents will light fires near the quarters of the key communist leaders and the main Red Army forces, munition factories, arsenals and grain storage sites to guide the bombers where to drop their bombs. Meanwhile other secret agents will lead shock troops in Red Army uniforms to go and mix with the Red Army troops and civilians who are fleeing the bombing, and to conduct sneak attacks on the residential courtyards of the Red Army leaders and kill them, as well as to set up explosives to blow up every important military site.

After analysing the telegram, RSU2 reckoned that the KMT clearly knew that the Red Army had no air defence capability; even if they came in the day, they had no worry that their bombers would be shot down, however they still chose to operate at night. This might have been because it would be easier for their shock troops to take action in the chaos of darkness. Pretending that they were helping to put out fires and save lives, they could easily mix with the Red Army troops and get near to key Red Army leaders, so that the success rate for their action would be high. The Red Army's important officials and main forces had no assignments to go out at night and they were all in their quarters, so bombing and shooting results would be good. It would also be easier for the KMT secret agents and shock troops to hide and withdraw after they had finished their mission.

The message was remarkably shocking. For a while, all over the Jiangxi Soviet Area people took every precaution as if they were anticipating a fierce enemy attack yet not knowing what to do.

Ruthlessly and resolutely the bombing began, and in a few days the bombing ended.

One day Chen Xiaohua reported in alarm, "I couldn't hear any signals on the frequency used by *QI*. I searched all the frequencies but could not find that familiar signal. I think it indicates the enemy has stopped using that cipher." Then she formally presented her reason, "I suspect that the enemy has discovered that *QI* has been cracked by us."

Ji Zhenren did not agree with her conclusion. He went to read through some of the interrogation materials gathered a few days previously, trying to find out the true reason why the enemy had stopped using QI.

· · ·

THE SECRET AGENTS' INTERROGATION FOR THE '11 JULY' BOMBING

The people being interrogated:

- **Ding Yiquan:** son of Ding Ji, the owner of the Yuhe mountain goods shop
- **Zhang Caifang:** Ding Ji's daughter-in-law
- **Li Zike:** the liaison of the enemy frontline shock troops

Ding Yiquan

At midday on the 5th of July a young couple came to my shop. They dressed like mountain goods dealers and spoke with a southern Jiangxi accent. As soon as they entered, they handed me a shopping list, asking me if I had these items in stock. I let my wife Caifang receive them while I went to the inner room, where I dug out the different parts of a book from a few holes. I put them together, and this was the code book for QI we used to contact the people from above. I used the codes for the incoming messages and decrypted the shopping list. It was a line of Du Fu's poem 'In August the autumn wind is howling'. I then used the codes for outgoing messages and encrypted a line of Li Bai's poem. I came out of the inner room and handed my note to the young couple. The husband precisely decrypted it as 'Heading east for Yangzhou among willow catkins and flowers'. The contact passwords were exchanged. The husband took out another shopping list, saying it was the order his boss wanted for next month. On it were the item names, prices and quantity. I knew that those numbers were encrypted by using QI, so I took the paper and went to the inner room and decrypted them. The information was about a secret arrangement: to inform the seventeen hidden agents and nine local contacts in all townships to assemble at Tian Dahu's house that evening where important tasks would be assigned. I then wrote a question by using the code for outgoing messages: Can the nine landlord and rich peasant elements who joined us recently come tonight? He wrote using the code for incoming messages: "All of them can come." In the past it was generally my father who received the contacts. But yesterday he was involved in a big deal on another side of the mountain. As for the young couple in front of me, I did not suspect them at all, because I noticed that the whole QI code book seemed to be ingrained in the young man's head.

Only the elite secret agents of the party and the state could manage to possess such a skill.

Zhang Caifang

As soon as the young couple left, my husband and I hurried to different townships and villages to inform the twenty-six agents. Among them seven were in the Red Army, so informing them took up most of our efforts. We finally managed to notify everyone. But when it came to eight o'clock at night, none of them came. My husband, the members of the Tian family and I were captured on the spot. Afterwards we knew what had happened. Now I want to know after you tricked my father-in-law, is he still alive, or is he dead? To tell the truth, if he hadn't left the shop, you could not have successfully played those petty tricks on us.

Li Zike

On the 6th of July, around sunset, I went to Yuhe mountain goods shop where I was met by Ding Ji's son and daughter-in-law. In the previous two years I went to the shop twice and Ding Ji received me on both occasions. I didn't know Ding Ji's son and daughter-in-law. In the shop, the contact passwords were our shopping lists. After the passwords were matched, I presented them with my master's outstanding bills for June, which was actually the action plan for the '11 July' bombing. The couple went to the inner room to decrypt the message, then they gave me the statement of account, which was a question encrypted by QI for outgoing messages: Is it possible not to bomb our house and the houses of those nine families? I wrote down in code: Very hard to avoid being bombed; if you are hit, the higher-ups will compensate you in full. They set their minds at ease, cooperating with the hidden agents and undertaking preparations for a few days. On the 11th of July, I went to the shop again at eight o'clock in the evening. Although we had met last time, we still followed the procedure and used the passwords, the sole identification for us, which was an iron discipline. Then I walked out of the shop, quietly followed by the couple. After we walked out of the township, one after another, more people came and followed us. He nodded to me every time a newcomer joined, meaning he was one of us. When we reached the gathering point at Xiangquan mountain, we met seventy-eight members from our shock troops, who were then divided into thirteen groups. The twenty-six agents were also divided into thirteen groups in charge of taking the shock troops to specific locations for bombing, such as the quarters and warehouses of the Red Army. We used a transceiver and sent messages to our higher-ups, telling them that everything was ready. At about 11 o'clock that night, the thirteen teams went to hide near the bombing targets, and at each target three piles of firewood were ready. One hour later, we heard aircraft coming. We lit the fires. But surprisingly, after the first bomb dropped, Red Army soldiers suddenly jumped out from the woods. We were wiped out on the spot before we could carry out our action. The two hidden agents in each team pulled out their pistols and began to shoot, but at the shock troops who should have been their own people. Especially the commanding team, which carried a transceiver with them, was pressed hard by the Red Army force. The Dings' daughter-in-law was very brave and fierce. With three shots she killed those nearest the transceiver. Her husband then held the transceiver and went to hide behind a rock. Our commanding team was wiped out in a flash before our eyes. Luckily I wasn't killed but captured alive. Then together with your people I stood on a mountaintop and witnessed the whole bombing process. I realised that the thirteen lighted locations were all empty spaces or unoccupied houses, not real targets. Then I heard a man, the others called him Chief Gao, commanding the Dings' son and daughter-in-law (now I know they are your people, posing as the Dings' son and daughter-in-law) to send out four telegrams. Although I was tied up, I could still hear. The contents of all four telegrams were given orally by Gao. The man posing as the Dings' son encrypted the messages using the QI cipher, then the false daughter-in-law sent out the messages using our transceiver. The first two telegrams said, falsely, that the air raid had successfully hit several important targets. The third telegram said that our first shock troops had suffered heavy casualties, thus requesting the second group of shock troops to go to the Laoyeling gateway to meet the remaining troops. You know this was our plan B. The second shock troops' commander and assistant commander were Li Kezhong and Ji Zhenfu. The fourth telegram said that the aircraft had dropped bombs on our own people, and they suddenly switched the transceiver off. Although our higher-ups lost contact with the shock troops, the next day during daylight hours they still sent aircraft to drop more bombs. I guess that you must have put mirrors on the roof of the unoccupied houses or on the top of the hillocks. The reflection of the sunlight guided the airplanes to drop their bombs on false targets because we had originally planned to use fire at night but mirrors in the day. As for our second wave of shock troops, they must have been ambushed when they went to the Laoyeling gateway to meet the remaining members of the first team. Yet I don't know the details about this.

The Red Army beat the enemy at their own game, and the operation and the fraudulent link were carefully prepared. The enemy, except for two members of the shock troops who made a successful sortie, were killed or captured. Deliberately and cleverly the Red Army let the two escape, which was actually part of the plan to cheat the enemy. After the whole fraud was completed, the enemy must have made the following judgement: their shock troops' transceiver was mistakenly bombed; it was possible that the loose copies of the *QI* code book had fallen into the Red Army's hands, therefore they had to stop using *QI*. The enemy would therefore have concluded that the likelihood that *QI* had been cracked by the Red Army was slight.

Ji Zhenren used the above self-analyses to convince himself. He also went against Chen Xiaohua's conclusion that 'the enemy suspected that *QI* had been broken'. As early as before the bombing raid started, Chen Xioahua had moved thirty-two kilometres away to Shiyun mountain with the central organisations, the main Red Army forces and the whole of RSU2. As soon as the bombing raid ended, she returned and found Ji Zhenren, saying only, "Your self-persuasion is nothing other than to help you achieve your aim of satisfying your professional psychology of a cryptographer, or I call it vanity: I've cracked *QI* but the enemy did not see through it. But what realistic significance does it have?"

"You can never be a cryptographer but a monitor," he replied.

Chief Gao walked up to them, saying, "The cracking of *QI* allowed us to move our important departments to Yunshi mountain to avoid the enemy bombing, allowing us to capture twenty-six hidden enemy agents, and to almost completely wipe out two teams of enemy shock troops. Ji Zhenren and Song Daxiong made a first-class contribution to this operation. You two did a very good job of playing the Dings' son and daughter-in-law. Besides, Daxiong did a perfect job of imitating the enemy transceiver operator, and deserves to be called a telegraph expert. However, Ji Zhenfu, the assistant commander of the enemy shock troops, was shot dead. He died in retribution for his sins. Ji

Zhenren, you must restrain your grief. Take a break. Daxiong can be with you for a few days. I feel that you two can progress your relationship one step further. Despite our disciplinary regulations, I will turn a blind eye."

In front of Chief Gao, Ji Zhenren did not show excessive sadness for his brother's death. Composing himself, the thought of Song Daxiong warmed his heart.

Later, he found a quiet place, wanting to cry his eyes out. He felt sad and depressed, but he could not cry. Knocking his head against a tree trunk, he bruised his forehead badly. Going back to his room, Song Daxiong's words lessened the sadness in his heart, "This time, you and I have done our utmost! We don't know how many Red Army soldiers have been saved because of our action. Our efforts were worthwhile!"

12 /THE GROUP A AND B CIPHERS

IT WAS from the cryptographers that the anxious and irritated atmosphere in RSU2 began to spread. Or speaking from a certain angle, RSU2's cryptographers were the first group of people in the whole of the Jiangxi Soviet to become restless and disturbed, as they knew about the enemy activities before everyone else and felt the onset of a hopeless situation for the Red Army.

With his powerful ideological work, again and again Chief Gao suppressed this foreboding, but again and again it was aroused by intelligence they intercepted. The perilous situation in the Jiangxi Soviet got worse day by day, striking unprecedented fear into the hearts of the cryptographers. This fear was caused by pages and pages of enemy telegrams and more and more of the tense *click-clacking* sound of telegraphic code. With trembling hands the cryptographers wrote down what they had deciphered and passed it to Chief Gao.

Some officers and other ranks also felt uneasy, but were not aware of the scope, timing or extent of the devastation. Yet the cryptographers knew everything. In those days one phrase had become Chief Gao's favourite saying, and whenever he met someone he would say, "Calm down, calm down." To some extent his unusual calmness comforted everyone in the unit.

Ji Zhenren was simply not anxious at all. At first Song Daxiong thought that his mind might have been occupied by codes and ciphers, so he was slow to react, being indifferent to things and people, resulting in him never being in an anxious state of mind. But slowly she found this was not the case. The following two comments of his changed her opinion about him.

"Now we must be ants and we can only be ants now. However, we will never be ants under Chiang Kai-shek's feet, but ants that can topple an elephant! We at RSU2 are a group of ants who can overturn Chiang Kai-shek! When you hear about it, you may think it unimaginable. Your habitual thinking makes you believe that ants can never bring down an elephant. But think about it from a different angle. This group of ants is going to cleverly use the elephant's limbs and climb up to its eyes and ears, causing it to be blind and deaf, so it will bump into trees and fall into a ditch, or even fall off a cliff and die, isn't that so? Yes, this is definitely possible. Our job is to work on the enemy's eyes and ears. It is an issue of confidence, as well as an issue of tactics and technique. Of course, we also need to defeat our enemy with our convictions."

The second comment was voiced when the Red Army first began to break out of Chiang Kai-shek's encirclement. At the time the Red Army general headquarters issued orders every day asking troops to get ready and act the next day, but no actions were really taken because no one told the troops on exactly which day the action should be taken, and how. The vast number of generals and soldiers had no idea at all where to go, how to get there, how long to go for and why! Although it was a passive strategic breakthrough of an enemy encirclement and the destination could change at any time, the tendency and the signs for moving away had been evident for several months. The military advisor Otto Braun and Bo Gu, who was generally responsible for the Red Army, had kept silent toward the Red Army generals. Only at the last moment before their departure did Otto Braun and Bo Gu circulate a notice to the troops that they should go to the west of Hunan and Hubei provinces.

It was at this moment that Ji Zhenren said,

"Daxiong, look at the situation. The 5,000 porters from the troops and conscripted civilians are carrying on their shoulders the whole Chinese Soviet Republic. This chaotic and colossal column extends over thirty to thirty-five kilometres, carrying all sorts of items on their backs or between their shoulders, moving the whole state on the journey. Put aside for now if this moving-house-style military action is right or not, but for a military operation of this scale, the leadership should tell the generals in advance of all the routes of the basic elements of the operation. This is common sense. If such information is not forthcoming, how can the generals command their troops? They don't know what the strategy is, nor do they know what the prepared plan is, so how can they fight the battle? The higher-ups do things in such a way. Humph! It obviously has aspects of a typical Prussian military style! This is military mysticism, and it will bring calamity to the army!"

Listening, Song Daxiong was stupefied. Looking around, in a low voice she reminded him, "I feel that such remarks should not come out of the mouth of a cryptographer. The trouble you got into last time made your brother Kailai suffer. Disaster comes out of one's mouth. We have to speak less but do more to keep mishaps away."

Later the Red Army leadership voiced criticism of the 'military mysticism'; furthermore, later the Red Army general headquarters paid attention to sorting out the problem of information being held up, and began to inform the troops of their own situation and the enemy's situation; much later the Red Army repeatedly suffered heavy defeats. The whole of the Red Army troops began to question the central leadership and its command, and the prestige of Bo Gu and Otto Braun fell to an all-time low.

After becoming aware of these circumstances Song Daxiong admired Ji Zhenren even more. Those complaints from his mouth, which nearly caused him trouble, were so right. She wondered if all cryptographers and intelligence experts had such formidable insight.

While she was thinking about this, the central organisation and the majority of the Red Army's main forces, after experiencing all kinds of hardship and peril, finally crossed the Xiang River in Hunan; but their military strength had reduced from about 80,000 when they left Jiangxi to about 30,000.

In the days before crossing the Xiang River, on a rapid march Ji Zhenren met his mother and youngest sister.

Talking of rapid marches, in RSU2's case, it was really 'rapid'. In order to keep on monitoring the enemy wireless communications, Chief Gao adopted an effective and flexible method, namely, to divide the staff into two echelons, marching in turns. According to the general distance for the day, they calculated the times of departure and encampment for the two teams. Team One would leave three to four hours earlier than the main troops, usually leaving at two or three o'clock in the morning. Team Two stayed on the spot monitoring; then they started marching three to four hours after the main force departed. After Team One had stopped halfway, or arrived at the destination for the day, they set up aerials and began to work. Team Two then packed up their equipment and began their march, passing Team One and marching on to the next stop. So the RSU2 staff would often travel fifty kilometres per day. Working overnight was the norm; on average they only had about three to four hours' sleep each night. Marching, working, staying up late at night, yet having no time for food or drink. The strenuous schedule badly drained their physical strength, which had reached the limit. Some broke down from the constant overwork, while some died of exhaustion.

All the RSU2 staff knew profoundly that at many critical moments time was truly a matter of life and death. Whether they could transcribe and decipher the enemy telegrams in time and quickly and precisely ascertain the surrounding enemy's routes of advance affected the safety of the whole Red Army. For instance, every night the Red Army headquarters would issue orders to the troops. Mostly they only issued the departure time for the next day but no route or destination. The decision as to where the troops should go had to be decided after RSU2 had intercepted the enemy intelligence and when the Red Army knew about the enemy's operational plan. This had become a scene frequently experienced during the Long March. For the relay, the speed with which the two teams exchanged roles, as well as how one team joined the other team in an orderly fashion, was the key. No matter what difficulties they encountered, they had to ensure that all the team members arrived at the designated place on time.

That day, mounted and with their equipment and weapons on horseback, Ji Zhenren, Song Daxiong and Chen Xiaohua raced against the clock and hurried on their way.

Riding to the left and right behind him, Song Daxiong and Chen Xiaohua were safeguarding Ji Zhenren. Song Daxiong then noticed that something was wrong with him. Sitting on horseback, he was rocking back and forth, left and right. From time to time he took out some paper with code written on it and read it, and several times he nearly fell off his horse. She knew that he was, once again, immersed in his work.

This was too dangerous. She needed to find a way to help him.

They reined in the horses. Moving the equipment from Ji Zhenren's horse onto hers, Song Daxiong mounted Ji Zhenren's horse. The two of them were skin and bones, so the horse was able to bear their weight. Song Daxiong sat in front while Ji Zhenren sat close behind her and held her waist. They used one belt to tie themselves together. It was safe no matter how fast the horse galloped, so that Ji Zhenren could work as much as he wanted.

Hitting on an idea, Ji Zhenren needed to do calculations urgently, so he said, "No desk. I have to borrow your back to write on."

Song Daxiong didn't get it, calling out, "Talk sense."

"I need to write," he said. Taking out pen and paper, he began to write on her back, which was too soft to write on. He then saw a wooden board at the roadside. Reining in the horse, he picked up the board, transforming it into a proper writing board. Tying a rope through the board he hung it on Song Daxiong's back, which was much more comfortable for him to write on.

On the main roads and narrow paths the horse galloped and trotted. Ji Zhenren held Song Daxiong's waist, letting his thoughts roam free. When the horse slowed down, he would lean on her back and write on the board. This scene became a particular feature on the Long March. Whenever they met troops, the soldiers would throw sidelong glances at them and talk in whispers.

One day they heard someone calling out on the roadside, "Brother, Ji Zhenren! Ji Zhenren, Brother!" Ji Zhenren was too deep in thought to hear the call.

Song Daxiong saw a girl waving at them. She hesitated to stop the horse. The girl threw herself on her knees, giving out a heart-rending wail, "Ji Zhenren, help!"

Song Daxiong quickly reined in the horse.

A mother and her daughter stood by the roadside, both in rags; two shabby wraps were on the ground.

Song Daxiong woke Ji Zhenren out of his reverie and helped him to dismount.

He recognised the two women before his eyes as his mother and youngest sister.

Before the troops had evacuated from Ruijin, he had gone home once. His mother didn't say much, only asking him to set his mind at ease and go. But no sooner had the troops departed, than Zhang Chengfeng took her daughter with her and followed the withdrawing troops. Large in size and carrying many belongings with them, the speed of the column was slow. Besides, the troops travelled zig-zagged to avoid the enemy, so they did not throw the mother and daughter off.

Zhang Chengfeng was dead set on leaving with the Red Army. Before she left home, this very calculating woman made a good analysis. She figured out that after the KMT troops swooped back to the Soviet Area, they would cruelly kill the family members and supporters of the Red Army soldiers. She thought that during the land investigation movement, her family was indiscriminately eliminated as a landlord household, but the KMT army would also know that her family had made donations to the Red Army and her children were also in the Red Army ranks. The Jiangxi Soviet government might not remember the Jis' contributions, but the KMT would carry out punishment according to these 'contributions' and kill all the Ji family members. They suffered disasters under both parties, having pleased neither side. This was what Ji Huizhong was so muddleheaded about. He himself was driven out of his home, leaving his wife and young daughter to be slaughtered.

This woman, who had her own ideas and was inwardly staunch, chose the sole way of keeping herself alive, namely, to follow the Red Army and leave. Along the way there were some other families like hers, also secretly following the Red Army troops. They did not know where the Red Army was going or how long they would be on the road, but they were all determined not to drop behind, as dropping behind meant death. Because in addition to the KMT army's encirclement, pursuit, obstruction and interception, the reactionary landlord armed forces of various places were also very savage. They killed Red Army officers and ranks and their family members who dropped behind, beheading them, cutting open their chests, and hanging the head and torso on trees. Zhang Chengfeng and her daughter kept their wits about them. Every now and then they followed the Red Army, or hid in the bushes, thereby not losing their lives.

Right now she was as cool as usual, only her daughter Ji Xiaomin was crying her eyes out. She told her brother about their suffering on the journey, saying that their mother had injured her right foot, and the wound had festered, and that now she had difficulty walking. Zhang Chengfeng stopped Ji Xaomin, "Why say that much? Your brother is a man doing great deeds. No backtracking for him. Quick, let him go."

Before Ji Zhenren could enquire after his mother's and sister's well-being, Song Daxiong pressed him to go, saying they had to make a start, or they would not reach the next stop on time. Taking out all the silver coins and paper money from his pocket, Ji Zhenren pressed them into his sister's hands. Song Daxiong then helped him to mount the horse.

"Brother, if you leave our mother behind, you will not see her again in your lifetime." Standing before the horse, Ji Xiaomin bellowed, "Everywhere is desolate and uninhabited, can we eat money for food?" Ji Zhenren came to realise his error. Hurriedly he took the grain pouch off his shoulder. Song Daxiong also took off hers. When Chen Xiaohua tried to take hers off, Song Daxiong stopped her, saying, "Keep yours. Ji Zhenren must not starve to death."

Ji Xiaomin still refused to get out of the way, crying out, "Can grain pouches block the cruel landlords' sharp knives?"

Eyes moistened, Chen Xiaohua said, "How about this? We can leave behind a horse. Or all the horses can go, let me stay behind to look after Ji Zhenren's mother."

"Shut your mouth!" snapped Song Daxiong.

"Xiaohua, your task is to protect the equipment," said Ji Zhenren. "Without you there's no guarantee the equipment will not be damaged. Besides, when we arrive at each relay stop, we need you to transcribe messages and rotate the generator handle. It's a long way. If we leave a horse behind, our speed will be greatly affected, and we won't be able to reach our next stop on time; it's too much responsibility for any single person." Dismounting, Ji Zhenren knelt before his mother, knocking his head hard on the ground three times. Song Daxiong also went down on her knees and touched her head to the ground. Getting up, she left her medicine box near Ji Xiaomin's feet. She then pulled Ji Zhenren up off the ground and put him onto the horse's back. Giving the reins a jerk, the horse galloped away.

Behind them Ji Xiaomin cursed furiously, "Ji Zhenren, you are inhuman. You do not belong to the Ji family any more. You look after your wife but abandon your mother. You will be punished by thunder and God." Chen Xiaohua, who was following closely behind Ji Zhenren and Song Daxiong, sobbed uncontrollably.

After the horses had galloped some distance, Song Daxiong felt Ji Zhenren writing again, and she breathed a long sigh of relief.

Before long, a column of main troops were blocking the road. Song

Daxiong found the commander. Out of breath, she said in a low voice, "We are from RSU2! We need to pass immediately."

RSU2 was a top-secret unit, and the subordinate troops knew nothing about it. Feeling uncertain about these three peculiar people on horseback, the commander did not move. Song Daxiong took out her identity documents, saying, "We are really from RSU2, please make way for us."

The commander said, "Why have I never heard about it?"

"RSU2 is working alongside the senior commanders of the military commission," said Song Daxiong patiently. "Please do not delay us."

"We didn't come here for sightseeing, who is not in a hurry?" muttered the commander. "It's not that I'm trying to give you a hard time. I'm afraid I couldn't make way for you even if I wanted to." Then he called out loudly, "All make way, all make way!" The troop formation was tightly packed and enormous, with a sense of unease and a confusing mixture of voices. As expected the shout did not work.

Ji Zhenren was oblivious to everything going on around him. As soon as the horse stopped galloping, he could do his calculations and writing more easily. Full of curiosity the soldiers watched the man and woman on horseback, pointing their fingers at them and commenting. They found it amusing to see a man writing on a woman's back.

Suddenly Ji Zhenren struck the wooden board hard, shouting: "I've cracked it, I've cracked it! I've got it, I've got it!"

Song Daxiong, pistol in hand and red-eyed, gazed at the commander, asking, "The military situation is critical! Are you going to sort it out, or let me do it?" The commander hesitated a bit. Song Daxiong fired three shots in the air, spurring on the horse she directly charged towards the column of troops.

The head of the column instantly made way. The five-kilometre-long procession dodged either side of the road in an orderly fashion from the head of the column to the tail. Three fast horses galloped forward like a fast boat on the sea, braving the wind and battling the waves.

The officers and ranks in the front did not know what was happening. Hearing three gunshots and seeing the column dodging to the roadside, they followed suit and quickly jumped to the side of the road, seeing a man and a woman holding each other tightly on horseback speeding off. The woman held the reins with one hand and a pistol in the other. The man kept his face close against the woman's back. Behind them were two more horses and a woman. Soon another horse followed, and it was the commander, who carried on shouting, "Make way, quick, let the comrades of RSU2 go first!"

Three horses galloped all the way through the column, and muddy water splashed all over the soldiers. Everybody began to comment, "What backing does RSU2 have? A man and a woman were hugging each other on the same horse, and they were more domineering than Heaven! What a majestic bearing, that woman soldier was like a man; but that man was like a woman, dull-looking, thin and weak."

They arrived at the designated place on time. The other two teams also arrived. Ji Zhenren handed Song Daxiong what he had deciphered on horseback, asking her to report to the higher-ups immediately. He then set up the transceiver and, putting on the headphones, he began to monitor. Sorry at having abandoned Ji Zhenren's mother, Chen Xiaohua wound the handle of the generator so hard that the electrical current was unstable, making Ji Zhenren keep cursing.

The cipher he had cracked on horseback was YAN, an advanced cipher used between the Central Army directly under Chiang Kai-shek's control and the troops under the command of Hunanese warlord He Jian. From the intelligence, the Red Army discovered that the Hunan and Guangxi armies were changing their troop deployment. General Bai Congxi had ordered the Guangxi army's main forces to withdraw from Gong city and move south; however the Hunan army sent to take over garrison duty from the Guangxi army had not yet arrived, so the two armies failed to link up, leaving a 60-kilometre defence line north of Xing'an and south of Quanzhou along the Xiang River wide open.

Meanwhile several other important ciphers cracked by RSU2 gave the Red Army a more timely, broader and more comprehensive understanding of the overall disposition of the enemy.

Therefore the Red Army general headquarters acted on the intelligence, making a swift decision to order troops to make an emergency breakthrough of the enemy line. In breaching the enemy's defences, the troops stormed the river, speedily and finally crossing the Xiang River.

After crossing the river, the higher-ups specially sent people to take pork to RSU2 as a reward and a token of gratitude. Not standing on ceremony, Ji Zhenren ate half a bowl of pork braised in soya sauce. Song Daxiong gave her portion to him, which he did not decline.

Song Daxiong said, "When I went down on my knees to kowtow to your mother, I said inwardly that I would look after you like a mother would do. In the future, when I take care of you, you should be like today, you shouldn't turn me down."

Listening, Ji Zhenren put his bowl and chopsticks down. Turning in the direction they had come from, he knelt on the floor and wept. Only then did he remember his mother. Guessing that something bad might have happened to her, he couldn't help but feel sad.

One month later his sad feelings were aroused again after Chen Xiaohua told him that in the Qigou area she had met Ji Xiaomin who told her how their mother had died.

The next day after the mother and daughter had been left behind, they met a group of landlord armed forces. Seeing the cavalry galloping toward them, and that there was no time to hide, the mother showed resourcefulness in an emergency. She pushed Ji Xiaomin down the hill. She herself then ran with her wounded foot, drawing the cavalry toward a forest. After the cavalry came out and galloped away, Ji Xiaomin went to look for her mother, finding that she had been stabbed to death.

Ji Zhenren was so sad, asking where his sister was now. Chen Xiaohua said, "She did not want to see you. No matter how hard I tried, she refused to come with me. She went with several Red Army soldiers' family members and they moved on." She took out a piece of paper, saying Ji Xiaomin had written down the time and location of their mother's death.

For many days afterwards Ji Zhenren was in a foul mood. He would lose his temper, smash things and curse, mainly to curse himself. But no matter how his mood fluctuated, as soon as he picked up a telegram, he quickly calmed down.

Later, in Zunyi in Guizhou Province, the Central Political Bureau held an enlarged meeting, in which Mao Zedong's leadership of the Red Army was established. Excited, Ji Zhenren expressed his opinion, "This is good. With Comrade Mao Zedong in command of the Red Army, our intelligence will be put to good use. To be honest, we cryptographers want neither official positions, nor material gains nor official titles, and we can even abandon our parents. What we want is that someone pays attention to our work and uses the results of our work. Facts have proved that if importance is attached to the intelligence we gather and it is used well, then the Red Army sheds less blood. If we little ants can cause the elephant to tumble more, and harass the elephant's eyes and ears more, less Red Army soldiers will die! But much good intelligence was ignored, which bitterly disappointed me. But things will change for the better."

After his remarks, Song Daxiong nodded her head seriously. These days, not only did she often feel a close bond with Ji Zhenren, her mind was more and more inseparable from his. He never felt cold on horseback, because when he stretched his hands he could hold her warmth in his arms. When he needed to write, he could do it on her back to his heart's content. In the public gaze he could freely lean on her back to get some sleep, while she had to sit upright to maintain her balance so that his sacred dreams would not be disturbed. After he woke up, he would look satisfied, smiling mischievously and wiping his dribble off her back. Having already got used to the others whispering, she never bothered about their comments.

But Chief Gao did not allow the others to gossip. He maintained this distinctive scene on the march from the bottom of his heart. In front of the whole unit he announced, "Ji Zhenren and Song Daxiong are a revolutionary pair, a noble integral whole. Separating them, they are two weak halves; integrating them as one, they are as strong as steel. Either way is innocent revolutionary love. Song Daxiong is Ji Zhenren's transportation corps and safeguard; while Ji Zhenren is the tank, the trump card. The Red Army needs this blessed combined force. Therefore, we say they are a revolutionary pair and work partnership, needed by the revolution and permitted by the organisation. If anyone dares reproach them, I will never forgive them!" In fact, to those who were in the know, who didn't understand it?

Once, Liu Kailai privately made fun of Song Daxiong, calling her 'sister-in-law'. She did not show any shyness, maybe because she had already got used to this role in her mind.

"You addressed me this way but, firstly, you must not let your brother hear it and, secondly, you must not let Chief Gao hear it. Thirdly I like you addressing me this way very much. But I have never been treated like a 'sister-in-law'. Basically I am your brother's faithful friend, his good partner in work and life-and-death comrade-in-arms on the revolutionary road. In your brother's eyes, more often than not I am not a woman.

"However, recently it seems that he has been able to regard me as a woman, which happened when he was extremely weak and mentally stressed. He treated me as a mother, while I couldn't help treating him like a child who badly needed a mother's care. I unwillingly gave him motherly love. What I wanted to give him was the love between a husband and a wife. But when he had a cipher that was very difficult to crack, and he was on the verge of a nervous breakdown, only motherly love could comfort him. When I held him in my arms, it was like holding a dying child.

"It reminded me of an incident I experienced. In a battle, a colleague by my side was hit by a bullet in the heart. The instant he fell to the ground, what came out of his lips was a low and deep call for his 'mother'. That made me think about what is on someone's mind in the last moment before they die and, in this case, the last shadow must have been his mother who had given birth to him and raised him. Although only some people call out, more people die before they can get the words out."

She then thought of Ji Zhenren's mother and she began to weep. During these years few people had seen such a mentally strong woman wailing in such a way.

Liu Kailai did not know that his mother had died. But seeing Song Daxiong looking so sad, he could not help but wail too. After a long while he said, "You are my brother's benefactor and our Ji family's benefactor. On behalf of our whole family I am happy to leave my brother in your care."

Song Daxiong calmed down, saying, "Your brother often forgets himself, but that is all for the sake of saving more Red Army soldiers' lives. I am not talking big. This is what he thinks and what he does. Therefore, what I have done has nothing to do with the Ji family but is firstly for the Red Army and secondly for myself as I am passionately in love with him. You say that I am your family's benefactor. I cannot bear such a compliment; on the contrary I might be a guilty party toward your family." She was wondering whether she should tell him about the death of his mother and sister, but decided against it. Why should she be the cause of more suffering and pain?

In fact she did not tell Ji Zhenren about the death of Ji Xiaomin, either. Actually, he had brushed past his sister's dead body without seeing it.

That day, mounted, the three of them went past a junction. Chen Xiaohua cried out in fear. Song Daxiong then saw that on the roadside three women were hanging on trees. Among them was a young woman whose badly mangled breasts were exposed, with a small medicine box and two empty grain pouches slung over her shoulders. At once she recognised that they were the items she had left with Ji Xiaomin. She realised what had happened. At the time Ji Zhenren was deciphering codes, so she did not disturb him. After riding some distance, she said that she needed to relieve herself. Once they had dismounted, she let Chen Xiaohua go with Ji Zhenren first. She then went back to the junction and saw clearly that the dead young woman was Ji Xiaomin. She stopped several passing soldiers and together they buried the three corpses in the woods. She wrote down the time and place of the burial on a piece of paper, wanting to give it to Ji Zhenren sometime afterwards.

When she saw Chen Xiaohua, she asked her when she had last met Ji Xiaomin and why she had not taken her to join the Red Army. Chen Xiaohua said that she tried and tried but Ji Xiaomin would not come with her, saying that she did not want to see her brother again after he had refused to save his own birth mother's life, nor did she want to see his cruel and heartless woman whom he held in his arms all day long.

"It seems that she went to her death without forgiving her brother. There was no way she could view her brother's action from the angle of the revolution, and why he abandoned his mother and sister."

Quietly Song Daxiong said, "Even though I know something sad has happened, I still say that in a military emergency, personal feelings and family affairs cannot be allowed to delay our assignment. Do you understand what I'm saying?"

Chen Xiaohua cried out, "I don't have such a high political awareness as you do. Under the circumstances, if I were you, I would have stayed with my mother no matter how difficult it might have been."

"In times of disaster, it's not that Ji Zhenren didn't want to be with his loved ones. But he still chose to leave them. Even if he had chosen to stay, I would have tied him up and forced him to leave," said Song Daxiong with tears gushing out of her eyes.

In the following days she was in very low spirits and said little. Ji Zhenren tried to cheer her up by telling her some happy things. He went to Chief Gao and came back with a technical report, which did make her smile, "You think this report is guaranteed to cure every single disease in the world? Sometimes no medicine can treat a psychological ailment."

"But this report is a tonic for me anyway," said Ji Zhenren. "After one read, all my illnesses are cured."

Taking hold of the report, she began to read seriously.

(A) Cipher name: QING, JING, LU, YONG, KAI, YAN, FU, WU and SHAN.

Type
Self-compiled and dual usage.

Troops using it
The KMT Army's 'Encirclement and Suppression' Headquarters and its subordinate troops.

Time of cracking
August and September 1934

People who cracked the ciphers
All RSU2 cryptographers.

Beneficial results gained from the intelligence: By cracking the KMT Army's nine major ciphers, the Red Army acquired the most recent troop deployments, operational plans, instructions and orders from the field headquarters in Nanchang of the president of the KMT Military Council regarding the encirclement of the Red Army. Specifically, one month in advance the Red Army learned that the KMT Army would launch a fresh large-scale offensive to surround the Red Army in the Jiangxi Soviet Area in the last ten days of October. According to the original plan, the date for the Central Red Army to break through the KMT encirclement was at the end of October or beginning of November. After intercepting the enemy intelligence, the Red Army Headquarters took urgent action, adjusting its troop deployment and revising the original plan, with the result that they started to make a sortie at the beginning of October. In the words of the senior officers at the Red Army General Headquarters, this sortie and move were "suddenly decided" because of the urgent military situation, demonstrating how important the intelligence gathered from multi channels and by multi means can be.

(B) Cipher name: **QIANG, WEN, SHUN, HAI, TAO, YING, QIN, YAN** and **SHENG.**

Type
Self-compiled and dual usage.

Troops using it
The field headquarters of the president of the KMT Military Council in Nanchang, the Nationalist armies under the direct command of Chiang Kai-shek, as well as the Hunan and Guangxi armies.

Time of cracking
October to December 1934.

People who cracked the ciphers
All RSU2 cryptographers.

Technical significance: The Red Army took the difficult path of breaking out of the encirclement and were forced to either outwit and outflank the enemy or fight to the death. During the Long March, the military situation changed constantly and the troops had no fixed whereabouts. There was no base to reply to, and ground surveillance was difficult, with no way of contacting the underground and intelligence stations, so the RSU2 system had become almost the Red Army's sole intelligence source. During this period of time, the ciphers used by Chiang Kai-shek's field headquarters, the KMT Central Army and its subordinate troops were all compiled by their Chinese expert cryptographers. They were complicated, with a high level of confidentiality, hard to break, and new ciphers were frequently issued to replace the old ones.

Luckily the RSU2 cryptographers had followed the enemy's cipher compiling techniques for a long time and knew about the rules and understanding at their core, and were consequently able to handle the job with ease due to their previous experience. Basically their achievement was that as long as they received the telegrams, they could crack the ciphers and decrypt the messages. In this respect, there was no special technical importance, but when they were trying to crack TAO, a significant thing happened.

It turned out that after the majority of the Red Army troops passed the Jiufeng mountain bordering Guangdong and Hunan, Chiang Kai-shek eventually realised the Red Army's large-scale shift was not a mobile tactic but a strategic shift; not scattered and temporary mobile or guerrilla warfare but the abandonment of their home and running away. So he held an emergency military meeting and made a major deployment of five columns of troops to coordinate in combat, planning to create the chance for a decisive battle on favourable terrain east of the Xiang River, in attempt to deal a devastating blow to the Red Army. His deployment order was composed of five parts, very specific and detailed. But he was worried that his troops would not seriously carry out the order, so in his telegram, he quoted four sentences from the ancient military strategist Wei Liaozi to express his thirst to find the enemy and convey his expectations to his subordinates, "Once the troops have been assembled, they must not be broken up carelessly; once the troops have gone into action, they must not return without accomplishing anything; the desire to fight should be like a parent being determined to find their missing child, attacking the enemy should be like rushing to rescue a drowning person regardless of one's own safety." This order was encrypted via the advanced MI cipher and sent to all components of his army.

After Ji Zhenren intercepted this telegram, he began to decrypt it at once, but he remained perplexed despite much thought. He seemed to have encountered the second half of the telegram before, but he just could not catch hold of its tail. Seeing him scratching his head anxiously, to keep his mind off the cipher, Song Daxiong took him with her and they strolled along the road out of the camp site. They met an old woman who had a piece of paper with 'My son Li Dingfeng comes home'written on it, stuck on both her front and back. Moving along the road with her bound feet, weeping and wailing from one troop to another she was searching for her son. Someone said that Li Dingfeng had actually been killed in action, only that they did not have the heart to tell her about it. Seeing the scene, Ji Zhenren stood still like a tree stump. He then turned around, ran back to the campsite and started to work without sleep for two days.

He had learned quite a lot of the well-known phrases of the ancient military strategists. Inspired by the old woman searching for her dead son, all at once it reminded him of Wei Liaozi's four sentences. He gave it a try, feeling it was a mess, with countless ties and knots, but his

whole body was wriggling. As expected he saw the little tail. He held
the tail tight and pulled the whole body out of the hole. With a knife he
cut and skinned it layer by layer. He then saw the flesh, the bones.
Cutting open the belly, he dug out the heart and the lungs. In the end he
cracked the cipher.

When she had finished reading the report, Song Daxiong's eyes were
filled with tears. She muttered, "Reading the report, I feel it is
worthwhile even if you and I should die." She then cracked a smile,
"You are right. This is a miracle cure for all people and all illnesses!"

13 /THE FANG CIPHER

ONE DAY, as soon as they arrived at the camp site, Ji Zhenren suddenly felt terribly cold all over. Song Daxiong was tethering the horses outside. After she returned to the courtyard she saw no sign of him. Then, seeing a haystack trembling, she pushed aside the bundles of hay and saw him lying underneath, face dark purple and neck all covered with goose pimples. Touching his forehead, she could feel it was burning hot.

Not long ago, she had become acquainted with an old herbalist. Since then she would often carry with her some Chinese herbal medicines for ailments such as headaches, colds, fever and diarrhoea, and they were all prepared for Ji Zhenren.

Seeing how sick he looked, she thought he might have a cold. She boiled some herbal medicine for him. However, after drinking the concoction, his trembling became worse and he began to rave deliriously. His last sentence when his mind was still clear was, "I've got malaria, caused by mosquitoes."

Song Daxiong went to see Old Yang, the unit medic, who muttered, "Even Mao Zedong had to hold out with all his might when he suffered malaria. I have no medicine to treat this disease. Yes, someone may not be able to hold out. Particularly for those who are physically weak, they may have complications. The symptoms for malaria are abdominal pain and diarrhoea, which gives off an unbearable stench. Besides, the patient can be restless and mentally deranged, twitching and in a state of unconsciousness. You must be careful. If anything bad happens to our exceptional Ji Zhenren, Chief Gao will hold you responsible."

Song Daxiong gave Old Yang a ferocious gaze, "If he dies, I'll use your head to make a sacrifice for him." Hurriedly Old Yang picked up his medicine box and went to see Ji Zhenren. Knowing that there was no cure for the disease, he still gave him some medicine, fearing that if he died, Song Daxiong would point her gun at his forehead. It was well-known that on the issue of Ji Zhenren's safety this woman was uncompromising. Medicines were as precious as gold to Old Yang.

After giving Ji Zhenren the medicine, his heart ached so much that he told everyone, "That woman despot! She wasted my medicine on that exceptional person of hers. The amount was enough to save two wounded soldiers, which means she has brought death to two wounded soldiers!"

Each day Ji Zhenren was dripping with sweat, and his clothes were repeatedly wet through. Song Daxiong even gave him her own clothes to wear, but she still didn't have enough dry clothes for him to change into. It had been cloudy and drizzly for days on end, so she had to wear his wet clothes, drying them with her own body warmth.

Ji Zhenren felt too sleepy and struggled to stay awake. After picking up the telegrams, in the twinkling of an eye he would lean his head on one side and fall asleep. A sound sleep was what he had missed in recent years. Chief Gao ran into the room, shouting anxiously, "War is pressing! How can he fall asleep? It's so outrageous! Listen, Song Daxiong. I need him awake, and I hand this task to you. If he can break ciphers in his dreams, it's alright for him to sleep all day." Song Daxiong rarely flew into a rage when confronted with an assignment.

Pointing her finger at Chief Gao, she called out, "Don't step in the room if you've come here with an assignment. I cannot fulfil your damn shitty assignment. I only want to keep him alive, which is my sole task. Even if a high fever turned him into a fool, I would also want him to live. You want him to break ciphers for you 24 hours a day, 365 days a year. Old Gao, his condition is so wretched, can't you let him have a good sleep?"

Chief Gao was still flying off the handle, giving Ji Zhenren some hard pushes, he bellowed, "How many more soldiers will die on the frontline if we let him sleep for a few more hours? I'll say it again. I need him awake at any moment! This is a political assignment handed to you by the organisation!"

Song Daxiong pushed Chief Gao out of the room, yelling, "To hell with your political assignments. From now on, if any one comes here for anything other than to treat Ji Zhenren, I will kick them all out. I don't care who the shit senior officers are."

Ji Zhenren's mind was fuzzy, and he frequently raved. As soon as Chief Gao left, with difficulty he turned over in bed. Holding Song Daxiong's hand, he put it on his breast. Squeezing her hand harder and harder, he then pushed it between his chest and abdomen, twice moving it below his abdomen and nearly touching his private parts. Flushed and nervous, Song Daxiong felt that something would happen imminently. But it did not.

She cursed inwardly, "He doesn't even dare not to behave like a man in his illness and dreams." Suddenly she remembered something. "After all, is he a man?" Gritting her teeth, she removed all of his soaking clothes and underwear, changing him into a pair of dry trousers. With her face burning feverishly, she murmured inwardly, "Well, he is a man." After passing the test of changing his underwear, she went to every corner of the village and the township and finally found a large wooden tub. She boiled some hot water and gave Ji Zhenren a hot bath. His condition seemed to be improving a little, but before long he had a high temperature again, and for a few days he was vomiting and had watery stool, lying in a deep coma.

If his condition went on like this, he would definitely die. She went to see Chief Gao who began to weep after hearing her description. He thought of every possible solution he could think of and went to ask for help from anyone he could think of. She then went to see Old Yang. She went down on her knees, which scared the medic, so he also went down on his knees, telling her that he could do nothing to save Ji Zhenren. Drawing her pistol from her waist, she pointed the gun at the medic's forehead, screaming, "No more nonsense. If he does not live, you will not live either." Old Yang knelt there for a long time, simply swallowing the grief into his belly.

Several days later, more dead than alive, Ji Zhenren looked like he was at the end of his tether. Unable to control himself any more, Chief Gao burst into tears. Summoning up his courage, Old Yang walked over to Song Daxiong, saying, "He's had a high fever for many days and the complications are getting worse day by day. I'm afraid he will not pull through. At the moment the enemy is vicious, chasing and pressing us very hard. The number of wounded soldiers is increasing, and our medical unit is struggling to cope with them all. If we cannot take Ji Zhenren with us, we can leave him behind with the villagers. I promise that after the victory of the revolution I will come back here and pick up Comrade Ji's bones and bring them to you. Please trust me!" Giving Old Yang a kick, Song Daxiong carried Ji Zhenren away on her back.

It was the beginning of 1935. The Central Red Army withdrew from Zunyi via left, right and central routes and advanced westward towards the area of Guizhou's Chishui and Sichuan's Luzhou. Travelling while fighting against the enemy encirclement, pursuit, obstruction and interception, their march was extremely difficult. Especially since all elements of the Sichuan Army launched attacks with terrific force, constantly checking the advance of the Central Red Army. In order to travel light, RSU2 had to throw away as much material and equipment as they could, and arrangements were made for some of the seriously wounded soldiers to recover in the homes of local villagers. But Song Daxiong did not allow anyone to touch Ji Zhenren. She carried him, who was now skeletal, on her back wherever she went.

That day the headquarters decided to surround and annihilate the chasing enemy in a mountain valley east of Duqiu township, starting a battle between the Central Red Army and the KMT's Sichuan Army.

Because the operation began in haste, there was not enough time for RSU2 to prepare any intelligence. Besides, Chiang Kai-shek had begun to get a better idea of the Red Army's wireless interception capacity, saying, "The red bandits particularly eavesdrop on our wireless communications. Although we have ciphers, it is still easy for them to secretly decrypt our messages." He gave urgent orders to all troops to strengthen their security in respect of secret information. So the Sichuan Army had gathered together some expert cipher compilers and their self-produced ciphers were unbelievably difficult to crack. RSU2 failed to crack any of them before the battle began, so the Red Army had to rely on either the ground scouts, or the monitoring of the enemy's plain-text messages. The intelligence gathered from all sources showed that the chasing enemy force only consisted of four regiments.

After exchanging fire with the enemy, RSU2 still could not manage to undertake an overall monitoring of the enemy's wireless communications, so the Red Army did not know exactly how many of the enemy they were facing nor their disposition. After the fighting had persisted for a while, they felt that things were not right. The enemy had much more than four regiments engaged in the battle, and they were not as easy to deal with as predicted, being high in combat effectiveness. The Red Army's original plan of an ambush turned into a seesaw battle, and they suffered heavy losses in one day.

RSU2 was working close to the command headquarters, not far from the firing line. From all sides the sound of guns, shells and battle cries were heard all day and all night. Batches of wounded soldiers were carried out of the trenches, groaning, howling, cursing; heart-rending sounds, too horrible to listen to. Chief Gao had deployed all his manpower and equipment. After giving assignments to the staff, he handed the management work to the other unit leaders. He himself dived into the messages; with a few key cryptographers they went all out to crack the ciphers.

The alien enemy transceivers, the ciphers that were extremely difficult to crack and the wretched crying and howling were all testing the monitors and cryptographers. If it were not for the peacetime training and cultivation, as well as the tempering under actual combat conditions, all these technical pressures, combat urgency, terror of death and injury, and horror of the battlefield could almost have wrecked their psychological defenses. But RSU2 was an excellent team. What they were presenting was a different scene: it seemed that nothing was happening, and everything was in good order.

Calmly and unhurriedly, Chen Xiaohua primed the generator. No matter how the battle was going, she kept her eyes on the indicator, keeping a stable supply of electricity. Sitting before the transceiver, Song Daxiong proved herself to be a dab hand at monitoring; using her good ear to listen, in absolute calmness she transcribed, and every message was good quality work. For Chief Gao, it seemed that he was working in a quiet room. One moment he quickly went through the telegrams, the next he gazed at the stone wall deep in thought; one moment he stood up and paced to and fro slowly, the next he suddenly sat down and wrote swiftly. One bomb exploded not far from them and the burning soil landed on the papers. He dusted the soil off and carried on writing.

In the headquarters next to RSU2, the sound of footsteps coming and going seemed to increase. Chief Gao heard someone shouting loudly, "The enemy has drawn near the headquarters. Order the Cadres' Regiment to launch a counterattack!" The shout startled Chief Gao, because he knew that the Cadres' Regiment had a very high combat effectiveness and they were the general headquarters' last trump card. Dispatching them heralded that the battle had reached a critical moment. Soon, Assistant Chief of Staff Li ran to RSU2, shouting, "Things are in a bad way. Even comrades Zhu De and Liu Bocheng have gone to the front line. The headquarters urgently needs detailed enemy information and tactical intelligence. RSU2, pull your fingers out."

Chief Gao suddenly lost his temper, bellowing, "Don't you have eyes? Are my people sleeping?"

Before he had finished shouting, a shell whizzed at them and several people were thrown to the floor. Chen Xiaohua threw herself on to the transceiver and shrapnel hit her in the back and pierced her heart. She died instantly. At the same time, Song Daxiong jumped up, throwing herself on top of the nearby Ji Zhenren, while Assistant Chief of Staff Li lept onto Song Daxiong, who then felt Ji Zhenren underneath her moving a little. She pushed Li away, holding Ji Zhenren in her arms, and saw that his eyes were slightly opened.

A weak voice floated from his mouth, which had not opened for many days, "Is it the Sichuan Army coming? Quick, give me the telegrams." Tears streaming down Song Daxiong's cheeks, quickly she passed him a pile of enemy telegrams. Before he could take hold of them, he went into a lethargic sleep.

Only then did Song Daxiong find that Assistant Chief of Staff Li was leaning to one side and his left shoulder was bleeding. Trying to express her gratitude, she saw that he had stretched out his right hand to touch his wounded shoulder, pulling out shrapnel. Holding it in front of his face, he blew hard on it and the blood spattered everywhere. Giving a sneer, Assistant Chief of Staff Li staggered away.

Soon he came back again, shouting blusteringly. Chief Gao was about to fly into a rage, but he restrained himself after seeing the bearded senior officer had also come.

Looking around, the bearded senior officer was surprised to see Ji Zhenren holding the enemy telegrams in his hand. He squatted down next to Ji Zhenren, asking, "You can read telegrams again?" Ji Zhenren was still in a lethargic state.

The bearded senior officer called out, "Ji Zhenren, wake up! If you don't wake up, I'm going to fix the bayonet on my rifle and engage in hand-to-hand combat with the enemy!"

Ji Zhenren shivered. Opening his eyes, he struggled to sit up. Holding the enemy telegrams before his eyes, first he murmured to himself, then he cried hysterically, "The senior officer will also go into hand-to-hand combat with the enemy!"

News that the bearded senior officer was to go into hand-to-hand combat with the enemy spread all over the trench, bringing tremendous shock and pressure on RSU2.

During an interval in the fighting, Song Daxiong came to see Ji Zhenren who had a dazed expression in his eyes but could speak clearly, "I'm so cold. I feel like I am leaning on an iceberg. Yes, this Sichuan Army's cipher is like an iceberg, with only the tip showing above the water, but there's no way for me to approach the giant body underneath the water. Can it be that my brain has been truly damaged by the high fever?" He began to shiver again, stretching out his hand, he grabbed some food and pushed it into his mouth.

After opening his eyes, he did not close them again for the following day and night. Twinkling weirdly, his eyes did not move away from the codes even for a moment. He knew the damned illness could not beat him, but he worried that the cryptography could infiltrate his blood like a virus, step by step driving him to a nervous breakdown. Again he seemed to feel that he was nearing the end. When he relaxed, he went into a lethargic state again.

A big, powerful dog appeared beside him. It kept him at arm's length, looking ferocious but did not bite him. Flustered and exasperated, he recklessly pounced on the dog! Through valleys, forests and lakes, he chased and chased. Finally he blocked it inside a room, both of them pouncing on each other. When the dog's teeth bit into his throat, he seized it by the throat and killed it. He saw the word 'Cipher' on the dog's back. Throwing the dog on his back he walked toward the forest. He wanted to hang it on that century-old tree, skin it with a knife and dig out its heart. Walking on the slope, he felt the load on his back get heavier and heavier. Turning around, he saw a larger dog's giant head biting into his throat. Waking up with a start, he looked around the trench and dropped into lethargic sleep again. Surprisingly, the same nightmare resumed. The dog was clinging to his back and it turned into a sack of stones. The weight nearly pressed him to the ground but the slope was endless.

A voice said to him, "When you see a pebble on which grass is growing, you can take a stone out of the sack and throw it away." Not bad, he saw countless pebbles with grass growing on them. Slowly the sack became lighter and lighter. When only one stone was left, the voice said again, "That grass you saw was not growing on the pebble but in the mud on the pebble, so you must go back and start again." The stones that had been thrown away all returned to the sack. Like carrying a mountain on his back he crawled with difficulty along the slope.

After Chief Gao, who was working intensively on the codes, heard that Ji Zhenren had taken on the enemy telegrams for a whole day, he choked with emotion, "Thank god the illness has not turned him into a fool." Walking over to Ji Zhenren, he saw that he was having a nightmare. Shouting and wrangling, it seemed that he was fighting fiercely with somebody. Shaking Ji Zhenren, he woke him up.

Still looking sleepy, Ji Zhenren was not aware that someone was at his side. He was sitting at the bottom of the ditch, his back leaning on the side of the pit. He wobbled and rubbed his head in the mud in rhyme, while playing with a piece of stone in his hand. On the wooden board beside him the papers with code were blown by the wind and scattered on the ground. Gently Chief Gao picked them up and put them in order. Ji Zhenren's lips moved. Chief Gao put his ear close to his lips and heard him saying, "It's time. Call Chief Gao."

Chief Gao called out, "It's time for a full-scale encirclement and annihilation of the enemy!"

His call gave Ji Zhenren a start. At once he sat up, murmuring, "It is a relay of thought and a decisive battle of intelligence, urgent and momentous. Success or failure hinges on this one action."

"Can you cope with it?" asked Chief Gao.

Ji Zhenren exerted himself, "I did feel I was about to die. But I simply would not die. What will die are the Sichuan Army's ciphers!"

The decisive battle for cracking the ciphers was launched immediately. Those who were qualified and capable of joining the battle were not ordinary cryptographers. They had to have years of cipher-cracking experience and extremely high-level imaginations, and to be in possession of a special way of thinking, and such a special way of thinking was very difficult to define clearly. Chief Gao had once designed a test to screen the special, natural endowment of an excellent cryptographer, but he had failed. A person's ability for language and words, techniques and skills, and knowledge of military affairs and politics, could all be tested, but whether a person had a 'cipher brain' or not could not be precisely tested. He said that only actual combat could test who had a genuine cipher brain.

At this very moment, five cipher brains sat in a circle in the bottom of the trench, with neither paper, nor pens, nor any one to keep notes. Every one of them had the relevant knowledge and they collectively tackled the cipher using magic and accurate mental arithmetic.

The experienced, careful and sharp thinking of Chief Gao and his superb ability to crack ciphers stood out forcefully in the twinkling of an eye.

Ji Zhenren found seven stones which had relatively distinct characteristics. Pointing to one, he thought it was a stone on which grass could grow. Another cryptographer followed up, stating his basis. For the other three cryptographers, two were silent, while one clearly did not agree. Ji Zhenren then gave his reasons from a different angle and he gained one more support, making it three to two. The stone was struck with a hammer. Each of the five picked up a broken piece, polishing and examining it.

Li Qingyun described a labyrinth; in fact a huge labyrinth made up of many small labyrinths. He thought the surface characteristics for this large labyrinth, which was complicated and confused and multiplying in endless succession, tasted strongly of Sichuan flavour, hot and spicy; however, its internal mechanism was a variant of the cipher used by the KMT Central Army, and a hybrid cipher between the Guangdong and Guangxi Armies, yet covering the common property of mountain streams, rivers, forests, cities and towns, and with one of the paths extending to the summit of the mountain. The other four cipher brains first listened enthusiastically but generally, then one opened his eyes wide, one kicked his legs, one struck the floor with his hand, and one sat still with his eyes blinking fast. They all expressed the feeling that there was a great possibility that a monster was hidden in this labyrinth; but that it could be explored and dug through! Let us damned well do it!

Outside the trench, there was continuous gunfire, with bullets showering down like rain and battle cries being raised one after another; inside the trench, there was the train of thought docking, a contest of intelligence, the collision of skills and smart techniques linking up in an orderly fashion. Either in a roundabout way, or via a direct attack, or via a crack or gap in the zenith, or by diving deep into the bottom of the cave, link by link they advanced faster and faster in succession.

While a fierce battle was being fought outside the trench and the opportunity to win was in a state of confusion, inside the trench suddenly a blue sky finally opened wide.

It really was a monstrous cipher system! And the five cipher brains truly had a taste of the sturdiness and craftiness of the Sichuan Army's ciphers.

Alternately, the system used substitution, shifting positions and carving-up encryption methods. The mixed use of substitution and shifting position had already reinforced the cipher density. It then blended with many transfigured groups of code and meaningless reserved empty spaces. These two factors, irregularly spread in the encrypted codes, further increased the trickery of the cipher; yet most noteworthy was its clever use of carving-up encryption, the technical backbone to secure this cipher. The process was that when sending a message, a cryptographer first cut the message into two, three or four parts, then encrypted them separately via different methods, followed by blending and reorganising all the parts. Only after these things were done could the message be sent. To decipher such messages, the telegram's beginning and end were always the most valuable elements.

No matter how difficult the Sichuan Army's ciphers were, they failed to escape RSU2's effective assault. Under the tremendous pressure that defeat was irretrievable, and the enemy had dug bayonets into their chest, the Red Army cryptographers were still able to hold their breath and crack the enemy cipher, ripping open this ferocious 'dog' alive, smashing the 'rock' and destroying the whole labyrinth.

When reading the enemy telegrams, the Red Army commanders at the general headquarters were all dumbstruck. Large numbers of enemy troops had been deployed and basically the Red Army had been surrounded by a formidable enemy force. They were in a precarious situation except that one opening had not been closed up.

Based on the intelligence, the Red Army headquarters quickly made the decision at the last minute to pull their troops out of the battle through that small opening, thus successfully evading danger.

What the five cryptographers had broken was the Sichuan Army's number one cipher - FANG. The intelligence gathered helped the Red

Army break out of the enemy encirclement at Wugong, thereby avoiding the total annihilation of their troops.

The complete demolition of the Sichuan Army's cipher system was carried out during the Red Army's continuous sorties and long-range raids on the enemy camps.

When the sortie at Duqiu township began, Song Daxiong consulted the general headquarters and she got five stretchers to carry the five exhausted cryptographers. Closely following the advancing troops, they broke out of the ring of encirclement, leaving those at the headquarters behind.

She had obviously received instructions from a certain senior leader, otherwise she would have had no authority to organise such a special team to escort the five precious cipher brains of the Red Army.

What a formation they were! Four soldiers carried each stretcher, one after another, and on either side of the five stretchers a reinforced platoon guarded their advance. Song Daxiong would now run to the head or to the tail of the procession to make sure there was no hold-up at the front, nor any falling behind at the tail.

The procession ran for some distance. No matter how loud the guns and shells were thundering, and with danger rearing its head everywhere, the five cryptographers had a sound sleep on the stretchers. Then Chief Gao asked to change the formation of the stretchers. He was in the centre, with the other four closely positioned on either side of him. Surrounding the five stretchers the two platoons formed a circle. This was a unique work formation. The five cryptographers were cracking ciphers while making a sortie. In order to hear each other, centred on Chief Gao's head, the other four lay on their stretchers head to head. All the ciphers after *FANG* were cracked in this formation.

Although all five heads were close to each other, talking day and night made their throats sore and they lost their voices. Song Daxiong found some wooden boards, the cryptographers each had one. Whenever they had an idea, they would write it on a piece of paper and then pass it among them. If it was out of reach, Song Daxiong would pass the paper among the stretchers. Throughout the journey, only the footsteps and the sound of writing could be heard.

One day Chief Gao said to Song Daxiong, "We can get some sleep on the stretchers, but you were on foot and were busy for several days and nights. I worry your health will suffer."

Close to Chief Gao, in a low voice, Song Daxiong said, "If you are truly concerned about me, you should give me permission to marry him. I don't know how long he will live. In this world the only person I worry about is him. If one day I am shot dead, my biggest regret will be that he and I are not husband and wife."

"Wait for the victory of the revolution," said Chief Gao. "I promise the first couple to be granted approval to get married by the organisation will certainly be you and Ji Zhenren."

Song Daxiong gave a wry smile, "When will the revolution victory come? Anyway, I will not die as long as there is hope. I will not die, nor will I let him die." Saying no more, tears rolled out of Chief Gao's eyes.

One day the unit rested for a night at Qishan township. Ji Zhenren suddenly began to sob. After Chen Xiaohua died, his mind had been deep in ciphers, thereby forgetting about his feelings. The break made him remember her, so that he was swamped by emotions.

Song Daxiong walked over to him. Holding his head in her arms she cried along with him, "Your crying today sounds like a man."

He stopped weeping abruptly, saying, "Aha, in Chiang Kai-shek's secret order the groups of codes that were hard to decipher turned out to be these words." He began to mutter, his voice rising, falling and pausing, "The red bandits are very resourceful and cunning; they are skilled at exploiting cracks between our troops, so we must emphatically and jointly defend these linking areas."

"Shit, ciphers are your ubiquitous lover," mumbled Song Daxiong indignantly.

Ji Zhenren's condition was sometimes better and sometimes worse, the illness attacking repeatedly. Before long he started having a high fever again, and Song Daxiong kept watch over him at his bedside.

That day he lost consciousness yet raved to himself, "The Holy Spirit sends out notices to his commanding generals by telegraph; the Tianjin Incident is the Wing King; donkeys rolled in mountains of flames; roast me to death he does not pay his life; an imperial army of twenty thousand enters Sichuan; at the Dadu river bank fires burn wildly; one pot boils the imperial army to death; capture the old man and burn the wings; nothing left, neither cowards nor heroes; a double-edged steel sword briskly shovels coals; flames are roaring and roaring; bathe in the cool water at the natural barrier; have a sound sleep; who is the next Wing King; fire burns at the Dadu river bank; burn all, burn all; naked bodies, burn them all; your body is icy cold, your mind is itching; you are a fire pan, burn everything; hey, hey, clang, clang."

Song Daxiong knew that Ji Zhenren's delirious talk had something to do with Chiang Kai-shek's mention in his telegram of letting Mao Zedong be the next Shi Dakai. She felt somewhat relieved, as it meant that the high fever had not damaged his brain. In desperation she was resolved to save Ji Zhenren's life.

Pushing her work to one side, she spent three days and three nights travelling among villages and townships, and in an old town she finally found a veteran doctor of traditional Chinese medicine. She told the doctor, "If you can cure his illness, the Red Army will regard you as a hero."

The doctor thought for a long while, then said, "A hero to the Red Army is a sinner to the White army. After the Red Army leaves, the White army will kill me."

"I came to see you at midnight because I did not want the others to know of my visit," she explained. "If you give me the prescription, only Heaven, Earth, you and I will know about it."

"I have a secret prescription handed down from generation to generation to treat malaria," said the doctor, "but it is highly poisonous. Normally I dare not use it because the hairs would completely fall off the patient's head. Being bald, he will have difficulty in finding a wife."

"I'll marry him," muttered Song Daxiong. She got the prescription.

The troops marched on. After three townships, she found every ingredient for the prescription. After five doses, Ji Zhenren's hair fell out but he made a full recovery. The illness did no damage to his brain. His bald head was as intelligent and worked as well as before, except for him being thinner and more frail. He would often mount his horse using only one arm.

She began to treat him like she was his wife. In the past she looked after him with no complaints whatsoever about what she had done for him. Now not only would she look after him, she would also be grateful to him from the bottom of her heart.

That day enemy aircraft strafed them wildly, and everyone ran to the bushes and fields to hide. After the enemy aircraft flew away, the troops were assembled and a head count was made, finding one person missing. A search was made and Song Daxiong was found sleeping in a barley field in the sunlight; an unexploded bomb was stuck in the ground beside her. She was too fatigued. Ji Zhenren woke her up, saying, "How do you have the guts to hold a bomb and sleep in broad daylight, while the aircraft are hovering above your head?"

"You are more scared than the bomb," she muttered quietly. "No one dares to hug you."

When she released the blanket roll from her back at night, she found a bullet had gone through the clothes and the blanket. Fortunately she was carrying the thick writing board on her back so the head of the bullet did not pierce it, but got stuck in the board. She credited this to Ji Zhenren. If it were not for him deciphering codes all the time, she would not have carried the board on her back, which had warded off disaster. After all it was Ji Zhenren who had saved her life.

She went to see him that night while he was deciphering codes. Throwing herself at him she kissed him passionately. Then the head of a bullet was in his mouth. Stupefied, he panted heavily. "This is fate," she said. "Even Heaven is helping us." Seeing that he failed to get it, she said, "You may have no idea that I have bathed you." He was very surprised.

"You've bathed me?"

"I've changed your trousers for you as well," she replied. Having no patience to argue with him, she pushed him onto the straw mat. Struggling, but to no avail, he was pressed tight under her body. He felt that she was on the verge of going insane, and no force could block her from what she wanted to do.

Suddenly she stopped moving. A cold gun muzzle was dug into her chin. "You always have the habit of using a gun to solve a problem," said Ji Zhenren. "I'm giving you a dose of your own medicine. Only this metal stuff can calm you down. Don't move. People will die if the pistol goes off; however, people will live if a man and a woman become too intimate, resulting in a fresh new life being born, which will make you unable to march and put me in no mood to crack ciphers. This is a major principle and general politics. Let's wait until the victory of the revolution, OK?"

Backhandedly, she disarmed him. Grinning exaggeratedly, her embarrassment had gone completely: "Ha-ha. I didn't expect that you would have invested all your talent into this pistol. You thought I was going to do something to you? You wish! I only wanted to test if you had the guts. As expected, you are really not a man. At this moment you could have misused the gun and dug it into the wrong place."

While speaking, she pulled his trouser waist and dropped the bullet head into his crotch: "These two are quite matched! Good-looking but good-for-nothing!"

Getting up she strode off, seemingly humming a tune. Listening, tears welled up in Ji Zhenren's eyes.

14 /THE COLOURFUL CIPHER

AMONG THE MANY ENEMY CIPHERS, the Colourful (*LAN*) cipher is particularly noteworthy. When it was presented to Ji Zhenren, he had a premonition that it could be a stinking and fathomless pool. Without the slightest hesitation he dived into it, but a rock gave him a hard knock.

This hard-to-crack cipher failed to scare him, but the pressure from Chief Gao to decipher it as soon as possible was unbearable. He wrote 'I Exert Myself Without Being Pushed!' on a piece of paper and stuck it on his back. When Chief Gao came again, seeing his arched back before the piles of codes, he turned around and walked away. Actually Chief Gao himself felt vexed and resentful, mainly because he was being scolded by others, but he had no one whom he could vent his frustrations upon.

This had something to do with the situation in the preceding stage.

For three months in succession, the Red Army had crossed the Chishui river four times. In the dangerous circumstances when large numbers of enemy troops were trying to encircle, pursue, obstruct and intercept the Red Army, all RSU2's talents were devoted to tackling problems collectively and effectively, virtually controlling all the enemy transceivers of all routes. One after another they cracked nearly a hundred enemy ciphers, timely and accurately acquiring a large amount of important intelligence about the enemy commanders' intentions, operational plans, troop deployments and changes of action.

During this period of time, the most distinguishing feature of the

Red Army's tactics were the words: if the enemy changes, I change. The Central Military Commission's battle plan and deployment changed almost every day, or even several times a day. What they based their tactics on was detailed intelligence of the changing enemy situation, to ensure that the Red Army avoided defeat on their Long March and rescued themselves in desperate circumstances. Therefore it could be said that the whole process of the operation of crossing the Chishui river four times was also the whole process of how the Red Army skillfully made use of the intelligence gathered by RSU2 from deciphering enemy telegrams.

RSU2 was the Red Army's top secret, and some of the commanders knew nothing about how the Central Military Commission fought battles with the aid of the intelligence intercepted by the unit. The officers and soldiers depended on their two legs to march and sometimes they repeatedly advanced via roundabout routes. Coming over today and going over tomorrow, many of them were too fatigued to crawl any more. On several occasions they were in low spirits and cursed profusely. General Lin Biao, who was always good at fighting hard battles, had lots of complaints about their advancing by roundabout routes, going so far as to send a telegram to the Central Military Commission suggesting that the general commander be replaced. Of course some leaders blamed RSU2, "What rubbish intelligence they have provided! Even if we are not killed by the enemy, we may die of the exhaustion inflicted on us by the intricate ciphers and the mystical RSU2." However, no matter who it was, or how badly they cursed, no one can leak military secrets.

"Being cursed is nothing," said Chief Gao. "Winning battles is all that matters! Curses will not kill us, but it could be a bloodbath if we went the wrong way!"

At this moment Ji Zhenren was focused on cracking *LAN*, taking great pains to preset details and guess the mechanism. On and on he kept at it, trying to exhaust all the variables so that he could catch the sole constant factor. After a sleepless night, he worked from dawn to dusk as guns thundered, and he finally selected an almost impassable underground stream and dived into it. Via cunning logical reasoning and unreliable magic, he swam upstream under the water. A rarely seen fear grew out of his mind: if his deduction was wrong, he would definitely get suffocated in this underground stream which had a thousand twists and a hundred turns. Consequently, in his imagination he died several times, but the fear instantly disappeared.

When he held his breath and swam in the stream, a shell landed near his shelter. Song Daxiong ran over to him and pulled him out of the rubble. Covered in dust, he held his right buttock, screaming, "My buttock has gone." Song Daxiong called for medics but there was no reply. She treated his wound - a piece of flesh the size of the mouth of a bowl had been cut out of his buttock.

Grabbing a water can from Song Daxiong, he emptied it in one breath. Taking out a ball of crumpled paper from his chest and spreading it out, he dived back into his underground stream. She then understood that when he heard the whizzing of the shell, he must have thrown himself into the papers, rushing to gather them up and keep them on his person.

Chief Gao ran up to them. Seeing that Ji Zhenren was thinking, he said, "You must be quick." Turning around he began to leave.

Song Daxiong bellowed: "A shell has cut half of his backside."

Turning around again, Chief Gao darted a glance at her, muttering: "What a fuss you are making! I'm happy as long as it's not half of his head that was cut off."

Song Daxiong yelled again, "Yes, his head is intact so he can still crack ciphers for you. Demon, you are a demon."

"Witch. You're a witch," mumbled Chief Gao as he walked away, "but a revolutionary witch who can ensure Ji Zhenren will not die. Wait until the victory of the revolution. I promise I'll let him marry you."

"With a leader like you, I'd rather be a nun!" shouted Song Daxiong. After walking some distance, Chief Gao ignored her crying.

"It's broken, broken," muttered Ji Zhenren weakly. The distant shadow instantly turned around and ran back.

Song Daxiong sneered, "Humph! Chief Gao is always very sensitive to the word 'broken'. He can hear it a thousand miles away."

Staring at the papers, Ji Zhenren was talking to himself, "Broken, the bandage on my buttocks is broken. Fasten it tighter for me." Hearing this, Song Daxiong burst out laughing.

Soon Old Yang ran up to them. Ji Zhenren's thinking was at a critical moment, so he yelled to Old Yang when he touched him, "Don't touch me." Song Daxiong winked at Old Yang and they pressed Ji Zhenren onto a square-shaped stone. He struggled and shouted, "Don't touch me." Song Daxiong hurriedly put codes before him and he at once quietened down. Old Yang put medicine on his wound. Actually there was no medicine to apply but he simply treated the wound. Ji Zhenren shuffled through the papers and wrote down something from time to time. Everyone minded their own business, not interfering with each other.

"Damn it," muttered Song Daxiong. "Where are the war reporters? This scene is absolutely wonderful."

Old Yang finished and walked away. Ji Zhenren said, "It's broken! It's broken!"

Song Daxiong called out to Old Yang, "Come back, you didn't bandage the wound properly, what a lousy job." Walking back, Old Yang had a look and saw nothing wrong with the bandage.

Ji Zhenren spoke again, "Finally it's broken. I'm almost suffocated. No one would believe that the origin of the fragrant stream is that stinking pool."

Old Yang did not understand, asking, "Your wound is not infected, where is the stinking smell from?"

Ji Zhenren grabbed Old Yang's water can and drank the water in one swig, saying, "Call the man who keeps pressing me to come." Then he cried: "Aiya, I'm so hungry. Dear Sister, please give me some food."

LAN, cracked by Ji Zhenren bending over a rock with a wounded bum, was recently used by two bodies of troops under the direct control of Chiang Kai-shek. Its encryption method was extremely unusual. After Chief Gao learnt how Ji Zhenren had cracked the cipher, he made a comparison, "It is as if Ji Zhenren first found a little red spot in the gap under its fingernail, then pricked the spot with a needle and pierced the flesh underneath the fingernail. He searched and decided on one blood capillary. He entered it and travelled along. Then one after another he entered the venule, vennula, medium-sized vein and vena cava, and finally entered the heart and seized its gate of vitality." He further commented, "Such odd encryption can only be decrypted by doing a long distance outflanking raid. If it were not for Ji Zhenren who is extremely skillful, experienced and thinks in an unusual way, *LAN* could not have been deciphered so quickly. The war was pressing. If it had been cracked a few months later, it might as well not have been cracked at all."

Ji Zhenren brought off the task of deciphering *LAN*, but his wound

got badly infected. Medicines were scarce for the Red Army so there
was no suitable medication to treat him with and he had a high fever
for days running. Chief Gao was extremely worried and the senior
officers above him also attached importance to his treatment, but they
could do nothing about it.

Turning to Song Daxiong, Chief Gao said, "To allay his fever by
indigenous methods, this is a political task I assign to you." Panting
with rage Song Daxiong said nothing. What would be the use of
indigenous methods without medicines? Rubbing his body with a wet
towel, or even soaking him in ice-cold water would not solve the
problem. A tiny spot underneath his fingernail could have killed *LAN*,
so the wound as wide as the mouth of a bowl, and seriously infected
could quickly have led to him kicking the bucket.

At this very moment, by chance she heard an interesting story. On
either bank of the Chishui river, the Red Army and the KMT troops
were thrown into confusion after constant manoeuvring. Amid the
chaos, the troops of both sides would sometimes walk on the same
path. Covered in mud, in darkness, rain or mist, they would mix, with
no one paying attention to who the others were and with no exchanges
of fire. Some Red Army soldiers wore the KMT army's uniform and
they penetrated in and out of the enemy lines. Daring and mischievous,
some of the underage soldiers even went to the enemy canteen for
meals.

The story was nothing to the others, but important to Song Daxiong.

One day she called upon a soldier called Zhang Guo. They rubbed
Ji Zhenren's body with wet towels again and again. Then they cleaned
the stinking wound, put on a clean bandage and carried on cooling his
body with wet towels. When they were ready to start moving, the
troops had already gone, leaving them behind. Taking out three sets of
KMT army uniforms, Song Daxiong described the circumstances to
Zhang Guo and briefed him on the task. Zhang Guo said, "It seems
you've been planning this for a while."

Song Daxiong explained: "Rather than letting him wait to die, we'd
better take the risk. It may bring a glimmer of hope, which could be the
only way for me to fulfil the political task assigned to me by Chief
Gao."

When they changed Ji Zhenren's clothes, he opened his eyes. Weak
of voice but with a determined tone, he said, "I've guessed what you
want to do. It's too dangerous, so you must make sure of two things.

First, tie a grenade under my clothes. When the situation is critical, I'll pull the pin if I am awake. If I am in a trance, you pull the pin, or you open fire to kill me. I must not fall into the enemy's hands alive. Second, the chasing enemy is the KMT's 4th Regiment of the 131st Division, the Commander is Liu Siyuan. Our identities are foot soldiers of the 3rd Company of the 5th Regiment. My name is Li Zhiguang, a new recruit, falling behind due to a serious injury. Learn by heart the following information in case we need it in an emergency. The commander of the enemy's 5th Regiment is Zhang Zili and the assistant commander is Liu Qingxiang, who is the sworn brother of Tian Hai, the assistant commander of the 4th Regiment. Many 5th Regiment soldiers are from south Jiangxi, so we are also from south Jiangxi. I learned this enemy information either from deciphering LAN, or from idle chats at night when the enemy wireless operators violate the rules." When he had finished speaking, he went into a trance again. Song Daxiong muttered inwardly: "This exceptional person is truly exceptional."

At dawn the next day, Song Daxiong and Zhang Guo carried Ji Zhenren on a stretcher, hiding behind a roadside rock. Before long a column of enemy soldiers went past them. Quietly they joined the column. After a conversation with the soldiers at the tail, they knew they were from the 3rd Battalion of the 4th Regiment.

At noon the procession took a break and ate lunch. With an easy manner, Song Daxiong and Zhang Guo went to the cooking pot of the 1st Company of the 3rd Battalion and got some food, which they enjoyed very much. For nearly six months they had not had a meal as good as this. Feeling a bit energetic, Ji Zhenren asked Song and Zhang whether they were ready. Song Daxiong replied, "Yes. Action."

Her attire and manner indicated that she was a male soldier, but her voice betrayed her when she spoke too much. So she briefed Zhang Guo about everything on the understanding that he would do the talking. They carried Ji Zhenren to the 4th Regiment's medical station. A medic called Huang walked up to them. Zhang Guo told him about Ji Zhenren's condition. Touching Ji Zhenren's forehead, Medic Huang said nothing but pointed to the operating table. Hurriedly Song Daxiong and Zhang Guo carried Ji Zhenren onto the table. A nurse came and gave Ji Zhenren an injection to stop the pain. Medic Huang treated the wound, giving Ji Zhenren one more injection. Song Daxiong helped to hold a white enamel plate, she then emptied the plate of festering flesh and blood into a large metal bucket. Having tried her best to bear the staunch smell, she failed to hold herself back when she saw the piles of severed legs and arms in the bucket. Her stomach churned violently, but she gritted her teeth and forced the food she had had for lunch back to her throat. She did not worry that she would waste such a good meal, but that the noise of vomiting would reveal her female gender.

Medic Huang said, "Three more days' treatment is needed for him before you rejoin your 5th Regiment, otherwise his life will be in danger."

"We have troubled you to treat him. Anyway, the 4th and 5th Regiments are brothers," said Zhang Guo, who intended to let the medic take Ji Zhenren seriously, so he stressed his identity, "This patient is the cousin of the assistant commander of the 5th Regiment, Liu Qingxiang."

Medic Huang said, "We are all brothers of the party and the state. No matter whose cousin he is, I will try my best to treat him."

Such words should have been satisfactory but, unexpectedly, Zhang Guo added, "Our 5th Regiment's assistant commander Liu Qingxiang is the sworn brother of your 4th Regiment's assistant commander Tian Hai."

Medic Huang had intended to leave, but he walked back, asking, "What is the name of this wounded soldier?"

Zhang Guo replied, "Li Zhiguang, a new recruit." Picking up the telephone, Medic Huang called the regimental headquarters, asking Major Tian Hai to answer the phone. Someone on that end answered the call.

"My fellow schoolmate," said Medic Huang. "You have a sworn brother called Liu Qingxiang, don't you? His cousin Li Zhiguang is wounded. He has an infection, so he has been falling behind. He is receiving treatment at my station. Out of courtesy can you find time to visit him?" He then put down the phone.

Soon the phone rang. Listening to the phone, Medic Huang turned around, saying, "Major Tian said that Liu Qingxiang does not have a cousin called Li Zhiguang." Song Daxiong's face went ashen. Quietly she cast a disdainful glance at Zhang Guo.

Then Ji Zhenren muttered: "In order to make a few coppers, I took another person's place and served in the army. Li Zhiguang is not my original name, so Liu Qingxiang knows nothing about it. Forget it. I'm from a poor family, so how can I seek connections with the assistant commander? Don't mention him any more."

A stalwart officer walked in. Medic Huang hurriedly stood to attention and saluted, "Good afternoon, Commander."

The guard who was following said, "Our commander injured his arm in action, treat him quickly."

Medic Huang asked staff to remove Ji Zhenren from the operating table. Ji Zhenren thought that this man might be Liu Siyuan, Commander of the 4th Regiment, so he opened his eyes, glancing at him. Startled, he quickly closed his eyes. Hands trembling a little, he held the pin of the grenade tightly in his sleeve.

The commander said, "It looks as though he is badly wounded. Don't move him. I only have a light wound and I can sit." Medic Huang went to treat the commander who fixed his eyes on Ji Zhenren, whose eyes were tightly closed but his eyelids trembled gently. The commander asked, "Which regiment is this wounded brother from? Where is your old home?"

"We are from the 3rd Company of the 5th Regiment," replied Zhang Guo. "His name is Li Zhiguang, from south Jiangxi. He was wounded so he dropped away from his regiment. We took him to your regiment for treatment. He had a high fever, often remaining unconscious."

"He was awake a moment ago, saying that Li Zhiguang was not his original name," said Medic Huang.

The commander seemed very interested in this wounded soldier, so he asked, "Then what is his original name?"

In a false voice, Song Daxiong replied, "He has been called Li Zhiguang since he joined the army. We don't know what his original name is."

"Everyone has something awkward to disclose, and he must have had his own reasons for not using his original name. An adult man should always be upfront about his identity. Since the name has been changed, there must be a reason for doing so. All right, I'm not going to ask about it any more. We are all fighting the Red Army, so we have a common cause; we are all military men of the party and the state. Everyone fighting for this cause shares a common responsibility to suppress the communists. Anyone who is wounded in action should be treated equally and receive good treatment." Commander Liu spoke with his eyes fixed on Ji Zhenren. Seeing that everyone felt ill at ease and was cautious, he said: "Ah, he is from south Jiangxi, so we are fellow villagers. A few years ago the hilly area of south Jiangxi was the main battlefield between the KMT and the Communist armies. The area has range upon range of hills and the mountain paths and passes are rugged. When it is foggy, nothing can be seen. The Red Army was good at using the natural barriers to fight battles and we suffered huge losses in the previous four encirclement campaigns until we won the fifth one. Did you take part in those battles?"

Worrying that Zhang Guo would make a slip of the tongue again, in a false, deep voice Song Daxiong replied, "I was in the 5th Regiment then and I took part in those battles. They are new recruits so they missed them."

After his wound was bandaged, Commander Liu walked over to Ji Zhenren. Standing before the operating table, he said with a smile, "This brother is awake all the time. Is it because you don't want to offer me the bed, that you pretend to be in a trance?"

Ji Zhenren had to open his eyes. No longer avoiding Commander Liu's eyes, he said, "Many thanks for the treatment I have received from your regiment. Half of my bum is cut off so I have to lie down on my side, or on my face. It is truly inconvenient for me to move, and I apologise."

Commander Liu's eyes brightened. Unusually kindly, he said, "Ah, once you open your eyes and begin to talk, you seem more like a blood brother of mine." His tone then sounded sad, "He worked in a telegraph office in Shanghai, but he was shot dead over a woman. Among my six brothers and sisters, he was the most intelligent and educated, but unexpectedly he died young in troubled times."

Grimacing with pain Ji Zhenren cried, "Ah, it's hurting. The drug is losing its strength."

"You have to grin and bear it," said Commander Liu. "We are lucky the shell only cut your bum and the bullet hit my arm. Who can be sure our heads will not be hit tomorrow? But even if we die, we sacrifice our lives for the party and the state; very glorious." Turning around he said to Medic Huang, "I feel that he is an old friend of mine. Please look after him like you are looking after my blood brother."

With a pained expression, Ji Zhenren couldn't control his emotions, and a few tear drops fell from his eyes.

Medic Huang went to receive a phone call. Coming back he said quietly to Commander Liu, "Major Tian is bothered about this Li

Zhiguang again, asking me to get to the truth about him and report back."

Commander Liu stared at the medic, saying, "Haven't I spoken clearly? Li Zhiguang is my fellow villager whom I'm congenial with, so no need for the others to bother about him. He is here to have a wound treated, so why should we differentiate between the 4th and 5th Regiment? Can't we have some affection between neighbours and brothers?! Humph, he has none of the interests of the party and the state in mind. Tell Tian Hai what I've said. Goodbye!"

Medic Huang saw Commander Liu off, telling him, "Don't forget to come and have the dressing for your wound changed, Commander."

Ji Zhenren's palms were wet through with sweat. Quietly he pushed the grenade pin back into his sleeve. Song Daxiong and Zhang Guo also broke out in a cold sweat.

In the afternoon they carried on marching along with the field medical station. They exchanged views whether to leave or stay: if they left, Ji Zhenren's wound would not be treated; but if they stayed, there was a danger of them being found out and they might lose their lives. Ji Zhenren said, "I'll stay, but you two find a chance to leave. The worst-case scenario is that my brother and I meet our deaths together. Anyway, without treatment for three days, I would still die if I left now."

"As far as I can see, your brother has no evil intentions, so it's not too dangerous for you to stay here," said Song Daxiong. "He has made his stand clear, so Major Tian shouldn't poke his nose into the matter. I think we should carry on as planned."

With a worried frown, Ji Zhenren said, "It is not unusual for a defector to change his name and seek an official post of some kind. But how is it that he is still alive? Chief Gao himself told me that my brother Ji Zhenfu had been shot dead by the Red Army."

"The KMT's medicine injection works like magic," said Song Daxiong, "and you have regained consciousness for many hours. But you'd better speak less, because I find that you are not like a new recruit." Giving a wry smile, Ji Zhenren closed his eyes.

The next day Commander Liu did not turn up to have the dressing for his wound changed. On the afternoon of the third day, wrapped in gunpowder smoke, he entered the medical station. Two guards helped him in. Medic Huang examined his wound, saying there was an infection and blamed him for not coming the day before. Tired out, he said, "It was so hard to fight this group of communist bandits. Our regiment fought for a day and a night but we could only manage to wipe out one hundred and thirteen of them. Such a result was achieved only after I personally went to the front line and supervised the operation."

Helped by Song Daxiong, Ji Zhenren was standing to one side. He saw Commander Liu's eyes were netted with little veins. "Little fellow villager, you look fine today. After you recover, go back to your regiment and fight hard. Your 5th Regiment is always cowardly, how can they be called troops? They should be ashamed to be called soldiers of the party and the state. For this battle the 5th Regiment should have supported our 4th Regiment by taking coordinated action, but it took them so long to come, otherwise no one from the two communist companies could have escaped."

"We have dropped out for several days, where is our 5th Regiment now?" asked Ji Zhenren. "We must rejoin them as soon as possible."

"In the direction of Xiaojiahe," said Commander Liu, "pursuing the Red Army's 3rd Regiment. With their combat effectiveness there is no chance at all for them to catch up with the enemy."

"In which direction is Xiaojiahe?" queried Ji Zhenren.

"Look, this is the quality of the 5th Regiment's soldiers. They've got lost and can't find their own regiment. Where is Xiaojiahe? In the sky," grinned Commander Liu, "because you look like my brother, and it lets me experience a warmth of affection on the cold, cruel battlefield, so I'll take care of you. When we take up quarters tonight, I'm going to make a phone call to your commander Zhang Zili, asking him to send people here to take back the muddleheaded foot soldier Li Zhiguang. I'm not joking. I'll really take care of you." Ji Zhenren then thanked him again and again.

When it was midnight, Song Daxiong and Zhang Guo held Ji Zhenren's arms and they went out of the medical station, making off with a stretcher, they quietly bypassed the sentry and disappeared into the darkness.

After they were out of the 4th Regiment's defence sector, they found a quiet place to take a break. Suddenly a black horse lept out from the darkness and galloped directly towards them. The dark shadow halted its advance not far from them, moving round the same spot twice and passing on the words, "Brother, have a good journey!" With a bang, something dropped to the ground. The dark shadow then galloped away.

"The voice is familiar," said Song Daxiong.

"It's really him," muttered Ji Zhenren.

Zhang Guo ran over, returning with a package. There were medicines, compressed biscuits, a map, a torch, some money and a letter.

Brother Zhenren,

I am sure it is you, my younger brother. I did not expect that you were still alive. I enquired about you in secret. The 5th Regiment does not have a soldier called Li Zhiguang, so I almost correctly guessed your identity. Besides, in the last two days several Red Army detachments constantly made surprise attacks on my regiment, and their way of attacking was baffling. Their operation target was ambiguous, seemingly they were looking for something. But they had no interest in materials and equipment, not even any interest in my headquarters. So I thought they might be searching for their people who had fallen behind. It's possible that they were looking for you. All right, my younger brother. In the prolonged combat and continuous gunfire, I cannot even ensure my own safety, nor can I keep you here. But as for the Red Army, you must not go back either. They may perish at any moment and at any location. There would be nothing but a dead end waiting for you if you follow them. So take the opportunity and leave them. Return to Ruijin. I have no news of our family. After this campaign ends, I will go home and visit the elders. On the map I have marked the general disposition of the troops on both sides, so bypass the troops and travel in the direction of Jiangxi. Destroy the letter after reading it. If I let the KMT army find out that I have contacts with the Red Army, I will lose my head. I am a sworn enemy of the Red Army, so I will fight them to the death. Brother, please listen to me and go home.

After reading the letter, they opened the map and searched for which route to take, then they chose a direction and marched away. Suddenly Song Daxiong discovered that they were being tailed. Hurriedly they hid behind some rocks, seeing that there were about a dozen silhouettes scattered on the slope, quietly moving towards them.

"Who can they be?" wondered Ji Zhenren.

"I don't know," muttered Song Daxiong, cocking her gun. "Quick, destroy the letter. Get ready for action."

"Without the letter we cannot explain ourselves to the organisation," said Ji Zhenren.

Then they heard shouting from the slope: "I'm Tian Hai, the assistant commander of the 4th Regiment. I know you three are Red Army soldiers. You can't leave now. Surrender, and I promise I will not kill you." Hearing no reply, he went on, "Only by following the KMT army can you have a future. Liu Siyuan came to us from the Red Army and he is now a regimental commander. Was it him who left you the medicine a while ago? Now, he feels that he has not fully fulfilled his wishes, and he wants to keep you and head for the future together. Red Army soldiers, come over to us, quick."

Moving close to Ji Zhenren, Song Daxiong said, "This guy is no good. He has something else in mind."

Ji Zhenren nodded, "He's trying to seize evidence of Liu Siyuan colluding with the Red Army. He himself wants to be the commander."

"If that's the case," said Song Daxiong, "he must catch us alive. It seems that we cannot force our way out and run for it. Let's quietly move backward to the slope, then jump and run."

As soon as they began to move, the enemy opened fire and blocked their retreat. Song Daxiong switched on the torch, waving it in a circle twice. Suddenly she stood up, directing the light towards the grenades tied on her breast, she shouted, "If you press us too hard, we'll meet our death together. If you want us to surrender, tell us your conditions." Winking at Zhang Guo, she let him pin down the enemy. Then she carried Ji Zhenren on her back and quietly crawled behind some rocks.

"Li Zhiguang is indeed Liu Qingxiang's cousin," yelled Zhang Guo. "When they were young, Liu Qingxiang suffered malaria and he almost died. It was Li Zhiguang's father who saved him. Now he dares not acknowledge his cousin who has joined the Red Army. Where is his conscience? Besides, your sworn brother has a Red Army cousin, you'll be implicated too."

Someone opened fire in the direction where Song Daxiong and Ji Zhenren were retreating. Zhang Guo called out again, "Don't shoot. What is there to be gained by us going over to you?" The fire was more fierce, pinning Song Daxiong and Ji Zhenren down behind a giant rock.

Then Song Daxiong saw something unusual. Behind her soldiers were quietly and stealthily taking cover on the right-hand slope.

"Raise your hands in the air and walk towards me," shouted Tian Hai. "Don't worry about the conditions."

"Let's discuss the conditions first," Zhang Guo shouted back. "After that we'll come to you."

Tian Hai was running out of patience. "You three bumpkins. What right do you have to talk about conditions? If you do not surrender, I will kill you all."

Suddenly, the soldiers on the right-hand slope behind Song Daxiong and Ji Zhenren opened fire in Tian Hai's direction and gunshots were also heard from the left-hand slope. Obviously these unknown soldiers were making a pincer attack. Tian Hai's side fired back, but seeing the situation was not good they withdrew and fled.

From the right-hand slope someone bent over and ran toward Song Daxiong while calling out, "Are you Song Daxiong? I'm Liu Kailai."

Song Daxiong, Ji Zhenren and Zhang Guo rejoined the unit. As soon as Chief Gao saw them, he waved his hand, "Lock them up!"

Ji Zhenren threw the wrap to Chief Gao, saying, "Everything is here."

"The medicines are exclusively for Ji Zhenren's use," said Song Daxiong. "No one else has the right to use them."

Chief Gao stopped her, saying, "That's not up to you to decide."

Chief Gao reported the circumstances to the higher authorities and the reply was: RSU2 should take charge of the political investigation of the three who dropped out.

After talking to Song Daxiong and Zhang Guo, Chief Gao went to talk to Ji Zhenren. "Zhenren, I have absolute trust in you three," he said, mentioning nothing of the matter but beginning to talk about the recent cipher cracking.

Shortly news got out that Chief Gao would discipline the three for leaving without permission as, although the incident had been scary and no harm had been done, its nature was so serious that they had to be punished.

Song Daxiong went to see Chief Gao, explaining, "Zhang Guo was only following my orders. We took Ji Zhenren by force to the enemy medical station for treatment, a kidnap, going against his will. Apart from this, he was in a deep coma, and when he woke up he was already on the operating table. So it has nothing to do with them. Punish me, not them." Before long RSU2 announced disciplinary action against her.

Her attitude was indifferent, and she looked like nothing had happened. Ji Zhenren went to see Chief Gao, but he mentioned nothing about Song Daxiong being disciplined.

"You have no conscience. For her sake you should at least make a complaint that she has been treated unfairly. What she did was all to save your life," mumbled Chief Gao.

"It is only right and proper for her to save me. Besides, she did it out of fulfilling the political task you assigned her. You forced her to do so, after all. You should be the first, if someone should be punished." Surprised by Ji Zhenren's complaint, Chief Gao turned around and began to leave. Holding him tight, Ji Zhenren asked why his brother Ji Zhenfu was still alive. Chief Gao then had to explain the situation to him patiently.

During the '11th July Bombing', as an assistant commander Ji Zhenfu came along with the enemy's second group of crack troops to the first group's aid. The Red Army wiped them out with only two escaping. Afterwards, an investigation confirmed that one of the escapees was Ji Zhenfu. Considering that if Ji Zhenren got to know that his brother was in the opposing army, this would put him under mental stress and psychological pressure, in order to let him focus on his work with no worries, as well as to let the internal personnel who knew about his brother's defection not to make things difficult for him in any future political movements, after the approval of the high officials, Chief Gao let it be known that Ji Zhenfu had been killed, so that Ji Zhenren had no connection whatsoever with enemy personnel. Such a measure was to protect Ji Zhenren politically. A few months later, when Liao Chengzhi, whose family had a KMT background, was accused of being a KMT spy and took part in the Long March under escort, he felt that he was right to have taken precautions to protect Ji Zhenren, despite the fact that he was personally taking a political risk. He believed that a defector, when considered worthless, would be abandoned, keeping silent and lying low. He never thought that Ji Zhenfu would change his name and that the KMT would put him in an important position; besides he would be extremely fierce in pursuing the Red Army.

After hearing Chief Gao's explanation, Ji Zhenren said, "Thank you for your thoughts on the matter. But there is not a shadow of doubt my brother is guilty of killing Red Army soldiers, for which he deserves to die ten thousand deaths. Although he took brotherly affection into consideration and let me, Song Daxiong and Zhang Guo off, he was never soft on our frontline officers and men. But to be honest, even if this is the case, if I met him again, I could not be vicious enough to kill him."

Chief Gao consoled him, "In the Jiangxi Soviet, after you deciphered YIN and QI, you accurately reported the related information to higher authorities, an action that placed righteousness above family loyalty, thus properly handling the relationship between family and enemy. And politically you are reliable, so I have trust in you. I have seriously told Song Daxiong and Zhang Guo not to leak the information that Liu Siyuan is actually Ji Zhenfu. But, of course, I have to report it truthfully to the senior officers."

Ji Zhenren's eyes welled up, "I have given my heart to the organisation."

As to Song Daxiong, her view on being disciplined was that a life for a disciplinary action was worthwhile! Before long once again she voluntarily accepted a charge on Ji Zhenren's behalf.

One day the movement of the 2nd Squad directly affiliated to the Central Military Commission was impeded by the enemy at Nanxi mountain. The battle went on for a day, yet the group made no progress in getting through the mountain. The enemy troops checking the 2nd Squad's progress was the KMT's 4th Regiment under the 131st Division, whose commander was Liu Siyuan. At night the squad changed tactics, giving up the shortcut via Nanxi mountain but advancing by a roundabout route through a narrow valley on Dongxi mountain. Liu Siyuan firmly believed that he had tightly sealed the area and that the Red Army could not have escaped even if they were given wings. In the latter half of the night the 131st Division headquarters discovered the tracks of the Red Army's roundabout route, and sent the 4th Regiment a coded telegram, ordering them to quickly take a shortcut to Xiaoqing mountain to block the Red Army's 2nd Squad.

The next morning when the 131st Division headquarters enquired about the battle result, the 4th Regiment was still guarding the same position on Nanxi mountain. Liu Siyuan took no action, so the 2nd Squad got through Xiaoqing mountain, successfully extricating itself from the enemy's encirclement. When the 131st Division headquarters called the 4th Regiment to account, Liu Siyuan said he had never seen the orders about launching an attack on Xiaoqing mountain. The division headquarters checked the records, confirming that the 4th Regiment had received the telegram. Tian Hai, who was in charge of wireless work certified that the telegraph operator had presented the telegram to Liu Siyuan right away. The situation was reported to Chiang Kai-shek. Letting a Red Army squad go was an undisputed crime invoking the death penalty. Soon the 131st Division received Chiang Kai-shek's orders and Liu Siyuan was executed for the charge of 'failing to carry out orders, defying orders by taking no action, and hindering military operations'.

The 2nd Squad owed their escape to the detailed map given to Ji Zhenren by Liu Siyuan, on which they discovered the narrow valley.

Soon after the squad escaped through the valley, Song Daxiong intercepted the coded telegram sent to Liu Siyuan by the 131st Division headquarters. She passed it to Ji Zhenren. It was encrypted via *LAN*. Reading it, an idea flashed through Ji Zhenren's mind. Grabbing the tapper, in the name of the 4th Regiment he sent out the signal 'QSL' to the transceiver of the 131st Division Headquarters. Any expert would know that it was the reply to confirm receipt of a telegram. After receiving it, the sender would not have sent the same telegram again. So it was to say that Ji Zhenren had received the telegram on behalf of the 4th Regiment. Because it was during fierce fighting, the 131st Division wireless operator sent out the telegram quickly and received the reply confirming receipt at once, feeling that everything was normal. But it was late at night and the operator of the 4th Regiment might have been tired and fallen asleep, so there was a strong possibility he might have missed this telegram. As expected, the 4th Regiment's wireless operator knew nothing about this telegram. Afterwards, when the matter was investigated, Tian Hai cleverly drew the content of the telegram from the investigators. Then he forced the wireless operator to commit perjury. The operator was in a panic for having missed the telegram. Seizing the opportunity to shirk his responsibility, he hurriedly forged a telegram. Previously Tian Hai had failed to secure any evidence against Liu Siyuan having secret communications with the Red Army, this time a sharp knife was sent by heaven and he hit Liu Siyuan when he was down. Finding it hard to defend himself, Liu Siyuan was dead and gone.

According to usual practice and discipline, RSU2 had only ever intercepted but never interfered with enemy communications. This time Ji Zhenren broke the rules and breached discipline. The idea came to his mind in the twinkling of an eye: the group had been blocked for a whole day with substantial casualties; if they had been checked again on Xiaoqing mountain, the consequences could have been disastrous; Ji Zhenfu (aka Liu Siyuan) was extremely fierce and malicious to the Red Army, and if he had stayed on as the regiment commander, he could have inflicted great harm on it. If his action had been successful, Ji Zhenfu would not have thrown his troops into battle, which meant he would surely have been removed from his post or demoted. With all this in mind, Ji Zhenren decided to do it.

As soon as he sent out the signal 'QSL', Song Daxiong gazed at him, knowing what his action meant. He gazed back at her, saying in a stern voice, "I'm responsible for the consequences. You don't need to be concerned about it! Hurry up and deliver this coded telegram; let me carry on monitoring."

She delivered the telegram to Chief Gao, and she also reported that they had signalled a receipt to the enemy transceiver, falsely claiming it was her who hit upon the idea of doing such a thing. Chief Gao flew into a rage, "How did you have the impudence to do such a thing? You acted like a fool!" Hurriedly he reported the related information and the coded telegram to the general headquarters.

Nevertheless, soon Chief Gao discovered from the enemy transceivers that the enemy's 4th Regiment had been kept back from the battle; and before long Commander Liu Siyuan was executed. Of course, he knew this was in fact Ji Zhenren's doing, so he went to see him, saying, "The distinguishing feature of wireless technology is to identify codes rather than operators. There must be no risks at all. Only under the most urgent circumstances, where there is no alternative, and after the prudent approval of the higher authorities, can we occasionally take the risk; otherwise, if the practice is exposed and the enemy is alarmed, the consequences are too ghastly to contemplate. This time you breached discipline and employed your consummate skill without authorisation. We should have dealt with it sternly, but taking into consideration that you've just lost your elder brother, I will not pursue the matter further but put it aside for the time being."

"My real intention was for him not to be in a position to confront the Red Army. I didn't expect... it would result in him losing his life." Tears were streaming down Ji Zhenren's face.

"Again and again the enemy forces encircled, pursued, obstructed and intercepted us but we survived. Chiang Kai-shek has been annoyed about this for a long time. Killing a regimental commander who defied orders and failed to take action achieved the aim of punishing one as a deterrent to the others," noted Chief Gao.

"It's my fault."

"To your credit!"

"To RSU2's credit!"

"To *LAN*'s credit!"

15 /THE XIANG CIPHER

THE TIME CAME to climb snowy mountains and cross grasslands. Surprisingly, Ji Zhenren did not feel any of the hardship that all the Red Army officers and ranks generally felt; what he agonised over the most was that his brain had become less busy.

The Red Army had thrown off the chasing enemy troops, thereby substantially reducing the work for monitors and cryptographers, causing everyone to experience some rare moments of relaxation.

"I've always worked intensively," mumbled Ji Zhenren. "Even in my dreams I never stop working. Once my brain is idle, I feel terrified about being thrown off the planet, making me feel that to live is no better than to die." Yes, the perilous conditions would never distress him, but his unoccupied mind could suffocate him. Therefore he needed to find some cipher-related things to do. Soon he began to examine people and his attention turned to his opponents on the cipher battlefield.

The ciphers used by the Sichuan Army were tricky and clever. Despite employing external assistance, they basically fitted the characteristics of the Sichuanese people, giving him a very hard time. Among the ciphers used by the troops under the direct control of Chiang Kai-shek, those used by the Sichuan Army were reckoned to be the most difficult to decipher. For years he had adopted the view that the enemy was the enemy, but also a teacher. So what could the creator behind the KMT Central Army's ciphers, his evil opponent and devil teacher, be like? He felt long ago that some of the ciphers had been written by an intersexual individual, neither male nor female, neither masculine nor feminine, very weird.

When climbing the high, snow-covered mountains, or taking a rest in the marshlands, his mind was fully occupied by this intersexual enemy teacher.

He had to find this intersexual cipher-compiler who had tortured him for so many years, and he had to kill him!

In those days, at night, he constantly had nightmares, either real or illusory. With grief and indignation as well as resentment, he set out to track down this opponent of his.

He held that in this world no one else could know this person better than him. Across the air waves, he had waged battles of wits with this intersexual individual for so long, having dismembered it and dissected it, and knew every inch of its flesh and every cell like the back of his hand.

He knew that this person was a prized talent of the KMT Army, a rare figure, and a backbone of their core sectors. This individual had to stay in a heavily guarded fortress, with their every movement protected by open and hidden agents.

Looking around the Red Army troops, only he was able to find this intersexual individual.

One day, in Xiaokouzi Street in the bustling area of Fuzimiao in Nanjing, a white-faced scholar set up a book stall. A list of 667 books were displayed conspicuously. They were all ancient books of past ages. No matter who it was, as long as they pointed at one on the list, giving a certain page and line, the scholar could recall the corresponding contents and recite fluently without missing a single word. The deal was that if he made one mistake, he would hand out one copper coin; if he made no mistakes, he would be paid one copper coin. The money was a negligible amount, but the matter was somewhat odd. In three days he had made about one hundred copper coins. Some scholars were not convinced. After the list they dug out the corresponding only copy extant from their own collections, yet none of them could put the white-faced scholar on the spot. They were taken aback inwardly, moaning that their treasured copy was not the only existing one; this white-faced scholar must have one, otherwise how could he recite it so fluently? For another three days people made random selections from the 667 books and his success rate was one hundred per cent. The matter caused a stir in Fuzimiao, consequently startling many scholars in Nanjing, where two main newspapers published the news for three days running. When it came to the ninth day, a mysterious person drove an army van with no registration plates to the site. Without listening to the scholar's protests, he put him and his stall into the van and drove away.

Blindfolded, the scholar was taken to a mansion. In a dark room, one after another, people came to test him, but no one could find fault with his answers.

The scholar put a nearly disfiguring make-up on his face. Standing behind the dark window the intersexual individual carefully observed his every movement and way of speaking.

Finally the intersexual individual showed its face. It turned out to be two people, a male and a female.

The scholar had hidden a specially-made pistol loaded with one bullet in the scroll roller of the book list. More bullets were useless, as he had only one chance to open fire. His original plan was to kill the intersexual individual with the bullet before he was captured. But now the situation had changed, as this intersexual individual was a man and a woman. Which one should he kill? No matter which, the other half would remain, and could find another partner to produce a new intersexual individual. He would generally not do such an incomplete thing.

The woman began to speak: "I will pick one from these 667 books. If you can recite, without making a single error, the chapters and sections I will name, I will give you a thousand yuan and let you go. But if you fail, or make more than ten mistakes, you must stay and work with me. You will not be yourself anymore, but a part of me. As with my present partner, we will form a new intersexual individual and work for the party and the state."

"Let me have a think, then answer you."

"No! You have no choice!"

The scholar did not panic, as he was confident that he could fluently recite 666 out of the 667 books, which had been in his own collection for many years. When he did the book list, he wrote down 666 books. But he fanned the breezes, thinking 666 was too auspicious a number, giving people the feeling that he had made up the amount, so better to add one more; 667 would seem more real to people. Such behaviour was dictated by his personality. In fact, except for these 666 books, he could not fluently recite any more. Trusting to luck, he added one which he could only remember part of the chapters. It was *The Sad Record of a Strategy for Peace*. Only two copies existed in the world and they were kept in the Shanghai Library. He thought that the book was far away from Nanjing, so the number of people wandering around Fuzimiao who had read it, would be very small. And it was even less likely that someone would hold it and examine him before his stand.

He, who never took action unless he was absolutely sure (apart from cracking ciphers), made a big mistake this time.

The woman threw an ancient book on the table.

Glancing it from a distance, he saw it was *The Sad Record of a Strategy for Peace*. Many years ago in Shanghai he had read it and indexed it. Up to this point he still trusted to luck, wondering if by any chance she might ask him something he could remember. Although he looked calm, his heart was pounding violently.

The result was that out of fifteen selections, he was able to precisely recite eleven, making errors with the other four. In other words he failed to be one hundred per cent correct, getting the general meaning right but some words wrong.

"That will do. Now you belong to me. Compared to my old partner, I think you are very wise and farsighted. My old partner is old and useless. Let him go and die."

Instantly the scholar knew who to fire his gun at. Killing the woman, the intersexual individual would no longer exist. Do it! This bullet belonged to her.

Then the woman spoke again, "You are beaten, so you can only be my other half in work. My old partner is still my other half in terms of affection, because we cannot bear to part with each other emotionally."

Because of this sentence the scholar changed his mind about shooting her dead but decided to shoot the man dead, as he was his rival in love.

It turned out that the woman was Jiang Xiaodian and the man was none other than Gao Q.

Jiang Xiaodian was dead, right? Never mind, anyhow she used to be my lover. He hesitated no more: how can I let that rat Gao Q have my woman?

He forgot his original intention of killing the intersexual individual but turned to killing his rival in love. So he said, "Please can this gentleman pass me the scroll of my book list? I can't remember if I have included *The Sad Record of a Strategy for Peace* in my list."

Gao Q presented the scroll to the scholar, who took it and examined it carefully. Suddenly he poked the scroll roll into Gao Q's chest.

In his mind he heard the gunshot, but the gun inside the roll did not fire.

Gao Q roared with laughter. Opening the scroll roll, he said that when he had put the scroll into the van, he had replaced the gun with a wooden stick. "Tell the truth and nothing but the truth. Who are you? And why did you come here?" he yelled.

The scholar did not speak for three days and three nights.

Obviously, Gao Q wasn't aware at all that the scholar, who had false facial features, was an acquaintance. But privately Jiang Xiaodian firmly believed that she knew his identity. When he was reciting *The Sad Record of a Strategy for Peace*, she had recognised him.

Ji Zhenren had been shot dead, right? So how could he still be alive? She did not tell anyone else about it, intending to keep the secret forever.

She said to Gao Q, "He is only a swot, defending himself clumsily, not plotting to murder anyone here."

The scholar stayed. But they only talked to him about the 666 books, day by day, book by book and chapter by chapter. Soon he revelled in the fun of books. It was hard for him, whose life revolved around books, to meet a soul mate, particularly as it was a great pleasure to chat with her alone. He wanted to spend days with her like this forever, letting the hard-to-come-by destiny in books extend to a thousand miles and all their lives.

Slowly he came to realise that this woman did not truly regard him as her soul mate in books. Her talking with him about books was a cover for some other serious work assignment.

She mistook him for a Red Army cryptographer, his other identity. The reason for her thinking so was that he had a super strong ability for languages and words.

The Red Army's ciphers had never been cracked by the KMT Army, which was Jiang Xioadian's greatest embarrassment. Her immediate superior had made the comment: "We've spent years studying the red bandits' coded telegrams but we have been unable to get a grip on it. What else can we do? Their encryption, decryption and code books are all carefully, remarkably and masterfully constructed. Internally they've done a lot of work on how to protect their telegrams with ciphers. They are highly vigilant. Rules and commandments for keeping secrets are exceptionally strict. Their security organisation is complex, extremely large in size and hidden, thereby ensuring the absolute safety of their coded telegrams. We are at our wits' end, and we don't know what to do."

She completely agreed with her superior, besides, she had her own thoughts but on a different angle. Deciphering capacity is closely related to the cipher creation level. If ciphers of party A are cracked by party B, that means party A's cipher creation level is lower than that of party B; if party A cannot break party B's ciphers, then there is a great possibility that party B can crack party A's ciphers. Therefore cipher construction must be guided by cipher breaking techniques, and the two are interdependent and mutually complementary. In view of this, she held that the Red Army's cipher construction and breaking ability were absolutely terrifying, but for many years she had never been truly afraid. Despite the fact that she had failed to crack the Red Army's ciphers, she still indefatigably and closely followed the Red Army, hoping she could crack their ciphers some day.

This time, possessed by the Devil, she firmly believed that this white-faced scholar was a drill rod for cracking the Red Army's ciphers. Therefore she had to hold on tight to this man whose identity was special. She had to study all the books he had read, his intellectual structure and everything about him, which was fundamental work if she wanted to crack her opponents' ciphers.

Once the white-faced scholar became aware of what she was after, he stopped talking to her and became mute.

Since it was hard to crush him mentally, she had to destroy him in the flesh. That day, the man and the woman again combined into one, threatening to kill him.

The scholar gave a grim laugh and still said nothing, but his facial expressions showed: I will greet your butcher's knife with a smile, waiting with pleasure to be killed!

The next day the situation was reversed. The intersexual pair suddenly disappeared, never to reappear again.

Later, the scholar was released. When he was sent off the compound he was still blindfolded, but he clearly heard the casual remarks from people in the van, which generally meant the two had got a dejected scholar who was making a living from guessing words. They were engaging in underhand activities to dodge their faults. Anyway, this scholar was not someone who could be easily dealt with and killed. The newspapers had reported his weird story for several days, and all walks of life in society were watching, resulting in us having to take the trouble to send him back. For a long time the damned pair had looked down their noses at everyone and had been extremely arrogant, regarding everyone else in our department as fools.

Now the scholar fully understood what had happened.

Quietly he rejoined his unit. From the deciphered enemy telegrams he knew that a Red Army confidential staff officer had been captured by Long Yun's KMT troops. He was searched and some decrypted scripts of the KMT army's coded telegrams were found on him. Chiang Kai-shek flew into a rage and he sent a telegram to the troops under his command, stating, "After an investigation, we know that most of the telegrams between our troops have been secretly intercepted and deciphered by the communist bandits. It is dangerous and worrying, and a crying shame." In a fit of anger, he ordered the execution of the man and the woman who were in charge of cipher creation and the safety of wireless communications, claiming: they are mediocre people; their technical level is not high and the security work has been shoddy; they neither owned up to their clumsiness, nor recommended better qualified personnel; for a long time they've been good at playing the game; holding up the great cause of the party and the state, while delaying the progress of suppressing the bandits. What is the use of keeping these idiots? Kill them!

That morning, after Ji Zhenren woke up, he wept nonstop. Song Daxiong asked, "Why are you so sad?"

"She has been killed by Chiang Kai-shek," he said.

At once Song Daxiong felt sour. "Didn't she die long ago? Humph! How can you cry so miserably after only seeing her in your dream? Is it worthwhile? During all these years I have never seen you cry over me once."

"Why should I cry over you? You didn't die."

"Bah!" She gave him a push and he fell into the swamp.

Politically, take the enemy as the enemy; technically, take the enemy as a teacher. This is an attitude and convention. But was the enemy side qualified to be my teacher?

Lying on his stomach in the swamp, this was the question Ji Zhenren was pondering.

The following was also a dream.

"Who am I? Who are we? Are we the kind of people who think that their every act and move concerns the safety of the world? Or who would like to go all-out in their work to stop wars from happening? Yes! In some people's eyes, no matter how you look at it, such people are only reckoned to be miserable wretches subject to some sort of sacred hallucination at the mercy of hypnosis. But you and I are the ones who rely on this sacredness to do our work, and we are sacred enough to have only actions and missions in our heart. Yes! These actions and missions are to prevent wars and bloodshed, to prevent the ugliest things from happening or spreading.

"A cryptographer must at heart be concerned about soldiers' lives and their fate. Every time they pick up a cipher, they are searching for a secret to keep soldiers from death. However, everyone understands that as long as war exists for just one day, death will extend for one day. Where would war be without death? Where is the secret that can truly help soldiers escape death? But as a cryptographer, one must neither lose heart, nor give up but disregard one's own life, family and loved ones, and all matters besides ciphers. One must spare no effort, even using every single hair on one's body to break ciphers, trying to make use of the strength of the armed forces with a just cause to prevent soldiers from being killed.

"Codebreaking is a profession with which cryptographers have to live with a mystical agony. The direction it points is clear, namely, one must crack it. Now one must be careful, because each step one takes may be in the completely wrong direction. And what is terrifying is that one is unaware of it when one is on the wrong path. A cryptographer does not move carefully along a flat road but explores an unknown barren mountain or a ferocious river, where the most common thing to happen is the explorers die a violent death by losing their way.

"To fasten a screw, one must turn the head in the same direction. Before it reaches the end, it does not change direction. A cryptographer must have the spirit of fastening a screw, but not adhere to its thinking. When they feel that it is not right, they must change direction as soon as possible, otherwise it will be difficult for them to clearly explore the numerous unknowns within a limited period of time. In theory any cipher can be broken as long as there is enough time. If a cipher, by normal means, needs eighty years to crack, yet the span of a war might only be several days, months, or years, then waiting for eighty years to crack a cipher, the efforts and value will be nil. That is why time is what a cryptographer must win. Speed is the lifeblood of a cryptographer."

As soon as Ji Zhenren heard these words, he felt a restless move deep inside his body that could not be seen or touched. They were thoughtful and profound. Although he and the speaker had never met each other, these remarks in his dream made him feel that they were friends with complete mutual understanding, true bosom friends. The speaker and he were of the same occupation, besides they were of the same ideological understanding, and therefore very agreeable confidants.

In recent years, during the development of the Soviet areas in Hubei, Henan, Anhui, Sichuan and Shaanxi provinces, the Fourth Front Army also had a unit like RSU2, doing the same kind of work, shouldering the same kind of mission, and with the same kind of creative brilliance, just like RSU2. Among their cryptographers, one was as talented as Ji Zhenren; his cipher cracking ability was much appreciated by the Fourth Front Army leaders, and his name was Li Mozi.

Two years previously, via wireless waves Ji Zhenren and Li Mozi had communicated with each other, and ever since then they have not been able to stop contacting each other. Despite being restricted by a confidentiality and that their communications be confined to stipulated business exchanges, Ji Zhenren still felt that he and Li Mozi could boil their souls in the same pot.

Recently, he constantly dreamt of Li Mozi, although his face was blurred in his mind, but his realm of thought and professional accomplishment in cryptography was outstanding.

The following chat between them was not in a dream but a reality.

One day after the First Front Army and the Fourth Front Army joined forces at Maogong, Ji Zhenren received an order to go to the Fourth

Front Army's wireless unit to cooperate with the cracking of an enemy cipher.

From a distance, the man called Li Mozi was particularly eye-catching, and 'paleness' was his most striking feature. For many years the Red Army officers and men fought and marched in barren mountains and wild forests, so it was normal for them to have tanned skin. But Li Mozi's skin was neither tanned nor toughened by exposure to sun and wind.

They felt like old friends when they first met and they chatted for three days and three nights.

Early in the morning on the fourth day, Song Daxiong came to see Ji Zhenren about something. As soon as she saw him, she cried out, "Ah! The good food of the Fourth Front Army has really restored your health. I haven't seen you so energetic for days."

"That's the result of good chats and the effect of having a close friend," muttered Ji Zhenren.

She cried out again, "Ah! All the years I've been with you, I've never heard you utter the words 'close friend'. Well, not bad, that sounds nice. Can you say it again, and let me enjoy it as well?"

Li Mozi laughed heartily, his pale face turning crimson, "Zhenren, you spoke about your 'close friend' at the wrong time, in the wrong place and with the wrong person. Look, you are in trouble now."

Before Li Mozi had finished speaking, a young and beautiful female Red Army soldier dashed over to him, muttering hurriedly but with tenderness in her eyes, "The communication between Hu Zongnan and Wu Guagua has resumed. Here are three coded telegrams I transcribed last night." In a low voice, she then mumbled flirtatiously, "Look at your red eyes. You must have stayed up all night. I wonder if you fail to crack this Guagua cipher, you won't want to live any more, will you?"

Ji Zhenren stifled his laughter, saying, "This place is really blessed, Sister Lin (Lin Daiyu, the heroine of *A Dream of Red Mansions*) is everywhere."

"These telegrams are of value to deciphering *XIANG*. What a timely assistance!" Li Mozi's expression showed that his mind was instantly in a different state. "Quick, call the other cryptographers to go to the Xicao House. Today we must crack it." At once Ji Zhenren was also in a state of combat readiness. He and Li Mozi ran to the building on the slope.

Song Daxiong and the young female soldier wanted to follow. Li Mozi stopped them, "Don't follow us. When it is dusk, you should come to collect our corpses at the bottom of the cliff."

Watching them running into the distance, the young female soldier muttered, "He swore again. If he fails to crack the Guagua cipher, he is going to jump off the cliff."

The deciphering work took a favourable turn, so Ji Zhenren and Li Mozi took a break and chatted for a while. Ji Zhenren talked about humanity's natural disposition:

"From how one speaks, we can judge one's natural disposition. Anyone who betrays others will have a guilty conscience when talking to them; anyone who feels uncertain about things will choose words carefully when speaking; anyone who is in luck does not talk much; anyone who is impetuous will talk too much; anyone who defames others will make the false evidence conclusive; anyone who is derelict in their duty will speak with remorse."

"These are obvious facts. Worldly affairs are like a puff of smoke and that has always been the case," responded Li Mozi.

"Anyone who is persistent speaks loudly. And I present this sentence to you," said Ji Zhenren.

"The level of this sentence is no lower than those from the *Book of Changes* you were talking about. I can see you were talking about yourself," Li Mozi remarked.

Ji Zhenren's eyes brightened, "A few days ago, I dreamt of an intersexual individual, so I linked the relations between *yin* and *yang* to the *Book of Changes*. Now I call to mind that the heart of the book is the character 象 (*xiang*). Is it related to the cipher we're trying to crack?"

"Yes. According to what I know, Wu Guagua has done some studies on the book. He is a man with a mind that is always suspicious, so he will not use the ciphers issued from above but invited an expert to write *XIANG*," noted Li Mozi.

"Ah, this old guy takes us by surprise. Probably he does have his mind on the book," muttered Ji Zhenren.

"The *Book of Changes* is full of dialectics and methodology and also ingenious mathematical relationships, so it's a smart move to use its fundamentals to write a set of ciphers, a surprise. How about we start from here and give it a try?" suggested Ji Zhenren.

When it was near dusk, they managed to find the trick to decipher *XIANG* - the *Ho Tu Diagram* in the *Book of Changes*. Inferring from the *Fu*

Xi Bagua, through the transformation between numbers and *yin* and *yang*, and the principle of movement of the opposing forces of *yin* and *yang* producing symmetrical numerical values, they got the substitute and shifting encryption of *XIANG*. Based on the *Ho Tu Diagram* and according to the internal relations contained in the five elements (metal, wood, water, fire and earth), the enemy cipher creator designed the key secretly to mount the mouth of the lock; following the principle of the mutual propagation and restraint between the five elements, filling the numbers and performing mathematical calculations to start the key. The application of the principle of the *Book of Changes* into writing ciphers broke with tradition, taking the Red Army cryptographers by surprise.

A girl's crisp voice was heard from outside, "Dinner is ready. It is diced chicken with rice, spicy and tasty."

"This morning I found that the expression in that young girl's eyes was not right," chuckled Ji Zhenren. "She seems to have taken a fancy to you."

"To know a girl's mind is harder than cracking a cipher," said Li Mozi. "Don't talk nonsense."

Walking out of the room, Ji Zhenren saw the young girl standing with Song Daxiong. He examined the two and witnessed a striking difference between them. Healthy and with rosy cheeks, the young girl had a well-rounded figure, while Song Daxiong had a famished and suntanned look, being a bag of bones.

Ji Zhenren cried inwardly: this is the sharp contrast in image between the Central Red Army and the Fourth Front Army.

He couldn't help thinking of the scene when the two armies first joined forces: Zhang Guotao had a ruddy complexion and a round chin, and was big and square, showing no sign of experiencing hunger, while Mao Zedong was haggard, his face withered and deeply wrinkled, being tall and thin, it seemed that a puff of wind could blow him over; Zhang Guotao was dressed in a new grey uniform, clean and trim, while Mao Zedong's old-fashioned uniform was loose and full of patches; proudly mounted on horseback Zhang Guotao was in high spirits, while Mao Zedong looked gloomy and solemn, holding a walking stick, he stood on the slope with his shabbily dressed officers and men. Back then, Ji Zhenren had the impression that Zhang Guotao was like an old master who was showing off his wealth to his poor relatives. But in a low voice Chief Gao shouted to his staff, "Don't be envious of their wealth. Although we at the Central Army are all skin and bone, as long as there is bone, we must not worry that we will not grow flesh. Once we've eaten our fill for three meals, we will be the same dragon and tiger as before."

Looking at the young female soldier, he felt that something was not right. Hadn't he met her before? Gazing at her, he slowly moved closer to her.

Stepping up to him, the girl grabbed his hand, tears gushing from her eyes, "Brother, I'm Hongmei."

Ji Zhenren was astounded, turning to Song Daxiong whose eyes filled with tears, "A girl changes eighteen times before reaching womanhood. You suffered so much on the Long March so the physical changes made you two fail to recognise each other. If it were not for my chat with her about her family, you two might have missed the chance to recognise each other."

Excited and leaping for joy Li Mozi cried out, "Yes, both of you have the surname Ji, why didn't that occur to me?"

Eagerly Ji Zhenren asked, "Hongmei, how is it that you also work as a cryptographer?"

That year, carrying their mother's letter, Ji Hongying and Ji Hongmei left home. They failed to find their brother Ji Zhenfu, but they met the Fourth Front Army, so they stopped at Xinji township, capital of the Soviet Area in Hubei, Henan and Anhui provinces. Just as in the Jiangxi Soviet, red banners, red arm bands and spears with red tassels were everywhere in Xinji. The revolutionary slogans on the walls and shouted from people's mouths were very encouraging. The Young Pioneers, the Youth League of the Communist Party and the Women's Union were very active and their methods for recruiting soldiers were unbelievably varied and their enthusiasm was extremely high. The two sisters really could not resist the temptation. When they were at home, due to the objections of their mother, they did not join the Red Army. But now they were far away from home, after a discussion they signed up to join the ranks.

Both of them were sent to the medical unit. Six months later, the higher authorities came to recruit educated people to work on technical jobs. Ji Hongmei put her name down. After a literacy test, she was taken to the wireless training class to learn how to operate transceivers.

Ji Hongmei visited Ji Hongying, telling her how good the wireless training class was, and that with her educational level she would have no problem being admitted to the class. Without thinking, Ji Hongying told Hongmei that she would not go, saying that she was applying for the Women's Independent Battalion and that it would be fascinating to fight in real battles, as she wanted to be a combat hero like Qiu Zihao.

On one occasion Qiu Zihao led two companies which held out against an enemy battalion for three days and three nights. He had multiple wounds and was carried to the medical unit. As soon as he opened his eyes, he saw the face of a beautiful female soldier. Grinning, he said, "Losing a few pieces of flesh was worthwhile! Comrade Nurse, what's your name? I'm Qiu Zihao, Assistant Commander of the 3rd Battalion, the 8th Regiment, the Fourth Front Army."

Touching his forehead, Ji Hongying was alarmed, "So hot. How many days have you been wounded? Why didn't you come for treatment earlier?"

Qiu Zihao joked, "I wounded my groin the day before yesterday, my chest yesterday, and my neck today in the blocking action. I've fought all these years, winning a basket of merit citations, and never getting wounded. But I got three wounds in the last three days. If I had known that the women here are as beautiful as paintings, I would have got wounded long ago and come here to be hospitalised." Having looked after hundreds of wounded soldiers, Ji Hongying had never come across one with such tedious banter.

Anyway, she could not get annoyed, so she said, "Comrade, please speak less. Can you cooperate with me?"

Qiu Zihao was a lucky man. One bullet went through his groin, one shell peeled off a piece of skin close to his rib and one bullet grazed the nape of his neck. He had avoided being hit in the sinews, bones or arteries. Besides being only lightly wounded, he was carefree, showing no signs of pain on his face but devoting his full attention to Ji Hongying, who pretended to see nothing but concentrated on treating his wounds. The wound on the groin was in the wrong place, only one centimetre away from his wedding tackle. In the beginning he covered his crotch with his hands. No matter how hard she tried, he just refused to let her change the dressing for him. She then held a pair of scissors and cut his trousers to the end. Calmly she said, "Don't move, or I will not take responsibility if your family jewels are cut off."

He stayed in the medical unit for thirteen days during which time he told her stories about the battlefield. She listened with great interest, feeling that it must be great to go and fight on the front line.

Looking for an excuse to be her boyfriend, he said, "Nurse Ji, my private parts have been viewed by you. It must not be for nothing. In my mind I am yours. When I first saw your face, and from the time when you first saw my groin, I had made up my mind that I would be yours in this life."

Ji Hongying was cutting a bandage. Pointing the scissors under his chin, she drove him to a quiet corner, grinning, "How domineering you are! Your reason is not convincing. I've seen many men's groins, wouldn't they all become my men? The Red Army does not allow its officers and men to have several husbands or wives."

Pressing his chin down a little bit, Qiu Zihao declared, "No matter what, I am yours. How about you give me a bloodletting so that I can sober up." While speaking he suddenly knocked his chin hard on the scissors and his chin began to bleed. The scissors dropped to the floor with a clunk. He held her in his arms and the blood was all over her neck. Then he said, "Let me make one more bet. In the next battle if I neither die nor get wounded, I will definitely be yours." When he had finished speaking, he marched out of the medical unit.

In the days after Qiu Zihao left, Ji Hongying was in an unsettled state of mind. One day, someone shouted outside, "The assistant commander of the 3rd Battalion is badly wounded. Get ready for an operation." A stretcher was rushed in and the wounded man was almost blasted to pieces. The operation was carried out on the stretcher. The damaged face was unrecognisable, but Ji Hongying knew that Qiu Zihao was the assistant commander of the 3rd Battalion. She was occupied with the operation, but her mind was in turmoil. He had said that he would be hers if he was not wounded or did not die in the next battle. It seemed that she could not have that day. Tears began to well up in her eyes.

With such extensive wounds, the effort to rescue him was only a formality. The surgeon said to those who had carried the stretcher into the room, "Comrade Battalion Commander, we have tried our best. The assistant commander has died." The commander covered the body with a piece of white cloth, giving a military salute and asking his men to carry the stretcher away. Patting Ji Hongying who was lowering her head and weeping, he said, "Comrade Hongying, the dead cannot come back to life. Please restrain your grief and accept the inevitable."

What a familiar voice! Raising her head, she saw that the battalion commander was Qiu Zihao, who was following the stretcher and striding away.

Later they fell in love, very, very much in love.

"To be a nurse may not be the best choice," he said.

"I yearn to fight in battle like men do," she replied.

"All members of the Women's Independent Battalion are heroines."

"I want to go, really."

He did recommend and transfer her to the Women's Independent Battalion, saying, "This is great. You won't be in the medical unit to view others' groins."

She laughed: "Ah! For this reason. What a feudal mind you have!"

Later, the troops were engaged in a campaign to eliminate counterrevolutionaries. In the Women's Independent Battalion Ji Hongying's educational level ranked as the highest, so she was investigated. Her ancestors of previous generations were landlords, so she became the target of a purge and was locked up. Meanwhile, Qiu Zihao was the captain of the shock brigade. Before he went to the front line, he carried his gun and rushed into the regiment's command post, declaring, "This time if I die in action, everything will be out of sight, out of mind. But if I should survive, and after I return, if I fail to see Ji Hongying in a one piece, I will take my shock brigade and find a place to argue it out. You claim that she is a counterrevolutionary, but if there is no evidence against her, my gun will not agree with you."

He led the shock brigade and won the battle completely. After returning to the barracks, and seeing that Ji Hongying was still locked up, he dashed across to the regiment headquarters with his gun in his hand. He was held down by several burly fellows. The regiment commander told him, "I will go and sort out the matter of Ji Hongying. If you don't behave yourself, you will never return."

The regiment commander went straight to see the senior officer of the army corps, who went to negotiate the release of Ji Hongying. It worked, but not that much. The person who had successfully spurred the higher authority to release Ji Hongying was Ji Hongmei, or more precisely Li Mozi, who knew that Hongying had been wronged, so he went to talk to the senior leader, who firstly explained to the very angry Li Mozi about the policy. Li Mozi had in fact heard of these policies long ago and he just resented them.

In the *Report to the Central Political Bureau* Zhang Guotao pointed out, "The target of the movement to eliminate counterrevolutionaries is mainly three kinds of people: those who came over from the White army, no matter whether they revolted and crossed over, or surrendered or were captured, all must be investigated regardless of their present behaviour; those who are from a landlord or rich peasant family background, no matter how they have behaved, all must be subjected to strict investigation; those intellectual and young students, every one of them who had attended a school, or been to a private school, must be subjected to a strict investigation. Those who are under investigation must either be locked up, purged or killed."

The report stipulated the rules for the movement, but the actual implementation went even further. Some troops listed all those who had received middle school education as targets for investigation. Some cadres engaged in security work even judged a person by how many Chinese characters they knew, whether they had any calluses on their hands, or whether their skin was suntanned. Anyone who wore glasses, or had a pen pinned in their jacket pocket could easily be suspected of being a bad person. Since they were bad people, they had to be eliminated.

The reason for Ji Hongying being locked up was even more ridiculous: this woman was too beautiful. Her delicate skin was milky and rosy, and everybody could see with half an eye that she was the daughter of a landlord or capitalist family lurking in the revolutionary ranks.

In front of the senior leader, Li Mozi threw his pen to the floor. Stamping on it he crushed the pen to pieces. "All the staff in my unit are intellectuals. They all have a pen or a pencil in their jacket pocket. Pens and pencils are our weapons. Besides, many comrades and I myself wear glasses, then kill us all!"

The senior leader said, "When you joined the wireless unit, every one of you underwent strict political examinations. No problems were found with any individual or their families. The higher levels trust you all. And Comrade Guotao trusts you all. Just set your mind at rest and do a good job in transcribing and deciphering enemy codes and ciphers. No one will dare to touch you."

Trying to finish what he wanted to say, Li Mozi went on, "Since everyone in my unit has passed the political examination concerning themselves and their families, Ji Hongmei's blood sister Ji Hongying should be in the clear too. In fact, Ji Hongying is a good soldier, brave and skilled in battle. If she is wronged, it will affect Hongmei. If Hongmei is affected, I will be affected, which means our unit's work will be affected. Is this a convincing argument?"

"Go back and wait for news," said the senior leader, who took out his own pen and handed it to Li Mozi. "If anyone dares to touch you, tell them that this pen is from me. By the way, it is a present from Comrade Guotao."

Two days later Ji Hongmei came to thank Li Mozi, "My sister has been released. I've told her that in future she must pay attention to her bearing, not dress so exotically; darken her face; wear loose and shabby clothes and stop speaking with the tone of an intellectual."

"But Hongmei, you mustn't be like that. Natural disposition cannot be hidden. Just be yourself. There is nothing wrong with looking beautiful. Who says that beauty is not needed in times of hardship?! Revolutionary optimism is still needed." Li Mozi really gave Hongmei a lot of encouragement.

She said no more but called to mind her first lesson after she attended the wireless training class. The instructor was none other than Li Mozi. At the time, she was so amazed that she cried out inwardly that the Red Army could have a man in its ranks with such a casual and elegant bearing.

Tall, thin and with a pale, square face, Li Mozi wore a pair of black-framed spectacles that could not hide his big eyes and bushy eyebrows. His hair was parted on the side and his chin clean shaven, slightly protruding, showing an overbearing manner. Dressed in a well-fitting grey uniform, enhanced with a wide green belt and a pair of shiny leather shoes, he looked particularly impressive behind the lectern. When he opened his mouth to talk, his voice was soft and pleasant to the ear. His professional level was outstanding. Before Ji Hongmei had any feelings about the subject, she was hugely interested in the lecturer. Later he personally taught her how to operate a transceiver. And later still the troops fought from place to place. Under his guidance, she slowly perfected the art of operating transceivers. Somebody joked that she had taken a fancy to Li Mozi. Angrily she replied, "I was engaged when I was at home." Afterwards no one made fun of her about this.

· · ·

Before the Baozuo campaign started, Ji Zhenren called together Ji Hongmei, Ji Hongying and Liu Kailai. Having not seen each other for many years, they chatted for a whole day and night.

He had consulted Song Daxiong about whether he should tell his brother and sisters that their mother and elder brother had died. She said that it was his family business and he should make the decision. Seizing the chance, she told him that Ji Xiaomin had also been killed. She handed him the note on which she wrote down where she was buried. The news of Xiaomin's death made Ji Zhenren extremely sad. He was thinking of cancelling the meeting, feeling it would be difficult to explain to his brother and sisters. In the end he mentioned nothing of their family members' death. He let himself shoulder all the pain of losing loved ones. Especially the true circumstances of Ji Zhenfu's death could not be revealed, because he knew that for a matter of such extreme political sensitivity, it sometimes cannot be explained clearly and it could also get them into trouble at any moment. Song Daxiong agreed with him, saying that he was a man with an incomparably strong heart, who could hold up the whole world, to say nothing of trivial family affairs.

"It's not just this," he said. "My main concern is that if I told them the truth about our elder brother dying by my hand, they would never forgive me, nor would they acknowledge me as their brother." As he spoke, tears rolled down his cheeks.

After the meeting with his siblings, he soon put aside distracting thoughts and sadness, and once again threw himself into the world of codes and ciphers.

The most difficult time of the Red Army's strategic shift also saw RSU2's most brilliant achievement in intercepting and deciphering enemy ciphers. Centred on deciphering and counter-deciphering, round after round the KMT and the Communists launched fierce competition, which later developed to such an extent that Chiang Kai-shek's Central Army and the armies of the warlords had prepared multiple ciphers, which would be changed every day; in one week each cipher was only used once and the date of use was not fixed. Normally they changed ciphers daily, and at crucial moments even twice or three times a day. 'While the priest climbs a post, the devil climbs ten.' The Red Army had several dozen senior cryptographers and excellent monitors like Chief Gao, Ji Zhenren, Li Mozi, Song Daxiong and Ji Hongmei. Facing the increasingly complicated and uncertain enemy ciphers and situation, they shone with the light of wisdom, always finding a way at the earliest opportunity to defeat their opponents.

One day Ji Hongmei captured a new signal. She transcribed three messages and handed them to Li Mozi and Ji Zhenren, who spent two days working them out individually. After exchanging views with each other for three days, they declared that they had cracked the cipher. It turned out that this cipher was a variant of the previous XIANG. Despite being more unfathomable, it still failed to escape from Ji Zhenren and Li Mozi's calculation. Ji Zhenren remarked that they had killed horses and donkeys, how could they not peel the skin off a mule?

Only after breaking the XIANG family of ciphers did they realise that general Hu Zongnan's confidential department thought that the XIANG created by Commander Wu Guagua of the 39th Division was pretty good, so they used the series as the communication means between the general headquarters and the 39th Division.

The intelligence gathered from deciphering messages encrypted by XIANG as well as some other important ciphers helped the Red Army senior officers finally make the decision to conduct an operation. Before long an assault on Baozuo was launched, and the result was that Wu Guagua's 12,000 personnel were carved up into three parts and were wiped out one by one by the Red Army. The victory at Baozuo opened the path northward to the south of Gansu for the Right Route Red Army who had just come out of the grasslands.

Ji Hongying, who had been promoted to Commander of the 2nd Company of the Women's Independent Battalion, and Qiu Zihao took part in the battle and they both cut dashing figures during the attack on Baozuo.

The Women's Independent Battalion was in charge of attacking the defending enemy at the Aji Temple, which was built with tall, thick walls. The strong defense works on the back slope dominated the commanding point. To take the temple, the south gate had to be taken first, and the task was handed to Ji Hongying's 2nd Company. Covered by firepower from higher ground, the south gate was easy to defend but hard to attack. She exercised her brains before the battle.

When the morning sunlight shone on the south gate, a big fire suddenly started in a nearby temple. Soon a dozen nuns dashed out of the temple gate and instantly chaos ensued. Some caught on fire, rolling on the ground to put the fire out; some were squatting on the ground holding their heads, wailing; some were holding tree trunks coughing. Then these wretched young nuns began to run to the Aji Temple.

Amid the miserable wailing, the Aji Temple's south gate opened. The nuns rushed in. The gate closed immediately, but just at this moment the Women's Independent Battalion launched a general offensive and instantly the sound of guns and shells was heard all over the place. Soon the south gate was opened and Hongying's company charged into the temple, closely followed by the 1st and 3rd companies from the east and the west gates respectively.

In less than an hour they captured the temple as well as the defense works on the higher ground behind it. A nun standing on the higher defense works was wounded in one arm. Throwing her gun to another nun beside her, she let the medic dress her wound. The battalion commander said to her, "Comrade Hongying, you are both brave and wise. After we return to our barracks, I will ask the higher level to record your meritorious service." Taking the nun's cap off her head, Hongying wiped her face which had been blackened by smoke and dust.

"Don't bother about that," she said, "It will be OK if they just don't lock me up again."

Qiu Zihao again won the battle without a scratch; however he fought the battle carelessly. As soon as the regiment commander issued the order to attack, he led his battalion to charge at the enemy's command post, killing the regiment commander and taking back a transceiver.

After the battle ended, he saw Ji Hongying dressed as a nun. He teased her, "It's fine if you don't want to marry me, but there is no need to become a nun. Ah, you are wounded. Is it serious? Have you hurt your bones?" As he spoke, he went to pinch her arm.

She patted his hand, saying, "Don't touch a nun."

He laughed, "I'm bringing you a gift from the enemy. Please pass this transceiver on to my sister-in-law Ji Hongmei."

"Who is your sister-in-law?" Ji Hongying scowled at him, "I will cut your chin off if you carry on speaking such nonsense."

The commendation was made good at the battlefront. Ji Hongying won a first-class merit citation for her strategy of taking the Aji Temple south gate and the enemy defense works. Yet there was no mention of Qiu Zihao's achievement in capturing the enemy regiment headquarters and killing the enemy commander. He also won a first-class merit citation but it was for bringing back the transceiver.

When he took the transceiver to RSU2, there was no sign of appreciation on Ji Zhenren's face at all. Gazing at him, Ji Zhenren asked, "Is this all? Where are the cables, chargers, batteries, or hand generator? At least you could have grabbed one of them."

"For this transceiver you can only earn half a merit," said Chief Gao. "It's like capturing a gun, but not the bullets. You are three bricks short of a load. Quick, go back and find them."

Ji Zhenren hurriedly said, "Send an educated person with him, or it will be the same."

Chief Gao turned to Ji Hongying, "Hongying is educated. Why don't you go with Qiu Zihao to the mountain again?"

Ji Hongying tried to avoid going, "Who says I'm educated, I will turn against him."

Song Daxiong laughed, "Once bitten, twice shy. All right, I'll go." Not daring to delay, Qiu Zihao took one company and went straight to the hilltop.

After entering the ruins of the enemy command post, Song Daxiong quickly dug out two batteries. Triumphantly she directed some soldiers to remove them. Then a gunshot was heard from behind a stone table. Turning in a circle, she fell forward to the floor. Qiu Zihao and the soldiers started shooting back at the stone table. It turned out that the commander who had been shot by Qiu Zihao had regained consciousness. He fired one shot at Song Daxiong.

Carrying Song Daxiong on his back, Qiu Zihao hurriedly dashed down the hill. Fortunately the bullet went through her left cheek. Two teeth were knocked out, but her life was not in danger. Qiu Zihao was extremely ashamed, blaming himself for not shooting dead the enemy, leaving trouble behind.

When Song Daxiong was in the medical unit receiving treatment, Qiu Zihao often went to visit her, where he would sometimes meet Ji Zhenren, who would say angrily, "What a half-baked revolutionary! You nearly got her killed. What are you looking at? Do you not understand what I'm saying? Humph! Poor marksmanship and deaf too."

Song Daxiong could not speak but she wrote down, "Zihao, don't pay attention to what he says. It's not your fault. Go and fight the enemy boldly and confidently."

This gunshot changed Song Daxiong's attitude to Ji Zhenren. From then on, although she took care to cooperate with him at work, as always, in terms of personal affection she kept him at a distance, expressing no affection toward him any more. Sometimes she was closer to the other staff than to him and they would ask her why. When pressed too hard, she replied, "My right ear is deaf and my left cheek is shrunken, so I am severing ties with you." Although she could not close her lips properly and her words were blurred, each word was like a knife stabbing into Ji Zhenren's heart.

Immediately he submitted an application to Chief Gao to marry Song Daxiong. But Chief Gao did not give formal approval, telling him that Song Daxiong absolutely refused to marry him and, if pressed, she might die. Chief Gao also told him that Song Daxiong had got herself into a dead end; besides she was a woman of strong character and integrity, the organisation dared not give formal approval, suggesting that he give her time to slowly accept the reality that she had a disfigured left cheek, and leave marriage for later consideration.

This made Ji Zhenren feel depressed for a long time.

16 /THE GU CIPHER AND THE MEIHUA
TELEGRAMS

SONG DAXIONG'S face was wounded, which meant she was as good as disfigured. A woman with strong character, she appeared not to care about it. Now and then she would say, "My left cheek is sunken and my right ear is deaf. I don't look like a woman." When Ji Hongmei heard her muttering, linking it to the fact that she had deliberately cold-shouldered Ji Zhenren, she knew how troubled Song Daxiong's mind was.

What an attachment there was between her and him! In the past she was so close to him, but now she seriously put forward the idea of severing ties with him, meaning her heart would die once. She knew perfectly well that he would never dislike her or avoid her, but she disliked herself very much. She knew that although her personality lacked femininity, her appearance and her figure were very womanly. In her early years, her breasts were full and round and eye-catching. Afterwards in spite of the fact that every day she marched, fought, starved, was as thin as a hemp stalk and flat-chested, she always cherished a hope that while there is life, there is hope, and after victory was won in the revolution and after eating steamed buns for three months, she would definitely turn into a fully rounded beautiful woman. But that was impossible for now. The evil bullet had robbed her of two teeth and cut a slice of flesh off her cheek, causing scarring and disfiguring her for life. She was deeply in love with him, so in love that everything she gave him had to be perfect all the time. Now the basic element of a woman - her face - had become incomparably ugly, how could she talk about perfection any more?

No one would imagine that a woman of such strong character could take such exception to her appearance. Ji Zhenren asked Ji Hongmei to talk to Song Daxiong. She went, talking, weeping and disgruntled, but to no avail. She went to sleep on Song Daxiong's straw mattress one night, refusing to leave but pestering her and keeping on at her all night.

That night RSU2 and Li Mozi's wireless unit barracked next to each other in two courtyard houses in Haotai village. When Li Mozi did the bed check, he failed to see Ji Hongmei, so he went to the next courtyard to look for her. Throwing her clothes on, Song Daxiong went out, mumbling, "Hongmei is here with me, please set your mind at rest." Li Mozi stopped asking any more, returning to his quarter to rest.

Too fond of sleep, Ji Hongmei slept soundly until she didn't know what time. Song Daxiong hastily woke her up. In a low voice she said, "The military situation is critical and we must depart immediately. No talking, no running around, no torches. One after another we will leave the village." It was still pitch black outside. They all got up and quietly busied themselves with getting ready to leave.

Out of the village they ran twenty kilometres in one breath. Only when they reached a mountain pass did they stop for a break. Ji Hongmei noticed that the people were all from RSU2, not a single person from the Fourth Front Army's wireless unit, nor did she see Ji Zhenren.

Song Daxiong explained that Ji Zhenren and some others had already left. What they needed to do was to go to the Third Army Group to find them. There were urgent orders from above that the Central Red Army depart for the north, while the Fourth Front Army was to go south. Ji Hongmei asked who had planned this! Song Daxiong did not explain too much. Ji Hongmei then made a scene, insisting on going back to her own unit. Pulling her to one side, Song Daxiong tried hard to help her get over her worries, but she was too stubborn to listen.

"All the Red armies are one family. We can undertake a revolution no matter whom we follow, and this is what I am going to say to you. Why must I take you with me? It is because of your brother. Who is he? He is an expert cryptographer and an exceptional man who can read obscure writing. You have learned that when he is working, he forgets everything, even his life. He does not eat when hungry, nor sleep when tired. Yes, he is a cipher-cracking genius, but he needs someone to look after him meticulously so that his talents can shine over and over again. For the sake of your brother and our cause, and the future of the Red Army, RSU2 needs you. Where the revolution needs your brother, you will also be there."

"I myself also need to work for the revolution! I must transcribe and decrypt codes and ciphers. I can also become a master cryptographer. Why should I play foil to him, to be his stepping stone? I will not do it. What he does is revolutionary work, not tilling our Jis' land. I have no obligation to work for him."

"Look, crunch time reveals true consciousness. Is that what you are worth? I can also tell you the truth. Not only that I don't love him any more, but also I am fed up with him, extremely fed up. Each day, it's like looking after a child, I worry about him too much. I really have had enough. If you don't take care of him, I will absolutely not do it either. I've done what I could and I've treated him fairly. I did not let RSU2 down, nor did I let the revolution down. I quit, I am not going to do it any more!"

Ji Hongmei did not want to listen any more. She got up and began to run. Song Daxiong grabbed her around the middle. Struggling hard, Ji Hongmei cried and screamed, "I have work to do, so why should I go with you? What right do you have to do such a thing to me? Only because he is my brother? But first of all I am from the Fourth Front Army, and my leader is Li Mozi. Without orders from him I will not go anywhere."

"Aha, you're telling the truth now. I worked it out long ago. You don't want to leave Li Mozi. But you'd better give it up. You have been engaged and your future husband is Ji Zhenfu. You are not the Jis' daughter but a child bride, which you must not forget. Anyway, even if you don't marry Ji Zhenfu you must marry Ji Zhenren. The Jis cannot raise you for nothing. Really, I have been thinking that you and Ji Zhenren are well matched and the most suitable couple."

"I am truly shocked by such an idea. Ji Zhenren has not become a fool but you have. It seems that he has told you about me and the Ji family. I've always felt that you treated him with the mentality of a Ji woman, so you'd better see it through. He has said a hundred times that he doesn't dislike you."

"From now on he is yours. You can either take him as your blood brother, or your husband. It's entirely up to you."

"Sister Song, I will not argue with you any more, because I take you for a mad woman who is speaking nonsense."

Ji Hongmei was intent on leaving, so she said, tactfully, "Sister Song, you are a veteran soldier, and your political level and conscience are both first class. You'd better think about me. I am a soldier from the Fourth Front Army and my membership credentials are with its wireless unit. How can I go with you? If I do the same with you, will you go with me? We are both Red Army soldiers and we have our own organisations, so when problems crop up we must think politically rather than abandoning ourselves to emotion."

When the political nature of the matter was mentioned, Song Daxiong pondered for a while. In the end she understood what Ji Hongmei meant. But she said, "Even if you must go back, you can't do it now. You must wait for daybreak until we have marched far away. If you go back too early, it might divulge a secret."

Ji Hongmei laughed, "All right, you can sit here with me. After daybreak when your unit has marched far away, you come with me. Once you are with us, you can then completely escape from the man you are feeling vexed with." Song Daxiong smiled but said nothing. Before daybreak, she decided to let Ji Hongmei go.

Throwing herself into Song Daxiong's arms, Ji Hongmei cried, "Sister Song, our Ji family is truly grateful to you. I'm afraid that in this life we cannot find another woman who could be as kind as you to my brother."

Song Daxiong urged Ji Hongmei to go, saying, "Go ahead, you and Li Mozi." In the end she did not tell Ji Hongmei that Ji Zhenfu had died.

The night in question was 10 September 1935. They were faced with a dangerous situation when Zhang Guotao ignored the Party Central Committee's warning that 'going south is taking the road to ruin', and used his military strength to coerce the Central Committee to head south. The Central Committee decided right away to secretly break away from Zhang Guotao that same night, leading the 1st and 3rd Army Groups and the Military Commission Column to march north. At that moment the leading officers of the central authorities were specially urged to take RSU2 with them. Some went personally to the barracks to take some of the key members of RSU2, while the other members sneaked away by starlight and they all arrived at the 3rd Army Group safely.

It was dawn when Ji Hongmei returned to the barracks and saw Li Mozi sitting in the quiet but messy courtyard, saying nothing but continuously smoking cigarettes. He looked as though he had a heavy heart.

Ji Hongmei went to sit down beside him. After a long while, he asked, "Your brother and the others have gone far?" She nodded. "They left in such a hurry," he said. "It must have been urgent and sensitive for them to have not even let us know about it. How has it come to such a state? A few days ago Comrade Guotao personally talked to Ji Zhenren, mobilising him to work in our unit. I thought I would be his colleague for years to come, never anticipating that they would leave overnight."

Ji Hongmei smiled bitterly, "Everyone has their own ambitions. We can't force others to do things against their will. Isn't it better that I've come back?"

Standing up, Li Mozi muttered, "It seems it is easier said than done for all the Red armies to be part of one family."

It was more than six months later when Li Mozi and Ji Hongmei saw Ji Zhenren and Song Daxiong again. The Fourth Front Army suffered a severe setback in its fighting in the south, suffering heavy losses. Zhang Guotao had to order his troops north to join forces with the First Front Army in Huining, Gansu province. After going through innumerable hardships as well as two partings and reunions, the two Red Army main forces finally joined forces again. Everyone was naturally elated and radiant with joy. However, the Ji brothers and sisters could not bring themselves to be happy.

Ji Hongmei brought them the grievous news that eventually Ji Hongying had been executed in the movement to 'eliminate counterrevolutionaries'.

After Ji Hongying was released from prison, her revolutionary zeal was not affected by the event; on the contrary, she was more courageous in combat. She was promoted to Company Commander and she also made contributions during the battle for Baozuo. Later she got into trouble because she wasn't happy with Zhang Guotao's decision to take troops south, forming a separate central committee and constantly being defeated in battle. The people who were grumbling were not small in number.

Others had kept their displeasure in their hearts, but she expressed hers on her lips, "Why fight our way to Chengdu to eat rice? If we carry on with the present course of action, we won't even be able to get a cold fart to eat." She also said, "Has anyone seen a monster that grows two heads? Can a man who grows two heads survive?"

Originally these were just some grumbling to vent her frustration as well showing concern for the future of the troops, nothing wrong in nature. But after her comments were passed on to the higher authorities, someone formed an association, making it terribly serious. 'Fight our way to Chengdu to eat rice' was Zhang Guotao's slogan for going south; 'a man with two heads' was insinuating 'the forming of a separate central committee'. The purge had not ended yet so they decided to get even with her. With her being the daughter of a landlord family, an intellectual and a counterrevolutionary element, if she could not be eliminated, then who could? During this period of time, Zhang Guotao invented a policy: if an intellectual commits a crime, increase the guilt by thirty per cent. If a worker or a peasant element commits a crime, reduce the guilt by thirty per cent. Therefore, Ji Hongying was classified as one who should be punished severely. This time no one dared, nor was able, to block it. On a certain morning, along with several bad intellectuals and KMT spy suspects, she was dragged to Dongshan hill and executed.

Worker-peasant-element cadre Qiu Zihao and Ji Hongmei went to identify and bury Ji Hongying under a big tree on the slope. Ji Hongmei cried her eyes out, while Qiu Zihao bit his lips until they bled. Eyes red with indignation, he dared not say a word. Feeling too suffocated to breathe, he fired his gun at the tree top. He then carried Ji Hongmei, who had fainted from weeping on his shoulder, down the hill.

Soon Qiu Zihao was demoted to company commander from battalion commander. The reason for his demotion was that he had fired a revolutionary gun when burying a counterrevolutionary element. But when the organisation dealt with his case, they adopted the principle of reducing his guilt by thirty per cent for a guilty worker-peasant element, otherwise he would have been stripped of his rank completely, or even locked up or executed.

Ji Hongmei wept and mourned a counterrevolutionary element, so she had to be punished. Li Mozi went to see the senior officer. When he went, he held a coded telegram in his hand.

It was encrypted by *GU*, used by the troops of the Qinghai warlords Ma Bufang and Ma Buqin. Ji Hongmei had learned how to crack ciphers from Li Mozi and she had made considerable progress. But this cipher was written in a disorderly and complicated sequence. The deciphering job was mainly done by Li Mozi and several other core staff, who had all agreed to use it to rescue Ji Hongmei.

Embarking on a career in cryptography, as well as the process itself, were not plain sailing for Ji Hongmei. Some people were against the idea, saying that women were not suited to be cryptographers because their physical strength and capability could not match the demands of the work. However, she happened to have a strong interest in cracking ciphers. It was said that she forced her way into the tent of the senior officer, boldly and assuredly talking to the officer who nodded his head and said, "I am waiting for our wireless unit to have a female hero."

Li Mozi put the telegram in front of the senior officer, saying, "Ji Hongmei played the leading role in cracking this cipher. She has great potential and before long she will be an expert cryptographer. It is hard for us to get good cryptographers. Those who willingly dedicate themselves to the work must not be punished, and specially not wrongly punished, otherwise one case could have a knock-on effect."

The senior officer laughed, "This threat of yours will not scare those who have killed so many intellectuals. Tell me clearly how important this *GU* is. The importance of Ji Hongmei is linked to the importance of this cipher. Then let me deal with the other matters."

The intelligence gathered from the telegrams showed that in order to prevent the Fourth Front Army from entering Qinghai, Ma Bufang and Ma Buqin had dispatched a 1,500-strong cavalry force, each having two fast horses, riding in turn and carrying food and forage with them. They travelled about fifty kilometres each day toward Xining. But before they reached Xining, this cavalry unit had been worn down; the force was down to half strength and they had lost over 2,000 of their 3,000 horses.

So where was the significance of the intelligence?

"Zhang Guotao does not agree that the Fourth Front Army should go north to rejoin the First Front Army in Shaanxi and Gansu. He still favours going west, insisting that his troops start for Qinghai from Ganzi in Sichuan. Then the question is: is the route passable for the Red

Army troops? Even the Mas' cavalry who had horses and grain struggled to manage, how is it possible for us with neither horses nor food or forage to do it? Apart from this, the meticulous Hongmei analysed the related information and discovered that from Dege to Qinghai there are about seventy-eight horse stations, meaning that it takes seventy-eight days even for horses to travel the distance; and the roads are all narrow paths, with no inhabitants, no food or forage, and not even any sources of water in many of the sections on this route. The insurmountable dangers were obvious. At the moment our officers and men either openly or secretly resist advancing to the west, so what will they think when they get to know what Mas' cavalry suffered? Surely we in the Red Army never fear death, but the command level must not let people die in vain." After he had finished speaking, Li Mozi turned around and began to leave.

The senior officer said, "You've spoken in a rational and convincing way!"

Li Mozi said again, "I leave Ji Hongmei's fate to this intelligence."

"No. We leave the fate of tens of thousands of Ji Hongmeis to this intelligence." Holding the telegram in his hand, the senior officer rushed off.

A few days later the outcome arrived: cracking GU prevented Ji Hongmei from suffering misfortune - she would not be punished. And the substantial related intelligence gathered also played a role in preventing the Fourth Front Army from suffering misfortune. After the other leaders and commanders tried very hard to dissuade Zhang Guotao, he had to cancel his plan of sending his troops to Qinghai but agreed for them to go north.

To thank Li Mozi for saving her life, Ji Hongmei bought some raw wool from a shepherd. After washing and spinning the wool, she knitted a jumper and a pair of ear protectors for Li Mozi who happily accepted the gifts.

After Ji Zhenren listened to how Ji Hongying was killed, he looked gloomy, neither saying a word, nor shedding a tear. Leaning on an old elm tree, he stood there the whole afternoon. His stamping foot, kicking, broke two tree roots and dug a big hole in the ground.

The relationship between Ji Zhenren and Song Daxiong became more strained because of a political event.

At that time, the Central Revolutionary Military Commission gave orders to the Fourth Front Army to get ready to carry out the Ningxia Campaign, which was then abandoned due to changes in the enemy situation on the east side of the Yellow River. But as for the troops that had already crossed the river to the west, the Military Commission named them as the West Legion. Li Mozi and Ji Hongmei were staff of RSU2 which was on the east side of the river, but because of a temporary task they were dispatched to the Fourth Front Army headquarters. They could not withdraw after the campaign was cancelled, so they stayed on with the West Legion.

Before long the Mas' blocking action inflicted heavy losses on the West Legion. To rescue them from the hopeless situation, the Military Commission dispatched reinforcements. Ji Zhenren and some other staff were ordered to join the relief troops to safeguard intelligence for the operation.

Previously, the main targets of their monitoring were the KMT's Central Army and the surrounding warlords' armies. They had never monitored the Mas who were thousands of kilometres away. In the beginning they failed to catch the wireless signals of Mas' troops. After an urgent improvement to their existing equipment, they finally managed to receive the enemy signals, which were so weak that the sound of a pencil writing could be a disturbing noise. The staff met with unprecedented difficulties, either catching no signals or transcribing some incomplete messages, the so-called '*Meihua* telegrams' (meaning fragmentary messages)'.

Fortunately Ji Zhenren and his colleagues did a superb job. Facing the situation, they marched with the troops at high speed while undertaking monitoring and deciphering. After some strenuous round-the-clock work, they gradually got things into shape.

The difficulty was that these messages were encrypted by ciphers written following the customs of the language of the Hui nationality. The style was completely different from that of the KMT regular armies. Furthermore, the missing parts of the messages made it extremely difficult to decipher them. But no matter how challenging, these outstanding cryptographers were not beaten. What seriously concerned Ji Zhenren was that the intelligence gathered could not be passed onto the West Legion because, from the enemy telegrams, he knew that the whole West Legion had been destroyed and that several hundred survivors had withdrawn to the west. At the last moment the

West Legion wireless staff had destroyed their code books and smashed the transceivers. Picking up guns and swords they had launched a life-and-death struggle with the enemy and their fate was unknown.

After rejoining RSU2, Ji Zhenren's heart was heavy. One day he heard by accident that a staff member called Zhan had behaved strangely when on the relief mission and he might have secretly kept some enemy telegrams.

Ji Zhenren reported it to the organisation. People were sent to talk to Zhan who said that he had never touched the Mas' telegrams. On hearing it, the monitors were angry. Striking hard on the table, Song Daxiong threw the record book for everyone to see. Zhan's signature showed that he did take away telegrams. So he was searched and six telegrams were found. Although the evidence was before everybody's eyes, he stubbornly refused to admit his mistake, claiming that he had treated them as useless telegrams, and had no intention of keeping them.

Song Daxiong told the authorities, "At the time nearly all the telegrams we transcribed were incomplete. The situation was special and the conditions were difficult. The unit treated these incomplete telegrams as complete and good ones, so Comrade Zhan has unarguably kept telegrams in secret."

One day later, after lunch, Ji Zhenren invited Zhan for a walk outside the courtyard. He wanted to help Zhan straighten out his muddled thinking. Unexpectedly, Zhan adopted an extremely bad attitude toward him, grumbling, "At that time some of the incomplete telegrams could not be deciphered. Why are you fixated on my six telegrams?"

"We collectively deciphered these telegrams," said Ji Zhenren. "If our collective efforts failed, we gave up. But your case is different. You kept them without permission, simply not intending to hand them out for collective deciphering, so that's a completely different issue."

Zhan was enraged, shouting, "Someone died and that's it. Why should I feel sorry for them?!"

Hearing these remarks, Ji Zhenren flew into a rage. Pouncing on Zhan he swung his arm and began to beat him. Dodging the blow, Zhan grabbed Ji Zhenren's collar.

At this moment Liu Kailai came off sentry duty and passed them. He hurriedly pulled Ji Zhenren away. The villainous Zhan was ferocious, taking the opportunity to slap Ji Zhenren on the face, cursing, "You spoiled wolf, you can't bear the sight of others being safe and sound. And yet you give me a hard time. Isn't it because the organisation will offer you another reward? You are addicted to being an exemplary person, aren't you?" Turning round, he began to walk away.

"Stop!" yelled Ji Zhenren. "You shut your eyes to our men who were dying, and you neglected your duty. Heaven and Earth do not tolerate such behaviour!" Grabbing the rifle from Liu Kailai, he cocked it. With his sharp eyes and nimble fingers, Liu Kailai stretched his arm across the gun, deflecting the shot which rustled the leaves of a willow tree ahead.

Howling, Zhan held his ear and squatted down, blood dripping between his fingers. Raising his head, he saw smoke still rising from the muzzle of the rifle. Wounded, Zhan was a very calculating man. Calmly he walked to the willow tree and dug the bullet from the trunk.

Liu Kailai snatched back his rifle. Zhan turned around with a cold smile on his face and walked over to Liu Kailai. Grabbing Liu Kailai's hand, he yelled ferociously, "Ji Zhenren, how dare you fire at your own comrade? My half ear and the bullet in the tree trunk are evidence. I will make sure you really regret this!"

Liu Kailai shook off Zhan's hands, shouting, "Open your eyes wide and see clearly, I'm Liu Kailai. Do you know why I fired at you? First, because you are a bully and raised your fist at my brother, for which I cannot forgive you; second, you shut your eyes to our men who were dying, causing my sister Hongmei to lose her life under the swords of the Mas' cavalry, for which I cannot forgive you, either. Let me fire another shot at you." As he spoke, he held the rifle and aimed at Zhan.

Zhan was stupefied, not by the rifle aimed at him, but by the person holding it. A moment ago he clearly felt that it was Ji Zhenren who had fired the gun at him. How all of a sudden had it changed to Liu Kailai? He looked at them right and left, and the two really looked as though they had come out of the same mould. He could not tell who was who. He rushed to grab the gun barrel, saying, "No matter who you are, you have been caught in the act."

Calming down, Ji Zhenren went to examine the wound on Zhan's ear. Sure enough a piece of ear the size of a broad bean had been severed by the bullet. He realised the seriousness of the matter. He hurriedly helped Zhan over to the medical unit for treatment. But Zhan refused to go, grabbing the rifle with one hand while the other grasped Liu Kailai's collar tight.

Song Daxiong walked toward them from a distance. She took out a handkerchief and wrapped the wound for Zhan, then took the three of them to the unit office.

Pointing at Liu Kailai, Zhan said, "He opened fire at me. I ask the organisation to back me up."

"Speak!" said Song Daxiong, glancing at Ji Zhenren.

Liu Kailai muttered, "I was wrong to open fire and wound comrade Zhan. I request punishment from the organisation."

"Speak!" reiterated Song, still gazing at Ji Zhenren.

Ji Zhenren had to say, "It was me who opened fire!"

"We are all comrades," said Song Daxiong. "Is it worth firing weapons at each other over a disagreement about work?"

The deputy unit leader's face took on a grim expression. He yelled, "Liu Kailai, send Zhan to see a doctor. Song Daxiong, you go and inform the unit leaders at all levels to come for a meeting."

In the meeting an agreement was reached on three punishments.

First, for a difference of opinion about work, Ji Zhenren pointed a gun at his revolutionary comrade resulting in injury, and the nature of the incident was very serious, so he was immediately reported to the Political Security Bureau for punishment according to the law.

Second, during the campaign to relieve the West Legion, Zhan hid the fact that he had secretly kept the enemy telegrams, intent on deciphering them himself so that he could win a first-class merit citation. Because the Mas' ciphers were extremely difficult to crack and because the messages were incomplete, and due to Zhan's limited capability, he was unable to decipher them. However, he was unwilling to follow the rules and stipulations, and failed to report to the unit leader so that more resources could be applied to decipher them. Instead, he allowed the six telegrams to stay in his hands, resulting in them missing the opportunity to immediately decipher them collectively. Probing the reason, the trouble was caused by his egotism and his grave intention of seeking fame and fortune. He treated the telegrams as his private resource for gaining personal honour and rank. He was now to be handed over to the Political Security Bureau to be investigated according to the law.

Third, Liu Kailai failed to strictly manage his gun or to do his best to stop the incident, so he was to be transferred to the combat troops in the front line to temper himself as a foot soldier.

Ji Zhenren countered, "The unit has made a serious error in the understanding of Zhan's problem, which was neither about individualism nor about seeking fame and fortune, but dereliction of duty resulting from his narrow-minded and disgusting thought of revenge. In the grassland when Zhang Guotao insisted that the Red Army go south, some First Front Army members were left behind with the Fourth Front Army where they suffered wrongs and became the target of attack. This time the Fourth Front Army comrades were cornered in a hopeless situation, and Zhan deliberately slacked off in his work, hiding the enemy telegrams but making no report to the unit to decipher them. What he did was actually a retaliation."

Song Daxiong, who was sitting beside him, gritted her teeth and said, "After investigation, it is true that Zhan slacked off in his work; but it's not true that he deliberately played dirty and prevented the telegrams from being deciphered. Comrade Ji, you should not express your opinion based on assumptions. In order to crack ciphers, it is necessary for us to think more profoundly. But for political issues it is absolutely wrong for us to be suspicious for no reason."

Ji Zhenren was more resentful, saying, "Wanting to retaliate is a bane. Zhan is narrow-minded and something is wrong with his political ideology. To speak bluntly, he has a problematic political sentiment toward the West Legion."

In a low voice Song Daxiong muttered, "As I see it, it might be that you have such thinking. Ji Hongying was executed in the purge by the Fourth Front Army, so you want to take revenge on them, don't you? Otherwise, why did it take you so long to crack the Mas' ciphers when you were in the front line?"

Ji Zhenren was furious, yelling, "How can you also use sentiment to judge right and wrong? Ji Hongmei was slaughtered by the Mas' troops when she marched with the West Legion, so who should I hate? I am always open and aboveboard on how to deal with my personal feelings and major issues of principle. When in the front line, everybody knows that it was purely because of the objective conditions that we could not crack the Mas' ciphers quickly, not that we subjectively delayed doing it. Song Daxiong, can't you stop making unfounded and malicious attacks on me?"

"So that is why no one should be swayed by personal emotions or resentment, or become suspicious without grounds," said Song Daxiong calmly. "Zhan behaved badly. He sought fame and fortune, yet his capability was below expectations, which was why he got into trouble. However, his trouble is not a weighty political one as you have suggested but based on 'narrow-minded and disgusting thoughts of seeking revenge'."

Ji Zhenren did not want to argue any more, asking, "Chief Gao has gone to study for so long, when will he come back?"

Song Daxiong stared at him, mumbling, "Don't count on him to save you. You must save yourself."

Ji Zhenren and Zhan were detained by the Political Security Bureau.

Two weeks later the bureau announced Ji Zhenren's punishment: considering the conclusive evidence against Ji Zhenren, who opened fire and wounded his revolutionary comrade, as well as his abominable conduct of refusing to acknowledge his mistake, we now give him a disciplinary warning and sentence him to six months' forced labour.

In May 1937 Ji Hongmei followed the surviving West Legion troops numbering about 420 personnel. After passing through many different places, they broke through the enemy encirclement and finally withdrew to Xinxin Xia. Soon they were rescued and returned to Yan'an. Ji Hongmei rejoined RSU2.

Only then did people come to know that Li Mozi went missing during the battle of Hongliuyuan and no one knew if he was dead or alive.

One morning, six months later, a beggar came down a yellow muddy road, unkempt and in rags. In front of the RSU2 courtyard, he called out 'Chief Gao' and then fainted.

A sentry called Chief Gao who had the sentries carry the man into the courtyard. After a wash, Chief Gao recognised that the man was none other than Li Mozi, who was only skin and bones; besides, he was suffering from disease. Li Mozi then stayed in the medical unit to receive treatment and nursed his health for over a month.

According to related regulations and procedures, the organisation made investigations and examined Li Mozi's political behaviour during the time when he was missing. Finally they confirmed that he was not captured, nor did he defect to the enemy. Only then was he allowed to rejoin RSU2, resuming his work as a cryptographer.

17 /THE XIN CIPHER

IN THE LABOUR camp Ji Zhenren stood out among the others. Every day at dawn he would stand bolt upright on the empty ground to respectfully receive his job assignment, and at dusk, smilingly and earnestly, he would hand the form signed by all the overseers to the camp leader.

Swallowing the hardships into his belly, he quietly waited for the arrival of the happy moment in the darkness. But one, two, three nights passed, and the happy moment did not come. He had thought that it might be the same as when he was sent to do hard labour in the Jiangxi Soviet, that someone would quietly bring him the enemy telegrams, so that he did not miss his duty but happily did his professional work at night. But this time the unit had decreed that anyone who had committed errors could not touch enemy telegrams and not a single code word was allowed out of RSU2's office.

Ji Zhenren did hard labour during the day while he suffered mentally at night. It went on like this for three months, yet one day he suddenly vanished. Song Daxiong went to see the camp leader, asking to know where Ji Zhenren had gone. The answer was that he had returned to RSU2 for some very urgent work. She found Chief Gao who looked surprised, saying that Ji Zhenren had not finished his six-months hard labour, so he must still be in the labour camp. She stopped searching, as she sensed that it must be a confidential matter because everyone was dodging and shirking her enquires.

It was mid-summer when she found out where Ji Zhenren had gone. Along with another two people, she went to see him in the Anti-

Japanese Military and Political College. At the entrance they were stopped by the sentry. Then a message came, saying that it was inconvenient for Ji Zhenren to meet visitors. She thought it was natural for him not to have freedom because he had been locked up to receive education and reform. A few days later they went again, but again they could not meet him. However, she discovered that RSU2 had formally recommended Ji Zhenren for admission to the Anti-Japanese Military and Political College and the reason for him being there was not because he was a bad element receiving education and reform.

After the peaceful settlement of the Xi'an Incident in December 1936, a new atmosphere emerged in the cooperation between the KMT and the Communists. In Yan'an, although life was hard, the political environment was stable and relaxed. No more constant marches and battles, so everyone felt more at ease. Some comrades began to desire to go to colleges and universities, and such a trend was closely related to the environment at the time in Yan'an. On the one hand, waves of spontaneous reading and study had surged dramatically and reading books had become the main spiritual and cultural life for everyone; on the other hand, Mao Zedong encouraged as well as took the lead in reading; besides he had specifically given instructions regarding RSU2's reading and study, so some unit staff were sent to the Anti-Japanese Military and Political College to study.

Song Daxiong already knew about this great development. What interested her was why Ji Zhenren, who had made mistakes and should have been in a labour camp for another three months, had openly entered the college to study. And others returned to the unit after completing one term (six months) of study, but Ji Zhenren went on with his study for two terms (one year). What was more extraordinary was that the college had given him special tutoring in Japanese military terminology, whereas others had to learn it in a training class run by RSU2 itself.

In the meetings for the unit cadres, with regard to the punishment of Ji Zhenren, she complained several times that the unit was unprincipled and failed to be fair, stubbornly requesting an explanation.

Chief Gao explained, "In the first three months Ji Zhenren thoroughly acknowledged his mistake and he behaved well in the labour camp, so he was transferred to the Anti-Japanese Military and Political College to carry on reforming while attending classes. After the six-month term ended, we let him carry on for another term. For such an arrangement the higher authorities must have had their own long-term considerations."

She was not convinced, "He has completely acknowledged his mistake on the issue of Zhan? I don't believe it."

"The current situation requires him to make progress in his skills to crack Japanese invaders' ciphers and he is the one we must use," said Chief Gao.

"I believe he can do it," she acknowledged. "But he has committed an error, so he must pay the price for it. Especially since he failed to admit his error, he must be punished severely. This is a completely different issue to that of selecting him for a job, and the two cannot be lumped together."

One day she ran into Ji Hongmei who said bluntly, "Sister Daxiong, if you don't love him any more, that's the end of it. But why must you turn love into hate. He has been punished and sent to a labour camp. What else do you want? What Zhan did was a typical offence of dereliction of duty, but why don't you keep a close watch on him and uncover the whys and wherefores?"

Glaring at Ji Hongmei, she said, "The root of Zhan committing a crime was because he was deluded by fame and fortune, what else is there for me to uncover?"

Ji Hongmei walked away, leaving behind some harsh words, "You can only snap at Ji Zhenren, and not loosen your bite. To me, it is obvious that you are suffering from low self-esteem since your face was disfigured. Turning love into hate, you are a psychopath!" After Ji Hongmei had walked some distance, a fit of sad and shrill weeping came to her ears from behind.

No matter how the others complained, nothing and no one could hold up Ji Zhenren's study. In June 1936, he rejoined RSU2 without a hitch. He went straight to see Chief Gao, who said, "Zhenren, go through the enemy telegrams for the last year and start work as soon as possible."

"No, I must meet her first. You agreed that I can meet her."

"I almost forgot about it. It's OK for you to meet her, but you must observe proper restraint. Consider Daxiong's feelings. After all, you will date that woman under her nose."

"I understand. The proper restraint is for personal feelings, not for politics, because this woman has no political issues."

. . .

Following is what happened after Ji Zhenren was sent to study in the Anti-Japanese Military and Political College. His punishment was lifted, and at the weekend he went to the bookstore in town.

There was a reading area in the bookstore. After buying a book, customers were able to sit down and read the books they had just bought. It was always packed with readers and he had met some veteran Red Army soldiers, but most of the readers were passionate youths from all over the country. The brand new Eighth Route Army uniform could not conceal the vigour of their youth. Unsophisticated, these student soldiers were high in cultural attainment and had a particularly strong thirst for knowledge. They all entered the bookstore with great eagerness.

Sitting down, Ji Zhenren was reading Zou Taofen's *A Wandering Message*. From time to time he raised his head and his eyes fell on the backs of several readers in the front row. A female soldier sat down in an empty seat, bringing an extra back into his view. As she dropped into the seat, she carelessly threw a glance at the back row. This gaze caused his mind to drift from place to place. His eyes blurred, then glistened. The scene in the library in Shanghai appeared before his eyes, and his heart began to pound fiercely and irresistibly. He sensed that in the last two to three years he had never been like today in that he was so eagerly and strongly yearning for her. The sudden glance instantly opened the floodgate of feelings he had shut off for many years. Taking out a notebook and wielding a pen, he wrote down: Books and Life.

The whole morning he wrote passionately, as if he was narrating some soul-stirring stories. As midday approached, feeling satisfied he breathed out hard, and his writing came to an end. Under the title he wrote down a pen name: Caesar.

Then he saw the female soldier stand up and walk to a row of book shelves, with her back toward him. At the behest of supernatural powers he stood up and walked to the other side of the bookshelves, searching for that figure through the gaps.

She came into his view. Lowering her head, she was turning over the pages of a hardback book. Her eyes gazed softly at the pages, looking absorbed and delighted. It seemed that even if the bookshelves had fallen over, she would not have been disturbed. Her reading posture looked so much like HER, which was HER landmark appearance and also the scene grasping his heart the most.

Just at that moment, through a gap, her eyes fell on his. She did not turn her eyes away from him. Like reeling in a big fish that had taken the bait, she slowly tightened her grip. Bypassing the bookshelf she walked toward him with a mixed expression on her face. With her unusually piercing eyes, she gazed quietly at him for a while, then asked, "Are you looking at the book in my hand? You have stared at it for a long time. It is the *Collected Works of Lu Xun*, really worth reading. All the copies have been sold out except this one. If you like it, you can buy it first."

He came to his senses. Avoiding her eyes, he muttered, "No, I am reading Hu Yuzhi's and Zhang Hanfu's anti-Japanese series. They are very good. You might want to have a read." As he spoke, he walked away, flustered.

Sitting down and turning the pages, he could not calm down for a long time. Then a steamed bun stuffed with meat was put beside his book, and a soft voice said, "It's lunch time. I bought one for you as well." She sat down to eat her steamed bun while turning the pages of her book.

Pushing his hand into his pocket, he grinned with embarrassment, "I'm sorry, I spent all my money on books. I'm not hungry."

She smiled lightheartedly, saying, "It's only a steamed bun. Eat it while it's still warm. By the way, which unit are you from? You look like a civil official."

Chewing and swallowing a mouthful of the bun, he said, "Cavalry Regiment, a horsemanship instructor. My name is Niu Sangen."

"I'm Lan Keqiao, from the newspaper office, working for the *Liberation Weekly*."

He was so pleasantly surprised that he cried out, "What good luck! I've just finished writing an article, can I have it published in your magazine?" She took the manuscript and had only read the title when he took it back, muttering, "Forget it. It's too long. I don't think it is suitable for your magazine." Then he said, "I will find time to send the money for the bun to your office."

"Don't bother about it," she muttered.

A few days later, Chief Gao sent Ji Zhenren a message, asking him to return to RSU2 for something important. When he arrived, it was lunch time so he went to the mess first, where he unexpectedly met Lan

Keqiao. Song Daxiong introduced them to each other, "This is Ji Zhenren, our cryptographer. This is Gao Yuncao. Her previous name was Jiang Xiaodian. She's a new recruit to the preparatory class of our training team."

Ji Zhenren was so in shock that he nearly dropped his rice bowl onto the dinner table, while Gao Yuncao dropped her chopsticks on the floor, "You? How can you still be alive?"

In a trance, Ji Zhenren muttered, "You? Didn't you jump off the roof?"

Standing up, Gao Yuncao said, "Zhenren, let's go for a walk."

With a pained expression on his face, Ji Zhenren said, "I don't feel well. How about another day?"

After quickly having some food, he went straight to see Chief Gao. Song Daxiong also came. Chief Gao said, "We called you back just for this matter. We plan to employ a new student in our preparatory class but we found out that she worked in the Shanghai Telegraph Office at the same time you also worked there. In her biodata, she mentioned that she had escaped from the Shanghai underworld by pretending to have committed suicide by jumping off a building. She had a copy of the *Da Wan Bao* newspaper which reported the incident. I recalled that you were shot in Shanghai, which was connected to the incident. She was Jiang Xiaodian, now Gao Yuncao."

Ji Zhenren then gave a detailed account of what he knew about Jiang Xiaodian. "But as to how she had come back to life, or what had happened afterwards, I have no idea at all," he added.

Chief Gao said, "This Gao Yuncao has worked in telegraph offices. She knows English and Japanese, besides she used to secretly decipher customers' coded telegrams. A rare person, hard to find. We think she has indeed the makings of becoming a talented person. Speaking simply from a professional angle, after going through some training, there is a strong possibility that she will become an expert cryptographer. But the key issue is that she must be absolutely politically reliable."

Song Daxiong then introduced the initial examination of Gao Yuncao's political record.

Gao Yuncao (Jiang Xiaodian), was a technician in the Shanghai Telegraph Office before December 1931. Because her family had a secret society background, in the same year some old hostility and grievances surfaced and a fierce fight took place between her family and the underworld. In the end her grandfather Jiang Jinzhi was forced to flee Shanghai and live incognito in Guangzhou. Their enemies wanted to stamp out the source of trouble. It was the underworld power, the Gao family, who secretly planned the scheme and where Jiang Xiaodian pretended to be dead. She was saved and fled to Nanjing where she was recruited by the telegraph office. In 1937, after the Lugou (Marco Polo) Bridge Incident, she took part in protest marches organised by the young students in Nanjing. Cherishing the ideal of resisting Japanese aggression and saving the nation, she came to Yan'an, carrying with her a 'travel permit', a letter of introduction issued by our Party's office in Guangzhou. We firstly arranged for her to receive two weeks' training (actually for screening) in the 'Youth Salvation Federation' of the Central Committee of the Communist Youth League in Sanyuan County. She worked in Nanjing, so how could she have had a reference issued by Guangzhou? Her own explanation was that she came to Yan'an from Guangzhou where her grandfather was living, therefore her 'travel permit' was issued in Guangzhou.

In accordance with our relevant rules for youths from all over the country coming to Yan'an, as long as they have a letter of introduction or recommendation from the offices of our Party, or from a person of note, they can come directly to Yan'an. If they don't have one, they must go to the 'Youth Salvation Federation' in Sanyuan to receive training and screening, which was mainly to prevent the KMT, the Japanese and puppet government spies from sneaking into Yan'an. Gao Yuncao worked in Nanjing but she had a letter of introduction from Guangzhou, so she was regarded as having no letter of introduction and was sent to Sanyuan to be screened.

Song Daxiong had been in charge of the internal security of RSU2 for many years, so she was qualified to speak in this respect, "Under normal circumstances that apply to ordinary people, after screening, examination, training and education, we can use them. I have absolutely no problem with it. But my instinct tells me not to trust her. So I strongly advise we start a special investigation of her."

From a different angle, Chief Gao explained the necessity for doing so. His main thought was that Gao Yuncao might have the potential for technical development and the prospect of becoming a pillar of RSU2, thereby encountering core secrets. Therefore, they could not treat her as an ordinary person but had to subject her to a special investigation.

The so-called special investigation meant that the Political Security Bureau of the Military Commission and RSU2 joined forces, going to the ancestral home of the target of investigation as well as the places where she had worked and studied, cooperating with the local Party underground to carry out a secret investigation. They were effective means to ensure that the target of investigation would be absolutely reliable politically. Such investigations had been carried out before, but with restrictions.

Song Daxiong's mind wandered. She muttered, "Jiang Xiaodian was dead. How could she have come back to life? He is really lucky to be in love with beautiful women. Outside he has a girl from Jiangnan; at home he has a child bride. In any case he has someone to love."

"You are completely lost as long as you consider the issue of love with Ji Zhenren," said Chief Gao. "We are discussing proper business, but you are messing things up. You want trouble for Gao Yuncao, don't you!"

Ji Zhenren expressed his opinion at once. From the security point of view, he said, "We should send people to Shanghai, Nanjing and Guangzhou to investigate her. I suggest Song Daxiong goes with the comrades from the Political Security Burerau to accomplish this task."

Staring at him, Song Daxiong said, "Since you say so, I will go. I will smash this full, round and eye-catching Gao Yuncao to pieces, crushing her to a pulp and picking out the bone fragments to see whether she is actually black or red."

Pointing his finger at her, Chief Gao said, "This kind of fortitude can get the job done. You are the one to go! But everything must be done under absolute confidentiality. You must not disturb her or her grandfather, still less the KMT side; they mustn't know that we are investigating her."

Ji Zhenren knew very well what he had to do, so he said, "Before the final result of the investigation comes out, I will do my best to minimise contact with her."

"Not less, but absolutely no contact," said Chief Gao, pointing at him. "Focus on your study. You cannot come back before I call you. Wait for the investigation result. As long as there is no problem with her, I will let you see her publicly."

Two months later Song Daxiong returned. The investigation

materials were placed on file in the Political Security Bureau, while one copy was sent to RSU2. The main points were:

1. Jiang Xiaodian's grandfather, Jiang Zhijing, changed his name to Gao Fuhai. He opened a cotton mill in Guangzhou where he had close relations with a store selling textiles, which became our underground liaison post and would often receive financial help from Jiang Zhijing, who had completely extricated himself from the underworld's nagging, gradually becoming open-minded in his political awareness. He accepted the new ideology passed onto him by the store staff and also did good deeds for our underground. He often visited his granddaughter Jiang Xiaodian in Nanjing. She also went to Guangzhou on holiday. According to the store staff's observations, Jiang Xiaodian was strongly influenced by her grandfather, having a strong mentality of saving the nation, a typical progressive youth. Our underground organisation in the store trusted them both. Jiang Zhijing and the store staff had supported both Gao Yuncao's active engagement in anti-Japanese activities and her departure for Yan'an. Our store staff introduced her to our Party's office in Guangzhou to receive necessary examinations, where she went through related formalities for going to Yan'an.

2. Her stated reason, the sequence of events and the details of the incident which led Jiang Xiaodian to leave Shanghai and look for a job in Nanjing, matched exactly what the Shanghai underground had learned. She also mentioned this incident in her written material when she joined the training class, which was also consistent with what the Shanghai underground had learned; besides which, there was a newspaper report as evidence. Now it seems that Ji Zhenren had seen her jumping off the building with his own eyes. According to Jiang Xiaodian, the reason for her not to inform Ji Zhenren of the truth beforehand was so that he would act realistically at the time. She had intended to explain to him afterwards. But no one could have foreseen that he would also be hit by a bullet in the chaos of the gun fight, still less would any one have expected that our Red Brigade and Liu

Kailai would have saved Ji Zhenren, as well as faked someone's death. In her written material, Jiang Xiaodian mentioned "unfortunately my boyfriend was shot dead accidentally in my fake death scheme".

3. After Jiang Xiaodian arrived in Nanjing, through the recommendation of Gao Q, a former colleague in Shanghai, she was employed as a technician by the Nanjing Telegraph Office. Gao Q was originally the deputy head of Section Two, Telecommunications Department, Ministry of Communications of the KMT government. He was dispatched to the Shanghai Telegraph Office to be in charge of technical work, a colleague of Ji Zhenren and Jiang Xiaodian. The Gao clan has an underworld background in Shanghai and they saved the Jiangs when they were in dire peril. Gao Q was clearly the power behind this Gao clan. Later he was transferred back to Nanjing and has worked in the Nanjing Telegraph Office ever since. To avoid being hunted down by the underworld from Shanghai, Jiang Xiaodian changed her name to Gao Yuncao and worked in the Nanjing Telegraph Office. Some of our underground comrades in Nanjing secretly photographed her personal file and her monthly pay slips, which had her signature.

4. Regarding Gao Yuncao's personal love life (originally the comrades from the Political Security Bureau thought there was no need to include it in this material; it was Song Daxiong who insisted that it be included). When she was in Shanghai, Jiang Xiaodian had a boyfriend called Ji Zhenren. Meanwhile she also had a dubious relationship with Gao Q, consequently her two love rivals fought a duel before a big crowd. At the time the 'Da Wan Bao' newspaper determined the nature of the incident as being that she had died for love. Although we now know that the duel was a scheme set up by Gao Q and Jiang Xiaodian, we cannot rule out the fact that Jiang Xiaodian had a foot in both camps. After arriving in Nanjing and learning that Ji Zhenren had died, she openly chased Gao Q. The love affair only ended because Gao Q already had a lover. In this respect her own account matches what our underground learned.

Song Daxiong had put her trust in Gao Yuncao in every possible way. Unusually excited, she said to Chief Gao, "I'm confident there is absolutely no problem with her. Successively the Youth Union and our training class have examined her using routine methods. Then the Political Security Bureau and the related underground organisations investigated her by unusual means. She has passed all the screening, so you can trust her and use her boldly. She has a professional foundation in telegraphy and knows two foreign languages."

After the investigation ended, Chief Gao did not call Ji Zhenren back to RSU2.

Anxious yet unable to ask Chief Gao about it, Ji Zhenren constantly went to the bookstore, going every Sunday and hoping to meet that familiar face.

Finally he saw it, but she was with Song Daxiong, whom he was also eager to meet. She told him, "She is a very good person. We found nothing wrong with her, so you can rest assured and enjoy yourself." He understood, saying inwardly: "The true her, after all, is still alive."

He completed his studies at the Anti-Japanese Military and Political College and rejoined RSU2. The first thing he wanted to do was to meet Gao Yuncao. Not refusing him this time, Chief Gao handed him a pink pen, saying, "When we were in the Jiangxi Soviet, you handed this pledge of love to me to keep. Now I return it to you. You are indulging in love, but I hope you can still perform your duty scrupulously." Taking the pen, he saw the name 'Jiang Xiaodian', turning around he left in a hurry.

No one could witness what it was like when he and Gao Yuncao met and recalled the past. But when he ran into Song Daxiong at the basketball court, they got angry with each other during their conversation, which was witnessed by many people. He was heard saying, "The fourth part of your investigation material is not serious and precise. There was no love between her and Gao Q, so where did the fighting for love and dying for love come from?"

Song Daxiong deliberately raised her voice, "Two men came to blows over a woman, what do you call it?" When he was about to say something, he was hit on the chest by a basketball that flew at him, and the person who had lost the ball was none other than Gao Yuncao. The spectators sighed. A beautiful cut-off in the half way line, she finished her run and was about to raise her arms to shoot, but the ball flew straight toward Ji Zhenren, who was struck dumb.

"Did you see?" said Song Daxiong. "She wants you to shut up."

His eyes popped with surprise: What a rare thing! How can she play basketball?

"Her ball skills are superb and she has a consuming passion for basketball,"muttered Song Daxiong. "It is said that some years ago when she went to Jinling College for Girls to see friends, by chance she watched a basketball match played by students from the sports department. Afterwards she was mad about basketball. After she came to RSU2, she could not restrain her love for the game so she taught many female colleagues how to play it. Chief Gao gave his permission for us to organise a women's basketball team and she was the captain, often leading the team to play against the men's team. As captain and playing forward, all the men's eyes were on her. Whether their minds were on the ball or on her breasts was hard to tell; besides, players would often knock arms and run into her chest so one day such knocks may set off some sort of spark. Ji Zhenren, you must keep an eye on it."

Watching the game attentively, Ji Zhenren's eyes were fixated on Gao Yuncao and he was oblivious to what Song Daxiong was talking about. "Hey, your eyes are glued on that sleeveless shirt," she grumbled.

Gao Yuncao ran three steps and took a shot at the basket. The spectators were stunned, not by her beautiful shot but by her knocking down an opponent. Taking a look, Song Daxiong saw that the player knocked to the ground was a senior officer. Everyone knew that he liked playing basketball, but to be knocked down by such a powerful move was a rare scene. Song Daxiong called out, "Foul! Send her off!" But the referee let the score stand.

Bending down, Gao Yuncao held her knees, puffing and panting. With a smile on her face she said to the senior officer, "Sir, you wanted to stop me but you couldn't do it. Why don't you go and take a rest."

Jumping to his feet, the senior officer said, "There should be reasonable body contact. You bullied me, an aged player; but gentlemen's revenge will not be late coming after ten years."

Still puffing, Gao Yuncao said, "No need to wait for ten years. I concede your next shot. Why don't you take a long-range shot at the basket?"

"No, two shots," said the senior officer, laughing. From a distance he shot the ball into the basket twice. The spectators cheered loudly. Not knowing what was going on, Song Daxiong still cheered hard for the senior officer, while inwardly she was jealous when she saw Gao Yuncao whispering head to head with the senior officer.

That was not the first time Gao Yuncao had played basketball with the senior officer. When she first met him on the basketball court, she did not know him. They bumped into each other several times. She muttered to herself, "This uncle can play basketball very well, but he can also foul opponents savagely, like a black bull." She stopped him from shooting the ball at the basket, while cleverly making use of the match rules she bumped against him, making him fall to the ground head over heels.

Instantly a few players sprang on the senior officer and pulled him up, asking anxiously, "Officer, are you all right?" Gao Yuncao was stunned.

Walking over to her, the senior officer asked, "Are you all right, young girl?"

"Are you really a senior officer?" she asked.

The officer pointed at the number on his shirt, saying, "Player Number 10, an ordinary soldier." She bowed hurriedly and apologised. The senior officer laughed, "In sport players on the field should not respect each other like guests, otherwise how can we play matches? You brilliantly stopped me from passing the ball and your tackle on me was also very clever. You did not break the rules so I have to keep my complaint to myself."

She regained her composure, saying with a grin, "You are so broad-minded and generous. So I will have a free hand in my playing to make sure you enjoy yourself to the full."

The senior officer laughed again, "Do what you want."

She instantly warmed to this basketball friend, muttering to herself: "There is such a senior officer in the world. I like it!"

Before the 'Grasshopper' plan was put into practice, those who devised it made some very meticulous preparations.

The Special Secret Wireless Section of the Military Council of the KMT government directly drew up the plan. After discussion and deliberation, it was submitted to three higher levels for examination and approval. An official called Tang added one particular detail: to let 'Grasshopper' learn to play basketball. His reasoning was that when the KMT troops went to stamp out the Red Army, after capturing the ground of the Red Army's headquarters which was relocated several times, they always saw simply-built basketball courts. On one occasion they captured some weaponry, among which there was a folding basketball board with a hoop. In such a brutal war and under such harsh conditions, those who had such a refined mood and were able to carry on playing basketball on the life-and-death battlefields had to be rather extraordinary people. Later they discovered that these people who were so passionate about playing basketball were some Red Army senior officers, who had been running the central headquarters basketball competition for several years running. Therefore, letting 'Grasshopper' learn to play basketball was not a bad thing.

It was so prudent in minor details that we could imagine how comprehensive the whole plan was.

'Grasshopper' was none other than Gao Yuncao. The heart of the plan was to dispatch her to infiltrate RSU2, to find out about the technical circumstances inside the unit, to make use of her technical superiority to cleverly throw the unit's work into disorder, to mislead the deciphering work onto the wrong path and prevent the Red Army from cracking the ciphers of the KMT army at the crucial moment. It has to be said that this was an extremely special mission, and those in the know were restricted to several main officials of the KMT Military Council, as well as Gao Q and Zhen Yanli who were cryptography experts.

The plan had long been at an embryonic stage, making no substantial progress. After the KMT and the Communists began to cooperate with each other from the spring of 1937, the KMT Military Council sent a delegation to Yan'an on an inspection visit. They demanded to visit RSU2, intending to see what the unit, which had cracked the KMT armies' ciphers time and again, looked like; particularly to see who the cryptographers were. The Yan'an side readily agreed, welcoming the delegation's visit to the unit. But what they saw were a few rooms with some desks and chairs and some student soldiers sitting here and there. When they asked about the numbers of staff, the answer was that all the staff were present. After the delegation returned home, the Special Secret Wireless Section was determined to adopt special measures to find out RSU2's interception strength, deciphering methodology and inside information. Only then was the 'Grasshopper' plan activated.

Viewed from the actual effect, the reason for 'Grasshopper' to be able to successfully hide in Yan'an's core confidential department depended on four factors.

First, the ability of Gao Q and Gao Yuncao to make themselves invisible for a long time. For years they were permanent staff of the Nanjing Telegraph Office, using false identities to carry out the duty of secret agents, secretly monitoring the wireless communications of all circles and factions while cleverly camouflaging their activities. When Gao Yuncao had to go and attend training for secret agents, or go and execute some secret military assignments in other parts of the country, she had invented all sorts of plausible excuses, such as sick leave, compassionate leave and technical training. The other staff felt such leave was normal, and when the underground made investigations, they found nothing wrong about her either. Even her own grandfather had no idea that she was a KMT secret agent.

Second, the authenticity of Gao Yuncao's files in Shanghai and Nanjing. Not a single falsified account was found in her files and every item was true. She did not talk ambiguously in her written statement to RSU2, still less did she tell any lies, including her relationship with Ji Zhenren and Gao Q.

Third, the early preparation of a sure-fire plan to secretly pave the way to collude with the Communists. The KMT secret agents had kept a close watch on the textile store, a communist underground stronghold in Guangzhou. But after they found out the ambiguous relations between Jiang Zhijing and the store, they withdrew their surveillance, allowing the store to carry out activities as it pleased, besides, ordering that Jiang Zhijing must not be disturbed for his anti-Chiang Kai-shek and anti-KMT remarks and deeds. The purpose was obvious, letting Jiang Zhijing, a former underworld member who had turned over a new leaf and become a Communist, create a favourable family environment for Jiang Xiaodian to enter Yan'an. Of course, when Jiang Xiaodian pretended to be a progressive in Guangzhou, the KMT had helped her to achieve her aim. Eventually the underground formed a good opinion of the Jiangs and came to trust them.

Fourth, Gao Yuncao's telegraph office experience and her professional strength, which were the main objective qualifications for her to gain a foothold in Yan'an and also the main thing that made her attractive to RSU2.

Therefore, when Ji Zhenren unexpectedly appeared before her, returning to life after death, Gao Yuncao did not feel it was a crisis. Of course the stupefied expression on her face when meeting the 'live ghost' was real.

After taking root at RSU2, Gao Yuncao finished phase one of the 'Grasshopper' plan. Of course she came here not to play basketball or have fun. For phase two she had to rely on her technical strength and rise through the ranks into a key technical post in the unit.

Her technical level was already quite high. In the Special Secret Wireless Section, Gao Q, Zhen Yanli and herself were notable staff and core technical personnel. But now in RSU2 she had to hide her real level, making it appear as though her technical level in telegraphy was only average and that at most she had deciphered some customers' coded telegrams in secret. She could not suddenly reveal her superb technical ability, otherwise she would let the cat out of the bag. So when RSU2 assigned her as a trainee monitor, she was extremely careful, trying to make the others believe that she was truly a trainee, new to her job and made errors from time to time.

She warned herself that she had to progress slowly, in accordance with the pattern of development of a monitor progressing from trainee to intermediate to top performance, waiting for the chance to be a cryptographer, then a top cryptographer. She had to choose an opportunity to achieve instant fame, then crack a few ciphers in a row to lay the foundation for being an expert cryptographer, finally becoming a core member and an authority of the unit to control the whole deciphering work. Only then could she meet the requirements of fulfilling key tasks of the 'Grasshopper' plan. Of course, during this long process, she had to remember her other task, namely, to ensure her own safety while sending out important intelligence she had gathered about the Communist troops to the Special Secret Wireless Section. But if RSU2 was heavily guarded and she could not send her intelligence out, she was allowed to halt her spying activities and go into hibernation.

As soon as she took on her work, she displayed immense zeal for it and great interest in learning. On Sundays, she would get up early, do her laundry, then spend the whole day in the bookstore in town. She knew the unit rules. No matter whether for business or personal matters, nobody could go out of the compound on their own. There had to be a minimum of three people going out together, so she invited

Ji Zhenren who in turn invited Song Daxiong, who agreed to accompany them. But when she saw Gao Yuncao, she found an excuse to decline. Gao Yuncao then found Ji Hongmei and they went to Chief Gao to ask for permission to go out.

Once out of the compound, Gao Yuncao was so excited that she suggested they walk around the town first. Ji Zhenren said, "We asked to go to the bookstore when we sought permission to leave the compound. It is not right if we change the route."

"Yuncao is new to Yan'an," said Ji Hongmei, "We'll only have a quick walk around, so there shouldn't be any problem if we mention nothing about it."

Ji Zhenren, by not allowing a change to the permitted route, showed his overcautious character. In this respect he was the same person as years before. However, Gao Yuncao still noticed changes in him, as now he was often fervent at heart, but icy cold in appearance. Anyway all the other staff were the same. They always liked to handle affairs in a very low-key way, which added a dignified tranquility to the solemn environment; patiently putting up with things became subconscious daily behaviour for them. Gao Yuncao had repeatedly warned herself that she had to fit into her new surroundings and new habits and that she must never display her individuality, but endure whatever she could.

But she did not want to restrain herself today. Everything was novel in her eyes; she stopped constantly, easily getting surprised and excited.

There was a forge in an open shed.

A furnace and two anvils stood in the centre where two masters and two apprentices were wielding four hammers of different sizes. Holding a large hammer, each apprentice forged hard on the metal. Turning the metal over with pincers in his left hand, each master held a smaller hammer in his right hand, striking the metal with a specific rhythm to command the apprentice to forge, while tapping lightly to correct the key positions. Finally they forged the semi-finished product into some kind of utensil.

Ji Zhenren used his ears to 'see' the hammers, which were different in size for different jobs and used in different forging stages, flying up and down. Listening, he then understood something. Calling Gao Yuncao and Ji Hongmei over to him, he said, "Close your eyes first and listen strike by strike; then open your eyes and watch strike by strike. What can you discover?"

The blacksmiths had made three utensils. Shaking her head impatiently, Ji Hongmei grumbled, "I only heard the disorderly sound of *ding-dong* noises. My mind is in chaos."

Gao Yuncao smiled, "There is a pattern in the sound, but I don't know what sort of pattern."

In a low voice, Ji Zhenren said, "A monitor's listening skill can be judged by their sensitivity to sound, which not only applies to the sound of telegrams being sent. Listen, the hammer's striking sound implies a scientific principle. You don't believe me? Well, let's have a test." Borrowing a scale from a butcher, he weighed every hammer, while Ji Hongmei marked the hammers.

Three more utensils were made. The two girls looked on wide-eyed. Yes indeed, the hammers' sound did mean something.

Holding a small hammer, one master said, "I have been a blacksmith for thirty-five years. For the first twenty years or more I used dozens of hammers and I did not discover the regular pattern of this sound. Afterwards I realised this particular characteristic." Seizing Ji Zhenren's hand, he continued, "It is either that your ancestors were blacksmiths so they passed this wonderful ability on to you, or that you are an exceptional man with an exceptional ear. You only watched us for a short while but you caught on to this profound theory. Come on, what you are doing? Where did you get your amazing hearing ability from?"

"Both my father and grandfather were blacksmiths," said Ji Zhenren, hastily.

One apprentice looked at his skinny physique, muttering, "You don't look like the son of a blacksmith."

Gao Yuncao pulled Ji Zhenren to her, crying, "Hey, you are not your father's son, whose son are you? You've got yourself into trouble."

Ji Hongmei gave her a smack, snapping, "Shut up! Let's go, we need to go and buy books."

Looking anxious, Ji Zhenren said, "Let's go back to the unit!"

"I was only kidding," said Gao Yuncao. "How can you take it so seriously?"

"Let's go back immediately!" shouted Ji Zhenren.

He hurried away. Half way, he called Ji Hongmei to him, "Let's discuss that cipher." As soon as she heard this sentence, Gao Yuncao sensibly kept some distance from them. The unit had its security regulation that they should refrain from reading or listening to anything they were not supposed to. Despite the distance, she could still hear bits and pieces of their argument. To an outsider these off-and-on words would have been blurred and indistinct, but Gao Yuncao was able to get the general gist of what they were about: these two cryptographers had been enlightened by some outside factors and they had suddenly hit upon an idea of how to crack a certain cipher. In other words, they might have found the solution to a specific cipher. Pretending to walk leisurely behind them, she pricked up her ears and tried hard to listen.

She knew that when they passed the forge, from the noises Ji Zhenren heard a harmonious blend of sound emitted by the hammers forging pieces of iron. This remarkable man had discovered that some hammers could make a harmonious sound, while others could only make a racket. After an analysis of the hammers, he had discovered that there was an internal mathematical relationship between the hammers that could make a harmonious sound, namely, that there was a ratio between their weight and the sound they made. That is to say, the hammers that weighed half, a third or a quarter of a particular piece of hammer, could produce a harmonious sound. However, the hammers with no such relationship when struck together only produced random noise.

Gao Yuncao overheard fragments of the conversation between Ji Zhenren and Ji Hongmei. Linking in her mind the mathematical principles learned from forging iron, she was terrified. This cipher was XIN! Yes, the Ji brother and sister will soon decipher XIN.

She cursed inwardly: "That stiff-necked Sheng Keneng, a fool who always regarded himself as infallible. Why did he rush into using his creation XIN?"

Sheng Keneng was a cipher compiler for the KMT troops commanded by general Hu Zongnan. When Gao Yuncao was appointed as the candidate to infiltrate Yan'an and intense preparations were under way, Sheng reported that General Hu's troops were planning to use XIN. At the time she did not have enough time to determine the cipher's degree of difficulty, but judging from her experience and instinct, she reckoned it would not be very difficult to crack. But Sheng insisted that his cipher was unbreakable, suggesting that the Special Secret Wireless Section give permission to use it, and also saying that it was General Hu's wish as well. She was about to set out for Yan'an, so she did not argue any more but handed the matter to her successor. Now it seemed that the Nanjing side had failed to make strict checks before letting *XIN* out of the bag.

From the conversation between brother and sister Ji, Gao Yuncao overheard that RSU2 had intercepted messages encrypted by *XIN*, and that they had accidentally been enlightened by the blacksmiths forging iron, giving them an insight into what made *XIN* tick. Then she called to mind that Sheng might have been the son of a blacksmith in Xi'an. Now it could be said that he might have grown up among his father's *ding-dong* sounds and already knew about the relationship between the weight of hammers and the sound they produced. With such inspiration, when he compiled ciphers, he had incorporated the profound lessons forged by his father for decades into a cipher, giving it its name *XIN* (鑫), a Chinese character derived from combining three metal (金) radicals, indicating that his family had a specific affinity with ironware.

XIN was about to be annihilated!

As expected, that night became the end of *XIN*.

It was impossible for a trainee monitor to be told of such a secret. Gao Yuncao speculated about it based on the temporary adjustment of the monitoring assignment. Early the next morning, Song Daxiong hurriedly arranged for the monitors to monitor the signals on a certain frequency used by General Hu's troops. Chief Gao also came, saying, "My instinct tells me that Hu's many radio frequencies and transceivers are using this cipher. Cast the net wide and search for the pattern of the signals to catch every one of them."

Gao Yuncao stayed at her desk for a day and night, no one could persuade her to take a break. She said, "I'm a new hand. If I don't push myself, when will I become an old hand?" Constantly she tuned the frequencies, searching for the few needles in the haystack, but in fact her mind was in turmoil. She repeatedly asked herself, "What should I do?" In the end she focused her mind on one question: what was the real possibility of Song Daxiong and the other monitors finding these needles? Her judgement was: they can capture them all in one haul in the next day or two.

So she searched for a new radio frequency and found it before everyone else. She transcribed a message. She found another new frequency three hours later and transcribed a message. Again a few hours later she transcribed another two messages on the third and fourth new frequencies. Pretending that she had no idea about what she had transcribed, she handed the messages to Song Daxiong, saying, "I have transcribed four messages on four frequencies. They look to be encrypted by the same cipher but I don't know what."

Song Daxiong said nothing but went straight to see Chief Gao. Returning to the office, she was very excited, "You've achieved a rare feat of correctly guessing the enemy radio frequencies by relying on a mathematical ratio, the knowledge gained from the blacksmiths forging ironware. Yuncao, you are a very good trainee, showing great promise at monitoring radio signals. With this foundation, you just go full steam ahead with your work!"

The intercepted messages showed that the KMT had not changed its trick of false cooperation but was truly anti-Communist. The intention of seeking opportunities to create anti-Communist friction was very obvious, and they had begun to take military action to encircle and crush the Eighth Route Army troops.

After detecting and cracking *XIN*, Ji Zhenren called on Gao Yuncao and Ji Hongmei and they went to the bookstore to make up for the trip they had missed last time. On the way Gao Yuncao said, "Blacksmiths forging iron and cipher cracking have no relevance whatsoever to each other. A cryptographer, relying on their remarkable powers of observation, imagination and aggression, combined the two together and smashed *XIN*. Ji Zhenren, you are really an exceptional person. More inspiration for today?"

"In our profession, sometimes we do rely on a flash of inspiration based on our rich experience," said Ji Zhenren.

"The enemy cipher compiler might be like you, also the son of an old blacksmith." Gao Yuncao laughed.

"I wonder if there is someone who would like to be the daughter-in-law of an old blacksmith?" teased Ji Zhenren, also laughing.

"Don't think too much about this. You were Song Daxiong's man a long time ago and everyone in RSU2 knows it," countered Gao Yuncao.

"She didn't agree with it before, still less so now. She intends to return me to my former girlfriend," said Ji Zhenren.

"Song Daxiong has had such a close relationship with you for years. Any novelty with you has worn off, so who else would want you? You must not fancy yourself as being very attractive to the opposite sex," said Gao Yuncao, with a faint smile.

Becoming reserved, Ji Zhenren was quiet for a long time.

That night he invited Gao Yuncao to have a walk in the courtyard and they talked about Song Daxiong again.

"The profound feelings between Daxiong and I are mostly about revolutionary friendship and duty, which were determined by the professional characteristics of a cryptographer in the special war environment. Firstly, our mission required us to work as a team, so neither of us could take into consideration that I was a man and she was a woman. To put it simply, both of us had had our hearts broken and kneaded into one, giving everything, including our lives, to one another. But our relationship, like the one between men and women, is still a blank sheet of paper. This is mainly my problem. At the time our soldiers' lives occupied my mind, so I could not spare even a tiny bit of my mood and energy for anything but codes and ciphers. I regarded each cipher as the last one in my life to tackle, because I really did not know when I would die at my post. Every day I was like a fool, unable to look after myself. Involuntarily she gave me the same affection as between a sister and a brother, or the love a mother would give to her son. Each day was as if she was looking after a child. At the time the war was extremely cruel. I myself dared not imagine how she had managed to get me through it alive. So the feelings between her and me, how should I put it...? In my heart she was my right and proper lover and my diehard wife, but at the same time she was my elder sister and my mother. Naturally I would show how timid I was in front of her and went to her to pour out all my grief and depression. She said that after the revolution was victorious, and after she had eaten steamed buns for a month, she would present me with a plump and beautiful Song Daxiong. But now she feels that she has lost the hearing in one of her ears and her face is disfigured. She is no longer good-looking, so she does not allow me to love her any more. She feels that I should have a better companion. After Ji Hongmei appeared, like someone not right in the head, she wanted to push Hongmei toward me. Now you have come, so she is trying hard to bring us together, feeling that you are my best companion. No one understands her better than I do. Now she absolutely does not want to be my wife. With regard to the love between a man and a woman, she keeps her distance from me; but regarding feelings between comrades-in-arms, showing political solicitude for me and caring, she can't do without me. This has fallen into a pattern. In this life she will not take me as her husband.

Yuncao, this is everything you need to know about me and Song Daxiong. What should I do? Please help me."

Tears welled up in Gao Yuncao's eyes, but she managed to restrain herself, "The relationship between you and Song Daxiong is so rare and precious. I am so amazed by this kind of attachment. It is touching and a hundred per cent sincere. From you two I know that the feelings between a man and a woman can also be like this, which can never be understood in Nanjing, or in the telegraph offices, or even in other armies. What sort of army is this that can produce such a rare relationship between people!"

Ji Zhenren closed his eyes tight, tears streaming down his cheeks. Gao Yuncao's facial expression changed from touching to firm, and she said, "Just now you asked me what you should do. You make your own decision. Don't expect me to be able to help you. Don't dream of making me a second Song Daxiong. I will not concern myself with your personal affairs." She turned around and left.

Ji Zhenren caught up with her and handed her an article he had written, "I wrote this in the bookstore when I first saw you in Yan'an. These days I often think of my days and nights in Shanghai. I think about them very hard, in great detail and very imaginatively."

Taking the article, she read it, "You also mentioned me in it?"

He nodded, "I wrote about the relationship between us and books and life."

"I would like to have a proper read," she said, and went on with what she wanted to say.

"I think you should marry her, and you must marry her. Otherwise you will have no peace of mind for the rest of your life. If you do not marry her, everybody will feel that Heaven has treated her unfairly. If you marry a different woman, she will live her life always the object of other people's curiosity, and you will become a heartless and dirty person. Didn't you ask for my help? This is the solution I have worked out for you, the only bright and smooth road leading you to happiness."

"But at the bottom of her heart she ruthlessly dug up this road a long time ago."

"Where she dug it up, is where you build a bridge. She digs up endlessly, endlessly you build bridges."

Gao Yuncao did not return to her dormitory but hung around for a long time. She was clear in her mind that in this mysterious courtyard and in everyone's eyes, she was only a trainee. She had to make sure that she fitted into the circumstances, avoiding any of her words and deeds from giving her away involuntarily. Although she was experienced, smart and was able to see through inexplicable things, she had to pretend to be the opposite.

However, in Yan'an was she really a smart woman who could see through inexplicable things?

In the years when she served in the KMT army, because of her profession, she knew more about the Communist Party and its army than the KMT's combat troop commanders did. But her understanding of this army's intrinsic quality was from the days after she came to Yan'an. Despite the fact that she could not discover any more secrets, but was only able to observe through the eyes of an ordinary person, it was not a hard thing to make out something substantial. And some of these things were enough to change her way of thinking to some extent.

For instance, the Communist army fought with the KMT army for many years. Most of the time, their operational plans were all made on the basis that they had extremely precise knowledge of the KMT army's intentions. Conversely, when the KMT army studied the Red Army, they virtually never pondered a problem from this basic point. Therefore the countermeasures they formulated lost their factual basis. Detailed information and intelligence had changed the original concept of this war, yet the KMT army failed to realise it for a long time.

Once she asked Ji Zhenren about the relationship between intelligence support and winning a battle. By using some generals' views, he said, "The commander of an army must either have the right determination, or have comprehensive, timely and accurate intelligence. Without them, it is difficult for the commander to make a correct decision. However, although intelligence is available, without a commander who is good at using it, the intelligence is only a piece of waste paper."

In the past what she heard most was that the Red Army was an army with a low literacy level synonymous with being a bunch of 'country bumpkins' or 'clodhoppers'. After she arrived in Yan'an, her personal experience told her that this army's commanders were extremely cultured, and their mastery of Chinese traditional culture and their understanding of China's actual situation were generally higher than those in the upper strata of the KMT army. Meanwhile there was a

military presence that could not be ignored - RSU2. This unit was an elite
team imbued with traditional Chinese culture. If one picked out a
cryptographer at random, one could see that their mastery of the
connotations of traditional Chinese culture was not inferior to that of the
KMT's high-ranking officers, and their studies of actual Chinese
conditions were no less than the KMT army's policymaking level. RSU2
was very well aware of the soldiers' morale and the will of the generals in
the KMT Central Army and the warlord armies; they knew as much
about them as they knew about their own family members. They read
their coded messages as though they were reading letters from home,
being able to quickly sense what was in these generals' minds behind the
words. The central leaders in Yan'an knew many rarely known inside
stories at all levels of the KMT army, and quite often they were able to
know whatever they wanted. However, even many of the KMT high-
ranking generals knew nothing about these circumstances for a long time.

Thinking about this, Gao Yuncao felt a heavy responsibility on her
shoulders, complaining inwardly: for these years one of the biggest
miscalculations of the KMT was that they had taken no notice of the
need to maintain the secrecy of wireless communications, and that they
had looked down on the Red Army's wireless reconnaissance force.

As if in a daydream, she murmured to herself: "What should I do?"

A human shadow suddenly darted out of the corner of the wall
from behind. To act in accordance with the usual practice, when under
attack by someone in the dark she should quickly have moved one step
to her righthand side, then turned around and pinned the assailant to
the ground. So with a conditioned response, she quickly side-stepped
to her right, ready to turn around and pin the person down, but she
suddenly remembered that she must not let the others see that she was
a well trained secret agent. Halting her movement, she dropped to one
side onto the floor, mumbling, "Ouch, who is this? You scared me
terribly!"

It was Song Daxiong. Helping Gao Yuncao to her feet, she said,
"You're very distressed, aren't you? I heard you asking yourself what
you should do? What else can you do? It is only right and proper that
you and he reunite after the separation. No, look at my lousy mouth.
You two have never been separated. I have an intimate understanding
of Ji Zhenren. All these years after you 'died', he always had you in his
heart. He never accepted my affection."

Standing still, Gao Yuncao mumbled, "Don't you think that I should not have come back to life? And you don't want to see me, a living ghost, in the loess plateau, do you?"

"Yuncao, I'm speaking from the bottom of my heart. I truly wish you and he can be together as soon as possible. After life and death experiences, it is not easy for him to live, and less easy for him to see his former lover. This is destiny and Heaven's will."

"You two came through life and death together, if you don't become husband and wife, none of the citizens in Yan'an will agree. If I take your place, those Red Army veterans will draw their pistols to kill me," said Gao Yuncao.

"To tell the truth, he and I fought shoulder to shoulder, sharing weal and woe, as well as love. If I ask him to marry me, he will neither demur at it, nor have any complaints whatsoever. And here you are, still alive, so let's stop arguing. This is a decree by Old Heaven that he is yours."

"It seems that I must die again. But even if I should die, I will not marry him. You can set your mind at ease, Daxiong. A while ago he wailed and whined, saying that he simply had to marry you."

"Really? I know that he cried because he felt grateful to me, which had nothing to do with love. The seed you sowed in Shanghai should have bloomed and borne fruit a long time ago, so what are you waiting for? These days he might have lost sleep because he was thinking of you. I am skinny and bony, besides I am disfigured and mute, so I can give him nothing."

"Sister Song, what are you talking about? He is not that kind of person. He would never forsake you."

"Is it you, or I that understands him? Quick, decide to marry him, so I can set my mind at rest."

"Now that I'm dead, I'll die forever. Will I marry him? Absolutely impossible. No matter who would try to force me or how, it's still impossible. You'd better give up the idea. If it were not for the revolutionary ideal that drew me to Yan'an, I would leave you. But not yet. I came here not for him, but for the revolution. Therefore, let me do my revolutionary work, and let him marry you, so neither will be abandoned but mutually benefit."

"Let's wait and see. It is true that I have saved his life. But this time I must personally hand him to you, so as to thoroughly save his life.

His life is on you. Without you, he would rather die than live. Please do believe me this time."

"I don't love him any more. Jiang Xiaodian has died, do you understand?"

"But why did you come here if you don't love him any more?"

"He died in Shanghai a long time ago. I say it again, I came here to join the revolution."

Two months after the above conversation took place, one evening when Gao Yuncao walked into the mess, she noticed that two meaty dishes and half a bottle of sorghum spirit had been added to each table, all of which had been fully taken. As soon as she took her seat, and before she could ask what the meal was for, she saw Chief Gao walking in. In high spirits, he announced, "Today is a day of great happiness. A bride and a bridegroom are going to wed. Ever since Comrade Song Daxiong joined the revolutionary ranks, she has been standing together through thick and thin with RSU2, going through all the past struggles against the KMT's encirclement and suppression as well as the Long March. She has engaged with the revolution heart and soul and distinguished herself in action. Finally she is to resolve her personal issue. Our Daxiong is getting married today!"

No news about the marriage had been heard previously. How could it be that she suddenly was to get married? Completely in shock, Gao Yuncao's eyes swept from table to table, seeing no sign of Song Daxiong or Ji Zhenren.

In Yan'an it was not an unusual thing for the Red Army veterans who had gone through the Long March to suddenly announce who would marry whom, but Gao Yuncao still felt the announcement had come as a surprise. Although the marriage was within the bounds of reason, or a circumstance that would happen sooner or later, and although she had repeatedly urged them to do so, when the time actually came, it still took her by surprise. She felt lost, completely lost.

Song Daxiong was going to marry him. Was it real? Didn't she say that she would absolutely not marry him?

Her sense of loss then turned to resentment: you are going to be a bridegroom. But why did you mention nothing about it to me? You should at least have told me about it. I don't want you to get bogged down in our love affair in Shanghai. I also understand the love between you and Song Daxiong that was established in the flames of war. But, after all, I have re-appeared before you, alive and kicking. You are to give your love life a result, but you should also give me a simple explanation. I'd be happy even if it was only a few casual words.

You heartless man. Do you know how I have wished that we could resume our love affair in Shanghai. Since I saw you still alive, I have been happy in my heart every day, often being woken up at night by the laughter in my dreams. Although in front of you and her, I spared no effort to help you two to get married, that was all for show. I was saying one thing and meaning another and I spoke with my tongue in my cheek. In fact I need your love more than Song Daxiong does. My heart, my passion and my everything needs it.

Thinking and complaining, she couldn't help picking up the wine bottle. Raising her head she gulped down a big mouthful of liquor. Everyone at the table heard the noise. Their eyes turned from Chief Gao to her face. Not noticing it, she gulped down another mouthful. Only after someone gave her a pat on the back did she realise that she had lost control of herself.

The liquor stimulated her nerves. Feeling her spirits buoyed up, she forced a smile, saying inwardly: was it easy for the couple to get to where they are today? Do I really think that they should not be together? Gao Yuncao, what a mentality you have!

Chief Gao continued, "Today's meal has been paid out of Daxiong's allowances. She bought half a fat pig. Let us enjoy the food and then we can all go to tease the newly weds in their bridal chamber, which is a cave dwelling worthy of the name. The bridegroom spent three days and three nights renovating an abandoned cave dwelling into a bridal chamber. If we don't go and tease them tonight, will we have a second chance in the future?"

Someone shouted, "You are too long-winded as a speaker. Hurry and call out the bride and the bridegroom. Our mouths are watering for food." With a troubled mind and distorted thoughts, Gao Yuncao began to leave the mess quietly, not waiting for the arrival of the bride and the bridegroom.

As soon as she stepped out of the hall, she saw Ji Zhenren walking slowly to the mess. Surprised she said, "Hey, the play is about to begin, but the leading role has not arrived yet?"

"It's so noisy," said Ji Zhenren. "What are they doing here in the mess?"

With her head tilted to one side, she looked at him, "Playacting. You are still playacting. No wonder Chief Gao was prattling on and on. It turns out that he was waiting for the bridegroom."

At this very moment, a man mounted on a war horse galloped towards them. Halting at the entrance of the mess, he dismounted. Throwing his whip away, he dashed into the hall.

"What is Qiu Zihao rushing to our place for?" asked Ji Zhenren.

"What else could he have come here for? To attend your wedding banquet, of course," replied Gao Yuncao.

"What on earth are you talking about? I've been out on a mission and only just returned," grumbled Ji Zhenren impatiently.

Feeling that something was not right, Gao Yuncao took hold of Ji Zhenren and they ran into the hall.

The wedding ceremony had just begun. The bride and the bridegroom slowly walked into the hall, and Qiu Zihao and Song Daxiong were standing in the public gaze.

As jubilant as he was a moment ago, Chief Gao announced, "Bridegroom Qiu Zihao, Commander of the 2nd Regiment, also nicknamed Fierce Thunder, is a formidable combat hero. Even today he is too busy to find time for his wedding. He has just come from the front line straight to the hall. For the couple, the bridegroom has sworn that he would marry no one but Song Daxiong, who has also sworn that she would marry no one but Qiu Zihao. They swore their eternal love, even making their case to the senior officers. What a good woman Song Daxiong is. But she has been snatched away by the 2nd Regiment and there is nothing we can do about it. Anyway, it is RSU2's honour that we and the 2nd Regiment are joined in marriage. Tomorrow there will be a major battle to fight and Commander Qiu's Regiment is the vanguard force. Without further delay, let me announce that the wedding banquet begins. We also drink to bolster our bridegroom's departure. I propose a toast to Regimental Commander Qiu. Here's hoping he wins victory in the first battle tomorrow, and wishing him victory in the first battle in the bridal chamber tonight. Cheers!"

There was surprise as well as silence in the mess. The hall was slowly filled with the noise of guests raising their wine cups to congratulate the couple. It was obvious that people could not quite get used to the fact that the bridegroom was Qiu Zihao.

Ji Zhenren walked straight over to Chief Gao, shouting, "Give me an explanation."

Raising his wine cup, Chief Gao said, "No explanation but wine!"

Pulling Song Daxiong, who was accompanying Qiu Zihao to toast the guests, to one side, Ji Zhenren yelled, panting with rage, "Give me an explanation!"

Song Daxiong handed him a cup of wine, saying, "Didn't I clearly explain it to you a long time ago?"

"You said it to vent your anger," muttered Ji Zhenren.

Song Daxiong laughed, "The wedding ceremony is not a rehearsal for a play. Zhenren, give me your blessing."

Li Mozi walked up to them, pulling Ji Zhenren over to sit beside him.

No one noticed that Gao Yuncao had run out of the hall and was howling alone on the drill ground.

A few days later, after a major battle, Qiu Zihao made new contributions to winning battles. He then laid out a table of simple food and called Gao Yuncao, Li Mozi and Ji Hongmei for a meal. Song Daxiong went to invite Ji Zhenren, who resolutely declined her invitation.

Ji Zhenren found out why Song Daxiong and Qiu Zihao got married. It was quite simple, actually. Qiu Zihao had always felt guilty for the gunshot wound on Song Daxiong's face, so he often visited her to comfort her. Over the course of several encounters, they both fancied each other. When he expressed his intention to marry her, she agreed instantly and went to pester Chief Gao for permission. Chief Gao did not grant his permission, so the couple went to see the senior officer. But Ji Zhenren obstinately held that Qiu Zihao marrying Song Daxiong was to make up for his error and because he took pity on her; while Song Daxiong agreeing to the marriage was to avoid him and to let Gao Yuncao marry him, this marriage between Song and Qiu was a marriage without love. Song Daxiong had once 'tut-tutted' at him, "Stop imagining things without any basis of fact. I am neither a noble, nor despicable woman who would give Zihao a marriage without love in order to help you marry Gao Yuncao. Please remember, the love between Zihao and I is higher than the sky and deeper than the earth."

He had taken it to heart until today. Angrily, Song Daxiong stared at him, yelling, "If you do not go today, I will not take you as a friend of mine. Never!" Seeing that she was really upset, he followed her and went.

The six of them had a meal together, but in silence. Only Qiu Zihao spoke, "After I drink this wine, Zhenren will be my elder brother and Hongmei will be my younger sister." They all understood that he meant he would have Ji Hongying in his heart forever.

Gao Yuncao also said a few words that seemed somewhat ill-timed: "Mozi and Hongmei, you two should also hurry to get your things done." Unexpectedly Ji Hongmei slapped her chopsticks on the table, roaring, "Hurry to get what done? You'd better not worry too much about it." Gao Yuncao felt extremely embarrassed.

EARLY NEXT MORNING Song Daxiong appeared in the office. Someone remarked, "Bride, why not take a few days off?"

She replied, "We never saw the senior officers taking days off when they got married. What's more, I am taking on a trainee."

With her good ear, she had extended her extraordinary performance in monitoring radio signals, while tutoring trainees and producing good hands every year. At the moment she had one student, Gao Yuncao.

As a tutor, two things about her made a deep impression on Gao Yuncao: firstly, training and management were extremely strict, which could be described as a typically monstrous way of teaching, helping and leading. Every day only eight hours were put aside for trainees to eat, sleep, wash and tidy themselves up, while the other sixteen hours belonged to her, during which detailed training schedules were arranged for every minute which had to be implemented one by one with no exceptions. Even on her wedding night, when it was eleven o'clock she still went to check on Gao Yuncao, hand by hand supervising her until one o'clock in the morning when bridegroom Qiu Zihao, who had to go back to the battlefield at first light, was waiting in vain for her outside for more than an hour. Seeing her come out, without uttering a word, he held her with his arm and speedily went back to the bridal chamber. Secondly, her monitor tricks were complicated, unusual and weird. Compared to the instructors in the training classes, her method was like putting a square peg in a round hole; besides, it was diverged widely from the standard training plan of

the KMT armies as well. Gao Yuncao said nothing but silently accepted
Song Daxiong's tutoring. Gradually she found that although the Song
style of training was extremely rustic and countrified, it could produce
surprising results. She could see that these tricks were the essence of
what Song Daxiong had learned and refined her technique from years
of experience of monitoring enemy transceivers. Tutors who lacked
such practical experience, no matter how hard they tried, could not
present such effective, clever tricks to their students. She moaned
inwardly, "The Communists have many masters like Song Daxiong,
who had trained groups of brilliant students, whose skills are as good
as their masters. I will be surprised if the KMT army's transceivers fail
to be captured in one haul by the Communists."

Recently Song Daxiong had been leading Gao Yuncao on to a
strange radio signal. Apart from the normal enemy wireless signals,
Song Daxiong had discovered a slightly abnormal one, which was
always sent out between one and three o'clock in the morning, and
sounded like it was being sent by a business transceiver. But every time
when messages were sent, it was like someone was talking but did not
dare to talk loudly, as well as sounding hurried and sneaky. At first,
Song Daxiong gave up on it, so did Gao Yuncao. After the shift, they
looked into the signal, feeling that something was not right. At the
same time the next day, Gao Yuncao failed to find the signal, but Song
Daxiong found it on a different frequency. Listening, Gao Yuncao did
not hear anything unusual. Song Daxiong listened carefully and
transcribed the message, which was encrypted so she could not read
the content, but the basic feature showed that it was a commercial one.
She showed the message to Ji Zhenren, Li Mozi and Ji Hongmei and
they all agreed that it was a commercial telegram. This dispelled her
doubt at once.

Gao Yuncao, who knew the KMT armies' transceivers thoroughly,
could tell that the signal was neither from them nor from the KMT's
secret services. She judged that it was a commercial transceiver, so she
listened to the signal perfunctorily. But one day she suddenly called to
mind that Song Daxiong's ear was highly sensitive to wireless signals,
since she had felt something was wrong, it was better not to ignore it
rashly. Out of trust in Song Daxiong's ear, she began to pay attention to
this transceiver again. What she had in mind was that if she were to
confirm it was a well-hidden transceiver of the KMT army or secret
services, she had to try a clever way of covering it up, to completely

dispel Song Daxiong's doubts, thereby not letting RSU2 capture and monitor its signals. After monitoring the transceiver several times, she herself also felt something was up, guessing it was a transceiver with the KMT military and secret services background, but under cover of business use. However, the characteristics of the cipher were completely different to anything used by the KMT armies before. She could not make it out. Was it that the KMT army's communication department, or the secret services had had some extremely difficult ciphers created by some expert cipher compilers? Well, who cared? Since RSU2 firmly believed that it was a transceiver for business use, she'd better say nothing and pretend nothing had happened; that might be the best thing for her to do.

After the night shift and when they had finished breakfast, Song Daxiong and Gao Yuncao had a walk in the courtyard. On her own initiative Song Daxiong enquired about Gao Yuncao's relationship with Ji Zhenren.

Since her wedding day, Song Daxiong had been indifferent to Ji Zhenren. But anyone with discerning eyes could tell that she was cold-shouldering him deliberately, so that he could marry Gao Yuncao as she expected. In fact, inwardly she could not get him out of her mind. So either secretly, or deliberately or accidentally, she tried her bit to bring the two together.

Song Daxiong spoke straightforwardly as before. Also without reservation and sticking to her unchanged question, Gao Yuncao asked, "You hurried to get married so that I can marry Ji Zhenren, am I right? If you talk straight, I will go and love him in a spectacular way. If you don't, I'm sorry, I cannot develop my relationship with him."

Song Daxiong gave a wry smile, saying, "The fact is that I am married, which means my affection for him has ended. Except for comradeship, I have no other relationship with him."

"I am a newcomer," said Gao Yuncao. "I only want to know in these revolutionary ranks how novel the relationship between people can be. I felt that no other case could illustrate the situation more vividly than the one between you and him. Of course I have got a general idea, but I want to hear the precise answer from your mouth."

"All right. This will be our last word on this subject," explained Song Daxiong. "Let me put it this way, I know too well what you mean to him and the weight of your first love in his mind. You came back to life, and his feelings for you have grown geometrically. That is why, in this respect, I cannot occupy him emotionally, nor can I take him into my custody but have to release him, sending him back into the arms of the woman he loves and who loves him."

With tears in her eyes, Gao Yuncao earnestly nodded her head, "You've given him up but willingly help me marry him. I'll keep your kindness in my heart all my life!"

"No, no, no. I have deeper considerations on the matter. He is an unusual cryptographer who does not conform to standard. In respect of the affection between men and women, he is also different to ordinary people. He is a very stubborn man. I concluded that if he could not have you, it would mess him up mentally. His mind would be disturbed, as well as his brain. If his mind and brain are disturbed, his excellent inspiration and sharpness will suffer badly, even losing his ability to crack ciphers."

Relieved, Gao Yuncao smiled, "I understand. In short, what you have done is to keep his career in good condition. If these words had been said by someone else, I would not have believed them. But I believe what you've said."

Song Daxiong forced a smile, saying, "That's why there is no need for you to feel guilty or grateful. Promise me that you will not get entangled in this question again, and that you will love him from the bottom of your heart."

At this very moment, they heard an unusually loud rumbling sound coming closer and closer. Song Daxiong responded swiftly, jumping onto an earthen mound and climbing up a wall and then onto a roof. She saw a dark mass of airplanes, from east to west, heading straight to the town of Yan'an. Someone in the courtyard clapped their hands, calling out, "Is Chairman Chiang delivering money and goods to us?"

"Run to the bomb shelters!" shouted Song Daxiong anxiously. "They are the Japanese devils' planes!"

Hearing her shouts, people inside the rooms ran out and headed for the bomb shelters.

Climbing down from the roof, Song Daxiong ran straight to the cryptographers' office. As expected, Ji Zhenren was bent over a pile of telegrams, deep in thought. "Hurry and run!" she yelled. "The enemy planes are coming!" Seemingly hearing nothing, Ji Zhenren turned the pages and continued writing as usual. Carrying Ji Zhenren on her back, Song Daxiong dashed out of the room.

Inside the bomb shelter, Ji Zhenren shouted at the top of his voice,

"My coded messages. My coded messages." Struggling against Song Daxiong, he simply had to go back to the office.

Holding him down, Song Daxiong barked, "Wait here." She ran out and dashed into Ji Zhenren's office.

At this moment, everyone felt the tremendous force of bombs exploding on the ground.

According to people's descriptions afterwards, there were large numbers of Japanese bombers, flying low, dropping hundreds of bombs onto the small town of Yan'an, and instantly houses collapsed and fires broke out all over the place.

There were signs that the key target of the bombing was Phoenix Mountain where the CPC Central Committee and the Military Commission were stationed. The cave dwellings of Chairman Mao and the Party organisations were bombed, and over thirty Eighth Route Army officers and men were killed. People speculated that spies must have provided detailed intelligence to the Japanese.

During the incident, when Ji Zhenren's mind sobered up, he did not see Song Daxiong coming back. Like a lunatic he dashed to his office, which had been bombed flat and a fire was burning. Ignoring the enemy planes hovering above their heads, people did all they could to put out the fire and dig up the rubble. They finally found Song Daxiong.

A cross beam had rammed her head into the floor tiles, while her legs were buried under the collapsed wall. A door panel had stabbed into her back, nearly cutting her in two.

People turned her around, seeing that she was clutching a pile of telegrams in her arms.

On horseback Qiu Zihao rushed to the scene from his barracks outside the town. Chief Gao did not want him to see Song Daxiong's corpse, "Regiment Commander Qiu, it is better for you to keep an image of her as being complete in your mind." Raising his head to the sky, Qiu Zihao howled, flames of fury darting from his eyes.

Paralysed with shock, Ji Zhenren sat on the ground, holding the pile of paper in his arms. No tears, no words, he was staring hard at the white sheet.

Kicking Ji Zhenren hard, Qiu Zihao cursed, "I knew that she would die in your hands sooner or later." If the kick had landed on his chest, the force would have been like a bullet. Luckily Qiu Zihao only kicked the pile of paper out of his arms.

Waking up with a start, Ji Zhenren staggered to pick up the papers from the white sheet. He slipped and fell to the floor. Instantly his emotional defenses collapsed, and he wailed miserably.

Before Qiu Zihao realised it, Ji Zhenren was holding Song Daxiong's corpse in his arms. Choking on his sobs, he fainted. Kicking him over and lifting him in the air, Qiu Zihao slapped Ji Zhenren's face again and again.

Charging at Qiu Zihao, Gao Yuncao bellowed, "Qiu Zihao, if you treat Ji Zhenren in such a manner, Daxiong will die without closing her eyes."

Not until now did Qiu Zihao see clearly that Song Daxiong had been bombed beyond recognition. He threw himself on her and held her tightly in his arms. Ji Zhenren also threw himself on her and held her hand. Again Qiu Zihao punched and kicked him.

Chief Gao went to block Qiu Zihao, saying, "Regiment Commander Qiu, this is a wrong committed by the Japanese. You should not vent your anger on Ji Zhenren."

Qiu Zihao roared, "Ji Zhenren's guilt regarding Daxiong is inexcusable!"

"Don't bother about me," wailed Ji Zhenren. "Let him beat me to death."

RSU2 found a vacant lot and buried Song Daxiong. On the seventh day Ji Zhenren, Li Mozi, Gao Yuncao and Ji Hongmei went to the burial site and saw in the distance a man sitting in front of the grave. It was Qiu Zihao. Seeing someone coming, he mounted his horse. As he passed the group, he suddenly bent and lifted Ji Zhenren onto the back of his horse and galloped away.

Gao Yuncao called out, "Qiu Zihao, what is your problem? Why is there no end of it? Why not let it go? Are you still a man?"

On horseback at high speed, Qiu Zihao said to Ji Zhenren, "You are very familiar with this way of riding a horse, aren't you? The only pity is that the person in your arms now is a man."

"I understand where you're coming from," said Ji Zhenren. "Kill me or whatever, do as you please." Qiu Zihao whipped the horse on, while sentence after sentence of sentimental words flew past Ji Zhenren's ears.

"During the Long March, you and Daxiong were on the same horse. When troops blocked your way, she would draw her pistol and fire warning shots while spurring the horse to run like mad. At the time I was a company commander. Seeing the scene, I admired the bold and brave woman on horseback so much that I thought to myself how nice it would be if I could have such a woman as my wife.

"This image of her was engraved in my mind for many years. Later I met the same bold and brave Hongying. I didn't expect her to die so young. Furthermore, later I came to know about your relationship with Song Daxiong.

"Before she agreed to marry me, she spoke two sentences. One was that she and you were clean in your relationship. Although riding on the same horse, and even sleeping on the same straw mat, there was nothing more to your relationship and you were never intimate with each other. Her second sentence was that she could marry me, but that I had to allow her to have you in her mind. Of course, what she meant was that she would think about you like a sister would do for her brother, or a family member worrying about another family member. In the end I complied with her request.

"She was a good woman, but you did her a disservice. Actually, when I beat you on that day, it was for wasting this good woman's good intentions. In this respect she tolerated you and her tolerance somehow defied reason. But I will not forgive you. Off my horse, you excuse for a man!"

Throwing Ji Zhenren off the horse, Qiu Zihao spurred onward at full speed.

History records that the first Japanese bombing of Yan'an was on 20 November 1938, followed by a second bombing the next day.

The higher authorities assigned RSU2 the task of monitoring the Japanese and the puppet government's transceivers. For RSU2, the pressing matter was to capture the signals, to crack the ciphers and to get a clear picture of the spies hidden in Yan'an.

Song Daxiong was dead, but Gao Yuncao could not get her tutor out of her mind for a long time. What a nice elder sister she was to whom she could open her heart and her feelings were completely in synch with Song Daxiong. What a pity she had died; but before she died, she had assigned her to look out for that transceiver for business use, which she had kept in mind.

She monitored that transceiver again. Vaguely she felt that she seemed to have met the sending techniques and the 'handwriting' of the operator before. In the previous nights she had the same feeling but she did not form a concept about it. This time it suddenly occurred to her that the operator seemed to be the same operator from the Military Supply Bureau of the KMT government's Military Administration Ministry in Shaanxi. The sending techniques of the two were similar, and she was almost certain that they were the same person.

Soon, her experience as a veteran wireless operator made an impact. From the heading of a message she guessed that it was being sent to Shanghai, and this discovery was extremely important.

Normally, the telegrams of the KMT's Military Supply Bureau in Xi'an were sent to Chongqing, not Japanese-occupied Shanghai. One possibility might have been that the telegram was sent to one of the KMT's own hidden transceivers in Shanghai, which meant that the operator in Xi'an was a KMT spy. Another possibility was that it might have been sent to the Japanese military or the puppet government's spy organisation in Shanghai. If this was the case, then the telegram sender was undoubtedly a traitor or a secret agent, that is to say, a Japanese mole was hidden in the KMT's Military Supply Bureau in Xi'an.

With these thoughts Gao Yuncao secretly increased her efforts to monitor this transceiver, meanwhile she began to crack its cipher.

In these days, to avoid being bombed by the Japanese bombers, RSU2 constantly moved quarters. The staff were fed up with moving. That day, when Gao Yuncao inwardly cursed the 'damned bombers', her mind at once linked to the transceiver in Xi'an. If it was truly a Japanese spy transceiver, she thought, what would be its focal point in northern Shaanxi now? Of course, the bombing of Yan'an and to supply intelligence for the bombing. Yan'an had an extremely tight system to guard against secret agents, it was almost impossible for this Japanese spy to set up aerials in Yan'an. Could it be that after this spy stole intelligence in Yan'an, he delivered it to Xi'an where a transceiver would have sent the intelligence to Shanghai? Then what kind of intelligence did the Japanese need for their bombing? Certainly the weather and the location of the bombing targets. With this guesswork, the range that she must decipher the messages sent by the transceiver in Xi'an was greatly reduced.

A few days later in the small hours of the morning, she was lying in bed racking her brains. Suddenly she cried inwardly, "As expected, that's it!" Subconsciously, the words slipped out of her lips and the sound was not soft.

Ji Hongmei, who was sleeping beside her, sat up, "Who is it? What's the matter?"

Alert and resourceful, she turned over in bed, pretending that she was talking in her sleep: "Zhenren, wait for me." Once Ji Hongmei was sound asleep, she got up. Picking up a pen and some paper, she went to the toilet.

It was really that transceiver! What she had deciphered were the weather conditions in Yan'an and the locations of the Communists' key departments. Her guess was so correct that there were indeed Japanese spies in Yan'an. After gathering the information, they delivered it to a secret agent hidden in the Military Supply Bureau in Xi'an, who then sent the information in coded messages to Shanghai. Based on the intelligence, the Japanese headquarters issued orders for bombing missions.

The cipher cracked by Gao Yuncao in secret was *LAN*. From the messages, she discovered that it was used only between a Japanese spy called 'Delta' in Xi'an and the Japanese and puppet spy organisations in Shanghai.

To Yan'an this was a major piece of intelligence. But whether or not she should report it to Chief Gao, she was resolute that she must not do it. Because if she did, she might expose herself as a KMT spy; if she did not, she would be safe. This transceiver was for business use, which had been screened and decided by RSU2 as one of a thousand such transceivers. Only Song Daxiong had some doubt, but she was now dead, so no one would remember this transceiver. She also thought that if she held back the information, the effect would suit her real identity as well as her responsibility. To the KMT higher authorities, the bombing of Yan'an was also what they wanted. Making use of the Japanese to wipe out the Communist forces was also the need of the party and the state, so she thought.

However, more or less she felt awkward inwardly. Putting aside the nature of organisations and political identity, and purely viewing it from the professional integrity of an intelligence agent, she had to think of a way to let RSU2 know about it. Besides, although she had nothing to do with the bombing of the key communist locations, from the point of view of avenging Song Daxiong and ensuring the safety of Ji

Zhenren and the other friends, she had to report it. She would have felt sad if any one of them had died from the bombing.

But she slapped her face for these thoughts of hers. How could one be concerned about the wellbeing of one's enemy? What was your aim in coming to Yan'an? Wasn't it to prevent the KMT armies' ciphers from being cracked? If the cryptographers in Yan'an were bombed to death, wouldn't that have been what you wanted?!

Gao Yuncao was at a loss. But out of curiosity and professional habit, she began to think over one question: in which department would this Japanese spy have been hidden in Yan'an?

From the messages she intercepted, she saw the name of the sender from Yan'an was 'Luobilou', while the name of the sender from Xi'an was 'Delta' who used the transceiver in the Military Supply Bureau. A transceiver was always located in a confidential site with no outsiders near it. Judging from this, she was certain 'Delta' was an internal personnel of the Military Supply Bureau. But she could not make out where 'Luobilou' would be hidden in Yan'an.

One day she went to the bookstore with Ji Zhenren and Li Mozi, where she specially searched for a reference to 'Luobilou'. In the end she confirmed that only the Lius' library in Suzhou was called 'Luobilou'. Once again she called to mind her good friend Liu Hai'er and her sad but beautiful love story, as well as the origin of her own name, Yuncao. She chuckled to herself: of course the Lius' 'Luobilou' had no connection with the Japanese spy 'Luobilou'.

When leaving, she said to Ji Zhenren, "When I went through some ancient books, I suddenly called to mind a female friend of mine in Suzhou. She is called Liu Hai'er. Do you still remember her?"

Ji Zhenren laughed, "Didn't you send the one-word telegram for her? Friendship in those years was precious and unforgettable." While speaking, he took her hand. After Song Daxiong's death, this was the first time there had been any intimacy between him and Gao Yuncao.

She avoided his hand, saying, "In these years you haven't contacted Liu Hai'er and her husband, have you?"

He forced a smile, "I'm a dead man. How could I meet old friends in Shanghai again? Of course, you are the exception."

"I don't know when I can go to Luobilou library to feast my eyes. After all, the bookstore in Yan'an is not very exciting."

"We are at war, so it is hard for us to enjoy ourselves to the full by reading. After we win victory in the revolution, we can read as many books as we like and enjoy ourselves to the full."

She remembered something, saying, "Your article '*Books and Life*' is really good. It would be very interesting to have it published."

"Will you help me polish it?"

In the evening he handed her the manuscript. She made a few small changes, crossing out the detailed description of the Lius' library and the building names.

Using 'Caesar' as his pen name, Ji Zhenren submitted the article to *Construction Journal*, the institutional learning guide of the border government.

It was said that reaction to the article among young intellectuals in Yan'an was quite good. The editorial department made use of the circumstances to publish several readers' reviews; besides they launched a large-scale debate on reading and the result was also good.

One day Gao Yuncao led her basketball team to play a match. Because of the air raids, no decent games had been organised for a while. For this match all the teams participating were bursting with energy, fielding their strongest lineup to fight it out to see which was the better team.

Gao Yuncao's team was still the most splendid scene in the venue. For security reasons, they took part in the name of the logistics department medical unit. As the team leader, she did very well, winning cheers from the crowd.

A senior officer came to the match that day and he played two matches as a member of Headquarters Team One. Feeling that he had not enjoyed it to the full, after the formal games finished, he led his team to play a friendly game with Gao Yuncao's team.

As soon as she went onto the court, Gao Yuncao whispered into the senior officer's ear, "Officer, today I will not budge an inch, nor win the ball by tricks. Watch out. Don't offend me, or within the rules I will be free to knock you down."

The senior officer laughed, "Don't be stubborn and reluctant to admit defeat. Don't snivel when you lose the match."

The senior officer played the game really to his heart's content. It could be seen that he was very excited. In the first half he knocked Gao Yuncao to the ground twice, but the referee did not whistle for a foul.

At half time, someone was passing a glass of water to the officer. Panting with rage, Gao Yuncao walked up to him and intercepted the glass. Raising her head she gulped the water down.

"Officer, you knocked me down when you dribbled, but the referee did not blow the whistle. Do you admit your error?"

"The referee did not penalise me, so where was the error?" said the officer, laughing. "You blocked me savagely, it was you who violated the rules. You have also stolen my water, so you are doubly guilty."

"OK, in the second half, you wait," said Gao Yuncao, gnashing her teeth. "Don't curse me if I knock you down and hurt you."

The officer looked up at the sky and laughed out loud, "How can a man be scared by a woman? I certainly will let you suffer a crushing defeat."

At this moment, someone came and called out, "Jiang Xiaodian. Jiang Xiaodian." Gao Yuncao turned around and saw that it was a journalist with a camera round his neck, asking her, "Is that really you, Jiang Xiaodian? You don't recognise me?"

The blood in her veins rushed to her skull, while a cold sweat piled on hot sweat. For a secret agent, it was disastrous to be recognised under such circumstances. Her former psychological training tutor had told her that in such a situation she had to be calm and not panic but be natural. So she put on a smiling face and went to warmly shake hands with the journalist: "Hello. Hello. You are a journalist now, the king without a crown. Good, good…"

The whistle for the second half was blown and someone came to pull her away. But she was out of form for the whole second half. Her running was out of position and her shots were inaccurate. The spectators grumbled and sighed. Quietly the senior officer reminded her: "The spectators are watching our ball skills. Have you been frightened by my strength?"

She was still absent-minded, pondering who on earth that journalist could be? When the match neared its end, she finally called to mind Liu Hai'er, and then Zhang Jiayin. The journalist vaguely looked like Zhang Jiayin whom she had met several times many years ago. Great. So long as it was him, there would be no crisis for her.

Sure enough her team lost the match. Wiping the sweat from his face the senior officer pointed at her, saying, "Women refuse to be outdone by men. I am talking about your ball skills, but for this match you were beaten by lack of courage and spirit."

Pretending to be embarrassed, she grumbled nervously, "You wanted me to suffer a crushing defeat. Only ghosts would not be scared." Grabbing a ball from the ground and standing outside the court, she suddenly threw the ball and it fell straight into the ring, which caused the spectators to roar with applause.

The journalist came and called 'Jiang Xiaodian' again. Was he really that Zhang Jiayin? She was not so sure, so she said: "News of victory has been passed on to Jiayin, let us wait to watch the next game." As expected, the pun worked (*jiayin* literarily means good news).

The journalist smiled: "Xiaodian, you remembered me at last. A few days ago when I read an article in the *Construction Journal*, I felt that it was talking about Liu Hai'er and me. I wondered who the author could be. After thinking about it over and over again, I decided that the author could be no one but you or Ji Zhenren. But both of you were killed. So when I watched the basketball game, I wondered if I was watching a ghost playing. But when I saw you sweating, I knew you were still alive."

"How did you come to Yan'an?" asked Gao Yuncao impatiently. "How is Hai'er?" In a summary tone, he told her why he had come and that Liu Hai'er was fine in Suzhou. But Gao Yuncao held back the news that Ji Zhenren was also alive.

So he had finally come!

After she discovered the source of *Luobilou* in the bookstore, she thought of Liu Hai'er and her husband. She was clear that it was impossible for the 'Luobilou' in the telegram to have any relationship with Liu Hai'er and her husband. But as a cryptographer who was spending her time fiddling with codes and ciphers, she had a very lively imagination and was very suspicious. This time she also had an illusion. The rough and bumpy road of love for Liu Hai'er and Zhang Jiayin started from *Luobilou*. If the couple were truly spies, there was a strong possibility that they would have chosen the name of the building as their code name. The reason for her to encourage Ji Zhenren to publish his article was that from its contents the couple would have guessed who the author was and that the author was in Yan'an. So it was possible that they would have come to search for whoever it was. Although this was like trying to catch a specific fish in the ocean and the possibility of the fish biting the bait was only one in a thousand, or even one in ten thousand, it was still worth throwing the fishhook into the water.

So when Zhang Jiayin really appeared, it took her half of the basketball match to respond.

She then thought that she must employ a series of stratagems, so she asked Zhang Jiayin which newspaper he was working for. He replied that he was working for the *New China Newspaper*, the border government's official newspaper, and only for six months.

"Good, a journalist and a good camera. You must take nice photos for me."

"It seems that you are not from the medical unit. Hey, which unit are you from? Where should I send your photos?" asked Zhang Jiayin.

"You are worthy of being a journalist. Your vision is very sharp." In a mysterious and low voice, she said: "I know the senior officer very well, and we often play basketball together. So which unit am I from? I am working at the side of the senior officers. Aiya, this is not something convenient to talk about. Sorry, how about I come and find you in your office some day. You must print more photos of me. I will not let you off if my photos do not look nice."

The basketball match was played on ground levelled half way up a hill. There was a row of cave dwellings and a company of orderlies was stationed there.

An old GAZ truck came to pick up Gao Yuncao and her team. The players got on the truck, which drove down the hill along the winding road. But Gao Yuncao saw that Zhang Jiayin was climbing up toward the peak of the hill.

Sitting in the driver's cab, she chatted intimately with the driver who was a basketball fan. When the truck reached the foot of the hill, she let the driver drive the truck in the opposite direction to the RSU2 compound and enter a nearby barracks. Four sentries were guarding the entrance but what they were guarding was an empty building. To avoid air raids, the troops had moved to other barracks, but the outsiders knew nothing about it. Seeing the sentries guarding the complex every day, they thought that the troops were still stationed deep inside.

Once the truck entered the yard, the girls got out of it. Gao Yuncao asked the driver to take the truck out of the complex via the main entrance, then go to the small east gate at the back of the western slope to pick them up again. She led the girls on a walk around the barracks and then sneaked out of the east gate down a small narrow path. The other girls did not understand, asking, "You brought us here only to visit these bombed corners of the barracks?"

"I used to come here with Daxiong when she was visiting Qiu Zihao," she replied. "I miss her. We were passing, so I wanted to come in and have a look to recall my old friendship with her." Tears fell from her eyes as she spoke. She wiped away the tears, turning around to glance at the empty barracks, and got into the driver's cab.

Having learned the lessons, most of the Party and government organisations had moved into the cave dwellings in the mountains. Never before was awareness of the need for air defense as strong as it was now. The early warnings from the observation posts a hundred miles away from Yan'an were quick so that people from all parts of the area could evacuate in time, making the Japanese bombing raids quite ineffective.

From the messages encrypted with the Blue (LAN) cipher, Gao Yuncao saw that the Japanese espionage organisation in Shanghai repeatedly pushed Luobilou to collect precise information as soon as possible so as to optimise the results of the bombing. She thought: Luobilou's superior was impatient, so he would do something desperate.

As expected, a few days later, the Japanese bombers came again. The empty barracks she had led the basketball team to visit was a key bombing target.

People could not understand why the Japanese would have done this in such a big way and dropped dozens of bombs on an already bombed and empty barracks.

Gao Yuncao understood what this implied. Luobilou had put this empty barracks as a top priority on his list of main targets for the Japanese to bomb.

She patted her head hard. Just as she had expected, the guy who climbed to the top of the hill on that day would have seen the truck entering the barracks with the girls but coming out empty. He must have made the following judgement: he must have taken an ordinary barracks hidden at the foot of a remote mountain as the government head office; besides, this barracks had already been bombed, and such a practice was entirely in keeping with the Communist army's cunning way of doings things, so deceptive and concealed. Then, this Zhang Jiayin was undoubtedly Luobilou.

"What should I do?" she asked herself.

"What else can I do? Keep quiet, of course," she answered the question herself.

During the break, the staff went to the courtyard for a walk. Holding a newspaper in her hand, Ji Hongmei invited Gao Yuncao to view a photo. It was the *New China Newspaper* and it was a very beautiful photo. The senior officer was in the air about to shoot the ball, which had just left his hand; opposite him Gao Yuncao was also jumping in the air, both arms stretched toward the ball. Their movements were very coordinated and full of vigour. The senior officer was calm and composed, and the expression on his face showed that he was confident that the ball would definitely fall into the hoop, meanwhile Gao Yuncao appeared as though she was competing with all her might to stop the ball from falling into the hoop. Her beautiful eyes were wide open as was her mouth, and she looked as though she was shouting. The other players on both sides were doing their own movements, unintentionally they served as a foil to the two. It really had the flavour of a myriad of stars surrounding the moon.

Gao Yuncao cried out, "What a good picture! Zhang Jiayin does have a few tricks. I must meet him some time." While speaking, she gently folded the newspaper.

Afterwards another basketball match was organised and she was asked to lead a team. Finding an excuse that she was not well, she stayed behind. Her true intention for not going was that since Zhang Jiayin was a Japanese spy suspect, to avoid trouble she'd better not see him. However, before the players left for the match, she urged them, "Recently the Japanese bombers have frequently come to raid us, so certainly the cursed spies are tailing us. When you return, the truck must go round and round our compound. After making sure that you are not tailed, you can enter so as to prevent the cursed spies from locking in on RSU2." But suddenly she felt surprised for her remarks and said inwardly, "Why am I worrying about the safety of RSU2? How weird!"

One day Ji Zhenren returned to his dormitory after a meal, looking heavyhearted. Gao Yuncao said, "The dead will not come back to life. Only when the living are happy will the dead rest in peace."

He did not take up the thread of the conversation, but he began to talk about work, "In recent days the Japanese bombers have frequently come to bomb Yan'an, but the spy providing the Japanese with the intelligence has not yet been captured. We have monitored and searched but we've failed to find a suspect transceiver. We have focused on monitoring the signals with military and secret services' characteristics but with no result. I feel that we should expand our monitoring to include the transceivers for civil and commercial use in Yan'an and Xi'an, even taking radio broadcasts as the key targets. We must be searching full-time as if we are looking for a needle in a haystack."

"You dare to think about it. But fishing for a needle in the ocean and casting a net everywhere, can RSU2 handle such a large amount of work?"

"But can Yan'an bear any more Japanese bombing? We can mobilise the whole unit, so there is nothing that cannot be done." Ji Zhenren's eyes flashed weirdly, as he said, "In our profession, illusions and hallucination can sometimes solve some of the problems. At the moment my intuition tells me that this single spy, or group of Japanese spies, will certainly be unmasked, and we may even be able to ferret out some KMT spies."

Gao Yuncao was not scared by him; on the contrary she laughed, "If you can figure things out intuitively, it can save us from working overtime."

Failing to realise her irony, Ji Zhenren said, "From the Japanese bombing our empty barracks, it is certain that the intelligence provider is not from our key departments, which increases the possibility that the spy is hiding in some of the minor departments. Therefore we must not only focus our attention on our key departments, but take a wider view."

Suddenly looking for some excitement, Gao Yuncao muttered, "Tell me, where is the safest place for a spy to hide? No idea? Let me tell you, it is in people's hearts."

Staring at her, Ji Zhenren said, leisurely, "At this very moment an illusion is flashing past my eyes. It tells me that you Gao Yuncao have hidden in the depths of people's hearts, so you feel that you are the safest."

The excitement went too far. Feeling extremely nervous, she mustered her courage and muttered, "What do you mean? You mean that I am a spy? Such a joke cannot be made casually."

Pointing at her, Ji Zhenren said, "No matter how the situation changes, you are always the safest. You already had a well-thought-out plan and full assurance of success, feeling that as long as you appeared, Song Daxiong would surely be defeated. You always had this feeling, which came from the camphor forest by the Huangpu river eight years ago when you stole that heart."

Only after hearing these words did she suspend her worries. But she had to pretend that she was angry with his remarks, so she said, "Ji Zhenren, Sister Song has gone. So what's the point of being obsessed with the issue? You fancy yourself too much. Who was hidden in your heart for so many years? Who stole that awful heart of yours? Who wanted to have you for so long? Is this your so-called illusion, hallucination or intuition? I now understand. Genius plus illusion plus hallucination plus intuition equals a bad mental disorder!"

With her mind in tumult, she ran away. Returning to her dormitory, it took her quite a while to calm down. Soon she began to worry again. If all the monitors should cast a net everywhere to search for this transceiver and then chance on Ji Zhenren's lethal illusion, hallucination and intuition, the odds were against this *Luobilou* rather than in his favour, and the possibility of him being exposed was great!

She knew what to do now!

Quickly RSU2 lept into action and even cryptographers Ji Zhenren, Li Mozi and Ji Hongmei joined forces to monitor signals.

Ji Hongmei was in Gao Yuncao's team. That day they were on night shift. Gao Yuncao's pharyngitis recurred, so she coughed from time to time.

"Hongmei, what is the difference between asthma and pharyngitis? Have you ever seen an asthma patient?"

"Yes, I have. When asthma flares up, the patient wheezes and is out of breath. Sometimes the patient feels suffocated, and their face and eyes turn purple, like someone being hung by the neck."

"So my symptoms are for pharyngitis. I always worried that I would suffer from asthma. Well, some days ago between one and three o'clock in the morning, I often heard an operator sending telegrams as if his asthma had recurred, pressing the keys hurriedly and chaotically, as if he couldn't breathe and was being suffocated. As soon as I heard this sound, I felt pain and irritation in my throat, short of breath and I felt suffocated. Do you think I'm suffering from an operational disease?"

"The peculiar sound of sending telegrams can bring out certain physiological reactions on the part of the receiver. I've heard about it but I've never seen it."

They had barely finished talking when Gao Yuncao threw her headphones on the desk and began to cough non-stop, "Talk of the devil, here it comes. That sound has appeared again. My throat is so irritated, can you come and listen?"

They changed seats. As Ji Hongmei listened, she muttered, "It's fast and chaotic, a typical symptom of asthma. Your metaphor is very apt. But why is this operator sending in such an urgent and chaotic way?"

"Yeah," muttered Gao Yuncao. "I'm also wondering what critical situation is causing a commercial transceiver to send a message in such a way and at such a late hour. How annoying."

When she had finished her turn listening, Ji Hongmei looked deep in thought. Slowly she said, "Yuncao, when someone talks, no matter how fast or how chaotically they speak, their voice doesn't change at all."

"Of course not," replied Gao Yuncao. "Like Li Mozi, no matter whether he speaks lovers' prattle in a soft voice, or gives you orders in a deep, gruff voice, you can always tell that it is him speaking even with your eyes closed."

Ji Hongmei delved deeper into her thoughts, "Don't talk rubbish. I'm being serious. Yes, this operator was surprisingly identical to the operator of the KMT Military Supply Bureau in Xi'an whom I monitored a few days ago. They seem to be the same person."

Immediately Gao Yuncao became serious. "Which means this operator was initially the operator from the Military Supply Bureau, but camouflaged as a commercial transceiver. They often sent telegrams anxiously and chaotically late at night. What do they want to do?"

"Let's focus our monitoring on this transceiver," said Ji Hongmei. "It is extremely urgent. I have transcribed two messages; let me have a look at them first."

After a while, she said, "I remember that Song Daxiong asked me to read some messages sent by this transceiver. At the time I thought it was a commercial transceiver so I let it pass. Reading these two messages, they do not look as though they have been encrypted by a KMT cipher."

"Whose cipher can it be? Is it a Japanese cipher?"

Patting her own head, Ji Hongmei muttered, "Neither commercial, nor the KMT, who else can it be? It is definitely connected with the Japanese and the puppet government. Yuncao, you know Japanese, have a look at the messages."

"You know that I only know a little bit of cryptography. Go and find Ji Zhenren and Li Mozi. Quick, don't delay."

Not long after Ji Hongmei ran out, she returned, bringing a monitor with her. Hurriedly she said to Gao Yuncao, "Chief Gao said that you know Japanese, and he asked you to go to the cryptographers' office."

It was the first time Gao Yuncao had taken part in deciphering work at RSU2, so she showed an obvious nervousness and excitement. In discussions she was cautious with her words, but following the others she would say something, making it sound as though it was not premeditated. To utter these few words, she had racked her brains. She could not let the others sense that she had already deciphered the messages, yet her remarks had to be meaningful. Spontaneously and without any awareness, she would open a tiny corner to let the others suddenly see the light to discover the real gem and lift the lid. It was very difficult but she achieved it.

Three days later Chief Gao announced that the *LAN* cipher used by the Japanese and the puppet espionage organisations in Shanghai had been cracked.

After lifting the veil on *LAN*, they saw that although it had the characteristics of mixing Chinese with Japanese, it was a cipher that was mainly compiled in Chinese, suitable for use by treacherous espionage organisations. From the messages, they learned that a Japanese spy codenamed Delta was hiding in the KMT's Military Supply Bureau in Xi'an, meanwhile a second Japanese spy codenamed *Luobilou* was hiding in a certain department in Yan'an, providing the Japanese with Yan'an's weather and information on targets for bombing. RSU2 was more concerned about who *Luobilou* could be and in which department they were hiding?

The issue could only be resolved via two channels: firstly, by make use of the KMT-CPC cooperation mechanism, letting the KMT arrest Delta in Xi'an, from whose mouth they could dig out *Luobilou*. But there were difficulties. The KMT would not turn down a request to arrest a Japanese spy. But the matter involved their own people, so they would not allow the CPC to mess things up. Secondly, by resolving the issue in Yan'an. But *Luobilou* had no transceivers. So long as he did not send any messages, RSU2 could not make a breakthrough. If they only relied on coded messages, no matter who it was, it would be difficult to find this specific person.

One day while having a walk, Gao Yuncao gave Ji Zhenren the *New China Newspaper* to read. After he had read it, he remarked, "The photo is very nice. Good Lord, no cover up, your shining white flesh has been published in the newspapers."

Seizing the newspaper from him, she said, "Why is the photo very nice? It should be that the real person is very beautiful. Hey, guess who took this photo."

Scornfully he said, "Who else could it be? A priggish journalist who specially took photos of a leading cadre's face and a young girl's breasts."

"You know this journalist. There was a Liu Hai'er in Suzhou whose family had a library called *Luobilou*, where a sad but beautiful love story took place, and the male protagonist was called Zhang Jiayin. Do you still remember him? He was that priggish journalist. He recognised me while I was playing basketball."

Standing still, he stared at her curiously. Seeing the expression in his eyes, she knew that he had fallen into her trap. But she went on with her pretend performance, saying, "I have always been aware of keeping secrets so I did not tell him that you are still alive."

Looking at her with the same weird expression in his eyes, he yelled, "Liu Hai'er, Zhang Jiayin, *Luobilou*. I have always said that a cryptographer should often let their illusions, hallucinations and intuition shine." When he had finished speaking, he left with vigorous strides.

What happened next was not complicated. After the approval of the higher authorities, the Political Security Bureau attended to the matter personally with the assistance and cooperation of RSU2. The work was done in three steps.

Step one: they organised a basketball match where Gao Yuncao met Zhang Jiayin again. Unintentionally, she revealed the new site where the central organisations were stationed. After obtaining the information, Zhang Jiayin got in touch with a shoe shop assistant in Gufang Street, who then went to Xi'an on the pretext of purchasing some cotton material. In Heshun Noodle Bar he sat eating noodles at the same table with a man who came to collect information from him. All this was under the surveillance of the Political Security Bureau. As expected, when the Japanese bombers came again, the false new site revealed by Gao Yuncao was bombed flat.

Step two: to arrest and interrogate Zhang Jiayin. In the beginning, he refused to open his mouth. The interrogators employed some torture methods for dealing with traitors, but they still got nothing from him. A traitor would 'rather die than submit'! After hearing about this, Ji Zhenren wrote a note to the interrogators: "This man has two weaknesses. One is that he loves books very much. The second is that he loves his wife very much. In his heart, the love developed from life and books is above heaven."

Therefore, when the interrogators questioned him again, they said, "If you want to save Liu Hai'er's life, you must open your mouth and speak." They then brought in a basket of books that they had got from his room. In front of him they began to burn them one by one. When they started to burn the fifth book, he opened his mouth and confessed how he had been recruited as a Japanese secret agent.

"In those days my wife and I knew nothing about the death of Jiang Xiaodian and Ji Zhenren. Several times we went to the Shanghai Telegraph Office to look for them, which drew Director Yang Tianhu's attention. At that time, Director Yang had been recruited by the Japanese and the puppet government's secret services, and he was looking for young people to serve the Japanese. At the time the headquarters of the puppet government's secret services had not yet been established, so Yang was put into an important position by the leading Japanese intelligence officer, Doihara Kenji. In secret he discovered that my wife and I would always go to the library when we came to Shanghai, so they knew that we truly loved to read books. He warmly received us, telling us about the deaths of Jiang Xiaodian and Ji Zhenren and asking us to stay for a meal. From then on we got to know each other. Later he put his cards on the table, but we refused him. After that, he gave each of us an ultimatum, saying, 'If you don't comply with my request, I'll kill your loved ones and burn down the Lius' library.' At the time the Japanese had occupied Suzhou. To kill and burn would have been as easy as turning his hand, if he had wanted to. We had no choice but to submit and became traitors. After receiving training to become secret agents, Liu Hai'er was sent to infiltrate the KMT's Military Supply Bureau in Xi'an and I was secretly sent to Yan'an."

• • •

After Zhang Jiayin's confession, Chief Gao put forward a stratagem: they would not disturb Delta but let Zhang Jiayin carry on working as a journalist to provide false intelligence and draw the Japanese to come and bomb false targets. Later on the Japanese found out that the features of the loess mountain slopes were difficult to distinguish from the air, the Yan'an town area was narrow and small, and the bombing indicators were not easy to spot. And because the Communist Party and the government organisations frequently moved from place to place, it was harder and harder for the bombing to be effective, so they stopped bombing Yan'an.

During this period of time, Number 76, the secret services headquarters of the puppet government in Shanghai, was established. Through Doihara Kenji's recommendation, Yang Tianhu became the right-hand man of Li Shiqun and Ding Mocun, the chiefs of Number 76. Because he had successfully recruited and used Delta and *Luobilou*, who had provided intelligence for the Japanese aerial bombing of Yan'an, he was rewarded handsomely by Number 76.

As to how the Political Security Bureau dealt with Zhang Jiayin, and how they negotiated with the KMT to arrest Liu Hai'er, although Gao Yuncao and Ji Zhenren very much wanted to know about it, that was beyond what RSU2 was authorised to know about the case, so they dared not violate the rules to enquire about it. However, one thing was for sure. Ever since then, Gao Yuncao and Ji Hongmei never heard the breath of that 'asthma sufferer'.

"Before duty, friendship is not worth a cent," said Gao Yuncao, feeling a little bit sad.

"They aided and abetted an evildoer, how can we feel pity for them? We cannot even feel pity for our own blood brothers, let alone old friends and feelings of the past," said Ji Zhenren.

"Like Yang Tianhu, your skills to catch others' weaknesses are also extraordinary," murmured Gao Yuncao.

"Love of books like love of life and passionate love are two of the purest things in the world. From this point of view it seems that I am as filthy as Yang Tianhu," sighed Ji Zhenren.

Gao Yuncao breathed a long sigh of relief for herself. In this incident not only did she avoid being exposed as a spy with cryptography knowledge, but in Chief Gao's eyes she had made notable progress in her technical skills, displaying a rare power of understanding when she had first touched ciphers. Therefore she was officially transferred to do cipher-cracking work.

During that period, she would often think of Zhang Jiayin and read that part of the newspaper. She really loved the photo of herself and the senior officer.

What she did not expect was that her superior far away in Chongqing also liked the photo.

The *New China Newspaper* was the official newspaper for the government in Yan'an. It was naturally the target of information to be collected by the spies in the city. One day a minor spy mixed this section of the newspaper with dozens of other newspapers and it was passed on to Chongqing, the den of the KMT. By chance Gao Yuncao's direct superior saw her photo in the newspaper.

Since she had infiltrated Yan'an, her superior had heard nothing from her, leading him to guess that she had either failed in her mission and had been captured and executed, or that she had failed to infiltrate RSU2 so she was not in a position to gather any information, or that she had succeeded in her mission, but because RSU2 was heavily guarded, she had had no opportunity to make contact with the outside, or that for the time being she had been unable to gather any important information, so there was no need to take the risk of contacting the liaison officer and she had gone into hibernation.

Now seeing her playing basketball with a Communist army big shot, that put his mind at ease. 'Grasshopper' had not only successfully infiltrated Yan'an, but had also made close contact with high-level Communist officials.

IT WAS before RSU2 moved to Ansai, a county north of Yan'an, that Gao Yuncao decided to come out of hibernation.

During the Japanese bombing of Yan'an, RSU2 had moved to Ansai and camped in Youhulu Ravine, which had a small mouth but a wide body that extended ten kilometres in depth flanked by high, steep hills, closed off by a ridge; so it was an ideal location for security. From the way they dug their cave dwellings and the exchange of houses with local civilians, they obviously planned to stay there for a long time.

Since spies had been uncovered in Yan'an, all the key departments of the Party, military and government had begun to implement unprecedentedly strict security regulations and precautionary measures, and RSU2 adopted even stricter and more stringent measures of its own. Apart from moving the unit to a location far away from Yan'an, the security force guarding its compound had been strengthened, while more personnel with rich experience of guarding against spies were dispatched to the unit. RSU2 was tightly protected. For the key confidential departments, all sorts of rules and regulations were quickly established and perfected. The mechanism of mutual supervision was particularly strict. Everyone and everything could get stuck in this multi-precautionary web. There was absolutely no chance for any individual activities, and eyes were everywhere, either in the open or undercover.

Gao Yuncao considered herself lucky to have been able to send out her first intelligence before the move, because it was much more difficult to do it now. In fact she had taken a great risk to get it done, but she told herself no matter how risky, she had to take the first step, or she would have been unworthy of the party's and the state's trust in her if she had taken no action for so long.

On that occasion, she had exploited loopholes in the regulations regarding 'permission from three levels of authority and three people going out together'. She had gone with Ji Hongmei and the pregnant Ding Lili to buy eggs in the downtown market, where she got in touch with her liaison, a one-eyed chicken peddlar, and cleverly took into the RSU2 compound a carrier pigeon with instructions hidden in the boiled eggs. She had released the pigeon and sent out her intelligence that night.

After the pigeon had flown away, she had been uneasy for a long time, worrying that if something had happened to the pigeon half way, the intelligence would not have reached her superior, or that after her superior had received the intelligence, what measures would he take against RSU2, or whether Ji Zhenren's life would be threatened.

With these hidden worries in mind, she was ill at ease when she met Ji Zhenren who sensed her anxiety. One day he said to her, "You seem to have something on your mind, something serious."

She was stupefied but her tone was calm, "Why do you think that? Is it because of the ghastly expression on my face?"

"Your face is normal, but your mind is restless. My intuition senses it."

"Your time-tested intuition again. But I'm afraid it won't work on me."

"The other teams have made progress on cracking the Japanese ciphers, but you are still wandering on the edge. You have a good foundation in the Chinese, Japanese and English languages, and Chief Gao also places high hopes on you, but you have achieved nothing."

She laughed inwardly, "Oh, I see. His intuition can sometimes also be rubbish." So she said, "I know the significance of cracking the Japanese military ciphers, and I am also very enthusiastic about working on it. I have the basic skills and I have spent a lot of time and energy. Why am I anxious? Because a breakthrough has not yet been achieved."

Gazing into her eyes, he said, "Something in your mind is still in hibernation. Is it time for it to wake up?" Hearing the word 'hibernation', Gao Yuncao's eyes popped out. He said again, "Have a think about your father Jiang Daming." She lessened her uneasiness and began to think of him, going on submitting a report calling for a consultation on the material her late father had left her.

According to regulations, all the books and written material brought in by staff when they first joined RSU2 had to go through a security examination and registration. The books were returned to their owners, but the written material had to be kept in the office for classified material.

Ji Zhenren and Gao Yuncao explained to Chief Gao that the material under their names was an organic whole. The part under her name had been deciphered, but the part under his name had not yet been done. It was very valuable material which might be useful for cracking the Japanese army's ciphers.

Chief Gao signed off his permission, giving them two weeks to decipher the papers.

Seeing the papers, what first aroused Gao Yuncao's emotions was her late father's last words to her. She told herself, "In the current Chinese situation, anyone who was deeply conscious of the righteousness of a cause, no matter if they were KMT or Communists, had to have the determination to resist Japanese aggression to the end and to act on it." When Ji Zhenren blamed her for having achieved nothing in cracking the Japanese army's ciphers, she felt that she had been wronged. Because it was not that she did not want to achieve something, but her ability was beyond her power, therefore she was unable to achieve anything.

But now her late father's material gave her hope, firstly, giving her the courage and strength to strike down the enemy ciphers; secondly, allowing her to see if she could find technical enlightenment from them. When Ji Zhenren tried many years ago, he was an amateur cryptographer so he failed to decipher them. In recent years he had fought up and down the country, carrying them with him by mixing them with his books, showing that his determination to decipher them was everlasting.

Now they were in a better situation to get the job done. Recently RSU2 had cracked some Japanese troops' ciphers, thereby providing the initial experience that could be used as reference. For many years they had accumulated much occupational inspiration under a variety of technical circumstances, which was also a precondition for cracking ciphers.

On the first day they reviewed the already deciphered material and the related scenes floated before their eyes. Gao Yuncao was badly upset by her father's misfortune during the Sino-Japanese war of 1894-1895 and the underworld attempts at putting her grandfather to death. In earnest Ji Zhenren warned her and his words changed her state of mind, "Yuncao, if you cannot control your emotions, we will waste these two weeks." On the second and third day, they studied the Japanese military and political situations before and after the Sino-Japanese war of 1894-1895, as well as the relations between the two countries. The information in this respect was rare to see in the days when they were in Shanghai, but was plentiful now, because Chief Gao had asked people in the reference room to get it ready for them. On the fourth day and thereafter, they began to work on the undeciphered materials, sleeping only for three to four hours a day. Except for the time to eat their meals, they immersed themselves in the dark world created by Jiang Daming.

On the fourteenth day Jiang Daming vividly walked out of the darkness and the deciphering was a success. In fact, of all the material in the package, not a single code was Jiang Daming's but the Japanese and the Qing government's coded messages that he had collected. He sorted them out, summed them up and made some analysis, of which some was reasonable, while some inadvertently led people to a far-away place and down a wrong path.

Before their eyes the actual circumstances were clear: many years later, the coded messages of the Qing government deciphered by the Japanese were exposed. Jiang Daming was made a scapegoat and was put in prison. What had he done before he was put in prison? Firstly, he felt that the Japanese might have juggled things in the Chinese coded messages, so he nursed a hatred towards the Japanese. Taking advantage of his position as a telegraph operator, he began to secretly collect the Japanese coded communication material, which included the messages during the war and the day-to-day communications after the war, as well as the transcription of the original Qing government telegrams. His objective was very clear: to give the Japanese a taste of their own medicine. Since the Japanese had implemented the incident of Japan severing ties with China, he also wanted to compare the messages from the Qing government at all periods of time, in an attempt to decipher the Japanese messages. Afterwards he was released from prison. At home he did nothing but focus on deciphering those Japanese telegrams. He was overwhelmed by his hatred for the

Japanese which lasted the whole latter half of his life. His mind was driven into a corner. He spent days and nights in his study fiddling around with those papers that no one knew anything about. The result was that he came to be regarded as a lunatic in the eyes of his family members and until his death he failed to solve the mysteries in the package.

Several decades had passed since the navy battles between China and Japan in 1894-1895. Comparing the Japanese ciphers used today to those used decades ago, there were fundamental changes. However, they shared a common root and the same culture, and the influence of their cipher creators' thinking and their language structure and pattern could not be dismissed. So the material in the package could be used as a reference for the cracking of the present Japanese army's ciphers, particularly for Gao Yuncao who was coming across the Japanese ciphers for the first time, they were even more rare material.

With the inveterate hatred inherited from her father, and the fresh hatred accumulated by the death of Song Daxiong, as well as the national righteousness originating from her awakened consciousness, she was unshakable in her determination to go all out to tackle the Japanese ciphers.

After all the material was deciphered, Chief Gao spoke about a circumstance which greatly astonished her, "As early as a few months ago, Ji Zhenren had deciphered your late father's material in that package. For your last technical training session as well as the ideological initiation before you enter the battlefield of cracking Japanese ciphers, he had wholeheartedly accompanied you for two weeks. I don't know if you noticed that for those few technical breakthroughs, he did not play a crucial role. It was all you who spotted the problems; seizing upon them, you resolutely made your move and solved several thorny issues. In the end it was you who controlled the deciphering process. For the other material gathered by our underground as well as our frontline troops, he did in fact study them thoroughly. He kept this from you but let you do the work, while giving you assistance from time to time."

After thinking deeply about it, she sighed, "At the time I was only concerned about my own feelings and went all-out working on the ciphers, giving no consideration to other things. Recalling it now, it was indeed exactly as you said. In his trap I worked hard for two weeks. He really gave it a lot of thought and I must thank him for his good intentions!"

"Expressing your gratitude is a matter between you and him. But you must wait until you come back from the frontline. Including Li Mozi and Ji Hongmei, all of you must put your personal affections aside." He then talked to her about how to share technical competence among the staff and maintain tacit cooperation with each other.

Sending staff to the frontline was an unusual measure taken by the unit. Apart from increasing the surveillance of the Japanese military transceivers in the Yan'an area, RSU2 needed to expand its surveillance range and resources, so it decided to dispatch three contingents to the north China region where the Japanese and their puppet armies were active, meaning that they would monitor and transcribe right under the enemy's nose.

Ji Zhenren was leader of Team One where Li Mozi, Gao Yuncao and Ji Hongmei were team members. They left Yan'an one morning under the escort of a squad of soldiers in plain clothes.

Their destination was the Beiyue anti-Japanese base area bordering Shanxi, Chahar and Hebei. They disguised themselves as either mountain goods dealers or coal deliverers. They had six mules when they left Yan'an, and later added three more. The transceiver and the pistols were hidden in wicker baskets or inside their quilt rolls. The twelve soldiers had fought battles outdoors throughout the year so their complexions were no different to those of local labourers. Ji Zhenren and his team members had to put ashes and mud on their faces and limbs to make them look smudgy and tanned.

Clearly this was a very dangerous and arduous mission. The whole team put all their energy into the task, while Gao Yuncao had something else on her mind. After leaving the heavily guarded Yan'an, she now had a lot more personal freedom, so it was time for her to think about her mission as a KMT secret agent. She had two options: either to continue to hide in Yan'an, or to flee and return to her organisation in Chongqing.

Now she was far away from Yan'an, there was a golden opportunity for her to escape. But as a strategic spy, she had to hide for the long term in RSU2. Yet through the one-eyed chicken peddlar, she knew that her superior had issued an order that 'she could fight at the risk of mutual destruction and kill the Communists' key cryptographers'. Now she had an excellent chance to take action and then take to her heels. Ji Hongmei was a key member while Ji Zhenren and Li Mozi were pillar-level cryptographers of RSU2. So by killing them and returning to Chongqing, she would certainly achieve success and win recognition. Chief Gao, who had leadership responsibility, would also be finished after the incident. For Chongqing this would be an exceptional and outstanding achievement. What was more significant was that if she succeeded in escaping, she no longer had to wrap herself in a world of being a two-faced person. A two-faced life in the enemy camp was really hard to bear!

But if she were to take action, would her mind be at peace? After all, did Yan'an have anything worth remembering? Or was it worth staying on there? Besides, was Chongqing destined to be her final settling place? Why was she dithering? Because to dedicate her life to the party and the state, she had no other choice. Except for the fact that her beliefs had driven her to become a spy, her grandfather was being 'looked after' secretly by the party and the state. If she did not remain loyal to them, he would definitely be killed.

Yes, in order to devote herself to the lofty goal, she had come and blended into the enemy camp. It could be said that she had been closely associated with her enemy body and soul, and slowly she had developed a relationship with everything here and their feelings had become her feelings. Gradually she sensed the existence of a ruthless test of faith, and the battlefield was in her heart. Yan'an was a completely different world to her own camp in Chongqing. People here were not ordinary people but masters; while leaders here were not leaders but public servants, or ordinary soldiers, or brothers with whom you could play basketball and wrangle with. Here the leaders' power was based on the foundation of being inseparably linked to their subordinates. Her strong but also fragile heart! When the senior officer knocked her down on the basketball field, he also nearly knocked her heart into the enemy camp. How could her beliefs be so fragile? No. It had nothing to do with beliefs. She only felt that life here was leisurely and free, and that this kind of interpersonal relationship was great, that was all.

The enemy camp had exerted a subtle influence on her character before she had realised it. Or to put it bluntly, between hibernation and death, then a withered tree coming back to life was also a choice. Here no one knew that a spy called Gao Yuncao was hidden among them. In their eyes she was not a bad colleague and a good cryptographer. Deep in her heart she also regarded them as her comrades-in-arms, with whom she shared a common goal. Go and erase her past, but let a brand new Gao Yuncao grow. To Chongqing, she was either dead or still in hibernation; to Yan'an she was standing up to be counted and becoming a fine Communist army cryptographer.

But was it feasible?

"You're daydreaming. You have been made to measure. Is it still possible for me to choose and reestablish myself? No, absolutely not! Since there is no other choice for me, let me do a great deed: kill them to help myself to achieve my goal."

So she had an idea. Finding an opportunity when they encountered the enemy, suddenly and from behind, she would shoot the three of them dead and then quietly run away.

But such a chance was hard to come by. Later an unrelated incident forced her to shelve her plan.

Except for working together, Ji Hongmei always avoided Li Mozi; besides she had declined him several times when he had shown that he liked her. She had a clear-cut stand that she was Ji Zhenfu's child bride and the notion of 'childhood sweetheart' had become deeply rooted in her mind. However, although she had declined him, her admiration for him had become deeper and deeper. Because she was handicapped by that mental shackle, she was unable to give free rein to her true feelings.

Ji Zhenren's intention was to bring Ji Hongmei and Li Mozi together. In fact, if he had wanted to make things simple, he could have told Ji Hongmei that Ji Zhenfu had defected to the KMT and had been executed. But the true circumstances about Ji Zhenfu could not be leaked, under strict orders from Chief Gao. Neither did he dare to reveal that his elder brother had died by his hand. So he tried to find another way. He could tell her that their mother and younger sister had died, with the intention of letting her realise that no news of Ji Zhenfu for so many years meant that the possibility of him also being dead was fairly strong.

It was a very painful thing to do. He didn't have the courage to talk to Ji Hongmei to her face, so he told Gao Yuncao about how his mother and younger sister had died during the Long March. Gao Yuncao was completely shocked and sad. During his narrative, he had no tears in his eyes, but his heart felt as though it was being pierced by a knife. He asked Gao Yuncao to explain this to Ji Hongmei.

"It's hard for me to comprehend, so how can Hongmei forgive you? It's better if we don't mention anything about it to her," said Gao Yuncao.

"Immediate agony is better than chronic pain; sooner or later she will get to know about it. Once she knows the truth, it may help her to develop her relationship with Li Mozi."

"All these years you've heard nothing about Ji Zhenfu?"

"Ever since the guerrilla detachment in Wushan of east Hubei was crushed, there has been no news of him. It seems the odds were against him rather than in his favour. You must properly remind Hongmei of this possibility."

Gao Yuncao went to talk to Ji Hongmei, who cried her heart out after hearing about the death of her mother and sister. She dashed to a shabby temple where Ji Zhenren was sleeping. Lifting him in the air, she gave him two hard punches on the ear, "From today you are not my brother, nor a son of the Ji family."

Holding his face in his hands, Ji Zhenren thought, "If I tell her that Ji Zhenfu has died, she will definitely kill me."

In the following days Gao Yuncao did not see any development in the relationship between Ji Hongmei and Li Mozi; on the contrary she noticed that Ji Hongmei had distanced herself further from Li Mozi. She thought that until she knew exactly what had happened to Ji Zhenfu, the very stubborn Hongmei would not make any realistic choices.

Ji Hongmei became estranged from Ji Zhenren. Except for work, she would not say a word to him. When Ji Zhenren tried to talk to her, she said, "You only want assignments but not your family, where are your human feelings? I will never mix with someone who has no human feelings. I am ashamed that the Ji family has a son like you who has violated filial obligations, and a brother who has been heartless to his sister."

"Under the circumstances, you would have done the same if you were in my position," argued Ji Zhenren.

"You think everyone is like you. To me you have been groomed and demoralised by the political hen, Song Daxiong," cried Ji Hongmei.

"You can curse me, but I will never allow you to smear Song Daxiong! She had a noble character in her moral and Party spirit. She was the noblest person I have ever met in my life. No one has the right to criticise or insult her," said Ji Zhenren, annoyed.

"How do you have the nerve to talk about it? Then why did you push that good woman into Qiu Zihao's arms? In order to have your new love, you abandoned the woman who had looked after you every day in the heat of war. She gave you all her love, even her life. Tell me, have you treated Song Daxiong fairly? In this life of yours, have you behaved worthily to those closest to you?" countered Ji Hongmei.

Gao Yuncao followed Ji Hongmei to the temple. Unable to take any more she turned around and left, quickening her pace and with her mind in turmoil, "Is Ji Zhenren really so heartless? How can I comprehend what he has done and how he has behaved toward his family members? I cannot understand him now, but will I be able to understand him once my realm of thought reaches a higher plane? How high must it be before I can understand him?"

The one with a sinister scheme in mind began to berate herself, "Don't forget you're a KMT secret agent who renders service to repay the kindness of the party and the state. A few days ago you were plotting to kill them, but due to minor personal sentiments for Ji Hongmei, Li Mozi and Ji Zhenren, your interest in your mission flagged easily, and even your self-belief wavered again and again. Gao Yuncao, what has become of you? How terrible!"

Before long the Japanese armies started a winter mopping-up operation of the Communist bases in the mountains of Shanxi, Chahar and Hebei, attempting to find and annihilate the Eighth Route Army's main forces. Major General Token Toshihide, Commander of the Independent Mixed Brigade and an expert in mountain warfare was leading the operation.

Yan'an sent Ji Zhenren and his team a telegram, ordering them to take advantage of the situation whereby the Japanese troops were communicating with each other via wireless, and to go all-out to monitor and transcribe their coded messages; and, meanwhile, to cooperate with the Shanxi-Chahar-Hebei Military Command to battle against the enemy.

The difficulty for the team to cooperate with the combat troops was that when they moved around the area where the Japanese troops were operating, they could capture and transcribe their coded messages. However the cipher level was very high and many of them were compiled by machines, so it was unrealistic for them to achieve what they had achieved in the past by using manpower to crack the KMT armies' ciphers in hours or days. They had to transcribe a large number of high-quality messages and gather their wits to make a breakthrough; only after using enough abacuses to carry out tens or even hundreds of days of calculation was there a possibility, and only a possibility, of them cracking the ciphers.

With years of experience and a good command of the Japanese language, despite the fact that Ji Zhenren and Gao Yuncao could not decipher whole messages, from the headlines, the ends and the communication characteristics of infantry and artillery, they could still get a whiff of the Japanese units, distinguishing their transceiver signal features so as to lock on to their positions. Besides, all the team members knew English, which was also a help. They knew that the Japanese armies were using a Latin alphabet for their telegraphic code, not like the KMT troops who were using numerals. Two Latin letters represented a Japanese katakana, and by using irregular-multiple changes the Japanese set up traps and the structure of their ciphers. Most of these changes were complicated. Despite the difficulties, Ji Zhenren and his team still managed to discern some regularity. According to the codes in Japanese characters and the frequency of appearance of certain phrases and their habitual usage, they made a graph of the data. After analysing the graph, they slowly got to know some of the Japanese frontline transceivers' call signals, wavelengths, communication times and the contact relationships between the transceivers. They generally knew the designation of some of the enemy units, their positions and deployment circumstances. Yet they could not immediately decipher full messages, so it was difficult to obtain sufficient detailed information except for the enemy positions and movements, which were passed on to all the units under the Shanxi-Chahar-Hebei Command to directly support the Eighth Route Army's combat operations.

During the whole process, Ji Zhenren and Gao Yuncao coordinated their thinking and judgement of the situation surprisingly well. Several times Li Mozi quoted idioms such as *'Lovers' hearts are closely linked'*, or *'Great minds think alike'*, or *'Breathe through the same nostrils'* and *'One mind in two bodies'*, to make fun of them.

One day Ji Zhenren said, "In the last few days the Japanese messages featured one word which appeared in a sensitive place many times, followed immediately by a time: 20:00 on the second day."

"I feel the same. It is 'GM'. Does it represent an army unit, a kind of weapon, an event or a location?" Gao Yuncao echoed.

"Correct, 'GM'. Although we cannot decipher the full text of the messages containing this phrase, I can confidently make the judgement that it refers to a certain element of the enemy. I also vaguely feel that it is the name of a place. Two enemy units had 'GM' appearing in their coded messages several times, which location is it connected to?"

"The time is particularly puzzling. In a place called 'GM' and at 20:00, what do the two enemy units want to do? We have intercepted messages showing enemy positions, we might as well compare them to where our troops are stationed and make a careful study of the circumstances."

Finally they discovered that these two Japanese units were close to our 3rd and 541st Regiments. The Japanese might have been planning to attack them. If this were to be the case, 'GM' must have been where our troops were stationed, yet the Japanese telegrams showed that it was where their own troops were stationed.

Standing in front of a map, Ji Zhenren gestured with his finger among the mountain ranges. Watching his finger moving, Gao Yuncao suddenly clapped her hands, crying out, "Let's go back to Token Toshihide. This general is an illustrious expert in mountain warfare in the Japanese army. His forte is to fight battles by exploiting the terrain."

"That's right. This 'GM' could probably, possibly, may be the Hugou township at the foot of Huyong mountain," said Ji Zhenren, tapping the map.

"To hell with your probably, possibly and maybe. How can we report these evasive, ambiguous conclusions to our headquarters?" grumbled Ji Hongmei.

"We can't decipher the full text of the enemy messages yet. Seizing useful intelligence from fragmentary bits of information to draw an ambiguous conclusion is not easy. I know what he is thinking," said Gao Yuncao.

Ji Zhenren threw her a smile, saying, "This mountain warfare expert will probably not launch an offensive on either our 3rd or 541st Regiment, but exploit Huyong mountain to launch a surprise attack on our New Eighth Regiment stationed in the hinterland on the back of the mountain. Huyong mountain is two thousand metres above sea level, seemingly not suitable for a large contingent of troops to march over. But there must be small narrow paths for troops to travel on.

Once they climb over the mountain, after a 130-kilometre long-range raid, they can reach where our New Eighth Regiment is stationed. This will have the effect of surprising our troops by stabbing them in the back with a knife. We have always regarded our New Eighth Regiment as the safest garrisoned troops by stationing them in the hinterland with a mountain behind. Besides, its combat strength is the strongest among our regiments. Token Toshihide likes to tackle arduous tasks, so trekking over mountains to launch a surprise attack conforms to his character. What he relishes is precisely the unexpected."

"If there really is a path to cross over the mountain, then two enemy battalions could be driven to Hugou township to assemble before 20:00 on the second day of the month. They would then trek over the mountain to make a surprise attack on our New Eighth Regiment. What is crucial for us now is to make sure about the intelligence. We should go to Huyong mountain to investigate," suggested Gao Yuncao.

"If there is a path over the mountain that is accessible by troops, we need to find a way to examine if 'GM' stands for Hugou township," said Ji Zhenren.

They set off the same night, arriving at Huyong mountain on the third morning. At once they trekked up the mountain and asked the villagers for information. They went to a few mountain passes to carry out an on-the-spot investigation and their final conclusion was that troops could cross the mountain via three gullies and small paths. Although some sections were dangerously steep and difficult, they were not impassable to the well-trained Japanese soldiers.

Then how to confirm 'GM' was Hugou township? They spent a long time wandering around the hills near the fortified Hugou. Ji Zhenren then called to mind the fire on Limao mountain in the Jiangxi Soviet.

Gao Yuncao asked him if he wanted to start a bush fire to force the enemy to use their transceiver to contact their headquarters. He said yes, but starting a bush fire could be a problem. Because to prevent the Eighth Route Army from raiding them with the aid of the mountain forest, the Japanese had cut down all the trees within a kilometre of the township. If the bush fire failed to affect the enemy fortress, a transceiver could not be used by the enemy to call for outside help. However, we could have started a bush fire on the left side of the hill with the aim of making the enemy in the Hetaokou fortress sixteen kilometres away mistakenly think there was a big fire in Hugou township. Hugou was in front while the bush fire was at the back, so the three happen to be on the same axis. Watching in the dark from Hetaokou, it would look like Hugou township was on fire, so there was a strong possibility that the enemy in Hetaokou would send telegrams to Hugou asking for information.

The four of them had a discussion and all felt that the plan was feasible. At night they started a fire on the hill. In winter the trees were dry and the wind was strong, and before long Ji Hongmei caught strong, clear radio signals, which had obviously been sent out by the transceivers in Hetaokou and Hugou to enquire about what was going on and the replies. Before the woods burnt out, the team quickly withdrew from the site.

They studied the messages. As expected they discovered that both the header from Hetaokou and the ending from Hugou had 'GM' appended. Yes, 'GM' was undoubtedly the name of Hugou township!

At once they reported their prediction that the Japanese armies would raid our New Eighth Regiment to the military command, who took the intelligence seriously. "Generally the intelligence from RSU2 is believable. Although they have no full texts to confirm it, their prediction is also valuable. Send our ground scouts to this area. We must also formulate a corresponding battle plan as soon as possible. If this prediction is proved, the battle must be fought and won. Token Toshihide is a general who is good at doing big things, so we must be fully prepared for battle."

What happened afterwards was not complicated. More radio interceptions and the information from the scouts confirmed that our New Eighth Regiment was the primary target of Token Toshihide's attack.

The military command's battle plan was excellent and cunning. Using the New Eighth Regiment as bait, we fought a beautiful battle, ambushing and wiping out more than seven hundred of the enemy. Next, we made full use of Token Toshihide's 'eye for an eye' mentality, as well as his impatience. We used a small force to draw the enemy into the depths of a gorge near our base where we laid the biggest ambush since the countermopping-up campaign started.

During the fierce fighting, Ji Zhenren and his team provided two lots of weighty intelligence to the headquarters. They found out afterwards that one of the regular intelligence reports had brought a surprising battle result.

The team had two monitors and both had caught radio signals coming from a village on the north face of the mountain range. These signals were extremely strong and concentrated. Although they could not decipher the full text of the messages, from the circumstances they judged that the village must have been the enemy's headquarters. They reported their judgement to the military command who took the information seriously. Before long the military command received intelligence from the frontline scouts that there was an independent courtyard in the village and they saw Japanese army officers going in and out of it. The military command at once called a mortar company to shell the courtyard and its surroundings.

The second weighty bit of intelligence was that after the enemy command post was shelled, enemy reinforcements rushed toward the village from all directions, seemingly with the intention of encircling our attacking troops. The military command stopped at the right time, ordering our troops to withdraw from the battle.

Gao Yuncao and Ji Hongmei had been monitoring and transcribing messages. Before they withdrew, they were itching to kill a few Japanese devils. So when the others were pulling out, they moved close to a horde of Japanese soldiers. At first they fired their pistols, then they picked up rifles and enjoyed themselves to the full by firing at the enemy. Gao Yuncao had received regular training at the KMT's spy training base, so she feared nothing of the scene. But Ji Hongmei trembled with fear as soon as she heard gun shots. However, when she saw Gao Yuncao enjoying herself so much, she summoned up the courage to also fire at the enemy. Gao Yuncao then winked at Ji Hongmei and they moved closer and threw a few grenades into the enemy crowd. Seeing the scene, Ji Zhenren hurriedly ordered the team and the guards platoon to give the two girls covering fire so that they could extricate themselves and pull out. Furious, he pointed his pistol at them, bellowing, "You wretched bastards. You want to get yourselves killed?"

Quickly they pulled out of the fighting with no one dropping out. Since leaving Yan'an, they had travelled across mountains and rivers, marching day and night. Their skins were as tanned as those of the local farmers. Having developed the ability to run fast, they became physically stronger with each passing day. When they were in Yan'an, Gao Yuncao had tried hard to get Ji Zhenren to build up his physique, even trying to wrestle with him. But he had refused. If the story of him wrestling with a woman had broken in Yan'an, people would have laughed their heads off. She argued that if the senior officer could compete with her for basketball, knocking each other down on the floor, why couldn't he wrestle with her? Wasn't he more privileged than the senior officer? As he spoke, she went up to him, grabbed his shoulders and threw him to the ground. Angry and embarrassed, he got up and scuffled with her but her wrestling prowess meant she was instantly able to subdue him. Yet she didn't display her skills too openly but let him retain some confidence. After grappling with each other, she threw him to the ground. Refusing to accept defeat, he often found her to do some wrestling. Once they had physical contact, their relations deepened swiftly.

In the retreat, to punish Gao Yuncao for her mistake, Ji Zhenren tied the heaviest equipment on her back, saying, "From now on you are responsible for looking after this machine. You must carry it wherever you go." Seeing that he was still angry, she dared not say no. Dejected, she began to run with the machine tied on her back.

By arrangement, they retreated along a small path. After climbing over a hill, a group of Japanese soldiers appeared ahead. At once both parties scattered onto the slopes and began to exchange fire. Quickly Ji Zhenren judged that these Japanese were the remnants escaping from the ambush. According to the established ironclad rules, they were not supposed to zealously continue fighting when they engaged with the enemy, and under no circumstances could they fail to prioritise protecting the machines, the intercepted enemy telegrams and the technical personnel. There were around sixty to seventy of the enemy, who clearly outnumbered them. What were they to do? Everyone turned to Ji Zhenren, who felt that these Japanese were routed troops who must have had their own psychological issues. He whispered into Li Mozi's ears, then ordered his side to stop shooting.

Then a grenade flew at them and landed beside Gao Yuncao and Ji Hongmei, who jumped up from the slope and threw herself on top of Gao Yuncao.

Their cease-fire surprised the enemy. In a low voice, Ji Zhenren ordered everyone to withdraw to the east slope of the hill. He then stood up, calling out, "You little Japanese devils, come and chase us." They began to run toward the east slope.

A miracle occurred. Not only did the enemy not chase Ji Zhenren and his team, they retreated toward the west slope. Clearly the enemy thought that this Eighth Route Army's plainclothes contingent was luring them into a ring of encirclement, so they turned around and fled by a roundabout route.

Holding Ji Hongmei in her arms Gao Yuncao was weeping. Soaked in blood, Ji Hongmei had lost consciousness, while Gao Yuncao was also wounded in the leg.

Ji Zhenren was so anxious that his face was streaming with sweat. He discussed the situation with Li Mozi, "We must send the wounded to our 3rd Regiment for treatment. But we must pass the checkpoint in Tuobei Village, a Japanese fortified point. If we take a roundabout route, we'll have to climb two mountains. I'm afraid Hongmei cannot afford to wait that long."

He then remembered that each of them had a Japanese army uniform in their blanket roll, so he asked everyone to dress up as Japanese soldiers, falsely claiming that they were escaping from the ambush ring and carrying wounded soldiers to the medical unit of the Tagi Regiment for treatment. Ji Zhenren analysed the situation and he believed that two favourable conditions might bring about the success of the action: firstly, the enemy had just suffered a defeat so the enemy in the village were all badly frightened, therefore they were unlikely to come looking for trouble; secondly, they were in Japanese army uniform, and could also speak Japanese; in particular, from the intercepted telegrams they knew the commander in Tuobei Village was called Shinko Ichiro. If they shouted at him under the wall of the fortified point, there was a strong possibility that they would get past.

So they cut down some trees and made two stretchers. Carrying Gao Yuncao and Ji Hongmei, they ran to Tuobei Village where four Japanese soldiers stopped them at the checkpoint. An army officer stepped out of a blockhouse. In fluent Japanese Ji Zhenren called out, "Are you Major Shinko? We are from the 1st Battalion of the 2nd Regiment. Our commander is Itada Kozan. These two were badly wounded, please let us pass without delay."

Without hesitation Major Shinko called back, "I'll let you pass right away, as well as send you a medic to meet your urgent need!"

Saluting, Ji Zhenren said, "I will come and thank you another day."

Carrying a medical box across his shoulder, a Japanese soldier ran out of the fortified village following Ji Zhenren and his team. After passing a grove, Ji Zhenren asked the Japanese medic to treat Gao Yuncao and Ji Hongmei.

Before reaching the place where our 3rd Regiment was garrisoned, to avoid being mistaken as Japanese soldiers, Ji Zhenren and his team took off their Japanese army uniforms. Li Mozi had disarmed the Japanese medic before he realised what was happening.

Ji Hongmei's wounds were serious. Shrapnel had pierced her right ribs, luckily missing her internal organs. Her left arm was also wounded. Gao Yuncao had a piece of flesh sliced off her right thigh, but the wound was not serious.

Before long, from a Japanese radio broadcast, Ji Zhenren heard the bulletin issued by the Japanese Imperial Army about the death of Token Toshihide, the highest-ranking commander killed in the small courtyard on the north side of the mountain by our mortar company. Prior to the news bulletin no one would have thought that Token Toshihide would be among the dead, let alone that his death would have shaken the Japanese government.

After this battle experience, Gao Yuncao thought a lot. She had finally answered her late father's last will to her. Besides, she was wounded, so she gave up on the idea of running away and going back to Chongqing. In particular, the fact that Ji Hongmei had risked her own life to save her, that had a huge impact on her. She was deeply grateful and would never forget it.

After they returned to Yan'an, Chief Gao went to see Gao Yuncao, who was bent over her desk sorting out documents. In fact her mind was not on the papers. She was thinking what a pity it was she could no longer wrestle with Ji Zhenren once they returned to Yan'an. The thought of the happy moments when they held each other's arms and wrestled made her face flush when she heard Chief Gao saying, "Comrade Yuncao, you can write your application now." Hearing it, her mind followed her happy memories of the wrestling between her and Ji Zhenren, and her face turned redder.

"If an application is needed," she murmured seductively, "it should be him that writes it. Go and ask him to do it."

"It has to be you that writes it. He can only be your sponsor."

"What? My sponsor? He will introduce me to…? But…, but I don't know who that man will be. Is it appropriate for me to write the application?" She was startled.

"Who will that man be?"

"No one can make me marry anybody else. Humph! I never thought that he wanted to introduce me to somebody else. Who does he want to introduce me to?" She was very angry.

Suddenly it dawned on Chief Gao. Laughing out loud, he said: "It's my fault that I didn't make myself clear. What I am asking you to write is not an application for marriage, but for joining the Party."

Gao Yuncao's eyes welled up, holding her face she ran out of the office as Ji Zhenren was entering. He asked Chief Gao, "Are you sure she's all right?"

"Why not? Will becoming a party member frighten her to death?" grumbled Chief Gao, staring at Ji Zhenren.

Finally Gao Yuncao decided that she would join the Communist Party of China (CPC).

She then examined her conscience:

Is this change an issue of faith or morality? Am I the kind of person who can easily give up my beliefs? No. This change is only an issue of morality, and a process for an old-fashioned person to abandon the old and seek the new, and to break away from degeneration to become a new person in pursuit of freedom.

But it is a sin to betray one's faith. My sin is that I have developed compassion and reverence for these outstanding people. I admit that when I saw the army with so many talented people like Gao Yueming, Ji Zhenren, Song Daxiong, Li Mozi and Ji Hongmei, who were repeatedly under threat of being wiped out by the KMT government, I developed compassion for it. I also admit that I have seen through the decadence of that murderous KMT government as well as the well-regulated political environment of the Communist troops. Ji Zhenren and the others have only seen the solid integrity of the Communists, they have not had a chance to see the evil corruption of the KMT. But I am different. I have worked on both sides, so I can make a comparison, and under such circumstances, my allegiance has changed.

The political studies organised by Chief Gao to imbue the staff with revolutionary theories every day and every year have slowly taken root, germinated, blossomed and borne fruit in me when I was adopting the attitude of half-declining and half-accepting. I was completely unaware of the change in me. As the saying goes, anything in the world can become the seed of a person's transformation; that's right. A boring lecture in the classroom, an empty-sounding slogan, emotional humility, a carefree basketball game, an innocent collision on the sports ground, a heroic feat of saving another's life at the risk of one's own and vigorous love, all these can drive people crazy, transform them and enable them to be reborn.

Everyone yearns to obtain all the experience they can get, and everyone fears that their infinite expectations will be shattered a little. I will inscribe on my application form the days when I gained my enlightenment and the moments I acquired the most satisfaction. When I put pen to paper to write down my oath, I will feel that a dream is not only day in night but also night in day for a person. "All failures may also be mystical victories." The phrase I have been turning over in my mind speaks this truth. I must reestablish my image. But my new image has not been fully developed and it needs time to reach perfection. What I lack for the time being is confidence and willpower.

One day she suddenly said to herself, "I joined the Communist Party to hide more deeply to seek greater political advantages and for me to serve the KMT and the state better one day." Unexpectedly, she was frightened by this idea of hers! "No matter what, I have been in fact admitted to membership of the CPC!"

Ji Hongmei also submitted her application but her membership was rejected because Ji Zhenren opposed it resolutely, stating, "Regarding the relationship between sacrificing individual interests and safeguarding overall victory, in other words, whether the individual interests or the work and task have priority, Ji Hongmei has an incorrect attitude and a low level of understanding. She is not up to the standard of being a Party member." What he meant was that on the issue of the death of their mother and sister, Ji Hongmei had an incorrect prejudice against him, and her understanding of the issue was to a certain degree politically wrong in principle.

In the face of Ji Hongmei's complaints and blame, Ji Zhenren had always listened quietly, never arguing with her. Several times he even looked ashamed and shed tears of remorse. There were two occasions when he slapped his own face. But this time he took the matter so seriously that he set himself against her, "To be honest, speaking from the angle of being related by blood, no matter how she complains, blames, even bears grudges, or hurls abuse at me, I can understand her. But from a viewpoint of political consciousness, her ideological understanding is truly not up to the standard required for a Party member. It is in the public interest that I object to her joining the Party. I also want to use the opportunity to arouse her desire to speed up her ideological progress. Because she is so obstinate in her views that if we can use this solemn event to give her a push, it may be easier for her to sober up and undertake a self-examination. I am doing this for her own good."

However, Ji Hongmei not only refused to change her attitude to him as he had hoped, but reduced her relationship with him to freezing point. She had her name Ji Hongmei changed to Liu Hongmei and she even refused to put 'Ji Hongmei' in the column for 'other name(s)' in her personnel file or on other forms. She felt that her feelings had been repeatedly and badly hurt by Ji Zhenren.

Although Gao Yuncao wanted to marry Ji Zhenren very much, she was in two minds. The knot in her heart was her hidden identity: after they became husband and wife, if by accident her identity as a spy was exposed, it would cause him fatal damage.

Later, in a mentally demanding and highly intensive push for a solution to the enemy ciphers, Ji Zhenren suffered a serious illness, coming within an inch of his life, which precipitated Gao Yuncao's decision to marry him.

She proposed to him. Although he felt pressed but was too embarrassed to write the application. "Battles are fought one after another, how can we ask for a favour for a private matter?"

She was insistent. "If you are needed to fight battles all your life, you're going to be a lifetime bachelor, aren't you? This doesn't make any sense." She hurried off to see Chief Gao, calling out, "I like him, I love him and I want to marry him. If you don't grant us permission to get married, I will go under your window and bang my washbowl every night."

Chief Gao was startled, then laughed, "You have made your intentions so clear, presumably it's a matter more urgent than battles, so I give my approval." Give her an inch and she takes a mile.

"Another couple is also in urgent need of getting married," said Gao Yuncao. "Can you also give them approval?" She went to find Liu Hongmei, "You and Li Mozi must not wait any more. Let us hold our weddings together."

Still angry with Ji Zhenren, Liu Hongmei muttered, "Stop your unwarranted concerns about others. Anyway, if I were to get married, I wouldn't stand on the same platform as Ji Zhenren for my wedding ceremony. It's bad luck to be near him, a man with no human nature!"

Pointing her finger at Liu Hongmei, Gao Yuncao said, "I'm going to marry a man with no human nature, what have I become? I will never allow you to insult him like that or I will not attend your wedding when you get married!"

Liu Hongmei sighed: "I don't know if that day will ever come for me."

The wedding banquet was very simple. Ji Zhenren and Gao Yuncao paid the canteen that bought some pork for them. Each table was allowed two meat dishes and the wedding ceremony was done. Next to their office, they built an eight-square-metre bridal chamber with walls of rammed earth and a bridal bed by putting a few willow tree boards on a pile of stones at two ends. Carrying their quilts to the room, they spent their honeymoon in the still damp bridal chamber. After the honeymoon was over, they moved out and returned to the cave dwelling dormitory. Ever since then this small room had become a public 'room for lovebirds'. RSU2 would arrange for married couples to take turns living in it for a week every three months, which became a unique benefit for married people.

Gao Yuncao had finally harvested love, but she was uneasy in bed on the wedding night. Only after an inward self-talk, did she eliminate her uneasiness.

"My marriage to Ji Zhenren is so that I can be better hidden in RSU2, an excellent cover for me and a basic support for my mission. Of course it is the result of love and emotional need. We married purely for love. This is a question of principle and I must explain it clearly to myself, otherwise I will be uneasy and unable to sleep."

Sleep, sleep, but she could not sleep. She then thought of Liu Hongmei, "I owe my life to her." Liu Hongmei risking her own life to save her, the relationship between the members of the Communist armies and the reason why Ji Zhenren was opposing the move to grant Liu Hongmei membership of the Party brought her to reach the conclusion, "In the place of Yan'an, there are many things people have to think about but often find hard to understand. However, it is because these things are so attractive that my heart has been tightly attached to this loess plateau, making me unable to escape or leave. Since I cannot leave, I must stay and take part in the revolution like a real local!" In the end she returned to the question of principle and managed to sleep for a little while.

Gao Yuncao did not sleep well and Liu Hongmei was also agitated that night. She got up and went to the courtyard for a breath of fresh air, where she saw Li Mozi also taking a stroll. Giving a wry smile, she said, "Seeing others married, you can't sleep?" Li Mozi said nothing.

Liu Hongmei went on, "When we were on the front line, we were together day and night for several months. I experienced something that I had never experienced before. It was a mysterious experience, which I defined as a terribly happy feeling. Of course, it was from you that I had this feeling. Mozi, quietly you walked into my heart, and without noticing it, I also accepted you. This is how terrible a happy feeling can be. To tell the truth I grew up in the Ji family and I did have some hazy feelings for Ji Zhenfu. So before I have precise news about him, I will not have the peace of mind to accept your love. If one day he were to suddenly appear before me, you and I would not have a future. Mozi, I am telling you about this because I don't want to keep you waiting for me. You are a Red Army veteran, so go and find a suitable girl and get married."

In the dark she could not see his facial expression, but she heard him mumbling two words, "I'll wait!"

Before their wedding, Ji Zhenren and Gao Yuncao had participated in a remarkable battle to crack an enemy cipher.

It was an unprecedented joint effort. RSU2 submitted a written request which was approved by the senior officers who confirmed the leading team with Chief Gao being the chief commander and Ji Zhenren, Li Mozi, Gao Yuncao and Liu Hongmei the team members. The other participants were 298 cryptographers carefully selected from the cryptography system in Yan'an. Ji Zhenren and Li Mozi were jointly responsible for organising the daily work.

Before the battle commenced, people from all departments of RSU2 had clarified the basic nature of the target cipher, a special mechanically-created cipher. RSU2 had never cracked a cipher like this before. Technically speaking, the coding principle of this type of cipher was formulated by using multi-functional and multi-group coding machines, through constant changes to form different internal coding installations, and one installation could produce a million or more variables. That was to say, ciphers created by coding machines could be differentiated monthly, daily, hourly, message by message, paragraph by paragraph and even word by word. In the past, one cipher for one message or for one use was the most difficult thing for them to deal with, but this cipher before their eyes could achieve one cipher per word, which meant each word could be encrypted in a different cipher. For instance, if a message had five hundred words, it could be encrypted with five hundred ciphers. If one cipher was cracked after some strenuous work, it meant that only one word was deciphered, and 499 ciphers and words still needed to be cracked and deciphered before the whole message could be read. Therefore the degree of security defied the imagination.

Chief Gao explained the significance of the operation to the 302 cryptographers, "At the moment we mainly depend on manual operation to crack enemy ciphers. This time we must smash the myth that manual techniques cannot crack mechanically-encrypted ciphers. If we succeed, it will have an epoch-making significance on the history of cipher cracking. This is truly a hard nut! The degree of difficulty is equivalent to that of a man stepping on another man's shoulder to pick up a star in the sky. But my intuition tells me that although the possibility is extremely small it can be done! You must believe me as you believe the sun rises in the east every day. I can do it, you can do it, RSU2 can do it! From now on, let the beads of abacuses begin to sound non-stop twenty-four hours a day, every day. The operation may last for ten to fourteen days, or six to twelve months, or three to five years! How long will it take? I have no idea. But we must do it regardless! If we don't do it, we have none of the beliefs that a Communist Party member should have. If we don't do it, there is no need for RSU2 to exist!"

Chief Gao named twenty senior cryptographers to shoulder the main responsibility. Each was in charge of ten ideas and led fifteen cryptographers who each worked on two abacuses round the clock until they cracked the set of ciphers. Ji Zhenren and Li Mozi were not among the twenty senior cryptographers. Li Mozi assisted Chief Gao to look after the whole work, coordinating all affairs between higher and lower levels, while Ji Zhenren only strolled among the sound of abacuses every day. His eyes swept through all sorts of facial expressions of the three hundred cryptographers and the ever changing beads of the six hundred abacuses. He was thinking and calculating and clear about every small change in numbers. He could scatter his thinking at any moment, like numerous invisible fine threads sticking to or intertwining with dozens or hundreds of abacuses, while at the same time, and for the same element, coming to the exceptionally identical conclusions as three hundred cryptographers' changing thoughts and exquisite calculations.

The operation was carried out in a shed built along a slope with sun-dried mud bricks, wooden beams, straw, straw mats and mud, large enough to hold three hundred people working there. When it started, 421 abacuses began to work noisily. The awesome might terrorised the birds in the sky and on the tree-covered hill. The twittering of the birds and the sound of the wind were all gone. In this mysterious valley, only the clacking sound of abacuses became more and more intense.

It was a contest of intelligence and a call for inspiration of intuition as well as a test of physical strength. By the fifteenth day, nearly half of the cryptographers had broken down; by the dawn of the twentieth day, less than a hundred were left; by midnight on the twenty-fifth day, only seventy-one were still sitting in front of the abacuses. At this moment Ji Zhenren suffered back pain, causing numbness in his lower limbs. He was in so much pain that he could not walk but had to crawl among the desks. Once he was at work, his face never showed the agony he was in or how tired he felt.

Each of the twenty teams was given ten possible ideas, so two hundred in total. These ideas were decided after Chief Gao led Ji Zhenren and the other three members of the command team to discuss them over and over again. They sincerely believed that the ciphers had to be hidden among these two hundred probabilities. But after three hundred people had worked for twenty-five days, 181 ideas were confirmed wrong. Nearly all the cryptographers lost confidence. Because the most likely solution was among these 181 ideas, they saw no prospect of victory in them. The remaining nineteen were the least promising ideas, where hope was even slimmer.

Sighs were heard behind the *clacking* sound of abacus beads. Like everyone else, Ji Zhenren almost gave up hope, too. After a fit of coughing, a few drops of blood stained his handkerchief. Seeing the blood, he felt chilled, saying inwardly, "The sound of abacus beads is my funeral music. I will die in this shed." Suddenly he got up from the floor, shouting, "That damned cipher is hiding in the remaining nineteen ideas. It must be there. Definitely there." Before he had finished shouting, he had another fit of coughing. Everyone's eyes were on the abacus beads, so no one paid attention to his sickly appearance. In a weak voice he muttered again, "Now I announce that everyone should go to bed. At eight o'clock tomorrow morning anyone who can crawl on their hands and knees to the shed will form a death squad with me. Then we'll launch the final assault. Success or failure hinges on this single action. Dismissed!" He then sank onto a camp bed.

At midnight he had a nightmare. He was flying down the mountain ranges with a sharp knife in hot pursuit, flashing and whistling. A bottomless chasm appeared ahead. As soon as he stopped, he heard the knife ferociously whizzing toward him. In desperation he closed his eyes and waited to die. Once, in desperation, the ear-piercing sound disappeared. Turning around he saw what was flying toward him was not a knife but a fine needle. He laughed, "Heaven does not want me to die. What can a little fine needle do to me?" Suddenly he felt pain in his heels. Spontaneously he jumped into the air, but he lost his balance, falling off the cliff and was smashed to pieces.

He woke up, dripping with sweat. His sleepiness had all gone. He went to sit at the desk, raising his face and closing his eyes. He sat there motionless for a long, long time. Suddenly he grabbed pen and paper, quickly going through the 181 dead ends. Of course he only glanced over each key point. He then reorganised the remaining nineteen ideas and designed a new one. He told himself: "This is the one! This is definitely the one! This is the last straw, also the only wire to go across the steep cliff and precipice. If we don't want to be crushed by it, we must walk across this wire."

At eight o'clock the next morning, sixty-eight cryptographers came, haggard and with bloodshot eyes. Some were even still half-sleep, coming in by holding the door frame.

Sitting cross-legged on the camp bed, Ji Zhenren issued orders for the last assault. Throwing into the air the fourteen pages covered with the detailed ideas and solutions he had written down, he said, "You sixty-eight warriors all step on this piece of wire. Charge!" When he had finished speaking, he dropped onto the camp bed face-up and went into a trance.

During the days of the fierce battle to tackle the ciphers, Ji Zhenren had little time to sleep. Every waking moment he was searching for solutions. Even in his sleep he went on searching in corners he could not reach when awake, attempting to make a breakthrough in his dreams. Yes, 24 hours a day, his mind never left ciphers by half a step. He was no longer the master of his brain, it was out of control.

When his dream was in a tense state, he was woken up by some noises. Eighteen more cryptographers withdrew from the battle, lying on the floor tiles sleeping. Then a dying voice came to his ears and it was Gao Yuncao's voice, "Old Ji, this is another dead end!"

Grabbing the fourteen pages, he took a quick look, crying out, "Impossible! That demon must be among them. Continue." But the remaining fifty cryptographers stopped flicking the abacus beads. There was complete silence.

Tearfully, someone yelled, "Ji Zhenren, how can you be so certain that the answer must be in these fourteen sheets of paper? The number fourteen (read *yao si* in Mandarin, the same sound as the characters for 'about to die'); this time RSU2 will surely die. Your wretched Ji Zhenren has got a fourteen-page solution. Humph! What bad luck!" When cryptographers were in a hopeless situation, their nerves were very fragile. Filled with complaints, the shadow of an unlucky number could knock down many a genius. Ji Zhenren knew very well what it would be like for a cryptographer when a problem was beyond his mental capacity. At this critical moment, he needed to add a little bit of fresh confidence and courage to the men whose backs were about to be broken by that piece of straw.

Therefore he said, "Fourteen is an unlucky number, but fifteen is a good number. Fifteen (read *yao wu* in Mandarin, the same sound as the characters for 'making a show of strength') has always been RSU2's style. There has never been any place for cowards in RSU2. All right, let me add one more page, making it fifteen."

At this very moment, the nightmare he had had a while ago attacked him again, "Well, when a tiny needle wants to bring death to a strong man, all it can do is to stab the man's heel by surprise, making him jump in the air, lose his balance and fall off a cliff." So he thought more profoundly about the previous fourteen pages, and along with the magical effect of the one-needle thinking that occurred to him, he wrote down his fresh thoughts on a piece of paper. He then showed it to Gao Yuncao who was buoyed up by a sense of hope. Without a word she stroked his face hard. This stroking demonstrated her tender feelings, affection and loving care as well as approval and encouragement. Throwing the page into the air, Ji Zhenren called out, "This is it! Anyone who is still breathing begin to work by following this route." Taking two abacuses, he went to sit between Gao Yuncao and Liu Hongmei and began to flick the beads with both hands.

It was another sleepless night. By six o'clock in the morning, holding back his wild joy, Ji Zhenren commanded each group to organise their results systematically. Then he said, "Keep calm, no hurry!" He signalled Gao Yuncao and Liu Hongmei to work with him for the last link. Sitting in a row, each of the three worked on two abacuses. Based on their memories, they noisily flicked the beads and did the calculation. Forty-eight cryptographers were watching. Following the dancing abacus beads, their eyes flashed and jumped, fearing that the six hands would flick on a wrong bead. The noise of the six extraordinary abacuses went on for more than two hours. At eleven minutes past eight a surge of husky and choking cheers replaced the sound of the abacus beads.

The lifeline of the damned cipher series had finally been seized and all the ciphers had been cracked. Of the fifty-one cryptographers, some were crying, some were laughing, some were shaking hands, some were hugging each other and some were dropping to the floor and falling asleep. Ji Zhenren, Gao Yuncao and Liu Hongmei hugged one another, choking with sobs.

After calming herself down, Liu Hongmei saw Ji Zhenren leaning in Gao Yuncao's arms who was holding one of his hands tightly. She had had no oral communication with him for a long time, let alone such a tender and intimate movement toward him. Calling to mind his inhuman treatment of his own blood relations, hatred came to her mind again. Vigorously she pushed Ji Zhenren's other hand away, leaving him to slip to the floor. Gao Yuncao lowered her head to see that blood had stained her shirt and Ji Zhenren had passed out.

People cried out in alarm. They hurriedly carried Ji Zhenren to the medical unit while Liu Hongmei stood there motionless.

"The previous train of thought and calculations we made day and night were like a chasing dagger. When we were exhausted and both our legs were shaking with fatigue, the prick of the needle made us fail to hold on but fall off the cliff. That is to say if there had been no hard calculations in the previous days, the fifteenth page could never have produced the magic effect."

After his health improved, Ji Zhenren made the above comments to Gao Yuncao. Seeing that Chief Gao was also at his bedside, he said, "A strange thing happened to this set of ciphers. The demon gave birth to a brood of babies, but didn't give them any names."

"Why don't we call them the 'Nameless Cipher Array'?" suggested Chief Gao.

The cracking of the 'Nameless Cipher Array' created the miracle of picking stars from the sky and broke the myth that manual techniques could not crack ciphers created by machines, thereby going down in RSU2's history. Ji Zhenren's every word and action in the process was deeply embedded in Gao Yuncao's mind.

He was absolutely extraordinary and her god. His endless imagination and everlasting stubbornness, his two most distinct qualities, had seized her heart. For cipher elements he had an incredible inspiration, instinct and memory. It often happened that he listed the calculations in his mind, without writing them down on paper, he could carry on performing the mathematical calculations swiftly and clearly on and on until he reached an accurate result. He was an exceptional man who could blend life, intelligence and ciphers very well. His mind followed ciphers, which were cracked by his mind. The magical power of ciphers was like blood incessantly infiltrating his brain and organs.

This exceptional man had done a great job. But despite the stunning effect, it soon became insignificant to him. Brushing it off lightly, he said, "These ciphers could have been cracked in the first place. As long as there were enough texts and necessary technical personnel and enough time, at a certain point we were certain that we could crack them. That is because among the stars in the sky there are always three, four or even more stars whose light overlaps the others' on a certain straight line. Once there is an overlap, there will be reflection. Once there is a reflection, there will be contrast between different light beams. Once there is a contrast, there will be a chance. On the other hand, although ciphers created by machines are difficult and unfathomable, overall they have a comparatively weak point, that is, the mechanism itself. When the machine runs fast to a point where there appears to be a mutual self-identification between an elder brother and a younger brother, or between an elder sister and a younger sister, or between father and son, or between uncles and nephews, although the time is the blink of an eye, it happens, therefore objectively making it possible for it to be caught."

Gao Yuncao understood the crux of the issue, saying, "How can you talk about such a grand and profound project so casually and inconsiderably? You thought it was you who had cleaned out your family's cesspit for pigs. No! This was the hard work of three hundred people for nearly a month. Many of them used up their life-long wisdom, even all the senior officers at the headquarters were astonished by our achievement, so how can you conclude with such casual remarks?"

"I haven't finished yet," said Ji Zhenren. "The facts proved that this time the probability of catching the demon was one in ten million. But you mustn't forget that what RSU2 does is this kind of small-probability job."

Gao Yuncao broke into a wide smile, "Your first part was spoken too modestly, but your second part showed your imperiousness. I like this overbearing manner of yours. Remember not to speak of yourself as insignificant in the future. Genius is genius. Don't be foolishly modest and pretend that you are a coward."

Ji Zhenren had been in hospital for over a month to treat his serious lobar pneumonia. If it were not for the senior officers issuing orders to dispatch the best doctors and to apply the best medicines, he might have died. When he was in hospital, almost everyone who took part in the operation had come to visit him.

After he was fully recovered and the formalities for his discharge were completed, he did not want to leave. He was looking around as if he was waiting for somebody.

Straightforwardly, Gao Yuncao said, "You didn't die, so she won't come to see you. But even if you were dead, she may not necessarily have come to see you off either. Sometimes you mustn't hurt blood relations' feelings."

As he listened, tears streamed down Ji Zhenren's face.

Holding him tight in her arms with tears welling up in her eyes, Gao Yuncao said, "Zhenren, don't feel sad. There is still love between you and me."

A senior officer came to visit Ji Zhenren. Seeing the scene, he laughed, "What has made Old Ji throw himself into a woman's arms and cry like a child?"

Flushed, Gao Yuncao pushed the tearful Ji Zhenren away from her, saying, "He felt hurt because you didn't come to see him."

Wiping tears from his eyes, Ji Zhenren quickly grabbed the senior officer's arm while taking out a few sheets of paper from his pocket.

It was an intelligence analysis report.

"When he was in hospital, his mind never stopped thinking about intelligence," said Gao Yuncao. "Look, he's now focusing his attention on the development of the war in the Far East and the strategic movement of the Japanese armies. He thought there was a strong possibility that the Japanese would advance south to the Pacific. I also studied the related information and I had a similar view on some key points. This report is about this matter. I know RSU2 is never short of master intelligence analysts. You may already have several such reports in hand."

Flicking through Ji Zhenren's report, the senior officer laughed, "Yes, RSU2 has presented us with three such reports. The intelligence resources were rich, and the analyses were meticulous and scientific, so the conclusions were solid and reliable. The strategic motive for the Japanese troops to advance south to the Pacific does exist, and the probability of them doing so is great. This is extremely important intelligence. Ji Zhenren has spared no efforts to assist us to gain military secrets. He is a hero of rare talent and wit!"

"I did not mean to describe him as a mastermind who is good at intelligence analysis. What I mainly wanted to say was that his mind was on ciphers every minute of the day. He may one day get suffocated by ciphers, and never come out. I won't wait any more! Absolutely not!"

Raising her voice, Gao Yuncao said, "Sir, I want to marry him."

The senior officer's mind was still on the report. He was startled at first, then laughed, "Your request is as important as this report. Both are urgent and need to be handled urgently. If Chief Gao does not give approval, I will grant it directly."

Ji Zhenren smiled, "Look, Sir, for these years the relationship between you and I has been so good. I'm now going to get married, you ought to give me a present. How about your radio set?"

Staring at Ji Zhenren, the senior officer said: "No. That radio set is a premium item given to me by an American friend. We need it to listen to operas. I was worried that you might feel lonely when you were in hospital, so I lent it to you to relieve your boredom. So now that you have been discharged, hurry up and give it back to me."

"This radio set is the best one I've ever seen. Sir, you must give it to me as our wedding present, or I will not let Yuncao play basketball with you."

The officer's eyes widened even further, and he said, "You are too greedy. Not only do you want to rob me of my premium radio set, but also to have my high-quality basketball mate all to yourself. Let me see, you'd better not get married, otherwise other people's interests will be robbed. I will never let you have your way."

"Too late, Sir. The rice has been cooked," said Ji Zhenren earnestly.

The senior officer became serious, "Ji Zhenren, you get bolder and bolder. You have received neither approval nor a marriage certificate, so how can the rice have been cooked? And you have the audacity to speak out shamelessly in front of a senior officer. Leading a dissipated life is also breaking discipline regulations. We must not allow you to run wild as you please."

Blushing, Gao Yuncao hurried to explain: "Don't be angry, Sir. Even if he is not a decent man, I am not that kind of careless woman. You have misunderstood him. When he said that the rice has been cooked he means that he has dismantled your radio set and modified it. While in hospital, he let people find him some wireless equipment and he reassembled the radio. The room was full of the parts, an aerial was even erected on the roof. Day and night he monitored the radio signals, which the doctors and nurses were not happy about at all. Since he was discharged, he has removed the aerial. But he has let someone hide your radio set somewhere, as he is determined not to return it to you."

"You even dared to dismantle my premium radio set given to me by the Americans. You forcibly seized private property, it's robbery. This is outrageous!" Then the senior officer asked, "Is it true that from this radio set you can hear voices that cannot be heard on the other radio receivers? Is there any technical use for it?"

In detail Ji Zhenren said, "Before it was modified, I could hear voices from many places around the world. After it was modified, I could hear voices from nearly all over the world. Our job is to guess about the world. To guess it you must first hear it. When I was lying in bed in hospital, I relied on this radio set to hear the whole world. I could hear many, many radio signals and information from all the Japanese islands and the information about their relations with the outside world. I could hear clearly the broadcasts in Japanese, English and Chinese. Of course, I could also hear some coded signals sent by some other transmitters. I could hear much of the Japanese official news about important matters, market conditions and business news, music from entertainment circles, the whispering of private transmitters, the howling of the militarists, the breathing of the royal palace and folk anecdotes."

Staring at Ji Zhenren, the senior officer asked Gao Yuncao, "Is this radio set really that magical?"

Gao Yuncao hastened to add, "For instance, in his report he listed eleven reasons for the Japanese troops advancing south to the Pacific. Three of them were from information he gathered from the Japanese recruiting sailors with South Sea sailing experience and Japanese businessmen buying petrol and rubber. All this information was gathered from listening to this modified radio set."

The senior officer put the report in his jacket pocket, saying, "Great. I am giving you this radio set as a wedding present, or precisely, to RSU2!"

It was on the 7th of December that Ji Zhenren and Gao Yuncao moved out of the room for honeymooners. And on this same day the Japanese air and naval forces attacked Pearl Harbour, starting the Pacific War. That senior officer came across Ji Zhenren holding his quilt roll under his arm. Giving him a punch on the chest, the officer said, "It seems that you did not fall ill in vain. That report of yours is absolutely top quality. I am now rewarding you by allowing you to live in the room for honeymooners for another month."

"Forget it, Sir. Don't waste the room. His mind was on ciphers every second of every minute when we lived there. It makes no difference where he lives. Boring, truly boring. Ciphers are his eternal bride," muttered Gao Yuncao with a shy laugh.

The senior officer laughed as well. "Being married to Ji Zhenren is like being married to ciphers. I am sure you mentally prepared yourself for this a long time ago."

20 /THE FOUR GENTLEMEN CIPHERS

THE CODED telegrams of the Japanese Secret Intelligence Services in North China, after being intercepted and transcribed, were first delivered to Gao Yuncao and Liu Hongmei who spent seven days and nights working on them and managed to decipher several headers. They were so excited that they wrote a progress report at once:

> We have now deciphered the headers of eleven coded telegrams in package number eight. Our preliminary prognosis is that these ciphers are being used by the Japanese Secret Intelligence Services stationed in North China, four in total, code names Plum, Orchid, Bamboo and Chrysanthemum, and that encoding is undertaken manually. We expect to crack them in one month's time. We suggest this series of ciphers be named 'The Four Gentlemen Ciphers'.

After she had finished writing the report, Liu Hongmei spat hard on the floor, "How could the notorious Japanese Secret Intelligence Services use such fragrant plant names to name their ciphers, really tarnishing the four plants' reputation."

Gao Yuncao said confidently, "No matter what they are called, or if they are sweet-smelling or foul-smelling, let us strip their garments, open their chests and remove their hearts. The key is that we must be precise, fast and ruthless!"

After another seven days and nights, they submitted an application:

"The Four Gentlemen ciphers do not live up to their aromatic names but are stinking and hard. We clearly knew that the encoding was done manually, but after several hundred attempts we have failed to decipher them. Time waits for no one. We request technical support."

Chief Gao quickly sent Ji Zhenren and Li Mozi to aid them. Gao Yuncao emptied package number eight on the table, ready to give them an introduction to the basic circumstances. Ji Zhenren waved at her to stop, signalling Li Mozi to speak, who laughed, "Plum, orchid, bamboo and chrysanthemum are actually dishes for female comrades. Chief Gao asked us to come, which was not my original idea, so sorry we have offended you. How about we four share the four ciphers, cracking them separately, so no one can bully anyone else?"

"Your pedantic nonsense will not solve the problem at all," said Gao Yuncao, banging the package noisily, and Liu Hongmei slapped Li Mozi hard on the back.

Ji Zhenren said, "Let's analyse the disposition of the four plants first. What nature and character do they possess? The female comrades are experts on flowers, so can you two speak first please?"

Liu Hongmei still refused to speak to Ji Zhenren; straightening her neck, she jerked her head around.

Ji Zhenren said again, "I remember when I was little, my family had all these four plants in our back garden where my siblings and I often played. So Hongmei should be most familiar with the plants, can you speak first?" Seemingly she heard nothing. Liu Hongmei noisily rummaged through the pile of paper, ignoring Ji Zhenren.

Gao Yuncao ran out of patience, and said, "No need. We are cracking ciphers, what is the use of analysing if a flower smells nice or if it stinks?"

Ji Zhenren turned to Li Mozi, "Can you first tell us about the nature and character of these flowers?"

Taking the lead, Li Mozi said, "The plum blossoms are noble and unsullied; the orchids are serene and elegant; the bamboos are open-minded, modest and straight; the chrysanthemums are coldly elegant, pure and loyal."

Gao Yuncao cut in, "Braving snow, proud and unyielding, the plum blossoms represent noble-minded people; releasing a delicate fragrance in deep and secluded valleys, and remaining aloof from the world, orchids represent the prominent and worthy people in society; dancing in the breeze, tall, straight, elegant and refined, the bamboos refer to modest and scrupulous gentlemen; braving frost, natural, unrestrained and never fawning on the rich and powerful, chrysanthemums represent recluses and hermits."

Liu Hongmei grumbled sourly, "The plum blossoms are proud and unyielding! The orchids are serene and elegant! The bamboos are peaceful! The chrysanthemums are reclusive!"

Patting his thigh, Ji Zhenren cried, "Excellent! Let us fit the flowers' characters into our own personal character and divide up the work. Then let's make a concentrated effort to finish the job quickly. Afterwards, according to the circumstances, we'll do it together. The specific division of the work is as follows: I will be responsible for Plum, Gao Yuncao for Oochid, Li Mozi for Bamboo and Liu Hongmei for Chrysanthemum. Let us closely represent the character of each plant and imagine as much as we can. Let's start!"

Li Mozi agreed, "You've divided the work very precisely, particularly to give Orchid to Yuncao and Chrysanthemum to Hongmei."

"Stop talking rubbish! Let's get started!" Liu Hongmei cast a disdainful glance at Li Mozi.

Burying themselves in the office, they worked like crazy for over a month. In the last few days, the dawn of victory frequently appeared. Chief Gao was attending a meeting at the headquarters in Yan'an. They were too excited to report progress but pressed on to the finish without letup. Cutting weeds and flowers, all four ciphers were cracked.

Only then did they see clearly that for this series of ciphers the headers of the messages were encoded manually, while the texts were encoded mechanically. Such encryption could easily have misled cryptographers into treating the telegrams as manually encrypted telegrams, resulting in a failure to decipher the core texts. The significance of cracking these ciphers was that for the first time they saw through the unusual character of 'being unable to see the wood for the trees' of the Japanese secret services.

It was late at night and the office was as hot as a steamer basket. Too hot to be concerned about anything else, in underpants and vest Ji Zhenren and Li Mozi flicked the abacus beads for over three hours.

After they cracked the ciphers, they felt no excitement at all as they were shocked by what they had deciphered.

The messages revealed that a certain Pan who was an important person in the KMT party and government departments in the Taihang region, and a certain Qi who was in charge of the KMT Military Statistical Bureau in North China and a certain Sun who was the assistant commander-in-chief of a certain KMT Army Group had turned traitors and had gone over to the Japanese and the puppet government.

This was a major and most urgent military situation!

But, according to regulations, the telephone could not be used for such a top secret. RSU2 only had receivers for monitoring signals. The main transceiver and the spare transceiver were only for contacting headquarters in Yan'an for urgent and important matters. They were kept in the room for confidential materials and the tappers were locked in Chief Gao's safe. Besides, if a transceiver was needed, there had to be approval from three levels for only a specific person to use it. The time to communicate with Yan'an was fixed and messages outside the contact hours could not be received. Now there were four hours to go before the morning contact. But time waits for no man and the military intelligence had to reach the high command as soon as possible. Now there was only one solution: to send messengers to deliver the intelligence. But at such a late hour it was not safe to travel with a top secret written on paper, an action not allowed by security regulations either.

Ji Zhenren made a prompt decision. He and Li Mozi would ride their horses to meet Chief Gao in Yan'an where they would submit the intelligence to the headquarters in person. They would not take anything with them because all the intelligence was in their heads. Besides they could inform headquarters about some more related circumstances and background to help the high commanders to expedite their decisions.

Ji Zhenren urged Gao Yuncao, "You and Hongmei hurry up and organise the paperwork and write a detailed report on what was deciphered. Li Mozi and I will start off now. You go and wake up a squad of guards, and ask them to catch up with us and escort us to Yan'an."

Dashing to the stable, Ji Zhenren and Li Mozi mounted up and galloped toward the barracks' main gate. They then realised that except for the pistols across their shoulders, they were in their underpants and vests. But they didn't care that much. They spurred the horses on, shouting, "Open the gate! Open the gate!"

The sentry knew Ji Zhenren very well. Seeing him dressed like that did not surprise him because this unconventional guy had run to the office without his clothes on several times before when he had had a flash of inspiration, so he opened the gate.

At this very moment, even Heaven had no idea that a major crisis had tightly engulfed RSU2. A squad of eighteen enemy secret agents were hiding outside RSU2's barracks, waiting for their chance to raid the compound. At the foot of the hill two had swung into the compound using a rope fastened to a tree on top of the cliff and ten more were doing the same one by one. Outside the main gate six agents were hiding in the dark, waiting to back up the twelve agents inside.

Suddenly the gate opened and two horses with two riders galloped out. By moonlight the agents saw the riders were neither officers nor soldiers, spurring their horses on in their underwear. To shoot or not to shoot? If they had opened fire, the shots would have alerted the enemy.

Inside the compound a guard squad was quietly having an emergency meeting. But the neighing of the horses woke up the whole guard company. Some monitors and cryptographers also got up, leaning on the windows to see what was happening.

The two enemy agents who had got in and the ten who were waiting to get in did not know what had gone wrong. Looking at each other in surprise, they halted their action.

The guard squad dashed out of the gate, trying to catch up with Ji Zhenren and Li Mozi. The six waiting agents saw the cavalry coming out, thinking that the other twelve agents must have succeeded in getting in, so they opened fire.

Instantly three guards fell off their horses, while the others dashed past the gate. The squad leader was very experienced. He did not order his squad to fire back, but whipping his horse he chased Ji Zhenren and Li Mozi. He judged that the enemy activity was closely related to the journey of Ji Zhenren and Li Mozi, who were ahead of them and might have got into trouble.

When the enemy agents at the top of the cliff heard the gunfire, they hesitated no more. One by one they swung into the compound, heading straight for the cryptographers' offices and dormitory.

If anyone had been watching, it would not have been difficult for them to have discovered that these agents were coming for predetermined targets. They wanted to kill RSU2's cryptographers!

Because the guard company had woken up before the gun shots, they were in action in the shortest time. Implementing plan B for an emergency, their priority was to protect the cryptographers.

Hearing the gun shots, Liu Hongmei was highly vigilant. Quickly she gathered the papers on the desk and pushed them into the safe. Before locking the safe, she reset the combination to a random number, hence even she herself would not know the key. This was RSU2's rule for preventing staff from telling the enemy the key when under threat of being killed. Before she could pick up her pistol, an enemy agent broke into the room. Pointing a gun at her, he motioned to her to open the safe.

Pretending she was opening the safe, she suddenly turned around and grabbed a pistol. She fired at the enemy agent who had expected such an action, so he kicked her pistol away and pointed his gun at her forehead. Liu Hongmei said, "No key but my life. You can take it." She closed her eyes waiting for the shot. But nothing happened. She opened her eyes, seeing that the agent was quietly retreating toward the door.

Gao Yuncao stepped into the room. The agent turned around and fired at her. Almost at the same time Gao Yuncao also fired her gun and the bullet hit the agent's chest, while her own left arm was dripping with blood. Liu Hongmei grabbed a towel and used it as a tourniquet to wrap her arm. Locking the office, they ran out of the building.

At a bend, an enemy agent was lying in a pool of blood. Gao Yuncao said, "I shot him dead."

"Japanese or KMT?" asked Liu Hongmei. Gao Yuncao shook her head meaning she did not know.

In fact she was clear in her mind who the enemy agents were. Merely a moment ago, after she went to wake up the guard squad and on her way back to the office, she bumped into an enemy agent at a bend. Pointing his gun at her, the agent did not pull the trigger. Bending down she put her gun on the ground. But suddenly she swept her leg and the agent lost his balance. Swiftly she got up and gave him an upper cut, hitting his ear and the agent's gun was in her hand. The series of actions were completed almost in the same instant, which amazed the agent.

Pointing her gun at him, she said, "I will spare your life if you tell the truth. Hurry up, are you Japanese or Chinese? Why are you here?" His lips twisted in a contemptuous smile, the agent jerked his head round. Gao Yuncao took out a dagger from under the agent's left arm, turning her wrist she pressed the dagger on the artery of his neck.

Then the agent opened his mouth, "From your movement I can tell that you definitely did not learn your *kungfu* skills from the Communists. The skill of taking the dagger from under my arm is a skill mastered by our agents only. Ha ha, I don't want to ask who you are. But I can tell you that we came here to kill your cryptographers. Before we departed for the mission, our superior urged us not to kill women after we entered your compound. If it were not for this command, you would have been dead." No sooner had the agent finished saying this than Gao Yuncao pulled the trigger of her gun.

The enemy action lost the element of surprise, thus failing to achieve its goal. Only one cryptographer was killed when he ran out of his room. Among the three soldiers who were shot and fell off their horses at the barracks gate, two died and one was wounded. Two sentries guarding the confidential area were killed by the two agents who entered the compound first, but all eighteen enemy agents were wiped out.

At first light, Chief Gao, Ji Zhenren and Li Mozi returned to RSU2. A special group came with them. The general headquarters wanted to carry out an investigation of the incident.

At the time the rectification movement and the examination of cadres' personal histories were gaining momentum in Yan'an. RSU2 had already carried out its campaign and no problems were found among its staff. But the raid on its compound made the higher authorities realise that there were hidden problems, so things had to be straightened out and hidden troubles had to be eliminated as soon as possible.

The special group held that the enemy agents had chosen an excellent spot to enter the compound with a precise route and clear target. They knew very well where our cryptographers worked and lived, so it was obvious they had detailed knowledge about RSU2 and had made preparations before they came. Therefore, it could not be ruled out that spies were hiding in RSU2.

Considering the current situation, the special group decided to carry out the investigation along with the rectification movement. In the beginning, they delimited a key investigation area, that was to investigate the school graduates who had come to Yan'an from the Chiang Kai-shek-ruled or Japanese-occupied areas. After some investigations, except for some comrades who feared hardship or fatigue or boredom and failed to adapt to RSU2's nature of work and the confidential environment, nothing related to enemy secret agents was found. The special group had no choice but to extensively rouse the masses to action. They carried out a large-scale investigation and everyone and everything had to pass the test. The specific method was to combine public observations with private investigations, large-scale meetings with small-scale meetings, and individual talks with mass exposures.

One day, the special group called all the cryptographers for a meeting. On the stage, the group leader was briefing on the investigation and raising demands; under the stage, thirteen active elements, who had been selected in advance, were in every corner of the assembly hall to carefully observe every cryptographer's reaction and the expression on their faces, then record what they had seen. After the meeting, they went to submit their reports to the special group who then decided the key suspects based on these reports. During this period of time, the method of mobilising the masses had been applied in the extreme. The active elements sprang up and they voluntarily cooperated with the organisation to 'sniff out spies', to 'keep watch on spies' and to 'testify to a spy's guilt'. They targeted the vulnerable spot, and on persuasion they racked their brains and invented techniques of 'how to persuade, to persuade in person, to persuade by oral or written method, to make either a tough approach or a soft approach', attempting to find any clues to uncover a spy. Once a suspect was identified, they would be brought to the assembly hall, where the masses would form a circle. Standing in the centre and jostled by the people around them, the suspect had to answer all the questions raised by the masses who then made an on-the-spot analysis to find any flaws.

After such an action, RSU2 finally decided on eight suspects who were handed to the special group for examination. Ji Zhenren and Li Mozi were among them.

In the examination, someone initially suggested that the aim of the enemy agents' raid on RSU2 was to wipe out the cryptographers, and two cryptographers happened to escape the disaster that night. So was there a connection between them and the enemy raid?

Before Ji Zhenren and Li Mozi opened their mouths to argue, Chief Gao stood up, saying, "There was another person who was far away from the disaster and it was me. Two days prior to the incident I went to Yan'an to attend a meeting. If you put them under suspicion, you can add me as well."

The special group stopped him: "Comrade Gao Yueming, as a leader, you must let the masses speak out. Ji Zhenren and Li Mozi did leave the RSU2 compound under strange circumstances, an unbelievable coincidence."

"Ji Zhenren and the other three cryptographers cracked the Four Gentlemen ciphers that night," explained Chief Gao. "He and Li Mozi hurried to the general headquarters to report an urgent military situation, which the senior officers can prove," explained Chief Gao.

"The difficulty in dealing with RSU2 is that you can easily call in the senior officers of the general headquarters and the leaders of the central authorities to put pressure on us," said the special group leader. "You're right. RSU2 is extremely important and in the eyes of the senior leadership you are all treasures. And many of you grew up under their favours and spoils. But to me, on many occasions it was yourself who had increased your importance, feeling that you could not be provoked. Yet this time I must provoke you! We will focus on examining Ji Zhenren and Li Mozi and be strict with our investigation."

Pounding the table, Chief Gao bellowed, "It is your right to decide who you want to investigate, but you must not talk nonsense. Who has been given favours and been spoiled? Who? Say the names if you have the guts."

"You wait! The time will come."

Therefore Ji Zhenren and Li Mozi were locked up, as there seemed to be some 'ironclad evidence' against both of them that it was hard for them to refute.

The special group dug out a question of a political nature in Ji Zhenren's past record. In his early years in the army his elder brother Ji Zhenfu defected to the KMT. When his brother was the enemy regimental commander, he once met him and ganged up with him. To this question, Ji Zhenren found it hard to defend himself. Song Daxiong and Zhang Guo were dead and no one could testify about his circumstances. Regarding his signing an enemy telegram on behalf of the enemy, an act of placing righteousness above family loyalty, no written evidence remained. He could not explain it clearly, besides, he had to avoid talking about it. So, facing a bombardment of criticisms and questions, as well as the endless examinations and mental torture, he chose silence. It was not that he had no means of getting assistance, as he could have asked Chief Gao for help, but he did not do so. He felt that he had no right to use this sole evidence to defend himself, because it involved the secrets of the Red Army's code deciphering and related skills. Apart from this case, the special group kept picking on the matter of his firing at comrade Zhan. And this case involved the intelligence support to the West Legion; it was even harder to explain it clearly. Under such circumstances, he simply kept his mouth shut.

As for Li Mozi, his problem was that when the West Legion was broken up, he lost contact with his unit. After trekking and begging for six months, he returned to Yan'an on his own. Who could verify what he was doing during these six months? Nobody. With no witnesses to prove his innocence, the suspicion that he may have defected to the enemy could not be removed. Li Mozi knew that it was useless for him to argue, so he too chose silence.

Ji Zhenren was under strict investigation and examination, so as a matter of course, Gao Yuncao could not escape being investigated either. According to procedure, the special group carefully went over her history when she had lived in KMT-controlled cities. Because she had been repeatedly and seriously investigated in the past, she passed the test. Her performance in RSU2 was also approved by the organisation and the masses. As to how she behaved on the night in question, the special group screened the information gathered and they found nothing wrong with her but that she had taken part in a heroic undertaking. When running into the enemy agents, she had handled the emergency with ease, killing two all by herself even though she was wounded in action. The conclusion given by the special group was that Comrade Gao Yuncao had a clean personal record, and that there were no questions of a political nature in her history.

Liu Hongmei, Ji Zhenren's sister, who had broken off relations with him, and was a good friend of Li Mozi with whom she had a dubious relationship, was naturally put under strict investigation. The conclusion given by the special group was that on the night when the compound was under attack, she was resourceful in the emergency, hiding the material in the safe and destroying the safe lock combination. When the enemy pointed a gun at her, even death would not make her yield. She kept the material safe.

Before the special group talked to her, Liu Hongmei had a small question which she secretly exchanged views about with Gao Yuncao. She remembered that on that night the enemy pointed their gun at her, forcing her to tell them the safe lock combination. But then he quietly moved away from her. Why? Of course, Gao Yuncao could not tell her that these enemy secret agents had been given orders not to kill women. So she said casually, "When I entered the room, I did not see any sign that he wanted to withdraw from the room. Seeing his clean, pale face, he might have been fearful that he would be spattered with blood and thought of moving two steps away from you, then firing at you. It was me who startled him, so he turned around and fired at me."

Liu Hongmei passed the investigation smoothly. However, to complain about unfairness to Ji Zhenren and Li Mozi, she raised havoc in the special group's office.

She was so obstinate in her support for the innocence of the two men who were close to her, she neither ate, nor drank, nor slept. Day and night she squatted down before the office door of the special group to make her complaint. For her behaviour the special group came to the conclusion that this woman had gone insane.

Chief Gao then said that he had a way of testing whether she was mad or not. Carrying a package of coded messages he issued an order, "These transcribed messages are not difficult to decipher. The general headquarters urgently needs us to get the job done. Now I order Liu Hongmei to lead a team of eleven cryptographers to start working at once. You must decipher them within twenty-two days without delay!" Hearing Chief Gao's order, Liu Hongmei wiped the saliva from the corner of her mouth, got up and tottered unsteadily to her office. She had been on hunger strike for three days. Chief Gao mumbled to himself, "This comrade, her military and political quality, individual character and professional skills are all first class, particularly politically she is absolutely trustworthy."

Eighteen days later Liu Hongmei and her team deciphered the contents in the package. But she resumed her complaints, sitting on the floor outside the special group's office again. She said to whoever came her way, "You in the special group think that the food of RSU2 is delicious, so you hang around here and refuse to leave. You have even investigated the sows in the pigsty three times, but you failed to catch a spy cat or a spy mouse. What does this mean? It either means RSU2 is a very clean place, or the enemy spies are too cunning, hidden too deeply, but you are slow-witted, have poor eyesight and a confused mind. You cannot do it, so go and find someone better qualified. Please don't stay here, wrong decent people and earn your salary without doing much work."

Liu Hongmei's act made RSU2 a showcase and some busybody would often stand in the dark to watch the fun.

That day she was sitting outside the special group office complaining tearfully. A group of men and horses galloped into the RSU2 compound. A senior officer dismounted, shouting at Chief Gao, "What's the matter with that female comrade crying over there? The movement has caused injustice all over the place. Organisations at all levels must not investigate any more. They should stop and examine themselves."

Liu Hongmei dashed over to the officer, burning with rage as usual, and said, "A cryptographer who has had no affection between blood relations but only has ciphers in his heart, and who only wants the Party spirit but the normal human feelings, how can he go over to the enemy and betray the Party and become a spy, a traitor and a counterrevolutionary? I can't get my head around it! Ji Zhenren has been wronged. Sir, you must back him up."

"Did you really lock him up?" the angry senior officer asked the special group. "He is a major suspect. We will report to you in a moment," the special group replied.

The senior officer became more angry, "If he is a spy, a traitor or a counterrevolutionary, then some of our revolutionary ranks and revolutionaries were finished long ago. There is nothing wrong with him. I give my word! Ji Zhenren is beyond doubt and his work must not be disturbed. Anyone who has difficulty with him has difficulty with the Chinese revolution!"

Then Chief Gao said, "I also thought that Ji Zhenren was clean. But now it seems that he is truly a suspect. No matter how great a contribution a man has made to the revolution, he must be investigated if he is suspected of wrongdoing, and be punished if found guilty. No matter how great a revolutionary he has been, no one can guarantee that now or in future he will not become a counterrevolutionary! Therefore, we must carry out a thorough investigation of Ji Zhenren!"

The senior officer's anger subsided, and he said, "Since you have had such a great idea, why did you ask me to come? Guards platoon leader, let's go!" He mounted his horse, pointing his whip at Liu Hongmei, saying, "You have used inappropriate words to describe Ji

Zhenren. How could you say that he does not want to have normal human feelings? He is just the opposite. He radiates with noble humanity!" Having said that, he rode off.

Chief Gao yelled at Liu Hongmei, "You lunatic. You won't give up before you make RSU2 stink."

Liu Hongmei was angry and yelled back, "A fragrant man smells fragrant; a stinking man stinks. What has it got to do with me?" As she spoke, she went to sit outside the special group's office again.

Fed up with her, the special group informed Chief Gao, "Liu Hongmei is disturbing our work, so she is a spy suspect. We are going to detain her for interrogation."

Chief Gao hastened to say, "Wait a moment. There is a major assignment adjustment. We are preparing to transfer her somewhere else, so she won't disrupt your work any more."

A few days later Liu Hongmei was transferred away from RSU2. She was dispatched to a place over a thousand kilometres away.

It turned out that the Eighth Route Army office in Chongqing urgently needed wireless staff. The requirements for the job were: three or more years' work experience; politically trustworthy; technically multi-talented; not a meddlesome person in character. Liu Hongmei met three of the four requirements. Regarding the last one, her kicking up a fuss was probably not an issue of character. Chief Gao had a talk with her about the new assignment. She thought about it for two days and two nights and at last came round. She cried and poured out her grievances to Gao Yuncao, "Out of sight, out of mind. Since I can't change the reality, it's better to stay away from it. Let me leave, so I can be carefree."

"It's good to have a change of environment and adjust your mood," said Gao Yuncao. "If you stay here and stubbornly stick to your ways and complain, not only will you not be able to save Ji Zhenren and Li Mozi, but you will be detained for interrogation sooner or later. Moreover, letting you go to Chongqing shows that the organisation trusts you. So go."

On the eve of her departure, Liu Hognmei went to bid farewell to Chief Gao. With tears in her eyes, she said, "No matter how far away you send me, I will still say it. Ji Zhenren and Li Mozi have been wronged."

"Whether or not they have been wronged is a matter for the organisation to clarify," said Chief Gao. "After you arrive in

Chongqing, you must keep your mind on your work and do not poke your nose into other people's business again."

Sir Zhou's Mansion (or 50 Zengjiayan) was located on 4 Zhongshan Road, Yuzhong District, Chongqing. It was part of the Eighth Route Army's office, but was also the main office for the South Bureau of the CPC Central Committee whose identity in Chongqing was confidential.

When Liu Hongmei first arrived, she was amazed by the city's beautiful scenery. From childhood to adulthood, the only big towns she had ever been to were Ruijin and Yan'an. She had never walked through a flourishing metropolis. When she arrived in Chongqing and got off the steamer, lights were just being switched on. The beautiful green and red scenery and the hazy view of Chongqing by night was something she could never have imagined when she was in the ravines in South Jiangxi, or on the Long March or on the loess plateau. The next morning, as soon as the first light appeared, she got out of bed. Standing on the top of the building, the streets and lanes and the city's unique beauty were more clearly in view. The early morning noise was also intoxicating. The calls when shops opened for business, the cries of the peddlars, the squeaking noise of the peddlars' shoulder poles, the children's giggles, the birds' twittering, and even the sound of the wind sweeping through the city was completely different to the wind blowing through the loess ravines.

Liu Hongmei cried out earnestly, "How nice a big city is!" Unexpectedly her cries set off some chuckles from below. Lowering her head, she saw on the first floor balcony a woman who was looking into a small mirror and combing her hair. She was completely captivated by the charms of the woman. One word jumped out of her head: seductive. The city was bathed in the first rays of the morning sun, but the attraction failed to weigh down the glamour of the seductive woman downstairs. Like eating something delicious Liu Hongmei watched the beautiful woman and enjoyed the scene.

The sight of the city women in the morning took over whole streets and lanes. She suddenly called to mind that it might have been this sort of seductiveness that had lured that orderly into running away some time ago. Even a woman could be enticed by such coquettishness, let alone an eighteen-year-old young man.

Before she left Yan'an, Chief Gao had told her that not long ago an orderly working in the Eighth Route Army office in Chongqing had been seduced by a woman living in the compound where all sorts of people lived. Some of the guards and orderlies were from the country and had only recently joined the army. They had never seen the seduction of a city woman, so it was quite natural that some individuals failed to resist the temptation. The purpose of telling her about the matter was to remind her that inside and outside the office in Chongqing, the enemy situation and the spy situation were very complicated so she had to be sure not to let her guard down.

Suddenly she woke up from her fever to that woman's seductive charm. Looking at the courtyard on the right, it was the residential compound for Dai Li, Director of the KMT's military secret services, Juntong. Looking at the left hand side, it was the local police station. Looking down, the courtyard seemed even more odd. The Eighth Route Army had rented all the rooms on the ground floor and the second floor, as well as three rooms on the first floor on the east side. These rooms secretly accommodated the Communist South Bureau's organisations of military, culture, women, foreign affairs and Party. The first-floor corridor was divided into two parts. The tenants living on the left were a man called Li from the KMT upper circles, a man called Huang who was the secretary of the KMT Commission for Consolation and Compensation, and the organisation of the Wartime Women's Services Group which was led by the mayor's wife. The first floor was connected to the courtyard terrace, as well as the turf of the Wartime Women's Services Group. When people stood on the terrace and looked up, they could see the South Bureau's office on the second floor. When looking down, they could see the South Bureau's reception hall on the ground floor.

This was the mysterious feature of 50 Zengjiayan, that the KMT and the Communists shared the same courtyard and the same building. But the two sides harboured a grudge, and therefore had no contact with each other. In fact, the South Bureau knew very well that this was a special arrangement by the Juntong in order to keep the Communists under surveillance. Some of the KMT agents were scrupulous to the extreme, not only secretly keeping watch on the South Bureau, but often playing some small tricks. In shorts and vests, the women from the Women's Services Group would often play merrily on the terrace, taking chances to strike up conversations with the young men of the South Bureau and doing their best to seduce them. That orderly, a new recruit, was lured away by this very act. In fact, by luring away an orderly they were not able to get any secrets but to spread humiliation.

Thinking of this, Liu Hongmei felt deep reverence for the South Bureau. Working in such a dangerous environment and surrounded by enemies, it was really not easy for them to keep cool-headed as well as to maintain their integrity for many years. But to be realistic, not all the people living in the west quarter of the building were spies or bad elements. Taking the Women's Services Group as an example, the goal of the organisation was still to serve the War of Resistance against Japan. Each day they were kept busy with anti-Japanese affairs; this is what she was told by an old staff member of the South Bureau.

She had another look at the balcony downstairs where a woman had finished dressing. Fashionably dressed, she looked up at Liu Hongmei, smiling amiably, showing no hostility at all.

Again, Liu Hongmei felt that in this place even women had to constantly beware of temptation, let alone men.

Somewhat flustered, Liu Hongmei fled to her own room. Instantly laughter could be heard downstairs. But she felt that it was neither caustic nor dissolute.

Later, on many clear and bright mornings she could see that woman on the terrace, and she felt that her every smile, movement and expression was attractive. Inwardly they became friends over the course of several encounters. Although they never talked to each other, they felt they came to know each other very well. Privately Liu Hongmei even gave the woman a name: Yan Mei'er.

Liu Hongmei was not exactly sure what the Women's Services Group did. Every day Yan Mei'er would leave early and come back late, and she could only see her on the terrace in the early mornings and on Sundays. She sensed that although Yan Mei'er's confidence stemmed from her beauty, she was already a beautiful woman, but she did not neglect her dress sense. She would not go out until she had made herself perfectly beautiful. She always wore a new dress, which made Liu Hongmei very jealous.

Liu Hongmei worked in the confidential office on the second floor. The strict discipline and the security rules meant she was confined inside the small room so she rarely walked around freely in the courtyard. Considering that she had recently come to the city from the country, Lao Ding, who was in charge of the military group, requested approval from the higher authorities to allow her to go out. So three girls from the bureau, Zhang Li, Zhao Feixia and Wang Tiantian, went with Liu Hongmei to visit the streets a few times on Sundays. They told Liu Hongmei they were going sightseeing, but in fact they wanted her to get to know the surrounding area. The reason for the bureau's choice of office in the downtown area was for the convenience of communicating with people from all walks of life. In Chongqing, it was common for staff to go out for business, and going shopping in their spare time was not absolutely restricted either. Lao Ding said that the original intention of the security rules was not for physical restraint but for their minds. So long as the staff were highly vigilant mentally and exercised strict self-discipline, they were relatively at liberty to move around. But the bottom line was that there had to be no incidents, particularly not of a political nature.

After going out several times, Liu Hongmei had carefully viewed the charms of the wartime capital, Chongqing, as well as experiencing the KMT spies' tailing skills.

Zengjiayan was a narrow lane. On either side there were many grocery stores, small eateries and cigarette stalls. The stores at several key spots were guarded by secret agents. As soon as someone walked out of the gate of number 50, the agents would tail them. That day Liu Hongmei and the other three girls were buying clothes in a store. Taking a fancy to a bodice, Zhang Li then waved to a man standing nearby. He walked over to her. She asked his opinion of the bodice. Perfectly calm and collected, he took the bodice and examined it, "Not bad," he said. "It matches your yellow blouse very well." She asked which yellow blouse, and he said the one she wore the week before.

"You shameless man," she said. "Alright, I want this one." Smiling, he nodded and left.

Then Wang Tiantian needed to pee. She found a toilet and, turning around, she said to a man, "You really are a good dog, following me even to the toilet."

Liu Hongmei then understood that the two men were secret agents who were tailing them. Zhang Li told her that as time went by they and the secret agents got to know each other. When she cursed them as dogs, they would smile at her, making her feel annoyed.

Coming out of the toilet, Wang Tiantian and the girls went straight ahead. Then three hoodlums approached them, even asking Liu

Hongmei to change into her new clothes in the street. She was so scared that she hid behind her friends. Zhang Li tried to keep the hoodlums away from them, but one of the hoodlums raised his hand to touch her breast. Then two men came, punching the hoodlum about the ears. The hoodlums would not let it go at that. Drawing out knives, they surrounded the two men who raised their arms and pointed pistols at the hoodlums' foreheads. Showing no appreciation, Zhang Li muttered, "Sometimes dogs can also do human things." The two agents forced a bitter smile and moved away.

Occasionally they managed to cast off a tail. One Sunday they went to the editorial office of *Xinhua Daily,* and the secret agents had to wait at the gate. They left the building from the rear door. Zhang Li said, "If we want to throw off a tail, we can go to the public organisations first. There are several places we often go, like the KMT international news office, the American news office and the Sino-Soviet Cultural Association. We can sneak out of the back door, and after we've finished doing what we want to do, we can return by the back door, then stroll out of the main gate. We can slip out of the predicament like a cicada shedding its skin; this trick is time-tested and it's fun."

This time, after they sneaked out of the newspaper office, Zhang Li and Wang Tiantian went somewhere else while Liu Hongmei and Zhao Feixia went to buy shoes. Liu Hongmei was indecisive, hating to spend money, so Zhao Feixia left the shop and looked around on her own. Unsure whether she should buy high heels or pumps, Liu Hongmei raised her head and saw another woman was also trying on shoes. Instantly she recognised her as Yan Mei'er, yet the latter did not see her. She tried to strike up a conversation with Yan Mei'er, as in respect of aesthetic judgement she was far inferior to her, but she restrained herself. She should not have started the conversation because after all they were from two different camps. Even if this beautiful woman was not a spy, the contact between them was still sensitive, particularly since Zhao Feixia was nearby. If she saw her talking with a woman from the enemy camp, how could she have explained herself?

She tried both high heels and pumps. In the end she decided to buy pumps because she was uncomfortable in high heels, staggering when walking, neither nice nor stable.

Finally Yan Mei'er saw Liu Hongmei. They greeted each other with a smile. Seeing that Liu Hongmei was buying pumps, Yan Mei'er said, "You're a tall girl. Wearing high heels will accentuate your strong points. For a woman, choosing the correct pair of shoes is equivalent to changing herself into a new person."

To help Liu Hongmei try on high heels, she half knelt and tied the laces for her. She tied a very nice knot, saying, "Come on, tighten your legs..., flatten your belly..., lift your hips..., don't force your hips to stick out. Be natural. Good. Straighten your posture..., chest out..., chin down..., look ahead. Good, very good. Move a step..., not too big..., walk in a straight line..., don't turn your feet out. Yes, one more time. Hey, you're a quick learner, one touch makes a beautiful woman. Excellent. Go to the mirror and see if you can recognise yourself!"

In front of the mirror, Liu Hongmei walked back and forth. Putting her hand over her mouth, she was amazed by what she saw. She was bashful but her spirits lifted at once. She uttered her first sentence to Yan Mei'er, "Is this really me?! Yan Mei'er, thank you so much."

Surprised, Yan Mei'er said, "You called me Yan Mei'er?"

In a low voice Liu Hongmei said, "I've used this name to myself for a long time."

Yan Mei'er laughed and, holding Liu Hongmei's shoulder, she said, "All right. Thank you for giving me a name so pleasing to the ear. But I dare say if you pay a little bit of attention to your clothing, you will be several times more beautiful than me."

Liu Hongmei was even more bashful, "You are beautiful, and your words are also beautiful. You only choose good words to praise me."

"You gave me a beautiful name and I praised your beauty, both from the heart," said Yan Mei'er, straightening Liu Hongmei's collar. "Hey, why must we contaminate this good human thing with political elements of the KMT and the CPC? I really don't understand it." Liu Hongmei saw Zhao Feixia walking towards them. She hurried to the counter to pay for her purchase while Yan Mei'er made herself scarce.

Early the next morning, after washing up, Liu Hongmei put on her new clothes and shoes. She went to the walkway and strutted back and forth. Yan Mei'er was pleasantly surprised, yet she couldn't shout "Bravo". A gust of wind blew up her robe. Through the cover of the fluttering robe, she gave a thumbs-up to Liu Hongmei who saw it and muttered inwardly, "Yan Mei'er is very thoughtful. She is worried that she may cause me trouble."

"Why?" asked Zhang Li, laughing when she saw Hongmei. "Are you going on a blind date today? Look at your chest sticking out. I assume the boy will take you straight to bed."

"You mean I've straightened my back too much?" she said to Zhang Li, but her eyes were looking downstairs where Yan Mei'er quietly raised her thumb again. Feeling assured, she said to Zhang Li, "Every bit of me is perfect. I'll dress like this in future."

"Stepping out of number 50 in such an outfit, you'll definitely not be tailed by secret agents, because they would think that you are one of them," said Zhang Li.

Feigning anger, Liu Hongmei said, "Does a piece of clothing have to be contaminated with political elements of the two parties? How absurd!"

At twilight, the sunset enveloped the first-floor terrace, from where cackling sounds travelled upstairs. A few women were fighting for a letter and a photograph.

"This little bitch ran away to Nanchang and ate all the good food. Look at her, full and round. That deserter soldier can't live without her any more."

"What a lovely, chubby baby, very much like the father, that young Eighth Route Army soldier. Aha, I reckon the little bitch got pregnant when she was in number 50. The couple were really awesome."

"We had eyes everywhere. You tell me in which corner did that young man, a sentimental type, get our Yingmei?"

"Quiet. If everybody in the building hears us, can the two illicit lovers have an easy life?"

"The Eighth Route Army is busy resisting the Japanese. How would they have the time to go to Nanchang to catch the adulterous young man."

The speaker had no particular intention in saying it, but the listeners read their own meaning into it. In her room Zhang Li vaguely heard the conversations downstairs. She guessed correctly what they were talking about and reported it to Lao Ding at once.

At night, Zhang Li was very excited and talked to her roommates about those two illicit lovers. "Once, when I went to fetch boiled water in the boiler-house, I heard some strange noises in the storage room for firewood. I had never heard such a noise, so out of curiosity I went to the door. Through a crack between the door and the frame, I saw a man and a woman hugging each other. I was terribly frightened. Yet I could not move my feet, so I stayed there watching for a while before I slipped away."

"How could you stay there watching?" laughed Zhao Feixia.

"In the following days, whenever I thought of the scene, my mind would be in a whirl and I would become flushed," said Zhang Li. "But before I could report them to our leaders, they had eloped. Now it seems they ran back to her hometown to give birth."

The four girls lived in a room on the shady side of the second floor, so small that it could only accommodate four bamboo beds. With a small table, it was completely packed. Liu Hongmei slept head to head with Zhang Li whose excited saliva fell on her face, yet she was cheerfully listening to Zhang Li's stories. She got up early next morning and washed her face three times. She didn't mean to dislike Zhang Li who was doing publicity work. Along with Wang Tiantian whose job was in public relations, they engaged in open activities in the name of journalism. The four roommates were close and on good terms despite doing different jobs. Every night, before they went to sleep they would lie in bed and whisper their private thoughts, exchanging what they saw and heard, as well as news and their opinions about the current situation. Liu Hongmei was a new arrival, besides, she was involved in confidential work, so there was little she could talk about. She had one little secret yet she could not show off: she had heard from Yan Mei'er that the two illicit lovers had no spy background. They merely eloped and went to Nanchang to live a happy life as a small family.

A few days later, Zhang Li talked about the couple again, "Lao Ding has told me that the organisation has let the underground in Nanchang undertake a secret investigation. They found the couple were indeed in Nanchang. They gave birth to a chubby boy, opened a small shop and were living a good life over there. The underground found they had no political intentions, they had purely eloped for love, so the underground didn't touch them."

"Zhang Li, you must be careful," said Zhao Feixia. "Don't let what happened in the firewood room corrupt your mind."

"You underestimate me," said Zhang Li. "How could I behave as disgracefully as that little bitch?" Liu Hongmei stopped listening to the tiff between the two women, thinking that Yan Mei'er was speaking the truth. It seemed that not all seductive women were spies.

Afterwards, Liu Hongmei became more and more particular about her appearance. She spent all her savings and allowances on buying clothes. Working in number 50 the staff had to wear plain clothes. The girls dressed up in all kinds of clothes and nobody felt it was inappropriate. Liu Hongmei also held that she had spent her own money, nothing wrong with that as long as it did not affect her work. If one day the revolution should need her to die, she would go to her death without hesitation. But before she died, she had to be in her most beautiful clothes.

She appreciated Yan Mei'er's eye for pretty things to the extent that she began to worship her. She would follow how Yan Mei'er dressed and took her advice to heart. One Sunday morning she walked back and forth twice in the walkway. Pretending she was watching swallows in the sky, Yan Mei'er cast a side glance at her, quietly pointing at her hair, then to the west direction of the street. Yan Mei'er went back to her room. Soon she went out of the compound. Liu Hongmei went to the street with her roommates, but soon she turned up in Han's Hair Salon where Yan Mei'er was waiting. Looking at Liu Hongmei carefully, Yan Mei'er exchanged words with the hairdresser. She then asked Li Hongmei what hair style she wanted.

Liu Hongmei muttered, "Your opinion is always the best." The hairdresser did Liu Hongmei's hair while Yan Mei'er chatted with her. All they talked about were clothes and they even talked about the plain clothes worn by the female Eighth Route Army soldiers in Yan'an. Liu Hongmei said that the intellectual youth in Yan'an were from all over the country, and their clothes were of a wide variety. In short, chaotic.

When her hair was done, once again Liu Hongmei could not recognise herself. Considering her professional identity, Yan Mei'er did not recommend that the hairdresser dress Liu Hongmei's hair in a curly and wavy style, but straight which could be either tied into a bun or hang loose on her shoulders, except that the ends were slightly curled, and therefore looked nice either way. Blissfully happy, Liu Hongmei was very pleased. After they walked out of the hairdresser, they had a hot, spicy chicken meal before going back home.

Occasionally, from then on Liu Hongmei secretly went out with Yan Mei'er. They had become intimate friends who kept no secrets from each other. One Sunday Liu Hongmei saw Yan Mei'er wearing a sapphire necklace and she envied her very much. Yan Mei'er said that the necklace was her cousin's and she had borrowed it for a while. Liu Hongmei tried it on. Looking into the mirror she was reluctant to part with it. Cracking up, Yan Mei'er let Liu Hongmei wear the necklace for a couple of days. One day Liu Hongmei met Yan Mei'er in the street and they went window-shopping together, strolling here and there.

When it was lunch time, Liu Hongmei was dumbfounded. The necklace had gone. Yan Mei'er was so anxious that she started to cry. She then took Liu Hongmei's arm and they began to search the streets. They did not find it, of course. Liu Hongmei sat in the street weeping. Yan Mei'er did not blame her, but she could only weep too.

In the days afterwards, Yan Mei'er did not go to the terrace to comb her hair. Sloppy every day, she looked dejected. No longer a show-off, Liu Hongmei also felt bad when the alluring scenery downstairs was gone.

One Sunday they met in the street and began to weep again. Besides crying, they discussed what they should do. Both were single women with no valuables to speak of, so there was no way for them to reimburse the loss of the necklace. Then a few hoodlums approached them and harassed them, asking them to play with them. Not for free, they said, the price was different for accompanying them for a drink or in bed. From nowhere Yan Mei'er fished out a pair of scissors, swearing, "Go home and sleep with your sister." Seeing that they had met a hard nut, the hoodlums tried to slip away. Yan Mei'er suddenly remembered something. She stepped forward and grabbed the collar of one of the gang members. Sticking the scissors against his belly, she yelled, "You guys stole my necklace, didn't you? Hurry up and give it back to me, or I will fight it out with you."

Stupefied, the hoodlums swung their fists and knocked Yan Mei'er to the floor, cursing, "You bitch. It's fine if you don't want to play with us. How dare you blackmail us! We always rob in the open, never steal in the dark." While cursing, they gave Yan Mei'er a violent beating. Picking up a cleaver from a butcher, Liu Hongmei shouted while brandishing the weapon at the hoodlums. Seeing the scene, the hoodlums turned and ran.

Beaten black and blue, with blood dripping from the corner of her mouth, Yan Mei'er sat on the floor weeping. Liu Hongmei helped her get up and they began to walk home. "We can't find a way to get money, it's killing me," muttered Liu Hongmei.

"Now we have two choices," said Yan Mei'er. "Either we get money from the hoodlums, which means we have to sell our bodies, or from the spies, which means we have to sell military information."

Liu Hongmei did not get it.

Yan Mei'er explained that the Chongqing underworld had a profession called intelligence dealers. They made a living by selling intelligence, that is to say they get some information about the KMT and sell it to the Communists, or get some information about the Communists and sell it to the KMT. More money could be made for information about the Japanese and the puppet government, because they could sell it to both the KMT and the Communists.

"Being a prostitute and selling our bodies, there is no road back to our former positions. How about selling information?" suggested Liu Hongmei. "When we've made enough money, we wash our hands of it."

Yan Mei'er said, "We can mingle the true with the false information, stuff of major and minor importance to make some money. If we take care and are smart, no accidents will happen. How about giving it a try? I'll go to the KMT to eavesdrop on something, and you get something from the Communist side, to see if we can get something we can make money out of."

Liu Hongmei had a think about it, saying they mustn't do it, because they would lose their heads if anything went wrong.

Yan Mei'er said, " Don't get something major, only minor. Even if it is sold, it won't cause suspicion."

Liu Hongmei still said no, and she went back to her room.

A few days later, Liu Hongmei said to Yan Mei'er that she really had no way out, how about they go and sell their bodies. The idea made Yan Mei'er was sick. "Selling our bodies for half a year, we may get enough money, but our reputation will be tarnished, which will cause us mental suffering all our lives. We can't do it even if the alternative is death."

Liu Hongmei asked whether the names of places, hills and valleys in Yan'an were worth money. Yan Mei'er said a few years ago when the Japanese bombed Yan'an, that information was valuable, but now it was worthless. However, people's names might be valuable for a few coppers, besides, selling names ran no risks. She asked Liu Hongmei where she had worked in Yan'an, and she was able to list some names to sell.

Liu Hongmei maintained her basic vigilance. She set up a principle for herself which was to make some money for the lost necklace, but not to damage Yan'an's interests. So she said, "Since what we are selling are people's names, there's no need to mention what unit they are from. I can list some names." Alert and thoughtful, she did not want to leave any trace of her handwriting behind, so she mentioned the names orally while Yan Mei'er wrote them down. But Yan Mei'er said these names had to be listed by their departments, in full and had to be true otherwise the buyers would discriminate against them. If they were false, not only would the dealers not pay them a cent, but they would not trade with them any more. Liu Hongmei said the names were all true. The first 137 were for one department and the later 189 were for a different department. But again she was alert and thoughtful, because she did not list anyone who was close to her, so Chief Gao, Ji Zhenren, Li Mozi and Gao Yuncao were not among the names on the list.

However, Yan Mei'er failed to bring any money back. She said that the buyers had discriminated against the list, saying it was not a full list, so they refused to pay. She asked Liu Hongmei to have another think to see if she had missed someone. Patting her head, Liu Hongmei said, "Aiya, I forgot my chief. Add him on. It's Gao Yueming."

"That's all?"

"Yes, that's all."

A few days later, Yan Mei'er came back with money, 270 yuan in cash.

"Names are not worth much money. When will we have enough money for the necklace?" grumbled Liu Hongmei.

"I was paid 700 yuan for the information about a KMT infantry division shifting somewhere else for garrison duty. The more important the information, the more money there is to be made," said Yan Mei'er.

"How about ciphers, can I make a lot of money for selling them?" Liu Hongmei asked.

"Of course! But you must be very careful not to let the cat out of the bag. I heard that ciphers are worth nothing once the game is given away. Then you are finished. I think you'd better not touch that stuff," warned Yan Mei'er.

"I only send telegrams" said Liu Hongmei. "I don't know what the contents are. The code book is kept by the director who hides it somewhere where no one can steal it. But I can have a try if there is a chance, otherwise when can I ever pay back the money for the necklace?".

"No hurry. Safety first," said Yan Mei'er.

Some days later, a dejected Liu Hongmei told Yan Mei'er that she could not get the code book, and she was worried to death for failing to gather enough money for the necklace.

"What's the use of worrying?"

"Aha, can we sell the Japanese ciphers?"

Yan Mei'er's eyes brightened, "Yes, we can. We can make big money if the goods are good."

Liu Hongmei moved closer to Yan Mei'er, and said in a low voice, "I also did confidential work in Yan'an. Before I came to Chongqing, I knew that Yan'an had cracked the Japanese ciphers codenamed 'Four Gentlemen'. From the intelligence gathered, they knew that a KMT assistant commander-in-chief had defected to the Japanese with his troops." She then gave a detailed account of it.

Yan Mei'er got very excited, "If the 'Four Gentlemen' has been cracked, this information is worth big money to the Japanese. The money for the necklace is settled."

As expected it was settled. A few days later Yan Mei'er told Liu Hongmei that the information had been sold at a fair price and she had got the money. Seeing the big bag of money, Liu Hongmei's eyes turned green. They rushed to the jewellery shop and bought a sapphire stone similar to the one they had lost.

A great weight was lifted off Liu Hongmei's mind. Squatting down at the entrance of the shop, she cried her heart out. Then she stood up and, taking Yan Mei'er's arm, they went straight to the Huangma Hotel, which had the most famous restaurant in Chongqing. "Let's eat all the remaining money to get over the shock," said Liu Hongmei, as she kept on thinking about the remainder of the money.

During the meal, Yan Mei'er took out the new pendant and examined it. "What a nice sapphire," she remarked, asking Liu Hongmei to have a look.

As if she had stepped on a snake, Liu Hongmei jumped up and waved her hands, "I don't want to touch it. If it gets lost again, it has nothing to do with me." However, as she spoke, her eyes fell on the stone. "We should have washed our hands of it as we've paid for the lost sapphire. But if there is another chance, we can wangle some money and buy one for ourselves, which would be very nice," said Yan Mei'er.

"Don't just think of good things. Hurry up and return the necklace to your cousin. The anxiety these days makes me feel that I have already died once," said Liu Hongmei, hurriedly.

"Isn't it like nothing bad has happened? As long as we say nothing about it, the seller and the buyer will definitely not leak that we are the informants. It's safe."

"You're right. We made money so easily. How about we buy ourselves a stone not quite as good as this one? It won't cost much, will it?" said Liu Hongmei.

"No matter how much it costs, we must have money first. Stop thinking of good things. Let's eat our fill. You won't get a second chance to eat such good dishes in your life," said Yan Mei'er.

When Chongqing entered the rainy season, Liu Hongmei wanted to buy a raincoat. Again she sent out signals downstairs to Yan Mei'er. As soon as they met in the shop, Yan Mei'er said, "Want me to tell you what raincoat to buy? You never have to worry about bothering me too much."

Liu Hongmei laughed, "Bother produces affection. I feel that I'm more and more inseparable from you. If you were a man, I would marry you. In Chongqing you are the most intimate friend I have."

"What's the use of being intimate with me? I can't give you anything, besides, I brought you trouble with the necklace," said Yan Mei'er.

Eyeing Liu Hongmei up and down, Yan Mei'er went on, "Well, I understand why you're thirsty for that necklace. Look at you, only lacking a necklace. With one on your neck, you will look most refreshing and energetic."

Liu Hongmei had a think, then said, "How about we get one? Will the information of Yan'an's deciphering of the KMT armies' codes be worth big money?"

"Of course! Can it be that you have access to it?" asked Yan Mei'er.

"Yes. Let me tell you about it. After selling it, we can each buy a necklace to wear. Then we'll wash our hands of the matter," said Liu Hongmei.

"So it will be the last chance for me to benefit by associating with you. Well, haha, I'm so pleased to even think of the necklace," laughed Yan Mei'er.

Liu Hongmei then told Yan Mei'er about Yan'an's deciphering of codes used by the KMT troops under the command of general Hu Zongnan. Yan Mei'er asked Liu Hongmei to write them down, saying that the buyer would only believe the information written by her in person, so they could sell it for a good price. Liu Hongmei wrote down which ciphers used by Hu Zongnan's troops had been cracked and what the intelligence was from these messages. She wrote it down in minute detail and very professionally. Yan Mei'er said she could not understand what she had written. Liu Hongmei told her it was all professional jargon so, of course, she would not understand.

This time it was even quicker. The next day Yan Mei'er came with money and a big bag. Too impatient to wait, they went to buy themselves sapphire necklaces the same day. Yan Mei'er warned Liu Hongmei that she had to cover it when she wore it, otherwise it would arouse suspicion.

A few days later, at nightfall, Yan Mei'er sent signals, asking Liu Hongmei to go out. She told Liu Hongmei that she had just read the news in *Xinhua Daily*. The *Xinhua News Agency* in Yan'an had released important news about Chairman Chiang Kai-shek's secret order to the 400,000 troops commanded by Hu Zongnan and Yan Xishan to prepare for a surprise attack on Yan'an, as well as troop deployment plans and action orders. The intelligence dealers had passed on the word that among the information published by the Communists, many messages were sent by the KMT armies via telegrams encrypted with the three ciphers revealed by Liu Hongmei. Therefore, it was natural that the Communists deciphered them. For another two ciphers sold by Liu Hongmei, although they were not used for encoding these messages, through other channels, it was proved that they had also been deciphered by the Communists. So the buyers praised her intelligence as being very authentic and important, wanting to know if she had any more in stock. Someone was happy to pay a high price for them.

In a daze, Liu Hongmei seemed unable to get it. Yan Mei'er continued, "Those guys are really despicable. Now it is not just an issue of buying and selling. They've gone so far as to threaten me by saying that if you don't cooperate with them long-term and provide them with intelligence, they'll spread the news to number 50 courtyard that you have sold intelligence to them."

Liu Hongmei trembled with fright, muttering, "Except for my brother, my sister-in-law and my lover, I have nothing else, I have no extra information to sell even if they hound me to death."

Looking ashamed, Yan Mei'er said, "In short, it's me who has done you harm. I should never have let you wear my cousin's necklace. It's pretty tough on you, but whatever happens, you must not sell your brother, sister-in-law and lover. Anyway, people's names are worthless now."

Mentioning her brother, sister-in-law and lover, Liu Hongmei felt pain in her heart. She began to cry and cried harder than when she lost the necklace. She then told Yan Mei'er everything about how she had become a child bride, how her future husband Ji Zhenfu had defected to the KMT army, how Ji Zhenren had been implicated and how Li Mozi had become a target of suspicion. She had sold information about the Communists. If Yan'an found out, it would leave the Ji's with no decent people but her sister-in-law Gao Yuncao, who was clean.

With her eyes wet, Yan Mei'er was very sympathetic, "Your brother is married? Luckily the Communists did not implicate all your close relatives, or your sister-in-law would definitely have come to a bad end."

"She has a clean record, with no connection to the Ji's. She still worked hard although she might not be very happy with the treatment her husband had received. I myself was not implicated, otherwise I would not have been sent to Chongqing. I was allowed to come to Chongqing because my organisation took into consideration that both my brother and my boyfriend were under criticism and investigation, so they sent me here to take shelter from the campaign to eliminate spies. To tell the truth, the Communists' political movements are always ruthless. A few days ago some people from Yan'an arrived in Chongqing. They secretly told me that the special group had badly tortured my brother and my boyfriend. Now I'm falling into intelligence dealers' hands, life will be very hard for me." Again Liu Hongmei began to weep.

"It seems that you truly have no way out. You've done it, so it's hard for you to stop. You know that those intelligence dealers must have ganged up with the KMT's secret services, or they may even be one family. Now you are faced with two choices: either let them give you away to the Communists, or cooperate with them. A long-term cooperation is also a way out; money can be made and there is no big risk as long as you are careful," said Yan Mei'er.

Wiping tears from her eyes, Liu Hongmei said, "No, there is a third way. You and I can run away to a quiet place. We can each find a husband and live the life of a small family. I don't mind if you laugh at me. I'm quite jealous of that pair of illicit lovers. How about we also run away?"

Yan Mei'er laughed, "Two fragile women, where can we run to? What can we do afterwards? Probably we can only be prostitutes. I'd rather die than doing that to make a living. All right, Hongmei, watch out for your mood. Don't give yourself away before the others get suspicious about you."

The upsurge of the KMT's anti-Communist activities broke out in force and the situation in number 50 Zengjiayan was becoming increasingly grim. The office had to readjust work and one thing they did was to reduce the number of staff and send some of them back to Yan'an. Before long Liu Hongmei was informed that she might be one of them. In fear and trepidation she went to ask Yan Mei'er what she should do. Yan Mei'er had a think, telling her that she could do nothing but let nature take its course.

Yan Mei'er laid her cards on the table, "From the first day you sold intelligence, you became a non-staff secret agent of the Juntong. The difference is that the treatment you received was for a dealer, paid for each deal. Now there is no road for you to go back. If you choose not to cooperate, nor to submit, your loved ones will all be killed. The reason is simple, so there is no need to say any more."

She then revealed her KMT secret agent identity, which made Liu Hongmei dumbstruck at first, then cry her heart out. Yan Mei'er felt that this woman, who was seeking vanity, had been firmly in her grip, so she passed an assignment on to Liu Hongmei, "After you return to Yan'an, you must make contact with medical officer Liu Jiacheng and his wife, nurse Zhang Qianqian in RSU2. You will pass on to them the intelligence you gather, and they will hand you the money for the intelligence. But there is another way to pay you, which is that I keep the money for you. My true name is Zhen Yanli, and my address is 178 Xiangnaohe Road, Chongqing. Before you depart, I will take you to this address. In the future, no matter how many years pass, when you come to me for the money, I will acknowledge this debt. There is organisational discipline, so I dare not embezzle your hard-earned money. You can set your mind at ease." Liu Hongmei had no choice but to let Yan Mei'er keep the money for her because she was worried that the money might arouse suspicion in Yan'an.

Yan Mei'er gave Liu Hongmei a contact password, instructing her to form a spy group with the medical officer and his wife, codenamed 'Team Eagle', she being the team leader. Yan Mei'er also said, "The medic and his wife are in a junior position in RSU2, doing field work, so their range of activity is limited. Only you can get into the core departments to get important intelligence. If you do a good job, the party and the state will not forget you; but neither will they forgive you if you do your job badly."

Liu Hongmei made some strange remarks, "We've become sisters. One day when we meet again, you must give all my earnings to me, not a single penny short. I have exchanged my life for this money and I will use my life to claim it back. After I return to Yan'an, I am going to practice my gun skills, and one bullet will be kept for that money of mine."

Like a man, Yan Mei'er looked up at the sky and laughed out loud, "A money-grubbing woman is a hundred times more frightening than a man."

Throwing herself at Yan Mei'er, Liu Hongmei held her tight and sobbed. Then emotionally she kissed Yan Mei'er's cheeks and neck hard. Yan Mei'er pushed Liu Hongmei away, flushed, with breath rasping and voice trembling she said, "Ah, this kiss is more sweet than a kiss from a man. Why, you really want to elope with me? In this world all men are obscene, only the love between two beautiful women is the cleanest, purest and best. What a pity we have to part. Well, I am in Chongqing waiting for our reunion."

Liu Hongmei dashed away, sobbing.

What happened afterwards was simple.

Liu Hongmei rejoined RSU2. Immediately Chief Gao took her to the Central Department of Social Affairs, the CPC's counter-intelligence and intelligence department, where Liu Hongmei reported in detail on her dealings with the KMT secret agent Zhen Yanli (aka Yan Mei'er). In fact, as soon as she had arrived in Chongqing, she had secretly reported to Lao Ding on her every contact with Zhen Yanli, and Lao Ding had also promptly reported them to Yan'an.

It turned out that both the special investigation group of the Central Department of Social Affairs and Chief Gao felt that KMT secret agents were hiding in RSU2. But after all sorts of methods, they had failed to catch anyone. Therefore, they had decided to dispatch Liu Hongmei, who had a close relationship with Ji Zhenren and Li Mozi, to Chongqing, feigning to be a defector seeking opportunities to approach the KMT secret services and to find out the circumstances surrounding the KMT's dispatching of secret agents to Yan'an. When the decision was made, in RSU2 only Chief Gao knew about this secret plan.

The main problem now was how to deal with medic Liu Jiacheng and nurse Zhang Qianqian. After a discussion, the Central Department of Social Affairs and Chief Gao decided to turn the two enemy agents to serve us. Two methods could be adopted. One was not to arrest the couple, but let Liu Hongmei use the password to contact them. Afterwards, at some critical moments and for some critical events, she would feed some false intelligence to the couple, to either disturb the KMT's military deployment or benefit ourselves militarily through this false intelligence. The other method was to arrest the couple, forcing them to confess and desert the KMT, so we could recruit them to work for us. In the end, the higher-level authorities made the decision to use the first method and to keep the second method as a back-up, depending on how the first method went.

After some days' rest, complaining of a stomach ache, Liu Hongmei went to the medical unit several times in a row. Seizing the opportunity, she got in touch with the spy couple, and the process was natural and flawless.

According to the rules she could not ask the couple who their contacts were. With Chief Gao's permission, she passed onto the couple the intelligence of a certain KMT regiment garrisoned in Handan having defected to the Japanese and the puppet government, and in the role of being the leader of 'Team Eagle' she ordered the couple to send the intelligence out of Yan'an quickly. Medic Liu Jiacheng dared not be slack. The next day he left the barracks supposedly to purchase medicines. This intelligence relay was under the surveillance of the Central Department of Social Affairs, from which the Communists got a clear map of the KMT's intelligence transport stations from Ansai to Yan'an to Xi'an. The Central Department of Social Affairs planned to capture them in one haul in the future.

Returning to the matter of Liu Hongmei kicking up a fuss with the special group, it was the prelude to the Central Department of Social Affairs and Chief Gao sending Liu Hongmei to Chongqing, making it look as though she was extremely unhappy with the organisation, thereby creating a reasonable motive for her to defect to the KMT.

A cryptographer who knew all the secrets, besides she harboured resentment toward Yan'an, the KMT secret services would not let the opportunity slip to recruit her. Chief Gao reckoned that if there was a spy hidden in RSU2, he or she would report this information about Liu Hongmei to Chongqing. After she arrived in Chongqing, if the KMT secret services approached her to persuade her to defect, this would in turn confirm that enemy agents might truly be hiding in RSU2.

Facts later showed that when Zhen Yanli had her eyes on Liu Hongmei, our people in Chongqing had found out that she had a KMT secret agent background. So everything that happened between her and Liu Hongmei was under our side's control.

The implementation of this plan was extremely skilful and breathtaking.

Between June and July 1943, Chiang Kai-shek sent multiple coded telegrams to Hu Zongnan and Yan Xishan, ordering their 400,000 troops to get ready to make a surprise attack on Yan'an.

In this period, from the decrypted messages between Chiang, Hu and Yan, RSU2 in a timely fashion obtained their detailed operational plans and information on troop deployment. Meanwhile, the underground hidden in Hu Zongnan's troops also obtained related information. The intelligence from two different sources confirmed that Yan'an was faced with a serious crisis. At the time the Eighth Route Army's main forces were fighting the Japanese far away from Yan'an. The ratio of forces between the KMT and the Communists in the neighbouring regions of Yan'an were ten to one. The outcome for the battle of Yan'an had already been decided even before it began.

In view of such a grim situation, the Communists made a significant decision: to win victory without firing a single shot and force the enemy to retreat by its wits, to make the KMT's telegrams public, exposing the KMT's sabotage of the anti-Japanese united front and their plot to make a surprise attack on Yan'an. Serving as evidence, these detailed telegrams would make all circles of society believe beyond a shadow of doubt that the KMT would launch an attack on Yan'an. This in turn would lead domestic and international public opinion to condemn the KMT, thereby foiling the powerful enemy's attack on Yan'an.

Obviously this was a major leak of secrets, done as a last resort, but it simply had to be done. To Yan'an, such a measure might have been able to prevent the KMT troops from attacking Yan'an, but it would also have made the KMT suspect that Communist spies were hiding in their key departments, or that the Communists had cracked their major ciphers. The direct outcome could have been that the KMT would either have taken vigorous measures to ferret out the Communist spies, or have changed all the ciphers in use. Once the spies were ferreted out, their lives would be hard to save and years of achievement would have been destroyed in an instant; while the enemy changing ciphers meant that the Communists' major source of intelligence would have been cut off and RSU2's work would have suffered badly, which would have made it more difficult to crack the enemy's new ciphers.

But Chief Gao thought that compared to Yan'an's safety, partial loss was next to nothing, and that the sacrifice and leaks were necessary and worthwhile. After some hard thinking, he meticulously did one thing. With the approval of his superiors, he sent a telegram to Lao Ding in Chongqing, asking him to let Liu Hongmei reveal ahead of time to the enemy the information that the Communists had cracked the ciphers used by Hu Zongnan's troops, making the KMT side believe that Yan'an had obtained the information through the deciphered telegrams, so they would not suspect that Communist spies were among them. This would either protect the Communist spies, or raise Liu Hongmei's value to the KMT.

Just as Yan'an had expected, this tactic achieved the hoped-for results. The KMT's plot was exposed to the light of day. Due to protests and condemnation from all sides, Chiang Kai-shek had to give up the operation. Taking "we are relieving a garrison, please don't misunderstand us" as a response, he ended his third anti-Communist upsurge.

A few days before Yan'an made the enemy plot public, Liu Hongmei revealed and sold the intelligence that three ciphers used by the troops under Hu Zongnan's command had been cracked by the Communists. Part of General Hu's orders for troop deployment were sent by these three ciphers. Meanwhile, in order to prevent the KMT from linking Liu Hongmei's sale of intelligence to Yan'an's exposure of the KMT's plan to attack Yan'an, Chief Gao let Liu Hongmei sell information about two unrelated ciphers being cracked. In fact, these two ciphers were to be updated automatically and eventually abandoned.

As to what had happened to that sapphire necklace, there are four possibilities. First, Liu Hongmei broke the chain by accident; second, a thief made off with it; third, to force Liu Hongmei to sell intelligence,

Zhen Yanli stole it; fourth, Liu Hongmei herself stole it, thus paving the way for her to sell intelligence. Later, someone remarked that the most likely possibilities were the last two, but whether it was the KMT or the Communists, no one could say clearly.

Besides, the KMT Special Secret Wireless Section obtained much wanted information from Liu Hongmei, namely, that 'Grasshopper' Gao Yuncao had not been exposed, but was still in deep hibernation.

For some time after they received the intelligence sent by Gao Yuncao via carrier pigeon, they had heard nothing else from her. Gao Q and Zhen Yanli were very worried for her safety. Because the 'Grasshopper Plan' was specifically approved and operated by the Special Secret Wireless Service alone, other people in the Juntong knew nothing about it. For Gao Yuncao's personal safety, the Special Secret Wireless Service did not want the Juntong system to get involved. But Gao Q and Zhen Yanli knew that two agents from Juntong's 'Spy Training Class in Hanzhong' had infiltrated RSU2, so they intended to get some information about Grasshopper from this channel. However, they could not tell the agents about Grasshopper's real name or what she was doing, so they only asked the agents to collect the names of RSU2's members of staff. But the two agents only did some field work in RSU2. They could not get any information about the cipher department, not even a name list. So Gao Q and Zhen Yanli did not know whether Gao Yuncao was still alive or not. Later, the 'Spy Training Class in Hanzhong' planned to attack RSU2. The superior of Gao Q and Zhen Yanli asked them if there was anything that the 'Spy Training Class in Hanzhong' could do for them. Gao Q requested: "Don't kill women after the agents enter the RSU2 compound."

"It concerns the long-term, overall situation of the KMT armies' military secrets in wireless communications," added Zhen Yanli. The Juntong knew that it was a sensitive matter, so they asked no more questions and acted accordingly. For the surprise attack on RSU2, the medical officer and his wife provided a detailed map of the compound. They had planned to operate from inside in coordination with the forces from outside, and after they had killed RSU2's cryptographers, the couple were then to withdraw and rejoin the Juntong. But the unexpected still happened. That night they did not know why the guards had woken up early. Hiding in the dark, the couple discovered that the operation had been a failure, so they decided to carry on hiding, waiting for an opportunity to kill Ji Zhenren and Li Mozi, and then to withdraw.

Gao Q and Zhen Yanli urgently needed news about Grasshopper. After doing deals with Liu Hongmei, Zhen Yanli dared not ask directly about Gao Yuncao, so she couldn't wait to get the full name list of RSU2's cryptographers. It puzzled Liu Hongmei, because she thought that the Juntong should already have known the name list from Zhang Guotao, the defected Red Army leader. But she did not know that when Gao Yuncao infiltrated RSU2 and made a name for herself, Zhang Guotao had long since defected to the KMT, and therefore had no idea that RSU2 had a cryptographer called Gao Yuncao. At first, Liu Hongmei did not put Ji Zhenren and Gao Yuncao on the name list. Gao Q and Zhen Yanli were very worried about the fate of Grasshopper. Later Liu Hongmei accidentally mentioned Ji Zhenren and Gao Yuncao to Zhen Yanli, besides, she said that they had got married, which set Gao Q and Zhen Yanli's minds at rest.

As to whether Liu Hongmei should establish contact with Grasshopper by the identity of a covert spy, Gao Q took a firm stance, "The Grasshopper Plan was specially approved by our superior, so we must not rush to make changes. Furthermore, Grasshopper is a rare talent for us. It has been really hard for her to achieve what she has achieved. We must not let that impulsive and money-grubbing woman Liu Hongmei upset our plan and spoil our game. It is better to send Liu Hongmei to the 'Spy Training Class in Hanzhong' to reinforce the strength of the medical officer and his wife."

In the end, Gao Q handed Liu Hongmei to the 'Spy Training Class in Hanzhong' who listed her as a top-grade source for intelligence. They put her under key protection and stipulated that she could only contact the medical officer and his wife but not their other contacts. If an accident should happen, anyone in the line would be sacrificed, including the medical officer and his wife, so that Liu Hongmei would not be exposed, or meet with a mishap.

For this Gao Q was very complacent, "While there is life, there is hope. To make contributions and accomplish great tasks for the party and the state cannot be done in a single day. Grasshopper, who is in hibernation, will wake up sooner or later. For the time being the priority is her safety. It is all right if she does nothing as long as no accident happens to her." In a fit of jealousy, Zhen Yanli sneered, "This doesn't sound like you, a spy elite, used to say. If she keeps hibernating all her life, what use is she to the party and the state? Safety is the priority? In your heart her life and death is more important than the party's cause and your wife's life and death."

Gao Q was annoyed. Pointing a finger at her he said, "Our superior decided that Grasshopper is a strategic spy. She is needed to fulfil her mission without her identity being revealed. So she is absolutely right to keep herself safe but not to seek quick success. But you and the others can only see what is under your noses and are eager for quick success and instant gratification. Through a one-eyed chicken peddlar called Li, without authorisation you ordered Grasshopper to 'fight at the risk of mutual destruction and kill the Communists' core cryptographers'. You should know that what you did runs contrary to our superior's intention of making the Grasshopper Plan a strategic and long-term one. Besides, your action has also put Grasshopper's personal safety under serious threat. At the time you did it, for fear of hurting your feelings, I did not report you to our superior. Now you are making a fuss about my comments about her, you're just a narrow-minded woman!"

"This is truly outrageous!" said Zhen Yanli, dashing into the bedroom, coming out with a photograph and throwing it on the dining table. It was taken by Gao Q of Jiang Xiaodian in a swimming pool in Shanghai. He hid it in a secret place, not knowing how his wife had found it.

"How many photos of her have you hidden?" shouted Zhen Yanli. "Didn't you say that when you pursued her in Shanghai, it was for the sake of the party and the state and it was a game? It seems that they were all lies. In fact, in your heart you still love this woman deeply," shouted Zhen Yanli.

Gazing at the photo, Gao Q had a pained expression on his face.

"Look at your face, all the compassion and care for that woman. You really make me sick!" cried Zhen Yanli.

Looking pensive, Gao Q said, "In such a difficult environment she can still hold on and stay, neither impatient nor rash, for this she is an unbelievable woman. Could you achieve that? You can't even bear that one garment is not fashionable, or one meal is not tasty. So to Grasshopper, we have nothing else to say but to show our admiration. Please watch your words, you jealous woman."

With her eyes red, Zhen Yanli breathed a long sigh, "Her loyalty to the party and the state deserves reverence. But I really want to know if you two truly fell in love when you were in Shanghai?"

"Love or not, what is the difference? Over there in Yan'an she may die at any moment. It is hard for us to see each other again," said Gao Q, then he murmured to himself, "Keeping a photograph of her is natural and normal in human relations."

Before Liu Hongmei returned to Yan'an, the special group had been recalled from RSU2. Because she had passed on the precise news of the hidden KMT spies, there was no need to lock anyone else up for interrogation. Giving the public some feedback, the special group announced, "After investigation, no spies have been found in RSU2."

Thereafter, all those arrested were released and Ji Zhenren and Li Mozi resumed their work. The public was puzzled and had a lot of complaints about the special group. Someone went to Chief Gao to demand an explanation, accompanied by Gao Yuncao.

"After several rounds of screening, we failed to find any bad people, which means that everyone in RSU2 is a good person. Gao Yuncao, you are also a good person, a very good person, and your husband is an even better person. This is the conclusion we have reached. What other explanations do you want?" said Chief Gao.

Liu Hongmei still ignored Ji Zhenren when she saw him, yet he had something to say, "Only at the critical moment can the feelings between you and I as brother and sister be reflected. You went every day to the special group and complained loudly about the injustice I suffered. I heard you weeping. I was so touched that tears streamed down my face."

"I didn't do it for you but for Li Mozi," mumbled Liu Hongmei, poker-faced.

21 /THE YU CIPHER

It was in the second month after Liu Hongmei and Ji Zhenren went to the frontline that Gao Yuncao met with a crisis back home.

Since the intelligence leak initiated by Yan'an in July 1943, the KMT's wireless communications had had an overall reorganisation. The ciphers in use were terminated, the degree of technical difficulty for new ciphers was unprecedentedly high. The operating instructions and the security regulations and measures were much stricter than before. Therefore RSU2 encountered unparalleled difficulties in intercepting and deciphering the enemy codes and ciphers. Someone described the situation as Yan'an becoming mute and blind overnight. An over-exaggeration, but RSU2 were in a situation where they could neither receive any signals nor crack any ciphers.

Therefore, Chief Gao decided to dispatch scout teams to get close to the enemy. For Team 2, he appointed Liu Hongmei as the leader and Ji Zhenren as deputy. They were to go to the areas surrounding Hu Zongnan's KMT troops, hoping to put an end to their passive situation. A considerate boss, Chief Gao wanted to give Liu Hongmei and Ji Zhenren more of a chance to work together. Liu Hongmei's leadership ability was not inferior to Ji Zhenren's, so she fully deserved the title. Also, a team leader had to discuss work with the deputy.

When she was full of vigour and led the team at the frontline, in the RSU2 barracks in Youhulu Valley, the spy medical officer and his wife encountered a major situation and decided to handle it themselves. In fact, the matter was major, but not complicated. No matter if Liu Hongmei was at home or not, it had to be dealt with in the same manner as the couple had done previously. However, they had violated the orders given to them by Liu Hongmei before she left, "When I am not here in the barracks, we must halt all activities for Team Eagle and go into hibernation. Those who dare act without authorisation will be severely punished. The measure is to ensure we save our strength, also we need to consolidate our safety. You must bear it in mind." The couple promised to obey orders and not to act rashly. But they failed to stick to their word.

In the barracks there were three mess halls and the staff ate their meals in different halls according to the nature of their work. Hall no. 1 was for monitors and cryptographers, hall no. 2 was for the unit leaders and other cadres and hall no.3 was for the guards and orderlies. The RSU2 staff were involved with secrets at different levels and there was a separation system; for meals they had to eat in their own designated halls.

Nurse Zhang Qianqian and cryptographer Gao Yuncao worked in different categories, so their paths never crossed in either work or daily life.

One day Zhang Qianqian had her meal early. She then wandered toward hall no. 1 and hid in the bushes near a fork in the road, waiting for Gao Yuncao to come out. After Gao Yuncao walked past her, she came out of the bushes and quietly caught up with her.

"Are you comrade Gao Yuncao?" asked Zhang Qianqian.

Although it was inside the barracks, and Zhang Qianqian was in army uniform, due to her habit of 'not talking to strangers', Gao Yuncao did not admit that it was her, but said, "I think you're confusing me with someone else."

"I'm Zhang Qianqian, a nurse from the medical unit. An old friend called Zhen Yanli sends you her regards."

The name 'Zhen Yanli' jumped out of Zhang Qianqian's mouth like a bolt from the blue. An expert spy, Gao Yuncao did not panic at all but said calmly, "I'm afraid you've confused me with someone else."

Zhang Qianqian pulled up her right sleeve a bit, exposing a photo. Pretending to stroke her hair, she mysteriously revealed it to Gao Yuncao. It was the photo taken in the swimming pool in Shanghai. Gao Yuncao cursed inwardly: "This damned Gao Q, he has really held onto this photo for all these years."

Straight-faced, she threw a glance at Zhang Qianqian and carried on walking.

Zhang Qianqian stroked her hair again and a photo of Zhen Yanli and Gao Q was in her palm.

Gao Yuncao laughed, cheerfully and naturally, "What are you doing? Performing magic?"

"A photo is an inanimate object. I have something that can move." Zhang Qianqian opened her palm and a grasshopper jumped out and hopped into the roadside bushes.

Still laughing charmingly, Gao Yuncao said, "Are you really a magician? Will you turn something into a snake and scare me?"

"Zhen Yanli is right. It seems you really are a crafty grasshopper, calm and composed. But I earnestly tell you that I am one of you," said Zhang Qianqian, then her tone became fierce, "You had a bad tummy after supper, didn't you? Come to the medical unit at nine o'clock tonight. Military doctor Liu Jiacheng will be on duty and he is my husband. I'll be the nurse. Rest assured, as long as you come, the symptoms will vanish. If not, they will turn chronic, and no medicine will cure you." She walked away from the fork in the path.

Subconsciously, Gao Yuncao looked around, seeing nothing unusual.

After returning to the dormitory, she went to the toilet several times. "Something was not right with the food, I've got a bad tummy," she said to Wang Lan, her roommate.

Squatting over the hole in the toilet, she mulled over the critical situation that she was facing. In the end, she concluded that the situation could only be one of two possibilities, "Either I have been exposed, Zhang Qianqian works for Yan'an and she is testing me by setting a trap; or I have been in hibernation for too long, and my superior in Chongqing is impatient, so he has sent people here to wake me up and press me to do my job as a spy. No matter which is the case, visiting the medical unit is a must. Then I'll act as circumstances dictate."

She went and got some medicine. Quietly she threw the pills away. From somewhere she got a handful of wild beans and ate them. When it was midnight she suffered from both vomiting and diarrhoea. In the second half of the night she went to the toilet four to five times. As soon as the day broke she had to go to the medical unit again. This time medic Liu and nurse Zhang gave her some good medicine. Unwillingly, medic Liu said, "This medicine is meant for the senior officers. What a shame it has to be taken by a voracious eater."

Holding her painful belly, Gao Yuncao yelled, "What do you mean? The senior officers are human, but I'm not? Why is it a shame when I take them?"

Medic Liu laughed inwardly, "As expected, she is a master spy, good at playing games."

After taking the medicine for three days, Gao Yuncao's vomiting and diarrhoea stopped. Her anxious heart calmed down for the time being. Very soon she gained a clear picture of medic Liu and nurse Zhang.

Not long ago, the couple's friend Zhang Yuhe had returned to Shaanxi from Chongqing, bringing with him two photographs. When he was in Chongqing, by chance he had had a meal with Zhen Yanli who was not on good terms with her husband Gao Q and felt unhappy at the time. Zhen Yanli got drunk. In wine there is truth. She spoke about her husband and the fact that, although they were sleeping in the same bed, they dreamt different dreams. Gao Q always had in his heart a 'Grasshopper' tart, an undercover agent in RSU2 in Yan'an.

As for the few remarks after the wine, the speaker said them intentionally and the listener took them to heart. Zhang Yuhe turned them over in his mind, thinking that a spy who could hide in RSU2 for so many years must have been exceptional. If he could make contact with Grasshopper, he could certainly obtain some high-value intelligence. He was only a petty spy and for many years he had been operating in northern Shaanxi. It was hard for him to get any worthwhile information, neither being able to make money nor being promoted. Therefore Zhen Yanli's drunken remarks made him devise a plan regarding Gao Yuncao.

Zhang Yuhe was not the supervisor of medic Liu and nurse Zhang but an ordinary friend engaged in the same profession. Yet he knew that the couple were spies hidden in RSU2. This time, after he got the information about Gao Yuncao, he secretly went to see the couple who were also obsessed about winning promotion and getting rich. They went along with his scheme, which was in fact quite simple. Using the two photos that Zhang Yuhe had stolen from Zhen Yanli and the codename 'Grasshopper' or 'Grasshopper Tart' that he had deduced from Zhen Yanli's drunken words, medic Liu and nurse Zhang were to establish contact with Gao Yuncao. Afterwards they could slowly get some important information from her. By chance, Liu Hongmei was away so they had the chance to do a few deals and make some money. It was a private matter, making a small fortune on the back of Liu Hongmei. The three also inferred that Gao Yuncao had to cooperate; if not, they could threaten her by saying that they would betray her. She was a clever woman, so she would be aware of the consequences.

Gao Yuncao had loose bowels for three days, meanwhile she thought about the problem she was facing. In the end she decided to establish an underground contact with medic Liu and nurse Zhang. After all, she was a senior spy and her ability to win people over was amazing. After a few sincere conversations, medic Liu and nurse Zhang regarded her as their bosom friend. The couple not only told her about the appearance of Zhang Yuhe who was a secret agent and the boss of Jixiang Pharmacy in Ansai, but also revealed that Liu Hongmei was one of them. Wearing a cheerful smile, Gao Yuncao said, "Great, there is strength in numbers. From now on we can join hands and do more deals to honour the party and the state." She then applied RSU2's security education to the couple, giving them a lecture and making them realise that they were partners; no matter how much danger they were in, as long as they were of one mind and clubbed together, they could achieve great deeds.

Gao Yuncao found that Zhang Yuhe did not have much detailed information about her, except for the vague knowledge of her codename 'Grasshopper', or 'Grasshopper Tart'. But what was most terrifying was that he and the medic couple were absolutely certain that she was a KMT Special Wireless Secret Service agent. If Yan'an knew about it, the counter-intelligence department, Central Department of Social Affairs, would employ all its hidden contacts inside the KMT to check and verify it. If they were able to confirm the facts, it would be a disaster and pose a true danger to her. Meanwhile she called to mind Liu Hongmei. She had not expected that she could have become a KMT spy. Medic Liu and nurse Zhang did not know the details of when and how Liu Hongmei had become a Juntong secret agent. She dared not imagine what could happen once Yan'an found out that both Ji Zhenren's sister and wife were KMT secret agents, nor could she dare to imagine what it would be like when Liu Hongmei returned and found out her true identity.

In the end, the crisis-ridden Gao Yuncao made up her mind, "Success or failure hinges on this one action! Before Liu Hongmei returns, I must completely settle the matter once and for all."

Her basic thinking was that she must not become a true enemy of Yan'an. Although mentally she did not regard herself as a sworn enemy of the Communists for a long time, once her KMT spy identity was exposed, she would have no route of retreat. Meanwhile she did not want to get Ji Zhenren implicated. Because he lives to crack ciphers. To him RSU2 is everything, his political life must not be terminated because of his wife's problem.

So she decided to risk her life to fight it.

At the moment her main job was to crack YU for Yan'an. Before Liu Hongmei and Ji Zhenren went to the front line, RSU2 had already intercepted some enemy messages encrypted by YU. Because there were only a few messages, several top cryptographers failed to crack the cipher. One month later Liu Hongmei sent back some more transcripts but the cryptographers at home had still failed to crack it. Meanwhile Liu Hongmei and Ji Zhenren made no substantial progress either. Thinking of this now, it might have been that Liu Hongmei had secretly hindered the process, misleading Ji Zhenren to prevent the cipher from being cracked.

YU was a high-grade cipher recently put to use between the KMT Military Council in Chongqing and General Hu Zongnan in Xi'an, a key cipher for RSU2 to tackle at the moment. Gao Yuncao was of a mind to tackle it, and her purpose was to do some bedding down and preparation to put an end to the dangerous situation she was in.

When she was in Nanjing, she and her colleagues had compiled many ciphers for general use for the KMT armies, so she knew very well those cryptographers' thinking on how to create ciphers. But she felt profoundly that YU was completely different to the other ciphers they had created in the past. The characteristics of the man-made cipher appeared indistinctive while the distinguishing features of a machine-created cipher were beyond their reach. She couldn't sleep at night. She called for intuition and inspiration, but what appeared before her eyes were her former colleagues' ferocious faces and sneers. No one would give her a single pointer. She then picked the most ferocious and abominable face and, shaking her fist, she hit it with a sudden force. It cleverly dodged her blow, yet the expression was more abominable. In the end, she saw clearly that it was Gao Q's face. Experience told her that when intuition did not work effectively, she had to focus on one spot of the problem and dig deep, then suddenly outflanking the problem on the edge to identify the sound and search for the trace. Therefore, she aimed at Gao Q's thinking on cipher creation and his habits and characteristics. She began to think hard, deeply and broadly. She recalled all the previous technical exchanges between them, and analysed many of the favourite ciphers he had created. She pondered how much of his thinking on cipher creation had been adopted in the creation of *YU*. Could the grasp of one point cause the collapse of the whole structure of *YU*?

She worked on it for several days and nights without success. She looked up to the sky and let out a long, mournful cry. Inwardly she cursed her former colleagues, "You are all very capable now, aren't you? Why did you create such a damned cross-breed cipher to beat me? Aren't you truly ever-victorious? Isn't this cipher of yours unassailable? You damned men and women, can't you leave a crack and give me a chance?" In the end she vented all her anger on Zhen Yanli, "You bastard narrow-minded woman, you've really given me a hard time. You couldn't bear that Gao Q had kept a photograph of me. You're jealous even when I am a thousand kilometres away. Next time I meet you, I'll tear your lousy mouth apart." Cursing repeatedly, she suddenly stopped. She turned her attention from Zhen Yanli's jealousy to her hatred of Gao Q. Zhen Yanli was a woman who was always clear about what or who to love or hate, and she would take revenge for her grief. Emotionally she had a grudge against Gao Q, so inevitably she would bring this mood into her work. So when she worked on *YU*, it was possible that she had put on a rival show, doing exactly the opposite to what Gao Q meant to do. "Since I failed to make any breakthrough with Gao Q, let me try with Zhen Yanli. As long as *YU* had any input from her, I'll be able to spot it. If I keep on working, there is a possibility for me to crack *YU*. Zhen Yanli, you jealous woman, the success or failure of cracking *YU* is all due to your narrow-mindedness," Gao Yuncao murmured to herself.

Another two days and two nights went by. As expected, Gao Yuncao caught a pinch of a feather and tore a piece of skin and flesh off *YU* from where she found the vital direction, and finally realised a total breakthrough.

But she restrained her excitement. Holding back this significant progress, she mentioned nothing to the others.

She was biding her time.

At one o'clock in the morning, she suddenly jumped up from the bed, crying, "I've got it. I've caught the tail of YU. Wang Lan, get up quick. Let's go to the office to crack YU."

They ran out of the room. Calling on Li Mozi who lived next door, they hurried to their office.

It was common for cryptographers to suddenly be inspired at midnight, get up and go into action. Gao Yuncao talked excitedly as she walked. The more Li Mozi and Wang Lan listened, the more excited they became. They would constantly chime in and exchange ideas.

Obviously the deciphering work had already begun on the way to the office.

Their thinking gushed out like a fountain, with everyone joining in and relaying their ideas. When they arrived at the main gate, they showed their documents and were let in by the sentries.

They arrived at the cryptography office. Taking out the key, Li Mozi went to open the door. But he suddenly jerked his head around and gave an alarmed glance at Gao Yuncao, who called out, "The door is unlocked. Something has happened!"

In such a confidential department, to forget to lock doors was something that should have been impossible. Because even if someone had forgotten, the security guards would check every room to ensure it was locked. At such a late hour the cryptographers' office was unlocked, so they were all very vigilant.

Swiftly they drew their handguns. Pulling Li Mozi to one side, Gao Yuncao broke into the room first. Holding a lantern, she viewed the room. A shocking scene was presented before her eyes: a masked man, with a pile of paper in his arms, was stretching out his hand to grab a pistol on the desk.

Gao Yuncao and Wang Lan, who was close behind, opened fire almost at the same time. The masked man fell in front of the desk.

Quickly sweeping her eyes over the whole room, Gao Yuncao did not see any accomplices of the masked man.

Just at this very moment, two gun shots were heard in the corridor outside. Li Mozi, who was dashing into the room, fell to the floor.

Gao Yuncao and Wang Lan hurriedly turned around, firing in the direction where the gun shots were heard.

Gao Yuncao dashed over. The human shadow lying on the floor fired backhand and the bullet hit Gao Yuncao's arm. Wang Lan then fired three shots at the human shadow.

The one they had killed was another masked person.

Guards then swarmed into the room. Removing the black cloth from the heads of the two bodies, they quickly recognised that they were medical officer Liu Jiacheng and his nurse wife Zhang Qianqian.

Hurriedly Gao Yuncao commanded the guards to carry Li Mozi to the medical unit for emergency treatment.

A nurse came and treated Gao Yuncao's wounded left arm. She then ran back to the office.

The two dead bodies were laid in the corridor. Inside the office Chief Gao was leading people to examine the intercepted enemy telegrams, saying that another two rooms had also been broken into, but the safe was not opened so the material inside was safe.

Looking grave, Gao Yuncao said to Chief Gao, "I urgently need Team Two and Team Three to decipher YU tonight. That deeply-hidden inspiration has finally appeared. I feel that's it. Li Mozi and Wang Lan also agree with me. I request that we tackle the cipher collectively and instantly. Let's start now! The damned opportunity is fleeting, we can't delay any more."

Burning with impatience, even the fact that people had just died failed to disturb her determination.

Chief Gao at once issued orders to the cryptographers who had already gathered at the gate after hearing gunshots. They quickly entered, stepping over the two dead bodies. As soon as they sat down, they heard Gao Yuncao's clear and resolute guidance of thought and step-by-step illustration.

As soon as the work began, in a spectacular way it became white-hot. Drawn by Gao Yuncao, the cryptographers' fast-working brains battled breathtakingly.

After who knows how many hours had passed, people from the Political Security Bureau and Central Department of Social Affairs arrived. As soon as they entered the room, they demanded the cryptographers move away, while blaming Chief Gao for failing to preserve the crime scene.

The battle of wills continued vigorously, yet the sudden appearance of the security people disrupted it. Looking at each other in surprise, the cryptographers' excitement slowed down and their active thinking was diminished by the sudden change of situation.

With her left arm in a sling and standing in front of a blackboard full of her writing, Gao Yuncao's high-spirited expression turned to anger. She stamped her feet hard and a thick layer of chalk dust flew up.

She yelled, "A most urgent military action is in progress here. Those who have nothing to do with the action please leave immediately. I need three days and three nights, during which time no unrelated personnel are allowed to step into this room. At this critical moment, any intentional offences or unintentional disturbances might cut off our basic thinking. If it happens, it's possible I will shoot to kill. Now all cryptographers follow my order. Go back to your work immediately. Target: stage two, proposition three. Go!"

Looking angry, the person in charge of the investigation pointed at Gao Yuncao and yelled, "Nonsense! Don't exaggerate things just to scare people. The priority now is to investigate the shooting incident, which must not be delayed. Throw this woman out!"

Restraining her fury, Gao Yuncao said, unhurriedly and clearly, "I'll say it again. This military action is the number one priority. Because in the frontline our officers and men are being wounded or killed all the time. They are waiting for us to crack the enemy ciphers and to obtain the enemy intelligence so that they can win battles. I solemnly warn you, anyone who interrupts our work again is helping the enemy to eliminate our officers and men. I will fire my gun at anyone who acts in a hostile way." Drawing her pistol and loading it, she put the gun on the table with a loud bang. She then went on with her guidance to decipher YU.

The investigators went to push her out. Picking up the pistol, she fired twice at the ceiling.

"Gao Yuncao, stop acting recklessly!" shouted Chief Gao.

Picking up a piece of chalk, Gao Yuncao wrote on the wall beside her: "If YU cannot be cracked, I would rather die! I will kill anyone who dares to obstruct our work. Anyone who is killed gets what they deserve. I'll pay for their life with my life." When she had finished writing, she pointed her pistol at the investigators who then withdrew from the room one by one.

After working continuously for three days and three nights, the two teams strictly implemented Gao Yuncao's guidance and in the end they deciphered YU.

The instant eighty-seven abacuses abruptly stopped working, the cryptographers shouted and jumped for joy. But Gao Yuncao did not feel any excitement, she cursed, "The damned cipher, the dirty trick.

You've made us suffer so much." She then took Wang Lan and they ran to the medical unit.

A nurse stopped them outside the mortuary, saying, "Chief Gao has instructed us not to let people in to disturb the martyr." Pushing the nurse away, Gao Yuncao burst into the room and lifted the white sheet from the bed.

Li Mozi looked serene, as if he was sleeping soundly. Shaking him, Gao Yuncao wailed, "Wake up, Mozi, you can't die." The director of the medical unit came to pull her away, but she pushed him against the wall, yelling, "Hurry up and bring Mozi back to life, or I'll shoot you." The director said: "Comrade Li died at the scene."

Someone brought in Chief Gao, who said, "Comrade Yuncao, hurry up and write your report about deciphering *YU*. This afternoon you can go and attend Mozi's funeral."

With an indescribable feeling of rage, Gao Yuncao yelled, "You can only order me about. You can't ferret out the spies, letting Mozi die in vain. Who is to blame? Well, I should be blamed. It was me who called him to the office at midnight. I'm a murderer, a sinner." Wailing, she ran out of the room.

Gao Yuncao did not expect that Li Mozi would be shot dead. Originally, according to her detailed plan, she was confident that such an accident could not happen.

A few days before, she had given medic Liu and nurse Zhang a big piece of bait, "I've secretly collected a big pile of coded telegrams, which had escaped security checks, which means there are no records or sources for them. If they are lost, no one would know or go to check. But it is difficult to take them out of the office and more difficult to escape the eyes of the sentries. The cryptography office has a rule. During office time there must be more than two people in the room, so it is impossible for anyone to be in the office alone. Besides, for the confidential office block, nothing, not even a satchel, a paper bag, or even a roll of newspaper, is allowed to get in or out. So I can't take out this material which can be sold for big money. There is only one choice for us. We will have to go and steal it at midnight. I have a roommate so I can't leave my room at midnight. But you two live in the same room. There is no one to keep watch on you, so you two can go and steal the material. As for profits, we can share them half and half. If you agree, let's take action." The couple agreed.

She assigned a route for them, "Outside the rear courtyard of the confidential area, and five metres from the wall there is an old tree. No one has been to this place for many years, besides it is a dead corner hidden from the line of sight, so it is safe. Climb the tree, then throw a thick rope to a tree inside the wall. Here you must be careful. The rope must be long enough and then throw both ends together. Then stretch and tie the rope. After that, fasten a piece of string tied with a hook and slide down along the rope into the yard. At the foot of the wall, walk along the grove and go to a bush, then crawl on hands and knees to the back wall of the toilet of the office building. The toilet window is usually shut. But I will open it and leave it unlatched. Climb into the toilet. Outside the toilet is a corridor leading to a row of offices. I will put the pile of material in the drawer of the second desk next to the window. You can also open the other desks, but you must restore them to their former state. After you get the material, lock the door and return to the tree by the original route. Climbing over a wall and entering a house to pick a lock and steal are always the strong points of Juntong spies trained in Hanzhong, so this mission should be a piece of cake for you two."

She then instructed, "One o'clock in the morning is the best time for you to take action. I know recently the cryptography work has been at a stalemate, so no one will work overtime in the office. Although the sentry is always on guard, you can get in from the opposite direction, a dead corner overgrown with trees and weeds. No one will set foot in that corner, so there is no danger at all at midnight. But pay attention to the first room on the east of the corridor. Usually two staff sleep there, we nickname them the 'sleeping sentries'. They are always young or middle-aged men. But at one o'clock in the morning they are sound asleep."

When she had said her piece, she cheered them up, "The security in RSU2 has always been tight inside, loose outside; strictly guarding against our own people, but slack in preventing outsiders from getting in. All the facts have been laid before you, what to do or what not to do, it's your decision."

In the end they did Just as Gao Yuncao had analysed, and their operation went very smoothly. Having searched two rooms and got something, they moved on to room 112 to get the material mentioned by Gao Yuncao. They found it. Holding the papers in their arms and using a torch, they looked at the first two copies, seeing that they were ordinary magazines. Thinking that what they wanted must be at the bottom of the pile, they turned the copies one by one. But they were all magazines, not a single copy was the material they had come for. At this moment, they heard talking in the corridor. It was Gao Yuncao's voice. Before medic Liu realised what was going on, he saw two people dashing in. He stretched his hand to grab his pistol, but the two people opened fire first.

Gao Yuncao had sensed that something was wrong then. Initially she thought that medic Liu and nurse Zhang would go to the room together to steal the material. When she saw the door unlocked, she deliberately opened her mouth to talk, intending to let the couple hear her voice, causing them to pause for a second, so that she could quickly enter the room and open fire. The result was achieved, but she only killed one person. Inwardly she cursed: "Damn it, Zhang Qianqian is on the lookout outside." As expected, Zhang Qianqian opened fire behind them. Li Mozi, who was about to dash into the room was hit by two bullets. Zhang Qianqian probably realised that they had fallen into Gao Yuncao's trap, so she fired one shot at Gao Yuncao as well.

Gao Yuncao did not expect that one neglected detail would have cost Li Mozi his life and herself to be wounded, which was a heavy blow to her. In fact, over and over she had deliberated over every detail of the plot. She called on Wang Lan and Li Mozi to go with her as required by the regulations, as well as for them to be witnesses.

Eliminating the medic and his wife in such a way, she did not worry too much if she would be subjected to suspicion. She felt that she had acted flawlessly; furthermore she had just played the leading role in deciphering YU, having rendered outstanding service, for which she fully deserved the credit. Besides, the facts turned out to be more positive than she had thought.

The next day after the accident, the Central Department of Social Affairs instantly arrested the superiors of medic Liu and nurse Zhang. These people had been under surveillance by the department for a long time, and no one escaped the net. Immediately the Central Department of Social Affairs carried out interrogations. From the verified confessions, none of the contacts knew anything about the couple's operation for the night and nobody had assigned such a mission.

But Zhang Yuhe, the owner of Jixiang Pharmacy in Ansai, was not among those arrested. That was because he was not a contact of the medic couple, neither above or below them, but an ordinary friend of theirs. Besides, they had only met once or twice in Ansai, unknown to Yan'an.

In fact, as a link in her tight plan, Gao Yuncao had already killed Zhang Yuhe.

As early as one week before medic Liu and nurse Zhang went to steal the material, Gao Yuncao asked Wang Lan and another colleague to go with her to the bookstore in Ansai. On the way home, she had the runs so she went to use the toilet next to Jixiang Pharmacy. A fodder warehouse for a horse-drawn cart shop was behind the toilet, and next to the fodder warehouse was a primary school. Gao Yuncao loosened her belt and grabbed some rough straw paper. But she did not squat over a pit to relieve herself. Seeing that there were no other people in the toilet, she lit the paper and from the wide opening she threw the lighted paper into the fodder warehouse. Then she squatted down and carefully listened to what was going on outside.

A strong north wind was blowing, and soon a large fire was burning. In a moment she heard the chaotic noises of people coming to put out the fire. Taking advantage of the chaos, she quickly got out of the toilet. All the shop assistants of Jixiang Pharmacy went to put out the fire, because the fire would have spread to them if it had not been put out as soon as possible. Thick smoke was pouring into the pharmacy. Under cover of the smoke, Gao Yuncao slipped into the manager's room and slit Zhang Yuhe's throat with a knife. She took away a large amount of bank notes, creating a crime scene of killing and robbery. Then she quietly slipped back to the scene of the fire, going all out to put out the blaze, while she threw the bank notes into the flames.

The fire was finally put out; luckily it wasn't a disaster for the primary school.

Gao Yuncao's face was covered in black soot. The fire had burnt a few holes in her clothes and one of the holes was not in the right place. It was just at her breast. When she held her breast and came out of the building, she saw that Wang Lan and her other colleague were in the same bad state as her. When the three black faces looked at each other, they all burst out laughing. Wang Lan remarked, "The fire put the lives of students in danger. We acted bravely for a just cause, which is the true quality of a soldier."

Gao Yuncao chimed in, "Absolutely. The wind was so strong and the fire was so large. I was almost engulfed by the flames."

After Liu Hongmei returned from the front line, it pained her to learn that Li Mozi had died in the accident. However, she could only weep. She made no remarks about the whole incident. In fact, she could not express what she wanted to say. She understood that she herself was also a pawn in the event. As far as Team Eagle was concerned, as the leader, she had failed to manage the team members properly and strictly, resulting in medic Liu and nurse Zhang pursuing their personal interests and fortune, disobeying her orders and acting wildly. As far as RSU2 was concerned, from the organisational point of view she had never questioned their reverse usage of the spy couple, thinking that she had enough authority to keep the couple under her complete control. Now Li Mozi had paid with his life for her over-confidence. She could only cry silently and swallow the humiliation.

Seeing Liu Hongmei crying, Gao Yuncao did not cry with her. On the contrary, she did not shed a single tear but cursed Liu Hongmei deep down.

"You are living a perfectly good life, how can you walk on this path? You turned into a spy and brought death upon your sweetheart. Why have you done such a thing? There is a difference between you and me. When I became a spy, I had no capacity to make political distinctions so I chose to put my faith (in the KMT). After I arrived in Yan'an, I had a fresh understanding about beliefs, and it was this comparison that changed me. However, you chose to be a Communist at the very beginning. How could you have changed your mind? How could your heart have walked into the enemy camp? My decision to get rid of medic Liu and nurse Zhang was to free myself from a crisis, but also to remove future trouble for you."

She said all these words to herself. When she and Liu Hongmei sat facing each other, she refused to say a word, not even a word to comfort her.

Liu Hongmei sensed Gao Yuncao's icy coldness and silence. She said angrily, "Aren't you my good friend? Would saying a few words to comfort me kill you? But you haven't even broken wind." Gao Yuncao still said nothing. Liu Hongmei said again, "I remember when I blocked the shell for you, you didn't treat me with such an attitude."

Gao Yuncao opened her mouth. With an icy smile on her face, she muttered, "Don't beg others to take pity on you. Go and have a think about whether you deserve sympathy first."

Looking baffled, Liu Hongmei watched Gao Yuncao walk away in a huff.

Ji Zhenren returned, giving Liu Hongmei a target to vent her anger upon.

Initially their relationship had improved a lot during this front-line mission. Not only could they sit down together to talk about work, but they could also talk about the Ji family's affairs. Ji Zhenren was upset by one thing, and that was Liu Hongmei's marriage. So one day he told her that her future husband Ji Zhenfu had died many years ago. Hearing the news, Liu Hongmei was unusually calm. From that day on she would squat down in the trench and write letters to Li Mozi. No matter how busy she was, she would write one letter a day. Although they could not be sent, she just carried on writing. She had written all her life's sweet words to him. In the end she realised that words were superfluous. One sentence would be enough, "Mozi, I will marry you as soon as I return, I can't wait to marry you!" But a completely different ending awaited her. She sat beside Li Mozi's grave all day long burning the love letters she had written to him on the battlefield.

Ji Zhenren! Why didn't you tell me earlier that Ji Zhenfu had died? If you had told me about it earlier, I would have married Li Mozi long ago, so I would not have had to harbour this eternal regret of mine.

Therefore she vented all her pent-up resentment, pain, depression and dissatisfaction upon Ji Zhenren. As long as there was a suitable location and a suitable environment, she would make a tearful scene. The more she did it, the worse her mood became, and the more scenes she made. No matter how she behaved, Ji Zhenren would always patiently comfort her. He explained, blamed himself and cursed himself. He knew that at this moment he was her punch bag.

After Li Mozi died, Ji Zhenren did curse himself for not being a good person. For the sake of that lousy overall situation and the lousy security discipline, as well as for the sake of his brothers and sisters not harbouring grudges against him for his ruthlessness, he blocked the news of Ji Zhenfu's death for so many years, thereby completely ruining Hongmei's personal happiness. He felt deeply grieved, but it was too late for regrets.

22 /THE HE AND XUE CIPHERS

ONE DAY, with the high commander's eulogy, Chief Gao excitedly returned to RSU2. At once he organised an informal discussion for all staff.

"RSU2 can be rated as the shadow of the KMT army's supreme command." After the end of a campaign, in a summing-up meeting, a leading cadre made the above remark and its significance was self-evident.

In the past, in similar meetings or discussions of a political nature, if Ji Zhenren was asked to say something, no matter what the subject was, he could master his speech, as though he was attending an academic seminar on the subject of cryptography techniques and habitually elevate the technical issues to the fore, prevailing over everything else. But today he seemed different, "Being praised 'as the shadow of the KMT army's supreme command' was gained by cracking the KMT army's ciphers. To a cryptographer, or to the whole of RSU2, this praise means that if we cannot crack ciphers and obtain information, all our actions are for nothing." He then switched the conversation to another subject, "I agree that it's important to crack enemy ciphers to obtain the enemy's secrets, but it's even more important not to let the enemy know that their ciphers have been cracked. Cipher intelligence is a special intelligence source. All parties should make full use of it and also tightly guard it. Last time we published intelligence we had deciphered about the enemy's plan to attack Yan'an, it made the enemy more vigilant, and on our side more people now know what RSU2 is all about. So, if we don't protect this source of intelligence, soon no such valuable source of intelligence will be available, and all our work will come to naught. Then, the praise given by the leading cadres will turn into an undeserved reputation. Therefore, we must strictly restrict the number of people that have access to cipher intelligence. Not only must RSU2 pay attention to the issue, but also the senior commanders. However, I have found that the recent use of intelligence in the upper levels of the organisation has been a bit chaotic."

Chief Gao sniffed a different smell. Standing up, he hurriedly stopped Ji Zhenren, "Today we are here to discuss the instructions given by the leading cadres. How could you drag up the subject of keeping a secret?"

"We are all given such high praise because everyone in RSU2 has done a good job in keeping secrets, and the cipher information source has been well protected. But recently the higher-level organisations have used the intelligence carelessly, which is indeed a sensitive subject to talk about. But we must not only enjoy their praise, we must also dare to pour cold water on them. The following are my suggestions to them," said Ji Zhenren.

Although he had noticed that Chief Gao's facial expression had hardened, he did not want to shut his mouth. In one breath he put forward four suggestions, which from the angle of security discipline strictly restricted the qualifications of the senior leaders and organisations from reading cipher intelligence, and limited the categories of personnel who could access the information.

In one suggestion, he said, "The number of senior officers who can read the intelligence should be strictly restricted, and what they can read and know must be defined. At certain levels in the commanding headquarters, those who can read and know the deciphered intelligence must not be more than eight people at most. And attention must be paid so that these people must not be at risk of being captured by the enemy. If a situation is dangerous, we must resolutely take extreme measures at any cost."

It was this remark that got Chief Gao into a rage, "Ji Zhenren, you have been arrogant and conceited in the extreme. Wow! Not more than eight people at most. What right do you have to restrict senior leaders' access to intelligence? Wow! Resolutely take extreme measures, and at any cost. Are you going to shoot the top leader dead if there is a danger of him being captured? Do you mean this? Why don't you have any faith in the leaders' political and moral integrity?"

Ji Zhenren gave Chief Gao a hard look, saying: "If you like to stick labels, or to make accusations without foundation, there is nothing I can do about it. I only want to stress that there must be no grey areas with regard to keeping secrets! A secret in your head must not let your hat know. We must not forget that 100 minus 1 = zero, an equation we have learnt and paid for with blood!"

The hall was so quiet one could have heard a pin drop. Then a junior cadre called Zhu Kexin stood up and applauded, "I wholeheartedly support comrade Ji Zhenren's proposals. Maintaining secrecy is to maintain life. Before this rule all men are equal, so from high commanders to grooms or foot soldiers, we all must strictly abide by the security regulations. As a confidential officer, I have secrets hidden in my heart. If I am in danger of being captured, I will point my pistol at my head and pull the trigger. This is the due obligation mentioned in the examination questions for security discipline."

"That's all! That's all for today's meeting. You are dismissed!" yelled Chief Gao.

After the meeting, Chief Gao went to see Ji Zhenren, "Your intention of putting forward suggestions was good. However, these suggestions should not be raised by us, but by the leaders who are in charge of security work. If we do it, we will offend them. I am never afraid of offending anybody, but your suggestions involve the senior leaders and organisations, and that's too sensitive. It's not a small matter, so we must be extremely cautious. Our duty is to do a good job ourselves. As to the upper levels' problems, it is not for us to talk about them too much."

"It is fundamental to correct errors in our work so that we can improve. This must not be divided into an internal or external responsibility, otherwise when we have an accident, the consequences will be disastrous," replied Ji Zhenren.

"Different professionals are in charge of different aspects of work. Your duty is to do a good job in cracking ciphers. Let sleeping dogs lie," urged Chief Gao.

Later, Ji Zhenren got to know that his speech was deleted from the report sent to the senior leaders.

One day, a senior officer came to inspect RSU2 and Ji Zhenren handed him several sheets of paper.

The senior officer had a read and said nothing. Caught unprepared by his trick, hurriedly Chief Gao said to Ji Zhenren, "In fact, there is no need for it to be done in such a way. Give me back these sheets of paper and let's have a rethink."

The senior officer did not agree, saying, "How can you take your proposals back after you have submitted them?" Turning to Ji Zhenren, the senior officer said, "Ji Zhenren, what a man. Wait!"

Many days passed but nothing happened. As usual Ji Zhenren was absorbed in his work and forgot everything else. But Chief Gao was somewhat anxious. In the end, the senior officer came again. As soon as he saw Chief Gao, he said, "Good news. The majority of Ji Zhenren's four proposals have been adopted. The related department has made the detailed rules and regulations, which have been issued to all related leaders and departments to execute. Where is Ji Zhenren? Call him to come and see me."

Chief Gao sent people to call Ji Zhenren, who failed to come but sent a message, "My work is at a critical stage. I promise I won't put forward any more suggestions to make trouble for people."

"I'll go and see him," said the senior officer. When he arrived, he saw that Ji Zhenren's face was streaming with sweat, each of his hands was vigorously working an abacus and his fingers were flicking the beads so fast, it was as if sparks were flying. Behind Ji Zhenren sat sixty-seven cryptographers, who were also flicking abacus beads swiftly.

Quietly the senior officer walked out of the room, saying, "In the future no one is allowed to cause Ji Zhenren any trouble, but he can cause us leaders trouble any time anywhere." Standing at the door and pricking up his ears, he listened for a long time. Slowly tears fell from his eyes. He sighed with emotion, "The sound of RSU2's abacuses can completely rival the sound of our bullets on the battlefield. You cryptographers are all unknown heroes who fight bloody wars against adversity all-year-round, not knowing if you will live or die from one moment to the next." As he spoke, he bowed low toward the room.

Surely Ji Zhenren would make no trouble for his superiors, but before long he began to create trouble out of nothing in RSU2.

Zhu Kexin was an office worker dealing with paperwork. He had two distinguishing features: he was extremely scrupulous, sharply vigilant and too ready to suspect. Each day he kept exhaustive records of every document and matter he had dealt with. For years he had written in over a hundred notebooks. Wherever RSU2's confidential documents went, he brought these notebooks with him. Clues to facts relating to things that had happened many years before could be found from him. His second feature was actually an occupational disease. Anything involving a secret, he would not let it go until he was one hundred per cent sure.

After medic Liu and nurse Zhang were identified as spies and the situation was brought to light, Zhu Kexin suddenly recalled something, namely, that Liu Hongmei had borrowed documents from him about the defection to the Japanese and the puppet government of a certain KMT regiment garrisoned in Handan. After she had borrowed the documents from him, the next day he went to see a medical officer in the medical unit. As soon as he entered medic Liu's room, he saw that medic Liu was feeling Liu Hongmei's pulse and he vaguely heard Liu Hongmei mention 'Handan'. Seeing someone coming in, Liu Hongmei instantly shut her mouth. At the time he thought of her borrowing the documents, so he said, "You two are having a good chat, what happened in Handan? Was there an earthquake or a flood?"

Chuckling, Liu Hongmei quickly said, "Medic Liu's hometown is Handan. We are talking about his hometown's speciality, the stuffed bun with donkey meat."

He also cracked up, "It seems that the donkey meat from medic Liu's hometown can be used as a medicine. What illness will it treat for comrade Hongmei?"

Chuckling again, Liu Hongmei said, "How can you ask so casually about a woman's illness?"

The matter then passed. Many days later, when he thumbed through the registration book, he noticed that medic Liu was not from Handan in Henan but Yancheng in Jiangsu. He began to worry. Afterwards, he discovered that Liu Hongmei had made contact with medic Liu and nurse Zhang many times. Yet, he did not give it any further thought. Only after medic Liu and nurse Zhang died did he begin to ponder about the matter. He went to see Chief Gao. But Chief Gao told him that there was no question about Liu Hongmei. He argued that Liu Hongmei had been to Chongqing and there was a possibility that the KMT secret agents had incited her to defect. Who dared to say that she was definitely beyond reproach? Chief Gao declared that he dared to say that, unless Zhu Kexin distrusted his words. Ever since then, Zhu Kexin was more careful with material handled by Liu Hongmei. He would treat her much more harshly than he treated anyone else, sometimes even to the extent of nit-picking. RSU2 stipulated that the confidential office worker had the right to check on every cryptographer without informing them beforehand. Therefore, Zhu Kexin carried out several quick checks on Liu Hongmei's desks and cabinets. At one time, he even broke into her dormitory and one by one he examined her personal items, even her underwear. Eventually, Liu Hongmei was driven beyond the limits of forbearance. She made a complaint to Chief Gao, who called in Zhu Kexin for a talk. Again, Chief Gao assured Zhu Kexin that Liu Hongmei was clean, urging him not to be oversensitive, so as not to hurt Liu Hongmei's feelings.

Zhu Kexin held back his suspicion of Liu Hongmei for almost a year. In the end, he couldn't keep it to himself any longer, but secretly told Ji Zhenren about it. Ji Zhenren pondered over what he had heard, then said, "Cryptographers can sometimes crack a cipher intuitively; while confidential office workers can sometimes ferret out a hidden danger intuitively. You might as well prove how true these two sentences are. Leave it to me. To catch a spy I have more tricks than you. I know that you cannot say what you want to say. But set your mind at ease. The feelings between Liu Hongmei and I as relatives will not stop me dealing with the matter fairly. Please believe me."

"I came to you because I trust you completely," said Zhu Kexin. "I know you will never allow spies to hide in RSU2."

Patting Zhu Kexin on the shoulder, Ji Zhenren went off to find Chief Gao, asking him for permission to read the files on an unbroken cipher. Chief Gao was unaware of the ins and outs of the matter, so he signed his name on the application form.

Ji Zhenren spent two weeks looking into the files and analysing the circumstances, and he really found something: it seems that Liu Hongmei's confederates, medic Liu and nurse Zhang, were hiding in RSU2. Of course, he could not tell Zhu Kexin about it, so he went to Chief Gao and laid his cards on the table. According to regulations, Chief Gao could not tell Ji Zhenren about Liu Hongmei's hidden identity, so he insisted that she was clean.

"She is your sister, how can you suspect her without any grounds?" said Chief Gao.

"I never expected such words to come out of your mouth. What difference does it make if she's my sister or not? If she's a spy, can I turn a blind eye because she is my sister? In those years, when my elder brother defected, I did what I had to do. This case must be reexamined. If she is a spy, she must be put to death!" announced Ji Zhenren.

Chief Gao had to take Ji Zhenren to visit the senior leader in charge of counterespionage work. After returning to RSU2, Ji Zhenren told Zhu Kexin that Liu Hongmei was not a spy, and from the bottom of his heart he praised him for his conscientious work. Only then did Zhu Kexin set his mind at ease. He went to apologise to Liu Hongmei who felt embarrassed. Shaking his hands, Liu Hongmei said, "Nothing is small in confidential work and there are so many things for you to worry about. It is really tough for you. I appreciate it very much. Please carry on with your work spirit. I support you."

Due to Zhu Kexin's suspicion, Ji Zhenren had the opportunity to learn the truth about Liu Hongmei, being only the third person in RSU2 to know about her secret identity.

But Gao Yuncao knew nothing about it. She had always thought that Liu Hongmei was a true KMT spy, so she kept a closer eye on her, trying her best to leave Liu Hongmei no chance to do anything bad, and wholeheartedly helping her to wake up and turn herself around.

In fact, she kept a close watch on Liu Hongmei everywhere. Of course, such observation had to be done cleverly, neither revealing her intentions, nor letting Liu Hongmei sense that she was being watched. She applied all the skills she had learned in the spy training class in Nanjing and was very professional in her surveillance of Liu Hongmei. She had mentally prepared for the fact that it would be a long-term task, and that she would observe her for one year, two years, ten years or even all her life. As long as Liu Hongmei didn't change, she would carry on watching her. She thought she was duty bound to do so. Deep down she laughed at herself: Bound? Duty? Based on what? What do you think you are? A KMT spy in hibernation who wants to turn good. How dare you watch Liu Hongmei? No, no, no, I had intended to wash my hands and stop working for the KMT secret services, but she refused to realise her error. No matter what, I must not slacken my watch over her. I am duty bound to do it!

During this period of time, according to the general headquarters' strategic plan, RSU2 again sent its wireless surveillance forces to the bases in North China to cooperate with the Communist forces in a major counteroffensive operation against the Japanese and the puppet government.

Gao Yuncao, Liu Hongmei and 130 other members were dispatched to the base area bordering Shanxi, Chahar and Hebei provinces. Led by Chief Gao himself, one day before dawn they arrived at the headquarters in Fuping, Hebei Province.

Before leaving home, they had comprehensively gone through the enemy situation in the region, so they knew quite a lot about the enemy situation there. After they arrived, they listened to the military command's introduction about the enemy, then Chief Gao gathered the key members at all levels for discussions and assignment of tasks, thereby establishing a work schedule for the team.

After learning about the enemy situation, Gao Yuncao was completely shocked. She completely lost confidence in the KMT army. With such a mentality she began to ponder over Liu Hongmei. She wanted to use facts to persuade her, and make her realise how badly the KMT armies had been demoralised, so that she would give up her belief in the KMT, and secretly transform her into an Eighth Route Army intelligence officer.

She only explained one fact to Liu Hongmei. In North China, in rapid succession some of the KMT troops and other local armed forces had defected to the Japanese. These puppet troops hoisted the flag of the Republic of China - a 'Blue Sky with a White Sun' - to deceive the honest peasants into joining them, and rapidly their number increased to 470,000 in total. Some of these defected troops acted by following the KMT authorities' 'guidelines for action' sent through wireless services, so it could be said they did it by following orders. And earlier or later the KMT regular troops, numbering around 150,000, went over to the puppet government. Many of these troops had already had an illicit relationship with the enemy, and after defecting, their unit designations and garrison locations all stayed the same. Most of these puppet troops encircled the Communist anti-Japanese bases, serving as lackeys of the Japanese in their mopping-up campaigns against the Eighth Route Army, and their acts were extremely cruel and shameless.

Gao Yuncao intercepted such information when she first arrived in the area. She would talk about it resentfully with Liu Hongmei, who at first joined in with the curses, but slowly she noticed that whenever

Gao Yuncao was with her, she talked about nothing else except cursing the KMT.

Not just in words but also in action. In order to rescue Liu Hongmei, Gao Yuncao took a great risk and personally did one thing. The so-called risk was either to be captured by the Japanese, or for her true identity as a KMT spy to be seen through by RSU2.

Soon she received orders and led eight people to go with the Eighth Military Subarea in central Hebei to wipe out the enemy strongholds along the Wugong highway. Her team was assigned to capture enemy transceivers and collect any wireless communication material.

When they attacked Guojiazhuang Village, she closely followed the vanguard troops and dashed into the village. But she only captured a heap of scrap metal and a table of wastepaper. The enemy had destroyed the communication room. She went to see the vanguard regiment commander Ma Qiutian and complained, "You're too slow. When you attack, can't you make it a surprise? And do it without interruption and capture the village in one swoop. Don't give the enemy time to destroy their property. But of course, this is only if no extra soldiers should die."

"Next time we attack the Tu'erduo stronghold, let me have a good think about our tactics," said Commander Ma. "Actually, we don't have any other brilliant ideas. We can only lay an ambush around the stronghold at night and make a surprise attack at dawn when the enemy are still fast asleep. It may work if we can take the stronghold. Comrade Gao, do you have any better ideas?"

Gao Yuncao laughed, "I would be the commander if I had any."

At the crack of dawn the troops launched a fierce attack on the enemy. Gao Yuncao had her own ideas. She took two male colleagues and they secretly followed the vanguard platoon leader, charging after him into the fortified village. Usually a wireless office was set up on high ground, so they climbed ladders and dashed to the top floor of the enemy building. She followed the aerial cable and found the room for the wireless service, then the main forces arrived. The vanguard platoon began to take rooms one by one on the ground floor, while the majority of the enemy didn't even have time to throw their clothes on but looked for rifles to fire back with. Two wireless operators held their trousers and ran to the office. They were shot dead by Gao Yuncao, who blew open the office door with a grenade. She dashed in. Pushing the code book into her jacket pocket, she cried out to her two colleagues, "The code book is not here. Hurry to the dormitory and the officer's room. Quick!"

She shut the shattered door. Switching on the transceiver and tuning the channels, she held the tapper and began to send messages at high speed. The sound of the tapper was buried amid the intense gunfire. If anybody had broken in, they would have witnessed a strange scene: Gao Yuncao was sending messages with her left hand, while in her right hand she held a revolver and her eyes swept over the door from time to time. No matter who should break in, the enemy or her own people, she was subconsciously primed to pull the trigger.

It was hard to imagine that the reason she sent messages using her left hand was not to release her right hand to hold a gun, but to avoid letting others recognise her 'handwriting'. When she was in Nanjing, either in training or at work, she always used her right hand to send telegrams. Those who knew her were familiar with her right-handed sending sound. For the Yan'an mission, she specially trained her left hand, so that she could use it in an emergency. The reason now was not for her to confuse the operators in Chongqing, but her fear that Ji Zhenren, the only person who could distinguish her right-handed sending sound, might intercept the messages. Although the probability was very small, she still wanted to take preventive measures.

When her two colleagues returned, she was carrying the transceiver in her arms and was about to leave the room. They shook their heads. Putting down the transceiver, she dashed outside and stumbled over the dead bodies of the enemy wireless operators.

"Have you searched them?" she asked.

"We went to chase those still alive but forgot the dead."

She made a thorough search of the two dead operators. Then she cried out, "Here's the code book. Mission accomplished. Let's go."

At this moment the platoon leader rushed up firing his gun. Gao Yuncao swore at him, "What are you fucking shooting at? Your bullets nearly hit my leg. Hurry and cover us to get the transceiver out of here." Regimental Commander Ma walked up to her, laughing, "No need now. The stronghold has been taken. But I'm giving you a stern warning. Next time you must not follow the vanguard platoon and dash into the enemy barracks. The order given by those above is that I must firstly ensure the personal safety of your team, then ensure that you can accomplish your mission. Otherwise, I will be punished. Please don't cause me any trouble."

Gao Yuncao went downstairs, muttering, "I promise I won't do it again. But I haven't enjoyed myself to the full today. I didn't see a single Japanese devil. It seems that there is nothing to capture in a puppet troops' fortress."

Two weeks later the Eighth Route Army went on to capture the enemy stronghold in Xulihu Village, where two Japanese companies and three Chinese puppet companies were stationed. The assault troops were from the 9th and 10th Military Subareas of the Central Shanxi Military Command. Political commissar Guo Yi personally went to the frontline to command the assault. Back at headquarters, the commander of the Central Shanxi Military Command was ready to lead the 6th, 7th and 8th Military Subareas to ambush the enemy reinforcements.

Any experts with a general knowledge of military operations could have seen immediately that capturing the enemy stronghold was only one of the aims. To be really successful, the campaign also had to ambush the enemy reinforcements. This meant that no matter how brave and vigorous the 9th and 10th Military Subareas were, their aim was not to fight a quick battle. They had firstly to build up momentum, making the enemy inside the fortified village feel the situation was extremely urgent, so that they would request reinforcements by sending wireless messages to the Itakon Regiment that was stationed on Guyuan Mountain. Then our 6th, 7th and 8th Military Subareas would lay a ring of ambushes, waiting for the arrival of the Itakon Regiment. The operational targets were both to capture the fortified village and to ambush the enemy reinforcements. Such tactics and combat objectives were obviously not conducive to the task of Gao Yuncao's team to dash in and capture the enemy transceivers and code books. Yet, they had no choice but to submit to the overall interests of the operation.

It was a rather complicated process, but generally in keeping with the plan. In the end, it was a success and the enemy reinforcements sent out by the Itakon Regiment were wiped out. Guo Yi's assault went smoothly and he gradually redoubled his attack. The good luck desired by Gao Yuncao did not come. If the fighting went on like this, even a fool could see that the fortress would be captured in seconds or minutes. Thinking that in the last minute of desperation the enemy would definitely destroy their transceiver and code book, she dashed over to Guo Yi and hastily requested, "Comrade Commissar, you must not make the enemy in the fortress feel desperate, otherwise I cannot accomplish my task. Anyway, victory is already decided, so please find some good ideas to help me."

Guo Yi had a think, then said, "Your matter is also important. I have an idea but I don't know if the enemy will bite. In fact, it's simple. Let me withdraw some troops and lay an ambush at Zhanglidian, thirty-two kilometres away. We'll keep a gap open here. When the enemy tries to break out again, we'll pretend that we cannot hold out and let them flee. Afterwards we'll wipe them out in our ambush."

"Great!" said Gao Yuncao, understanding the tactics. "But you must withdraw your troops in a natural manner, making it look as though they are urgently needed for another battle. Besides, the ambush must be carried out suddenly, leaving no time for the enemy to destroy their transceiver and code book."

Guo Yi laughed, "It seems that you are an intelligence officer but also a tactician."

"I'm waiting for good luck," said Gao Yuncao. "Success or failure hinges on this one action." Having said this, she took eight team members and they followed the retreating troops to ambush the enemy.

The remaining enemy in the fortress finally broke out. They were out of danger after being chased by the Eighth Route Army troops for a while. As Gao Yuncao had expected, the moment they didn't feel desperate, their communication with the outside would not stop. Among the fleeing enemy, there were two wireless operators, each carrying a transceiver on their back.

Metre by metre the remnants of the enemy troops entered the killing ground of the ambush. Gao Yuncao watched them with her binoculars. From a distance she recognised two high-power transceivers. She said to Guo Yi, "Strike when the enemy is closer. Let snipers hit the soldiers surrounding the two wireless operators. Make sure you don't damage my transceivers." Not remembering when she had last held a *Sanpachi* rifle in her hand, she bent her back and ran some distance. Quickly adopting a prone position, she rolled along left and right. Then she crooked her left foot under her right leg, with her right hand holding the rifle while looking in the enemy's direction. Suddenly she lept to her feet and quickly advanced to the front line of the ambush killing zone.

Guo Yi was amazed, crying out, "Aha, your leaping forward movement is very professional, an instructor level."

Almost at the same time Guo Yi fired a shot to signal action, Gao Yuncao's rifle also sounded. Two shots. The two enemy wireless operators instantly fell to the ground, followed by the surrounding soldiers hit by Guo Yi's men. Soon a large contingent of troops jumped out from all directions and completely surrounded the enemy. Running at the front, Gao Yuncao charged at the enemy. She only fired at the soldiers close to the transceivers. In less than half an hour the battle was over.

As Guo Yi approached the two dead enemy wireless operators, Gao Yuncao was searching their pockets and bags. Triumphantly she waved the code book in her hand. Guo Yi turned the two operators face up, exclaiming, "Good gracious! Both bullets hit their foreheads. A woman sharpshooter! Comrade Gao Yuncao, our military command welcomes you to join us. I will let you coach a class of women sharpshooters."

Gao Yuncao was gathering together the transceivers and getting ready to rejoin her team. "It's getting dark," said Guo Yi. "The remnants and skirmishers will appear at any time. Why don't we hold a banquet and a performance tonight to celebrate the victory. Your team has taken part in the battle, so you must stay and join our celebrations. Tomorrow morning I'll send people to escort you back to your unit."

She turned round to look at the eight team members. The expressions in their eyes told her that they all wanted to stay and relax a bit. So she said, "Commissar Guo, will you please make a phone call to Chief Gao?"

"No problem. But I want to take joy in your marksmanship one more time." He let his people hang ten enemy helmets on a row of trees two hundred metres away. Nine sharpshooters were selected. Along with Gao Yuncao, they stood in a row. As soon as Guo Yi gave his order, ten shots fired. Except for the one Gao Yuncao fired at, all the other nine helmets had a bullet hole in them. She felt relieved, and said, "Look, I'm no good."

Guo Yi ran to the trees, then ran back, saying, "Let's go and enjoy the banquet and the opera performance. Today, apart from the successful military operation, we have captured a woman sharpshooter."

With an air of confusion Gao Yuncao said, "I'm good at banqueting and watching opera, but not at firing a gun."

"Come on, I saw you pointing your gun an inch below the target. The bullet hit the fist-sized tree trunk right in the centre under the helmet. So, you are our man when you are alive, and our ghost when you are dead. That's settled. I will go and talk to Chief Gao. I'm going to use a brand new communication car to exchange for this beauty of his. I don't believe he'll refuse me. If he does, I'll turn that car into a transport vehicle," said Guo Yi.

"I was lust lucky when I shot those two enemy wireless operators," said Gao Yuncao, laughing. "But since you think highly of me, I'll take you at your word. I'll go with you. Forget things further away. Tonight, you must reward my eight brothers handsomely with food and drink."

At night, there was good food, good drink and good theatre. The theatre was the Beijing opera *Three Assaults on the Zhu Family Village*, an adapted historical drama performed by the Taihang Theatrical Troupe. When the performance reached the tense part when Song Jiang led his men to make the second assault on the Zhu family village, Gao Yuncao quietly sneaked back to her accommodation. Shutting the door tight, she set up the transceivers. Holding a tapper with both hands, she pressed first with one hand, then with the other. Linking up the two transceivers, she smoothly sent out a message, sending one sentence with her right hand and the next sentence with her left hand, thereby completely changing the sending signature for the whole message. She was very adept at masking her true identity from others. When she had finished sending the message, she sneaked back to the theatre where in the play Lin Chong had just captured Hu Sanniang alive.

Early the next morning, when she and her team were about to leave, Commissar Guo Yi saw them off in person. "Comrade Yuncao, go back and wait for your transfer order," he said.

Holding Guo Yi's hands, Gao Yuncao expressed a thousand thanks, "I will. But why don't you send us back in your communication car, otherwise it'll be hard for me to tell RSU2 that I want to join you."

Guo Yi had a think, and said, "OK. Last night, I had a discussion with the commander. The car is a spoil of war and the best destination for it is RSU2."

Once again Gao Yuncao expressed a thousand thanks.

"Don't be polite," said Guo Yi. "You and we will soon be one family."

Happily Gao Yuncao brought back a communication car, two

transceivers and a code book. Chief Gao was so glad that he wanted to pat her on the shoulder.

He said, "Guo Yi has just phoned, saying that you are a sharpshooter. As soon as I heard his remarks about you, I knew his cunning plan. How can you be a sharpshooter? It's obvious that he has taken a fancy to you. Among the leaders of the second-level military command, he is still a bachelor. I told him that the beauty is soon to be a mother. Didn't he see it? Well, before you arrived, he phoned me again, saying that he had seen you run fast in the forced march and your leaps and bounds were amazing, not like a pregnant woman. He said that I was looking for excuses not to let you go, saying that he must take the communication car back. Humph! wishful thinking of his. I won't mess up a sure thing."

"You need to write them a letter to formally express your gratitude, otherwise it's going to be hard for us to make contact with them again," Gao Yuncao hurriedly reminded him.

"Of course, I will go and thank them in person," said Chief Gao.

Taking the opportunity when the troops were in action and without anybody noticing, Gao Yuncao sent two messages. Both were sent to the KMT's Special Secret Wireless Service in Chongqing, using the frequency and cipher fixed before she came to Yan'an.

The Special Secret Wireless Service had accepted Gao Yuncao's suggestion about what cipher to use for their wireless communications. At the time, she thought that the Communists were very capable at cracking ciphers. She could not even be assured that the KMT's special self-compiled cipher edition would not be deciphered for long. The typical problem for her espionage activities in Yan'an was that there was little or no chance for her to send out messages. Even if she was lucky enough to send a message, it could not be a long one, therefore she suggested that they use a book-based cipher. This kind of cipher was different to the shift cipher or substitution cipher. In a book, for the same character there could be many different combinations, meanwhile they could be double or triple encrypted. The use of statistical analysis was not effective in deciphering messages encrypted by such a cipher. If there were not enough messages or only a few, the possibility of deciphering them was nil. And in Yan'an, it was impossible for her to change ciphers frequently, so a book-based cipher was more suitable for long-term use. Hibernation, wake up, hibernation again, wake up again, nothing could be serious if the same cipher was used.

Her superior adopted her suggestion and let her pick a book. She selected *The Sad Record of a Strategy for Peace*, which she had read in Shanghai. Gao Q also felt that there were only two copies of the book in existence and very few people had read it. It would have been impossible for the cryptographers far away in Yan'an to think of this book. Even if they had remembered it, there would have been no way for them to access it. Therefore, this book was chosen and the cipher was named *HE*. Later, Gao Q secretly went to Shanghai. Through some special channels, he got the only copies of the book. He then started a fire and burnt down the room for special collections. The library staff thought that the fire was started by accident, never thinking that it was arson. Afterwards, the investigation showed that over two thousand ancient books were destroyed by the fire.

Returning to Nanjing, Gao Q locked one copy in the safe and handed the other copy to Gao Yuncao, who spent two months memorising the whole book thoroughly. She then burnt the book. Therefore, only one copy of *The Sad Record of a Strategy for Peace* remained in the world. After Gao Yuncao came to Yan'an, the message she delivered via carrier pigeon was encrypted using HE, and the same applied to the two recent messages she had sent out.

As Gao Yuncao had expected, RSU2's monitors transcribed her two messages, but they classified them as messages sent by the Japanese and puppet troops. Chief Gao even took them to the seminar for newly intercepted enemy telegrams for collective discussion. In the end, they were stored in the box for dead messages and sent back to Yan'an. The reason was that there were only two messages, no following up and they could not be deciphered.

In his office in Yan'an, Ji Zhenren always screened and analysed all the messages sent back by the teams out in the front line. After he read these two messages, he didn't get a wink of sleep for a day and a night. After a lot of calculation and comparisons, he confirmed that these two messages were definitely not encrypted by any known Japanese or KMT armies' ciphers. He was able to roughly determine that it was a rarely used book-based cipher.

Many days later, Gao Yuncao returned to Yan'an with her team. She had been secretly following Ji Zhenren to see what progress he had made deciphering her two messages. She was well aware of his ability to dive deep and probe for clues. What she feared most was that he would suddenly remember the good book *The Sad Record of a Strategy for Peace*. Although he could not remember every word of the book, once he became suspicious about it, who could be sure that he would not suddenly be inspired to decipher the messages? So, before he could react to the two messages, she suggested to him, "I judged they were encrypted by a book-based cipher. Although there are millions and millions of books in China, the messages are short, so objectively there is no solution for them. Therefore, we can't put all our eggs in one basket." Ji Zhenren agreed with her.

Opportunity knocks but once. Resolutely she set a trap. She used a different cipher she had intercepted and successfully diverted Ji Zhenren's attention. She knew that she had come to Yan'an with a mission, but she had not accomplished anything. Before experts like Chief Gao, Ji Zhenren, Li Mozi and Liu Hongmei, any hidden attempt of hers to mislead them would have been seen through instantly. Even though she had become a technical authority in RSU2, she had never made any attempt to undermine its overall deciphering situation. At first, she dared not take hasty risks; afterwards, she was reluctant and unwilling to do such a thing. This time, she racked her brains to divert Ji Zhenren's attention all because she had no other choice.

This cipher was *XUE*, an important cipher used by the Japanese armies in North China. She began to bend Ji Zhenren's ear about *XUE*.

"The distinguishing feature of *XUE* is that it melts into a pool of water as soon as it encounters sunlight. But the water can corrode bones and tendons and in the end kill people. The structure of *XUE* is scientifically perfect. I presume it has at least twelve ways to encrypt messages. I'm certain that the Japanese firstly use one method to encrypt the beginning of a message. They give it a technical coordinate, then jump to another method to encrypt some more words, giving them another technical coordinate, and so forth. For a single message, all the dozen methods must be used, so you can imagine how difficult it would be if we want to decipher these messages. I'm getting lost. I have not been able to deduce any of the coordinates. But I'm sure my gut feeling is correct. I had the same inspiration as you, but mine didn't work. I'm requesting your assistance to crack *XUE* with your wits.

How about we work together as husband and wife to create a classic example of cipher cracking?"

On hearing her words, Ji Zhenren muttered, "Let's do it!"

They went to Chief Gao to get the project registered and authorised. Then they began working round the clock. Two weeks later, Ji Zhenren found the most hidden clue. How many other clues were there? He had no idea. He felt that the time for collective tackling of the problem was ripe.

Chief Gao personally commanded the attack on *XUE*, and the battle began.

Firstly, Gao Yuncao briefed about sixty-nine cryptographers on her thoughts about the cipher. Then Ji Zhenren gave a talk about his views.

"Among the twelve methods assumed by Comrade Gao Yuncao, we have confirmed three and also found three technical coordinates. From this we can see why *XUE* is so difficult to crack. It is very scientifically constructed. On the surface, I have noticed that telegrams encrypted by *XUE* are not very different from the other telegrams. They all have groups of eight letters, however, I can't decide the true length of the *XUE* codes. I have reorganised the eight letters in every code, but haven't been able to sort it out. Yesterday, by chance I discovered that there were a small number of five-letter codes, while all the other codes could be divided by two. These five-letter codes flew like flies, and they confused Gao Yuncao's and my eyes. We were often led to a dead end, causing us to make no progress for several days. It is evident that the longer codes are very misleading to cryptographers. We must draw on this lesson. Now we have removed the curtain covering its bottom. But, if we want to defeat this demon, all of us must work our magic. Now let me talk about specific methods."

The twenty-three-day collective assault on *XUE* was soul-stirring. Chief Gao, Ji Zhenren and Gao Yuncao truly experienced the crafty and sinister nature of the Japanese. Working with all their might, the sixty-nine cryptographers finally conquered *XUE*.

Quietly Gao Yuncao breathed a sigh of relief, not for *XUE* being cracked, but for *HE*. She murmured inwardly, "Ji Zhenren will stop focusing on the two telegrams I encrypted with *HE*."

Actually the two telegrams she secretly sent out were typical 'Red Telegrams'.

The first telegram read: *"Liu Hongmei, Liu Jiacheng, Zhang Qianqian and their assistants were all wiped out in one go."*

The second telegram read: *"Our CHU, HUAN and YU have all been deciphered. I am in the enemy den, so it's inconvenient for me to send messages. But I never dared to forget my duty to serve the party and the state heart and soul. In this life I ..."* Deliberately she did not finish the message, meaning to tell her KMT spy superior in Chongqing that in Yan'an the conditions for her to transmit messages were extremely bad, so she had to stop sending it halfway through.

The purpose of sending the first telegram was that she wanted to stop the KMT secret service from sending more agents to contact Liu Hongmei. Otherwise, Liu Hongmei, a dead piece in the game, would have to come back to life.

For the second telegram, RSU2 had failed to decipher the KMT's *CHU, HUAN* and *YU* for a long time, which nearly drove the senior cryptographers mad. She herself also wanted to decipher them, but she had failed too. From the intercepted messages, she could see that these three ciphers were frequently used by many departments of the KMT armies. She predicted that after she sent out this telegram, the Chongqing side would certainly stop using them at once, and use other ciphers. Most of these ciphers had been deciphered by RSU2, therefore, this trick of hers was of huge significance to RSU2.

Before long, RSU2's monitors no longer received any enemy messages encrypted with *CHU, HUAN* and *YU*. Quietly Gao Yuncao felt delighted. She had finally made a direct and significant contribution in Yan'an. Although this contribution would never be known, it was enough to show that she had moved one step closer to her new beliefs. Later, when she thought of her identity, she laughed at herself inwardly, "Who the fuck do you think you are? A secret agent sent by the KMT. But now you're helping the Communists to harm the KMT. An action of a typical double agent! Yet an offbeat double agent."

After a few threatening but not dangerous matters were over, Gao Yuncao's relationship with Liu Hongmei was closer. In Liu Hongmei's eyes, Gao Yuncao was almost like a political commissar, who often couldn't help preaching to her. Liu Hongmei never understood Gao Yuncao's real intentions in doing so.

"For some people, their inner hearts sometimes blend seamlessly with the real world or Yan'an's political environment, but sometimes it seems that they have been cut off from the outside world for a long time, as if they are living in two different worlds. They live with two opposite ideologies every day. They are happy but mentally in pain.

They are persistent and have no choice. Sometimes they struggle desperately in giant swirls, and sometimes they climb up the banks, resting, looking and waiting."

Listening, Liu Hongmei's eyes popped out, as she asked, "Do such people exist? Are they around us?"

Gao Yuncao wondered, "You don't know them? But I know and God knows!"

Liu Hongmei seldom spoke to Ji Zhenren. But one day she said to him, "Recently Yuncao seemed not to be in her right mind. She constantly gives me political lessons, but I can't make head or tail of her words. What's wrong with her?"

Ji Zhenren's spirit was lifted, and he asked, "Can you repeat what she has said to you?"

Liu Hongmei repeated Gao Yuncao's preaching to her.

"That's nothing unusual," he grunted, while thinking inwardly that they were not just simple remarks at all. Hadn't Yuncao been aware of Hongmei's special identity? Or were there some deeper and more complicated traps?

Seeing that Ji Zhenren was puzzled and losing his concentration, Liu Hongmei turned and left. She then tackled Gao Yuncao head-on.

"I didn't sleep well last night," said Gao Yuncao. "I had a nightmare, in which the scene where you saved my life by throwing yourself on top of me reappeared. The dream reminds me that repaying a debt of gratitude is an everlasting obligation, and I'll spend the rest of my life accomplishing it."

Liu Hongmei was truly worried, "A trifling matter has upset you so much. You're so boring." Gao Yuncao looked embarrassed.

Seeing Zhu Kexin running toward her, Liu Hongmei called out, "Kexin, aren't you going to check my dormitory? I just bought some new underwear. Quick, let me go with you to examine them."

Zhu Kexin's face blushed scarlet. He muttered, "Hongmei, why don't you give me a break? I've made a self-criticism to you many times. What else do you want me to do?"

"I'm going to break off my relationship with Gao Yuncao, but I want to be your friend," replied Liu Hongmei.

Zhu Kexin's eyes lit up, "I thought so a long time ago, only I dared not talk about it."

Liu Hongmei halted her steps, and asked Zhu Kexin, "What did you think a long time ago?"

Returning to their dormitory, Gao Yuncao asked Ji Zhenren, "Hongmei and Kexin behaved sneakily, what is the comment about underwear about? What are they doing?"

"Why else would a man and a woman behave sneakily?" replied Ji Zhenren. "They're dating."

Gao Yuncao's worried expression disappeared, "I'd feel better if Hongmei has truly found her Mr. Right. If they can talk about underwear, I presume their relationship has developed quite well."

"A good thing," said Ji Zhenren with a sigh. "Hongmei deserves to have a decent man."

SOON AFTER THE victory over the Japanese, the Central Department of Social Affairs organised a summing-up seminar about the intelligence support work during the war. Representatives from all levels and channels attended this top-secret conference, and the organiser arranged Chief Gao and Ji Zhenren to give keynote speeches.

Ji Zhenren talked about the significance of cryptanalysis and code deciphering during the revolutionary wars. When he was talking, his eyes accidentally fell on two people sitting under the podium, who watched him open-mouthed, causing him to pause his speech many times.

They were Zhang Jiayin and Liu Hai'er, the captured Japanese spies. After Ji Zhenren, Zhang Jiayin also went onto the podium and gave a talk about his own experience, entitled *The methods, characteristics and rules of the Japanese secret services using the Chinese as their spies*. And when Liu Hai'er gave her speech, the audience's eyes were brightened. No scripts, no sitting down and no rush, she spoke for about half an hour, and several times she looked Ji Zhenren in the eye, seemingly she was only talking to him. Her topic was about how to make use of the Japanese and puppet government's spies to serve our own. Her speech sounded as if she was the leader and also the organiser of this scheme.

As soon as the seminar was over, Ji Zhenren saw the couple walking toward him. He turned around and waited for Chief Gao, because he wanted to know how the enemy spy couple could have become intelligence experts on their own. Chief Gao went to the leader of the Central Department of Social Affairs, who told him that the couple had just reported to him that they had seen a live ghost, saying that the man called Ji Zhenren had died many years ago in Shanghai. Always on guard against leaking secrets, Chief Gao did not expose to the leader about Ji Zhenren's unusual experiences and related information.

After persistent questioning by Chief Gao, the leader said a few more words about Yang Tianhu, the director of the Shanghai Telegraph Office. It was RSU2 who had reported the spy couple to them, so the leader said that the couple had taken our secret agents to Shanghai, contending with the Japanese and the puppet secret agents for seven and a half months. One after another, they killed 29 die-hard traitors, including Yang Tianhu, but our side had no casualties. Chief Gao recognised that the leader was flaunting so he resolutely refused the couple's request to meet Ji Zhenren.

Returning home, Ji Zhenren told Gao Yuncao that he had seen Zhang Jiayin and Liu Hai'er. Instantly Gao Yuncao rattled on about her views on the issue of a conviction.

A few days later, Gao Yuncao met Liu Hongmei and she told her about the couple. Liu Hongmei said, "How could the traitorous couple have become favourites of the Central Department of Social Affairs? You're imagining things. Those who have a secret agent background are the most dangerous. We must be very cautious if we use traitors to serve ourselves. These people lack perseverance and determination. You don't know when they will defect again."

Stopping Liu Hongmei from speaking, Gao Yuncao flared up without reason, "Be straight about it, you have no trust at all in those who have left the reactionary camp and crossed over to the side of progress. I tell you, those who have genuinely crossed over to the side of progress have basically changed their beliefs. Once they abandon their former faith, they can also be firm and unshakable in their new beliefs, which can be everlasting and unchanging. Facts have testified that Zhang Jiayin and Liu Hai'er have become key members of our intelligence department and they have taken on major responsibility for the organisation. How can you doubt their belief? Are you covering your misdemeanours by employing distracting tactics? Dare you cut open your heart and let it bathe in the sun under the Yan'an sky? Traitors and spies can be transformed, why not? You must have confidence in this!"

Liu Hongmei squeezed some words through her teeth, "I'm a cryptographer born loyal and raised in a proper way. I joined the revolutionary ranks much earlier than you, do I need you to instil lofty ideals in my mind?"

Turning around, she went to find Ji Zhenren, saying, "Your wife is very ill. The day before yesterday, in a seminar to discuss technical issues she broke away from the topic but unexpectedly talked about how she believed in communism and admired the Communist Party of China. She talked very emotionally. Apart from that, last night she woke up from her dreams. She ran out of bed to the office. But she was stopped by the sentry. In her underwear she squatted down beside the sentry post. Under the barn lantern she began to do calculations until she was allowed in. It was not the first time for her to squat outside like that. Do you think a normal person would do such a thing?"

Ji Zhenren replied: "Let me comment on the second issue first. I think nothing could be more normal. We cryptographers at RSU2 spend our flesh and blood, life and soul, and every second of every minute cracking ciphers, including during our sleep and dreams. When the craziness reaches a crucial moment, inspiration keeps appearing in dreams. Sometimes, a lightning flash or thunder bolt can connect trains of thought and open up many key crucial links. One gets out of bed and begins to work and the job is done. The most difficult cipher can be cracked in a dream, and that is why I don't feel there is anything wrong with Yuncao."

"I'am also a cryptographer, how can I not understand this? What I mean is that her exposure of her neck and shoulders, and her shameless countenance are not normal," said Liu Hongmei.

"As long as she can crack ciphers, what is wrong if she bares her body and squats down at the main entrance?" mumbled Ji Zhenren. "She won't lose a piece of flesh even if the others see her body, but more lives will be lost if ciphers cannot be cracked. Humph! Who wants to see her naked body, just go and see it. This is selfless devotion of body and mind. Do you understand?".

"It is really fish for fish, shrimps for shrimps and toads for turtles, a pair of psychopaths," grumbled Liu Hongmei.

"Let me come to your first question," said Ji Zhenren. "That's her trouble, but a trouble tormented out of her pondering over beliefs. Nobody can do anything about it, neither are there any medicines to cure it. I cannot interfere, nor do I want to."

Liu Hongmei was serious, "She always seizes on the issue of faith and often makes a fuss about it without any reason. You are her husband, don't you realise that she's a little bit weird?"

Speechless, Ji Zhenren walked away. Bringing the question home, he said to his wife, "If you don't explain it clearly, Hongmei will think that there is something wrong with you mentally."

Gao Yuncao was inwardly surprised, but she said, "I don't feel that I have said anything odd about belief. To be frank, I was worried that she would have a crisis of faith."

Puzzled, Ji Zhenren asked, "Her faith can go wrong?!"

Ever since then Gao Yuncao dared not raise the faith issue either to someone's face or behind their backs. If she did it again, she might give herself away, she thought to herself.

Affected by Liu Hongmei, Ji Zhenren began to secretly spy on his wife for her odd remarks and beliefs. But before he could find out the whys and wherefores of her behaviour, he encountered something unexpected during a mission to the front line.

The mission was to collect intelligence about the movements of KMT troops stationed in North China. Ji Zhenren and Liu Hongmei went with the team. RSU2's security was stricter during this period so, in accordance with the rules, everyone going to the frontline had a pseudonym: Ji Zhenren was called Wang Qiangui and Liu Hongmei was called Zhang Lihong.

Originally this mission had nothing to do with Zhu Kexin. After he heard about the mission, he wrote an application and nagged Chief Gao in his room for half a night. Ji Zhenren also spoke out for him, "No matter what, we need a clerk. It's the same no matter who is dispatched. If Zhu Kexin goes, it may be helpful for his relationship with Liu Hongmei, whose marital situation is my concern. So I hope the unit can show some consideration for it. Besides, with Zhu Kexin going, we can be more assured of the security of our work."

Chief Gao then said, "It has been proved. Anyway, Hongmei has made special contributions to RSU2."

In the beginning, the mission went rather smoothly. They passed many places and collected large numbers of coded messages. Afterwards, they settled in the town of Hujiayu.

Hujiayu was where the headquarters of certain PLA troops was located. A strategic point since ancient times, the small town was militarily important. All the KMT troops in North China had been eyeing it covetously, conspiring to gobble it up and bring the town under their control.

Stationed there for only a few days, Ji Zhenren and his team became awarere of a strong gunpowder smell. They clearly felt that the KMT was getting ready to send an army to invade Hujiayu.

The sudden tense atmosphere was invoked by the successive intelligence intercepted by Ji Zhenren and his team. The ground scouts also brought back information that the enemy was gathering troops in large numbers in areas south of Hujiayu, seeking to attack the town. They concluded that the enemy would undoubtedly attack Hujiayu from the south. The conclusion reached by Ji Zhenren and the other cryptographers tallied with that of the scout company.

So the headquarters decided to defend south Hujiayu. Based on this decision, they redeployed troops and got ready to do battle.

During this time, RSU2 was focusing on cracking three enemy ciphers - *YAN*, *YI* and *DUAN*. The KMT wireless services had recently issued these most secure ciphers to the KMT troops in North China, so they were used most. However, RSU2 had failed to decipher them.

Ji Zhenren was in low spirits. Zhu Kexin dragged Liu Hongmei in to console him. The relationship between Ji Zhenren and Liu Hongmei was still icy cold, so she didn't say much.

"Although we failed, from *ZHI* we still gathered the important information that the enemy was assembling troops in the areas south of Hujiayu. So you mustn't be so depressed," said Zhu Kexin.

Glaring at Liu Hongmei, Ji Zhenren asked, "You also think so? Kexin is only a clerk, so he doesn't have the sensitivity. But you are a cryptographer. Don't you feel that something is not right?"

Staring back, Liu Hongmei said, "The information from different sources was the same. It was precise and collected in time. In terms of information value and professionalism, this was a perfect result."

"But my feeling about this conclusion is like what I feel about my wife. I've always felt that there's something not quite right about her, but I just can't tell what it is. Yes, she's too perfect, that's her problem. The problem about this conclusion is that it is too perfect. It looks like the enemy has deliberately falsified it. Hongmei, I do have such a feeling," confided Ji Zhenren.

"Typical paranoid, delusion!" said Liu Hongmei, leaving in a huff.

When it was supper time, Ji Zhenren talked to Liu Hongmei, "This afternoon we intercepted a few more messages. They were still encrypted via ZHI and sent to all troops by the enemy headquarters. The contents were the same as we had gathered, to amass troops in the south and to advance north. I am thinking of one question these days. ZHI is an out-of-date cipher, rarely used by the enemy since the end of last year, even if it was only used for sending some unimportant messages. But this time it is being used frequently and all the messages encrypted with it are about assembling troops south of Hujiayu and advancing north to attack the town. Why?"

Listening, Liu Hongmei gave him a rare grin, "Why bother wondering which cipher they used to send what messages? To me, it suggests the enemy headquarters is worried that their troops might lack efficiency in carrying out the plan, so they have repeatedly sent messages to press them."

Ji Zhenren saw that despite Liu Hongmei's harsh words, her tone was much milder and warmer, so he said, "Hongmei, think about it. At this critical moment the enemy is reusing an old cipher, is there anything in it?"

Liu Hongmei giggled loudly, "Tell me, what's it about? I want to know."

Encouraged by her laughter, he said enthusiastically, "I think the reason they're using the old ZHI to encrypt messages is not for their subordinates to see, but us, because they're not sure whether their YAN, YI and DUAN ciphers have been deciphered by us or not. However, they're sure that ZHI has been cracked by us. So, to make sure we can read the contents, they have reactivated ZHI to encrypt their messages in the last few days."

"Eat your meal first, eat. The food has gone cold," said Liu Hongmei, pushing the food to Ji Zhenren, while saying, "You mean the enemy is deliberately putting on a show for us, and what our ground scouts saw was all untrue. The purpose is to make us firmly believe that their main forces are gathering south of Hujiayu and are preparing to attack the town from the south, so as to draw our main forces to the area, causing our other areas to be weakly defended. Afterwards they will select a time, as well as a direction, to make a surprise attack on Hujiayu."

Raising his chopsticks Ji Zhenren tapped Liu Hongmei's hand, laughing, "Your professional sensitivity has appeared. I vaguely had this feeling in the last few days, but to reach this conclusion we still lack some evidence."

Liu Hongmei stopped giggling. Moving closer to Ji Zhenren, she gazed attentively into his eyes. Unhurriedly and clearly she said, "Then let me provide you with some information. This morning, although I cursed you for being paranoid, I felt you might be right. To be honest, I have always admired you for your intelligence and inspiration for cracking ciphers. So, I thought your suspicion about things being 'too perfect' was not groundless.

"Therefore, I went and sat in the office to monitor all day. I discovered that all the enemy troops were using ZHI-encrypted messages to reply to their headquarters and reported their progress in implementing the plan to advance north. I didn't feel there was anything wrong with it. But I captured an abnormal event: transceivers used by the enemy's 1st and 2nd Cavalry Divisions were changed to higher-power transceivers.

"Of course, it was a small change. If a monitor wasn't careful, or suspicious, they would not have known the difference. But why did the two cavalry divisions change their transceivers? In the afternoon the answer was self-evident. The signals from those two transceivers tended to gradually decrease.

"Which is to say that their communications with headquarters didn't stop, and the operators' sending style as well as the contents of the messages didn't change, yet they were slowly moving away. Three times they increased the power of their transceivers to cover the fact that their signals were decreasing in strength, giving us the false impression that they were still moving troops to the south of Hujiayu. However, I saw through it. But why did the cavalry divisions move away when the other troops were preparing for battle in the south?"

Pounding the table, Ji Zhenren stood up, "An experienced monitor with good technical skills can judge the change in distance of a transceiver through power, signal strength and wavelength. The enemy also know this. That's why they took such a measure. At every post house, they changed their transceiver to a higher power to deceive us, trying to fool us into failing to detect the change in signal strength. This could indeed have deceived and confused us. We don't have the equipment and the technology to test the direction of radio signals, but only rely on our ears. It is very difficult for us to hear any tiny changes in signals. Well, the enemy never knew that we have someone like

Hongmei, who is highly skilled and has a talent in monitoring radio signals. Haha, let's go to the monitors' office."

"I haven't had my dinner yet," complained Ji Hongmei.

Pulling her arm, Ji Zhenren said, "Our heads are going to be blown off. How can you be in the mood to eat? We only know that two enemy cavalry divisions have gone, but where? We can't tell yet."

In the office Ji Zhenren carefully listened to all the transceivers and enquired from the monitors about the circumstances. He then called the monitors and cryptographers together for a three-hour-long meeting to discuss the situation. In the end, they came to a unanimous conclusion: the enemy's main forces were gathering south of Hujiayu. But the impression they were advancing north to attack the south of the town was false. Their true main forces, led by two cavalry divisions, had firstly withdrawn west to Yanping County, then travelled eight hundred kilometres north. They had made a detour to the north of Hujiayu. Then, from Yubian County they would make a stealthy detour south, and finally carry out a surprise attack on Hujiayu from the north. This line was extremely well hidden and would take people by surprise, so it was the best plan to attack Hujiayu. Therefore, we had to adjust our troop deployment urgently, to strengthen our defences north of Hujiayu.

With this conclusion, Ji Zhenren went straight to headquarters. He found staff officer Gao who was in charge of intelligence work, telling him about his team's judgement on the enemy situation. Ignoring the information, staff officer Gao said, "The enemy would not be so foolish as to make a detour of several hundred kilometres to attack Hujiayu from the north. The reality is that the enemy is assembling its main forces in the south, so it's a foregone conclusion they will attack from the south! Our ground scouts have seen this clearly from several directions, plus the enemy telegrams you've deciphered, word by word, code by code, the black words on white paper clearly show that. But now you come to me with a different conclusion."

"The enemy also thought in this way. Our scouts saw the evidence in person, the messages we deciphered also confirmed this, so we would accept it as true," explained Ji Zhenren.

Staff officer Gao was impatient, "To be honest, I've always had questions about your team. You are confined to the house and do your work behind closed doors."

Hearing the remarks, Ji Zhenren calmed himself down. With his character and temperament, if in the past he had heard such humiliating remarks, he would have forgotten the relations between higher and lower levels and would certainly have flown into a rage, and even begun to curse. But this time he put up with it patiently, trying to present facts and reason things out.

Staff officer Gao still refused to believe him, "Don't talk nonsense. If you can show me the specific telegram which says that the enemy is planning a surprise attack on Hujiayu from the north, show me one word, or one piece of code, black words on white paper, then I will believe you."

Again unhurriedly and clearly Ji Zhenren explained, "Yes, usually the intelligence we intercept is all written on paper, word by word and section by section, which can be used directly to serve the commanders. But in many cases, intelligence is not a ready-made meal that you can take and eat. We must put together many factors, such as accumulation of experience, career inspiration, monitoring work, message deciphering, comprehensive study and judgement of the enemy, our own situation and the battlefield situation, deep and thorough unearthing of the clues and traces, scientific analysis and sound comprehension, and only after careful extrapolation, can any information become effective intelligence.

"You are right, the scouts you sent out personally witnessed the enemy deployment. But what I want to say is that what we see with our own eyes may not necessarily be what we think we have seen. What we have seen may not be true. Yes, the information I intercepted from the *ZHI*-encrypted messages that the enemy was to attack Hujiayu from the south may not be true, either. Because the enemy was suspicious that we had deciphered their *ZHI*, they sent out false messages to deceive us. Therefore, we must not be taken in!

"In fact, I don't want to force you to completely adopt our new judgement, either. I only want to hear from you that you would like to take our views into consideration. If you don't even give me such an assurance, then give me special permission to carry a machine gun to the tower of the north gate of Hujiayu, and I will die together with the enemy!"

With his utmost patience, staff officer Gao heard Ji Zhenren out. He then sneered with a loud shout, "I'll say it again, I believe what I see with my own eyes. Of course, I can also believe your intelligence, but you can't show me any evidence written in black and white. What you have given me is your analyses, guesses, assumptions. They are hallucinations you dreamed up behind closed doors. Hallucinations! I don't believe them! Neither dare I report them to the headquarters. You'd better walk out of this room and go to the battlefield. The hostilities are urgent and I have no time to argue with you pointlessly. Somebody come in. Give cryptographer Ji a light machine gun and see him off!"

Someone ran into the room with a machine gun and threw it at Ji Zhenren's feet. Raising a glass of water high in the air and slowly lowering it, Ji Zhenren raised his head and gulped the water down. Dashing out of the room, he howled furiously in the open field until he had used up all his energy. Lying flat on his back, he mumbled, "Words and numerals written in black and white, where are you?"

Then he looked like he was sleeping. His eyes closed but he was racking his brain, "The current reality once again tells me that I cannot blame others. Basically, a cryptographer depends on what is written in black and white to speak. Without any real stuff which can be seen and understood, what is the use of smashing cups to the floor, cursing or wreaking havoc? At the moment, deciphering YAN, YI and DUAN is of paramount importance."

Suddenly he sat up. Taking out a notebook, he swiftly wrote down something. Instantly YAN, YI and DUAN occupied his mind. His desperate expression showed that if he should fail this time, he would die with these three ciphers.

He realised afterwards that this time the headquarters' view was indeed that 'seeing is believing'. Many ground scouts reported that they had seen the enemy main forces assembling south of Hujiayu. These troops advanced north by truck for days, obviously they were to attack Hujiayu from the south.

But the truth was, this was the enemy's scheme of 'doing one thing under cover of another'. They only dispatched one regiment, disguised as the main force. In the daytime, they advanced north in trucks and tanks, but at night, they moved back to their starting point. For days and weeks, they pretended that their main forces were to advance north to attack Hujiayu from the south. Meanwhile, the enemy sent out people to earmark rooms and purchase army provisions, threatening to assemble more crack forces to attack the city from the south, which made our side firmly believe that this was the enemy's attacking route. But the true enemy main forces were: two cavalry divisions as vanguards, followed by two tank brigades. They first traveled west, then raced north, then turned south. After twisting their way through several hundred kilometres and making a detour at many places, they came straight down to the north of Hujiayu.

Basically, this route and plan of attack were identical to what Ji Zhenren had anticipated. The only pity was that the headquarters failed to adopt this intelligence.

The enemy's vanguard cavalry wore their padded jackets inside out and wrapped the horses' hooves with cloth. As they noiselessly and suddenly arrived at Yubei, our defence line in the north was unprepared and had insufficient manpower, so our defence force fought desperately to block the enemy. In the end, they suffered a crushing defeat and withdrew from their position.

Soon, a large enemy force was bearing down upon north Hujiayu. Although our forces put up a strong resistance, in the end, they could not defend the city and had to withdraw. Instantly groups of carts with rubber wheels drawn by donkeys hurriedly moved goods and equipment out of the town.

Before this happened, Ji Zhenren had been bent over the desk and was concentrating on cracking ciphers. Twice he was driven mad. Jumping out of his chair, he attempted to go to the north gate and kill himself by knocking his head against the wall. He could not decipher YAN, YI and DUAN. When he was held by somebody and rushed out of the city gate, bombs exploding beside him woke him up from his dumb state. He had to admit that he was defeated by these three ciphers, while also realising that the city had fallen into enemy hands and was in chaos.

At this very moment, all the team members' sole task was to throw away their luggage and items for daily use, to carry the wireless equipment and boxes of cipher material and run away as quickly as possible.

As the sun was setting, they entered a forest in the eastern hills, but they met the enemy head-on. Immediately, they took cover in the bushes so the enemy did not see them, yet they carried on moving closer and closer to them.

Ji Zhenren was scared into a cold sweat. But he saw the situation clearly: the enemy outnumbered his team; besides his team was carrying wireless equipment and confidential documents. If they were exposed, the consequences would have been disastrous. He dared not think any more. Along with Zhu Kexin who was beside him, they quietly crawled toward the woods on the south side of the hill. Then he stood up, bending his back he ran fast for some distance. He stood up again, deliberately shaking tree branches and noisily running along the slope. Zhu Kexin gave out a heart-wrenching cry, "Regimental Commander, Commissar, wait for us." Hearing the noise, the enemy moved to the south slope.

After running a few miles, the enemy closed in on Ji Zhenren and Zhu Kexin, who fought back while looking for a chance to escape. But soon they realised escape was impossible. Again, Zhu Kexin gave out a heart-wrenching cry, "Zhang Lihong, you must live and live well." Without hesitation, he pointed his handgun at his head and pulled the trigger. When Ji Zhenren pointed his revolver at his own head, he remembered that he had a piece of paper with coded messages in his jacket pocket. It must not fall into enemy hands. He took it out of his pocket and tore it to shreds. Pushing the shreds into his mouth, he swallowed them. When he raised his revolver to his head again, the enemy fired first. The bullet hit his right arm and his gun fell down the slope. He then smashed his head into an old tree. Instantly blood cascaded down his forehead without stopping, yet he did not die. When he got up and threw himself again against the tree, two enemy soldiers dashed to pin him tightly to the ground.

Only after reaching a safety zone did the wireless team stop to count heads. Ji Zhenren and Zhu Kexin were missing, but not a single item of equipment or document was lost. They sent a report to the headquarters. On the same night, people disguised as local mountain residents were dispatched to search for Ji Zhenren and Zhu Kexin. Under the slope, they found Zhu Kexin's body, but they did not see Ji Zhenren. They went on searching for three more days and nights, but they failed to find him, either alive or dead.

Staff officer Gao panicked, "If comrade Ji was captured alive by the enemy, and he confessed, it's the equivalent of taking the pants off our intelligence department."

Liu Hongmei made it absolutely clear, "No one knows Ji Zhenren better than me. He is a man who would rather die than submit. I request that the organisation set its mind at rest."

Staff officer Gao said, "He is truly a cryptographer who can either precisely predict the enemy situation or has a strategic vision. But now we don't know whether he's dead or alive, while to our great sorrow comrade Zhu has died. I feel extremely guilty."

Angrily, Liu Hongmei said, "You should feel guilty for the loss of the whole of Hujiayu." She then wailed loudly. When she buried Zhu Kexin, she forced back her grief and did not shed a single tear, but now she could no longer control herself.

The frontline headquarters tried to locate Ji Zhenren on many channels, but to no avail. After Ji Zhenren had been missing for over a month, they had to report it to Yan'an.

When Chief Gao received the news that Ji Zhenren had gone missing, a sense of fear flooded through his body, but quickly he calmed down. He promised the central leaders, "Ji Zhenren is firm in his faith. He is an outstanding and dauntless fighter, an iron-mouthed gourd who regards keeping secrets as his life. Even if he has been captured by the enemy, he would never betray the revolution and sell out the Party's secrets." The leader said absolutism is the most harmful thing and it was better to find a completely safe plan as soon as possible.

Chief Gao quickly prepared for the emergency. Firstly, he established the extent of Ji Zhenren's knowledge of RSU2's secrets; secondly, he worked out a remedial plan B if any secrets were leaked; thirdly, he discussed what RSU2 would do if the enemy stopped using the ciphers that had been cracked by RSU2; fourthly, he analysed and made a prediction about the enemy's new type of ciphers, as well as new ideas in cipher creation and how RSU2 could respond to such a change; fifthly, he discussed with the Central Department of Social Affairs, requesting them to ask our hidden agents in the enemy camp to find out where Ji Zhenren was and his circumstances. He proposed that if Ji Zhenren was found to have been captured and showed any sign of defection, our hidden agents ought to kill him immediately.

The plan B was available and the preparation for an emergency situation had been done, yet Chief Gao firmly believed that some of the measures would never be used because Ji Zhenren would never betray the revolution.

Before long news came from the Central Department of Social Affairs: it has been established that one man from our army was arrested alive by the enemy's 31st Division. He has a head injury and is in a confused state of mind, suffering from a serious language disorder. He can only manage to say his name 'Wang Qiangui'. He moves with difficulty, so he stays in bed all day. Along with the other prisoners, he is being held in the enemy's 31st Division barracks.

Immediately Chief Gao understood that Ji Zhenren was in full possession of his faculties, because he could say his name 'Wang Qiangui', only pretending that he was seriously wounded and unable to speak. This gave Chief Gao more confidence in Ji Zhenren. When someone suggested they be on guard against Gao Yuncao and Liu Hongmei, he flew into a rage, bellowing, "No need. You are letting your imaginations run away with you. Ji Zhenren, Gao Yuncao and Liu Hongmei are absolutely reliable!"

Therefore, he did not put Gao Yuncao and Liu Hongmei on the name list of RSU2 staff who were barred from touching any confidential work. He even blocked the news of Ji Zhenren being taken prisoner by the enemy from reaching Gao Yuncao.

Then the situation in North Shaanxi underwent a major change. Chiang Kai-shek assembled thirty-four brigades and launched an attack on the border region of Shaanxi, Gansu and Ningxia, attempting to wipe out the CPC Central Committee, the PLA's general headquarters and the communist forces in the region.

In view of the situation, the CPC Central Committee and the Central Military Commission decided to carry out a defensive operation, withdrawing from Yan'an on their own initiative. Mao Zedong, Zhou Enlai and Ren Bishi would lead the central organisations and the departments of the Military Commission, along with the Central Guards Regiment, totalling about six hundred people to stay in Yan'an to command the whole liberation war. For the sake of maintaining secrecy, this special force of a few hundred people was externally known as the 'Kunlun Column'. Its duty was to draw the enemy in deep, checking the several hundred thousand troops under the command of Hu Zongnan and warlords Ma Bufang and Ma Hongbin on the highland plateau of north Shaanxi. RSU2 organised sixty cryptographers to work alongside the Central Committee and the Military Commission and they were codenamed 'Kunlun Column Unit 2'.

Gao Yuncao also became a team member. During this period, she had close contact with the central leaders, and the mien of Mao Zedong giving a speech would often flash through her mind, "When fighting a war, we must not care about the loss of one town or one place. If we lose a town for the sake of preserving men, we can have both the men and the town. If we lose men for the sake of preserving a town, we will lose both the men and the town. I am going to exchange Yan'an for the whole of China!" What a breadth of vision, strategy, astuteness and resourcefulness! Admiring Mao Zedong from the bottom of her heart, Gao Yuncao blended her worship-inspired zeal into her work. In the depth of north Shaanxi, hundreds of thousands of KMT troops were unable to do anything to the Kunlun Column of six hundred men and women. Calmly and unhurriedly, Mao Zedong led the enemy in circles around the loess plateau. What was the magic? She knew that it was closely related to RSU2, namely, the Kunlun Column knew everything about the enemy situation and knew in good time. Where was the enemy? Where would they go next? This was the information that RSU2 could lose no time in delivering into the leaders' hands.

RSU2 closely monitored all the KMT troops in greater northwest China. They deciphered large amounts of enemy codes and ciphers, and coordinated with the PLA Northwest Field Army to achieve several major victories in succession. Because it had precise intelligence to go by, the Kunlun Column dared to march in parallel with the enemy at a distance of merely eight to ten kilometres away. Sometimes, the enemy marched on the mountain while the Kunlun Column marched at the foot of the mountain, which the enemy was totally unaware of. The senior leaders were very satisfied with RSU2's work and praised them many times.

In those days, Gao Yuncao worked with soaring enthusiasm. She displayed superb ability and rendered outstanding service in cracking enemy ciphers. She would often talk about the leaders' compliments and people could see that her excitement and pride came from the bottom of her heart.

At daybreak one morning, she finished her night shift. Before going to wash the kerosene lamp's black ashes off her nose and face, she went to see Chief Gao. Eagerly she asked, "Chief Gao, does the central leaders' praise for RSU2 also include me?"

"In the early morning you came to me just to ask this question?" replied Chief Gao. "Let me tell you, the glory belongs to all the RSU2 staff, so it naturally includes you who have distinguished yourself in action. Those ciphers you cracked and the beneficial results in combat operations are worthy of the leaders' praise."

"Can I really become a good soldier of Chairman Mao?" she asked again.

"There is no question about that. You are Chairman Mao's excellent cryptographer, a loyal intelligence soldier," Chief Gao assured her.

Excited like a child, Gao Yuncao grinned broadly.

Seeing that she was happy, Chief Gao told her about Ji Zhenren being captured by the enemy. He stressed that the Central Department of Social Affairs had taken strong measures, and they had secretly sent a special force to hide near the enemy's 31st Division for several weeks. Through underground contacts they were trying to rescue Ji Zhenren. The people from the Central Department of Social Affairs who had gone to carry out the mission were Zhang Jiayin and Liu Hai'er, the organisation's crack agents.

Hearing the news, Gao Yuncao was dumbstruck, then she wailed non-stop. She dried her tears and said, "Ji Zhenren will not betray the revolution. He and I have sworn to be one heart to the Party. But Zhenren will suffer."

Gao Yuncao kept true to her pledge to be one heart with the Party. Afterwards, she thought that when she followed the Central Committee and fought from one place to another in north Shaanxi, she never thought about betraying Mao Zedong and the Central Committee, not in the slightest. She often marched under the eyes of the KMT army. If she had been even slightly half-hearted, the Communist Party could not have had the results of today.

But she, who was absolutely loyal to the Party, had undertaken a major 'secret business' behind the back of the organisation.

It happened after the Yulin campaign.

The Northwest Field Army used a small force to entice the enemy to carry on going north, while dispatching another force to cover the rear organisation, who were to disguise themselves as the main force and cross over to the east bank of the Yellow River to confuse the enemy, while the genuine main force secretly gathered east of Yulin and west of Jiaxian to wait for an opportunity to wipe out the enemy.

According to the plan, RSU2 was divided into two parts to provide intelligence. The main part stayed in north Shaanxi with the main forces, while the smaller part followed the rear organisation, pretending to be the main force and crossed over to the east bank of the Yellow River. To pretend to be the main force, they needed firstly to make an empty show of strength in appearance, making the enemy aerial reconnaissance believe that they were the true main force; secondly they had to send messages continuously through the headquarters' high-powered transmitters, making the enemy radio direction finders believe that they were the genuine main force.

Gao Yuncao volunteered to go to the rear organisation headquarters and take on the job of dealing with the enemy RDFs (radio direction finders) and to lure the enemy to take the bait. Her reasons were that recently, the KMT armies had been equipped with some advanced American RDFs. She wanted to do some exploratory work on the reconnaissance detection as well as counter reconnaissance, so she needed to collect some data. This seemed like a good idea, so Chief Gao granted her request.

As soon as the campaign began, the enemy RDFs detected the signals sent by the PLA's high-powered transceivers, showing that from Jiaxian County, the Communist forces were moving east close to the Yellow River. This attracted the attention of the KMT troops under Hu Zongnan's command. Several times, Gao Yuncao was on duty operating a transceiver to confuse the enemy. She sent out some error codes and miscellaneous messages, and under the nose of her colleagues, she accomplished a 'magnificent feat' that she had planned for a long time. She skilfully tuned the channels and cleverly sent a message to the KMT's Special Secret Wireless Service in Nanjing. The message was encrypted via HE. She was sure that this 'feat' was perfectly safe, because there were no receivers able to receive the miscellaneous messages that she sent out to confuse the enemy. RSU2 already knew that these were error codes and miscellaneous messages, so they would not waste their time trying to decipher them. She mixed this HE-encrypted telegram with the other messages, so RSU2's cryptographers would naturally deal with it as an error message.

The specific operating steps were: after she sent out three error-coded telegrams, she quickly tuned to the channel that she used to contact the Special Secret Wireless Service in Nanjing. She mixed her HE-encrypted message with an error coded telegram. After sending it, she immediately tuned back to the original channel and carried on sending more messages. The RSU2 monitors had no idea at all that the operator had changed channel, so they stayed on the same channel. Besides, it was normal for operators to pause between messages, so the monitors thought that the operator had paused after sending three messages, and then went on sending some more.

In fact, Gao Yuncao had made sure that her action was perfectly safe. After the Special Secret Wireless Service in Nanjing received her message, they quickly deciphered it with the help of *The Sad Record of a Strategy for Peace*, and it read as, "Prisoner of war Wang Qiangui in north China has been secretly fostered by Grasshopper for many years. He is soon to be recruited yet he knows nothing about it. Be sure not to reveal to him the secret Grasshopper mission, but to order the 31st Division to tactically set him free, allowing him to flee back to the Communist side, so that he can assist me in accomplishing great deeds. Be sure to bear this in mind. P.S., the communist main forces are soon to cross to the east bank of the Yellow River..." She played the same trick as she did the last time, ending the message at the critical moment to create a false sense that she was in a dangerous situation when sending it.

She had made a last desperate effort and risked her neck to save her husband from the den of demons. For a hidden agent, what had to be avoided most was to act out of a sudden impulse. But she was very calm, thinking it was worthwhile even if she were to lose her life.

Her gamble paid off. In Nanjing, after Gao Q received the message, he immediately sent a telegram to the 31st Division, ordering them to release Wang Qiangui; meanwhile he analysed the incomplete sentence of 'the Communist main forces are soon to cross to the east bank of the Yellow River...', thinking that the RSU2 Communist wireless services had been following the Communist central organisations, and the message sent from a high-powered transmitter illustrated at least one aspect that the Communist Northwest Field Army was to cross the Yellow River. So he telegraphed the situation to general Hu Zongnan, who had already made the judgement that the Communists would cross the Yellow River by following the track of the Communists' high-powered transceivers, as well as the intelligence gathered by aerial reconnaissance. However, a suspicious man by nature, it took him a long time to make up his mind, and Gao Q's telegram played a certain role in hastening Hu Zongnan to finally dismiss his doubts and worries.

This erroneous judgement laid the groundwork for Hu Zongnan's troops' defeat. As for the 31st Division, after receiving orders to release Wang Qiangui, they didn't think much about the reason behind the order, but racked their brains to find a way to release him in a natural way, letting Wang Qiangui know nothing about their plan, but making him think that he had actually escaped by himself.

Soon the 31st Division was ordered to move somewhere else. One day, on a winding path in the forest on Xinan Mountain, the procession escorting the prisoners of war was blocked by other troops for half a night. They could not move a step and complaints were heard everywhere among the officers and men. Taking advantage of the chaos in the dark, Ji Zhenren rolled into a trench that was thick with grass. Crawling into a forest, he ran away.

One month later, he found RSU2 in Linxian County in Shanxi province.

Ji Zhenren would rather have died than surrender. He escaped and came back on his own. But real trouble soon followed. The Central Department of Social Affairs and some RSU2 staff asked Chief Gao, "Ji Zhenren was heavily guarded by the enemy, how was he able to escape so easily?"

While people were puzzled, Ji Zhenren himself added an explanation, "That night, I accidentally heard the enemy battalion commander, who was in charge of escorting us prisoners, quietly complaining to an enemy company commander, saying it was ridiculous that to enable a prisoner of war to run away, the higher command lets them go round and round the mountain at midnight. I didn't know how many prisoners of war had run away that night, even less did I know if I was the one that they intended to let off deliberately. But I did feel that they were slack with their guard, so I was able to escape quite easily."

Immediately, Chief Gao went to contact the troops, asking them to report to him the names, ranks and job titles of the missing and captured personnel, particularly if there were any prisoners of war who had returned recently. After all the reports arrived, he discovered that there were no such cases. Among the name list of the missing and captured, except for Ji Zhenren, no one else was involved in confidential work.

Chief Gao judged that if what Ji Zhenren had said was true, the possibility of him having been released deliberately was great. But why? Had he defected? So, he had come back to be a secret agent for the enemy? But why did he confess to it himself? Chief Gao dared not say any more.

After a rigorous investigation, the Central Department of Social Affairs came to a conclusion, "The circumstances in which Ji Zhenren was captured by the enemy are unclear; so transfer him away from RSU2, and subject him to supervision while waiting to be restored to his former post." So Ji Zhenren was assigned to be a porter in the odd-job section.

Gao Yuncao's mind was in tumult, but she looked as peaceful as usual. She thought, "Unless I bare my unsavoury past to Chief Gao, there is no way to explain why Ji Zhenren was able to escape so easily from enemy capture." Then she thought again, "Luckily, he has come back. His life has been saved at least, as to what will happen in the future, I'd better watch quietly."

After a few days, she did not see anything unusual in RSU2, nor was there any mention of the matter in the KMT armies' telegrams. She was free in her movement and carried on working as usual. She judged that she had not been suspected by either side. So, she began to pester Chief Gao to tell him that Ji Zhenren was innocent.

Chief Gao clarified his stand, "As a senior cryptographer, Ji Zhenren has undergone tests for many years and he is most trustworthy for keeping secrets. If he had defected, our army's confidential system would have already suffered heavy losses. But after many examinations, from the enemy transceivers we were monitoring and the enemy use of ciphers to our own situation and the enemy situation, there have been no unusual changes since his arrest. The Central Department of Social Affairs also learned that the other intelligence fronts were normal. So, our preliminary judgement is that he did not defect to the enemy. But the fact that he had fled back easily, however, aroused suspicion that he was deliberately released by the enemy, therefore, it is difficult for the high command to completely set their mind at rest, nor can RSU2 vouch for him."

Understanding Chief Gao's reasonable remarks, Gao Yuncao refrained from mentioning the matter any more.

A few months later, after approval, Gao Yuncao and Liu Hongmei went to see Ji Zhenren, who was physically stronger but in very low spirits. He asked them to pass on his words to Chief Gao that life with no ciphers to crack was as good as being dead, and asking when he could go back to RSU2. He also told Liu Hongmei, "I witnessed comrade Zhu Kexin's loyalty. He died a worthy death, a glorious death." The mention of Zhu Kexin touched Liu Hongmei's sore spot. She ran away, wailing.

Then the war situation changed significantly. The People's Liberation Army turned from defence to strategic offence. All the PLA field armies went from victory to victory, while the KMT armies kept on retreating. As usually happened in wartime, the more whole army units were wiped out, the more frequently the losing side changed their ciphers. After every defeat, the difficulty of ciphers used would be ratcheted up a level. That is what happened to the KMT. All its armies and secret services were now using an extremely difficult cipher system.

RSU2 reorganised its cryptography resources, scientifically rationing and tightening the rhythm of work. Sleeping time for each cryptographer was limited to no more than four hours per day. Gao Yuncao and Liu Hongmei ate and slept in the office. For several months they were in a state of fighting to the death.

"Why do I feel that I am putting up a last-ditch struggle every day? For every cipher, I feel that I have used up my last breath, I feel like I'm dying," grumbled Liu Hongmei.

"We are indeed facing an enormous task," said Gao Yuncao. "But I cannot exclude the possibility that there is something wrong with your health. You must manage both work and rest well."

"The fighting has been so intense. Having a good sleep has become a luxury. When the war ends, I will sleep for three days and three nights," remarked Liu Hongmei.

During this period, Ji Zhenren twice requested to crack ciphers, but he was refused permission. No longer keeping quiet , he would yell at the guards, "I came back to serve the Party. Why do you deprive me of my right to work? The other troops even used Japanese prisoners of war to work for them, why not me? I might as well have been killed by the enemy! I came back alive, but you treat me in such a way. The fact is that you can only accept a dead Ji Zhenren, isn't it? All right, I'll die. After I die, everyone has a clean slate."

Later, RSU2 made a major breakthrough. All cryptographers reported on their practical experience and their deciphering routine, after improving their techniques and methods, and making the most use of themselves, they exploited the loopholes, contradictions and weaknesses in the enemy's wireless communications under specific conditions, and held onto the enemy's mistakes and flaws, thereby successfully solving a series of technical problems. Gao Yuncao and Liu Hongmei became heroes. The cooperation between them and their mutual complementarity worked surprisingly well. Besides, many other RSU2 cryptographers also worked wonders.

Chief Gao had paid close attention to the circumstances of Ji Zhenren. He failed to discover any bad effects or damage inflicted due to his capture by the enemy. But the Central Department of Social Affairs again consulted several hidden contacts in the enemy camp, and they could not rule out the possibility that he had been deliberately released by the enemy. Time might prove his innocence. But Ji Zhenren could not wait, neither could Chief Gao. So, under the circumstances whereby Ji Zhenren almost had a nervous breakdown as well as attempting suicide, Chief Gao tried all possible ways to plead and he finally got Ji Zhenren back to RSU2 to do some assistance work under the watchful eye of the security people. Chief Gao arranged for him to organise the old telegrams. Seeing codes and ciphers again, Ji Zhenren's mental state improved immediately.

Gao Yuncao breathed a long sigh of relief. Some time ago, when she heard of Ji Zhenren's attempted suicide, she went to Chief Gao to confess. As soon as Chief Gao saw her, he told her about the decision to transfer Ji Zhenren back to RSU2 so she did not take her confession out of her pocket.

How dangerous it was! If Chief Gao had spoken about it a minute later, she would have handed him those few sheets of paper. But could a self-confessed spy have saved her innocent husband?

Although Ji Zhenren returned to RSU2, he was under watch and lived separately. He was not allowed to make contact with anybody, not even his wife. He seemed to have no desire to reunite with his wife at all. As soon as he picked up a coded message, his desire to crack it quickly returned. Except for four to five hours sleep a day, he devoted himself heart and soul to cracking ciphers, and those who watched over him had to work in shifts.

But a miracle happened!

From the fragmented and disused telegrams he was able to pick out gold nuggets. Every week or two, he was able to crack a dead cipher, including those he had pronounced dead previously. No one had expected that after several life-and-death experiences, his brain would be even sharper. According to the guards who were watching him, every day he was like a patient with a mental disease. He did not know to eat his food when it was put in front of him. When he was asleep, he would wake up suddenly, only in his underpants and he would begin to work for five to six hours. These unused ciphers he cracked had no realistic significance. Some might have had a slight intelligence value, but that did not affect his soaring enthusiasm.

Later, the other cryptographers were swamped with work. When they encountered some odd ciphers that they could not crack, Chief Gao would secretly bring them to Ji Zhenren, and he would crack some of them. Of course, Chief Gao and Ji Zhenren were like thieves under the watchful eyes of the guards. But for such little tricks, Ji Zhenren was very proud of himself. He would often giggle, then picking up the food that had gone cold for hours, he would wolf it down.

His playing the fool went on until the war situation in Northeast China became urgent. Cryptographers were desperately needed in the front line of the battlefield.

Chief Gao submitted a report to the high command, "Ji Zhenren is a skilful cryptographer who is crazy about his work. He is very capable and sharp in deciphering codes, but he has lain idle for a long time, which is a loss to our intelligence venture. If we transfer him away from North China where he was captured by the enemy, there will be no worries about any side issues and it would be a completely safe measure. Therefore, I suggest he be transferred to the Northeast Field Army to work as a cryptographer under the watch of the security guards. We should also transfer Gao Yuncao, Liu Hongmei and another seven cryptographers to the Northeast Field Army to give technical support."

Soon the report was approved. Yet RSU2's investigation into the Ji Zhenren incident carried on, and Ji Zhenren was put under long-term observation. If he was found to be behaving abnormally or improperly, resolute action had to be taken, then a report sent to the higher authorities for the record.

So with a mandate from the high command hanging over his head and multiple chains shackling his feet, Ji Zhenren went to the Northeast battlefield. Very soon, he, Gao Yuncao and Liu Hongmei became the 'Three Musketeers' of cryptographers, displaying their abilities to the full and conquering the enemy ciphers time and again. Particularly, after they skilfully and profoundly mastered the enemy's advanced encoding techniques and cipher compilation rules, they were able to make precise predictions about the enemy's cipher creations. They could often pre-set their cracking methods in advance and get the technical requirements ready. Whenever a new enemy cipher was put to use, they could immediately make arrangements to swiftly crack it. What often happened was that when the enemy's receiving side took time to decipher the messages with their code books, our side had already deciphered them. What had been deciphered was written clearly on paper and delivered to the frontline commanders, creating a miracle that we knew the enemy information before they knew it themselves.

The trio had been lucky to be together with Commander Lin Biao from morning until night. Very soon, they became very well acquainted with General Lin Biao's attitude toward battle. He never went into battle if the enemy's circumstances were not clear. He said that a battle is actually a battle for information. Once we have intelligence, we can be absolutely sure that we are winning. Gao Yuncao would say, "This is a commander who places importance on cipher intelligence. He never lets go of a chance provided by cipher intelligence to deliver heavy blows to the enemy. But he has always been sensitive about intelligence and maintains an extremely cautious attitude toward intelligence work."

But she could not enjoy the happiness of success, because her mind was taken away by a scene that unfolded before her eyes.

It was when she went to the office to pick up some material, she saw a female monitor about to breastfeed her baby. Someone brought the crying baby in. As soon as the baby heard the *dih-dah* sound, he stopped crying. A colleague helped to unfasten the mother's buttons and press the baby to her bosom. When work was pressing, she would feed the baby while transcribing messages. The baby had got used to the *dih-dah* sound, holding her mother's bosom he sucked the milk greedily, as if nothing else was happening, while the mother concentrated on working as usual.

Suddenly, two security guards entered, taking away the baby, they then escorted the mother out of the room. The cries of the baby and the screams of the mother shocked everyone present. Gao Yuncao then found out that the female monitor was the wife of a traitor.

She was dumbstruck. At once she thought of herself, murmuring inwardly, "Ji Zhenren is not a traitor. I am not a spy. I am not the wife of a traitor."

This shocking scene stayed in her mind for a long time until one day she intercepted a special coded message, only then did she gradually forget about it.

Before the Liaoning-Shenyang Campaign started, about eighty transceivers closely monitored every movement of hundreds of thousands of KMT troops throughout the Northeast and nearby regions. A hundred and thirty monitors monitored the enemy transceivers round the clock and ninety cryptographers buried themselves in cracking the enemy's constantly changing ciphers. Large-scale war was around the corner, and victory or defeat depended on this test. Every cryptographer was tense, and their wits and inspiration flashed constantly. One after another, new ciphers were cracked and intelligence was quickly delivered into the hands of commanders.

XIANG was cracked in the daytime when the cryptographers on the night shift had fallen asleep. Liu Hongmei, who could not sleep for a day and a night, stared blankly at the ceiling. Suddenly, she sat up. Grabbing a pen and paper, she began a fierce attack on the flash of inspiration in her head.

A new enemy cipher was cracked by her. At first she was in a trance, then burst into wailing. Gao Yuncao jumped up and covered Liu Hongmei's mouth tightly. Grabbing the paper, she had a read and then gave it a go herself. Yes, Liu Hongmei's decryption was right.

She rushed to see Ji Zhenren who immediately became absorbed in it. From beginning to end, he did his own decryption. Then three of them did it again together, and the answer showed that they were absolutely correct.

Wild with joy, Liu Hongmei pounded the table noisily. Gao Yuncao held her tightly, muttering softly, "Calm down. Calm down."

With a commanding expression, Ji Zhenren said, "This cipher has no direct relationship with this campaign. Store it and report it afterwards. Now you two go and crack more ciphers."

Liu Hongmei's eyes popped out, as she shouted, "This cipher is of great significance. We must report it now! Do you understand?"

"Look at you, not like a cryptographer before a battle. For some personal concerns you fail to see what is urgent and important. Absolutely muddleheaded!" Throwing the papers on the table, Ji Zhenren left the room. Gao Yuncao consoled Liu Hongmei, "We must not hurry with this cipher, better to leave it alone for the time being."

This cipher, XIANG, only started to be used by the KMT's Baomiju system under the Defence Ministry. The first message Liu Hongmei decrypted was a general telegram to all war zones, and its content was like a grappling iron suddenly thrown out that gripped her heart.

A few days ago, after a thorough investigation, we found out that our 31st Division had neglected their duty at the battle for Hujiayu. They turned a blind eye to the bizarre behaviour of two Communists. They failed to see that the two, one who killed himself and one who swallowed paper into his belly and dashed his head against a tree, were Communist special elements, but regarded them as ordinary prisoners of war and tried to exact a confession through torture. Afterwards they were abandoned and ignored. Now we suspect the two were actually Communist cryptographers. However, the chief of our special secret wireless section sent the 31st Division an order by telegram without authorisation, asking them to release the suspect Communist cryptographer Wang Qiangui, causing us to lose the opportunity to seek him to cross over to our side, which had a negative impact. Now we inform all war zones, this special secret wireless section is only an institute for professional guidance, not in possession of power to issue orders to war zones. In future, for anything involving secret services, you must take orders issued by Baomiju as the standard."

Liu Hongmei was extremely relieved, "Although we don't know the intentions of the enemy's Special Secret Wireless Section in getting involved in the matter, this telegram is enough to prove that Ji Zhenren and Zhu Kexin are clean. Their professional integrity and natural instinct to keep secrets and loyalty to the Party are so touching." Yet she also understood that this telegram did not have much to do with the current combat operation, so she decided not to report it to the commanders to divert their energies.

After Gao Yuncao read the telegram, she cried out inwardly, "Not bad, this telegram mentioned neither Gao Q nor his codename, otherwise, if Ji Zhenren knew that Gao Q is the chief of the KMT Special Secret Wireless Section, he would associate many things with it, even me, which would threaten my true identity as a spy." Then she thought about it again, "Because the Grasshopper Plan is a secret within the Special Secret Wireless Section, Gao Q would never tell Baomiju the true reason for the release of Wang Qiangui. But Baomiju has direct access to the highest authorities and they can call him to account on the pretext of discipline. From this telegram, both Baomiju and Gao Q had no idea that Wang Qiangui is Ji Zhenren, otherwise, it would have been more troublesome."

Since XIANG was deciphered, Liu Hongmei could not help wondering, "Why did the enemy release Ji Zhenren?"

She went to ask Gao Yuncao about it, who deliberately confused her and said jokingly, "Doesn't Ji Zhenren have a relative in that Special Secret Wireless Section?"

She then went to ask Ji Zhenren, who yelled, "You idiot! Don't you know what relatives our family have?"

Then, wave after wave of battles in the Northeast intensified. Gao Yuncao was secretly watching over the matter of Ji Zhenren and Zhu Kexin, trying to discover and react as soon as possible if something was about to happen. In Baomiju's telegram the name of the Special Secret Wireless Section was mentioned, which meant danger was one step closer to her. Her uneasiness grew, mainly for fear that Ji Zhenren would pay attention to her. Such fear from deep inside her heart had not been seen for a long time, because she often forgot about her dark identity. All along, she considered herself a Communist.

In this period of time, RSU2 in the Northeast went all out keeping a close watch on the enemy situation on the battlefield. Wave after wave, the cryptographers launched attacks and they decrypted many of the new ciphers used by the enemy, acquiring prompt intelligence for the Tashan blocking action, the battle for Jinzhou and the peaceful liberation of Changchun.

However, the situation on the battlefield was still not good and there were constant urgent and dangerous circumstances. One day, the radio signals from the enemy's main forces under the command of General Hu Yan, which were monitored by RSU2, suddenly disappeared. In a field operation, losing track of the movement of an enemy's main division was a very serious matter. Commanders pressed for information and the pressure on the whole of RSU2 became extreme. All cryptographers took turns to tackle ciphers, some collectively, some individually working on one, or some working on several at the same time. Everyone had brought their wits into full play, as though they were preparing to exhaust their last ounce of strength.

Although it took the cryptographers a great amount of effort, the information gathered was generally useless. How absurd! The enemy transceivers were busy sending each other messages, but it was all women's gossip. The contents were all irrelevant odds and ends, not a single item involved military secrets.

RSU2 had never come across such a lousy situation. The atmosphere was tense, nearly reaching the point of explosion.

Ji Zhenren had been appointed leader of Team Three because of his excellent performance during this period. Yet he was still under close observation. Wherever he went, there were two people following him. Those not in the know might have thought that they were his bodyguards.

His pen slipped from his fingers and fell to the floor, as he himself fainted and dropped to the ground. No one noticed, nor could they spare their hands to wake him up. Only after Gao Yuncao settled one of her calculations did she stand up and pour a mug of water onto his face. Chilled by the cold water, he woke up. Getting to his feet, he picked up the papers and carried on working.

Seeing that Ji Zhenren was not looking well, a guard brought him a mug of warm water. He gulped it down. Suddenly, he swept his arms and all the papers fell on the floor. Stamping his feet hard on the papers, he cursed, "What do you think you are? Go away, you fucking empty-shelled egg! Go and drink your fucking spirits. Go to fucking sleep."

Ji Zhenren had not used foul language for many years. Liu Hongmei shot a glance at him and buried her head in her own work. She was one of the main cryptographers to crack the ciphers used by Hu Yan's troops so the pressure on her was tremendous. She looked deathly pale, beads of sweat rolling down her face. She checked the decrypted messages, but she did not see any shadow of Hu Yan's troops. She went to the other teams but saw nothing either. She mumbled, "Hu Yan, the old devil is driving us mad." Gao Yuncao brought a mug of water to her. Expressionless and in a weak voice, Liu Hongmei said, "I really feel that I am putting up a last-ditch struggle."

Gao Yuncao helped her get up, saying, "You haven't had a good sleep for a few days, go and take a nap."

But Ji Zhenren was angry. Staring at Liu Hongmei, he shouted, "What? You want to go to bed? You are the team leader, won't you feel ashamed if you step out of the room? Tell me, where are Hu Yan's troops?"

Tears welled up in Liu Hongmei's eyes. Sitting down, in a faint voice, she said, "OK, let me carry on. I have a feeling that the devil Hu is hiding in a corner somewhere laughing at me ferociously." Suddenly she was motionless. Her face turned scarlet, her mouth opened and blood burst out.

In shock, the other team members stood up and rushed over to her. Ji Zhenren was as angry as minutes ago, shouting, "This is a battlefield. Why are you surprised to see some blood? Go back to your seats and find the devil Hu. Hygienists, come here!"

Gao Yuncao wanted to help send Liu Hongmei to the medical unit, but Ji Zhenren held her arms, yelling, "Go back to your seat! Your post is your desk! Your job is to search for Hu Yan without stopping for a second!"

"No wonder Hongmei cursed your lack of human feeling," snapped the furious Gao Yuncao, breaking away from his grip and involuntarily slapping his face.

Dumbstruck, Ji Zhenren stood there motionless, his face burning. He stroked his face and blood covered his hand. It was Liu Hongmei's but on Gao Yuncao's hand. Subconsciously he smelt it. Seeing Liu Hongmei being helped away, a pond in his hometown in south Jiangxi appeared before his eyes. That dated back to their youth when he took little Hongmei to go and watch the adults catch fish. The water in the pond had been disturbed, it was muddy and the fish had all been caught. Suddenly, he and Hongmei saw a big fish quietly swim along the ditch and enter a small pool. Hongmei wanted to call people to come and catch the fish, but he stopped her. He pushed her to the ground, and her mouth hit the ground hard. Wailing, her blood spurted all over his face. But she forgot all about the fish, so that it survived its fate.

Again, he pushed his blood-stained hand under his nose. Suddenly he linked it to the battleground, "Could it be that, like the fish, that old devil Hu also thinks that the most dangerous place is also the safest place to be? Can't he use plain telegrams or a local dialect to send his messages?"

So he called out, "Keep a close watch on Hu Yan's troops' plain telegrams. Report the information to me immediately!" Then he shouted again, "Quick, go and find Hu Yan in the waste bins."

Kicking over the bins for waste telegrams, he emptied dozens of kilos of paper on the floor. He shouted hysterically, "Find Hu Yan in the waste bins!"

Under normal circumstances, after careful screening and

processing, if the cryptographers could not decipher them, or the messages were meaningless, all the fragmentary and plain text telegrams were put in the bin. After a battle ended, they would be registered and destroyed.

After a search, they found nothing from the bins.

Ji Zhenren shouted, "Hu Yan, where are you?" On the brink of collapse, he lay on his back on a pile of paper with arms and legs outstretched. In two shakes of a lamb's tail, he moved his fingers among the papers and began to go over the messages one by one. In fact, he did not read them, but only acted out of habit.

Suddenly, he sat up, two fingers pinching a sheet of paper and shaking it noisily.

This telegram had only eight numerals: 11662570.

Having memorised all the codes for nearly ten thousand Chinese characters in the codebook for plaintext telegrams, at once two characters came to mind: 女昽 (nǚlóng) .

His eyes popped out and the expression in his eyes was like that of a psychiatric patient. Losing control of himself, he went to shake the arms of all the cryptographers in the room. His lips and voice trembled, "Tell me, is the fish that keeps to the edge of the pond definitely the King Fish?

"Who is 女昽?

"Will the one that sneaks under our eyes be a big fish?

"Which place is called 女昽?"

He knew clearly that his questions were superfluous. Because the names of the above-mentioned enemy officers of regiments, townships, famous mountains, rivers and lakes throughout the northeast region were all in his head. There was not an officer nor a place called 女昽. But as a rule, he had to listen to the opinion of the majority.

With blood-stained face, he walked across to Gao Yuncao. Grabbing her hand, he pulled it to touch his face, "Don't you feel that Hongmei's blood has become the glue between you and me? Ha-ha, only she is right! Where has she gone hiding to shirk her work? Hurry and let her tell me who is 女昽? Where is 女昽?"

Looking baffled, Gao Yuncao shouted, "You neurotic, what are you trying to say?" Snatching the paper from him, she saw it was an extremely ordinary plaintext telegram.

Of course she understood that in the intense fighting, each day a monitor and a cryptographer would deal with thousands of coded, plaintext, commercial and private telegrams, as well as some telegrams with neither senders nor receivers. So there was nothing strange at all about throwing such a plaintext telegram into the waste bin.

Staring at him, she said, "You're so strange. What's the point of being fixated on these two characters?"

Grinning weirdly, he said, "On the battlefield, have you ever seen a telegram with two words? How could a two-word telegram not be significant?! A one-word telegram could have accomplished a love between two lovers in Shanghai. Why can't a two-word telegram become military intelligence in the Northeast? Why can't it deliver Hu Yan into the palm of my hand? Somebody come! Go and check all the names of the officers under Hu Yan's command, and the names of every place in the entire northeast region, to find out what this 女胧 is about. Quick! Go and find it!"

Soon the person checking the enemy plaintext telegrams came to report, "In the last few days, Hu Yan's troops mostly used telephone operators from Guangdong. They use Cantonese to communicate with each other. Our monitors from Guangdong are monitoring them, but we haven't intercepted any useful information yet." He then added, "However, another dialect also appears, but only spoken by the enemy's female operators. The messages sent in this dialect are very few, appearing no more than three to five times a day. All our monitors have had a listen, but no one could understand what they were talking about, so we didn't bother about it again."

Throwing the paper into the air, Ji Zhenren cursed, "Idiots! No more monitoring because there are only a few of them?" He dashed straight to the monitors' room, followed by Gao Yuncao.

In the end, they returned crestfallen. Fuck it, no one can understand that dialect!

At dusk, someone came to report that after a thorough check, there was no officer or place in the northeast called 女胧.

"胧 means obscure, dim or hazy, but 女胧 literally means nothing," said Ji Zhenren to Gao Yuncao, "yet my intuition tells me that this is not a wasted or half-finished telegram, but a full message. It means something." Turning around to face everyone, he stood still. He became lost in deep thought for a while, then he called out, "Yes, that's it! That must be it! Who or where is 女书 (nüshu)? Go and check the dictionary."

Gao Yuncao told Ji Zhenren that while she was checking all the names with the character 女 for people and places, there was no person or place called either 女眬 or 女书. She then asked, "Where do the two characters 女书 come from? Oh, I understand. You suspect 女眬 is a mistake, either in sending or transcribing. You're right. The code for 女 is 1166 , a double-digit code. Verifying each other, normally a mistake shouldn't be made when pressing the tapper or writing down on paper. There is a greater possibility of error for 眬. The code for this word is 2570 and it is very easy to mix up 0 and 9 because there are four clacks and one click for the number 9 and five clacks for 0. When a wireless operator transcribes very fast and hears four clacks for number 9, it is easy for the brain to misjudge it as five clacks, thereby missing the last clack and writing 0. In that case 11662570 could actually be a mistake (instead of 11662579). However, this is only one of many possibilities."

Ji Zhenren cried out, "What you are saying is correct. Since 女眬 is meaningless, let us ponder 女书. If we have no alternative we have to give this small possibility a try. Then what's the significance of 女书?"

After a moment, Ji Zhenren threw the paper into the air, saying, "There's no way this telegram was sent or transcribed incorrectly. This KMT operator couldn't be so inept as to have an error rate of fifty per cent, neither would our monitor transcribe it wrong. So, I judge the enemy has deliberately sent the wrong word to confuse us. They have already taken us by surprise by sending plaintext telegrams in war, now they have deliberately sent two meaningless words, which is a more confusing trap. OK, everyone go and think about 女书. Whoever can think of an answer, I'll tell them a love story behind a one-word telegram, including my first love and kiss."

"Ji Zhenren, in such an urgent military situation, how can you still be in the mood to crack a joke? You really are insane, aren't you?" As soon as Gao Yuncao had finished speaking, her anger disappeared. Her expression turned soft, murmuring, "Zhenren, actually I remember every detail of our love in Shanghai, including our kisses in the camphor tree forest."

This sentence beat Ji Zhenren awake like a stick. He hurried to stop her, "Yuncao, you're mad, too. How can you talk about it in front of everyone? Don't do it, please…"

"OK. I won't talk about the camphor forest. Zhenren, let me talk about another time, which was also unforgettable."

Ji Zhenren's face took on a ghastly expression as Gao Yuncao said,

"In that library we chatted about books all day. We enjoyed our chat so much."

Ji Zhenren pulled her, "Everybody here is working. If you really want to talk about it, we should go somewhere else. Don't interrupt their work."

Throwing off his hand, she said, "Didn't you say that you wanted to let them hear about our first kiss? Ha-ha, don't be nervous and set your mind at ease. I won't speak about anything embarrassing, I'll only talk about what we did in the library. That day we chatted about books, and we chatted about all sorts of things and thoughts that thronged our minds. I remember we chatted about Liu Zongyuan's reference to 'strange snakes growing in the wilds of Yongzhou' in his fable *Discourse of the Snake Catcher*, then about Zeng Bei passing Yongzhou in the period of the Taiping Heavenly Kingdom, then about a thrilling thing that happened to women in Yongjiang County, south of Yongzhou."

It was her last sentence that enlightened Ji Zhenren. He cried like a child, then with a smiling face he chanted, "The writing on the dancing fans is in very small characters which look like Mongolian. No male in the county can read these words, and this is 女书!"

Gao Yuncao had a broad grin on her face, "The force of love has brought your old memories back to mind."

Everyone in the room looked at one another in surprise.

Ji Zhenren explained, "Since ancient times, in the Nanling mountain area of Jiangyong County in Hunan Province, there has been a kind of writing that exists only for women. It uses the syllables of the local dialect to express the pronunciation of the words. The tunes are many in number and they are complicated. They are extremely local and difficult for non-locals to understand. The circulation of this dialect is very small. The local women are accustomed to singing folk songs. They often gather together doing needlework while singing and chanting. They also embroider this language on fans, handkerchiefs and cards, so this dialect and its writing form is called 女书 (*nüshu*, literally meaning women's book, style of calligraphy or document). According to records, this dialect and writing used exclusively by women is unique in the world and those who know of its existence are very few in number."

Ji Zhenren was intoxicated by the library in Shanghai. Unhurriedly, he talked about this peculiar 女书 culture. The next moment, he jumped up and dashed to the telephone.

Picking up the phone, he said, "There's no secret about this enemy coded message; they set a trap to confuse us. The 'women's calligraphy' is the only type of its kind in the world and the cipher is created by using this strange dialect."

Impatiently, the leader on the other end called out, "Speak human language."

Then he said, "We intercepted an enemy plaintext telegram with only two words; 女肶 . After analysis, we're sure this is Hu Yan informing his troops to start using 'women's calligraphy' (女书) to communicate with each other, which means that the enemy had planned it beforehand. They had secretly recruited and trained a group of women from Jiangyong County to be their wireless operators. Hu Yan is from Hunan Province. He must be particularly fond of this odd and rare local dialect. This communication method is secretive and safe, and took us by surprise. Now we request all our troops and the local underground liaison posts to immediately search for and recruit women from Jiangyong County. This is urgent!"

Three days later, from all channels five women from Jiangyong County were secretly sent to RSU2 and one of them mastered 'women's calligraphy'. After a test, the result was extremely good.

Because RSU2's cryptographers could crack whatever enemy ciphers they came across, it forced Hu Yan to find a new way. He took risks and came up with such a rare method.

Ji Zhenren presented his smiling face to Gao Yuncao, "Comrade Yuncao, we at RSU2 are awesome."

With an icy cold expression, she said, "You'd better go and see Hongmei. She's still unconscious."

Ji Zhenren stared at her, "How do I have the time for that?"

Then he called to mind that plaintext telegram: 女肶 . During wartime, it is not rare for troops to use plaintext, or local dialects or the languages of ethnic groups to pass on important information. But Hu Yan's was a rare case. At the critical moment, he used the coded telegrams as a signboard, in a disguised form he sent secrets via plaintext messages and used the 'women's calligraphy' for communications and liaison. RSU2's cryptographers often nicknamed this sort of plaintext telegram sent under the circumstances of putting up a last-ditch struggle as 'netherworld telegrams'. Facts proved that it was this special 'netherworld telegram' that was directly responsible for sending Hu Yan's troops to hell.

Many years later, Ji Zhenren went to Jiangyong County to visit the retired female monitor who had rendered outstanding service in this campaign. Through her guidance and explanation, he enjoyed the unique charm of the traditional culture of 'women's calligraphy'. When he held a handkerchief embroidered with the 'women's calligraphy' characters, his eyes were red. He called to mind Liu Hongmei who had had a nervous breakdown from constant overwork and had spat blood in the office. Because of the urgency of war, he did not arrange to send her to hospital in the rear. She stayed in the arms of RSU2's medics and was unconscious for a few days. She nearly lost her life.

When Chief Gao, who was far away at general headquarters, heard about it, he said emotionally, "Comrade Liu Hongmei collapsed on the battlefield of cipher cracking. For the sacred cause of deciphering code, she used up nearly all her energy and wit. Although she was on the verge of death, the fine qualities she displayed as a cryptographer supported RSU2 to carry on its miraculous and unceasingly glorious work."

However, in the final phase of the Liaoning-Shenyang campaign, Ji Zhenren and his team made a major mistake, leaving an unfavourable mark on their former 'miracles' and 'glory'.

At the time, all the Communist Northeast Field Army troops were going all out to encircle the main forces of the KMT's Liao Yaoxiang Army Corps, under which Pan Ting's troops were isolated and hidden somewhere in a faraway corner. They stopped wireless communications with headquarters, so RSU2 could not find out where these troops had gone. After some comprehensive examination and analysis of all the information, Ji Zhenren and his team reported their judgement to the Northeast Field Army headquarters that 'this group of enemy has advanced to the west'.

But the fact was Pan Ting had led his troops on a stealthy march east through the night. When the PLA Northeast Field Army headquarters discovered the situation, they quickly assembled forces to block the enemy. The majority of the enemy were wiped out, but several thousand still managed to get away.

After the campaign ended, the headquarters did not make enquiries about this misjudgement of information, there was not a word of blame. But Ji Zhenren blamed himself. He searched for reasons and requested that the organisation punish him severely. Besides, he kept picking on Gao Yuncao, because she was one of the people in charge of monitoring Pan's troops.

For a while, again and again he asked her the same question, "Why did you make the judgement that Pan's troops would go west rather than east?"

One day, when he asked her again, she suddenly felt stupefied and was scared into a cold sweat, "Obviously, he suspects that it was not a misjudgement, but that I did it deliberately, and that I deliberately let the enemy escape. If he truly has this opinion, he wrongs me terribly. I am not the Gao Yuncao of the past. So how could I deliberately have let the enemy go? If he does think so, it is very dangerous for me because it means that he has begun to suspect my true identity." So she decided not to answer his questions, which was the safest thing for her to do.

But later she decided to turn from defence to offence. In a cold voice, she said, "I've been thinking of one question recently. The defeated enemy fled east. Did someone deliberately leave one side of the net open, leaving the enemy a way out? Who could have done it?" Seeing no reaction from him, she continued, "Who is the man who always advocates not going on the offensive but universal love, spurns the use of force, sympathises with and pities defeated remnants, and tries hard to oppose being ruthless to enemies? Humph! Misjudgement? Was it a true misjudgement?"

In fact, it was after she had weighed the pros and cons that she decided to say these words, knowing that they could easily remind Ji Zhenren of the historical figure Kai Qie, and *The Sad Record of a Strategy for Peace*, thereby putting HE at risk of being deciphered. She could not think that much. She had to strike back in such a way. But of course, she knew that he was not the kind of person to deliberately let the enemy escape.

After hearing her words, Ji Zhenren was speechless for a long time. Then he said, "To reflect too much on a mistake compounds the mistake. As long as we have turned bad into good, there will be no way for maggots to become flies!"

Liu Hongmei, who had fallen ill, also thought a lot about this misjudgement of information. When she heard the news that several thousand of the enemy had fled east, she turned the matter over and over in her mind. Although she was ill and weak, one day she walked nearly fifty kilometres to see the senior commander. What she and Gao Yuncao said was as if they had been cut from the same cloth.

The senior commander said, "RSU2 has provided us with thousands upon thousands of fragments of intelligence with few misjudgements. So some occasional carelessness is normal. Especially when the situation on the battlefield was extremely complicated, besides, the enemy had stopped using transceivers for a long time, and later they completely gave up using wireless equipment, so it was easy for others to make a misjudgement. I'm afraid it is not good to elevate the matter to the level of principle and ideology."

Liu Hongmei had a fit of bad coughing, spitting out sputum with blood. She said, "This misjudgement is not a small matter. Ji Zhenren was in charge of the team. What caused him to make this error? I suggest the higher authorities investigate it. It's not that I want to show I'm totally impartial before blood relations, but in my heart of hearts, I object to any uncertainty existing in intelligence work."

Very soon the higher-ups sent a team to investigate this case. After enquiries, examinations and studies, they came to the following conclusion, "There is no evidence to show that the enemy was let off deliberately, or that the error was committed subjectively." They publicised the investigation's conclusions for everyone to supervise.

Liu Hongmei and Gao Yuncao stopped suspecting Ji Zhenren, who also stopped suspecting Gao Yuncao. He asked himself, "Driven by professional habits, everyone doubts everything, is it a good thing or a bad thing?"

One day, he asked Gao Yuncao and Liu Hongmei, "You two have always firmly believed that I could never be a traitor, but why did you suspect that I had let the enemy escape?"

"They are essentially two completely different things," replied Liu Hongmei.

"For twenty years the KMT army has never put down its butcher's knife to slaughter us. One more enemy runs away, one day later peace comes. You tell me what reason is there for me to let them run away?" asked Ji Zhenren.

"Set the enemy free for one day, suffer for generations. Everyone knows about it. Don't you see that we were conscientious about this matter? It was to play a joke on you, to seek some fun on the lonely field of battle," chuckled Gao Yuncao.

"Be serious," yelled Ji Zhenren.

"Who was playing a joke with him? I was serious!" grumbled Liu Hongmei.

After the Liaoning-Shenyang campaign ended, RSU2 followed the Northeast Field Army and took part in the Beiping (Beijing)-Tianjin campaign. As key cryptographers, Ji Zhenren, Gao Yuncao and Liu Hongmei continued making new contributions to cracking enemy ciphers.

Only then did RSU2 submit a telegram to the higher-ups to prove that Ji Zhenren did not defect when he was captured by the enemy.

But the higher-ups thought this telegram also proved another fact, namely, that Ji Zhenren was indeed deliberately released by the enemy. No one knew the enemy's motive, so one telegram could not remove the question mark hanging over him. After he returned to RSU2, he had to work under observation.

For this, Liu Hongmei raised havoc in the office of the Central Department of Social Affairs. One of her remarks lacked logic, so the others seized upon this mistake. She said, "How is the telegram not good enough to prove his innocence? In these years, it happened often that one telegram saved this revolutionary army. Why can't a telegram save a devoted veteran Red Army cryptographer?"

The people from the Central Department of Social Affairs sent to talk to Liu Hongmei were Zhang Jiayin, who had become the leader of the organisation, and his wife Liu Hai'er. Hearing Liu Hongmei's remarks, Liu Hai'er went into a rage, "In your mind, Ji Zhenren equates with one revolutionary army. Has RSU2 always dealt with personal problems in such a way? What political awareness is this? Is a telegram from RSU2 a decree of special pardon? Or a death exemption card (a certificate of exoneration dating back to imperial times)?"

Pounding the table hard, Liu Hongmei stood up angrily. She bellowed, "What you said is right. RSU2's telegrams are sometimes indeed a death exemption card! Because they have saved countless revolutionary officers and men from losing their lives. This is an iron-clad fact. Liu Hai'er, it seems that you are prejudiced against RSU2! Listen, you can smear and denounce me by using whatever words you want, or make things as difficult as you can for Ji Zhenren, but you can't make improper comments about RSU2. You have no right to do it.

If this attitude of yours represents the Central Department of Social Affairs, then let's go to the senior leader and ask him to judge who is right and who is wrong."

Soon after this incident, Gao Yuncao, Liu Hongmei and some of the RSU2 staff took part in the ceremony when the PLA entered the city of Beijing on 3 February 1949.

The truck they were in drove into the city from the Yongding Gate. Gao Yuncao saw a sea of people inside and outside the gate. The sound of firecrackers, drums, gongs, cheers and shouted slogans resounded in unison. This ancient city was seething with excitement. When passing the Legation Quarter, the column of trucks was surrounded by the welcoming masses. Some students climbed on the trucks and pasted up slogans. Gao Yuncao had two strips of paper stuck on her back. Brimming with happiness, she was unusually excited. She asked for another one with 'Long Live the Communist Party' and stuck it on her breast. Suddenly, she shivered a bit and she couldn't help but tremble.

Chief Gao, who was standing beside her, asked, "Comrade Yuncao, why are you excited?"

She blurted out, "Although I am among the army entering the city, I still feel that I'm a spectator."

"You're wrong," said Chief Gao. "How can the people from RSU2 be spectators? Not only this city, but even the new China that is to be established has bricks added by you. You and every comrade in this column are worthy masters of the new Beijing and the new China."

She was inwardly startled. Hurriedly, she covered her mouth with her hands; blowing out a cold breath, she then grinned broadly, "Masters of the new China? Worthy masters? Is it true? How glorious I am."

Then she heard Liu Hongmei muttering indignantly, "Ji Zhenren and Zhu Kexin should have also been in this column. They are also masters of the new China and the new Beijing. They deserve it."

PART 3
KEY WORDS

I FEEL that among the women of the Ji family, Liu Hongmei had the most wretched life. A child bride, after she grew up and joined the revolutionary ranks, her fiancé died, so did her later sweethearts Li Mozi and Zhu Kexin. When I went through these historical records, before I could feel sorry for her, I discovered that she was nearing her end herself.

At the time, she did not expect that the following intelligence she gathered would be her last as a cryptographer:

> Between April and May 1949, after Nanjing and Shanghai were liberated one after another, Chiang Kai-shek attempted to use Chongqing as his 'wartime capital' once again. He was planning to take the southwest as a 'base for resurgence', pulling back the main forces of the Bai Chongxi and Hu Zongnan cliques to the southwest and waiting for a change in the international situation to stage a comeback.

This was the comprehensive intelligence she submitted to the high command after she had analysed enemy telegrams at all levels. Although brief, the appendix was very detailed, amounting to 37 items, totalling 6,283 words.

After receiving intelligence from all sources that Chiang Kai-shek was planning defence affairs in the southwest, the high command immediately carried out preparations for combat operations in the southwest region. Before long, a secret mission was assigned to Liu

Hongmei. She was to lead a team to sneak into the city proper and the outskirts of Chongqing to carry out wireless reconnaissance.

It was a routine action they knew well and could manage with ease, so there was nothing special about it. No one knew that a sub-task was hidden behind the main mission, or to put it another way, that the main mission was designed to cover the sub-task. Liu Hongmei shouldered another secret mission, namely, she was to independently fulfil a secret task codenamed 'Owl One'.

That evening, she walked out of the place where they had taken cover. Turning in and out of two lanes, she went to a snack store and pretended to buy food. After confirming that she was not being tailed, she beckoned a rickshaw. After many turns through lanes and travelling via a roundabout route, the rickshaw arrived at the gate of 178 Xiangnaohe Road.

The rickshaw did not stop but dashed into a dark alley. She called out, "Stop! You've driven past it." The rickshaw stopped and turned around. Realising that things were not right, she drew her revolver on the rickshaw puller, but it was too late. She was hit on the head by a blunt instrument and she lost consciousness.

The rickshaw puller quickly ran to the bottom of the hill. Liu Hongmei faintly felt that she was on the puller's shoulder and was being carried to a deep valley.

When she recovered consciousness, she saw the rickshaw puller looking through a pile of paper. She knew that they were the documents she was carrying. Blood streaming down her head, she struggled to sit up and stretched one hand out to grab the papers. The rickshaw puller gave a peculiar smile and pushed her to the floor. She struggled with all her might, trying to rip the mask off the rickshaw puller's face. She wanted to see the true face of the evil man. She missed but locked her hand on his throat. The rickshaw puller had quick reactions. Pulling a button off his jacket, he pushed it into Liu Hongmei's mouth. She fell on her back, feeling her arms and legs go weak and limp. But her mind was clear. She saw the rickshaw puller pushing the papers back into her jacket pocket. Then he walked to a dead tree blown over by gales, where a deep hole had been created when the tree was uprooted.

"What is done by night appears by day. In the last few days, you sneaked into the demon's den. I was secretly watching you. Today, I let these documents be buried with you, because I want to let the King of

Hell know that you did not die unjustly." With a mixed expression in his eyes, the rickshaw puller muttered something else and his tone was chill, "You only have yourself to blame, but you must die. You are so incurable that you can't blame me for this. Luckily, an excellent naturally-made grave belongs to you." While mumbling, he carved *YI* on the tree trunk.

As soon as the puller opened his mouth to speak, the familiar voice was like a thunderbolt. Liu Hongmei was in an absolute panic. As her eyes popped out, she lost consciousness.

'Owl One' was an operation of the intelligence department of the Central Department of Social Affairs. Within RSU2, except for Chief Gao, only Liu Hongmei, who was to execute the task, knew about it. After arriving in Chongqing, she had ordered her team to carry out the set reconnaissance work, while secretly she made preparations for 'Owl One' alone.

First, she needed to approach the KMT's secret service bureau, the Baomiju. Chief Gao had prepared a big bag of confidential documents for her to use as bait for the KMT secret agent Zhen Yanli, the occupant of 178 Xiangnaohe Road. With these documents, Zhen Yanli could take her to knock open the door of the Baomiju.

Taking these confidential documents to 178 Xiangnaohe Road was the key link of the whole operation, so she went to the address twice before bringing the documents with her.

For Chief Gao and her, every link in the operation had been devised perfectly, so there could be no reason for Zhen Yanli to be suspicious. In fact, it went quite smoothly.

However, unexpectedly a third eye was watching in the dark. Before Liu Hongmei could step into the gate of number 178, a rickshaw puller killed her.

When the rickshaw puller carried her to the tree hole, she was still conscious, so she immediately guessed how the operation would end, "Operation 'Owl One' has only just started, but it has met an early and untimely end. I am dead before the ship even sinks."

The disastrous situation could not be remedied, yet Chief Gao knew nothing about it. He thought that Liu Hongmei had successfully infiltrated the enemy camp.

Following the original plan, he went to discuss with the Central

Department of Social Affairs and the PLA Headquarters the issuing of a secret order, "None of the troops entering Chongqing must go and disrupt the occupants of 178 Xiangnaohe Road."

Then he ordered, "Put off the reconnaissance operation. The team needs to withdraw from Chongqing at once and return to RSU2 headquarters and await further orders."

He gave no explanation to the team members, but he wrote a secret report to the Central Department of Social Affairs, "The first stage of operation 'Owl One' has been completed without any trouble."

For Liu Hongmei and operation 'Owl One', this outcome was a disastrous mishap; for RSU2, it would be an empty wait into the distant future; for 178 Xiangnaohe Road, it was a remarkable escape by the skin of its teeth because, before the offensive on Chongqing, the PLA troops had originally planned to capture this KMT spy stronghold.

One evening several days previously, an uninvited guest had visited 178 Xiangnaohe Road.

In the dark, Zhen Yanli examined the visitor for a long time before recognising that the visitor was Liu Hongmei whom she had not seen for a long time.

Just as when they had parted several years ago, Liu Hongmei passionately kissed Zhen Yanli on her cheeks. Mixed feelings welled up in Zhen Yanli's mind. Pushing away the passionate Liu Hongmei, she said, "Stop it. You are as coquettish as ever, no change at all in all these years. I can't stand it."

Again Liu Hongmei threw herself at Zhen Yanli who turned and went to her bedroom. With flushed cheeks and shyness in her eyes, Liu Hongmei followed Zhen Yanli into the room.

Immediately Zhen Yanli took out a bag and pushed it toward Liu Hongmei. "Shameless girl. Is it worthy for you to play such a game for this small amount of money? Everything is here, not a penny less."

Taking the money, a new light flashed in Liu Hongmei's eyes. Zhen Yanli laughed, "A moment ago, it was a sensual desire, but now it is a material desire. You have not changed, full of desires as before. I have indeed made a correct judgement about you. I was waiting for you to bring a gun to my house to collect your money, never expecting you to be as coquettish as before."

When Liu Hongmei went to the address the second time, Zhen

Yanli and Liu Hongmei closed a deal for a large intelligence trade. If this were to be a success, apart from making money, Liu Hongmei would fulfil a wish of hers, which was that she would not go back to the Communists. She had formally proposed to Zhen Yanli that she wanted to cross over to the KMT side.

After Liu Hongmei left, Zhen Yanli immediately reported the deal to her superior, who then recalled that Grasshopper Gao Yuncao had sent him a telegram, saying that Liu Hongmei, medic Liu and nurse Zhang had been captured by the communists in one haul. But now Liu Hongmei had come back to life, and in the name of a Communist cryptographer she had come to Chongqing to sell intelligence. So he decided to beat her at her own game. He would take her, then carefully scrutinise her identity, mainly to see if the goods she was providing were true or fake, or weighty enough.

Zhen Yanli murmured to herself, "I hope she will not miss the appointment. I'm hoping that before we retreat to Taiwan, I can hook a big fish and bring her to Taiwan."

For many days, she had stayed at home waiting eagerly for Liu Hongmei.

25 /I AM NOT MYSELF

ON THE EVE of the liberation of Chongqing, Liu Hongmei's life came to
an end. I really don't have the heart to carelessly write this ending to
my story. For many years, I had tried my best and wholeheartedly to
find out the truth about her death. In the end, after reading a confession
from a pile of historical documents, I suddenly understood it.

It was the second day of the New Year in 1953. Gao Yuncao walked
into Chief Gao's office, handing him a 48-page document.

Rather than giving Chief Gao a salute, she bowed deeply to him.
She then stood there bolt upright, her body as stable as Mount Tai, her
expression solemn, respectful, resolute and steadfast.

Yes, these are very appropriate words to describe her at the time.

Regarding her unusual behaviour, Chief Gao was not afraid but
calm and composed. This RSU2 founding father, who had led the unit
for dozens of years and experienced many big events in the process of
the Chinese revolutionary wars, had toughened his firm political
convictions and first-class psychological quality. Nothing in the world
could startle him any more.

"What? You said that you are a spy, an enemy of ours? I tell you I
don't believe it! Comrade Yuncao, have you been driven insane by the
damned GUANGFU-11? Or scared out of your wits? You want to beat a
retreat?" Sweeping his eyes over the title on the first page, his tone was
as steady and unhurried as usual, "Cryptographers are always weird
and neurotic. I give in. Put it here. I will find time to read it. Go."

Gao Yuncao did not move. She called out, "I want to make a
confession!"

Chief Gao maintained his composure, saying, "Haven't I accepted your written confession? Go, go."

"Where do you want me to go? I should go to the military court! You should send me to prison!" Gao Yuncao was enraged by his indifference.

Chief Gao was angry, shouting: "Your mind has been confused by GUANGFU-11. I can wait until your head is cleared. But I tell you, GUANGFU-11 waits for no one. If it cannot be deciphered, you can't go anywhere. Go back to your work now."

Gao Yuncao's confession, which she had planned for many years, was dismissed as a trifling matter. What was more, in the following months Chief Gao did not mention a single word about it.

She thought that she might be arrested after GUANGFU-11 was deciphered. After all, in Chief Gao's eyes deciphering code was the most important thing. Nothing could shake this fundamental principle of his.

In the following days, she felt that she was being secretly watched. She knew that they were Chief Gao's informers.

Three months later, GUANGFU-11 was deciphered and, of course, Gao Yuncao had played the leading role.

GUANGFU-11 was an advanced cipher the KMT put to use at the beginning of the year. The intelligence obtained from the messages encrypted by it was extremely important, because it was all about Taiwan launching a counteroffensive on the mainland. Therefore, RSU2 awarded Gao Yuncao for her meritorious military service.

When Chief Gao handed the certificate to Gao Yuncao, she fixed her eyes on him, thinking, "I know what he's got up his sleeve. He's so funny. Before he throws me into prison, he hangs a medal round my neck." Then her eyes welled up, she said inwardly, "This is the last time I'll stand with everybody here as a 'comrade'. My life as a cryptographer is ending, but I can finally walk into the light."

After the victory meeting ended, she got her blanket roll ready. She sat on the edge of her bed, solemnly waiting for the moment to arrive.

But nothing happened.

She could still move around as usual.

She had kept a copy of her confession. Before long, she bypassed Chief Gao and presented a 50-page confession to the higher authorities. The two additional pages were to report Chief Gao for shielding his subordinate, and for keeping a case from being reported and for the fact that there was a spy, but he did not arrest her.

She waited and waited.

In the end, two people came. One was Zhang Jiayin and one was Liu Hai'er. Without the usual ferocious look of investigators, they presented her with two smiling faces.

Gao Yuncao yelled, "I'm a criminal, comrades! Well, yes, I have no qualification to address you as comrades any more."

Still smiling, Zhang Jiayin said, "Before the Beiping-Tianjin campaign, Liu Hai'er and I witnessed in person your action toward the KMT secret agents in Tianjin, so we don't believe you're a KMT spy, comrade sister!"

Again she shouted, "You take such a perfunctory attitude toward my political life, and disrespect a criminal who opens her heart to the Party, you are neglecting your duty."

With smiling faces Zhang Jiayin and Liu Hai'er showed her a parcel, in which there was a shirt and a piece of paper. The shirt had a button missing, and the paper had a few lines which read: "About 760 metres into the valley on the south face of Caogang Ridge in Chongqing there is an old pine tree with the word 'joy' carved on the main trunk. From this carving, walk due south thirteen steps, there is a big withered tree tilted on the ground. In the hole under the tree root is buried a woman's skeleton with a poisoned button in its mouth."

As soon as she read it, she knew that this was the note she had sent to RSU2 anonymously six months ago. The matter had once been circulating among the unit staff, but in the end it went quiet. Later, she went to Chongqing on a business trip. Secretly she went to Caogang Ridge, finding that under that old withered tree, weeds and bushes were growing. It was obvious that no one had dug up the grave. She then knew that her parcel had been sent in vain, which let her finally make the decision to present her 48-page confession to Chief Gao.

"Did you send that parcel?" asked Zhang Jiayin.

She nodded. Zhang Jiayin asked no more, but said, "Tomorrow, come to Chongqing with us." The tone was indifferent, as if they were talking about letting her go on an unimportant business trip.

Helped by Chongqing's public security bureau, they did dig up a human skeleton with a button in its mouth, a leather bag under the rotten clothes and a pile of papers inside the bag. Some words on the papers were still recognisable.

Gao Yuncao thought that somebody would handcuff her, but it did not happen. Leisurely and carefree she returned to city B.

Before long, the investigation result came:

1. After a lab test, it was established that the button in the mouth of the skeleton was the one that had fallen from the shirt in the mail parcel. Potassium cyanide was found on the button.

2. After the confidential department's identification, the documents with the skeleton were identified as classified materials belonging to RSU2.

3. Coroners identified the skeleton as belonging to a female. The bodily form and height were basically consistent with that of Liu Hongmei who was suspected to have been murdered.

4. Although the word carved on the old pine was deformed, it could still be recognised as *'joy'*.

Chief Gao was dumbstruck by the news, then in front of Gao Yuncao he was in tears, sighing, "I thought she had gone to the place where she should have gone. I never expected that she had died a long time ago. Great hero, your death is so unjust!"

Gao Yuncao was in great shock, "What great hero? What unjust death? For that kind of person, wouldn't even death be too good for her? Yes, she did contribute to cracking enemy ciphers, and she was your great hero, but she changed afterwards. She turned into a bad person."

Chief Gao ignored her.

Looking blank, Gao Yuncao said, "It seems that I killed your great hero. But I had no choice. She had all the secrets of our party and army in her head, besides, she was carrying some extremely important documents with her. I could not sit and watch her defect to the enemy with our secrets. A cryptographer defecting to the enemy with confidential documents would have revealed every secret of RSU2. What I feared most was such a thing and it really happened. If it were something else, I could have turned a blind eye. But when such a thing happened, I had to kill her."

Then she added something that she forgot to write in her confession, "That button had been on my shirt for many years and its toxicity was greatly reduced. So, when I put it into her mouth, she didn't die immediately. It can be said that I buried your great hero alive. The reason for me killing her was that this hopeless evil traitor had enraged me. Although she had saved my life, in that urgent moment, I had no other choice."

"Did you really kill her?" Chief Gao's eyes were blood red. Glowering at Gao Yuncao, he shouted, "Evidence! I want evidence! If I have the evidence, I will never let you off lightly."

"Aren't they enough?" Gao Yuncao was at a loss, "Was I wrong to get rid of a traitor? I was a KMT spy then, didn't I redeem myself by ridding us of a traitor?"

No one would give her an answer .

In the end, she was taken into custody, but not formally charged for lack of evidence.

Zhang Jiayin and Liu Hai'er explained to her, "There is evidence to prove that you did murder Liu Hongmei at Caogang Ridge in Chongqing. But we need to investigate the motives. We can't just listen to your statement. You told us that you killed her to protect our army's secrets. But other people were of the view that, as a covert spy, you killed our unknown hero. So it's very important for us to find out your true identity. Is it true that you are a KMT spy, as you said in your confession? Currently we have no direct evidence. An ancient book that was used by the KMT as a cipher is the key evidence. We have sent people to several big cities to search in the libraries, but to no avail. Although people can prove that this book existed, and they can even remember the general content of it, memories cannot be used as direct evidence. So, the copy you wrote down from memory is naturally invalid. What we need is the original copy of *The Sad Record of a Strategy for Peace*. Currently, all we have is that you proved yourself to be a KMT spy, which basically means nothing. But due to the special nature of RSU2, as well as the fact that you claim to be guilty and, in addition to that, our higher authorities suspect that you are a spy, we won't take a *laissez-faire* attitude. If we cannot obtain direct evidence for a long time, you will be kept in custody for a long time to come. To be honest, for this case there is indeed not enough legal basis. However, we have no choice but to arrest you because you are a core member of RSU2. In view of this, the higher authorities have authorised a special policy for you: in the name of being a suspect awaiting trial, you will stay in the detention centre of the military confidential system until direct evidence is found to prove whether you are guilty or not. This is a special case among special cases and it only applies to you."

"I'll wait!" said Gao Yuncao. "No matter what happens to me, I'll have no complaints or regrets. You must believe me. After I presented my 48-page confession, I truly felt that I had been reborn. What is Phoenix Nirvana? What is a new lease of life? I have personally experienced it."

Zhang Jiayin and Liu Hai'er laughed, "Gao Yuncao, what can we say about you? Well, well…"

It was not until 1969 that Gao Yuncao was released from the detention centre. The first thing she did was to submit an application to the organisation for permission to change her name from Gao Yuncao to Xia Yuhe.

"I must change my name, to signify that I have put all those years behind me. Neither Jiang Xiaodian nor Gao Yuncao is as significant as Xia Yuhe. What is on the decline will wane, but what is to be reborn will be reborn eventually. I will use this new name until I die," she said.

26 /BEING INTIMATE WITH THE ENEMY

IF MY MEMORY serves me well, the material for the following story comes from three sources, *Selected Espionage Cases Involving Taiwan*, the oral account of my grandfather Ji Zhenren and an interview with the Dadongshan prison police.

Because the main characters play the same leading roles in the previous stories, I've decided not to describe too many of the minor details, but to narrate the gist of the story, as I feel that the details are not important. The key is to explain clearly the causality for result A, rather than result B.

What I am going to tell you about is an espionage case involving Taiwanese businessmen, which was cracked by the state security department in the early 1990s.

It is an odd case and the oddity lies herein:

A Taiwanese couple opened three businesses in succession in the mainland's Fujian area. They also set up an office in city B. The legal representatives were a young couple, but the true operator and manager was a rich old woman.

This elderly businesswoman looked about seventy years old. Everything she was selling was related to old people. Her business was in a slump, but she never bothered about it. She was busy, not with her business but with making friends with old people. In the beginning, people thought that she did so to sell her goods but later they found out that she had a special interest in former servicemen who had gone through the war years and was particularly fond of asking about those who had worked in the central organisations and what they had done.

The wind was blown into the national security organisation, so this Taiwanese-funded company was being watched by the national secret services.

It is not illegal to make friends and enquire about people, but the secret services found that the telegrams the old woman sent to Taiwan were strange. They were like account bills with messy numbers, seemingly she was reporting to headquarters about sales. But after a careful study, her company was not big and the business was half-dead, so how could it have been dealing with such large sums of money?

The secret services got a few telegrams and sent them to the related security department for examination. Soon the result came back. The cipher used to encrypt the telegrams was book-based. But they could not decipher it due to lack of deciphering conditions.

Therefore, the case was regarded as having no direct evidence. The reason was very simple. Not everyone who goes to a telegraph office to send coded messages is a spy, because what they are sending may be their business secrets.

So the case was put aside until one day, when the old woman enquired about veteran revolutionaries, she mentioned a mystical name: Ji Zhenren. This brought the case closer to being considered as a case of spying, according to the secret services. However, they found that she only enquired about him but with no practical actions. One can't say that anyone enquiring about Ji Zhenren must be a spy.

So they called Ji Zhenren back from his travelling lectures about revolutionary education, arranging for him to watch the old woman for a few days. He told them that he did not know her. Then, he suggested his wife Xia Yuhe take up the job, because she had sharp eyes.

Xia Yuhe stayed in a dark corner and watched the old woman for a few days. Her conclusion was that the old woman was called Zhen Yanli and had experience of being a KMT spy. Then she said, "If you believe me, you can tell me more about her recent circumstances. But how much I can help depends on how much you tell me."

The security people were extremely cautious. They said nothing but gave her the telegrams. She had a read, then she took out *The Sad Record of a Strategy for Peace*, a hand-written copy. She said that she had written it down from memory, but she could guarantee that compared to the original copy, her hand-written version was not a page short, had not a line wrong and not a word missing.

But with regard to this hand-written copy, the related department had already responded that they did not trust it.

Anyway, the telegrams were successfully deciphered and the contents were presented to the security department but their response was that "it's hard to tell if the hand-written copy is true to the original, so the deciphering is untrustworthy."

There was another reason for them not to believe her. There were no secrets at all in the telegrams. The contents were only about dates and which veterans of the Red Army and the Eighth Route Army she had met. One telegram was quite interesting, saying that after a long search she had heard nothing about Ji Zhenren, requesting if she could directly ask about of Gao Yuncao's whereabouts.

Patting the telegram, Xia Yuhe said, "This makes it clear that she's still a spy. You can arrest her."

But the response from the security people was as usual, "Why should we believe you?"

Xia Yuhe was enraged, shouting, "You don't believe anything I say. Alright, I've come up with an idea. Go to a telegraph office. In Zhen Yanli's name we'll encrypt a telegram via *The Sad Record of a Strategy for Peace* and send it to the head office of that company, telling them that the whereabouts of Ji Zhenren have been confirmed and let their head come to the mainland as soon as possible."

Seeing the listeners were responsive, she went on, "I know her boss is called Gao Q. Yes, in our telegram we state that he must bring the original edition of *The Sad Record of a Strategy for Peace* with him." Seeing the listeners nod their heads, she was more enthusiastic, saying, "The original edition of the book is important to this case, and more important to an unsettled case in 1953. Once we're in possession of the original edition of the book, many doubts and suspicions can be cleared up at once."

Although the security people nodded their heads, they still only half-believed it. So they told Ji Zhenren about the situation and took him to see Chief Gao who was ill in bed. But his brains still worked well. He cried out, "I agree! Do it and we can get twice the result with half the effort."

Cautiously the security department went through the procedure and they received approval from the higher authorities. Ji Zhenren drafted the telegram. After reading it, Chief Gao made some corrections. The security people went to a telegraph office and sent the fake telegram.

As expected, the Taiwan side took the bait. As soon as Gao Q entered the Chinese mainland with the book, he was arrested. Very soon the book was sent to the relevant state department to confirm its authenticity. The result was that the copy was printed in the early years of the Qing dynasty, the genuine ancient book that was out of print.

Soon, they announced the case had been broken. It was not a big case. In the years when Gao Q and Zhen Yanli were on the mainland doing business, they neither stole any state secrets, nor did anything illegal, nor did they engage in any espionage activities. Only their enquiry about the whereabouts of Ji Zhenren was considered as sensitive, to which they confessed everything.

In the end, the department with jurisdiction over the matter confirmed that as early as the 1960s, Gao Q and Zhen Yanli had broken away from the espionage organisation in Taiwan, so now they had no spy background. What the couple had intended to do was to find their old friends Gao Yuncao and Ji Zhenren to ease two troubles on their minds.

First, the KMT spy, Grasshopper, Gao Yuncao, was in hibernation for years, then she was exposed, and then she was turned by the Communists to serve them. How did this happen? And what were the details?

Second, after the Liaoning-Shenyang Campaign ended, the KMT armies were equipped with new portable transceivers with built-in encryption. Teaming up with the experts from foreign armies, Gao Q, Zhen Yanli and other KMT cryptographers meticulously did the research and developed such transceivers. After tests at multiple levels, they were put to use on the battlefield. The KMT Special Secret Wireless Section were very pleased with themselves, thinking that messages sent by such transceivers would be extremely difficult to decipher, so they could finally put an end to the problem of their ciphers being repeatedly cracked by the Communists. Until they retreated to Taiwan, these transceivers were commonly used and were praised by the KMT troops as 'life transceivers', 'never-die ciphers' and 'evergreen trees' to convey the KMT intelligence. For this achievement, Gao Q was awarded the highest grade of medal in his life. However, he could never have imagined that soon after these transceivers were deployed, the messages sent by them were deciphered by the Communists. Afterwards, messages sent by the improved model were also deciphered by the Communists. They did not know this fatal information until many years later in Taiwan, for which Gao Q was heavily punished. He and Zhen Yanli were puzzled despite giving it a lot of thought. Under the technical circumstances at the time, how did the Communists obtain and unlock the mystery of these new transceivers?

These two questions did not constitute any threat to the secrets of the mainland from a long time ago, so they wanted to resolve the puzzles, which had stayed in their minds for many years. In fact, it was because they could not forget either things that had happened in the past, or their old friends and old friendships. What they wanted was nothing more than to hunt for old friends, so that they could resolve old puzzles, renew friendships, untangle the knot in their minds, seek affinity and dismiss old grudges from their hearts.

From the viewpoint of settling a case, it was beyond belief but from a humanitarian point of view, it seemed understandable.

Although it could not be counted as a major case, the book brought in from Taiwan and some of the original telegrams solved the backlog of the KMT spy suspect case in 1953.

The whole truth of the thirty-year pending case had come out!

A key piece of evidence for this case was a letter delivered by a carrier pigeon. Gao Q and Zhen Yanli confirmed that they had received the original letter. They clearly recalled the contents, which tallied with what Gao Yuncao had confessed in 1953. The letter indeed contained some important information about RSU2. Now, a human witness was available, but the material evidence was lacking.

Through the arrangement of the related department, Gao Q, who expressed that he would cooperate actively, returned to Taiwan. He then brought some of the declassified material and files, including the original copies of that letter and two other telegrams to the mainland. The letter delivered by pigeon was enough to prove that Gao Yuncao was guilty; but the two telegrams (in one telegram she falsely claimed that *ZHE* and *YU* had been deciphered by the Communists, in another telegram she secretly supported the strategic trick of the Communists to cross the Yellow River and ask for the release of Wang Qiangui) could prove that she had rendered merit. Especially the second telegram that clearly told the truth about Ji Zhenren having been captured and released in the Battle of Hujiayu, thereby removing the historical doubt about Ji Zhenren.

In order to get this material to restore the truth, Gao Q had made strenuous efforts in Taiwan, employing special skills from his old profession.

No matter what, this case was finally clear. The party involved had confessed everything. Both witness testimony and material evidence were available and the facts of the crime and the motive were also clear. In view of this, twenty-two years after she was released from detention, Gao Yuncao was sentenced again. A two-year prison sentence was added, therefore this special prisoner, who had changed her name from Gao Yuncao to Xia Yuhe, served another two years in Dadangshan prison. Along with the sixteen-year detention, she was in prison twice for a total of eighteen years.

This was no ordinary case. The related matters were sensitive, so the related department limited the number of people who knew about the details of the case. Even the descendants of the party concerned knew nothing about the truth.

Two years later, Xia Yuhe was released from prison. Her son and daughter-in-law went to meet her. As soon as she saw them, she said, "Ha-ha. Two archaeologists have come to meet me, too wonderful for words! There you are, in the guise of archaeologists you often went to the mountains and islands to gather intelligence, having engaged in covert but glorious operations for half of your lives. Hey, why are you standing there staring blankly at me? Hurry up, let's go home."

The son came back to his senses and went to support her, "Watch your feet."

"I'm not that old, no need to support me." Pushing away her son's hands, she walked away with a steady stride.

The daughter-in-law laughed, "Mother is so high-spirited, like a general who has just won a victory."

The son also laughed, "Who ever saw such a person released after serving her sentence?"

27 /TAKING THE BLAME

ON MY GRANDFATHER'S 104th birthday, Central Television conducted a special interview with him. The host sincerely praised his amazing memory, saying that he was "a living archive of Chinese revolutionary war history" and "a forever young soldier on the hidden battlefront of the Chinese revolution".

He laughed heartily, "It's too much of a compliment. For me, what lives forever is my powerful faith, and the professional spirit that it engenders. They're not some high-sounding words but come from the bottom of my heart."

After the TV crew left, he held my hand; it seemed he had a lot to say. Standing before his painting *War Gallery*, he began to tell me a story.

Gao Q, who could only tell lies and boast, has died. Zhen Yanli, who was proud of her power to bewitch all her life, has also died. Zhu Kexin, the clerk who always regarded keeping secrets as his mission also died a long time ago, but he could never have imagined that many years later, his remains would be buried together with the remains of Liu Hongmei near an old pine tree in a valley in Chongqing, and that the tombstone would be inscribed with 'The Grave of Joy'. Xia Yuhe, who paid to have the grave built, would go every year to pay her respects to the dead. Each time, when she stood before the grave, she was grief-stricken. One year she suddenly had a heart attack and, leaning on the old pine tree, she died. She, who had lived in two different worlds for dozens of years, and was imprisoned twice for eighteen years, also died before me.

Gao Q and Zhen Yanli fought a battle of wits with me across the air waves. It's alright that they died before me. But how could Xia Yuhe have left me without holding on until the last minute. I regard her as a heartless woman, yet I am an infatuated old man. In the days after she died, I was heartbroken. Today I'm 104 years old, and I must talk to her about these things otherwise I will take them to the grave with me.

My old wife, do you want to talk about what happened in the past? Forget it, don't talk about them anymore. For us who know 'too much', the biggest taboo is to avoid being a regular chatterbox. It's alright if we don't talk about them.

Oh, but I feel we can still talk about the things between you and me.

Many years ago, in a shocking way, you put yourself in prison, thereby ending your political life. But you said this was self-redemption and repentance so that you were reborn. Good for you. To seek rebirth, you swallowed the bitterness of an eighteen-year spell in prison with no complaints and no regrets. You also dragged me in. I was held accountable, punished and removed from office. I paid such a high price for being related to you, yet you felt that you had no choice but to do it, and I could not avoid the consequences.

I remember at the time I made an unprincipled joke. I said, "Ever since I stepped over the threshold of RSU2, Chief Gao and the organisation overtly and covertly did their best to protect me. They resisted and prevented many political disasters from landing on me to ensure that I, RSU2's key cryptographer, was able to single-mindedly crack ciphers. In those years, the enemy secret services were also watching me closely. They wanted very much to kill me to break the sharp sword of the Communists, but they never got their way. Ha-ha, it was you, by giving yourself up, who ended my professional life, thereby cutting me off from my ciphers."

Hearing my words, you did not panic but said, "I thought about it on our wedding night. In the years afterwards I wasn't exposed. By following the trend of development, I was able to remain unscathed all my life. But I did not expect to subconsciously undergo a change in my political convictions. I never thought that beliefs could be so powerful. I analysed the situation before I made a confession, guessing that under the prevailing political environment you would be implicated. At least they would expel you from RSU2, or even put you in prison. But I could not restrain myself from confessing. After struggling for years, I was finally able to thoroughly cast off my old self, allowing me to walk to the light in politics and perfect my faith. I didn't mind about other people's comments on my choice. What I couldn't have borne was if the organisation and you had misunderstood me." OK, let me stop this matter here.

But there is one thing I have to say. You were bumptious. Failing to distinguish between true and false. You killed Liu Hongmei, making you doubly guilty and punishable by law. The motive for your killing was good, an error committed due to a strange combination of circumstances, but I failed to intercede with the organisation for you. I could have pleaded for you with favourable evidence, but I didn't. I'm very ashamed. You blame me, counting this as something I owe you.

Besides, the couple who loved books as life itself cannot be forgotten, either. During the Cultural Revolution, the rebel faction ignored the fact that Zhang Jiayin and Liu Hai'er had made great contributions to the revolution on the hidden battlefront but upheld their history of being traitors. The couple were no longer able to endure being paraded through the streets and being publicly denounced, so they fled to their old home in Suzhou. In front of the Luobilou library, in funereal clothes, they read ancient books. They died after an eight-day hunger strike. Just like their ancestor Yuncao, they became immortal among the pages of books.

Yes, another person died even earlier, but recently she often appeared in my dreams. Song Daxiong was another important woman in my life and my most respectable and closest comrade-in-arms. I dare not think about her. In 1949, Gao Yuncao and I went to Yangqu in Shanxi province. We dug up the remains of Qiu Zihao, who died in action in the Hundred Regiments Offensive in 1940. We moved them to Yan'an and buried them together with Song Daxiong. We rebuilt the grave and erected a tombstone. Ever since then either Gao Yuncao or I would go there to pay our respects every other five years.

I'm talking too much, yet I must add something important: after Gao Yuncao released that carrier pigeon in Yan'an, when it stopped at the KMT secret services post in Xi'an, the agents adopted a double safety measure. They dispatched an agent to deliver the original letter to Chongqing but put the transcribed copy in the original tube and used a new pigeon to deliver it to Chongqing. Not until 2013 did we know that this pigeon lost its way either due to bad weather or tiredness. It landed on the roof of a church in Chengdu to take a rest, and accidentally it died there. But the original letter was delivered into the hands of the KMT Special Secret Wireless Section.

My grandfather's eyes moved away from the painting. Then he seemed to remember something, saying, "Give me the hand-written book. My old wife saw the book like I am seeing you. How I miss you!"

Hearing this, I could not help thinking about my grandma, feeling sad. I handed him *The Sad Record of a Strategy for Peace*.

Seemingly lost in thought, he looked at me for a while, then muttered, "Grandson, my that chattering is nothing secret. Today, I'll break the rules and tell you a true secret."

I was overwhelmed by this unexpected favour. For dozens of years, it was the first time for him, who would turn pale at the mention of secrets, to voluntarily talk about them.

In the beginning he was calm. "On the battlefield of the Northeast I misjudged some intelligence, which resulted in the enemy under Pan Ting's command getting away. It was a major error, but the organisation did not investigate me. However, I knew it was my fault. How could a cryptographer make such an error? Why hadn't I more carefully, comprehensively and extensively monitored and studied the situation until I had gathered the precise information? I have regretted that my whole life. It has become the greatest pain in my heart. Whenever I recall it, my heart bleeds."

He became more and more emotional. Slowly, tears covered his face while he beat his breast and stamped his feet. I hurried to console him, "Things on the battlefield are complicated and change fast. It's impossible for intelligence work to be perfect. Besides, Pan's troops had imposed radio silence and you had no messages to hand, so you were cooking a meal without rice. Under such circumstances, it was excusable to have made an error."

He patted the book noisily, saying, "Don't stress objective reasons for the error! It was basically because my professionalism lapsed. I was not professional enough and failed to delve into it more deeply. In short, I wasn't good enough."

He then murmured to himself, "Why did no one blame me? I would have felt better if someone had criticised me."

Looking tired and with his voice trembling a bit, he said, "None of the leaders at any level blamed me, there wasn't even a word of criticism. But when I did a good job, they all remembered to praise me, not missing a single time. Oh, leaders, how could I have made that misjudgement? Why did the organisation not blame me?"

Seeing him in such a state, I was terror-stricken. He had gone down a dead end and sunk into another state of mind. I knew that he had been imprisoned by a distinctive, strange and densely packed sense of guilt. The psychological knot could not be untied for a while, or even forever. No one could undo it.

Worried about his health, I phoned for a doctor, but he stopped me.

He asked me to go home. Holding my hand, he said, "Don't worry, this old fart won't die. But if I do die one day, you must remember that regarding the error I made in the Northeast, although the organisation did not investigate it, I hold myself responsible. My biography must include this sentence: 'Because Comrade Ji Zhenren was not professionally competent and failed to devote himself to his work, he let thousands of the enemy escape, which was a serious crime.' Then along with the 199 words I drafted in 1953, these 228 words are for my biography. Not a word more, not a word less! Otherwise, I will not close my eyes when I die."

Slowly he calmed down. Holding the book in his arms, he closed his eyes and went to sleep.

Quietly I walked out of the room.

But Grandpa did not wake up again.

When I paid my last respects to my deceased grandpa, I was so sad that I slapped my face again and again. What a heartless and unworthy descendant I am! The night before, he was strangely talkative, but I ignored it. He died right under my nose, but I didn't even notice it.

Ji Shan held my hand, urging me not to be too emotional.

Choking with sobs, I said, "Your great-grandpa was depressed by the error he made in the Northeast. He regretted it for the rest of his life and he died of this regret."

Ji Shan said, "This has been written into his biography. This is how he asked to be punished so he would die without regret. Anyway, he was 104 years old and died a natural death. Dad, you shouldn't think about it too much."

I gazed at Ji Shan, then my sadness was replaced by a sorrowful feeling of a different significance — until he died, Grandpa did not know that his coded painting had been deciphered by his wife and his great-granddaughter. I was sure, before he closed his eyes, that he would have been very pleased with himself: I would really bring the secrets of all my life to the grave.

Rest in peace, Grandpa. The things in your painting are not secret any more. They have been declassified in different times by different means. All the signs show that to those core secrets little known to others, you did not paint them in the *War Gallery*. I know you never betrayed your principles about confidentiality. Although you were punished and out of a job, no longer involved with ciphers, your determination to keep your promise was unswerving.

So many feelings welled up in my mind. No matter how, I cannot express enough my sad memories of my grandpa. Let me stop here. I would like to add one sentence to the end of my story, which I spent seven years and worked my back off to write:

A Red Army cryptographer of our party and army, who made brilliant achievements in wartime as well as bearing professional regrets, passed away on his 104th birthday, holding the hand-written ancient book 'The Sad Record of a Strategy for Peace', and before his own coded painting 'War Gallery'.

When Grandpa left this world, my novel came to an end. However, I did not expect that the story had not ended yet.

Here I need to stress a concept. In Chief Gao's words, "RSU2's discipline of confidentiality has always gone beyond affection between blood relations and been strict about our own flesh and blood. Liu Hongmei had never leaked a word to her brother and sister-in-law about the real reason she was sent to Zengjiayan, the Communists' office in Chonqqing. After Ji Zhenren learned the truth from me and the Central Department of Social Affairs, he never let Liu Hongmei know that he knew about her secret identity, still less did he mention it to his wife Gao Yuncao. As husband and wife, except for the projects they worked on together, or what the organisation allowed them to communicate, they had never exchanged any confidential information with each other. They all strictly followed this iron discipline, the bottom line and the cardinal principle, and acted in an exemplary way."

I heard this from my son-in-law Wu Yuan. From some soon-to-be declassified files, he read a report submitted by Chief Gao to the senior leaders. I believed beyond a shadow of doubt the version in the file.

In 1953, a certain day after I (Chief Gao) took over Gao Yuncao's 48-page confession, I received Ji Zhenren's self-criticism, in which he reported that as early as at the end of 1944, he began to suspect that his wife Gao Yuncao was a KMT spy.

In those days, Gao Yuncao often behaved strangely, having verbal conflicts with Liu Hongmei for no reason. If not for some fundamental issues tangled in her mind, she ought not to have behaved in such a way. So what led to her mind being so disturbed? Ji Zhenren thought it over, and in the end he was certain that it was about faith. Because, every day she kept talking about it, and mostly she talked about it subconsciously. She always thought about things from the viewpoint of faith, even in ordinary situations, which surprised him.

Not knowing from when, she seemed to be harbouring a deep secret. Looking as though something was seriously wrong with her, she was always making an extraordinary effort to make a fundamental change, to realise some sort of internal impatient yearning. Meanwhile, she tried hard to conceal this change, seeking to calmly realise this secret yearning. It was this hidden hunger of the soul, enough to wither a life, that robbed her of the ability to remain as calm as usual. Naturally, this abnormality in her character was not easy for ordinary people to notice. Those who noticed it first were the ones closest to her.

Ji Zhenren managed to keep calm and composed. He did not say a word about his discovery to anybody. But he began to secretly watch her. No matter whether they were working together or were on separate assignments outside, he tried to learn about her movements, including by using certain technical means to watch her when she was on transceivers transcribing messages. With his technical skills and experience, no one else in RSU2 was aware of what he was doing.

When Gao Yuncao followed the team to the front line, although Ji Zhenren did not go, he was tracking her every move, including the two telegrams she sent to Chongqing, which he intercepted far away at home. She changed her style of sending messages, resulting in his failure to recognise that she was the operator. But because he paid attention to all messages sent from that direction, no matter whether they were transcribed by himself or by other monitors, he designated them as key telegrams to be deciphered. He deduced that if she were to contact the enemy, the only real possibility for her to do that was when she was out on a mission. Despite the two telegrams being buried among a large number of intercepted telegrams from the Japanese and the puppet troops, he still sniffed them out. However, he failed to decipher them for a long time.

One night, he had a dream. It was the third time in years that he had dreamt the same dream, very rare indeed.

It was about a white-faced scholar setting up a stall in the downtown area of Fuzimiao in Nanjing to make money by reciting 667 books. His purpose was to lure an intersexual individual out of hiding and then kill them. In the end, on the 667th book, he betrayed his weakness, and the intersexual individual seized upon his mistake. The book was 'The Sad Record of a Strategy for Peace'. His assassination was declared a failure. In his dream, he understood that the white-faced scholar was himself, but the intersexual individual was a pair, one was called Jiang Xiaodian and the other was called Gao Q.

As someone who had read 'The Sad Record of a Strategy for Peace' many times and knew its content very well and had written heartfelt and opinionated commentaries about it, and as a senior cryptographer who had deciphered numerous enemy ciphers, and as a husband who knew his wife very well, if he had not been able to crack this book-based cipher, it would have disgraced his professional reputation.

Ji Zhenren was Ji Zhenren. In the end, via only two messages, he cracked this book-based cipher.

In that instance, he reached a conclusion: under ordinary circumstances, this cipher would have been unsolvable based on only two short messages. In this world, only one person could have brought about its doom and that was Ji Zhenren, who knew this book and his wife, and who had a great ability to crack ciphers.

When he read the contents of the two telegrams, his tense heart relaxed a bit.

He understood his wife's hard thinking hidden behind the telegrams, and they were typical 'red telegrams'!

Immediately, a concept flashed through his mind: this is a

degenerate KMT covert agent, with none of the distinctive characteristics of a spy.

He reached the decisive conclusion: "Our revolutionary army has turned a KMT sleeper into a qualified Communist, an excellent cryptographer and a loyal nameless hero. She spared no pains to crack the Japanese armies' ciphers and racked her brains to crack the KMT armies' ciphers; she did not do a single bad thing to the Communists when she could have done. Especially when she had the best opportunity to betray the Communist Central Committee's Kunlun Column and she could have escaped unscathed if she had done it, she was not disloyal to the Communists. On the contrary, she was ready to die the cruelest death and cracked many of the KMT's important ciphers. She made a great contribution to the Kunlun Column escaping from danger and accomplishing its strategic goal."

Who could say such a person was a KMT spy? Were there such spies in the world? But incontrovertibly she was a 'damned spy'!

"Should I have reported her? What would the consequences have been? Needless to say this 'damned spy' would have died! I should not have reported her, and there was no need to report her. Let her emerge and perish herself, and then be reborn. Thinking it through, leaving the political aspect aside, but viewed from the practical needs of intelligence work, not reporting her turned out to be the best choice. Otherwise, it could have been a great calamity for her, yet of no benefit to the work at all. As for Chief Gao and the other leaders responsible, as well as her relatives, it would have caused fatal and irreperable damage, greatly reduced and damaged RSU2's deciphering capacity, and particularly have dealt a deadly blow to the professional reputation of RSU2, which was the lifeblood of the unit. Once your reputation was gone, who would have believed your intelligence?"

After the meticulous Ji Zhenren had spoken two more sentences to himself, he set his mind at rest:

"A counter-revolutionary spy had been cultivated by revolutionary forces into a revolutionary force. Under the influence of the sacred cause, she had turned herself into a loyal practitioner, which precisely showed that RSU2's revolutionary force was incomparably powerful and that the revolutionary cause was great beyond compare. It brought no harm to the reputation of RSU2."

"This revolutionary furnace possessed the power as well as the charm to transform decadence into magic. Since she had changed, why did I have to extinguish this magic and turn it into decadence? She was reborn, so why did I have to push her against the revolution again?"

In the end, he had decided for once in his life to be disloyal to the Party. It was the only improper behaviour in his life and the only political stain. But his action did not result in any negative consequences.

In the following days, he had secretly kept a close watch on her. But everything had remained normal for a long time.

In March 1943, Ji Zhenren had been captured by the enemy, and then he was released and allowed to decipher some abandoned undecipherable messages under observation by the security people. During this time, he had discovered the two telegrams that Gao Yuncao had sent to Chongqing and he had deciphered them.

Then he had truly understood her intentions in sending them, either out of impatience to save her husband, or to show the KMT that our Northwest Army had been about to cross the Yellow River to the east bank, thereby helping our army to achieve its strategy of deception. He naturally had nothing to say about this but only murmured inwardly: several times she had risked being exposed, but quietly did what was beneficial to the revolution.

Between the end of the Liaoning-Shenyang Campaign and the start of the Beiping-Tianjin Campaign, a special mission had been assigned to Gao Yuncao, which had again confronted her with a rigorous test.

At that time, the KMT troops had been equipped with a new type of transceiver, which caused a lot of trouble for RSU2's monitors and cryptographers.

Ji Zhenren had been clear that if they had wanted to solve this complicated mechanical encryption technology, they had to get hold of an actual transceiver for structural analysis.

The related department of the higher authority took the matter seriously and soon the decision was made for a special mission. The difficulty for the mission was that they had to ensure that the enemy were not aware of the true intention of the mission, otherwise the enemy would have taken measures, such as strengthening the technical difficulties, or terminating the use of this type of transceiver, to prevent their communications from being breached.

The higher authorities coordinated different sections of the Central Department of Social Affairs, a certain unit of the field army, RSU2 and the underground in Tianjin, to transfer people to form a special crack operation team to jointly accomplish this mission. For RSU2, one of the conditions for being selected was familiarity with the enemy cipher situation and mastery of the technology for both encryption and decryption, as well as a high level of English-language ability. Ji Zhenren, Gao Yuncao and Liu Hongmei were selected for the mission.

In Chief Gao's eyes, despite the fact that there was still a question mark as to why Ji Zhenren had been released by the enemy, he was the only proper candidate for the mission. Therefore he promised the higher authorities that Ji Zhenren had no political problems.

With regard to Gao Yuncao, Ji Zhenren had a question mark in his mind, but then he had an exclamation mark, "Give her one more chance to pass the test." Secretly he had taken some preparatory measures and he urged Liu Hongmei, "In the operation, no matter what happens, as long as there is a sign that Gao Yuncao is to be captured or is going to flee, you must shoot her dead. Don't ask why and don't tell anyone else what I've told you. Of course, there is a danger both you and I could be captured, Zhu Kexin is our example."

However, Gao Yuncao also had a question in her mind about Liu Hongmei's political reliability, so she also had an exclamation mark, "Give her the opportunity. Of course, I will closely watch her in secret. As long as she passes the test, that will allay my suspicion of her for many years."

In this operation, our side had no designs on the transceivers of the enemy's regular troops because, no matter whether by force or by cunning, it would have been hard to get a transceiver from the enemy's regular troops without exposing our intentions. So the team had their eyes on the KMT Juntong's station in Tianjin, where two new such transceivers had recently been allocated . One was on the station chief's desk, and the other one was in the hands of the captain of the tracking team, who was often away on official business.

Only when the team had been assembled did Ji Zhenren get to know that the Central Department of Social Affairs had dispatched Zhang Jiayin and Liu Hai'er for the operation, with Zhang Jiayin being the team leader.

The operational plan had been decided and all team members had been informed about it before they assembled. Several links had good foundations for the operation. First, through XIANG cracked by RSU2, they had a general knowledge about Juntong's station in Tianjin; second, the Central Department of Social Affairs had led the underground in Tianjin to make a thorough investigation of the environment of the operation; third, one of our divisions had been tasked with selecting a powerful force to fully cooperate with the operation.

The preplanned steps were: our planted agent had leaked information that seventeen Communist underground members in Tianjin would gather in the Jufeng Teahouse on 9 Hetan Road to hold a secret meeting at 10 o'clock in the morning on the 11th of the month. Under normal circumstances, Juntong's station in Tianjin would have sent a tracking team to arrest the Communists who had come to attend the meeting. A few days before the 11th, our special operations team went to survey the topography of the site, confirming three commanding heights where the enemy might have laid an ambush. One was the Qingzhao Restaurant, one was the northern building of the Zhang's residence and the other was Jiang's rice store. Then our underground people and the personnel from our 3rd Division, who were in civilian clothes, were to be divided into four groups to lay an ambush outside the three buildings. Our side predicted that the captain of the enemy's crack team would definitely have been in one of the three buildings to command the operation. Our side had enough force to be more certain of capturing the transceiver.

At the first glimmer of dawn on the 11th, as expected, the enemy agents had quietly entered the three buildings, and some had squatted down in hiding near the Jufeng Teahouse. Before 8 o'clock, everything seemed ready, which was in keeping with our side's expectations. At about 9 o'clock, one after another, 17 people had entered the Jufeng Teahouse. These were members of our special operations team disguised as meeting participants. At 10 o'clock the enemy agents had carried out their attack, and our side had also begun a counter-attack.

Ji Zhenren, Gao Yuncao and Liu Hongmei each followed the attacking force to the three buildings to examine the transceiver as soon as possible.

It was Gao Yuncao who first noticed a change in the circumstances. After following the combat team to enter the Qingzhao Restaurant, she discovered that no one was using a walkie-talkie to talk. She had held her pistol at the forehead of the KMT agent, asking him where their captain was. When the agent had refused to answer, she had shot him. She had then levelled her gun at another agent, who had replied that the captain had set up a command post in a van in the street. Grabbing a rifle and cartridge belt from the agent, she had dashed to the roof of the building. Looking around, she had not seen a jeep parked at the entrance of a lane. The distance was too far for her to shoot. She had lept over a row of roofs and quickly closed on the target. When the jeep was about to move, standing on the roof and aiming the rifle at the jeep, she had fired twice and two tyres were punctured by the bullets. Someone inside the jeep had fired back at her. Jumping down to the street, she had approached the jeep and, catching two fleeting opportunities, she had shot two agents dead in the vehicle. Then pointing her rifle at the last agent in the jeep, step by step she had drawn close. The agent inside had seen that she was an accomplished spy, so he had not dared to move. She had opened the door and seen that the agent was clasping to his chest exactly the type of transceiver she wanted. She had aimed the rifle at the agent, signalling him to give her the equipment. The agent had suddenly seen the light, realising that this woman had come for the transceiver. He had abruptly bent down to pick up his gun. A gun shot was heard and his hand was hit. She had called out, "The keyword!" He had hesitated, then his leg was hit by a bullet. He had told her the keyword. She had asked, "You were only provided with this machine for a short while, so you must have the manual with you." The agent had taken out a little booklet. Another gun shot was heard, the agent's head had dropped and he had died. She had torn away the cover of the manual, along with the leather cover for the transceiver, and thrown them back into the car. Taking out a bag from her pocket, she had scattered some transceiver parts and scrap pieces of the shell of a transceiver onto the car seat. Then she had thrown two grenades into the car. All her movements had been urged by Ji Zhenren beforehand. He had told her that no matter what, once they had got the transceiver, they had to make it look as if it had been smashed and burnt on the spot.

Carrying the transceiver on her back camouflaged as a blanket roll, she had run along the lane, trying to return to the building. Then a familiar figure had flashed past the entrance of the lane. It was Liu Hongmei. That had given her a start: hadn't Liu Hongmei been absolutely unrepentant and tried to flee to that side? She had dared not give it any more thought, but had quietly followed up. After they had run along three lanes, she had raised her rifle, and at the same time Liu Hongmei had turned around and also pointed her gun at Gao Yuncao. This time, from the entrance of the lane had run Ji Zhenren, Zhang Jiayin and Liu Hai'er. So everyone had quickly retreated by the arranged route.

Later, from the XIANG-encrypted telegrams sent by Juntong's station in Tianjin to the Counterintelligence Bureau under the Ministry of National Defence, our side had come to know that the enemy had not discovered the true intention of our operation. Besides, the Tianjin Campaign was imminent and everyone at Juntong's station in Tianjin was in a state of anxiety. They were all preparing to move south, so no one went to investigate why they had gone to arrest the Communists but suffered heavy loss of life instead, still less to think of having lost a transceiver because evidence at the scene clearly indicated that it had been damaged and burnt.

After Ji Zhenren had seen that the captain of the enemy's crack team and the transceiver were not in the building, he had pointed his gun at an enemy agent, who had told him that the captain was in a jeep in the street. Without hesitation, he had run to higher ground to search and by chance, from a gap between buildings, in the distance he had seen a woman walking toward a jeep. It was Gao Yuncao. Hadn't she planned to run away? Quickly, from the roof he had run in the direction of the jeep. As he he had approached, he had seen Gao Yuncao opening the door of the jeep. He had raised his gun and aimed at her. Soon the action of her opening fire, picking up the transceiver and throwing the grenades had taken place. He had then put away his gun, murmuring, "She finally deserves to be considered trustworthy. Hey, her movements were absolutely professional. She has proved herself to be an expert spy trained by both the KMT and the Communist armies."

After they had returned home, Ji Zhenren, Gao Yuncao and Liu Hongmei had joined hands and cooperated with the radio communication experts sent by the higher authorities. After eight days' and nights' continuous work, they had finally cracked the transceiver's voice and encryption principles.

This operation had helped Gao Yuncao to fulfil her wish of being reborn but had planted the root of Liu Hongmei being killed by her later. Having a stubborn preconceived opinion about Liu Hongmei, when in Chongqing and catching Liu Hongmei carrying 'proof of

guilt', she had 'laid murderous hands' on Liu Hongmei without
hesitation, directly resulting in the failure of operation 'Owl One'.

In 1953, after much mental struggle, Gao Yuncao had decided to
make a confession. The organisation had then punished my
grandfather Ji Zhenren by dismissing him from his post and
prosecuting him for 'hiding enemy activities for nine years'.

STANDING before the giant *War Gallery*, Ji Shan recalled her days with her great-grandfather, feeling sad. Despite tears blurring her eyes, she still noticed that a change had been made in the painting: in the middle of a river, a solitary island had appeared from who knows when. It was overgrown with trees and a temple was faintly visible; the scene and the scene on the banks added radiance and beauty to each other. If viewing the painting for the first time, it would have been hard to discover that this island had been added later.

She realised this meant that her great-grandfather had had some words to say before he died. Soon, by applying the same method to decipher the whole painting, she had cracked the message of this island.

She told me that they were her great-grandfather's explanations to two questions.

Question 1: In August 1947, our Northwest Field Army had succeeded in its strategy of deceiving the enemy. During that time Gao Yuncao had sent the KMT's Special Secret Wireless Section the telegram saying that 'the communist troops are about to cross the Yellow River to the east bank very soon' to deceive the KMT. After the campaign had ended, the KMT would certainly have realised that they had been deceived. Had the Special Secret Wireless Section ever doubted the status of Grasshopper (Gao Yuncao)?

In the early 1990s, after the Taiwan spy case had been cracked, Ji Zhenren and Gao Yuncao had been allowed to meet Gao Q and Zhen Yanli, and had found out the related circumstances.

At the time, Gao Q and Zhen Yanli's views were very divergent on the telegram sent by 'Grasshopper' Gao Yuncao.

Gao Q had thought that for such a confidential operation to deceive the enemy, the decision makers would not have let ordinary internal personnel know about it in advance. What was most probable was that the Communists had deceived the KMT troops as well as 'Grasshopper'. What 'Grasshopper' had seen was that the Communist main forces were going to cross the Yellow River. Her misjudgement was not intentional, so she had not sent the telegram deliberately. Therefore 'Grasshopper' was still the same 'Grasshopper' who was loyal to the party and the state.

Zhen Yanli was furious, saying, "This telegram is enough to prove that she has abandoned the party and the state."

Patiently, Gao Q explained, "In ordinary times, Gao Yuncao used her right hand to send messages, which you and I both heard. But when she sent this telegram to us, she had quickly and cleverly jumped on our radio channel and used her left hand to send the message. After it was done, she had quickly gone back to the channel and carried on sending messages using her right hand. Let me ask you why she did it this way? It was to evade their own monitors, particularly to deceive Ji Zhenren who could have distinguished her from the others when she used her right hand to send telegrams. Under the nose of the Communists, she had secretly sent out the message. This showed her high skill and courage, loyalty and daring. Speaking from a technical aspect only, she would not have acted in such a way if she had been turned against us by the Communists. This is my professional explanation to this question."

Zhen Yanli seemed convinced, but said, "If she had pretended it all, what would you have said?"

Gao Q shook his head, "I understand her as I understand myself. When I listened to her sending telegrams it was like sitting face-to-face with her and listening to her words, examining her expressions and watching her deeds. I am sure she sent the message out in a desperate situation. By her mentality of fighting to the death, resolutely but in a flustered way, she had secretly sent out the message. That was definitely not a pretence."

Zhen Yanli called out, "Gao Q, you finally admit that you are on intimate terms with her. Now I can see that her best ability is not hiding in the enemy camp for many years without being exposed but hiding and living in a married man's heart for many years."

Gao Q shouted, "No matter how jealous you are, Grasshopper is still our own agent who has not been exposed. No one can spoil my Grasshopper Plan. Anyone who dares to stir up trouble is guilty in the eyes of the party and the state. And I'll not treat them leniently."

Question 2: In Chongqing, on the eve of the founding of the New China, Liu Hongmei showed up at 178 Xiangnaohe Road. Gao Q and Zhen Yanli would certainly have been suspicious of Grasshopper's telegram about 'the military medical officer couple and Liu Hongmei having been caught at one fell swoop', and would have concluded that Grasshopper had been turned by the Communists. If that was true, Gao Q and Zhen Yanli would have known that the cipher based on *The Sad Record of a Strategy for Peace* had been cracked. But how could they still have used it in the 1990s and brought it to the mainland and hurled themselves willingly into the net?

To this question, Gao Q and Zhen Yanli had a confession to make.

When Liu Hongmei turned up at 178 Xiangnaohe Road in Chongqing in 1949, they had drawn their own conclusion about it. In those years, what they were able to confirm was that medic Liu, nurse Zhang and their other contacts had all been exposed and caught because Liu Hongmei, medic Liu and nurse Zhang were all direct, linear contacts. After the death of the medic couple, Liu Hongmei had become a dead piece, so they had no idea about her whereabouts. Later, from the telegram sent by Grasshopper, they had confirmed that Liu Hongmei's line was also finished. But now she had suddenly come back to life, which had made the situation more complicated. One probability was that Grasshopper had not been exposed, and the telegram she had sent years ago had been genuine. Then the Liu Hongmei before them might have been turned by the Communists, taking on their task and coming to Chongqing to try to achieve something. The second probability might have been that Liu Hongmei had indeed surrendered to the Communists, but that she had pretended to submit yet was unwillingly to be used in reverse against the KMT, and subsequently she had truly wanted to return to the arms of the KMT, therefore she was secretly carrying Communist secrets and had defected to them. The third probability might have been that

Grasshopper had been exposed and she had sent the telegram years ago under the instructions of the Communists.

Gao Q had concluded that all three of these probabilities were possible, so they should not make a rash decision on which one. But Zhen Yanli had insisted that Grasshopper had been turned by the Communists. Each had stuck to their own point of view so they had not reported the result to their superior.

One day, Zhen Yanli had asked Gao Q, "Do you have any brilliant ruses to examine and distinguish Grasshopper's current situation?"

Looking helpless, he had said, "This time I'm really at my wits' end."

Zhen Yanli's face had frozen at his remark, grinding her teeth, she had said, "Clearly you're unwilling to give your verdict that she has betrayed the party and the state." She then picked up a pen and drafted 'Report on starting to use *CHU*, *HUAN* and *YU* and trying to find out Grasshopper's current situation'. Then she forced Gao Q to sign his name on the report.

The plan Zhen Yanli had proposed was to use the *CHU*, *HUAN* and *YU* ciphers to send telegrams to Liu Guotian, Ran Yizhi and Li Fanglong, the Communist traitors who were performing a mission in Chengdu, Foshan and Deyang, ordering them to return to Chongqing immediately to go to 81 Xiaogang Sanlu Avenue at 9 o'clock on the 23rd, to attend a meeting in which the operational plan would be discussed and laid out to root out the Communist underground in Chongqing.

Before their defection, Liu Guotian was the key leader of the Chongqing Municipal Committee of the CPC underground, Ran Yizhi was the deputy secretary of the Municipal Working Committee and Li Fanglong was the leading cadre of the Municipal Organisation Department. After they had defected, they had provided the KMT with large numbers of secrets of the Communist underground, resulting in serious damage to the underground work in Chongqing and Sichuan. Large numbers of CPC members, such as Jiang Zhuyun, had been arrested. Thereafter, these three had become the most hated traitors whom the Communist underground were determined to kill.

Zhen Yanli had predicted that if the Communists had cracked these three ciphers, then their underground in Chongqing would have raided 81 Xiaogang Sanlu Avenue to eradicate the three traitors at any cost. If no corresponding action was taken, it could have proved that

Grasshopper's telegram was false and that she had been turned by the Communists.

The plan had been quickly approved by Director Mao Renfeng, in whose eyes the three Communist traitors had no more value, so there was a good chance for them to be used as bait by the Special Secret Wireless Section.

The end result was that after three telegrams were sent, there was no corresponding reaction from the Communist side.

Gao Q's last illusion had been shattered. None of the three ciphers had been cracked by the Communists, which meant that Grasshopper had really been turned by the Communists.

Among the trees on the island, Ji Shan had discovered a patch of camphor trees. At first sight, it was like the one on the Tangyan bend of the Huangpu River in Shanghai. Ji Shan had also cracked its hidden meaning in the painting.

It was a conversation between two old friends in the early 1990s. The codes had said that I had used the island cipher to write this conversation on the painting to commemorate the either silent, or grand and spectacularly weird years, as well as the love, friendship and hatred that had been engraved in my memory, as well as the remorse and faith.

"In those years in Taiwan, we had been trying to guess how Grasshopper had been exposed and how she had been turned by the Communists. There were many probabilities, but we had not been able to form our conclusion. In 1958, news had emerged from a spy case: as early as 1953 Grasshopper had been put in prison by the Communists. Later, you Ji Zhenren had also been punished and dismissed from your post. Only then did we get to know that you, you cunning old devil, hadn't died in the assassination in 1953. In view of this, we had written a special report which could have been regarded as a conclusion for Grasshopper: 'Under the Communists' extremely guarded environment, Grasshopper had plotted for ten years, wanting but unable to act. But her loyalty had been everlasting, being ready to sacrifice her life for the party and the state at any moment. In the end, she had had to use an extreme method of self-exposure, meeting their death together, jointly removing Ji Zhenren, the technical support of RSU2, breaking this sharp sword which was a huge threat to the secrets of the KMT, thereby accomplishing her mission.' Our superior had paid great attention to the report, and soon Grasshopper had been rewarded with a medal for her extraordinary service. A meeting was held and wide publicity was given to her heroic deeds. It can be said that the ending for Grasshopper in Taiwan was bright and satisfactory. However, we had never dreamt that in mainland China she would choose self-salvation, turning herself in to the police.

"This is resurrection, the high realm growing out of the special environment on this side. It is hard for those who have no personal experience to understand it. However, you two had hurled yourselves willingly into the net, and had come to the mainland to search for your old friends. This was beyond my expectation and more than exceeded the authorities' expectation. It seems that the most difficult cipher to crack in the world is the cipher of hearts.

"Now people can treat all things from the past reasonably. Some historical problems are no longer problems. Some years ago, many KMT key prisoners of war had been released by the Communists, and very good jobs were arranged for them. For my wife and I, since we are here, we may as well stay and make the best of it. If the four of us can live in the same city where we can joyfully spend our remaining years, it will be the happiest old age for us. We have spent half of our lifetime cracking war secrets, trying to fathom the ciphers in each other's minds for most of our lives. And in the end we can have this common understanding, which is not easy.

"We don't have to talk about war in our old age, but about love, I'm afraid we cannot avoid it.

"War does not exist, neither does love.

"Ha ha…"

In late spring and early summer of that year it rained continuously for seven days and seven nights. Ji Shan had gone upstairs to pick up something and she had found a slight bulge in the centre of the painting *War Gallery*. It looked like water had leaked through the wall, and dampness had caused some distortion in the painting.

She had touched the bulging area, feeling a regular rectangle in its shape. She had measured it, and the length was 130 centimetres and the width was 80 centimetres. How could it have been so regular?

Wu Yuan had gone to find a craftsman who specialised in mounting paintings. He had opened the frame and removed the painting from it.

There was another painting hidden between the painting and the frame.

In the foreground was a small pool; a small ditch connected the pool to a large pond behind. Faintly, one large and some small fish could be seen in the pool.

Wu Yuan had said the main painting had fully expressed the enemy's situation and our situation, as well as friendship among friends and love and affection among blood relations. He had not been able to think of any other secrets that would have merited Great-grandpa doing another painting.

Some days later, Ji Shan had burnt the small painting. Wu Yuan wasn't happy about it, and had asked, "Cracked? What does the painting say?"

"No secrets were hidden in it at all," Ji Shan had replied.

"I hope you can tell me those secrets. This is not my personal opinion," Wu Yuan had said seriously.

"No secrets in the painting, but you want me to crack them. I worried that I would have been pressed, so I burned it," Ji Shan had muttered.

In 1949, when in Chongqing, Ji Zhenren originally had not kept a wary eye on Gao Yuncao, but it had still hit him hard when he saw her sneaking out secretly. After all, they had been carrying out a mission in enemy-occupied territory and eventually the KMT armies would retreat to Taiwan. Ultimately, she had that hidden background. So he had begun to shadow her. But she was extremely skilled in counter-shadowing and he had lost his target. When he had found her, she was carrying somebody on her shoulder.

In the distance, he had followed her trail and had come to the valley on the south side of Caogang Ridge. After she had left, he had immediately dug open the hole underneath the dead tree. Fortunately the hole was large as a result of the tree having been blown over in a storm. After Gao Yuncao had put the person in, she hurriedly covered the mouth of the hole with some mud and dead tree leaves. But inside, it was hollow with twisted, intertwined roots. The person buried in it had not suffered any weight or suffocation.

After Ji Zhenren had dug the body out, he had realised it was Liu Hongmei, whose head had been struck by a blunt instrument but not sufficiently violently to have been the cause of death. He had carried out first aid by pressing her chest. In the end there was a faint breath. Carrying her on his back, he had hurried off down the hill.

Halfway, Liu Hongmei had woken up. After a fit of violent coughing, a button had burst out of her mouth. She had struggled to sit up and, in a weak voice, she had said, "The poison on the button has passed its expiry date. I am not destined to die." Impatiently she had wanted to leave, but Ji Zhenren had insisted on taking her to hospital. She had said, "Brother, in this world you are my dearest, most loved and trusted person. I believe in you as much as I believe in the Party. Brother, the urgent matter for now is to let me go." She had told him of her 'Owl One' mission. Then she had requested him to do one thing, "Try to find a dead female and put this poison button in her mouth. Then find some documents the same as the ones I'm holding in my hand and push them inside the clothes of the dead body. Bury it in that tree root hole. I am sure you can get it done. In the surrounding areas in Chongqing gun battles happen from time to time, so it is not difficult to find a dead female body. You're smart enough to go and find one, and make copies of the same documents; that's not difficult for you either. After that's done, I'll have no more worries. Yuncao doesn't know this hidden identity of mine. She tried to prevent me from going to the enemy yet without wanting to damage my reputation, so she used this method to place righteousness above family loyalty. Because of her relationship with me over the years, if one day she feels so ashamed that she can't bear it and she comes to rebury me in a coffin, but finds an empty hole, then there will be trouble. It may threaten my mission. But, if you do these two things, everything will be fine. This time I don't know when I can come back, my life and death is unforeseen. Brother, take good care of yourself." She had hugged him, then holding his shoulder, she had urged, "What happened today you must not leak to anyone else and be sure to keep it secret for the rest of your life. You must know this top-secret mission must not go wrong, no matter what." Holding the documents tight, she had turned around and left.

Ji Zhenren had tearfully watched her walking away.

Ji Shan had deciphered the small painting and obtained the above secrets alone, meanwhile she had also been mindful of Liu Hongmei's words: "What happened today you must not leak to anyone else and be sure to keep it secret for the rest of your life." On account of this sentence she had burned the painting. But some information had been engraved in her heart forever.

Great-grandpa had also said in this painting that in the 1990s, he had once been told by Gao Q that Liu Hongmei had been living an ordinary life in Taiwan, had many children and grandchildren, and had lived a very happy life. Not knowing for what purpose, Gao Q would not have mentioned Liu Hongmei again to anyone else on the mainland. Of course, he had no idea that Liu Hongmei's defection had been false. Great-grandpa had concluded that the significance and value of the documents Liu Hongmei was carrying with her, the gifts given to the KMT as bait, were so great that there was no reason for the KMT side to have suspected her intentions.

Great-grandpa had also described in the coded painting that in 1953 when he had undertaken a self-examination, he had not mentioned a single word about what had happened on Caogang Ridge in Chongqing. He had clearly known that if he had mentioned that Liu Hongmei had not died, it would have mitigated Gao Yuncao's sin, which might have reduced her sentence. But he had not done it. Because Liu Hongmei had told him that she believed in him as much as she believed in the Party. What respect and trust that was! Apart from that, according to the mission requirement and the security regulations, a man at his level should not have known about the secret mission 'Owl One'. Because he had come to know about it by accident, he had to keep it in his belly forever, which was in accordance with his natural instincts of keeping secrets and maintaining discipline.

In the painting Great-grandpa had also left behind a few questions: in 1953 Gao Yuncao had confessed how she had killed Liu Hongmei in Chongqing. At the time, Chief Gao had been bitter about the news, feeling sorry for Liu Hongmei who had died before achieving success in her mission, and he had even shed tears on the spot. Had he really not known that Liu Hongmei was still alive? Or had he known that Liu Hongmei had been successful in her mission, and his tears were put on for Gao Yuncao to see? In fact, there had been no sign that he had known Liu Hongmei was still alive. And wasn't it the case that for Liu

Hongmei's safety in Taiwan, he had taken great pains never to speak about her true situation?

Having been used to living with secrets, Great-grandpa, you had wanted to use this painting to be your mouthpiece, talking to yourself to relieve certain secrets, so as to seek a carefree state of mind. You had thought you were very mysterious and had freed yourself, without realising that it had made me a continuation of you. Your great-granddaughter, or even later generations that come after me will never walk out of your shadow.

Holding the ashes of the small painting, Ji Shan knelt on the ground for a long time.

NOTES

1. THE DUEL

1. In ancient times, bamboo slips were used for writing on and made into a book by linking the slips together.

3. XISHI

1. Juntong stands for the National Bureau of Investigation and Statistics, the military intelligence agency of the Kuomintang's Nationalist government before 1946.

Yu Zhiyan is a native of northern China's Hebei Province. He began writing in 1988, and is a working member of the Chinese Writers Association. His military and historical novels are widely published within the PRC, and several have been adapted to the screen. His work has received numerous honours and awards, including the China Book Review Society's Good Book Award, and the bronze medal in the first Chinese Print Art Biennale.

About **Sino**ist Books

We hope you enjoyed this tale of intrigue, love, espionage and counter-espionage set in the period of the Chinese civil war.

SINOIST BOOKS brings the best of Chinese fiction to English-speaking readers. We aim to create a greater understanding of Chinese culture and society, and provide an outlet for the ideas and creativity of the country's most talented authors.

To let us know what you thought of this book, or to learn more about the diverse range of exciting Chinese fiction in translation we publish, find us online. If you're as passionate about Chinese literature as we are, then we'd love to hear your thoughts!

SINOIST

B O O K S

sinoistbooks.com
@sinoistbooks